BANDI

Ricky though ut
the first man his
package, pulle ell
be a sword, and shouted over his shoulder. For
help, if the response from his friends was any
indication: three more of the raiders drew various
blades and started moving to meet the up-timers.

Ricky shouldered the Remington and dropped
the bead over the first bandit's naked torso. Pushing the safety off, he stroked the trigger with his
finger. The high-base shell made the gun kick him
in the shoulder, hard, and launch its load with a
heavy bark and flash as the buckshot exited the
barrel.

A spark went up from the man's sword, followed
closely by the swordsman himself slumping to the
ground with a wet, coughing sob.

The others, scattered in a loose group a few
steps from each other and behind the first, paused
a moment, then one of them started shouting.

Ricky cycled the action and drew a bead on
his next target.

The raiders were sprinting at him now, unaware
he had five more in the tube and thinking to cut
him down as he tried to reload.

Another man staggered, fell as soon as Ricky
pulled the trigger.

Ricky didn't bother to aim now, just cycled
and stroked the trigger. He was left unsure if
he'd hit or not, as the man now leading the pack
didn't slow. . . .

BAEN BOOKS by ERIC FLINT

THE RING OF FIRE SERIES

1632 by Eric Flint • *1633* with David Weber • *1634: The Baltic War* with David Weber • *1634: The Galileo Affair* with Andrew Dennis • *1634: The Bavarian Crisis* with Virginia DeMarce • *1634: The Ram Rebellion* with Virginia DeMarce et al. • *1635: The Cannon Law* with Andrew Dennis • *1635: The Dreeson Incident* with Virginia DeMarce • *1635: The Eastern Front* • *1635: The Papal Stakes* with Charles E. Gannon • *1636: The Saxon Uprising* • *1636: The Kremlin Games* with Gorg Huff & Paula Goodlett • *1636: The Devil's Opera* with David Carrico • *1636: Commander Cantrell in the West Indies* with Charles E. Gannon • *1636: The Viennese Waltz* with Gorg Huff & Paula Goodlett • *1636: The Cardinal Virtues* with Walter H. Hunt • *1635: A Parcel of Rogues* with Andrew Dennis • *1636: The Ottoman Onslaught* • *1636: Mission to the Mughals* with Griffin Barber • *1636: The Vatican Sanction* with Charles E. Gannon • *1637: The Volga Rules* with Gorg Huff & Paula Goodlett • *1637: The Polish Maelstrom* • *1636: The China Venture* with Iver P. Cooper • *1636: The Atlantic Encounter* with Walter H. Hunt • *1637: No Peace Beyond the Line* with Charles E. Gannon • *1637: The Peacock Throne* with Griffin Barber • *1637: The Coast of Chaos* with Paula Goodlett & Gorg Huff

1635: The Tangled Web by Virginia DeMarce • *1635: The Wars for the Rhine* by Anette Pedersen • *1636: Seas of Fortune* by Iver P. Cooper • *1636: The Chronicles of Dr. Gribbleflotz* by Kerryn Offord & Rick Boatright • *1636: Flight of the Nightingale* by David Carrico • *1636: Calabar's War* by Charles E. Gannon & Robert E. Waters • *1637: Dr. Gribbleflotz and the Soul of Stoner* by Kerryn Offord & Rick Boatright

Time Spike with Marilyn Kosmatka • *The Alexander Inheritance* with Gorg Huff & Paula Goodlett • *The Macedonian Hazard* with Gorg Huff & Paula Goodlett

TRAIL OF GLORY

1812: The Rivers of War
1824: The Arkansas War (forthcoming)

To purchase any of these titles in e-book form, please go to www.baen.com.

1637
THE PEACOCK THRONE

ERIC FLINT
GRIFFIN BARBER

A Baen Books Original

Baen Publishing Enterprises
P.O. Box 1403
Riverdale, NY 10471
www.baen.com

ISBN: 978-1-9821-9218-1

Cover art by Tom Kidd
Maps by Michael Knopp

First printing, May 2021
First mass market printing, October 2022

Distributed by Simon & Schuster
1230 Avenue of the Americas
New York, NY 10020

Library of Congress Control Number: 2021005965

Pages by Joy Freeman (www.pagesbyjoy.com)
Printed in the United States of America

10 9 8 7 6 5 4 3 2 1

To my parents, Bill & Donna,
for giving so much down the years
—Griffin

To Professor Stanley Wolpert,
December 23, 1927–February 19, 2019

Stanley Wolpert was my professor of Indian history at UCLA and the person who introduced me to that immense and fascinating field of the human past. I've now written eight novels which are in one way or another set in Indian history—the six-volume Belisarius series which I co-authored with David Drake and the (so far) two volumes set in my Ring of Fire series—and any number of other works in which Indian history and culture figures to some degree. That never would or could have happened without the impact and influence that Prof. Wolpert had on me as a young man. I have been thankful to him for decades and remember him very well, even though I never saw him again after I left UCLA in 1971.

Such is the fate of excellent teachers. They are remembered by their students long after the instructor has forgotten them. *Sic transit gloria mundi* is usually translated as "Thus passes the glory of the world." But I prefer to think of it as "Thus the glory of the world is passed on."

—Eric Flint

Contents

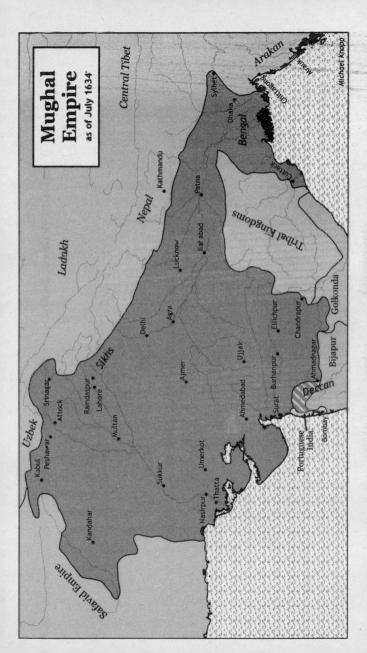

Mughal Empire
as of July 1634

Central Tibet

Arakan

Mrauk

Chittagong

Sylhet

Dhaka

Bengal

Cuttack

Nepal

Kathmandu

Patna

Ladakh

Lucknow

Ilahabad

Tribal Kingdoms

Golkonda

Delhi

Agra

Ellichpur

Chandrapur

Uzbek

Sikhs

Ajmer

Ujjain

Burhanpur

Ahmadnagar

Bijapur

Srinagar

Ramdaspur

Ahmedabad

Deccan

Attock

Lahore

Peshawar

Multan

Surat

Kabul

Portuguese
India

Bombay

Sukkur

Umerkot

Nasirpur

Kandahar

Thatta

Safavid Empire

Michael Knopp

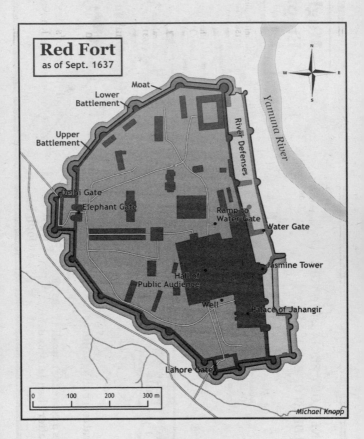

Red Fort
as of Sept. 1637

Moat

Lower Battlement

Upper Battlement

Delhi Gate

Elephant Gate

River Defenses

Yamuna River

Ramp to Water Gate

Water Gate

Jasmine Tower

Hall of Public Audience

Well

Palace of Jahangir

Lahore Gate

0   100   200   300 m

Michael Knopp

N
W   E
S

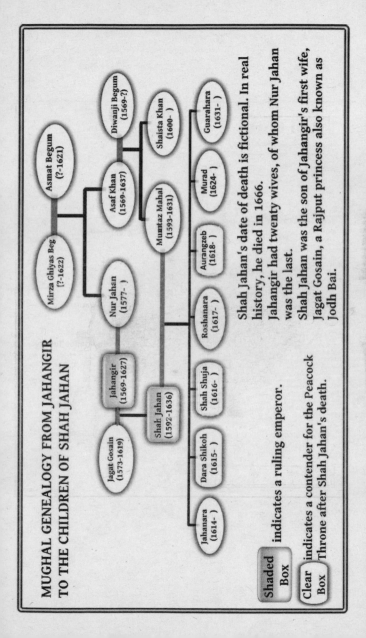

MUGHAL GENEALOGY FROM JAHANGIR TO THE CHILDREN OF SHAH JAHAN

Mirza Ghiyas Beg
(?-1622)

Asmat Begum
(?-1621)

Diwanji Begum
(1569-?)

Nur Jahan
(1577-)

Asaf Khan
(1569-1637)

Shaista Khan
(1600-)

Jagat Gosain
(1573-1619)

Jahangir
(1569-1627)

Shah Jahan
(1592-1636)

Muntaz Mahal
(1593-1631)

Guarahara
(1631-)

Jahanara
(1614-)

Dara Shikoh
(1615-)

Shah Shuja
(1616-)

Roshanara
(1617-)

Aurangzeb
(1618-)

Murad
(1624-)

Shah Jahan's date of death is fictional. In real history, he died in 1666.

Jahangir had twenty wives, of whom Nur Jahan was the last.

Shah Jahan was the son of Jahangir's first wife, Jagat Gosain, a Rajput princess also known as Jodh Bai.

Shaded Box indicates a ruling emperor.

Clear Box indicates a contender for the Peacock Throne after Shah Jahan's death.

1637
THE PEACOCK THRONE

Part One

February, 1636

Flame burns it not, waters cannot overwhelm
—The Rig Veda

Chapter 1

Jahanara stood in the stirrups and gave Azar her lead as they left their own half. The fierce little pony flowed across the turf like the wind. Enjoying the moment, the princess leaned over to strike at the ball. An instant later her mallet sent it spinning across to one of her new guards, Yonca.

"Bad pass," the princess muttered, seeing she'd sent the ball to where the Turkic warrior woman had been rather than where she was headed.

But Yonca showed great skill as Damla and Roshanara closed on her, coming to a complete stop that would have sent a weaker rider over pommel, mane, and mouth to slap face-first into the turf. Her opponents went by, forced by her sudden stop to move aside or collide with the rump of Yonca's mount. The talented horsewoman wasn't done showing her skill, however: she leaned well out of the saddle and clapped her mallet against the ball, sending it in a curving arc

3

that straightened along the boundary line ahead of Jahanara.

Roshanara, the closest rider from the opposite team, snapped her reins against her pony's flanks and set out in pursuit.

Jahanara lowered her head and again let Azar run. She had the straighter line and the faster horse, but Roshanara was smaller than her sister, and hadn't been riding her mount all that hard until the last few runs of play.

The other players were out of position, and could only join the shouted encouragement from the gathered women watching from the shade of the gardens. The birthday celebrations for Nadira's son had gathered nearly every wife, mother, sister, and daughter of Dara's *umara* to the gardens of Amar Singh Rathore's palatial home to participate, most of whom watched the two princesses compete.

The distance between the two players and the ball closed with exhilarating speed, making Jahanara's lips curve with feral delight.

Then the pair were riding flat out and side by side. The ball had stopped beside the boundary, meaning that Jahanara could only strike at it while riding out of bounds and from the left while Roshanara had it on her right, strong side. Jahanara quickly switched hands and dropped her mallet for the swing.

Roshanara's quick overhand swing of the mallet clacked against the ball, sending it rocketing back the way they'd come.

Jahanara's mallet tangled with her sister's as the momentum of the smaller woman's swing carried the shafts together. The impact sent a violent shiver up the wood that stung Jahanara's hands and wrenched her shoulder.

Roshanara was even more affected, as she'd stood in the stirrups and used every bit of strength in her body to make the hit. With her swing stopped so abruptly, Roshanara lost control of her mallet and struck her pony hard on the leg, making it stumble.

She overbalanced and started to topple sideways, away from Jahanara.

Jahanara dropped her mallet and snatched at her sister, hoping to stay her fall. She missed, but Roshanara caught her outstretched arm and used it to lever herself back upright.

As one, they slowed and turned back onto the field.

"My thanks, sister," Roshanara said, cheeks still flushed from exertion and perhaps, Jahanara reflected, from sudden fear.

Jahanara nodded, feeling the now-familiar surge of shame over the beating she'd given Roshanara the night of Father's murder. She wanted to apologize, but could not. To do so would be to admit *everything* that had happened that night, and that would only make her angry once again.

Instead, Jahanara nodded at the far end of the field where Damla and the rest of Roshanara's team were celebrating the final point and said, "Fine play, sister. You surprised me with that overhand strike, you delivered it so swiftly."

Roshanara's cheeks colored more deeply. "It was my only good play for the entirety of the game."

"Better to properly seize an opportunity once than attempt to seize every chance, however small, and fail."

Letting their mounts cool, the princesses rode in a

slow, silent circle before Roshanara departed for the accolades of the gathered women.

Sadness seized Jahanara as she watched her sister leave. Roshanara had been in virtual hiding since the night Jahanara had attacked her, and only come out for the day's events at Nadira's insistence. And if Smidha's spies and informants were to be believed, Roshanara hadn't been in contact with anyone outside the harem precincts. Jahanara dismissed as cruel rumor those reports that claimed Roshanara had not cried since that terrible night. Roshanara had never been a favorite sibling, and her younger sister's part in the events that led to Father's assassination had sent Jahanara into a killing rage.

Now, though, when her temper had cooled, Jahanara wished desperately for someone to speak to of her concerns, both political and personal.

Atisheh still recovered at Mission House and was not given to easy sentiment or concerted effort to unearth the meaning of life in the first place.

Smidha was an eternal help in most things, but sometimes the elder woman was just that: old-fashioned in her thinking and ... she was not inclined to speak of physical passions as anything less than a liability for her princess. And Jahanara had certainly not forgotten the feel of Salim's muscled flesh under her fingers, the interest in his eyes. The memory—and imagining what might come of his hands exploring *her* flesh—had kept her awake on more than one occasion in the last weeks.

None should be so well equipped to understand as her sister, and Jahanara was left wishing they had been closer as children so she might unburden herself without fear of betrayal ...

Knowing wishes would not reverse the established courses of their lives, she directed her pony to the waiting eunuch. And, as such melancholy thoughts would hardly serve in front of the collected ladies of the court, she sought distraction from her personal fears. As always, politics proved the easiest distraction to turn to; all she need do was think of the many challenges facing Dara's rule. Their brothers, the umara, the various religious and cultural factions, even the inertia of old policies and imperial precedent—each posed difficulties for her brother, whose health was also in question, the resultant pain of his injuries still affecting his moods and clarity of thought. That last was something she and the inner circle of Dara's court dare not speak of openly, even in the most private of circumstances. That Dara was often confused was something his enemies would trade upon mercilessly.

That Dara himself had used his infirmity to argue against taking another wife had been a surprise. A surprise that, upon reflection, made horrible sense: the betrothal ceremony alone could prove enough of an ordeal to force him to reveal his weakness before the court. Such would certainly prove disastrous for their cause, exactly the opposite of the purpose of marriage alliances.

No, they were wiser to wait in that regard.

She dismounted and handed over Azar's reins, who nuzzled her in search of sweets. Smiling, she patted the mare's neck and entered the enclosure set up to allow the players to bathe and change clothes before returning to the festivities.

"Begum Sahib," Smidha said, waving a bevy of servants forward to help Jahanara remove her riding clothes.

"Smidha," Jahanara acknowledged.

"You played well, Begum Sahib."

She shook her head. "Not well enough to beat Damla! That woman was born on a horse."

"She is no Atisheh, though."

Jahanara sighed. "No, she is not."

"Skanda's praises, but Atisheh was also born ahorse with a blade in her hand!"

"True enough," Jahanara answered, preferring not to think too much about the day Atisheh had proven herself so proficient with a sword.

Stripped, she stepped into the waiting bath.

"Oil or water, Begum Sahib?"

"Oil. My hair will never dry, otherwise."

Smidha set to work cleaning and untangling her hair with a comb and oils as her body slaves washed the dust and horse from their mistress.

"Are my sister's guests content?"

"It seems they are. They very much enjoyed the poetry, music, and of course, the pulu match. The betting was heavy, and some lost more than they should have bet."

Sensing a reproving note, Jahanara asked, "So, how much did you lose?"

"Nothing, Begum Sahib."

"You did not bet?"

"No, I bet on Damla and Roshanara to win. I earned quite a few rupees ... Though you gave me quite a scare at the end. I thought that I was going to owe our hostess, Paramjit, all my incomes for a week."

Jahanara snorted. "Never has my failure to win pleased me so. Are you done?"

A gentle tug at her hair. "Almost."

Jahanara sat through a few more minutes of being tended to before Smidha judged her presentable. She left the enclosure, Smidha following, and found Damla waiting outside, having eschewed the baths in favor of a skin of some drink. Truly, the woman was a slimmer version of her cousin, Atisheh. But lately come to service, Damla was young for her position as Atisheh's second-in-command, but had her kinswoman's full approval, at least until Atisheh could ride and fight again.

"Begum Sahib."

"Congratulations, Damla. You were magnificent on the field."

A shrug of armored shoulders. "I but tried to honor my uncle's teaching."

"My sister and I, unarmored, and on the finest ponies money can buy, were still outmaneuvered by you and your sisters as often as not."

Another shrug. "We have had more time to play than you, and do not have your . . . refinement in other arenas."

"Refinement?" Jahanara asked. She set out toward the dining area set up for the feast, intending to make a few final checks of the arrangements.

"I can swing a sword, shoot a bow, and ride, but my mother and aunts all despaired of ever teaching me proper calligraphy. My memory is also very bad. My father was certain I will never be married, as I could never recall the Prophet's words pertaining to the conduct of a proper wife."

"And Atisheh?"

A snort. "Hers was an even more difficult circumstance . . . but that is her story to tell."

Jahanara attempted to imagine what Atisheh's life must have been like as a child and found she could not. Then she tried to imagine the man the warrior woman might marry but could not think of one who would not be intimidated by her superior skill and proven strength.

"The lack of a husband certainly does not seem to cause you any distress," Smidha said.

"True." Another shrug of armored shoulders. "I do not feel the lack. God granted me my skills and set me this path. I serve. It is enough."

"And we thank God and you, humbly, for the service you give us," Jahanara said, heart suddenly so full she had to stop herself reaching out and taking the woman's gauntlet in her hands. Such would not be seemly, if for no other reason than Damla was a recent addition to the harem guards, brought on from this very house to serve the imperial harem. A moment's reflection allowed Jahanara to recognize the source of this sudden surge of feeling for Damla. The woman who looked, even sounded like, Atisheh. Atisheh, to whom Jahanara owed everything.

I must visit her soon, and to hell with the proprieties.

Her thoughts were, by necessity, silenced as their small group joined the other ladies attending the party. Moments after she was seated Nadira ordered the food be brought out. The feast was outstanding, and the company of the women exceptional, and lasted well into the evening. Varicolored lanterns were brought out as the first troupe of dancers entered and began to perform for the enjoyment of all.

After the remains of the repast were removed

and the dancers finished their routines, Nadira led a reading of poetry written by the very pinnacle of the ladies of the court. In preparation for the celebration, Nadira had asked each lady to compose a few verses with a woman's lot in life as the theme.

Jahanara's verses were well received, though she avoided speaking directly to the issue that drove Nadira's choice of themes. Instead, her poem focused on the search for wisdom in uncertain times.

At its end, Nadira launched into her own verses, which the accomplished poet had completed only last week. As she had heard her sister-in-law's poem already, Jahanara half-listened while considering Nadira's intent for the evening.

The celebration of her son's birthday had been planned, in part, to give Nadira an opportunity to silence a few rumors that had begun circulating about Jahanara. It seemed that Jahanara's management of Dara's harem had caused some resentment. The rumors complained that it had been one thing for Jahanara to manage Father's well-established harem of many wives and even more concubines, but quite another to do it for Dara, a young emperor with only the one wife and therefore very few close ties with his senior courtiers.

For her part, Jahanara could understand the ill will that fostered such rumors: if you, your parents, and your husband had spent a great deal of time and effort inveigling a position at court beside Nadira, it was understandable that resentment would follow upon discovery that Nadira was not the sole arbiter of who and what service was worthy of reward. No, the blackest rumors to reach her ears made her a power-hungry creature who refused to step down, only persisting in her position in order to exert undue control over her brother.

As her voice raised in protest would only serve to confirm the rumors to the minds of her detractors, it had been decided that Nadira would take the lead.

Her thoughts were interrupted as Nadira finished her reading and the ladies applauded enthusiastically.

Smiling, Nadira led a spirited discussion choosing which were the best couplets of the night. Jahanara participated, but less actively than she might have in order to allow Nadira all the attention she deserved. Instead, she sat quietly admiring her sister-in-law's ability to guide the conversation to her objectives.

Seizing on the couplet of one of her senior ladies, Nadira expounded a few moments on the quality of the verse before focusing on the matching of it to her chosen theme.

"In reading the verse, I love that it leads the reader down a certain path of thought to a crossroads. On the one hand, the joys of a life in service to another. On the other, the desire to be beholden and responsible only to oneself and to God.

"Now that I am a mother and feel the ever-present ache of love and duty toward my son, I want to devote all of my time to being the best mother I can be."

The other mothers among those gathered for the party expressed wholehearted agreement with the empress as she paused to drink her julabmost. While her courtiers nodded and spoke among themselves, the wife of the emperor met Jahanara's gaze over the rim of her goblet . . . and winked.

Jahanara covered a smile.

Lowering her drink, Nadira resumed speaking.

"Even at the cost of managing my husband's harem and its affairs. I told my beloved husband as much, and he agreed that while affairs of state occupy his mind and weigh upon his spirit, I should concentrate my efforts upon rearing our son.

"This in mind, my beloved husband asked Jahanara Begum"—she raised her goblet again, this time in salute to Jahanara—"to take up many responsibilities on our behalf. As a dutiful sister to both myself and my beloved husband, Jahanara Begum has resumed those duties that she discharged so well for Shah Jahan. I wish to thank her for this kindness, and for the many other kindnesses she has bestowed upon me since we became sisters."

The gathered ladies of the court joined their hostess in saluting the emperor's sister. For the rest of the night, the ladies were far warmer in their regard for Jahanara than they had been in the weeks since Dara had assumed the throne.

Over the next few days she saw a general increase in ladies asking for her advice, suggestions, and opinions on a wide variety of subjects. Soon after that there came an increase in petitioners and requests for intercession in certain matters that required the attention of the foremost lady of the court.

Nadira's message, it seemed, had been fully delivered.

Now it only remained to be seen how long the lesson would remain.

Chapter 2

Surat, on the Gulf of Khambhat
West coast of India

Lønesom Vind shifted at anchor as the tide raised the river under her, making her sweating captain sway on the ratlines lowered from her waist. The movement scarcely delayed Strand, who was far slimmer than he'd been when ship and crew had first been chartered by the USE mission.

Despite—or perhaps because of—the weight loss, he felt better than he had in years, and certainly far better than he had the last time he'd endured the Indian heat. In fact, the entire crew was, as a result of the up-timer's dietary regimen, more fit than any he'd served with.

Feet on the deck of the *Vind* again, Captain Rune Strand smiled.

And now, to go with our good health, great wealth! At long last, we have the firman of trade the up-timers sought for us! He spun the bag hanging from his shoulder around and opened it, drawing the beribboned

14

and medallion-strewn scroll into the light. Of course, the *firman* had also been accompanied by a request from John for two of the special shells the USE Navy had supplied for *Lønesom Vind*'s guns, but he was sure and certain they could be spared.

Eager to share the good news with his oldest companion, he looked aft and up. Loke stood looking downriver, out toward the open ocean.

Assuming the man was staring out toward the sea with the longing all of them felt, he quickly mounted the steps.

Loke didn't turn to face him, leaning hard on the rail. "Captain—"

"Loke, we have it! We have the—" The good news died on his lips as his eyes followed the path of the younger man's gaze.

Three small galleys were rowing, hard, upriver. Even at the distance he could see naked blades and no few bows were in the hands of those not hauling at oars. And they were approaching from the wrong direction to be soldiers of a local *zamindar*'s or even the *mansabdar*'s garrison troopers.

In fact . . . he turned and looked to the distant castle, city, and docks, which were just now reacting to the galleys. Poor sailors at the best of times, the local soldiery would be no help to the ships riding at anchor. Worse still, the crew had just completed a careening of *Vind*, and Strand, in an abundance of caution, had ordered *Lønsom Vind* as far from the castle as he dared. Sailors in the east never knew when the local potentate would decide that taking a European vessel was just the thing to solve a treasury problem, and being under the castle's guns made him twitchy.

"Pirates, in Surat?" Loke asked, his wave taking in the other ships just upriver and in the deepest part of the channel, including the vast bulk of the junk owned by Jahanara Begum Sahib for the use of pilgrims en route to Mecca. "Won't the emperor come down on them like the wrath of God?"

"With what navy? And, besides"—Strand gestured with the scroll—"we've had news from inland: the emperor is dead."

Loke nodded toward the approaching galleys. "They heard before we did?"

"Seems so." He considered shouting for his men to man the guns, but didn't want to precipitate an attack on his ship if the pirates had another in mind.

"Timed their approach to ride the tidal bore," Loke said.

"Eases the current they must fight and gives them an onshore wind," Strand agreed.

The galleys altered course, settling into a staggered line on a direct course for *Lønsom Vind*.

"*Fordømt!*" he cursed. *Just when things were looking up.*

Loke made better use of his tongue, cupping his hands and bellowing, "Pirates! All hands to arms! Light your cords!"

Lønesom Vind erupted in shouts and the pounding of feet and, within moments, the stink of match cords from the leader of each gun team.

Strand spent the next few heartbeats estimating time, distance, and numbers. Disgusted, he shook his head and spat over the rail. "Axes, Loke. Cut the anchor line."

"But—"

The captain cut him off. "You know I hate losing such an expensive piece of kit as much as the next ship's master, but we'll get perhaps one good broadside as she turns with the current, more than we would if we tried to bring it in." He left unsaid that anchors could be replaced far more readily than lives and, while she didn't have a great many, the cannon of the *Lønsom Vind* could very well even the odds, especially if the loads acquired just before they left Hamburg worked as well as the USE Navy man claimed.

If.

Loke nodded, relayed the orders.

Axes started falling as Strand bellowed to the waist of the ship: "Special load!"

"Special load, aye!"

One man of each gun team retrieved a heavy wooden cylinder and shoved it home atop the powder bag already packed in.

"Loaded-ed-ed." The shouts of each gun's team leader made a stammer as each gun was rolled into battery.

"Damn them," Strand muttered, watching the shadow of the mast as the ship started to swing. "Men aloft. We'll need some sail for after."

"Yes, Captain!" Loke again relayed his orders. "They make a brave show, eh?" he asked, watching the pirates again.

"That they do..." He calculated distances and angles, drew a deep breath, and called, "Make ready! Two guns to a boat, aye?"

"Aye!" the gun captains shouted among themselves, designating their targets.

The crews quivered, as prepared as could be expected.

"Think the Navy man was exaggerating?" Loke asked.

Strand shrugged. "That's why I'm going to let them get closer than he claimed necessary."

The lead galley had a small piece affixed across the bow. It boomed, belching off-white smoke and sending its shot skipping across the water to drown a few paces short of the *Lønesom Vind*.

Loke sighed, answered the look his captain shot him with: "I'd hoped they might try and parley."

The other two galleys turned slightly, angling to maximize the volleys from the mass of bowmen they carried along the raised walkway running the length of the little ships.

Arrows began arcing toward the USE ship.

"That's not a good sign."

Strand nodded and, judging the time right, bellowed, "Fire!"

The starboard side of his ship erupted in a series of horrendous bangs followed by a peculiar sound he'd never heard before, something like the world's largest, angriest nest of wasps flying very fast away from him.

The gun captains started their men on the reloading process as the smoke cleared.

Strand didn't think a second volley would be necessary.

All three boats were drifting, decks awash in blood and less identifiable remains of men, oars stilled and sails shredded.

He'd once been on the dock when a ship's magazine exploded at anchor, sending slivers of timber hundreds of paces through the air with man-killing force. A lighter had been approaching the vessel when it went off, and every man aboard it had been screaming for mercy.

Lønesom Vind's guns had each discharged a mass of lead balls with similar—and far better-directed—force to that explosion. The result was carnage so great, so total, the sharks that cruised upriver would struggle to find a morsel large enough to fight over.

The sound of Loke throwing up was loud in the silence that followed.

"Dear God," Strand breathed.

Men, like rats, often survive even the most devastating of blows.

So it was with the pirates: a few screams at first, then some slight movement from the galleys, men grasping oars or lost limbs, lathered in the blood of their companions.

The local mansabdar sent a small galley out to check on *Lønesom Vind* some hours after the—Strand dared not call it a skirmish, but couldn't bring himself to call it a massacre, either—and had finally settled on—volley. Strand didn't begrudge them the time: finding a translator was a time-consuming problem, especially since the English had their firman revoked and been forcibly evicted. In the end they used a local to translate Gujarati to Dutch, which Strand spoke passably well, even if he'd been told by his wife his accent was horribly thick.

He was surprised to see the expensive robe the leader of the delegation wore, and even more surprised as the man was introduced as mansabdar of the local imperial forces; so surprised it required him a few moments to catch up to the conversation and ask, "Beg pardon?"

"Who were these men that attacked you?" the

translator repeated as his client eyed the *Lønesom Vind*'s guns.

"Abyssinians, from their look," Strand said, shrugging. The distances involved made that unlikely, but he didn't know enough about the region's coastal communities to say otherwise.

"You took no prisoners?"

"We tried, but several jumped overboard, fearing we would fire on them again. The sharks..." He blinked to quell the memory, swallowed before continuing, "Well, the sharks had them before we could attempt a rescue. Their wounded did not survive the wait."

The mansabdar nodded, said something Strand didn't quite catch and the translator didn't deign to illuminate.

Biting back impatience, Strand asked, "What's that?"

"Swalley Hole. The English used it. Not best place, but enough to shelter one, two deep ships while waiting for firman. Mansabdar just had word from news writer: Now the English gone, pirates come. Try and take goods."

"What of the Portos?" The Portuguese had nearly a hundred years of history in these waters, and had long since established a system of extorting pilgrims and traders heading to Mecca. Sometimes they even did what they were paid to do, and protected shipping. Certainly they were an ever-present threat to everyone.

A waggle of the head that could mean anything. "Many ships at Goa, not so many north. Especially without monsoon wind to carry trade."

Strand pointedly looked to the shore and the many light galleys of the mansabdar's fleet drawn up along it and asked, "So, what will be done to ensure our safety?"

The mansabdar grinned, pointed at *Lønesom Vind*'s cannon, and said something to the effect of: "What, you're worried, even with those?"

Strand held up the copy of the firman. "Trade is made more difficult aboard ship, and this is the emperor's surety of our safety."

The man sobered, cocked his head, and said something lengthy and complicated. The translator, however, said flatly, "Which one?"

The captain resisted the urge to grab the translator by his robe and throw him overboard, but only just.

The translator must have realized how angry he'd made the big Dane because he quickly added, "Truly, all is in doubt. All *mansabs* must be"—he visibly groped for the proper word before finding it—"confirmed . . . by new emperor. Each recipient must declare their support for their preferred claimant."

Strand's brows knitted together, trying to piece together what that meant and hoping it didn't mean what it seemed to.

The noble went and said something more, grin reappearing in his beard.

Eyeing Strand warily, the translator dutifully said, "Do not fear, all things according to His will, in His time."

Damn, it does *mean what I thought.*

"This is not good," Loke said as they watched the galley head ashore.

"No, it is not," Strand said. "The fellow did say we could likely get away with trading on the firman we have, so long as we get it confirmed as soon as possible."

"But, isn't there going to be a war for the throne?"

"I assume so."

"So why was that man grinning?"

Strand shrugged. "What mercenary isn't happy at the prospect of a new contract?"

"But I thought mansabdar was a noble title? Such glee hardly seems fitting."

"I thought so, as well. But then so is a zamindar, and I have yet to speak to one of those . . ." He knuckled the rail in frustration. "I am not sure how they define such things, but suffice to say it must be very different to what we are used to."

"And what if the war comes here before the Mission returns?" Loke asked.

"It doesn't bear thinking on. Without a cargo . . ."

"We've been at anchor too long. The men are already about to lose their minds."

"That is so." He sighed. "No use borrowing trouble that has yet to come home to roost."

Chapter 3

Goa
Portuguese enclave on the west coast of India
Palace of the viceroy

"I've had disturbing reports from the local traders, Viceroy Linhares," Francisco Tinoco De Carvalho said, waving his glass of madeira toward the port. "Pirates all along the coast have grown bolder in the last few weeks, striking at places they never dared before."

"A direct result of the English being ejected from Surat, I'll warrant," another merchant said. "That, and the succession war everyone knows is about to break out."

The Conde Linhares, Viceroy of the Estado da India, nodded but kept silent. He'd heard it all already, of course, often from the lips of small traders themselves. But, aside from simply placating De Carvalho by hosting this feast for the baptism of the merchant's nephew, Linhares had hoped for fresh intelligence from those merchants and nobles in attendance. As De Carvalho was the head of the *Nuovo Cristao* merchant families in Goa, he had sources Linhares lacked, so it was best to pay heed to what the man said.

"You speak as if the Mughals controlled the sea-lanes in the first place," De Carvalho rumbled.

"Everyone knows that war breeds lawlessness like fleas on a mongrel dog!" the merchant, whose name escaped the viceroy, expounded as a slave topped De Carvalho's glass off.

"Everyone does know that," De Carvalho said, looking decidedly bored. "However, news of actual fighting has yet to reach us, and the princes were quite distant from one another at last report, so saying the pirates are already reacting to the news is a bit premature, I think . . ." He drank from his glass, pursed his lips and continued: "That said, I do suppose pirates will find it easier to get rid of stolen goods without Shah Jahan threatening every petty sultan with dire consequences should they interfere with his trade concessions."

"Exactly my p—!"

As their conversation seemed destined to provide no fresh intelligence, Linhares interrupted the merchant. "As to the increase in piracy: I have already sent out orders for each captaincy to set a schedule of patrols." Not that such orders would do much good, given that resources were perpetually thin on the ground—and even more so at sea—in the Estado da India.

"Father Cristovao De Jesus," Ambrosio whispered from the viceroy's elbow.

"Begging your pardon," De Carvalho asked, not to be put off by the whisperings of a servant in the viceroy's ear, "but does the crown have an official position on who among the Mughal princelings we will back?"

"For that, I have begun certain arrangements. As yet,

nothing is set in stone, however," Linhares said, eyes on the Franciscan father as the latter was introduced to the proud parents of the fresh-baptized child.

De Jesus was a slight man with the sloped shoulders and perpetual squint of the scholar, but Linhares knew him for an active fellow, having been hard at work in the church's efforts to convert the Muslims and Hindus of Goa almost as soon as he arrived. The delay had only been occasioned by one of the inevitable illnesses everyone suffered on arriving here. The churchman had also shown a gift for languages, evidently having picked up enough Konkani in his years in the back country to write the first Portuguese and Latin grammars.

De Carvalho turned slightly, following the viceroy's gaze.

Linhares did not miss the souring of his expression.

"You do not like our Franciscan friend?" he asked, quietly.

"I do not know enough of him to like or dislike him, but I think the Estado has enough churchmen. What we need are soldiers and sailors ready to defend the king's property and loyal subjects. I would even go so far as to think we could use more settlers, even with the problems they inevitably cause."

At least he's not a Jesuit.

"One can only make do with what tools God places at one's disposal," Linhares said, casting a significant look at the Franciscan.

"True, Your Excellency," De Carvalho said, looking from the priest to Linhares. "We will leave you to it, then." Taking his oblivious friend by the arm, De Carvalho moved off to circulate among the other guests.

The moment they had some privacy Ambrosio said,

"The Englishman is installed in your study, Your Excellency. He and His Excellency the archbishop were engaged in conversation when I left."

"Good. Inform His Excellency I will be up presently." Seeing De Jesus free, he started toward the priest.

"A toast to our host!" one of the celebrants called. His companions all raised glasses, turning to the viceroy.

Linhares nodded and added the appropriate returns to God and King before the toast was drunk, hoping they would leave it at that. Of course, some of the more reckless or drunk in the group moved in his direction, eager to be seen with the most powerful man in Goa.

The viceroy needn't have worried, for De Carvalho intercepted them before they could occupy any more of his time. He was able to give his full attention to the priest as he approached, assessing him in light of the plans he'd laid.

"Your Excellency," De Jesus said, bowing from the waist.

"Father De Jesus," Linhares returned. "Might you have a moment to attend me?"

If the fact the viceroy knew his name without an introduction surprised him, the priest covered with better skill than most, bowing again. "I am at your service, Your Excellency."

"Good. Follow."

As being a good host was not without its requirements, Linhares spent a few moments informing the younger De Carvalho that he would be returning momentarily. The process allowed him to see how the presence of De Jesus was received by his supporters and those of his opponents who were present. Some of the laymen eyed the priest with calculation, only a few with concern. Most of those were from the *Nuovo Cristao* families under Linhares' protection.

Those few Jesuits welcome at the palace bristled, of course.

Father Vittorio di Roma, the Dominican who had performed the baptism, was more genial, even greeting him personally. But then, Father Vittorio was always at great pains to appear a friendly sort, especially as the current archbishop of Goa was a Franciscan. Never mind that he was a principal judge of the Office of Inquisition in Goa and, in that capacity, frequently ordered the burnings of Konkans for returning to their gentile ways, not to mention his repeated—and secret, or so he thought—petitions to Archbishop dos Martires for the right to examine the De Carvalhos and the other *Nuovo Cristao* families for heresy.

Making the last of his excuses, Linhares filed away his observations for future review and took his leave of the crowd. He took the stair to his study two at a time, De Jesus scrambling to keep up.

A slave opened the door ahead of him, revealing the large, airy chamber the viceroy conducted much of his business from. Two men were already present, one sitting, the other standing at the sideboard, ridiculously tall lace ruff at his neck identifying him as English even if Linhares hadn't already known the fellow's nationality. His Majesty Philip IV had wisely outlawed such wasteful ostentation even before Linhares had left home more than a decade ago, but the English were a backward people in many ways.

On seeing the other man, Father De Jesus stopped at the entrance and was nearly clipped at the heel by the closing of the door behind him.

"Good evening, Your Excellency," Linhares said, thin smile creasing his lips at the younger priest's reaction. Everyone knew the archbishop was on a tour of the churches of the Estado, so it must be a shock for the father to find Archbishop Francisco dos Martires seated in the office of the viceroy, sipping from a glass.

"Greetings, President Methwold."

"Thank you for receiving me, Your Excellency," the English East India Company man said in passable Castilian, bowing low.

Ignoring both the Englishman and Linhares, Father De Jesus bent to kiss the archbishop's ring, receiving a benediction in return.

"Can we, perhaps, agree to set aside the social requirements of our individual styles for this meeting?" the archbishop said, smiling over the crown of his subordinate's bent head. "We'll be all night sorting out who is addressing whom, what with all the required 'Your Excellencies.'"

Everyone but Father De Jesus readily agreed and Linhares took the priest's delayed response as a result of either his movement to stand behind the archbishop's chair or simply being intimidated at the presence of his betters.

Impatient to get the preliminaries out of the way, Linhares addressed President Methwold in Castilian: "I trust you have been keeping well, Mr. Methwold?"

"Yes, Lord Linhares, I have been. Please accept my thanks on behalf of the Company for your hospitality and the generous favors you have rendered the Company's employees since we were so violently ejected from the Mughals' lands."

"You are most welcome. Indeed, it is on account of that favor that I asked you here tonight."

Methwold's expression didn't so much change as

harden, the lines of his face growing deeper as he looked from the priests to his host.

Linhares recognized the look immediately: Methwold was a fierce negotiator. Not two years past the two had sat across from one another and settled a peace between the Estado and the Company to better deal with the increased threat the Dutch posed to the trade of all nations in the waters of the East. That it had hardly made a difference in the face of Dutch depredations was neither here nor there; each knew the other for an honorable man.

"As and if the requirements of the Company allow it, you can be certain I will make good on those favors," the man said after an instance's quiet consideration.

"Good, good. I do not believe what I have to ask of you will conflict with the desires of the Company's investors. Quite the opposite, in fact."

The archbishop cleared his throat while Methwold thought that statement over. "For my part, I have a favor to ask of my young brother, here."

De Jesus came round the chair and knelt before the archbishop again.

"I would ask you to lead a diplomatic mission on behalf of Christendom and the crown to meet with the young man we hope will be the next Mughal emperor."

If Methwold had any objections to a Catholic priest representing "Christendom," Linhares couldn't see it. That kind of self-control was one reason the Englishman was here.

"To what purpose is my meeting with this Mohammedan prince, Your Excellency?" the priest asked.

Linhares was a bit taken aback by the direct question. His assessment of De Jesus' character increased in light of it. Not everyone could question authority with such apparent ease.

"To pledge our combined"—the archbishop nodded toward Methwold—"support, and secure the right to open churches and schools for the common people in the territory he commands, once he ascends the throne."

"Your Excellency, honesty makes me doubt I'm the best man for this. I am scarcely competent in Persian, have almost nothing of the courtly manners that such a mission would require..."

An expressionless Methwold looked sidelong at Linhares, who said, "The particular prince we would have you approach is rather ascetic in his religion. He does not hold much with ostentation in religion or philosophy."

"To put it bluntly: he doesn't like Jesuits. Thinks them arrogant and high-handed," the archbishop amplified.

A startled snort escaped William Methwold's control. While it was unlikely the man was unaware of the differences between the Orders and their respective methods of converting the heathen and the gentile, to have such division spoken aloud by a prince of the church in front of an Anglican of any rank was unheard of.

"But my work converting the local gentiles—"

"Commends you to the viceroy, to me, and to God. As does your gift of tongues."

The archbishop allowed a brief silence while his subordinate searched his heart.

"Your Excellency, I can find no reason that is not rooted in pride why I should not accept this mission," De Jesus said, at length.

"Very good, my son."

Linhares turned to Methwold.

"I'm not certain what I can offer on behalf of the Company," Methwold said.

"I propose we offer the prince supplies, free of charge or nearly so. Thanks to the hard work of men like Father De Jesus, the inland regions under our rule are finally producing an excess of foodstuffs."

Methwold cocked his head, making his ridiculous ruff sway. "For our part, I cannot see the Company agreeing to such a plan. The Company has never had much in the way of settled farmland. We've always relied upon trade to feed our crews and factory workers."

"Understood. Consider, then: What if our combined ships could cut off trade to his rivals and then transfer those goods as might be useful to him at limited cost and on agreeable credit terms?"

The archbishop didn't bat an eye at this oblique mention of usury, though Father De Jesus stirred a bit.

William Methwold scratched his chin as he considered. He nodded again, his collar having lost some of its rigidity in the humidity. "What you propose has merit. I do believe I can engage our various employees to this task without waiting for word from the Honorable Merchants at home."

Of course you can! Every one of you piratical bastards have been desperate to strike at the Mughals since the day they kicked you out and ambushed your caravan. The only thing staying your hand was the fear we might betray you to them and leave you without a safe harbor anywhere in India.

"Which prince do you propose to approach?" the president asked, though Linhares figured the Englishman knew precisely who the viceroy had in mind.

"Is that not clear from what has been said?" he asked, wishing to draw the man's thoughts out into the open, to better see if his own conclusions were sound.

"Well," Methwold said after a moment's thought. "Dara doesn't hate ostentation; he revels in theological, metaphysical and courtly display. He also controls the most ready cash and food supplies, as well as their most reliable port in Surat.

"Shah Shuja has a large army in the field, isn't terribly interested in religion beyond mouthing a few pious words at the proper moment, and will likely have a desperate supply situation sooner rather than later...

"Which leaves Aurangzeb, who is in an even worse position than Shuja, being farther into the famine-stricken Deccan. He is something of an ascetic, but he can't be the one you want us to approach, because I know from my own eyes that in addition to his asceticism he's likely the most pious Mohammedan prince the dynasty has produced since their great-great-great-grandsires converted in the first place."

"Everything you say is true. I have one or two pieces of intelligence you might wish to add, however:

"First, Aurangzeb, at last report, approaches Chorla Ghat where it debauches on the Deccan, and therefore will soon be in a position to receive our aid.

"Second, and perhaps of more importance: I have obtained evidence that Aurangzeb has inherited his great-grandfather Akbar's practical streak," Linhares said. "For I have received a message directly from him in which he asks us to send him a churchman and diplomat. Someone to speak to regarding arranging things to our mutual benefit."

Methwold looked from him to Archbishop dos

Martires. "Forgive me for saying so, Your Excellencies, but it seems to me that Father De Jesus may have been correct, that a Jesuit seems called for—what with all the diplomatic pitfalls that present themselves."

De Jesus looked on the verge of saying something, but the archbishop replied quite calmly before he could do more than look at the Englishman: "Prince Aurangzeb, from all that we hear, makes display of his humility. Aurangzeb does not encourage theological debates between heathen, gentile, and Mohammedan as his eldest brother does, and as his father and grandfather were known to do. He does not seek contradiction in his life. We will not send this prince, who makes prayer hats in his spare time, a priest who would challenge his way of thinking. Instead we will send him a man of God who is humble before both God *and* man. One who is educated, to be sure, but uses that education for the good of the common people, not to lord it over them. Someone who, when they offer guarantees that the pilgrims on Haj will not be molested, will be believed."

William Methwold spent a moment digesting the archbishop's words. "I see the value in defeating his expectations, Your Excellency. I withdraw my objection." He turned to De Jesus. "I hope I did not unduly insult you, Father De Jesus."

"With such praise being heaped upon me in result, I can scarce complain of its origin, can I?" the young priest said, a smile playing at the edges of his mouth.

Methwold smiled in return, then cocked his head as if just recalling something. "So, are we to agree to keep our hands off pilgrim shipping, even those ships not under the prince's protection?"

Linhares nodded. "Assuming Aurangzeb makes it a requirement."

"Understood." Methwold nodded, once, sharply, as if deciding on something. "God willing, I shall be ready to travel with the Father within the week."

Linhares smiled even as the churchmen stared in astonishment.

"Don't look at me so, Your Excellency. I have great interest in seeing this played through to our agreed-upon conclusion; the Company's captains do not need a president without portfolio jogging their elbows; and I can teach young De Jesus here my Persian, some of the various gentile tongues, and enough of court politics to avoid being killed, I should think."

Chapter 4

Agra
Mission House

"Begum Sahib, this is most inappropriate!" Smidha said, for the twelfth time.

Jahanara had been keeping count. She had also kept silent, planning... And dreading, slightly, seeing Atisheh once more. That first night after the attack Atisheh had been on the verge of unconsciousness when Jahanara had Mullah Mohan tortured. Even in such a state she had still cautioned the princess, nearly begging her to leave the Jasmine Tower while the deed was done. Jahanara would not be moved, however. This man had orchestrated Father's assassination, and if the torture of such a creature would stain her immortal soul, then Jahanara would gladly suffer it to discover what made such a man think he had the right to kill Shah Jahan, emperor of India.

In the end they had discovered only that Mohan was far stronger than he appeared. He would not admit to working for any of her siblings. He would not admit

35

to being manipulated into attempting the assassination, only that he had desperately wanted Nur dead along with Father. But Nur had fled to Aurangzeb, who had almost certainly been Mullah Mohan's secret patron.

Why flee to Aurangzeb if Mohan had been acting on Aurangzeb's orders? And if Mullah Mohan had been, why had Aurangzeb ordered Father's death in the first place? She could think of no reason for Aurangzeb to command his follower to do such a thing. Even one as sure of himself as Aurangzeb must know he had much to learn before he would be ready to rule. Unless he thought himself as exceptional as Babur?

Jahanara was drawn from her silent questions by a loud sniff from Smidha.

"Need I remind you, Smidha, that 'I am invited to come by their home at any time,'" Jahanara said, knowing that by repeating the up-timers' impertinent invitation, she was nettling her most faithful servant.

"But, unannounced?" Smidha said, scandalized. "You will put them in a very uncomfortable position, Begum Sahib!"

"It's not as if I am sneaking up on them unawares!" Jahanara said, gesturing at the howdah's curtains and the escort beyond them. That escort stretched back toward the gate for nearly a *kos*. Any member of the royal family on an outing always had a proper escort, but a princess must be accompanied by guardians sufficient to protect her virtue and enough servants to see to every need she might possibly have.

She didn't normally think about such things, but in recent weeks she had never felt so alone in the company of her servants and guardians. Perhaps that was a result of her constant contact with the up-timer woman,

Priscilla, and the strange ideas about how a just society worked that seemed to have infected the others from the United States of Europe, but she had felt discontented these last few weeks. It seemed the more power she obtained, the less content she was with the lot that Fate, Father, and God had ordained for her.

The drums in the advance guard changed tempo as one of her servants delivered news of her presence—as if that couldn't be determined by the size of her escort—to whomever was manning the entrance to Mission House. The drums changed tempo almost as soon as they had slowed, signifying that someone knew their business and was allowing them immediate entry. She heard the mounts of the guards at the head of her party set out but Ran Bagha did not move to follow after the expected interval.

She was about to ask Gopal what was going on when she heard him in a whispered argument with someone standing below and beside Ran Bagha.

Old ears must have prevented Smidha from hearing the whispers, because she loudly questioned Gopal's fitness to serve when they did not immediately start to move.

"I beg your pardon, Begum Sahib," the mahout said from his position before the howdah, "but there's no way we can get your howdah through the gate."

The look of recrimination Smidha gave her mistress was so expert that despite brimming with unspoken *I told you so*'s her expression remained entirely bland, even pleasant.

Happy that the afternoon air was relatively cool, Jahanara set about fixing her veil so that she could see for herself what predicament she had thrust upon her servants.

Smidha was far less sanguine and grumbled as she shifted position to help her mistress.

"Begum Sahib, if you'll give us a few moments we will sort this out," Damla said. "We had not anticipated the strange construction of this . . . palace the up-timers have built."

"I can walk, you know," Jahanara said, tempted to open the curtains and see for herself what this gate that so delayed them looked like.

"With respect, none has said otherwise, Begum Sahib. I ask your indulgence as I doubt your slippers would survive the experience. There is a great deal of filth and dung in the street outside the gate to Mission House."

Glad of her veil and that Smidha was behind her, Jahanara scowled.

Damla was being overly familiar but, to be entirely fair, the young guard commander had asked permission to scout the path before they went. Jahanara had refused her, wanting to be spontaneous and surprise the up-timers in their home.

Smidha was being very quiet, which served to annoy Jahanara all the more. Knowing that both activities would prove equally ineffective, she chewed her lower lip instead of barking at her entourage. Then again, barking at her entourage might have been more satisfying, but disgruntled servants rarely served well.

The exceedingly mild afternoon sun managed to slowly warm the howdah as they sat waiting.

Jahanara heard a rapid stream of English she thought might be curses then Damla speaking in a level voice to someone who either spoke very quietly or didn't speak.

Tired of waiting, Jahanara twitched the curtains aside and looked to the head of her entourage. Even at first glance it was plainly obvious Mission House had not been constructed with elephants in mind: the gate that pierced the wall before them was barely sufficient for a mounted horseman, and would never admit an elephant, let alone one surmounted by howdah. To add insult to injury, the gate was only twenty *gaz* or so from her elephant, close enough she could see Damla and another of her servants just beyond the gate speaking to the up-timer giant, Rodney. At least, she assumed it was Rodney, as his head was lost to view beyond the lower edge of the gate.

"Begum Sahib, we were just about to arrange for a litter," one of the new eunuchs promoted to her guard said, trying to be helpful.

"Forget that. Bring me a horse and let's get this farce done with."

Smidha tutted.

Frustration getting the better of her, Jahanara turned on her oldest and most trusted advisor. "One word, Smidha, and I will have you clearing the filth from our path home with your bare hands."

Smidha's answer was to bow her head in complete and perfect submission, which made Jahanara feel a good deal worse. Taking out her temper upon a servant wasn't proper, especially when all the servant had done was offer good counsel. Counsel she'd willfully chosen to ignore. Mother had taught her better.

"Forgive me, Smidha. I am anxious to see Atisheh and did not listen to your wise counsel regarding this visit."

"There is nothing to forgive, Begum Sahib. I felt your impatience, and should have done better to foresee this inconvenience rather than complaining or obstructing your will."

Jahanara reached out and took one of the older woman's hands in hers. "Nonetheless, I ask your forgiveness."

"It is given freely and with a full heart, Begum Sahib."

Wishing Azar, her pulu pony, was in the procession, Jahanara watched as a tall white Marwari was brought up beside the massive Ran Bagha.

Gopal directed the war elephant to kneel as two strong eunuchs stepped forward to assist Jahanara transition from howdah to horse. The well-trained horse stood still despite the unusual method of mounting, the nearness of the strangers, and the bull elephant casting a baleful eye over the entire process. In an almost laughable display, her drummers at the van struck up again as soon as her posterior touched the saddle.

Once again happy for the veil that concealed the flush that reddened her cheeks, Jahanara rode through the small gate of Mission House.

Mission House

Priscilla entered the bedchamber she and Rodney shared at the run. All of Mission House's servants were scrambling to make the place presentable for the princess. A runner had arrived fifteen minutes ago to inform Mission House that Begum Sahib appeared to be on her way.

Rodney and Bertram were downstairs and at least appeared ready to receive their visitor, but organizing both men and the household staff had required the full attention of both Monique and Priscilla, leaving little time to dress and prepare themselves.

"Mon Dieu, mais c'est vraiment la putan de merde!" Monique shouted from across the hall.

"I may have only had high school French, Monique, but I sure as hell understand that!" Priscilla said, trying to put on one of the incredibly expensive silken robes she wore for palace visits without messing it up.

From the muted huffing and puffing from across the hall, Monique was stuffing her own curvy frame into a similar outfit.

"Besides, how the hell was I to know she was actually going to take me up on the invitation?"

"You don't make the invitation at all unless you can be certain you have the means to entertain those you invite!" Monique cried.

"Well, shit," Priscilla said, frustration bordering on panic squeezing a tear from her eyes.

"Oh, Pris, I'm sorry!" Monique said. "It's not your fault. I'm sorry. There should have at least been *some* notice from the palace that she was coming."

The drums stopped.

Priscilla's and Monique's eyes met. Jahanara had entered the courtyard of Mission House.

"To steal a word or two from John, 'Shit! Shit! Shit!'" Monique said.

Glad that Ilsa wasn't here to complain of Monique's language, Priscilla checked her image in the very costly mirror Rodney had bought for her. She decided she looked as good as she could without the elaborate hair and makeup the harem seemed to require.

She heard Monique stepping out into the hall between their rooms.

Priscilla gave a final adjustment to her dress and joined the younger woman in the hallway. Monique looked stunning in a robe of pale blue silk that contrasted beautifully with her dark curls and pale skin.

"You have such lovely hair," she said, reaching a gentle hand to smooth one of Monique's wayward curls back into place.

Monique smiled. "If only it wasn't so unruly." She looked Priscilla over and nodded. "You look lovely."

"Thanks." She took a deep, steadying breath and said, "Shall we?"

"God, yes! Who knows what mess the men will get into without us."

The pair hurried down the stairs and into the central court of the villa. Their timing could not have been better, because Jahanara was just riding through the gate on a tall white horse.

Far too experienced to turn a hair at the unusual situation, Firoz Khan, the administrator in charge of Dara's harem, was already speaking with Rodney and Bertram.

"An informal visit, only. Begum Sahib wished to make this unannounced visit upon her court favorites and the harem guard Atisheh solely to show her favor for them and take them up on their kind invitation."

Rodney cast a relieved glance at Priscilla. "Should we leave the ladies to it, then?"

Firoz Khan paused in consideration, then nodded. "If that is the proper protocol when a visitor comes calling, then surely we can do that."

"Then let's go," Rodney said. He looked at Priscilla and smiled. "If that's okay with you, dear?"

"Of course. Jahanara and her ladies are welcome to stay with us for this visit." Just because her ladies were a troop of battle-hardened warriors, Smidha, and a maid or two didn't signify that West Virginia hospitality would not be equal to the task.

Firoz Khan rattled out several commands and then

followed a relieved Bertram and Rodney into the fountain room, where refreshments had been laid out for their visitors. The Mission House's male staff disappeared within moments of Rodney and Bertram leading Firoz Khan and the other eunuchs behind closed doors.

The female warriors dismounted in unison. One woman, almost as big as Atisheh, dismounted and sauntered over to Jahanara's horse. Taking the bridle in hand she offered her other to the princess, but Jahanara was already sliding out of the saddle to land on slippered feet.

Eyes bright, the princess sauntered to her hosts. Even veiled and covered head to toe, Begum Sahib's grace and poise were much in evidence.

Priscilla and Monique bowed deeply.

"Welcome to Mission House, Begum Sahib," Priscilla said.

The rest of her entourage dismounting behind her, Jahanara reached out with open arms and raised them both up. "Please, I but belatedly realized how much of an imposition this is upon you. I'm afraid I am a spoiled brat to descend on you so without prior notification. I hope I did not upset your men too much?"

"Firoz handled them admirably, Begum Sahib," Monique said. "I do not think Bertram even got a word in edgewise. And Lord knows Bertram likes to talk."

"And Rodney has always been uncomfortable when my friends would come by. Says he feels like a bull in a china shop when surrounded by my girlfriends," Priscilla added, smiling.

"I am much relieved to hear it. I'm afraid I've made everyone uncomfortable with this visit."

"Please, Begum Sahib!" Priscilla said. "We invited

you to drop by anytime, and meant it. We just didn't think about what an unusual invitation would mean for your . . . household."

"And Firoz Khan mentioned something about you wanting to visit with Atisheh?" Monique said.

Jahanara's eyes shone with interest over the veil. "If it is not too much trouble, I would very much like to see her."

"She is supposed to be resting right now . . ." Priscilla gestured at the second floor, uncertain why Atisheh had not appeared in response to all the noise.

"Supposed to be?" Jahanara asked.

Priscilla turned and led the princess and her party along the gallery to the stairs. "She can be stubborn as a mule, Begum Sahib." Priscilla gave a small shake of her head. "Of course, that stubbornness is likely the reason why we're all still alive, so I can't rightly complain."

"She does not want to take the advice of her physicians?" Jahanara said, the faintest edge creeping into her voice.

"Oh, she listens." The big warrior woman fell in behind them as they climbed the stairs. "She just chafes at the enforced inactivity. Not much worse than any active person would be in her place, I suppose, but I've rarely heard so many mutters and grumblings."

"She is a master mutterer," Monique said, grinning. "It helps none of us can understand what she's saying."

"I will be sure to admonish her to cease this muttering," Jahanara said.

"Oh, please don't, Begum Sahib! It's nothing she should be challenged on. Her mood is, frankly, fragile. Which I suppose is entirely understandable given the change in her circumstances."

"Oh?" Jahanara asked as they entered the hall leading to Atisheh's quarters.

"It couldn't have been easy to be plucked out of the harem, where she was certain of her place and power and be put here, away from everything she knows and understands."

"And told she can't even exercise the skills that set her apart from all others until she heals?" Monique shrugged. "Can't be easy."

"I suppose not. Still, she should be polite at the very least."

Priscilla chuckled. "If you only knew what trying to treat a meth head was like."

"A what?" Monique and the princess said at nearly the same time.

"Users of a particular up-time drug. They got on my last nerve. Mostly because they would not shut up. Not. Ever. That, and the fact that every time they opened their mouths they were lying."

Their conversation had brought them to Atisheh's door. Swallowing a sudden fear that Atisheh would be resentful of their intrusion, Priscilla raised a hand and knocked.

"Unless you're bringing me my armor and a blade, you can just turn around and go."

The elephant Jahanara had ridden here chose that moment to bugle a short challenge.

"Um, Atisheh, there's someone here to see you."

One of the mutters Monique had spoken of penetrated the door, closely followed by two other sounds: the noise of someone hurrying to their feet and Jahanara's sharp intake of breath.

Priscilla looked at the princess and saw a tightness around her eyes as Jahanara removed her veil.

"Atisheh, is that how you speak to your physicians?" Jahanara asked, lips a tight line.

Atisheh said something unintelligible but caustic as more fumbling noises reached their ears.

Taking pity on her patient, Priscilla said, "Shall we wait for you downstairs?"

The door popped open at that moment, revealing a disheveled, if dressed, Atisheh.

"Begum Sahib, I beg forgiveness. I did not know it was you."

"Do you often hear the drums announcing an imperial procession here at Mission House?"

Atisheh looked confused as she tried to explain, "I was dreaming, or so I thought."

"You look well, Atisheh."

It was only a slight exaggeration: Atisheh had none of the deathly pallor she'd had in those first days after her wounding, but she did look ready to punch something or someone, hard.

"Do I, Begum Sahib?" Atisheh asked the question of her princess, but directed a very pointed look at Priscilla as she did so.

Jahanara hesitated, probably realizing she had stumbled onto delicate ground. "You seem well on your way to a full recovery, I mean."

"I believe I would already be fully recovered if my jailers"—she nodded at Priscilla—"would allow me to ride, hunt, and practice at arms."

Priscilla shook her head and said, for maybe the twentieth time that week, "If we allowed that, your stitches would have torn and we'd be back at square one, Atisheh. You can't start working out yet. Not until those stitches are out and your wounds won't pop open under strain. Not on my watch. A few weeks more and you can start swinging whatever you want around."

"And still you did not answer my question, Atisheh. Do you speak to your physicians in that manner?"

Priscilla begged Jahanara with a look not to go after the other woman, but the princess was not looking at her, and likely would not have heeded the up-timer if she had.

Atisheh stared at Jahanara's feet and mumbled, "No, Begum Sahib. Or rather, yes, but I shall stop now."

"Indeed you shall, Atisheh. Now, apologize to them."

Opening her mouth to ask Jahanara to knock it off, Priscilla stopped when she saw the effect Jahanara's words had on Atisheh. It was confusing, but Jahanara's harsh words seem to have restored Atisheh's self-image rather than diminish it.

Atisheh had drawn herself up like a soldier at attention. In fact, the woman seemed more herself than at any other time since coming to Mission House.

Priscilla was still trying to digest the change when Jahanara said, "I'm still waiting to hear your apology, Atisheh."

"Forgive me, Doctor Totman," Atisheh said, instantly. "I have been muttering unworthy words in response to your care. I will do better in the future."

"Apology accepted, even if I think it unnecessary," Priscilla said, glancing aside at the princess in hopes she would be satisfied.

Jahanara nodded, once. "If I may have a private word with Atisheh? It will take only a moment."

"Of course, Begum Sahib."

Jahanara stepped into the room.

The door swung closed under the warrior's hand,

but not before they could hear Jahanara hiss, "You call these people goat-fucking pig-milkers in their own home?"

Atisheh's reply was muted, but the meek tone was unmistakable.

Priscilla stifled a giggle by clapping a hand to her lips.

Monique was less careful, and chuckled outright.

Jahanara's gaze slid past the oddly designed furnishings of the bedchamber and fixed on Atisheh as she waited for a response. Faintly, she heard someone chuckle in the hall.

Atisheh, thankfully, did not seem to hear it. The warrior would not look her patron in the eye. "Begum Sahib, please accept my full and abject apologies. I did not consider how poorly my words would reflect upon you. Please forgive my transgressions, I will do better."

Cold anger leaving her in a rush, Jahanara swallowed a lump in her throat as she had her first good look at Atisheh in some weeks. The older woman had a number of bandages swathing her torso, with matching ones on her left arm, right thigh, and right shin. None of them showed any color at all, meaning her stitches were holding and she was not bleeding. Priscilla had assured her that all of Atisheh's wounds were healing properly, but seeing Atisheh's slow movements and the sheer number of bandages on the indomitable warrior was sobering.

"A woman of your position needs to have better control over her tongue. Can I rely on you henceforth?"

Atisheh bowed her head. "Your will, Begum Sahib."

"Even when I am not present?" Jahanara pressed.

"Even so, Begum Sahib. I am your servant. I will not forget again."

"If I am understood, you may open the door and let our hosts in."

"Your will, Begum Sahib."

"On with it, then."

Atisheh opened the door and gestured.

Monique and Priscilla entered the room, the latter glancing warily from her patient to Jahanara.

"Forgive me for giving commands in your home, ladies," Jahanara said. "I want to make sure that Atisheh appreciates the care with which she is being treated. I have need of her once she is fully recovered, and if she has annoyed her physicians to the point where they cannot help her to that full recovery, then she will be of no use to me or my brother."

Atisheh's eyes narrowed, noticing her princess's emphasis on the word *fully*.

"Because I have asked Dara to confer upon you the title of Commander of *Urdubegis*, not just my personal guard."

The big warrior's expression rapidly cycled through suspicion to shock to joy before settling back to suspicion.

Stifling a laugh, Jahanara continued. "As part of fulfilling those duties is the testing of each applicant. I cannot see how you would prevail against the best candidates if you had to guard not only against their attacks, but against reopening your wounds."

"I'm afraid I must admit to some weakness. Perhaps Dara would be better served by one of my sisters?"

Jahanara shook her head vehemently. "There is no question who will best serve in this role. Dara would not have it otherwise. Nor would I. Nor any other who was there in the garden of the Taj Mahal."

Atisheh bowed her head.

Jahanara slowly realized that she had been too harsh for too long, and reached out to take the other woman's hand.

Atisheh, uncomfortable with such intimacy from the princess, went still.

"You are the best woman for this job, and I would have no other responsible for the protection of our family. Please, as you hold your oath to me sacred, heed the advice of your physicians and take care with your recovery so that it is complete and total. We will have need of your strong sword and discerning eye soon, but not so soon that you do not have time to make a full recovery."

Atisheh would not meet her eyes, but nodded.

And because the warrior might need to hear it, Jahanara edged her voice with the tones of command she had so often heard Father use: "I would have your word on it, Atisheh. Promise me you shall do as I command."

The warrior woman stood straight, met her eyes, and said, "Your will, Begum Sahib."

"Yes. My will." Jahanara released Atisheh, patting the broad, scarred knuckles of Atisheh's sword hand with her own finely manicured and hennaed one.

"Besides, I shall expect a full report of what goes on here in Mission House." She gestured at the comfortable chamber that Atisheh had been convalescing in. "Even their architecture is strange, though I do like the mosaic floor in the entryway. And the central garden is not entirely without charm."

"As to their architecture or how they choose to

decorate, I cannot speak intelligently. And, to be frank, their skill at arms—for hand to hand—is pathetic. Their firearms do seem to level the battlefield at any greater distance than melee, however."

"Let us hope that is true. Dara has already commissioned Talawat to furnish a great number of arms patterned after one of the weapons they brought from the future."

Atisheh's expression darkened momentarily at mention of the copies.

"What is it?"

"Your pardon, Begum Sahib, but the use of any weapon requires training. The more complex the weapon or skill, the more training is necessary to become proficient. It is harder to use a bow from horseback than while standing still. I cannot imagine that we have time both for the weapons to be made and the training of those who will wield them."

Jahanara smiled. "And this is why we need you fully healed and back in our service. You, my dear Atisheh, think a great deal more than any man will give you credit for."

Atisheh bowed her head, but Jahanara could see the remark had pleased her.

"If it is just my mind you wish returned to service, I can do it now," Atisheh said slyly.

"Look at you!" Jahanara said, laughing. "Outmaneuvering me in conversation!" She could laugh because she knew Atisheh's honor would not allow her to play such games, not after giving her word on it.

Atisheh gave a small, shy smile. "In truth, Begum Sahib, I have missed your laugh these last weeks. Even as I have missed all those under my protection in the harem. I am eager to return and thank you for visiting me."

Recognizing dismissal when she heard it, Jahanara smiled once more and turned to leave. She caught the barest hint of an approving glance from Priscilla before that woman bowed and turned to follow Jahanara from the room.

Jahanara paused in the narrow hall outside Atisheh's bedchamber. It was very crowded and growing quite warm.

Smidha gestured, indicating which direction they should go. The princess and her entourage descended a set of stairs into a large chamber with high ceilings that opened onto the central courtyard through tall wooden doors. A large, tall table laden with fruit and drink dominated the center of the room. Jahanara approached it, trying to give her followers room to spread out before turning to face Priscilla.

"I must thank you, Priscilla, for all that you've done for my family. My brother and I both know exactly how much is owed to you and the USE's mission. You do your king much honor."

Priscilla bowed deeply. "Begum Sahib, we have been well compensated for all services rendered to the crown. Frankly, it has been our pleasure to help you and your family."

"That is gratifying to hear, Mrs. Totman, especially in light of what I must ask of you now."

Priscilla cocked a brow and gestured for the princess to continue.

"I have been thinking a great deal on your skills, and how they might be best employed to help those soldiers wounded in my brother's service."

Priscilla shrugged. "My husband and I only have so many hours to treat wounded."

Jahanara smiled. "I am not being clear. I would like to employ you and your husband and perhaps Misters Gradinego and Vieuxpont. Not as physicians yourselves, but to train men and women to treat our wounded."

"Oh, like medics?" Priscilla shook her head and clarified: "You mean train people on the battlefield to treat the wounded?"

"Exactly so," Jahanara said, hiding her relief. Most court physicians would have considered the mere suggestion that they train random strangers in their rarefied skills offensive. "We can have some start with a small group— "

"And they will serve to train the next group!" Priscilla said, so excited at the prospect she interrupted the princess.

"Exactly so. I will have to secure funding from my brother as well as supplies, but I think it will be useful, no?"

Priscilla's expressive eyes were wide and her voice excited. "Oh, yes! When I was training to become a paramedic my training officer, a veteran of the Gulf War, was always going on about how the U.S. military did a better job of evacuating its wounded than any other in history, which made for higher morale amongst the soldiers. If you know that your wounded friend is going to be taken care of, you can put some of that fear out of your mind."

"I had not even thought of that aspect of it. I just thought we might help save lives. I shall recall that when I speak to my brother."

"We're going to have to talk to the men about

this too. They likely know a lot more about how the military organized it than I do. At least I hope so."

Jahanara nodded. "Of course. I just wanted to be sure the idea was practical and that you might be able—and willing—to do it."

Priscilla looked thoughtful as Jahanara turned her attention to Monique.

"Monique, would you attend me on my travels back to Red Fort?"

The young Frenchwoman bowed deeply. "It would be my pleasure, Begum Sahib."

Jahanara gestured at the table. "I'm afraid I have stayed too long. My brother needs me and I must attend him. Please forgive my intrusion, and my sudden departure. I will give you better notice next time?" She let the statement become a question to ensure they knew she understood, at last, that the initial invitation had been a polite fiction and that they would be expected to extend a formal one in future so that all parties were properly notified before this visit was repeated.

Priscilla and Monique both bowed and said, at the same time, "Of course you must come again, Begum Sahib!"

Part Two

March, 1636

To help the rolling wheels of this great world
—The Rig Veda

Chapter 5

Aurangzeb's army
The Deccan

"We must move faster," Aurangzeb said, teeth gritty behind dry lips.

"Shehzada, the horses have had no good grazing, the men very little food since we set out. All are tired," Sidi Miftah Habash Khan said.

Aurangzeb looked across at his newest noble. "I share their fatigue and hunger. Tired as I am, there will be time enough to rest when we overtake Shuja's army."

The *Habshi* clan leader waved a hand to encompass the vast column of tired riders. "Forgive me, Shehzada, but may I ask a question?"

Aurangzeb considered denying the chieftain's request, but he had included the man in his immediate company to show his favor for Habash Khan and his followers. Such accommodations had to be made. The *Habshi* were a new and valued addition to his forces as well as close allies of the Maratha chieftains who had come over to him with Shahaji. His treasury was

57

shrinking like a watering hole in the heat of the dry season and when it was completely gone he would have only promises of wealth and position to offer as coin for his troops. That being the case, Aurangzeb counted answering the man's questions a low price to pay, and waved permission.

"As loyal and God-fearing as this host is, will we not be too exhausted to fight, Shehzada?"

"Did I say we would fight?"

"What other reason, this forced march northward, if not to crush all opposition and secure the throne for you, Shehzada?"

"You do not know?"

"No, I do not."

"Good. It stands to reason my brother will wonder as well, and perhaps listen to my message."

"And what message is that, Shehzada?"

"It is for his ears alone."

A flash of white teeth behind the impressive beard.

"You smile?"

"I do, Shehzada."

"Why?"

"Forgive my impertinence, Shehzada, but I think I will enjoy learning if Shah Shuja will allow you close enough to speak your message."

Aurangzeb declined to comment directly, saying instead, "Have you given any thought to why you and the rest of my army continues to address me as Shehzada?"

"I assumed it is because you have yet to win the throne, Shehzada."

The prince waggled his head. "The throne is but a symbol of the wealth and power of the empire, and a minor one at that. The prince who causes prayers to be said at all the mosques under his control and has fresh coins struck in his name has made clear his claim to the empire."

"Yet, you have done neither of these things, Shehzada."

Aurangzeb nodded, watching Habash Khan from under hooded eyes.

"And why not, Shehzada?"

He had attempted to think of all the paths Shah Shuja's reasoning might take his elder brother down, and decided it would do no harm to try the various narratives out on the chieftain. "Perhaps I do not want to be emperor."

Another wave at the army around them. "Your many armed friends would indicate otherwise."

"Shah Shuja will see my arrival as a threat however many messages I may send to the contrary. Of that there can be no doubt."

"Just so, Shehzada."

"Perhaps I would have us return to the old way? Each prince a sultan in their own right, carving the carcass of my forebear's empire into petty sultanates and ignoring the inheritance laws Akbar set down for the dynasty."

Habash Khan's smile dimmed slightly. Petty sultanates and their many, many wars would mean easier pickings for some, but such unrest had already cost the Deccan untold lives and treasure, and was the reason the Mughal armies were in the Deccan in the first place.

"Or perhaps I will hand this army to Shah Shuja so that I might realize my long-held dream and retire to a life of study and contemplation of the Quran."

The deeply religious Habshi's smile disappeared entirely as he intoned, "A life would be well spent in such pursuits."

"Indeed it would."

"But yours will not, I think." The man said it quietly, so quietly his prince could ignore it if he wished.

He chose not to: "Let us hope that my brother does not see through me as easily as you."

"I am summoned?"

"Yes, mistress," Tara said.

"Quickly, then: my best robe," Nur said, getting to her feet. She swayed slightly, exhaustion weighing on her like a millstone. It was a well-earned exhaustion: she'd spent the better part of the last two months in motion. Not since the last days of Shah Jahan's rebellion had she been forced to ride so hard or so often. Pride kept her standing as much as the rest she'd snatched at every opportunity.

She mastered herself while the few servants she could afford busied themselves with her commands—showing fatigue was one thing, but showing concern and worry would be entirely unacceptable.

Within moments she was presenting herself before her grand-nephew.

Aurangzeb was as alone as any prince could be, his personal guards the only ones in earshot. He waved her forward with one hand, the other holding a sheaf of dispatches.

"You requested I attend you, Shehzada?"

"I did. Sit."

She did as he commanded.

He continued reading, ignoring her, the slave who

lit the lanterns nearly an hour later, and those others who entered bearing platters of food.

Nur did not take it personally, his ignoring her. Though she would have wished for more rest before being summoned to the stifling warmth and quiet stillness of the tent, decades of power had given her an abiding appreciation for the techniques, trappings, and challenges of its employment. If he was making her wait to render her off-balance and unsure, that boded well. And if he was instead applying his thought to thorny problems of state, so much the better. And finally: if he was doing both these things at once, then she had every confidence that the prince she had chosen to back would defeat his siblings and rise to be the greatest Mughal ruler since Akbar.

"What do you think of the Portuguese?" He asked the question quietly.

"In what context, Shehzada?" she asked immediately, glad she had not given in to fatigue and dozed off.

He held up a news writer's slip. "Their viceroy wished to convey to me his hopes that I prevail over my enemies."

She smiled. "You can be sure he sends such messages to each of your brothers."

He looked at her, expression unreadable. Such a youth should not be so proficient at hiding his thoughts. "Can I?"

"He does well to remember what happened at Hugli when your father took his vengeance for their refusing to aid him against my husband." Something about his attitude gave pause. "Though your question makes me believe I am not in possession of all the pertinent facts."

The faintest hint of a smile cracked his masklike expression. "What would you deem significant enough an event to make the viceroy of Goa sing solely for me?"

Put off by his reference to music, she hesitated. Aurangzeb's opinions on song and dance as unseemly and improper were well known, even to those who—unlike her—had not been responsible for his early education. "I merely hazard a guess at your command, but perhaps we are closest to the lands and people under his care and such proximity makes him fear you will decide Goa would serve as a base of operations?"

He cocked his head. "Setting aside the stupidity of marching farther from the sources of men and horses that make up the backbone of any army in the empire, fear is not outside the realm of possible reasons he would have to treat with me alone. Right below significant bribes."

Knowing how much silver he had been required to put in play to attract the allies that made his speedy victory in the Deccan possible, Nur knew that his treasury was much depleted, despite taking several small treasuries of the petty sultans and chieftains on the campaign south. There were only so many men Aurangzeb could finance out of his personal establishment, especially without additional fresh infusions of cash from the imperial treasuries at Agra, Surat, and Lahore, all of which were out of reach and under Dara's control.

That was another of the pressing logistical concerns underpinning their rush northward: Aurangzeb and the men of the army he'd marched south with were remunerated by *jagirs*—proceeds from land grants—in the north and east of the country. Jagirs allotted by Shah Jahan, and with the pretender Dara Shikoh sitting astride the imperial administration, any claims to those jagirs not already assigned were unlikely to be heeded until a clear victor emerged. All the brothers could issue new ones, but Shuja and Aurangzeb were not in possession of the paperwork, much less the coin, to make good on them.

"I might have suggested bribes, Shehzada, but did not think the *ferenghi's* power worth such notice this far inland."

"No, aside from their gunnery expertise, which is easily purchased without his approval, the viceroy has no significant military power inland."

"Then...perhaps he has some inkling of the histories that came to your father's notice?"

"Likely. He has a number of Jesuits in his company, and they carry news"—he hefted the papers in his hand—"for their pope."

"And so the viceroy makes certain the prince he has been told will win the war is content with his ferenghi neighbors," she said.

He nodded in seeming agreement, returning his attention to the many reports and messages spread before him.

Nur did not fully believe it: their conversation had the air of someone not so much exploring a thought but more of presenting facts already evident. She puzzled over it for a moment but made no headway. Her resources—mental and physical—were well and truly depleted.

"Have you eaten?"

"No, Shehzada."

"Please do. I will have more questions for you once I have finished reading."

"As you wish, Shehzada."

Nur ate sparingly, but as much as she could stomach, knowing she had to keep her strength. The camp around them slowly grew quieter as the men bedded down for the night.

Easing a cramp in her leg, she sighed.

He turned his head to regard her. "You are in some discomfort?"

"I find I am old for the rigors facing us," Nur said, instantly regretting it. *Do not provide truths to your enemies they might use to cut you, fool.*

He put one paper down and unfolded another without looking at it. "Why, then?"

"Whatever do you mean, Shehzada?" she asked, suddenly *very* alert.

"Why do you ride with me? You know I would see you well provided for should you decide to stay behind."

So you—and history—can conveniently forget me?
Not.
This.
Woman.

She smiled, hiding her anger. "What prompts the question now?"

"An idle question, but one I would have you answer." He looked at the paper in his hands, but his eyes did not move as they do when one is reading.

"I bear some small conceit that I might prove of assistance to you, much as your great-grandsire Akbar's aunts worked on his behalf."

Aurangzeb grinned, looked up at her. "I see. Should I expect you to find me a wife, then?"

"Not until you proclaim yourself emperor."

The smile disappeared as quickly as a snuffed-out candle. "I have made no claim to the throne."

"And you have been wise to avoid doing so, She-hzada. Not while Shah Shuja can destroy your army simply by stopping your supplies."

It was Aurangzeb's turn to sigh. "He need not even stop all of them reaching us, just a fraction."

"So again: I see the wisdom in your decision, just as I know you cannot persist in that position."

He refused to answer the implicit question, said instead: "Two weeks from now both our armies will be out of supply. Dara has already shut them off at the source."

Allowing him to deflect her question was easy; given the importance of the subject he offered instead: "Is Shah Shuja aware of that?"

"I assume nothing, but my brother's rate of advance—or, retreat, I suppose—from the Deccan is too slow to get out of the drought-afflicted area before he starts losing men and horses." He retrieved a chalice from the tray and drank, as if speaking of the drought made him thirsty.

"And even should he decide to give battle, such a fight would cost the victor too many men."

Nur nodded. "Your men wonder, Shehzada, what you will do when you meet with Shah Shuja."

He smiled. "My *men*?"

Sensing a trap, she proceeded carefully. "Yes, my servants say there is much wonder and consternation among the men."

"But *you* do not experience this consternation?"

She cocked her head and said, "You will do what you must, Shehzada."

"And what is it you think I must do, Nur Jahan?"

"Dissemble."

It was his turn to regard her sidelong. "All the world knows I am no good at that. Too devout, they say. Too rigid, they say."

I can almost hear Gargi's urgent whisper: "Careful, old girl, he has many spies, and he listens to them."

Nur leaned forward. "That you have made others believe such is why you will rise to rule them all, Shehzada."

Aurangzeb met her gaze with eyes steady, still, and dark as the deepest tank. "You will carry my words to Shah Shuja and negotiate our first meeting."

Nur bowed her head. "You honor me, Shehzada."

"You may now go and find your rest. I will have specific instructions and letters for you tomorrow."

It was only later, as she woke from a few hours of restless sleep, that she realized how thoroughly he'd made certain he would not have to answer her question.

Chapter 6

Agra
Mission House

It was around midnight when Priscilla was drawn from sleep by a noise. She lay there, listening carefully. Mission House, which she'd only moved into last week, still wasn't really *home*, so she had yet to have a catalog of the night sounds like she had back in Grantville.

There. A dull metallic ringing from the courtyard.

Gervais had designed the Mission like an old Italian villa; the second-floor chambers of the main building opening onto a balcony overlooking a central court of gardens and fountains.

Bobby has guard duty tonight. Poor guy looked tired when I went to bed. The boys have been stretched thin working security, but finding reliable guards who aren't scandalized by how we dress and act—even on our own property—ain't easy.

Suddenly fearful, Pris pulled the .38 from under her pallet and slipped from her bed. Taking a moment to don a silk robe that five years ago she wouldn't have dreamt of wearing, much less being able to afford, she padded across the cold tiles to a set of louvered doors.

Suppressing a shiver as the cool air seeping through the louvers bit through the robe, Priscilla reached for the latch. She could see someone had lit a lamp in the courtyard. The noise from below had settled into a rhythm, just not one she could identify.

She eased the latch up and stepped out into the night. Still unable to see the source of the sound, she approached the balustrade and looked down.

Priscilla relaxed, recognizing the figure in the lamplight below. A tall, broad-shouldered woman, Atisheh was hard to mistake for anyone else at Mission House. Better still, Atisheh's outstretched arms finally provided an explanation for the strange noise that had awakened Priscilla.

Atisheh had a number of horseshoes over each arm. The noise was a result of her holding those horseshoe-laden arms out to either side at shoulder height and then dropping into a squat.

The swordswoman stood straight with a hiss of effort, then repeated the entire process, vigorously.

"You sure you're up to that?"

The former harem guard and current patient of Priscilla's twitched in surprise, found the up-timer in the shadows above, and said, "Up? I not understand."

"I don't think you should be doing such heavy work."

Atisheh had been restive the last month, growling at her caregivers with an increasing impatience, volume, and grasp of English. The fact she'd been as near death as anyone Priscilla had ever seen—sword-cut in half a dozen places, battered so thoroughly she'd have been a single bruise from head to toe had she the blood to discolor flesh just a few months prior—made no difference to the woman.

Just as Priscilla's current qualms didn't stop Atisheh now.

"What time now?" She squatted low with her arms still out, breathed in, and stood again on the exhale.

"I don't know, after midnight?"

"Exact."

"What does that mean?"

Atisheh rotated her arms around and up, the shoes clanking, and raised her hands, then each individual finger until seven stood between them.

"Seven, what?"

"One week, you tell me. One week I start work. Seven days. I start soon I can and still follow orders you give."

Pris crossed arms over her chest. "Jesus."

"Why speak of minor prophet now? You miss prayers?"

Pris didn't even try to answer that question. "You are a machine."

"Machine?" Atisheh grunted, slowly lowering the weights, corded muscles standing out in her neck and shoulders, fresh scars angry in the lamplight.

"Never mind. I'm going back to bed."

"Good"—another lengthy hiss—"night."

Rodney returned late the next morning. Priscilla made a point of meeting him in the courtyard dressed in her favorite jeans and one of his old work shirts.

Ricky slid the bolt home on the reinforced gate as Rodney rode up to the stables. His fine robes and the sword in its jeweled sheath at his hip made him look every inch a prosperous warrior-noble of the Mughal court. Until you got close, saw how *big* he was, and how poorly he sat a horse. The nobles of the Mughal court rode like they were born in the saddle.

Her husband lifted his head to see her striding toward him and sent a tired but appreciative smile her way.

"Five nights in a row, now," Priscilla said, taking the horse's bridle in hand.

"He's in a lot of pain," Rodney said by way of excuse, dismounting and giving her forehead a kiss.

Her sigh tickled the nose of Rodney's horse, making the gelding toss his head. She patted its neck and said, "I don't dispute that."

"But?" he asked as she led his mount into the stable.

"Hard to say where the pain of his injury ends and the pain of loss begins."

"Sounds like a question for a priest, not a couple of certification-lapsed paramedics in way over their heads."

"I suppose it is, but I think we should watch him close to make sure he doesn't begin self-medicating," Pris said as she set about removing the horse's tack. The locals put much store in decorating every bit of riding gear with complex knots, braids, and what she could only call pom-poms. He could leave for Red Fort with a plain saddle and harness, but by the time he took his leave of the imperial stables, his horse and tack were always decorated to the ninth degree. The tack tended to bewilder a tired mind and his bigger fingers, so she handled it while Rodney removed the saddle.

"Gervais and I are doing what we can."

Knowing he was doing just that, she left off working at the tack to smile at him. On seeing his expression, she hugged him.

"You're still on cloud nine, aren't you?" he asked.

Priscilla released him and raised her arms, spinning in a circle. "God, yes! And who wouldn't be? There's a reason they call those in a harem 'inmates,' after all. A gilded cage is still a cage."

"Too true."

Pris caught him glancing at the high walls of the compound. "I know we're still behind walls, but just being able to wear what I want while I get some work done is huge. *Huge.*"

Rodney nodded.

"Speaking of working: How is Atisheh?"

She smiled. "Last I saw her she was beating the snot out of some eunuch trying out for a spot on Dara's harem guard. The woman's constitution is amazing. Barely a month out of our care and she's riding and fighting like she was never hurt."

Rodney's chuckle ended in a yawn. "Sorry. I don't think I will be good company for long." He yawned again, hugely this time, his jaw popping. "I'm dead tired."

She pulled him closer—really just pressed herself tighter to his muscular side, as she was far too small to move him—and said, "I'll just tuck you in, then."

He laughed, eyes shining despite fatigue.

"What's tickled you?"

"Just reflecting on the fact that some days it's real good to be a hillbilly named Rodney Totman."

"Monique." Bertram said her name with the slightest of smiles as he walked into the Mission's council chamber.

"Bertram," she replied. Gervais being present, she

kept her own, answering smile, locked away. Papa had always been strange about the men she favored, but Bertram was . . . special to her and, she suspected, to Gervais as well. Of course, her father would never admit such a thing publicly.

"Bertram, come here," Papa said, waving the younger man to join him. Gervais stood at a table strewn with papers and maps that dominated the center of the chamber.

"Of course, Gervais."

"Papa, Bertram may need a drink, or perhaps something to eat, before we figure out—in one evening—how to defeat the pretenders."

Gervais gave her a long look. "My lovely daughter: always encouraging her father to ever-greater accomplishments."

Bertram tried to head off their banter before it made a darker turn. "Perhaps later, Monique?"

She favored him with a smile and let it go. "As you wish."

"Right, now we've established you aren't hungry or thirsty, what news?"

Bertram leaned on the table with both hands, examining one of the maps Gervais had commissioned. "Dara has ordered the Banjaris to stop transport of all supplies to the armies of his brothers."

"Finally," Monique said. She'd been present when Jahanara had begged him to do just that—nearly a month ago.

Both men looked at her, but it was Papa who spoke: "A new monarch needs to avoid giving orders that will not be obeyed. Just because an order is given does not mean it will be followed."

"If they want to be paid, Dara holds the purse strings."

"Dara has access to the largest treasury, not all of it. His brothers have incomes and war chests of their own, saved against this very moment. Not only that, they have experienced and loyal courts full of warriors ready to fight for them."

When she didn't seem moved by those arguments, Gervais went on. "Besides, a great number of the Banjaris are strung out between here and Dara's brothers. What happens to them, and those actually in camp with Aurangzeb or Shuja, when the supplies stop?"

"Historically, the dynasty has proven very lenient toward those serving a princely master who subsequently loses, especially when those people really only declared for the losing prince because they had no choice, being in their power."

"But—"

She cut Gervais off. "This is not any of the courts of Europe, Papa. Princes here are *expected* to vie for control even before the succession comes to question, and so long as no one outside the dynasty tries to take power for themselves, changes of allegiance are seen as acceptable, even expected. It is yet another advantage Dara has—if he'll just *use* it! His treasury is massive, and neither of his brothers have anything comparable to the fortune at his fingertips. He also has all the imperial bureaucrats standing by, ready to do his bidding . . ."

Bertram cleared his throat. "Not all, Monique. Some have left the city. He has had the *khutba* said in his name, but only just ordered coins minted in his name, and was slow to confirm or remove the people in high positions under Shah Jahan. In the uncertainty, some left for greener pastures they imagine they'll find with either Shuja or Aurangzeb."

Papa crossed his arms across his chest and cast a knowing look at her, a good sign he was struggling to find some way to refute her points.

Bertram was looking at her with clear admiration. "I take it Jahanara is an excellent instructor on court politics?"

She nodded, smiling. "And I, an excellent student."

"Without question."

Despite herself, Monique blushed.

"Stop that, you two," Gervais said, glowering.

"Stop what?" they asked, in near unison.

Papa threw up his hands. "Just get it over with!"

"Get *what* over with?" she asked.

Gervais directed his words at Bertram, though: "You clearly wish to court my daughter."

"*Papa!*" she cried, so loudly she nearly missed Bertram's far quieter response.

"I do."

"You do?"

Bertram nodded, emphatic.

"Of course he does, girl! And now that I formally accept his designs on you, we can all get on with business without you two failing—miserably, I might add—to pretend you are not interested in one another."

"Damn you!"

Genuine shock flashed across Papa's face. She rarely cursed him.

"The one time I manage to upstage you with my education, you steal my thunder entirely!"

In a flash, Papa's infuriating smile returned.

She hugged him and leveled a stare at Bertram. "I am a woman of means, now, Bertram Weiman. You will need to win me."

He met her eye. "I shall endeavor to do so, Monique Vieuxpont."

Gervais cleared his throat. "Very well, now we have that out the way, may we return to discussing the present strategic situation?"

"Certainly...in a moment," Monique said.

"What?" Papa asked.

"Jahanara is..." She thought how best to describe the princess's mental state, sighed, and continued blandly, "The princess is at the ragged edge of her patience, ability, and power. She needs help covering for Dara's lapses. I offered ours."

Both men went silent.

Bertram was pale under his tan, but it was Gervais who eventually broke the quiet with, "To borrow an indelicate, yet precise term from John: shit."

Monique nodded. "Yes. Lots of opportunity to make a mess of things. Lots of opportunity to do a great deal of good."

"She agreed, then?"

"Readily, yes."

"Well, we shall have to prepare a few methods to make good on your offer to conceal his condition."

"And how do we do that, Gervais?" Bertram asked, a little sharply.

Gervais answered without rancor, "To begin with, we'll invert some of the swindles we've used in the past: while the one person feigns illness, the other accomplishes certain tasks while attention is focused on the supposedly sick person."

Papa's answer made Bertram look thoughtful, and perhaps a bit rueful as well.

"I will run possible ruses by you before Monique presents them to Jahanara. I'm sure you'll have a role to play in them, and that wicked sharp mind of yours will find embellishments we haven't considered."

"I'm not so sure about that, but it's probably a good idea to include anyone who will be in on it to be as knowledgeable as possible on the plan," Bertram said, pulling his lower lip in the way that told her he was worrying over something.

"What?"

"We need to run Jahanara's request past John, Priscilla, and Rodney, at minimum. More likely we need to bring everyone in all the way so that there's no surprises on our end..."

"Of course," Gervais said, though Monique was half-certain he'd not thought to ask. Papa could be *very* single-minded when he believed the stakes high enough. Single-minded to the point where he did not stop to consider the thoughts, let alone feelings, of others.

"I'm not sure Priscilla will like the idea of going back into the harem for any length of time. She chafes at it more than the rest of us."

"Regardless of what we decide on her request," Gervais said, "we need to finish going over the rest of the intelligence we have to present at the weekly meeting."

Bertram nodded. "Asaf Khan was my priority this week, but there's not a lot to report: word has it that his army is still inching its way back from Bengal. We have slightly more detail on Aurangzeb and his army, reports indicating his forces are somewhere south of Shah Shuja's in the Deccan. This is particularly alarming as Shah Shuja alone has three times the men Dara has raised so far, and if his younger brothers join forces against Dara, he will be unable to meet them in the field."

"Can we count on them to come to blows before they get here?" Gervais said.

"One can hope." Bertram shrugged. "I can see Aurangzeb handling it one of two ways: either he tries to bring Shuja to battle immediately and—if his victory is incomplete or Shuja evades battle in the first place—run the risk of starvation while chasing his brother. Then again, if they do meet, they may not have a pitched battle, but rather form up and negotiate some kind of disposition.

"Or he could hole up in one of the former Deccan sultanates and try to gather power to himself. But the governors assigned to the southernmost *Subahs* of the empire who served Shah Jahan have declared for Dara, so anything that allows Dara time to consolidate power is probably not Aurangzeb's first choice of strategy.

"Both ideas carry risks, and it's hard to say which way he'll decide, but everyone seems to agree on one point: Aurangzeb is the greater threat, even with Shuja athwart his logistics train." Bertram used the up-timer term with ease, knowing his audience would understand.

Gervais looked a question at Monique.

She nodded. "That's the essence of what Jahanara's people are saying as well."

Of course, it went unsaid that Dara's people were also Jahanara's, though Dara could hardly say the same about Jahanara's people. With Nadira Begum entirely occupied with Dara's care, and Dara himself still unsteady from his head injury, Begum Sahib Jahanara had become *the* power behind the throne—a status Monique and the other ladies of the Mission were *entirely* comfortable with but that the other ladies of the court were still adjusting to.

"Does anyone have any idea which way Aurangzeb will jump?"

"No," Monique and Bertram said, at almost the same time.

"And what about improving our knowledge of the whereabouts, goals, and condition of Asaf Khan and *his* army?"

"Certainly seems to be a great number of armies running about, eh?" Bertram said with a smile.

Monique had what she hoped would be, if less humorous, than at least more helpful, to offer: "Jahanara thinks we can help Dara on that particular score."

Chapter 7

"We are most pleased to raise you to the rank of one thousand *zat* and five hundred *sowar*, Abdul Khan."

Jahanara, shielded from the court by *jali*, winced. Dara had reversed the ranks he'd agreed, in consultation with his advisors, to give. Setting the young Afghan's salary at one thousand zat put him among the most respected of courtiers, while settling the maintenance salary for the number of sowar under his command at only five hundred meant Abdul Khan would not be obliged to recruit any of the additional men Dara—and his supporters—needed to bolster his forces. To be sure, Abdul Khan wouldn't have easily recruited enough kinsmen to fill his sowar in any reasonable timeframe anyway, but Dara's mistake had just removed the formal requirement for any further recruiting on Abdul Khan's part. Afghan fighting men were scarce on the ground at the moment, and not just from the recruiting Salim and his kinsmen had

79

done, but from the large armies both Dara's brothers had drawn up for their Deccan campaign . . . and then there were those recruited into Asaf Khan's army.

Dara only seemed to realize he'd made some error when Kwaja Magul shifted his bulk. Even then, he only glanced around and licked his lips, confusion scrawled across his features. Even from her place, Jahanara did not miss the glazed look in her brother's eyes.

She bit her lip in frustration. Dara was still having bouts of dizziness and terrible headaches from the mostly healed head wound concealed under his turban, but there was nothing for it. He'd had the khutba read in his name, and the coins struck. If a new-made emperor was uncertain, he must not be seen to be. And if he was weak, he must not show it. If Dara was to rule, he must be seen to publicly wield the power and majesty of the dynasty. To do otherwise was unthinkable.

And yet, Dara's thinking was slower. He was easily confused and quicker to anger than ever before. He was trying, but his efforts often led to frustration when progress wasn't as quick or as great as he believed it should be.

The emperor's closest advisors and family were left with a situation that, as the up-timer John Ennis had put it to his wife, was a matter of *fake it until you make it*. While she found the up-timer's speech often lacked the poetic beauty of the average courtier's, certain of their sayings were colorful, memorable, and, in this case, entirely apt.

The ceremony of elevation completed, Kwaja Magul led the freshly made courtier to his proper place in the ranks of nobles, adjusting on the fly to the emperor's departure from his plan. The heavy eunuch had remained with Dara after Father's assassination, and was already enjoying the traditional rewards of such loyalty: increased salary and power, not to mention increased proximity to the emperor's person.

Jahanara was reasonably sure the eunuch could be relied on, but the court's loyalty had yet to be tested. She suspected most of those bureaucrats of the imperial apparatus Father had appointed to her brothers' courts would find it easier to remain with whichever prince they had been assigned to than strike out for another's camp. At least until they were close enough to their preferred prince to defect: Mughal successions were replete with nobles changing sides on the eve of—or, less frequently, in the midst of—battle.

Dara brought the session to a successful conclusion without further lapses, and Jahanara departed the Diwan-i-Khas. Smidha fell in behind her with a slight grunt of effort. Her longest-serving servant and most trusted confidant, Smidha had taken to complaining of stiffness of late. Jahanara was not unsympathetic to her situation and slowed to accommodate her. A wordless sigh was Smidha's thanks.

Red Fort, the harem

As they entered the Rose Court, Nadira Begum called out a greeting over the head of her infant son.

"Greetings, Nadira. My brother will retire to the *Hammam-i-shahi* before joining us for further refreshment."

"Excellent," Nadira said, her tiny nod telling Jahanara she understood the coded message: Dara was not well.

Rising to join her sister-in-law, she handed the boy off to one of his milk mothers who in turn bundled him off to the nursery apartments with his *kokas*.

The cabal of Dara's inner circle had, of necessity, developed a coded lexicon in the weeks since Dara's injury. If Father's death had taught Jahanara anything it was this: Even here in the harem, that most sacred of places for the emperor's repose, there were those who would inform for their enemies. Everyone was watching—and listening—for signs of weakness, and the more Jahanara could do to conceal his condition, the better for everyone.

"Shehzadi Begum Sahib, the Amir Salim Yusufzai awaits the Sultan Al'Azam's pleasure in the *Hammam-i-shahi*," Firoz Khan provided as they entered the shade of the zenana.

"Very good," Jahanara answered.

Firoz Khan's gesture launched another trusted servant to find Rodney or Gervais and tell them to meet their patient in the *Hammam-i-shahi*—the imperial bathhouse, where only the emperor's doctors and closest advisors would have tongues to speak of what counsel was given there.

Smidha had carefully culled the imperial household for illiterate mutes who could be placed in service in the *Hammam-i-shahi*, and if they were not aesthetically pleasing to look on, nor particularly well trained to their tasks as yet, at least they were certain not to speak or write of what they heard there.

"Sister, my husband expressed the wish to have a quiet evening tonight, with only the very best dancers and his favorites in attendance," Nadira said.

"As he wishes, sister of my heart and light of my

brother's life," Jahanara said, pausing a moment to examine her brother's wife as they took seats in one of Jahanara's favorite chambers.

Nadira Begum was only four years her junior, already married, and mother to a prince. She had every right to assert control over her husband's harem, yet she allowed Jahanara to persist as head of the imperial harem and her appointees remain in their positions. What's more, she'd done so with grace and, more importantly under the current circumstances, without question.

"Firoz Khan?" Jahanara said, still watching Nadira.

There would have to come a time, though, when Jahanara would have to step aside and let Nadira be mistress of her husband's affairs. That moment would come sooner rather than later if, God willing, Jahanara's current plans came to fruition in timely fashion.

"Yes, Shehzadi?"

"Nadira Begum and the Sultan Al'Azam will dine privately this night, with only his favorite dancers, players, and body service. I will take my meal in my quarters with my nephew and anyone else that was to attend the Sultan Al'Azam's dinner tonight and will settle for my paltry company."

"Your will, Shehzadi." The eunuch bowed and departed. Smidha ordered refreshments and took a seat behind Jahanara to watch that all was done according to her command.

Nadira met her gaze, smiled gently and reached out with hennaed, lovely hands to take Jahanara's in hers.

"What is it, dear sister?"

"I marvel at you, who has so many cares, and yet carries through with such grace."

Nadira released Jahanara's hands to point at the jeweled ceiling above. "God as my witness, it is only because my husband's sister loves him so, and takes such pains to be of greater service than any save Him could possibly command."

Two women entered and deposited golden plates laden with dates and other fruits beside the women before retiring to sit just out of easy earshot.

"You are too kind."

"I only return the kindness given to me . . . perhaps with some polish upon it," Nadira said, an impish grin on her face as she mimed polishing one plate with the hem of her silks.

The very idea was so ridiculous, Jahanara chuckled. Smidha, too.

"Truth, now! You have some fresh worry, do you not?" Nadira asked, sobering.

"Beyond our already frequently discussed problems, no."

Smidha cleared her throat.

Nadira looked from her to Jahanara. "It seems your conscience has it otherwise."

Jahanara glanced over her shoulder at Smidha and stuck her tongue out.

Smidha, unperturbed, said, "I have asked my mistress repeatedly to let me send a letter to her old suitor, Nasr Khan."

"Oh?" Nadira said, smiling mischievously.

"He is rumored to have taken service with Asaf Khan, and would certainly return to fight for Dara."

Jahanara shook her head. "Nasr Khan serves our uncle, Shaista Khan," she said, hoping to shift the subject from old wounds.

"Who, in turn, serves Asaf Khan," Smidha insisted with a sniff.

"And both Dara and I have written Asaf Khan already, ordering his return that he might show the proper submission to Dara's rule. I see no point in muddying the waters with personal requests for men already in service to those who are honor bound to serve us."

"And yet..."

"And, as of yet there has been no reply." Jahanara did not want to think about what that meant, just as she did not want to think on Nasr Khan.

"Surely messengers would have reached him with the news."

"It is barely possible they have not. Bengal has killed many a horse and rider through the ages, imperial messenger or no."

And if not, the up-timers have promised to help discover what is going on with Asaf Khan.

An uncomfortable silence descended, each woman alone in her thoughts. Rather than let it persist, Jahanara decided to tackle yet another of the problems assailing her brother and caught Nadira's eye.

"Sister of my heart, there is another problem."

Nadira grinned. "Just one?"

"Indeed." Jahanara smiled at the joke. Nadira was in rare form today. Shaking her head ruefully, she plowed on: "Your husband has yet to approve any of the marriage prospects I have set before him."

Nadira's smile disappeared. "He has not?"

"No," Jahanara said, nibbling a date.

"But, he must!"

Jahanara waggled her head, grateful Nadira was on

her side for this. "As I, and all of his advisors, have told him. But he claims his love for you is too great to even consider another wife."

"Love!" Nadira scoffed. "He has love! He needs to secure life and throne before such personal considerations!"

"As I tried to tell him. Of course, he became quite angry with me when I did."

"Ah, that is why he was so short with me last night when I brought the subject to his attention."

Jahanara winced. "I did not wish to spoil your time with him, but the—"

"But these decisions are critical to our survival," Nadira interrupted, waving her protest down. "You will recall that I was present for your father's struggles, and the results of that for my father . . ." She looked down, but then appeared to take hold of herself. "Rest assured, I will make certain he hears my *full* opinion on the matter. We need marriage alliances to bolster our ranks, if for no other reason than I need him to take other wives if I am to be a proper tyrannical first wife!"

Jahanara smiled. Nadira did not seem the type to become an overbearing first wife, but one never knew exactly how the sexual politics and precedence of the harem would work out when adding new concubines— let alone wives—to the mix. Not until the deed was done, at any rate.

Regardless, she was glad of Nadira's full support, and would count that particular battle won, or nearly so, with her in the vanguard.

Now if only they had other generals as fine as Nadira to launch against the other problems assailing her brother.

Red Fort, Hammam-i-shahi

Amir Salim Gadh Visa Yilmaz sighed as he stepped into the steam-filled bathing chamber. A week of hard riding, another of negotiations, and then the return trip had him on the verge of exhaustion. He'd not had time to return to his own palace for a much-needed bath, so the summons to this particular place was most welcome, especially as it had come with express permission to bathe before the emperor arrived.

Slaves entered, peeling away his sweat and dust-caked clothing in an utter, and unnerving, silence.

When he was naked and the slaves had scrubbed the worst of the road dirt from him, Salim waded into the pool. The heat felt amazing, even on the fresh, angry, puckered scars from the wounds received while trying—and failing—to defend Shah Jahan from assassins sent by Aurangzeb's pet, Mullah Mohan.

Sitting on one of the submerged marble benches that formed the periphery of the octagonal pool, Salim leaned back and looked at the pattern repeated in the ceiling above. The heat quickly began to ease his aches and pains. He tried to let the warmth loosen the tightness that had dwelt in him since that terrible day without success. Meditating as Mian Mir had taught him so long ago also failed to work, as he kept slipping into a fitful doze plagued by images from that fight.

"It's clear he's recovering, my young friend, but why so slowly?" The question, in English, drew Salim from that place between sleep and consciousness. As his mind cleared, Salim recognized the speaker as Gervais.

"Well, I'm happy he *is* recovering." This from Rodney's

far deeper voice. "Slowly, sure, but he is recovering. Some guys I used to play football with, they got one too many cracks on the head and were never the same. I wish we could take an X-ray and see if there's something obvious we could do, but even back up-time brain injuries weren't easy to diagnose. Even for qualified experts, which I'm definitely not."

"So, we continue to ask him to take it easy, which he can't, and try to cover for his lapses where we can."

Salim decided it would be best to force them to change the subject. Ears were everywhere, even here, and it would not do for Dara's enemies to learn his condition.

"It's not ideal, but it's the best we ca—" The sloshing of bath water as Salim stood reached the pair, interrupting them. A moment later, Rodney's giantlike form fairly filled the archway leading to the cold bath in the next chamber.

"Hey, Salim! You're back!"

The attendant approached to towel Salim off, but he waved the fellow away as he exited the pool.

"Greetings, Rodney. Gervais," he said, walking past the big up-timer and directly into the cold bath where he submerged himself entirely. It was bracing, to say the least, and he felt more alert when he raised his head from the waters and sat on one of the steep steps of the pool.

"Good to see you, Salim! Did you have much success?" Gervais asked, clearly hopeful.

"I'm afraid not as much as we'd hoped." Salim shrugged. "Not so many of my kinsmen were in Delhi for the horse trade as I had hoped. A direct result of Shah Jahan's sensible policies..."

"What policies?"

Salim smiled and quoted from the law, "'Those who come into my kingdom to trade in horses shall not number more than one rider for every five horses.'"

Rodney looked puzzled, but Gervais' thoughtful expression quickly turned sour as he muttered a short curse in some language Salim wasn't familiar with.

"Not sure I follow?" Rodney said, looking from Gervais to Salim.

"That is because you do not think in terms of our armies. Horse traders coming overland use the same routes into India that every invasion force has used since the time of Alexander. Indeed, Babur, the founder of Dara's dynasty, was a sometime horse trader himself. So, since Akbar's time, at least, most emperors seek to limit the numbers of such traders coming into the country to avoid providing them with ready-made concealment for an invasion."

"Huh. Didn't realize you all imported horses."

"Oh, the empire imports something like eight in ten of its horses. The trade is quite lucrative," said Salim. "I myself came down from the high country with a herd to sell. India is not considered very healthy for most breeds, and the better areas have to compete with farming intended to feed the people rather than livestock. Besides, Uzbeks, Persians, Arabs, Afghans, and even the Turks provide better horseflesh than any domestic bloodline."

"The Rathores may differ with you on that, Salim. They do think the world of their Marwari breed!" the emperor pronounced, entering the chamber with a pair of attendants on his heels.

"Greetings, Sultan Al'Azam!" Salim said, unsure

how to proceed. His protocol lessons, while thorough, hadn't covered nakedness before the emperor.

"Did my doctors prescribe the cold baths for you, too, my friend?" Dara asked with a wave at Gervais and Rodney that almost struck one of the attendants removing his robes of state.

"Indeed, Sultan Al'Azam," Salim answered, watching closely as one silent eunuch raised his hands and waited for permission to unwind the turban covering Dara's head. The emperor leaned over slightly to allow the young slave to work. They made no sound as they finished disrobing the emperor. That part of his mind not examining the scar Dara had taken trying to save his father's life began to wonder after a moment if they were all mutes or something.

Dara's scar looked like some of his own, but Salim knew the head injury was more problematic. He had hoped to find Dara fully recovered, but knew from earlier conversations that the up-timers were concerned about the wound. A "severe concussion," they called it.

"We really just want you as rested, relaxed, and comfortable as you can be, to better speed your recovery, Sultan Al'Azam," Gervais said, approaching his patient with a smile.

"How are your energy levels? Your thinking remain clear?"

"Sultan Al'Azam, are you certain you wish your doctors to speak so freely—" Salim said before he could answer, glancing significantly from the emperor to the attendants.

"I am." He gestured at the slave to his right, who bowed and leaned his head back, revealing a thin white scar beside his Adam's apple. "They are all mutes, by one cause or another. I was told that Ishaan here was stabbed in the throat by some street rat when but a child, yet through the grace of God, survived."

The mute nodded, bowed, and withdrew with the emperor's clothing.

Dara lowered himself into the cool bath beside Salim.

Gervais bent to examine Dara's head from beside the pool.

"I apologize, Sultan Al'Azam. I should have guessed that you would be well protected in your own harem."

"I count it no sin to err trying to protect me, even from myself. I might have said Jahanara was being paranoid just a few months ago . . ."

"A wise thing, then, to take such precautions."

Gervais cleared his throat.

"My doctor wishes an answer, Amir." He pushed off from the bench, turned, and submerged himself. He came up, long hair dripping, and said quietly, eyes haunted, "I tire easily. I am easily confused. I cannot concentrate. My head aches abominably from time to time."

"What happened to make you confused?"

"I made a mistake today in court. Then, after, I could not recall what that mistake might have been, only that I had made one." Dara let himself sink beneath the surface again.

Salim looked over his shoulder and caught Rodney and Gervais sharing a look of concern.

"A complex task can exhaust even a well-rested, healthy brain," Rodney said as the emperor resurfaced.

"This was not complex. It was simple. I had only to carry through with what Jahanara and I agreed—not an hour before—was the best course. Instead I reversed the man's ranks, and then could not remember what my mistake might have been... Such mistakes frighten me, my friends."

"The brain is a mysterious organ, Sultan Al'Azam, and your recovery not yet complete. Be patient. Wait for it to heal," Gervais said.

Dara's expression darkened, scar pulsing scarlet. "The war for my throne will not wait for anyone or anything, least of all for me to recover my strength."

Chapter 8

Agra
Mansion of Jadu Das

"Jadu, my friend, how are you?" Salim said, dismounting and striding up to the shorter man.

Jadu bowed, smiling. "Welcome to my home, Amir Yilmaz. I am well enough. Well enough. Your friends are already present."

"Your friends, too, Jadu," Salim said, eyes on his host's stable hand as that worthy took charge of the Arabian Salim had just purchased at great expense. He had yet to decide whether he liked the tall black horse for his primary mount, but the stallion was certainly handsome to look upon. The other courtiers might say he was uncultured behind his back, though none would dare say it to his face. But none could say he was a poor judge of horseflesh.

"With all the upheaval caused by their coming, I wonder if they are truly anyone's friend," Jadu said with a note of sadness. "Though I suppose my brother would say that upheaval allows opportunity to take root like the fresh-tilled soil."

"How is Dhanji?" Salim asked as they mounted the broad, lengthy staircase.

"He is well, though I quote another of my brothers, not Dhanji."

Salim chuckled. "Well, many blessings on your father for having sired so many sons."

"My mother would argue that her six sons were less a blessing than a plague when we were young, but she now lives very well at our expense, so there is that."

Salim laughed, surprised to learn the many brothers of Jadu were not half-siblings birthed by some concubine or other wife.

"Wait, which brother?"

"Sundar."

Salim stopped dead in his tracks. "Sundar? Sundar Das? Would he be the same Sundar who was Shah Jahan's favorite munshi?"

Jadu paused on the stair. "He was the emperor's personal secretary, yes."

"I had no idea you were related! Mian Mir admired his talented pen a great deal, and gave us his works to read. Such poetry! A great many scribes and poets were greatly saddened to hear of his passing."

"He rose high, and quickly," Jadu said, looking away. But not before Salim saw tears in his eyes.

"Friend Jadu, I do not wish to make you uncomfortable or bring up painful subjects . . ."

Jadu waggled his head and resumed climbing to hide his expression. "I am too sensitive. Tomorrow marks the anniversary of the day of his death. It is an emotional time because some of the family, including our father, believed Sundar overstepped the bounds of proper custom and caste when he took employment with Shah Jahan."

Salim placed a hand on the older man's shoulder. "Even so, I am sorry to have upset you, old friend."

Jadu covered the hand on his shoulder with his own and stopped, still not looking at Salim. "My thanks for your concern. He was a good man and an even better brother. Our father was blind to those qualities, and a good many other things as well."

"Were any of your sons or nephews trained by your brother?" Salim asked. In the weeks since his return from Lahore, he'd learned through Firoz Khan's spies that the other nobles of court thought him uncouth, a man of the hills and mountains rather than a respectable man of education and learning. While his Persian was precise, Salim had no knack for the poetry and alliteration common to those educated at or aspiring to positions at the imperial court.

A munshi trained by one of such repute and fine education as Sundar Das would show the rest of the court that if Salim had not the skills himself, he was at least capable of recognizing and rewarding talent. It was a time-honored tradition at the Mughal court: newcomers, often strangers to the Persian literary inheritance of proper nobility, purchased the services of a munshi, a learned man of letters, poetry, and extensive managerial training, to assist them in their duties. The finest munshis also served as an ornament to the reputation of the courtier with their letters, histories, and manuals on subjects as varied as natural science and proper management.

Salim had considered approaching Jadu on the subject of hiring one of the merchant's family to manage his property but hadn't wished to impose on him for yet *another* favor. But now it seemed he might do Jadu a service that would also protect some of the wealth that was flowing to him as a result of his recent elevation at court...

"My nephews were, indeed."

Jadu continued after a moment's consideration. "For their part, my sons were too young and, frankly, more interested in mercantile pursuits like their father than in putting in the hard work to learn the skills of a proper munshi."

"I have need of a munshi to handle my correspondence and report the daily affairs of my estate. If you would write those of your nephews you deem properly trained and suitable for employment in my household?"

He paused and then added, "Indeed, if you or your brothers can spare a son or two, I might make use of their services in managing my estates. I am also looking to invest, as I have an inordinate amount of cash to spend, given the emperor raised me to five thousand zat last month. Having no wives, I have scarcely any expenses to speak of, and there are only so many horses and fine robes a man can buy."

Jadu turned toward him, eyes still shining. "I would be honored to present my nephew Ved Das, son of Sundar Das, as a potential munshi."

"And I know he shall prove more than worthy to serve," Salim said, finding himself inordinately excited at the prospect.

"As to diwans to assist in managing your growing portfolio, I have two sons of suitable age and training that I might spare for the work, provided you ensure they receive some education in the ways of the court."

"It is settled, then!"

Another waggle of Jadu's head was not—quite—disagreement. "My friend, you should be warned: no relative of mine will be paid less than appropriate to their talents, whether or not they are employed by my greatest friend. Especially when the potential employer just finished telling me how much loose cash he has to spend on fripperies."

"I would have it no other way!" Salim said, startled by the strong surge of affection, relief, and gratitude that rose up in him.

It required a moment's reflection to determine the reasons for it:

Firstly, he had not been comfortable handling such huge sums as he now had access to, never having had more personal wealth than could be carried on horseback or invested in a small herd, and the idea that any unscrupulous person he hired could take advantage of him had weighed on his mind more than he'd been willing to admit, even to himself.

Secondly, he hated the idea that his lack of courtly refinement might be a detriment to Dara's reputation. As his princely establishment had not been sufficient to staff the imperial apparatus on its own, Dara had been made to affirm many nobles that his father had raised to their positions. Nobles who, if things had been different, would have otherwise been shown the door. While Salim gave not a single fig for their views on his character, he wanted to forestall any whispers of, "Look at the uncouth louts the emperor surrounds himself with," at court if he could possibly avoid it.

❖   ❖   ❖

"They're on their way up," J.D. said from beside the balustrade overlooking the courtyard.

"About time he got here," Bobby said from his seat among the cushions across from Ricky.

Ricky, seizing on his apparent distraction, tossed a date at Bobby.

Without seeming to look, his target raised a hand and snatched it out of the air, popping the date into his mouth with an equally negligent movement.

Ricky grinned. Bobby had been the best shortstop in the county, and it was still damn hard to catch him off guard.

J.D. turned his head at the movement and chuckled. "Can't take you boys anywhere."

"Sure can't," Bobby said around his full mouth.

Ricky, glad to hear J.D. laugh even a little, let his grin widen.

John Dexter Ennis, or J.D. to his up-time friends, hadn't been laughing much since before...*Jesus, has it been two years since the pirate attack?*

Not that there had been a lot to laugh about lately, what with burying Randy and, in the last few weeks, preparing like mad for the latest expedition. All of them were a bit antsy, having long since been ready to move on, and this meeting was supposed to be the final one before they could pursue the actual mission they'd been sent to India for in the first place.

The world hadn't seemed so big as a kid growing up in Grantville, not before the Ring of Fire brought them back to this time and changed everything.

Bobby's date pit bonged as he spat it into the bronze container for the purpose.

It seemed to Ricky that it took a little longer than it should have for their host and the amir to emerge from the broad stair, but he entertained himself eating a mango. Another fruit he might never have known had Grantville stayed put in time and place, mangoes had quickly become his favorite. In fact, he'd decided only last month to see if a couple of the trees could survive transport back to Europe.

Salim and Jadu Das climbed into view, looking as if they'd been deep in conversation about something sensitive.

"Amir Salim. Good to see you!" J.D. said in English. Jadu was among those who'd taught Salim the language in the first place, as the Hindu was a long-term servant of the East India Company in Agra. John approached the pair, offering his hand.

The junior members of the Mission rose, uniformly smiling. As well they should: Amir Salim Gadh Visa Yilmaz had been their guide and champion at court since their arrival, and had served them honestly and well. Not that Salim was just some perfumed pretty, Ricky thought, remembering the blood-drenched man being carried from the gardens of the Taj. Most of the blood had been that of the assassins sent to kill the royals.

Most. Not all.

Almost all of the locals had doubted the sword-cut Afghan would survive his injuries, and even Rodney and Pris had been uncertain if he would recover, given the lack of proper medical facilities or supplies.

"And you, my friend," Salim returned, taking John's hand in his own and gesturing with his free hand for everyone to resume their seats.

Once they were all seated and Jadu's servants had brought more food, talk went from catching up on goings-on at court to the reason they were all here.

"So, is everything prepared, John?" Salim asked.

J.D. nodded, glancing at Jadu. "We think so."

"I think we are as well prepared as any caravan I have ever been part of." Jadu Das smiled broadly and continued, "It has been a long time since you rescued me from my tormentors, Salim. I learned my lesson then." He patted his healthy belly. "Age has made me realize that I like my skin too much to take such great risks with it."

Salim chuckled. "What route will you use?"

Jadu nodded at Ricky, who pulled a map from the bag beside him and unrolled it. "We plan on using the imperial road rather than barge our way along the river, as it gives us more mobility and better access to some of the markets north of the Jumna and west of the Ganges. With the number of guards we've hired, the quality of the Banjaris Jadu has contracted with, and the products we brought to trade with the locals, I think we should be able to purchase all of the opium and saltpeter you require, not to mention other trade goods we might want to bring back."

"And the other thing?" Salim asked, pulling a jade-hilted dagger from his belt and using the scabbarded weapon to weigh the top of the map down.

Ricky nodded, pulling his gaze from what had to be a fantastically expensive weapon. "We'll keep our eyes open once we get farther east, try and learn what Grandpa Khan is up to." He deliberately used the Americanism to confound any possible eavesdroppers—not that he expected any here, but one never knew.

Jadu waggled his head. "I will press my contacts as well. A personal visit from me should make them more amenable to speaking out than a note or verbal message would."

Salim looked from the map to Ricky and Bobby. "And neither of you has a problem taking your orders from Jadu should there be a fight or some other emergency?"

"No," they answered at nearly the same instant.

Bobby grinned, shaking his head. "We may have learned some Persian and the local lingo, but there's no way either of us could manage in all the different languages we're going to have to use to get this job done."

Salim looked back at J.D. "May I ask why young Bertram is not going with them? He has learned a great deal, and seems to find languages easy to learn."

"I am told the emperor has another task for him." The statement was accompanied by a look that told his friends he didn't much like the answer.

Salim must have mistook the look for anger because he said, "Meaning no offense, of course."

John waved a hand. "None taken. It would make sense, and I asked for him, but my wife said it was not going to happen, and I take her word on such things as gospel."

"It is a wise man that listens to the counsel of his wife," Jadu Das said. "I, myself, would have lost my fortune many times over had I not heeded my wife's advice."

"Speaking of which . . ." Salim cocked his head. "Where is that adornment of gardens, the woman I know you must have kidnapped and held to ransom to make her accept you as husband?"

"Surat, my friend. I would not have her here should our emperor's brothers arrive and take issue with his rule."

Salim grinned through his beard. "Over her protests?"

"No, on her insistence. We agreed our grandchildren

will be safest there under the protection of Dhanji and his wife. There is also the family business to see to, and she has a nose for deals."

"But Surat has hardly any defenses," John said, clearly confused.

Jadu nodded. "And they know it. Surat will go to whomever approaches it with an army, avoiding unnecessary fighting."

That produced some thoughtful expressions from the Grantville folks around the table and a sage nod from Salim.

"But won't that piss Dara off?" Bobby blurted, earning a quelling look from J.D.

Jadu waggled his head and answered without seeming to take offense. "It might. But then Surat serves the empire best as a conduit for trade, wealth, and Hajj pilgrims. Any long-term disruption of *that* trade from a sacking would prove far more problematic than a season or two of revenues going to another claimant."

"Seems very... practical," J.D. said. Rather diplomatically, Ricky thought. J.D. might say he was a simple, hardworking-if-ignorant hillbilly, but he was one helluva lot smarter than most people—including John Dexter Ennis—gave him credit for.

"Things will change once the empire secures deepwater ports along the mouths of the Ganges. But for now, the Assamese privateers and the outright pirates that infest Bengali coastal waters all the way up through the giant river valley of the Ganges make Mughal trade in the east a chancy thing. It's one of the reasons Asaf Khan was sent there with so many sowar."

And why we're to follow in his footsteps, trying to find out just which side he will back...

Part Three

April, 1636

Thorny and dark the path is!
—The Rig Veda

Chapter 9

Western Ghats, the Deccan
Southwest of Aurangzeb's camp

"And what does the comte want with me?" Carvalho asked as he shifted in his saddle, tone and bearing utterly insolent.

"The crown and Christ both wish you to provide an introduction for us at court, Captain Carvalho," De Jesus said.

"And this one?" the artillery captain waved a hand at William Methwold.

"Company business aligned with that of Father De Jesus," Methwold answered. More calmly than the priest, he hoped.

"And why, besides my *fierce* devotion to king and Christ, should I endanger my position with Shehzada Aurangzeb?" Carvalho asked, returning his gaze to De Jesus. Methwold was impressed with the man's ability to say such things with a straight face. According to the intelligence he'd had from De Jesus and the other papists, Carvalho's reputation was for mercenary self-interest first and foremost, with his skill as an artillerist a distant second.

De Jesus, an earnest priest if ever Methwold had met one, either didn't acknowledge Carvalho's irony or flat-out didn't recognize it, saying, "The Comte Linhares has authorized an offer of certain incentives and perquisites in exchange for your assistance, Captain Carvalho."

"Such as?"

"A title, lands, money, the blessings of Mother Church."

Carvalho's demeanor did not change. In fact, Methwold thought he detected some anger at the mention of Mother Church.

"You do not seem moved," De Jesus said.

"I was waiting to see if you were done."

Methwold hid a smile.

"I am."

Carvalho's mount twitched an ear, but the man himself sat still, expressionless. Eventually, he looked at Methwold.

"And you?"

"Me?" Methwold asked.

"What does the English Company's president in Surat offer?"

"What would you have of me?" Methwold asked, deciding not to correct the mercenary.

"What, you do not offer silver or gold for my service?"

"I await knowledge of what it is that you want in exchange for rendering us this small assistance."

"So you think it small, the assistance I can offer?"

"Without you to tell me differently, I can but proceed on my assumptions."

The corner of Carvalho's mouth turned up. "What manner of title can the English Company offer me?"

"None."

"And with your firman revoked, how much can you afford to pay?"

"Very little."

Carvalho nodded, seeming unsurprised with Methwold's honesty. He eventually looked back at De Jesus. "And the viceroy? What does he offer?"

De Jesus did not hesitate. "The comte will seek royal permission to elevate you to knightly orders, give you lands in Goa, as well as offering a healthy stipend of cash for your support."

Still the mercenary showed no interest. He had to be the coldest fish from the Iberian Peninsula Methwold ever met.

"What you fail to realize is that I have all these things already from Shehzada Aurangzeb."

De Jesus shook his head angrily.

Methwold covered an exasperated sigh that, despite his efforts, made his gelding toss its head.

"Will you tell us what would move you to assist our cause?" Methwold asked, laying a soothing hand on the gelding's neck.

De Jesus just grated out,"What, then, can we give you?"

"You may think it cheap, should I tell you . . ."

De Jesus colored, clearly impatient. "I tire of these games. What is your price?"

Carvalho dropped his insolent manner, his eyes flashing as he answered, "I will take what is offered, but I have one additional condition."

"And what is that?" De Jesus asked, anger sharpening his tone.

"That the viceroy find some pretext for the removal of Father Vittorio di Roma from Goa and the Estado," he snarled, deep-seated passions overcoming iron control. "That the viceroy put a stop to the burnings of the *Nuovo Cristao* in the Estado."

Father De Jesus must have flinched, because his mount sidled sideways in Methwold's direction.

The Englishman narrowly avoided having his leg pinned between the two horses. When Methwold looked up from controlling his mount, Carvalho was expressionless once more.

His own mount under control again, De Jesus apologized to Methwold, but his voice failed him and all color drained from his face when he looked at Carvalho once more.

Methwold wondered why the priest was so discomfited by the mercenary's requirement, but could not fathom it. He knew, of course, about the Spanish and Portuguese kingdoms' systematic persecution of Jews even after they'd converted to Christianity as the Catholic church and those crowns that bowed before such popery required, but didn't see any reason the priest should be so moved.

"My price too high for you, Father?"

De Jesus shook his head and visibly gathered himself. "I am not without feeling on this matter myself."

Carvalho's raised brows asked a question.

"The Konkani people of the interior, the ones I have been ministering to..."

"Yes?"

"Many of those who have converted, even those who have been baptized with by my own hand, have recently been threatened with investigation by the Holy Office of the Inquisition."

Carvalho's smile was bitter as he reached for a skin hanging from his saddle.

"So you see, we could agree to your stipulation, but any promises we make would not be binding on the viceroy until he and the archbishop decide the matter…" The mercenary seemed to ignore the churchman's answer, removing the stopper with red-stained teeth and putting it to his lips. The bulging skin shrank considerably as he swallowed several mouthfuls from the skin.

Only when he was done did he answer. "Well, if they—and you—want my continued support, then you will make every effort to see that he follows through on any promises you make here today."

"So you will help us?" Methwold asked.

"I will," Carvalho said, offering the wineskin to William.

"Thank God," De Jesus said as the Englishman took a long pull on the skin.

"For now," Carvalho said, looking the younger man in the eye, "and provided you can present sureties regarding those things you claim to be authorized to grant in order to gain my assistance."

"We have letters and grants sufficient to back our offers," De Jesus said, bristling slightly, clearly not happy with the mercenary's tone.

Aurangzeb's camp
Aurangzeb's tent

"A group of ferenghi seeks an audience, Shehzada."

"What manner of ferenghi?" Aurangzeb asked, refreshed in spirit if not in body. Prayer always steadied him that way.

"They are brought before you by your Portuguese umara, Carvalho. They include another Portuguese— this one a priest—and an Englishman I am almost certain your father exiled and that Mullah Mohan later caused to be attacked as he fled to Surat." A moment's thought. "Methwold, I believe he is called, though I cannot recall any titles or other names."

Interesting. I suppose I should not be surprised. The English would want to return to our good graces so they can resume trade. And yet, to come with the representatives from the Portuguese . . .

"Their stated purpose?" he asked, still musing.

"Carvalho claims they are here to offer the assistance of the Estado da India to your cause, Shehzada."

"The nature of that assistance?"

"They were not forthcoming with your humble servant, Shehzada."

Aurangzeb resisted the urge to smile as he arranged himself among the cushions. While the diwan he had selected from among the many munshi that applied for the position, the eunuch Painda Khan had certainly not been blessed by God with an overabundance of humility. And Aurangzeb was not inclined to reward such a lack with smiles or any other sign of indulgence.

"Bring them before me."

"As you command, Shehzada," said Painda Khan. If offended by the prince's curtness, he had the good sense not to show it.

Aurangzeb filled the time the heavy eunuch required to summon the ferenghi to his presence by reading the reports coming from the courts of Dara and Shah Shuja. As they were written by those who had already declared for one side or another, the reports generated by the imperial news writers were generally not the most reliable sources for intelligence—especially on the motives of his brothers—but they did provide information on the promotions and other announcements of the courts they reported on. From such information, he could deduce a great many things.

One particular report from Dara's court gathered his attention. It seemed that Dara had promoted the Afghan, Amir Salim Gadh Yilmaz, to command five thousand. The large number of men nominally at his command did not signify. It was never easy to find quality sowar to fill out that high a rank, and after the last year of heavy, repeated recruitment, it would be doubly difficult. And that was before considering mounts. Then again, Dara had access to Father's enormous treasuries at Agra and Gwalior Forts.

No, Aurangzeb's interest was more personal: by all reports from Father's assassination, Yilmaz was a warrior of great skill and courage. Given his ascendance, the man must have been more politically astute than Aurangzeb had originally given him credit for, having become first Father's confidant and now rising ever higher in Dara's service. Such men of quality were not common among those who were in Dara's service before he'd ascended the throne, and it was important to study those who might serve as his elder brother's chief general before ever meeting them on the field of battle.

The ferenghi party was ushered into the tent, distracting him with their mere presence. Unknown quantities were either opportunities or liabilities waiting to be identified by the wise.

Deciding he wished to begin determining which category his visitors would fall into, Aurangzeb nodded permission for them to approach rather than making them wait upon his pleasure.

Carvalho, wearing the robe Aurangzeb had given him on promotion to command five hundred, was first behind the diwan as they were led forward. The artillery captain had proven his worth on the campaign into the Deccan, commanding and being commanded without regard for race or religion. Such was rare among the ferenghi, who preferred adherents to their own religion in all things.

Thinking of Christians, Aurangzeb let his eyes slide to the man a step behind and to the left of Carvalho. The priest appeared an unimposing, slope-shouldered man. His robes were gray, and not cut in the same fashion as those of the Jesuits Aurangzeb had encountered in Shah Jahan's court. In fact, they were quite plain in comparison.

Such was the small size of the tent that Aurangzeb was unable to examine the third man before the diwan stopped and led the visitors in the proper obeisance.

"Shehzada Aurangzeb," the eunuch said, "I present Amir Carvalho, Father De Jesus, and President Methwold of the English Company."

"Peace upon you, Captain Carvalho."

"And upon you, Shehzada." The commander of five hundred bowed again. "Shehzada Aurangzeb, my associates have come from Goa in order to present certain offers from the viceroy of the Estado da India, the Comte de Linhares and the English East India Company."

"I have been expecting an answer from that noble person, though I did not expect the reply to be accompanied by a Catholic priest of an order I do not recognize and an Englishman my father banished from the empire."

The Englishman colored above the lace collar and the priest looked likewise discomfited, but it was Carvalho who spoke into the uncomfortable silence that followed the prince's pronouncement: "Shehzada Aurangzeb, I thought it wise to allow them to make their offers rather than send them packing without being heard."

Carvalho's quick yet careful response made Aurangzeb reassess the man's political acumen. The Portuguese might be worthy of more than simple field command.

"As you vouch for them, captain and commander of five hundred, I will hear what offers they convey immediately, and from their own lips, knowing that you only offer introduction, and not surety of the content of their message..."

The priest stepped forward and bowed again. His Persian was not polished, but was smooth enough for easy understanding as he outlined the viceroy of Goa's offer of assistance. Aurangzeb felt his hopes rising as the narrow-shouldered fellow spoke.

Careful now, do not show that this is exactly what you need before they have revealed the price of their assistance...

With such cautions in mind, Aurangzeb set himself to treat with the ferenghi.

Shah Shuja's camp
Shah Shuja's tent

The lavish meal complete, Nur watched her host from behind the jali as she waited for Shah Shuja to address her. Her niece's middle son, Shuja had never been among her favorites. Not that she knew him well, but his reputation for impropriety and pleasure-seeking had been well established by the time Aurangzeb had secured her return to Shah Shuja's court.

Now he held a goblet in hand, drinking wine from it as he watched the dancing girls perform with a hungry, lustful eye. His court were an extension of his own licentious nature, laughing and speaking crassly, each as deep—if not deeper—in their cups as their boy-emperor.

Interesting I should think of him as a boy when I have come to think of his even younger brother as a man, and a dangerous one at that.

The meal itself had been an unnecessary extravagance, given the supply situation. Of course, the livestock suffered more than people, having little water and poor forage. Why, she'd had great difficulty securing fodder for the few horses of the retinue Aurangzeb had provided for her mission.

It seemed to Nur that Shuja had decided to pursue all his grandfather's vices and few, if any, of his virtues. Too much a slave to his desires and still without a fine wife to guide and support him through the many pitfalls of ruling the vast empire of the Mughals, Shuja would never be a success as emperor—even if Aurangzeb were inclined to let him sit the throne for an appreciable length of time.

Nur shook her head. Never had she felt so old, so surrounded by inexperience and folly.

Interesting that I do not feel this way when at Aurangzeb's court. Jahangir—my own parents, for that matter—would never believe I would find comfort in the court of a prince so conservative he forbids dancing, and even some music.

As if her thoughts of Aurangzeb's policies had killed the music, the dance came to an abrupt climax with the dancers stretched in supplication to some Hindu god or other. Nur knew the tale; she just could not be bothered to place it just then. The gathered men roared their approval, more for the dancing girls' uniformly firm and shapely sweat-sheathed bodies heaving from their exertions than any proper appreciation of the tale they'd told, Nur was certain.

More like a pride of young lions watching a herd of antelope just emerging from an exhausting river crossing.

"Enough, my umara! Enough! Leave me!" Shuja's suddenly slurred command was missed in the tumult. He sloshed wine from his goblet as he gestured for quiet. It required a moment for his drunken entourage to quiet enough to hear the rest of what he had to say. "I must speak with my brother's emissary, Nur Jahan."

A few drunken umara mumbled protests, but were silenced by their more sober—or simply smarter—brethren.

"My kokas and diwan will remain, of course," Shuja slurred. "I will want their counsel."

What counsel does a drunkard heed when the fermented grape has poured its sweet song into his ears, blocking them from receiving any wisdom beyond that in the bottom of his own cup?

Nur remained silent and still as roughly half of the assembled umara slowly departed, reflecting that Shuja's "milk brothers" should be content to be allowed to stay, as most of them were unable to rise, having drunk far more than she or her late husband would have allowed even common sowar to have while on campaign, even after a hard-fought victory.

And my beloved remains famous for his love of intoxicants, even if the rest of the world does not know that I was chief among those... She hid a sigh, longing for the touch of a man long departed from this world.

Shuja was impatient, ordering the jali be removed before half those who were to depart were within a few paces of the tent flap. Nur affixed her veil as the slaves bent and removed the screen. Hardly necessary, as those who would remain to see her were family in all but blood, but it would not do to give detractors even a hint of impropriety, not while performing as Aurangzeb's intermediary and messenger.

"Well, what is it my brother wished of me, but was too frightened to ask in person?" Shuja asked, grinning at his sycophants as if he'd exhibited some great wit.

Setting her voice to cut across the tittering and chuckles that followed, Nur answered, "Sultan Al'Azam, Shehzada Aurangzeb desires only to meet with you in person to pledge his support for you as rightful emperor, and seeks your surety as Sultan Al'Azam that he will have the opportunity to do so."

Shuja blinked as if he'd been rapped on the nose with a stick.

Hiding her pleasure at holding the reins of an emperor once again, Nur waited for the drunken child to catch up.

"He doesn't want the throne?" Shuja murmured it so quietly that only those nearest him could hear.

"It is well known that Shehzada Aurangzeb is a religious man, his heart more suited to study of the Quran than ruling over the hearts of his fellow man. He wishes only to submit, first to God, and then to you, his elder brother."

Her reply drew nods from those of his kokas sober enough to follow the conversation. Nur ignored them in favor of watching Shuja. She could see him wishing he'd remained sober for this interview. Too late, of course.

"And what of Dara?" he asked after a moment's rumination.

"Shehzada Aurangzeb loves his brothers. Hard as it is to countenance, Shehzada Aurangzeb finds it hard to believe that Dara knew nothing of the plot against Shah Jahan, happening as it did right under his nose. Beyond that, Aurangzeb knows his eldest brother pays heed to all manner of idolatry and mysticism, where you are concerned with ruling wisely."

Shuja began to shake his head, but Nur went on before he could refute her words: "Aurangzeb bade me say that he wishes peace upon the kingdom of your forefathers, and that he knows only you are strong enough to end the war quickly and thereby hasten his own steps to Mecca and the life of contemplation and worship that has always been his sole and most fervent desire."

One of the kokas sniffed derision on that, earning a sharp, if unsteady, look from the Shah Shuja. A drunken young man blanched and muttered a muted apology.

Shuja looked again at Nur, a thoughtful look he was too drunk to hide crossing his features.

"Does Aurangzeb offer any sureties beyond these pretty words of yours, Aunt?"

"The words are not mine, they are his, as I have said."

"You do not answer my question."

"Shehzada Aurangzeb remains a prince. He does not order the khutba said in his name, nor order men to strike coins with his likeness nor name upon them. He remains a prince. He makes no claim to be other than what he is."

"For"—Shuja belched wetly—"now, at least."

Shuja's men chuckled.

He again shook his head. "You have given me much to think on, Nur Jahan. Present yourself tomorrow..." He picked up his goblet and drank from it. "In the afternoon sometime."

"Your will, Sultan Al'Azam," Nur Jahan said. Long reins were as useful as short for control of a well-broken mount, after all.

Chapter 10

Agra
The Red Fort

The gunsmith's factory was dark after the noonday sun, and loud with hammering and the constant hissing roar of several furnaces.

Unsure where to go, John led Atisheh and Bertram deeper into the gloom in search of Talawat.

"He said to meet him here, didn't he?" John asked. His Persian had improved to the point he didn't need a translator for most things, but he was glad Bertram was here to make sure he made none of the big mistakes of communication poor language skills often led to.

"He did," Atisheh said.

Talawat said something from Atisheh's elbow, startling them all. John and Bertram jumped. Atisheh's response was more practical: she turned, blades appearing in her hands.

"So sorry. I did not mean to startle you!" the thin gunsmith shouted as he backed from the warrior woman.

Atisheh checked herself with visible effort and a curse John didn't understand.

"Sorry, I didn't hear you," John said, interposing himself between Talawat and Atisheh to give them both a moment to recover.

If Talawat was offended, he did not show it. Lowering his hands, the gunsmith smiled and rendered another and lengthier apology to his guests.

Atisheh grunted and returned her weapons to their sheaths.

Bertram just nodded.

"I have the first of the guns ready, Mr. Ennis," the gunsmith went on, gesturing his guests toward a set of large doors leading out into a sunlit court behind the factory.

"So soon?" John asked as they walked into the long, narrow space between low walls. Aside from the color and quality of the stone, it looked like a lane at the shooting range his uncle used to take him to, right down to the wide bench at the near end. A trio of long lumps that John took to be guns rested under a silken sheet of some sort, something he never would have seen on his uncle's range.

"Well, I followed your advice and didn't try and recreate the pistol or even the Remington," the man said with another smile.

"You did?"

"Instead I copied the weapon your associate, Randy, left behind. The L.C. Smith." He pulled back the sheet, revealing his handiwork.

The first was, indeed, Randy's gun: a hammerless side-by-side double-barreled break-open twelve-gauge shotgun, lovingly maintained but still bearing the scarred wood of too many generations tramping through West Virginia in search of game birds. Randy had been very proud of the piece, it having been in his family for three generations. He'd lugged it all the way to India even though the pump action Remingtons they'd all trained with were far more practical for the kind of shooting they had expected.

The second gun was a stunning, nearly exact copy of the original. Nearly, because instead of the plain blued steel of Randy's shotgun, this one had the endless wave pattern of Damascus steel.

The third one had the same patterning, but looked odd. The same basic structure as the shotgun, but it was single-barreled, and had a ladder sight at the rear. Without looking down the barrel, he could only assume it was chambered for, at most, twenty gauge. On second glance, the barrel looked significantly longer, as well.

"Wow," John said, fingers twitching with desire to touch the magnificent-looking tools.

Bertram let out a low whistle, eyeing the odd-looking one. "The craftsmen at home would be hard-pressed to manufacture a copy, and never with this quality on the first try, and certainly not in a few months."

"Firearms are loud, and can fail at the worst moment. I prefer the blade or the bow," Atisheh opined.

Talawat's grin only grew wider on hearing her. "These are something entirely better than the usual products of my establishment, warrior."

"They sure are pretty. May I?" John asked, engrossed in the fine workmanship and the endless patterns in the steel.

"Of course."

John picked up the first copy, surprised that it wasn't heavier.

"Amazing," he said, flipping the gun up and enjoying the smooth action that ended in a deep clunk as the barrels locked against the breech. John sighted along the long groove between the barrels and smiled. Lowering the weapon, he pushed the breech lever sideways, releasing the barrels and watching as the shell extractor rose smoothly from the opening breech.

"I thank you for the praise, but this weapon itself was not the most difficult part of this particular weapon." Talawat waved at the open doors, summoning someone.

"The shells?" Bertram guessed.

"The shells," Talawat confirmed.

A younger version of Talawat emerged from the workshop. The young man was carrying a set of belts or bandoliers. One was studded with dozens of brass-based shells while the other long brass cartridges. He lay the belts with the shells on the table in front of John and the other in front of Bertram. Talawat retrieved two of the shells and presented them to John.

Taking them, John took a closer look. Each shell had a high brass base, but the hulls appeared to be something like an odd plastic.

"Shot?"

"Yes."

"And the"—he looked at Bertram for help translating, who supplied the word after a moment's thought—"hulls?"

"Waxed paper," Talawat said, pride evident in his voice even as he spoke slowly and more clearly than his excitement inclined him to in deference to John's language skills. "Settling the process was a great challenge. It still fails to extract the empty shells too often for complete contentment, but we are still making improvements to the formula."

"May I?" John asked again, holding the shells up and gesturing with the shotgun.

"Of course."

John dropped the shells in, closed the break and shouldered the shotgun, admiring how smoothly the action worked. Aiming down the lane at a man-sized target that looked something like a scarecrow, he took up the front trigger with his finger and squeezed.

The resulting bang was loud, the recoil tolerable, and the target gave a satisfactory shiver before smoke obscured it. He pulled his finger from the first trigger and took up the second with similar results. Thick, cottony smoke obscured the firing lane for a few seconds, but cleared to reveal still more damage to the target.

"See, loud," Atisheh said. John noted that, for all her disapproval, the warrior woman was paying very close attention behind that chain veil.

In answer, John pressed the lever to release the break. The shells extracted flawlessly, flying a few feet before tock-tocking on the tiles of the courtyard. John pulled another two shells from the belt with one hand and dropped them in, snapping the action closed with an almost negligent flip of the hand holding the gun.

"Just like that, I'm ready to shoot again."

"Almost as fast as a bow," Atisheh answered, the grudging respect coloring her tone robbing the words of any insult.

Talawat looked like he might burst with pride.

"And these?" Bertram asked, waving at the gun and cartridges in front of him.

"Well"—he touched the gun in front of Bertram with a prideful smile—"I looked at the cartridges for the handgun John showed me last year...and thought I might make something similar but that fire from the same basic principles as the shotgun."

"Wait, the barrel is rifled?" John asked, reverently returning the shotgun to the silk-covered table and picking up the gun in question.

"It is. I used the larger caliber pistol cartridges for the .45 revolver you showed me as the model for the cartridge..." He pulled a brass cartridge from the bandolier. It wasn't very wide, but was longer than a pistol cartridge, making it look like an absurdly long .45 round.

"So big?"

"I tried to use slugs through the shotguns, but they were not effective with the amount of powder I had to use. Nearly killed myself with one breech explosion among many," the gunsmith said, clearly excited to explain his craftsmanship to someone who might appreciate the technical achievement for what it was.

"Our black powder can't match the velocity of your smokeless powders, and the bullet from that gun, even when I lengthened the cartridge to add more powder behind it, was too light to do much at range, so I decided on the bigger round. The results were... more than satisfactory, I think you will find."

John smiled and reached for the cartridge in Talawat's hand, deeply impressed.

Talawat did not hand it over, however, shaking his head. "Not in here. This range is too short for shooting these."

"Really?" John said, surprised. The range was about a hundred feet long.

"Well, these are accurate, when aimed, to about two hundred and fifty of your 'yards,' and there is only stone behind our target here. I would hate for a ricochet to kill or wound one of us."

"Two hundred and fifty?" John said, incredulous.

"Well, a shot will likely kill a man at *sixteen* hundred yards, but no one could hit someone on purpose at that range."

"*Sixteen hundred?*"

"Yes. What use a rifle if not to reach out and touch someone from great distance, eh?"

"But, sixteen hundred?"

Talawat's smile was broad and happy. "You'd look like you were shooting at the moon, but yes."

Bertram looked thoughtful. "How many can you make?"

The smile faded as the gunsmith waggled his head. "Depends upon how much time the pretenders give us. Far fewer of the rifles than the shotguns, of course. The true challenge is making the primers for the ammunition. It is dangerous, painstaking work, and I despair of making enough shells and cartridges to make a real difference. Especially in light of the work I am doing to copy those delightful cannon shells your ship's master sent along."

John was sobered by the reminder that Talawat, genius that he might be, was still a lone man running one shop. He could never be expected to produce enough guns to make a real difference. The thought was depressing.

"Of course, I have all of the smiths of the Sultan Al'Azam's establishment working on producing these weapons and their ammunition. It goes slowly, as I am having trouble convincing my fellows to forgo treating the steel in order to best show off the lovely patterns."

"So, a hundred or so?" John said, gloomy.

"Of the rifles, yes. The shotguns: a thousand, perhaps more if given time."

"Holy shit! A thousand?"

Talawat's brows shot up as he asked for the meaning of the English words.

Atisheh coughed to cover a chuckle.

Embarrassed by his outburst, John shook his head. "Nothing, sorry. I simply had no idea you could make so many."

"Not me alone, of course. The emperor Dara Shikoh, long may he reign in wisdom and the light of God's good graces, has a great many artisans working for him, and I have some . . . small weight with them."

"A great many?"

A diffident shrug. "Seventy *Atishbaz* families, their servants, and their apprentices. Not to mention the European, Persian, and Afghan tradesmen who are not, technically, members of our caste or clan. Nearly four-hundred-odd tradesmen worthy of the appellation 'master,' all told."

John stifled another expletive. Even Bertram looked surprised.

Talawat looked at John in puzzlement. "Why this shock? Surely you knew the emperor for the richest man in all the world, and as such, the supreme patron of crafts, sciences, and the arts. It is only natural that he be the epicenter of all such things as interest him."

"Guess I never thought of it that way," John said, thinking that it was a wonder India hadn't become *the* leading world power up-time. Gooseflesh rose on his arms as he considered that with such men as Talawat, and knowledge of the weapons from the future he had supplied them, they just might.

South of the Red Fort

"So, you have all the men you need, John?" Salim asked, reining in. His entourage, trailing behind their master and the up-timer, halted as well. He'd told them to stand off a bit, wanting to have a private conversation with John.

To think I now have a flock of lackeys to do my bidding!

Then, because of his time spent in the company of Mian Mir and in study of Sufi wisdom: *Do not succumb to the pleasures of this fleeting world, Salim.*

All things from God, to God.

"Sure," John had said, rubbing his chin. "There won't be enough guns to go around for a while yet, anyway. Ammunition will become the real bottleneck once we get into live-fire training." His horse tried to sidle sideways, but the up-timer controlled him with barely a thought.

"John, I hope you'll forgive me for saying it, but you've become a far better horseman these last months than ever I thought you'd be," Salim said, smiling to overcome any insult the words might offer. Indeed, John seemed to be far more at ease than Salim had ever seen him before.

"Well, thanks. Still wish I had the Ford Mustang I bought in high school."

"What's that, a breed of horse?"

John laughed. "No, a car."

"Car? Oh, like the ones in Grantville?" Salim asked. The vehicles had been insanely fast and very loud. In short, something he would greatly enjoy.

"Only faster."

Salim's brows drew together. "Faster?"

"I had souped mine up. My family had some history running moonshine, see..."

He shook his head, gesturing at the men Salim had kept at bay. "Never mind. I assume you wanted to talk to me privately about something more important than missing my old ride."

Feeling the press of time upon them, Salim reluctantly agreed. Hoping his sincere desire to hear more came through, he added, "I do want to know, John. You'll have to tell me the rest when we have more time."

"But," John said, smiling.

"But," Salim agreed with a sigh. "For now: Dara assures me Talawat and the rest of his establishment are producing ammunition as fast as they can."

"Is that where you're taking me?" John asked, nodding at the tall berm rising up before them.

"It is. Talawat and Begum Sahib thought it wise to keep ammunition production some distance from the fort."

John looked along the mile or so upriver toward Red Fort.

Salim joined him. It was a grand sight, with the many manors and gardens of the court spread along the river to the cleared land near Red Fort, and beyond it rose the magnificent beauty of the Taj's proud onion dome. The umara of the courts of two great emperors had spent great sums to build ever-grander manors in the area, as proximity to the emperor was a physical representation of one's favor, so the gardens and mansions only grew more ornate and beautiful the closer one was to Red Fort.

"Is that stone at the top?" John asked, drawing Salim's gaze back to the berm, which John was examining with a builder's eye.

Salim regarded the berm as well. Each one rose to a height of about thirty *gaz* and had a core of stone walls, either previously existing or built from rubble.

"Yes."

"Where from?"

"Talawat used some preexisting structures to build the factory and its berms."

"Preexisting?" The up-timer looked again at the manors to the north and south. "You mean someone's mansion?"

"Exactly so," Salim answered.

"What, they get tired of it?"

"No. They were dispossessed for choosing to throw their support to Shah Shuja."

"I . . . see." John looked uncomfortable.

"Such are the risks involved in any succession war, John."

"But, what of the family that lived here?"

"This particular man is with Shuja's army in the Deccan. His wives, children, sister, and mother are now in the emperor's harem."

John looked alarmed.

"They are treated well and respectfully, John," Salim said, hoping to forestall an angry outburst. "We are not barbarians, and the keeping of wives, sisters, mothers, and children of those who support your opponent is considered a sacred obligation. They are almost never used as hostages unless that is their agreed-upon status before being brought into the harem. Akbar started with peace, and his descendants have kept it."

"Almost?" John asked, seizing on the qualifier as Salim had known he would.

He shrugged. "There are those who have done wrong, certainly."

Patting his horse's neck, Salim continued thoughtfully, "The men, of course, receive less mercy from the victorious. But even then, being stripped of rank and incomes is the norm, imprisonment uncommon, mutilations even more unusual, and executions rare. Admittedly, Shah Jahan was more . . . comfortable with bloodletting than his predecessors. At least, Asaf Khan was never punished for doing away with Shah Jahan's potential rivals."

"Seems like it's all been thought out," John said, irony twisting both tone and expression.

Salim chose to ignore his friend's tone. John was an up-timer, with an up-timer's strange ideas about some things. He answered carefully, trying to explain his own convictions on the matter. "The empire has had some recent experience with succession struggles. The dynasty that stagnates is soon to perish, and the way they've done it here tends to leave the common folk more or less alone relative to what I know of similar succession wars in Europe and elsewhere. Of course, our emperor and his siblings are relatively young. Why, Aurangzeb is nearly as young as Babur was when he started the empire, if I recall correctly."

"So, Salim, I really don't want to be rude, but why do you keep saying 'they' when you refer to the empire?"

He hiked a thumb at the cluster of messengers and servants. "Looks like you are an integral part of this empire's machinery by now..."

"I do, don't I?"

Seeing that he'd never had to explain it to someone else, he spent a moment collecting his thoughts before speaking further. "You may recall Shah Jahan informing you that he was Sultan Al'Azam of many peoples, not just one?"

"Sure do." John nodded. "Can't forget his angry look when I made that particular mistake."

"He got angry because it's important. The Mughals themselves are a mix of Turco-Mongol, Persian, Rajput, and other bloodlines. Your wife can tell you how many languages she hears daily in the harem. The Timurids rule over hundreds of different peoples, each with distinct dialects if not utterly different languages, differing religions and practices thereof, not to mention the entirely different lives the nomads, farmers, and the city-dwellers live. So many different languages are spoken that the very language of the empire's northern sowar is translated into the other languages as 'camp tongue' because it's a combination of so many local tongues.

"All bow before Timurid power. Some are happier with that state of affairs than others, but all recognize that the Timurids are, historically, excellent overlords who have, on the whole, improved conditions for everyone under their rule, not just Muslims, or Rajputs, or a particular caste. Everyone. And, in the successions the old order, those that supported the last emperor, are joined by those outsiders who threw in their lot with the victorious prince. My own people are not a bad example: Shah Jahan fought the Yusufzai when a young prince, and we have since fought for the empire against the Safavids under his command."

"I get it, it's a melting pot."

"No, it's not, not really." Salim struggled to ignore the dismissive tone and explain for his friend. "The Timurids themselves are, I suppose. They've assimilated so much of what it means to be Indian, in that they have more in common with the people here than many of their central Asian ancestors.

"Akbar's *Sulh-i-kul*, or 'peace with everyone,' is a fine example: rather than force all these people, with their different laws and customs, through the needle's eye of Mughal custom and legal precedent, Emperor Akbar chose to invite the religious leaders, the lawmakers, and the lore keepers of India to discuss what was fair and righteous for all. He wasn't trying to make everyone melt together, just provide them with a framework in which to prosper without tearing the empire apart or unduly repressing one group or another.

"The following generations have lived up to that ideal with greater or lesser success, so the lives and customs of the peoples within the empire are allowed to continue as they always have done, so long as they pay homage and taxes and offer no violence to their neighbors. That last is especially important, as it was not something that was common practice before Mughal rule. Beyond that, each person has their place in India, but the Mughal system allows the best talent to rise, and rewards those talented people who work within the framework of Mughal rule."

"For most people, anyway." John's smile was more honest this time, and took the sting from the words.

Salim returned the smile, adding, "I do believe your up-time democracies benefitted most people, most of the time. We can scarcely do better without the benefit of the three hundred and more years of experience your predecessors had."

"Lot of blood shed to learn from those mistakes," John said. He shook his head. "Don't mind me, Salim. I'm just some hillbilly from a small town in West Virginia."

"If I had a hundred rupees for every time I have been called a simple hillman by some fop thinking it an insult, I would be a—well, I would be even more rich than I am."

John chuckled. "You do dress better than any hillbilly I ever met."

"Or at least more *expensively*, my friend?" Salim said, knowing the up-timers thought the *khalats* and robes of distinction handed out by the emperor and eagerly sought after by courtiers garish and overly opulent.

The pair shared a moment of laughter, clearing the air between them.

Salim, careful with his words in case he shatter the mood, said, "We can only try to do better, and in order for us to be here to make those efforts, the man I believe to be our best chance at lasting peace and thoughtful change must emerge victorious." He pointed at the berm. "Hence, the work going on in there, and the work I ask of you."

"Salim, I know you need someone with experience in infantry stuff, but I am no drill sergeant. In fact, I got out of basic training back in the USE and felt like I hadn't learned anything about being a soldier."

"I know you think you are not qualified, but you are. At least, in all the ways that matter here and now."

"You said that when you first asked me to do this. I still don't get it."

"And I thank you for not requiring that I explain it in front of the court. They do not need to know the particulars of Dara's reasons."

"I can't believe I have to ask, but what—*exactly*— does he think he's getting in me?" John asked.

"The Mughals often recruit military specialists from outside the limits of the empire. There are not many here with Dara's military establishment, but Aurangzeb and Shah Shuja both have artillery parks and other specialist troops overseen by and composed of ferenghi."

John shook his head again and shifted in his saddle. "I don't know anything about cannons, friend."

"Let me finish, if you please, John."

The up-timer gestured apologetically for him to proceed.

"The common sowar and, possibly more importantly, the umara of the court are used to seeing foreign experts training their comrades. They were used to it even before the arrival of such technological marvels as those Talawat created in copying your L.C. Smith shotgun."

John's eyes widened. "Oh, hell."

"Yes. So you see, it is as important you are *seen* to be training the men as providing it in the first place, not because we cannot figure out a way to adapt to the technology ourselves, but because those who are in Dara's camp *expect* to see you in charge. If you, an up-timer, are not visibly in charge, then they will not have much faith the weapons will serve to redress some of the imbalance of forces we face. Without faith in that strength, Dara will be abandoned for one of the pretenders."

John nodded. "And word will get back to the brothers that I am in the thick of things, maybe making them cautious."

"Exactly so, my friend. Keeping the appearance of strength is as—if not more—important than actually being strong right now. Everyone is holding their breath, hoping to see who will make the first error and thereby indicate the eventual winner."

"I get it." A sly grin spread across his lips.

"What?" Salim asked.

"You're not going to insist I wear one of those silly robes, are you?" he asked, gesturing at Salim's clothing.

Salim laughed. Then laughed harder, making their horses shy.

"What?" John asked as he got his horse back under control.

"Dara may! In fact, I will suggest the very thing to him this afternoon if you cannot beat me to the manufactory!" Salim called over his shoulder, snapping heels to his horse and riding for the gap in the berm.

Chapter 11

Agra
Red Fort, Jasmine Tower

Drums rolled, echoing across the river and burying the snap of silken banners in their thunder. The soldiers beneath the banners and marching behind the drums were uniformly big, bearded, broad-shouldered men, with tall helmets wrapped in fine turbans making them appear even larger.

The two thousand men sent by Hargobind Singh crossed the open ground before the walls in solid blocks of several hundred each. Each battle was armed in different fashion: swords, spears, arquebus, and, leading the way, cavalry.

"I cannot believe you made Dara accept their offer of support," Nadira said, in tones of flat anger.

"Are we so strong that we can afford to turn anyone away?" Smidha asked before Jahanara could formulate a response more sensitive to Nadira's feelings.

Nadira's hands tightened into fists on the sandstone wall.

Inwardly sighing, Jahanara said, "Sister, he asked the guru for fighters, and these"—she gestured at the marching men—"are the result."

"But their leader nearly killed my Dara," Nadira said, more softly.

"That he did," Jahanara said, taking one of Nadira's fists in both her hands. "And then he treated Shehzada Dara Shikoh honorably, as he now sends his followers to serve upon request of the Sultan Al'Azam Dara Shikoh."

Nadira shook her head. "I do not speak of Guru Hargobind Singh. I speak specifically of that man." She nodded stiffly at the rider at the front of the cavalry contingent.

"Bidhi Chand?" Jahanara asked. Even without his place in the front, the man was not hard to pick out. His horse was a magnificent white beast, taller by a hand than the rest of the mounts. It was a gift from Dara, given before his ascension to the throne in respect for the warrior's great skill and chivalry. Aside from his mount, the saint-soldier was dressed no more richly than the riders following him. It was his bearing, handsome features, and personal charisma that drew the eye.

"Yes, *him.*"

"Surely Chand's presence, as one of the guru's greatest warriors, speaks of the strength of that man's desire to fully support your husband."

"I know it does." Nadira turned steady eyes on Jahanara. "Just as I know I must tolerate his presence. That does not mean that I must enjoy it."

Jahanara smiled at Nadira. "At least he does not have another prospective wife for Dara in tow."

"There is that." Nadira looked again at the men passing below. "There is that."

"At least, as far as we know," Jahanara teased.

Mission House

"Do you think it's enough?" Bertram asked, handing Monique a cup of wine as he sat among the cushions next to her.

"I think so, but I don't know how much proof will be required," she said, giving him a peck on the cheek.

"Proof of what?" Gervais asked, entering the chamber set aside for less formal meetings of the Mission members.

"We think Monique has uncovered a spy."

"Oh?" Gervais asked, collecting a cup for himself.

Monique waited until her father had settled among the cushions across from her and Bertram before speaking. "Jahanara was right to ask us to watch the harem. I think I've identified—"

"Think? Your daughter gives herself too little credit," Bertram said with an affectionate smile at Monique.

Monique tossed her dark curls. "I want to talk it out before I bring it to Jahanara's attention. I was not trained to this as you were, my handsome spymaster."

"Well, uh . . ." Bertram said, flushing pink as an idiot's grin spread across his face.

Gervais, choosing to ignore the byplay, waved away her concern. "Who do you suspect, then?"

"Mahroz, wife of Orang Khan."

"A Persian couple?" Gervais asked.

"Yes, though as far as we can tell, not related to the royals."

"Do you think they report to Nur even so?"

"A natural conclusion to draw, but without confirmation at the other end it's impossible to say with certainty."

"Certainty isn't a thing we trade in, daughter."

"No, I suppose not. Still, I *am* certain she is passing messages out of the harem."

"And not just sending love notes to her husband?"

"Not her husband, no," Bertram answered. "He's been home all week and I've set watchers on the family manor."

Gervais looked a question at them both.

"We compared notes last week and then again before you came in," Monique said, divining the question an instant before Bertram.

"And here I thought I was only giving you time to steal a few kisses."

"Well, that too, Papa!" Monique said, grinning impishly.

Bertram flushed again, cleared his throat, and changed the subject. "The messengers rode south while their mansion is to the north and on the other side of the river from the Red Fort."

"Some other paramour? Parents?"

"Doubtful in the first instance, and deceased in the second," Monique answered, instantly.

"For both of them?"

Bertram looked thoughtful, but it was Monique who answered, with less certainty this time. "Her parents are dead. Not so sure about his."

Gervais shrugged. "I suppose it doesn't really matter . . . though it would be nice to know who, exactly, is receiving the intelligence. Perhaps Dara can get us verification from one of the camps?"

"Possibly. I will ask Jahanara."

"Any idea what intelligence was passed?"

"Two items make sense: The first rumors regarding

completion of the munitions factory circulated at about the same time as the first messenger departed. The second messenger left the same day as Bidhi Chand and the Sikh army arrived."

"But why report that second bit? The arrival of the Sikhs has to be general knowledge."

"That's what I asked him," Monique said, looking at Bertram for an answer with a twinkle in her eye.

He cleared his throat, having been distracted at the time by her warm lips and nimble fingers. "Informants often feel they must report everything in order to be seen as reliable, especially ones seeking to ingratiate themselves with whomever they are spying for. And they have a point, to a certain extent. Just because a thing is common knowledge in one place does not mean that it will be reported in another..." He thought a moment and continued, "In this case, though, I think the former situation applies: Mahroz and/or Orang both wish to ingratiate themselves with someone, and seek to be first with the news."

"So probably not accomplished spies."

"Almost certainly not," Bertram agreed. "Which is why it would be useful to track their movements. We might identify the center of the ring if we can watch them long enough. Even professionals slip up, eventually."

Gervais considered a moment before asking, "Just what do you think Dara will do with this information?"

"He'll probably take them prisoner, remove their rank, and generally make them miserable," Bertram said.

"And Jahanara, what would she do?" Gervais looked at his daughter this time.

"Jahanara will likely set her own people, or give

us free rein to continue watching the couple in hopes they would lead us to roll up the rest of the ring."

"Then I suppose it makes sense that we tell Jahanara and let her decide whether and when to inform her brother."

Monique rolled her eyes and said, exasperated, "That was exactly my idea, Papa!"

"Why so vehement?" he asked, brows rising.

"I would like to think that you, at least, believe I know what I'm doing when it comes to this sort of thing."

"Did I show you differently?" he asked, looking to Bertram for support.

"Of course you did, by not asking me what I planned in the first place!" she snapped.

Bertram, aware that the lovely young woman he wanted desperately to please might not look favorably upon any support he showed for Gervais, kept his mouth shut. Gervais and Monique did this sometimes, arguing over what seemed to outsiders to be trifles. They rarely differed on matters of importance, and to be honest, Bertram found the pair were far closer than he'd been with either his mother or his father since becoming an adult, so who was he to judge?

Red Fort, Harem

"Do we know how large the network is?" Jahanara asked. Placing her carved jade *chaturanga* piece with care. She had lost three straight matches to the older woman. What had started as a way to engage in private conversation had become something of a grudge match.

"Three in the palace proper. Two more in the manors of nobles of the inner court... Damn these hot flashes," Smidha said. They were on a balcony, but the fitful breeze coming off the dry-season Yamuna had little impact on the older woman's temperature.

Jahanara gathered some ice from the bowl that chilled their drinks and, after a raised brow elicited a nod from Smidha, pressed it to the hollow of her servant's neck.

"Oh, that's wonderful, thank you, Begum Sahib." Smidha sighed, and then indulged in a moment of calm consideration of the board before making her move. "There are two in the harem, another among the umara of the court. The ring is rather large, but in identifying the ringleader, we think we know most of them."

Studying for her next move, and hoping to distract Smidha, Jahanara asked, "And how certain are we of this identification of the leadership?"

"As fully as one can be on such things. Two separate sources confirmed it and a third mentioned suspicions to that effect..."

"And do they know we have identified them?"

"Your move, Begum Sahib," Smidha said. "In answer to your question, it is doubtful."

"While certainty would be comforting," Jahanara said, making the move she considered the least detrimental to her game, "comfort in such matters is a sign we were being deceived."

"Exactly so, Begum Sahib. Discomfort and uncertainty are the bywords of intelligence work." Smidha grinned and made her move, seemingly without thought.

"What is it, beloved Smidha?" Jahanara asked, eyeing

her opponent, and then the board, with suspicion born of long experience.

The smile broadened. "Oh, nothing."

Jahanara took another handful of ice and pretended to throw it at Smidha.

Her servant sniffed, unmoved, and said, "Truly, Begum Sahib, it was only this: our familiarity and acceptance of those conditions of uncertainty and discomfort are inherent in what it means to be a woman and therefore, it seems to me, must give rise to women's supremacy in such work."

"Supremacy? Such a strong word," Jahanara said thoughtfully. She tossed the chips of fast-melting ice back in the bowl and preemptively waved a slave back to his position when that worthy thought to replenish the bowl's contents. Privacy was far more important to her right now than the temperature of her drinks.

"Oh?" Smidha prompted.

Jahanara shook her head. "It seems too broad a generalization. Perhaps it would be better to say that we inmates of the harem are trained by our experiences while those who are not immured in such circumstances have less experience to learn from and trade upon?"

Smidha considered. "It is difficult to say, as those not in these circumstances who are also close to power are not easily found in all the wide world."

"Unless they are from the USE, I suppose," Jahanara said, thinking of Monique, Ilsa, and Priscilla. "Or until, like Nur, we are beyond our child-rearing years."

"Even then, proprieties must be observed," Smidha said, smoothing the fringe of the pillow she reclined on.

Jahanara did not miss the sign. She glanced again

at the board, but realized she was beaten in three moves or less and decided Smidha's reaction had to do with something more important.

"What is it, Smidha?"

Smidha's good humor disappeared, replaced for an instant with a feral intensity Jahanara had last seen in the Garden of the Taj. "More than anything, Begum Sahib, I want to roll up this spy network like so much betel and burn it to ash. I want it, and everyone who threatens you, burned to the ground, made into ashes that can be placed in the sacred river and carried to the sea." Smidha's hands had curled into claws by the time she'd finished speaking.

Jahanara nodded, allowing the anger and heat of Smidha's outburst to pass without accepting it, wanting to make sure her advisor and ally was fully aware of her will when she chose to speak it.

The older woman's experienced, agile mind recovered from the fit of temper quickly enough, leading Smidha to bow her head respectfully and mumble an apology.

Jahanara ignored the apology to focus on the problem. "What you propose is a mere trimming of leaves. I want to uproot the brush, root and all, and slay those wishing to gather any harvest from it."

Smidha waggled her head. "I understand the desire to keep them in play, b—"

"It is not simply a *desire*, Smidha. It is necessary. All our hopes for the future may come to rely on a very few things, who knows what and when: the up-timer weapons, the strength of our resolve, and whomsoever earns that most precious of commodities—the blessings of divine favor."

Smidha, pale now, looked away.

Jahanara sat back. Giving Smidha another moment cost her nothing but time. She even made her move, knowing it was futile.

Smidha's eyes, following Jahanara's hands, fell on the board again.

"Your will, Begum Sahib..." She let her words trail off, and made the move Jahanara knew she would.

"But?"

A tremulous smile. "Not so much a 'but' as 'new thoughts occur...'"

"Oh?" Jahanara said, ceding the game by laying her emperor on his side.

"Amar Singh Rathore," Smidha said, picking up the pale jade horseman she'd captured earlier. The piece Priscilla said came to be called the knight in that future which was not to be.

"What of him?" Jahanara knew the young Rajput umara's reputation for prideful arrogance, but he had been nothing but supportive of Dara's rule.

Smidha reached across the board to Jahanara's remaining castle, placing the sowar beside it. "Your brother must send Amar Singh south to garrison Asirgarh."

"Why?" Jahanara asked, genuinely puzzled.

"Because he is as prickly as that new fruit from the Americas, what is it called...pineapple...yes, pineapple, that the court has enjoyed these last few years. Yes, prickly, and like to give offensive wind at the least opportunity."

"And?"

"And if Dara were to publicly give him an independent command as important as Asirgarh, it will swell his head with even more pride. That pride will tie him to our cause with chains forged of strongest steel yet he'll feel only pleasure at the recognition and responsibility received, not the collar we have placed around his neck. And here, at home, your brother will have one less potential headache."

Jahanara cocked her head. "But, why send him to Asirgarh? Why not to Gwalior?"

"Because Gwalior's zamindar is headstrong and still resents the way Shah Shuja and Aurangzeb snubbed him while pursuing Shah Jahan's campaign to the south. If Dara were to replace him, who knows which way the man would jump, and who he might back out of pure spite. Besides, Asirgarh is far enough away for both the semblance of independence such men crave and distant enough for Dara's general peace of mind. And, if common opinion and his own words on the subject are to be trusted, Amar Singh is at least a competent commander."

Jahanara smiled. "He does tend to wax poetic about his own exploits. Paramjit is a staunch ally, however. I would not see her offended."

Smidha waggled her head. "That she may be, but Amar Singh's mother, Raijada, is another matter entirely."

"Oh?" Jahanara asked. "Is she spying for one of my brothers?"

"Nothing so useful as that! No, she's simply a bitter old prune of a woman with a penchant for rumor-mongering. She was at the center of the web of rumors you and Nadira worked so hard to quell."

"She was?" Jahanara's tone made a statement of the question. Then the anger hit, filling her mouth with bitter copper. "She was," she repeated. Jahanara let the rage expand to fill her heart, then expand some more, and finally, let it expand beyond the confines of her body in hopes that, as it lost density, it would also lose power over her thoughts.

Smidha was watching her as one hunting cat watches another, not fearful—never that—simply...watchful.

Jahanara took a long, deep breath, then let it out slowly, sending the remainder of her anger and bitterness out into the world with the exhalation. She had room in neither heart nor head for such feelings, not if she was to win.

Chapter 12

Allahabad
Mission camp on the Great Trunk Road

"This is the biggest lump we've bought so far. I hope it's pure," Ricky said, the crickets just starting to sing their night song beyond the tent flap.

"How much more do you need?" Jadu asked without looking up from his ledgers.

"Not really sure how long it keeps..." Ricky said, looking uncertainly at the fist-sized lump of opium lying on waxed paper before him. They'd bought it at what Jadu assured them was a fair price in Allahabad just before departing this morning. Ricky had laid it out for repacking with the smaller amounts they'd obtained from previous stops.

"Kept away from damp and extremes of temperature, salt water, or immersion, it will last at least a year," Jadu said, quill never stopping in its glide across the pages before him.

"Extremes of temperature like you get in Allahabad during the dry season?" Ricky asked, glancing out of the tent at the last, lingering light of the sunset. The days were getting steadily warmer and there wasn't an air conditioner for thousands of miles.

"And we just have to keep it out of water as we cross the rivers bounding this *doab* and enter into Bengal, where the rivers abound?"

"So long as it's not left for hours in direct sun, it should retain its effectiveness. And the watertight chests I provided should be effective in keeping it from inundation."

"All right . . . Then I think I'd like to have twice what we got. Twenty chests or so ought to do it. I was told we wouldn't need anywhere near that much to make what we need, because of the process they plan to use, but I don't want to be the guy who came back without the goods, you know?"

Jadu nodded agreement. "Almost always, it is better to have mo—" The quill stopped. "Ricky, where is Bobby?"

"Lying down and trying not to shit himself."

"Arm yourself, Ricky."

"Wha—" Ricky stopped as a scraping sound reached his ears. It took a moment for Ricky to identify the noise: swords being drawn from scabbards were not among those sounds a youth spent in small-town West Virginia made readily identifiable.

"The night creatures have ceased making any noise," Jadu said, eyes wide.

Ricky snapped up the eight-seventy and chambered a shell with the obligatory, and comforting, *shick-shack* sound.

As the metallic noise faded, Ricky heard the thunder of hooves, a sound he had grown more accustomed to identifying since coming to India.

Jadu shouted something and ran into the semidarkness of the camp.

Unsure what the man had said, Ricky ran out of the tent and came to a stop to get a quick idea of what was happening.

Lights were approaching from the east, the closest just about ten yards from the first of the perimeter of the camp, if he remembered correctly. From the number of torches they carried, a dozen or more horsemen were attacking from that direction, climbing diagonally across the gentle slope toward Jadu's tent at the center of the camp.

The merchant's shouts were answered from all along the perimeter of the camp, followed quickly by pillars of flame as campfires were doused with oil. The merchant himself rushed toward where most of the guards were entangled in a melee with the riders, shouting further orders.

Ricky looked away from the sudden flare of lights. Seeking a patch of darkness, he looked toward the river. As luck would have it, he spied figures running among the caravan's supplies and trade goods stacked not fifty yards from his position.

A choking cry sounded from among the people there, followed by the fall of one shadowed figure.

Blinking, he realized the remaining figures were picking up the various goods and throwing them over the shoulders of their comrades. Somehow the second party of raiders had managed to get between the tents and the river.

They must have swum . . . The thought came slow. "Jadu!" he shouted.

No answer from the merchant, but Bobby appeared

next to him, his own shotgun at port arms, like they were taught.

"You see that?" Ricky asked.

"Yup." Bobby suddenly hunched over his gun, emitting a rumble.

"Stay here till you're feeling better," Ricky said as his friend straightened.

"I'm . . . good enough," Bobby muttered, looking green even in the red light of the fires.

"Let's go, then," Ricky said, comforted by his friend's insistence on joining the party.

They started trotting toward the . . . bandits or river pirates? Was there a specific term for them? Shaking off such thoughts, Ricky tried to get a count of the raiders. It was hard to judge in the limited light, but Ricky counted between a dozen and twenty figures. Most were moving back and forth to the water's edge with the caravan's goods in their arms.

Ricky thought about firing a warning shot, but the first man to see them coming dropped his package, pulled a knife so big it might as well be a sword and shouted over his shoulder. For help, if the response from his friends was any indication: three more of the raiders drew various blades and started moving to meet the up-timers.

"Couple more steps?" Ricky asked.

Bobby groaned, doubled over, and farted wetly.

Ricky would have laughed if he wasn't so scared his friend might have caught some deadly disease *and* the raiders hadn't started to charge at that moment.

Unable to see to his friend, Ricky shouldered the Remington and dropped the bead over the first bandit's naked torso. Pushing the safety off, he stroked the trigger with his finger. The high-base shell made the gun kick him in the shoulder, hard, and launch its load with a heavy bark and flash as the buckshot exited the barrel.

A spark went up from the man's sword, followed closely by the swordsman himself slumping to the ground with a wet, coughing sob.

The others, scattered in a loose group a few steps from each other and behind the first, paused a moment, then one of them started shouting.

Ricky cycled the action and drew a bead on his next target.

The raiders were sprinting at him now, unaware he had five more in the tube and thinking to cut him down as he tried to reload.

Another man staggered, fell as soon as Ricky pulled the trigger.

Ricky didn't bother to aim now, just cycled and stroked the trigger. He was left unsure if he'd hit or not, as the man now leading the pack didn't slow.

By now close enough Ricky could see his eyes glittering in the firelight, Ricky watched the growing round O of fear the man's mouth pulled into as he cycled the action once more and fired.

This time the man went down, sliding across the damp grass of the camp to a boneless stop almost at his feet.

Again he cycled the action, but the fourth man was already on top of him, swinging a sword overhand at his head. Ricky ducked, desperately throwing his shotgun up to parry the descending blade. The sword clanged against the receiver somewhere near the loading gate. The raider pulled back for another swing.

Bobby's gun barked at Ricky's hip, surprising both combatants.

The raider fell, revealing the back of the last man as he ran for the water's edge.

Ricky lowered his still-smoking gun. He felt a surge of excitement, a feeling of invincibility, of being entirely *there*.

Unnerved by the sensations, Ricky looked around, moving his head to be sure he could actually see what he needed to see. From the absence of torches at the edge of the camp and the fading hoofbeats, the horsemen were fleeing, having distracted the caravan guards.

He looked to where the other raiders had been on the shore and dimly saw shapes on the water. After a moment he realized it was a boat being poled rapidly downstream.

The sound of Bobby puking reached him.

He swung around and knelt beside his friend. "You okay?"

"No. Sick. Soooo sick." He paused a moment, then mumbled, "I think I shit myself."

"Me too!" Ricky laughed, a note of panic he didn't like edging the words.

"Reload," Bobby groaned, thumbing a shell into the loading gate of his own weapon.

"Oh, yeah." Ricky found his hands were steadying as he took the first shell out of the vest he wore and thumbed it into the loading gate. His thumb caught on the deep scratch in the metal left behind by the sword stroke he'd parried. The thought of how close he'd come to getting stabbed made Ricky's hands start to shake once more. The shells seemed slippery and the gun heavy and awkward, making the loading take longer than it should have. He managed, though, despite the stink coming from either Bobby or the bodies at his feet.

The pair of them ignored the moans of one of the men Ricky had shot. Not out of cruelty, but because there was almost nothing to be done for the man—and what did a guy ready to kill people just to take their property deserve in the way of care, anyway?

It wasn't the first time he'd had to kill someone, and he didn't know how he'd feel about it tomorrow, but for now he was okay with leaving the son of a bitch to die.

"Ricky? Bobby?" Jadu called.

"Here, Jadu."

The merchant strode up the slope, his footman and body servant, Vikram, carrying a torch aloft for him. Two guards were on his heels as he joined the up-timers.

He wasn't even breathing all that hard, despite the slight paunch he sported and the fact Ricky hadn't seen him exercise or train once in the weeks they'd spent on the road.

"Are you well?"

Ricky gestured with the shotgun. "Bobby's still sick, but we managed to keep from getting cut to pieces."

"So. Sick," Bobby groaned.

"But not injured in the attack?"

"No."

Nodding, Jadu knelt and examined the man dying at their feet. After a moment he stood and walked down to where the goods and supplies had been dropped when they turned to attack the up-timers.

Ricky helped Bobby to his feet, intending to take him back to his tent.

"No, man. I'm good enough here. Besides, I want to hear firsthand what's up."

"You sure?"

"Yeah, I have to wash in the river anyway."

Eyes tearing from the stink coming from Bobby's pants, Ricky said, "Yes, yes you do."

They took a few steps, and Ricky couldn't resist a jab at Bobby's expense: "But isn't that how you took sick in the first place?"

"Might be," Bobby mumbled, taking the question seriously. "But I won't open my mouth this time, not even if I have to scream for help."

"Right," Ricky said. Deciding not to make any more fun, he simply supported his sick friend on the way to meet the merchant.

Jadu addressed the up-timers as they approached. "Thanks to your intervention, it looks like they weren't able to get more than some of the indigo we bought and some cotton cloth I was planning to sell soon anyway, prices being cheaper nearer Bengal. I would have preferred not to lose anything, but with no one seriously injured and so little lost, I am content. More than that, I am thankful. I will make a great offering at temple when next I am able."

Vikram held the torch aloft as his master knelt next to the wounded man and asked a question.

Ricky couldn't hear the answer, but at a gesture from Jadu, the guards picked the wounded raider up and carried him toward Jadu's tent.

Jadu stood and walked among the other men Ricky had shot, examining them.

"What are you looking for, Jadu?" Bobby asked, wading into the river to clean himself.

"I hope to discover who sent them," Jadu answered, an odd expression on his face as he stopped what he was doing and watched Bobby.

"They're not bandits?" Ricky asked.

Jadu waggled his head. "Perhaps. But using horses and boats in such a well-coordinated attack speaks of more organization than we normally see from bands of criminals, especially here where there are more regular patrols by police on both river and road."

Bobby pulled his shirt off and started to weakly pull at his pants.

Jadu looked more uncomfortable, made a nervous gesture with his hand. "Could you . . . come out of the water?"

"Need to get clean . . ." Bobby paused a moment, his expression thoughtful, then asked, "Why?"

"There are a number of snakes in these waters and along these shores. If they should bite . . . That will kill you very quickly."

Bobby's eyes went wide enough the whites were visible in the torchlight. He appeared to levitate out of the water and to shore, looking to Ricky like nothing so much as a cartoon character running for his life.

Stifling a laugh, Ricky turned away. When he could keep a straight face he turned around only to find his friend shaking, eyes darting from the river to the ground at their feet.

"Who do you think it was?" Ricky asked, as much to distract Bobby as get an answer.

Another waggle of the head accompanied Jadu's reply. "Could be the local zamindar out to pilfer goods because he knows he's not likely to be investigated by the emperor's men any time soon. It could also simply be someone opposed to the emperor's rule... It is difficult to know."

"The wounded guy know anything?"

Jadu glanced after the man and gave a very Western shrug. "He might tell us something should he wake before we leave tomorrow." He returned his gaze to the two up-timers. "You should rest. We must leave earlier than I planned when we made camp."

Bobby nodded, worry and illness leeching the color from his expression, even in the torchlight.

"Why the hurry?" Ricky asked, worried that Bobby's condition would worsen without rest and easy access to clean water while on the move.

"If the local zamindar was involved in this attack, he may decide to complete our destruction and thereby guarantee there are no witnesses to interrogate if the Sultan Al'Azam or local governor gets around to ordering an investigation."

"I'll be good to go," Bobby said, bravely trying to mask his discomfort.

"I will arrange for you to ride in a litter at our next caravanserai, my young friend. In the meantime...and with your permission, I will use some of the opium we just purchased to make a remedy that I hope will prove helpful in arresting your digestive distress."

"Anything," Bobby said. It said a lot about how badly he must feel that he so readily agreed to take the drug that both young men had such a healthy fear of. It made Ricky feel bad, knowing he'd had fun at his friend's expense.

"I want to thank you for all your help and guidance,"

Ricky said, wishing to change the subject and acutely aware the older man's precautions, planning, and commands had been the difference between losing most of their goods—not to mention their lives—in the raid and suffering the minor losses they had.

"Thanks are not necessary." A small smile transformed the man's face. "At least not yet. We have not yet met with success, and to accept your thanks prematurely may call the disfavor of the gods upon us . . ."

He and Ricky helped Bobby up, and together they walked to the tents.

Chapter 13

The Deccan
Red Tent, Shah Shuja's camp

The drums rolled on as Shuja's *wazir* announced
Aurangzeb's arrival at the court of the emperor.

The court of an *emperor, at any rate.*

Aurangzeb did not allow the irony of the thought
to change his carefully neutral expression as he came
to a stop before Shuja's tent. Such would not be prudent, given the fact he was beyond the assistance of
the bulk of his army and deep in his brother's power.
Besides, smiling made him appear even younger than
he naturally did, something he had long cultivated a
calm and disinterested demeanor in order to combat.
Further, he had expended much effort and treasure
to gain this audience. Indeed, his fresh agreement
with the Portuguese viceroy had provided Aurangzeb
with the one thing Shuja could no longer do without:
supplies for his host. Food and fodder enough to last
them a few months, at least. So, however much he
disliked most music, only a fool would follow the

investment of treasure and time with a display of ill temper over such a trifling thing.

Aurangzeb did not count himself a fool.

Dismounting, Aurangzeb examined his older brother. Shuja wore an impressive robe sewn with pearls, rubies, and emeralds, and had a large diamond in his turban that twinkled in the early-morning light. His cheeks were flushed, whether with wine or excitement or a combination of the two, Aurangzeb could not say at this remove.

For his part, Aurangzeb had chosen his wardrobe very carefully: a simple robe of dark silks that would stand in contrast to his brother's ostentatious display and a *taqiyah* of red and black he'd fashioned for himself. The only jewel to adorn him was affixed to the hilt of the dagger that rode at his belt.

The drums stopped. After a long pause, the echo from the far hills did too.

As the pride of lions, or in this case, perhaps, a pack of jackals examines prey before the hunt, the eyes of all those present turned on him.

Aurangzeb stood tall under their collective gaze, glad that those who observed could not see the heart beating hard in the cavern of his chest.

With a pride bordering on the unseemly, he reflected that whatever reputation for austere habits, religious piety, and personal bravery he had obtained in his short life would certainly be enhanced by today's events, regardless of the outcome God had decreed.

"Brother!" Shuja called. The sun's rays scattered from jewel-studded sleeves as he raised his arms in welcome. That Shuja did not rise from his seat—Aurangzeb could not, in the privacy of his own mind, call it a throne—before the tent was not lost on anyone present.

Aurangzeb least of all. Of course, Aurangzeb had planned for these petty aggravations and, with the exception of the drums, Shuja had failed to act outside of his younger brother's expectations for the meeting.

Judging his moment to again gather all eyes, Aurangzeb approached his elder brother on steady feet, posture erect and perfectly proper. He stopped just short of the distance Shuja's kokas would be expected to order him disarmed in the presence of the emperor.

"Sultan Al'Azam," Aurangzeb said with a deep, respectful obeisance.

A collective sigh ran through the assembled courtiers as, with his first words, Aurangzeb publicly acknowledged Shah Shuja's claim on the Peacock Throne. Aurangzeb could not decide if it was relief or pleasure that made them exhale so, and quickly decided it did not signify.

Hoping to forestall some wise courtier among his brother's advisors ordering him taken prisoner now that he'd played what appeared to be his best gambit, Aurangzeb waited scarcely a heartbeat before continuing: "I wish to serve you, my brother. You, Sultan Al'Azam, are one I know will stand in righteous opposition to that misguided, irreligious fool, Dara! He, who knows neither respect nor grace, honor nor amity, and was unable to protect our father from his enemies must be returned to his proper place! He must be prevented from corrupting our storied lineage with error and idiocy! Kept from defiling your great empire with misrule and disharmony!"

Shuja was sitting forward and nodding as his younger brother finished. Belatedly realizing his error in showing interest—let alone affirmation—for what his brother had to say, Shuja sat back as silence descended.

Aurangzeb tried to gauge the effect of his speech without appearing to, and failed to find a friendly face among those closest to him.

The wazir fidgeted, drawing the eyes of both brothers.

As if the sight of the man brought him back to some prearranged script, Shuja looked again at Aurangzeb. "What then, brother?"

Aurangzeb bowed once more before replying. "All present here today know that I desire nothing more than a life of quiet contemplation, an opportunity to focus on pursuing a deeper understanding of the Word of God—" Some among the gathered nobles muttered. Aurangzeb, expecting it, seized upon their skepticism to fuel the fire of his tongue. "I would happily live out my days engaged in only these holy pursuits, but I cannot!"

The atmosphere of the crowd was changing, those closest hanging on his every word. "No, not so long as our feckless brother preaches of accord with all religions even while he reaches for *bang* and honeyed wine then rallies to his banner those 'up-timers,' men who profess no faith at all! These things he does in hopes of gaining some technical advantages over you, the rightful Sultan Al'Azam!"

The crowd was now, if not held entirely in thrall to his words, then approaching it.

Shuja's wazir seemed on the verge of advising Shuja to silence his brother before they realized they might have chosen the wrong son to back.

Aurangzeb did not allow him time to speak, however. "Why, he even allows our sister to rule his harem instead of the wife that should! That Jahanara is a wise and intelligent woman, I have no doubt, but my regard and respect for her quality does nothing to remedy this breach of tradition. Indeed, under her influence, Dara has not sought wives of his leading nobles as a Sultan should! The nobles of the court are left without the traditional guarantor of their sovereign's trust and love! Instead the influence traditionally wielded by the collective women in the harem is not even left in the hands of his lone wife—but rather, our sister!"

Many courtiers were nodding—the older among them, those with daughters of marriageable age—in particular.

That Aurangzeb had not taken a wife was one of the few things that made this interview possible. Had he wives, or worse yet, children, he would be too obviously a threat to Shuja's claim for his dissembling to have any chance at success. Every event was an opportunity, every crisis a lever to move the world.

That Shah Shuja himself had entered into negotiations for several wives in the last weeks had not been lost on Aurangzeb as he prepared this moment.

Indeed, Nur had served both brothers well in this regard: her rank and seniority making her the natural choice as go-between for Shuja and the families of prospective wives, and then duly reporting her observations from those meetings to Aurangzeb.

That she was also cautiously vetting several of Shuja's more prominent nobles regarding marriage prospects for Aurangzeb went without saying. The nobles she'd chosen were to be kept in the dark a little while longer, as it was not yet safe for her to approach them, regardless of how carefully they were selected for discretion as well as clear indications that they had joined their cause to Shuja's more because of proximity to his power rather than any earnest desire to serve Aurangzeb's older brother.

Even ordering Nur to assess such nobles had been a risk. But, while Aurangzeb must allay Shuja's fears, the end game also required that he had allies in place to secure a smooth transition of power. Marriage alliances were the best way to secure those allies. So, for now, he was unmarried, which only added to his reputation for asceticism for the conservative nobility and insured that Shuja would perceive him to be less of a threat.

"And, while he persists in resisting your rule, Sultan Al'Azam, I cannot but support you in putting a stop to his misrule. So I bring you those who have been loyal to my court, and place them, and myself, at your service."

Silence descended in the wake of Aurangzeb's final, ringing assertion. Not because those who heard him did not feel the pull of his charisma and skill at oratory, but because even the least discerning of Shuja's courtiers was aware that Shuja's reaction was the only one that mattered in this moment.

If Shuja waited a long moment before answering, Aurangzeb could not be certain as to his strained nerves each and every beat of his own heart required an eternity to complete.

"You speak wisely and well, little brother, and I thank you for your offer of service." He paused a moment, keeping his listeners in suspense, then continued. "I accept it, as I accept you: with my whole heart and open arms." He stood and suited actions to words. "Come, embrace me!"

Aurangzeb moved forward and stepped into his brother's embrace as the court erupted in approbation.

None were near enough to hear a smiling Shuja speak in Aurangzeb's ear: "I will gladly send you off to

Mecca with a glorious stipend when we have defeated Dara, brother. You are too dangerous to be allowed to remain, otherwise."

Smiling to the crowd, Aurangzeb said quietly, "You wound me, brother. I but serve at your pleasure."

Shuja released Aurangzeb and looked him in the eye. "Be sure it remains so, and I will not have you thrown into Gwalior Fort to rot."

"Your will, Sultan Al'Azam," Aurangzeb intoned as he gave another, deeper, and most solemn bow before his brother. That the movement concealed his pleasure was proper, as the thought resounding through his mind was a simple, incredibly powerful refrain:

All is accomplished according to His will, and in His time!

It seemed to Aurangzeb that his plans were in accordance with that Will, and were thereby rewarded with success.

Nur's tent
Shah Shuja's camp

Triumph stirred Nur's heart to an erratic beat as Aurangzeb and his brother retired to the Red Tent to plan Dara's downfall. Such a public display of amity and common purpose was useful for both men, and would, no doubt, be recorded by the many informants who dwelt in both camps.

Aurangzeb had not explicitly revealed his plans to her before embarking on this course, but she had suspected something of the sort. Instrumental in sounding out certain nobles on the subject of marriage, she had learned early on that he had long-term plans, His interest in seeking marriage alliances was the one factor that promoted her suspicions to absolute assurance: Aurangzeb had plans that reached *far* beyond this clever act of political theater.

Using her successful overtures and negotiations with Shuja on his behalf as a pretext for her elevation, Nur had been rewarded with high position in both courts as a result. That said, both of them knew the truth: By allowing her to do this on his behalf, Aurangzeb had ceded her some measure of power over him. Keeping secrets for a prince was the first duty of a loyal servant, and the first public show of trust a prince or emperor could bestow upon his subordinates.

She returned to the tent Shuja had set aside for her in his camp and ordered a light meal. The men would be at it long into the night, especially Shuja, who continued to drink and carouse far more than was wise for a fresh-minted emperor with brothers still alive and ready to contend for the Peacock Throne.

There was, perhaps, an opportunity there. She must see if someone could be suborned in Shuja's tent. Someone with access to his food or, better still, some of the vast quantity of wine the man consumed.

It seemed that by his every action, including today's acceptance of Aurangzeb's fealty, Shuja reaffirmed her decision to support Aurangzeb's claim on the Peacock Throne.

In contrast, Aurangzeb was a natural politician, charismatic in a way neither of his older brothers were, and wise beyond his years. In this, he most resembled his eldest sister, Jahanara.

Exchanging heavy robes of state for lighter silks,

she spied a fresh missive from Agra resting on a golden tray. Eagerly, she plucked it up and set to work decoding the cipher.

As she worked, a part of Nur's mind examined why she'd thought of Jahanara in the context of leadership. Of course, her own history of ruling alongside her husband made her more alert to the possibility of women wielding great power from the harem, but never before had the sister of an emperor been so powerful. Always before it was a wife, or perhaps concubine, who had risen to power. Jahanara's position in her father's court was perhaps unusual, but not entirely unprecedented, as there were other fathers who had doted on their daughters to some extent and gave them power and position. But Jahanara Begum's power and prestige under Dara was *entirely* new to the Mughal court.

As any court had more than its share of jealousies, Nur had chosen Jahanara's unique status as an avenue of attack.

And going on the attack had been, and continued to be, necessary. All her previous intelligence from Agra had it that the young woman was at the center of the intrigues and bedevilments that continued to make life difficult for spies and informants wishing to report the goings-on in Dara's court. Gaining private, insightful news of Dara's health or state of mind was well-nigh impossible these days, and Nur's overtures to those noble wives who had access to the harem had been slow to bear fruit. And even then, she was forced to admit, the product had been small and barely worth the cost in time and promises, as their information was scarcely more than what was available through official public channels.

The cipher cracked, and she had to focus all her

considerable mind on reassembling the message for a few minutes.

The corners of her mouth turned down as she finished and read the message through once more. The content was both timely to the subject of her thoughts and exceedingly frustrating: Nadira had, through clever manipulation of the court, put an end to the whisper campaign Nur had launched against Jahanara only a month past.

While the whispers had not cost her significant time or effort to begin, it was a gambit she'd used to great success in the past when attempting to draw the fangs of rivals, both within the harem and in the wider court. Such attacks were also not repeatable, at least for the foreseeable future. Those who had been most vocal in their complaining would not be as readily listened to should they essay some new complaint against Jahanara. Worse yet, those who might have been encouraged to raise their voices from other quarters would be discouraged by observing how Nadira had rallied to Jahanara's side to quash the whispers. Perhaps if she were there, things would be different. Most harem politics was reducible to a game of credibility and character, with the emperor's children and the emperor's time and affection among the critical pieces in play at all times, in all seasons.

Nur hoped the one piece she'd moved that had yet to report might still have success, but there was no telling when that play would bear fruit, let alone what that fruit would be.

She shook her head, acknowledging she was, perhaps, too distant from Dara's court to directly influence the full gamut of court play. It put her in mind of the years she had spent in quasi-exile after her defeat at Shah Jahan's hands.

After a moment spent in self-pity, she put her frustrations away and turned her attention to Shuja's court. Events here were more than enough to keep her mind active, thoughts focused, and her thirst for power whetted to a keen edge.

Yes. Nur would let Aurangzeb direct her to any active subterfuge in Dara's court and otherwise simply continue to monitor her sources for usable intelligence. It was time to focus on the work nearer to hand. Already she had planned two marriage bids for Shah Shuja. Now she must find a way to present them, first to Aurangzeb so that he could let her know if either choice would prove a detriment to his plans, and then to Shuja. It would be a delicate process, but one she'd managed before.

It would help if Aurangzeb did not keep his plans so close. The young man had a knack for political maneuvering, but in consequence he did not share his plans easily or often.

Perhaps she should not be thinking in terms of *what* he planned, but *when* he would execute them. She knew, with a certainty normally reserved for the sun rising in the east, that the end goal of all his maneuvering and plots was to rule as emperor.

Yes. That was it. She could spend time and effort trying to learn *what* he planned and get nowhere . . . Or, she could, instead, set herself to preparing for the *moment* of Aurangzeb's next move.

Yes.

She would make herself indispensable to his cause by being ready to assist him in that moment, whatever his needs might be.

Chapter 14

Agra
Red Fort, the harem

Heart hammering in her chest, Jahanara nodded at Atisheh as she approached the warrior's post.

The freshly appointed commander of the warrior women assigned to guard Dara's harem made a silent half-bow in return.

Sudden trepidation made Jahanara slow just steps before Atisheh. Even now, she could return to her quarters, call off this folly and act as if she'd had nothing to do with bringing a man into the harem precincts.

She stood on the balls of her feet, ready to turn and flee.

"You only wish to meet the amir because of the fire of your desire, Shehzadi. Please do not do this thing," Smidha had cautioned, only that afternoon. "It is dangerous, and gains you nothing you do not already have."

Jahanara had simply ignored her servant's cautionary

whisper, as arguing the point could provide listeners with proof she entertained the idea. Keeping secrets from everyone who did not have an absolute need to know seemed to have become the one constant of her existence.

The argument she would have given, had circumstances allowed, was primarily that her brother needed his closest advisors to know each other's minds. The daily requirements of court life prevented any real chance of that understanding between the amir and her, especially as their public conduct was the subject of constant scrutiny from all quarters.

Written missives were equally problematic, as they could too easily fall into the wrong hands, and all potential messengers were watched at one time or another.

She straightened. No, this had to be done. At least this once, she had to meet him face-to-face. To thank him for his service, if they could not reach some greater understanding.

Silencing the uneasy thought that Smidha's assessment of Jahanara's true motives for the meeting could be more accurate than her own, Jahanara squared her shoulders and strode forward on slippered feet.

Atisheh pulled aside the hanging and pressed a particular part of the wall. The section of wall opened, revealing a secret passage from which the smells of sweet tobacco smoke drifted out to enfold her.

Glad the scents of desperation and death that had permeated the chamber beyond when Mullah Mohan was tortured to his end had been cleansed, Jahanara entered the passage.

❖   ❖   ❖

Salim puffed at the water pipe, uneasiness stirring in his belly as he waited for the messenger he had been told was coming.

The secrecy he'd been ordered to maintain seemed... extreme.

For one, he did not like the location. Oh, the chamber itself was fine: small but hung with silks, plump cushions, and lit with scented candles. A chilled, golden carafe of some juice or another sat beside goblets on a gold tray, while a fine water pipe sat in the midst of the cushions. That it was loaded with the very best tobacco that Salim had ever smoked was besides the point.

For another, Salim was used to secrecy by now. He wondered what was to be gained by meeting with a messenger face-to-face here, rather than receiving the message among others, thereby concealing any importance.

Unless the messenger is more important than the message. The thought chilled him, as it called to mind only one, or perhaps two, people who might fit that description, both of them women.

And the location of the secret chamber took on an even more ominous meaning in light of that thought. During the time he'd spent in service to Shah Jahan, translating the up-timer documents almost nightly, he'd gained a fair degree of working knowledge of the layout of the harem precincts. He suspected he was very near those precincts if not within them even before Atisheh had shown him through the secret door he'd had no idea existed. The warrior woman, most trusted of Jahanara's guards, had told him she would be outside, to avail himself of refreshment, to relax, and that he should only have a short wait. That it had been Atisheh who showed him here made him more nervous, not less. Granted, the warrior woman would never betray her mistress, but Salim could not imagine Atisheh acting in so clandestine a manner for anyone *but* Jahanara, and that was a problem in and of itself.

He could not shake the remembered feel of Jahanara Begum's skin under his hands nor the touch of her body as she clung to him the night he'd tried, and failed, to defend Shah Jahan from the assassins sent by Mullah Mohan.

The sound of her voice issuing from behind the jali while giving counsel to her brother had been indicative of a sharp, inquisitive mind that was certainly superior to his, at least in regard to formal education. But that voice also brought to mind the shape of her nose, her eyes, her . . .

It required an effort of will to stop his thoughts from pursuing the path they'd turned to. He closed his eyes and offered an unspoken prayer: *God, please don't let it be Jahanara Begum who wishes this meeting, for I am weak, and she is exactly that which waters the parched plains of my desire.*

He heard a sound from the short passage he'd entered from. Dreading who he would see, Salim looked and then cast his eyes heavenward.

God, you make no effort to save this poor petitioner from himself!

She was veiled and swathed in silken robes that protected her modesty, but he recognized her from her graceful movements and, when she drew closer, her eyes—the color and shape of them as well as the lovely long lashes that she lowered demurely.

"Shehzadi Jahanara Begum," he said, coming to his feet for a deep, respectful bow that also gave him time to gather scattered wits.

He glanced surreptitiously beyond her in search of some escort, but was disappointed to see the secret door closing, and not so much as a maid or guard to protect her reputation.

"Amir Salim Yilmaz, honored commander of five thousand," she returned, gliding forward to the cushions opposite him. The smell of roses traveled the air in her wake, as if flowers bloomed in honor of her passage. She did not so much sit as gracefully fold herself onto the cushions.

Salim remained standing, frozen in place. Caught entirely unprepared for this private meeting and, frankly, unmanned by the strength of his reaction to her presence.

An instant later his mind thawed enough to run through the dire repercussions of discovery: repercussions that started with execution and ran heedless and fast down a mountainous slope from there.

The political ramifications alone could potentially cripple Dara when he needed to appear, at all times, to be fully in charge of everything that occurred in his household, especially to those of his followers—and they were in the majority—who set great stock in such things.

This meeting was breathtakingly dangerous—

"Do you like the tobacco?" she asked, interrupting his thoughts while picking up another of the water pipe's stems and slipping it under her veil. The pipe burbled as she drew on it.

Realizing he still held the other stem of the pipe in his hand, Salim said, "I do, Begum Sahib."

"It is my favorite," she said, regarding him through the smoke she exhaled. "You may be interested to know that it is from Nur's personal stores. Procured through some family connection in Persia, no doubt."

"Begum Sahib, I don't know how to say this..."

"Then don't." She gestured with a hennaed hand for him to sit across from her. "We do not have a great deal of time, and I would prefer to spend it speaking of important matters rather than your advising me that I endanger my brother's cause with this meeting, so please..." She waved again, eyes sparkling.

"Begum Sahib, I am your servant." He sat and took a long draw on the pipe to avoid meeting her eyes and losing himself in them.

"You have been a most worthy servant to me and my brother. I wanted to thank you once more for your efforts on the night my father was assassinated. Beyond that service, which nearly cost you your life, you have continued to aid my brother in his time of need, keeping our secrets and working consistently to secure our future."

Salim sat, silent, ruminating, drawing on the pipe once more.

When he did not respond even after filling his lungs, she said, "Say what you will. You will not anger me with sincerity."

Oh, I think I will, but as you ask...

"While I thank Begum Sahib for her kind words of thanks, I do not know that they required such risks as this meeting to convey," Salim said, each word punctuated by a puff of smoke.

Her beautiful eyes did not so much as narrow. "Salim... may I call you Salim?"

He nodded, mouth gone suddenly dry. He very much liked to hear his name upon her lips.

"Salim, we are in your debt. I wished to express my personal gratitude for the actions you took . . . openly, without the constraints of conduct any such expression would find were I to engage in it before the entire court.

"But beyond that expression, I thought it wise that we establish a dialogue now, an understanding that will permit us to work more closely toward our common goal: the preservation of my brother's reign."

Red Fort, Rosharana's quarters

"So, you should not leave it too long, Roshanara Begum."

Roshanara nodded. Then, realizing the man was not able to see the movement from behind the thick veils that had been placed over his head for this visit, said, "I understand, Doctor Gradinego."

"Excellent. Do you have other questions of health I need answer?"

"I do not."

"Very good. With your permission, I will withdraw, Shehzadi?"

"Of course."

Blindly, the Venetian reached out as he made to stand.

Roshanara caught the hand in hers on the pretense of helping the man to his feet. The note passed from his palm to hers smoothly. Slipping it into her sash, she handed him off to Sabah, the warrior woman Atisheh had set to guard her. Ostensibly there to protect her, Roshanara knew better: the woman was, if not a spy, then a watchdog reporting her every move.

"See the doctor out," Roshanara commanded.

As if to provide proof of the validity of the princess's suspicions, Sabah summoned a eunuch to escort the ferenghi from the harem instead of doing it herself.

Pretending a lack of interest in the guard's activities she certainly didn't feel, Roshanara returned to the calligraphy project she'd been working on before the Venetian had been admitted.

The *qalam* was light in her hands, the paper smooth and thick awaiting the ink. Roshanara tried to find the calm required for her best work, but the meditative state eluded her. Gritting her teeth and willing herself to calm, she began to copy out the passages from the *Akbarnama*, the chronicle of Akbar the Great's reign.

But thoughts of the note in her sash and the messenger who had delivered it intruded. Gradinego had been summoned to advise her regarding certain respiratory health issues. The time and skills of the up-timer physicians had been monopolized by her elder siblings, so Roshanara and Dara's other courtiers had been forced to settle for their hangers-on, of whom Gradinego was not only the most popular for his skills and close connection to the up-timers, but also the most eager to avail himself of the favor of lesser lights like Roshanara Begum, who was still in some disfavor with the court.

Most of the court thought it odd that there were not more men like Gradinego among the ferenghi, social climbers who used the reputation of their associates to improve their own situation. There was a man among the merchants, but he'd been Salim Yilmaz's man even before the arrival of the up-timers, and never claimed any knowledge beyond that of his caste and position.

Roshanara began the next page, irritated that none of her activities would bring her any closer to knowing the contents of the note the ferenghi had passed. A glance showed that Sabah was still watching her closely enough to observe any surreptitious move to retrieve and read the note.

She muttered an imprecation as her irritation and wandering attentions led her into error: the light, loose grip on the qalam had shifted into a tight, heavy hand, ruining yet another page with an ill-formed stroke. The qalam clattered in its cradle as she set it down harder than intended.

Seeking calm, Roshanara sat back on her heels. A gesture summoned a slave with a goblet of julabmost, which she drank without tasting.

She picked up the qalam once more, thinking to clean it, but delayed as she saw a messenger entering the chamber. Atisheh often used that one for ordering the harem guards about. Dipping her instrument into the ink once more and placing another thick sheet of paper before her, she watched the messenger approach Sabah from the corner of her eye.

As the child eunuch spoke in the square-shouldered woman's ear, Roshanara slipped her hand into her sash and retrieved the paper. She flattened the missive out on her work surface and quickly read it through.

> *Should this whisper reach your ears,*
> *I will not suffer the night's fears,*
> *Alone, four times and never alone*
>   *again,*

I have but to think of your eyes and
the wisdom seen there,
To be restored to my faith in love,
For word shall surely come to me—as
on the soft wings of the dove!

Heart skipping a beat as she sifted the possible meanings of the rather poor poem. To be sure she took the proper message from it, Roshanara reread it. Once certain she had it committed to memory, she gave another—false this time—sigh of frustration and used the message paper to clean the qalam, taking her time to be sure she obliterated the writing.

Her hands began to tremble as the ramifications of the message sank in.

Just months ago she'd been certain that Jahanara would have her executed for her part in Father's death. Certain to the point of asking that an architect be sent for in order to plan a humble tomb for her remains to find their eternal rest. But weeks had passed without Dara giving the order for her execution. Then she'd grown afraid to eat, thinking she would be poisoned, murdered to save the family public embarrassment. It was only in the days since Nadira's birthday celebrations that she had begun to breathe once again. In saving Roshanara from the fall, Jahanara had proven herself uninterested in her death. Her elder sister was not happy with her, and blamed her for Father's demise, but she was not inclined to seek vengeance on Father's behalf.

This one message would have wiped out any ideas of clemency from Jahanara's or Dara's minds at a single stroke. The very thin obfuscation of the true message, not to mention the source, would not stand up against even the most cursory of examinations, especially if discovered amongst her things. No, the poem could have proved to be her death warrant.

The audacity of using the ferenghi to carry such a thinly concealed message made the hand holding her qalam tremble with fear.

Aurangzeb wants me to inform for him. The thought rattled, reverberating through her mind, an echo of a bull elephant's trumpeted threat.

She took a deep, steadying breath and set the now thoroughly cleaned qalam down again, proud that it did not clatter against the cradle this time.

Briefly, she thought of telling Jahanara of the message, but then she'd already destroyed the poem and... sudden tears born of frustration and fear formed in the corners of her eyes.

No. Dara and Jahanara would never let me alone if I told them I'd been contacted by Aurangzeb. And certainly not if I revealed that I'd destroyed the message before reporting it.

But did that mean she must be Aurangzeb's creature? That she must spy for him in Dara's court? She had always liked him best of her siblings. He, at least, was steadfast in his manner with everyone, where Dara was always alighting on some new subject, some new way of seeing the world, and never seemed interested in the world as it was. Shuja—Shuja was the most predictable, but he'd also always been crass and wild, not given to speaking to his sisters regarding anything of importance or even mutual interest.

And then there was Jahanara, who so resembled Mother in her manner and behavior that when Jahanara grew upset with some minor infraction of hers,

Roshanara always felt Mother's stare issuing from her sister's eyes.

And then there was Father's death and Jahanara's knowledge of her role in it...

Shame made Roshanara's cheeks heat, and tears spilled free from her eyes. She sniffed, hands twisting expensive silks between her fingers, staining them black with errant ink from the qalam.

The dam she'd erected against the pain and guilt of the last few months shattered. With sudden, breathtaking speed, her heart flooded and her thoughts drowned in emotions she'd kept at bay for too long.

Unsure whether she was crying for Father, for the state of her own soul, or for some sin she had yet to commit, Roshanara could only let the tears flow.

She collapsed forward, sobbing uncontrollably.

It was nearly an hour before she could be convinced to lie down, and another hour before she would drink the calming elixir pressed upon her at Jahanara's direction.

At last, she drifted on a sea of unconcern, and eventually, into a deep, drug-induced sleep, plagued by dreams of being pulled one way and the next...

Part Four

May, 1636

As smoke blots the white fire
—The Rig Veda

Chapter 15

The Deccan Plateau
Aurangzeb's column on the march

"Shah Shuja has not seen fit to meet with us," Father De Jesus said, angry voice loud enough to carry through the noise of the column to reach Aurangzeb's ears.

The prince briefly considered ignoring the priest but decided it would prove counterproductive. He'd already been avoiding the ferenghis for some time, hoping they would press their claims on Shah Shuja. Unfortunately, Shuja—or, more likely, his advisors—had immediately seen what rode toward them, proven wise, and studiously avoided interfering with any and all of Aurangzeb's obligations to the Europeans.

Then again, the Portuguese priest must be kept content, and if he did not wish to field their questions in open court, where even the questions asked might raise suspicions among the brighter of those serving Shuja, then Aurangzeb needed to quietly bring this particular dog to heel as soon as possible.

"Bring them to me, then make certain none can hear us," Aurangzeb murmured.

"Yes, Shehzada!" the captain of his *nökör* said, ordering the other riders to chivvy the scribes, messengers, courtiers, and other hangers-on into a loose circle just out of earshot. The captain then went to collect the Europeans and bring them to ride alongside the prince.

"Shehzada Aurangzeb, you are kind to see us on such short notice," a red-faced Methwold said, after they'd all made their obeisance from the saddle. It was hard to tell if it was the heat of the day or some embarrassment that held the man's color so high in his cheeks, as his fluent and courtly Persian left no hint of embarrassment.

"It is you men who have been most kind to me, President Methwold."

A moment passed in relative silence as the ferenghi digested the platitudes sent their way. Relative, because even at the head of the army, the noise of thousands of men and horses riding to his will was an ever-present rumble, not unlike the thunder of an angered heaven.

Methwold seemed to take the platitudes and silence for the warning Aurangzeb meant them to be.

Father De Jesus did not: "We have only acted as we were instructed by the viceroy, Shehzada. Under the agreed-upon terms."

"Whatever do you mean to imply, De Jesus?"

Aurangzeb's cool tone and lack of honorific penetrated the priest's armor of self-righteousness. He swallowed audibly and glanced at Methwold for support. When none was forthcoming he said carefully, "I imply nothing untoward, Shehzada Aurangzeb. I ask the question as we have wondered when you will be in a position to return the favors the viceroy, the Company, and the Church have provided your cause these last weeks."

Aurangzeb, patience strained, curbed the desire to lash out at the impertinent foreigner. De Jesus, annoying though he was, had the ear of those in power in Portuguese Estado, making him someone who should not be offended, with or without cause.

Aurangzeb would not reveal plans to Europeans that he couldn't reveal even to his most trusted subordinates. So, instead, pretending a greater calm than he actually felt, Aurangzeb patted his horse's neck and asked a question he already knew the answer to. "How long have you been in India, President Methwold?"

"Some years, now, Shehzada."

He looked at the priest. "And you, De Jesus, how long have you been here?"

"Slightly more than a year, and almost all of that spent in Portuguese India."

Aurangzeb nodded as if their answers had explained something he hadn't already known. Looking off into the distance, he asked, "And within the first weeks or months of your arrival, President and Priest, did either of you have occasion to enter into negotiations for goods or services?"

Both men nodded, De Jesus seeming impatient with the seeming non sequitur.

Methwold's expression was more cautious, as if the Englishman sensed a trap.

"And when you negotiated, did our merchants or the masters of our caravanserai grow impatient with your lack of language skills?"

"Only when first we came," Methwold answered before the priest could do more than open his mouth. "As we became more proficient, then—"

Aurangzeb's gesture of negation cut him off.

"Shehzada?"

"Were they impatient with you, or, lacking understanding, were you impatient with them?"

Methwold's shoulders twitched slightly, then slumped.

"For my part, I suppose I was the first to grow impatient," De Jesus supplied when Methwold did not answer. The priest was clearly puzzled by Methwold's sudden silence, so Aurangzeb gave him a moment to think.

Once confident he had the man's attention again, Aurangzeb nodded, sagely, as if the young priest had explained something very complex to his complete satisfaction.

Methwold shook his head, irritation, and its subject, easy to see.

"What?" De Jesus' irritated mutter was directed at the Englishman, allowing Aurangzeb to decide to ignore his rude tone.

Explaining to the priest, Methwold said, "The prince kindly illustrates for us that we are but lately come into his camp, and therefore do not yet understand all the goings-on here. He implies we are impatient, and our impatience reflects poorly on us, and may, eventually, annoy even our most patient of princes..." He trailed off with a thoughtful look at Aurangzeb.

"But—"

"What's worse," Methwold went on over De Jesus' words, whatever they might have been, "I suspect that he cannot explain his precise plans to us"—here his eyes flicked to the clouds of dust kicked up by the army—"they are for us to learn."

A slight smile teased at the corners of Aurangzeb's mouth. The Englishman was clever and sensible. Too bad his was the lesser part in the delegation the viceroy had sent to treat with and observe him.

"But—" De Jesus tried again.

Methwold cut him off once more. "I suspect there is much the prince would *like* to tell us, but cannot. Circumstances forbid it. So we must practice patience, and have faith in Shehzada Aurangzeb."

"Speaking of faith"—Aurangzeb looked at the priest—"I think you may be familiar with the tale of Joseph, son of Jacob? Who was cast down a well by his brothers?"

"Old Testament," Methwold said, receiving surprised looks from both Aurangzeb and De Jesus for his trouble. "What?" Methwold said. "We of the Church of England know our Bible."

Aurangzeb smiled, assuming the man's defensive tone had more to do with the Catholic priest's confounded expression than his own.

"Indeed you do." He paused, looking De Jesus in the eye as he continued, "But the reason I bring up Jacob and Joseph's story is that they reveal for the faithful that patience is considered a great virtue... to both Christian *and* Muslim, alike."

De Jesus looked back and, eventually, slowly nodded.

Aurangzeb relented once he was sure he was understood: "In time, I will see to it that the largesse you have shown me is rewarded. I ask that you exercise the virtue of patience, so that we may all benefit thereby."

De Jesus looked on the verge of asking another

question, but Methwold's cleared throat made the priest subside once more.

Once certain he had Aurangzeb's attention as well, Methwold said, "We will continue to be patient, Shehzada, and trust in you..."

"I ask for nothing more, and no less," Aurangzeb said, hoping to end the interview there.

But Methwold had been formulating a diplomatic response, not letting himself be brushed off so easily. "Of course, we two men are not, ultimately, responsible for the quality nor quantity of the largesse you receive. The English Company will continue to offer its support so long as I am president, but the viceroy may not agree with our practice of that virtue you hold in such high esteem. And should the viceroy decide to withdraw support from our endeavor, the Company cannot make up the shortfall the departure of our trading partners would cause in your chain of supply."

He paused to let that sink in before continuing, a wry smile on his lips. "Furthermore, the Company's honorable merchants at home may have already determined I am to be replaced. A letter that removes me from my position and names my replacement could already be en route to us here."

Another brief pause, then: "Such is the uncertainty of the times we live in."

Aurangzeb could find nothing in Methwold's statement to seize upon as offering insult. Impressed despite himself, he cast a glance at the priest. The younger man's expression told him how neatly the Englishman had presented their collective concerns, even at the very moment it appeared those concerns would be dismissed.

He rode in thoughtful silence for a few moments. Wishing to avoid a repeat of this interview any time soon, he measured his own response carefully before speaking. "Thank you. I understand your position more clearly for this conversation. I understand that your positions and any personal desire you might have for patience may be superseded by the commands of those for whom you toil. Equally, I hope that you will understand that I work toward an end that will see *all* of our collective positions advanced, and you and your masters rewarded."

He paused, glancing at each older man in turn, hoping to assess their responses.

Methwold's expression was blandly pleasant and entirely unreadable, while De Jesus looked, if not mollified, then at least less inclined to make another embarrassing scene. Catching the prince looking at him, he opened his mouth to speak.

Aurangzeb smiled thinly and preempted whatever the priest had in mind, saying, "It seems we should all practice patience here, at the bottom of the well, treading water."

Tent of Methwold and De Jesus, Aurangzeb's camp

"I can't believe I let you silence me," De Jesus groused as Methwold's slave cleared the remains of their meal. "My orders were to get him to agree to allow us a permanent presence here, and he has yet to even tell us when he will be in a position to make good on his numerous pledges."

William, already impatient with his companion's recent behavior, knew De Jesus' concerned mention of "us" actually meant the Catholic Church and its interests, but let that fact sit without comment in favor of a more important point: "Press for that now and you'll see our collective cause ruined. His plans are in motion, and our position more delicate than I think you appreciate."

"Oh, I know exactly how 'delicate' our position is. He has given us only the vaguest assurances that we will be given what he promised, and then only when pressed! And I now know the viceroy has informed the archbishop that as we move farther and farther from Goa, he has—at great expense, mind you—had to arrange shipment of the supplies first by sea from Goa to Bombay before they are transported inland for the use of these ungrateful heretics."

That was always the plan, you fool.

"As you know, Father, the viceroy's plan has inherent financial risks."

"Oh, I know. What I do not know is how I will write the archbishop and viceroy with yet another rendition of Aurangzeb's vague and infrequent assurances that he will make good on his pledges. Still more reporting of such 'delicate' positions will eventually result in orders that we abandon Aurangzeb and approach Shah Shuja directly and without hesitation."

Methwold didn't bother to hide a wince. "Should they direct us to such action, I would think it solely the result of how little they appreciate the peril such a move would place their agents—that's you and me, Father—in. Aurangzeb is powerful, and very...*effective* in his politics. He would take umbrage, certainly, and that would result in our deaths and the death of our chances for success. No, we have the tiger by the tail, and must hold on or be rent and torn by the very power we wish to place in harness."

"All such earthly power pales before the will of God," De Jesus asserted, again testing William's patience.

"That's as may be, Father." Methwold had found the use of the honorific could placate the priest somewhat, and felt the need to do so now. "But we mortals can only work with what circumstances God places before us. I, for one, do believe Aurangzeb's assurances that he moves to attain those heights from which he can reward our support."

"Why believe him over the evidence of your own eyes?" De Jesus asked, an angry flush darkening his cheeks.

"That we cannot see those moves speaks to his skill at intrigue, not inactivity."

"But you must admit that such skill could just as easily be used to dupe us into continuing our support even as he pursues some goal other than the ends he proclaims to us."

"That I cannot argue, but consider: Why does Shuja rebuff our every attempt to approach him directly?"

De Jesus twitched his shoulders as if he thought little of such a question.

Methwold waited, having discovered quite early in their association that while the younger man was often impetuous, De Jesus was too intellectually honest to completely ignore any approach or line of questioning simply because he was angry. All that was required was time and patience, and the young priest would eventually apply his intellect.

"I believe that he," De Jesus said after an uncomfortable few moments, anger making a growl of it, "like Aurangzeb himself, does not want to be seen publicly placing himself in debt to foreigners."

"That is my belief as well...though I've come to believe that was not the entirety of his reason..." Methwold let the thought hang, marshaling his thoughts and giving De Jesus' anger more time to cool.

"I presume you have some new thoughts on the matter?" De Jesus asked, calm at last.

"I do." He sat forward on the cushions. "I grow certain that if we attempt to transfer our arrangement to Shuja, we will alienate both brothers, with results detrimental to our desires and ends."

"While I know it's a risk, I'm afraid you'll have to convince me how staying with Aurangzeb improves our position."

"The young prince is more astute than I gave him credit for when we first decided on this course—"

The priest smiled faintly, interrupting, "Did you mean to present me with further argument *supporting* Shuja over Aurangzeb?"

Methwold grinned. "No, I recognize that a powerful and wily emperor will prove more difficult to manage in the long term, but any pretender must first *win* the throne. And really—the Company's interests here are purely mercantile, whatever the up-timers say about our future...conquests."

That the Company had come to rule India had seemed absurd to Methwold when he'd first learned of it, but far less so since Shah Jahan had acted upon the merest possibility by first revoking their firman and then attempting the murder of the Company's representatives even as they fled for Surat. He'd lost a lot of good men in that debacle, including those of the natives he'd relied on most for their insider's views on the political situation at court.

Shaking free of memories of some of the darkest, most fearful experiences of a life of varied adventure and travel, Methwold resumed: "So I do not see a need to 'manage' whatever man sits the throne so long as we gain the concessions agreed to in exchange for our services."

De Jesus thought a moment before speaking his mind. "I am not certain the archbishop or viceroy would fully agree with you, but even if they were to do so, you still have not explained why you think it such a bad idea to even attempt to gain Shuja's favor."

Just as you have not spoken of your reasons for wishing to hurry. Do you think me blind? That I did not see the viceroy's messenger this morning?

Swallowing the angry questions as detrimental to his cause, Methwold explained, "Shuja will see such a move as feckless—as us fleeing the service of a prince who has already pledged his, and therefore our, service to the throne. We would be asked why we seek to leave, what assurances we offer that we will not abandon Shuja in similar fashion. While we proffered our answers and waited for his response we would certainly be at risk as Aurangzeb sought to murder us for our betrayal. In addition, if Shuja wanted us as his clients, I believe he would have made an overture while the two of them were negotiating with one another, to better assess our reliability and value to his opponent."

He leaned back, added one more point as his slave entered and lit the lantern: "If we decided to just cut and run, or are ordered to withdraw our support by the viceroy and archbishop, then Shuja—or Aurangzeb when he comes to power—may decide taking Goa and its productive land is worth the fight, then strike at Dara with secure lines of supply that he controls utterly."

"Could he do that?"

"We are still closer to Portuguese territory than Agra, and the interior is far less well defended than the port..." Methwold shrugged, leaving unsaid that it was a poor option for any would-be emperor, and Aurangzeb in particular. There were many reasons the Mughals had not already ejected the Portuguese from India, not least of which was the fact the place was simply not that desirable given the amount of fighting that would have to be done to secure it.

"I hadn't thought they would do such a thing, having made peace with earlier viceroys."

"That was previous emperors. Few things bind a new emperor to the agreements entered into by past emperors, as evidenced by your own people's experience at Hugli. It is yet another reason not to break faith with any of the royal family."

"As I understand it, Shah Jahan's actions at Hugli were a result of our having angered him by refusing to assist his bid for his father's throne, not supporting one of his siblings... So the circumstances are not entirely equal. I mean, the princes take on the followers of their defeated siblings upon emerging victorious, do they not?"

"They do, but those not of royal blood who break faith with a losing prince without first being asked to do so by the winner are often punished most severely."

De Jesus sighed. "Such a corrupt, venal system. It is a wonder they yet rule here."

Wishing he could give vent to his feeling on the hypocrisy of a papist calling the Mughal system of rule corrupt, William Methwold wisely kept his own counsel.

Deciding a change of subject was in order, he considered asking after the messenger. While De Jesus had kept him ignorant of the exact content, his outburst on approaching Aurangzeb had been a powerful signal the news from Goa was not good.

Deciding the priest had calmed sufficiently to take the question without exploding into anger again, he said, "Does your impatience with Aurangzeb have aught to do with the messenger this morning, Father?"

De Jesus looked away, color draining from his cheeks this time. "My passing along of Carvalho's... requirement for assisting us has been responded to. Neither the viceroy nor archbishop received the request positively..."

"No?" Methwold prompted.

"They haven't denied the request outright, but I..." The priest's thoughts trailed off again, probably remembering too late that Methwold wasn't Catholic, Portuguese, or a priest. The internal politics of the Estado and the Catholic Church were hardly suitable topics for any member of the Church of England, ally or no.

"But they are hardly likely to try and stop the Inquisition in the Estado," Methwold supplied, saving the young priest from having to say more. "Too many hot irons in the fire to grasp that particular one just now."

De Jesus nodded, expression clearing as he realized he would not have to explain further or, worse yet, lie outright to his only ally in this camp.

And he would not have to explain because, perversely, Methwold was a better student of men than the priest. De Jesus' character had seemed a muddle of contradictions until the day Carvalho had asked that the Inquisition be prevented from its work in the Estado. Judging from the way he'd agonized over the wording of the letter containing Carvalho's request, De Jesus was familiar with the dark and pitiless nature of the Holy Office of the Inquisition, and struggled to reconcile its activities with the espoused tenets of his faith.

Methwold, for his part, knew the more rabid members of the Anglican Church held views that were scarcely more tolerant of Jews and Gentiles, they just held less official power in the state.

"Even so," De Jesus said, "we must consider what Carvalho will do when he learns the viceroy and archbishop will not accede to his wishes."

Methwold nodded again. "I'm not sure what he *can* do at this point. The same web of obligation that binds us to Aurangzeb binds Carvalho's reputation to us. If he withdraws his support from the arrangement reached with the prince, Aurangzeb may ask uncomfortable questions of him."

A wry smile pulled at the priest's mouth. "Uncomfortable . . . That is a good way to put it. I can see how our situation is a double-edged sword poised at all our throats." The smile faded. "Though his request of us regarding the Inquisition has merits I wish my superiors would recognize and support."

"The people you have converted are that threatened?" Methwold asked, despite his earlier resolve not to.

De Jesus' brows snapped together as his shoulders slumped.

Methwold waited, carefully reining in the fit of temper that moved him to ask in the first place. On reflection, he knew why he'd asked the question: He was angry, too. Angry the young priest had been so reckless in his challenge to Aurangzeb, and angry that the Portuguese should continue with their claims on India while the Company struggled on without legitimacy. Angry that, in order to rectify the situation, he was made to tie his fortunes to those same Portuguese and accompany their impetuous priest into the camp of the prince who, while quite able, sat furthest from the throne.

"They are," De Jesus said after a long silence.

"Well, no one can say you fail to do your best for those for whom you work, and perhaps your superiors will find wisdom from your example."

"We can but pray," De Jesus said.

Methwold wondered, not for the first time, how such a fool could balance what seemed a very deep and sincere faith with such utter inflexibility.

Chapter 16

Agra
Red Fort

Bertram absently waved away another offer of refreshment from one of Dara's slaves, focused on the men drilling in the yard below.

The sun was a club that beat down on anyone forced to leave the shade. The men standing almost fifty abreast and two ranks deep had been beaten by its rays since dawn, but very few had fallen out. Not when they marched from one end of the square to the other; not when they were slapped and, later, when they did not learn the complex marching instructions fast enough from their leadership, struck with fists.

Their commander seemed, if not immune to the heat, then carved from stone: scarcely sweating despite conditions that had caused some half-dozen of his men to collapse from heat exhaustion.

Unlike a stone, Bidhi Chand shouted a command in Punjabi, punctuating the order with a slight motion of his heavy saber. That he held the weapon out—at shoulder height and motionless—for the hundredth time as if it were the first, spoke of the man's stamina and disciplined training.

In response to his command the second rank pointed their weapons at targets set up roughly forty yards to their front while the front rank knelt, opening the breeches of their guns, extractors ejecting shells. There was no tinkle-tock of brass-based shells striking the flagstones at this remove, but Bertram's memories of that fateful night on the Taj filled in the sound quite readily. Then again, the shells were not empty, either, as the shells were what John called "training dummies." Each shell had the same general weight and construction as real ones, but contained sand in place of powder and shot. Bertram understood the need very well: real shells were too dear to expend in drills just yet, though Bertram had heard Talawat assure John that production was scaling ever-upward even as Dara's craftsmen produced hundreds of shotgun shells each day.

A single-word command had each kneeling man pulling a pair of brass-based paper shotgun shells from the covered belt at his hip while the second, standing rank of men pulled one of the triggers on their guns. The weapons did not belch smoke and shot as they would with real shells, but the Sikhs remained stockstill, awaiting the next order.

That fresh command came quickly: a shout and movement of the sword summoned another trigger pull from those standing while the kneeling men placed fresh shells in their weapons and closed breeches.

Another, different shout, and new position for the sword.

The front rank, still kneeling, each rested an elbow on one raised knee and aimed at the targets while the second lowered their weapons and opened breeches. Brass winked in sunlight again as extractors launched shells into the hot, dry air.

Another shout. The kneeling rank mock-fired while the second reloaded.

Bertram was distracted by scattered sunlight as the diamond the size of a child's thumb stuck in Dara's turban caught the light.

"Bidhi Chand and his men appear to learn the up-timer weapons and training more quickly than the Rajputs, Amar Singh Rathore," Dara said to the man sitting at his right hand.

Bertram felt his gaze snap to the Rajput princeling, but managed to keep the alarm he felt off his face. The emperor should be more circumspect in his comments, or at least less loud in their pronouncement. Amar Singh Rathore was one of the most powerful nobles of Dara's court, with many warriors at his command and no few holdings to purchase the services of more. He was also a man more touchy of his honor than most Rajputs, which was truly saying something.

He glanced again at Salim, but the Afghan was as powerless to intervene as Bertram. Anything said now would only serve to undermine the emperor's authority and image, coming as it would unsolicited.

The Rajput's signature wide, curling mustaches trembled as he spoke. "Sultan Al'Azam, my people are fierce warriors, ready to fight to the death for your honor, should you command it! What they are *not* is dirt-grubbing farmers grown fat on easy living and but lately come to your cause! If they are slow to learn these new weapons, it is because they fail to see the honor in their use."

Thankfully, Amar and Dara had been reviewing the training privately—at least as privately as was possible for the Sultan Al'Azam. As a result, those on the balcony were, slaves and servants aside, mostly Mission people. Thus, while the angry tone of Amar's words might have carried, the words themselves were unlikely to reach ears that might report the umara's disparaging remarks to Bidhi Chand.

If Dara was slow to respond, it served him well. In the silence that followed, Amar seemed to think better of his outburst, bowing his head as if expecting an angry tongue-lashing from the emperor.

"Friend Amar Singh Rathore, I do not seek to impugn the honor of fine men that have given such good service for so long. I merely observe that you and yours now have some small competition at this particular drill..." Dara said, conciliatory message spoiled by a tic that pulled at one corner of his mouth, lending a mocking edge to his smile.

Desperate to prevent Amar from noticing Dara's expression, Bertram sprang to his feet. He gasped loudly and made sure to knock over a nearby tray of fresh fruit laid out for the courtiers. As intended, all eyes went to him as the tray thumped to the carpets and fruit rolled every which way, a complete pineapple rolling to a stop only after Amar Singh put his foot down on it.

Bertram bent double, massaging his thigh as if relieving a terrible cramp there while slaves set about picking up the mess.

A moment later, pretending sudden awareness of

everyone's attention, he stopped rubbing his thigh and cast a sheepish look at Dara.

"So sorry, Sultan Al'Azam! The heat made me cramp terribly."

Bertram hid his relief as Dara's tic subsided and his smile returned to its more natural, if forced, appearance. The emperor waved a languid hand to silence further apologies and nodded through the Rajput prince's disdainful comments on how ill suited the Europeans were to the climate.

The moment passed, Dara and Amar Singh turning to watch the men drilling.

Relaxing ever so slightly as he sat, Bertram became aware of Salim watching him. Once he was sure it was safe, he met the other man's eye behind the backs of the emperor and one of his most powerful umara.

Salim nodded silent thanks.

Bertram returned the nod, though Salim hadn't been thanked for the many times *he* had saved the emperor from more of the same over the last few months. Rodney and Gervais insisted Dara's condition was improving, but the many stresses of ruling slowed the emperor's progress and lent every setback that much more weight.

Gervais and Rodney could not attend Dara all the time lest the mere presence of the up-time-trained doctors provide irrefutable evidence of his condition to the watching court.

And they were watching.

All the time.

It was a miracle they hadn't already had some incident spiral out of control and into public view.

He covered a smile with a bite of mango, reflecting

that the miracles had two names: Jahanara Begum and, to a lesser extent, Monique Vieuxpont.

The princess carefully guarded all aspects of Dara's public life, paring down appearances to the bare minimum necessary to avoid comment and stage-managing those appearances that were absolutely necessary as closely as possible. That management required men she could trust. Bertram was proud to be counted among that very select group, especially as it was Monique's vouchsafe for his skills that moved Jahanara to approach him in the first place.

She'd made the recommendation just days after he and Monique had stolen some time alone at Mission House.

Thoughts of Monique led his mind down garden paths, air heavy with floral scents, dark curls in his hands, lips parting under his, breath and stolen caresses mingling in memory to heat his flesh even in the shade.

With effort, he turned his mind from pleasant memory and forced himself to focus on the future. As was often the case of late, he began worrying what would become of them all when the Mission concluded their business—successfully, God willing—and it was time to leave.

Their current efforts, while effective, left him feeling very much like the Mission had, in assuming such lofty responsibilities, taken a tiger by the tail.

The up-timers had become fixtures of Dara's royal court, with Rodney and Priscilla becoming indispensable to Dara—and his family's—health, while John Ennis had become a military advisor of sorts, working closely with Salim and the Atishbaz gunsmith,

Talawat, to develop the drills being practiced below. And it wasn't just the up-timers of the Mission who were deeply involved in courtly politics: Gervais, in addition to his role as the most in-demand of court physicians, had become Dara's diwan in all but name. That role gave him a greater range of reasons to have access to the emperor, allowing his native talent at what up-timers called "the long con" to work upon the court at large.

Monique had been instrumental in that, as well, presenting Jahanara with several options when the princess had been at her wit's end with how to prevent Dara's condition becoming common knowledge. Today's little folly being an example of one of those options in action.

His attention wandered again at the thought of her. He was continuously surprised that anyone so intelligent, so beautiful, and as talented as Monique would show any degree of romantic interest in him. He'd been selected by the family as a potential spy as much because of his bland appearance as any other specific talent for the job, after all.

God help us if Monique and her father get bored with the court and decide to leave with their loot! The thought made him smile, then shiver despite the heat.

They could do it, too. Have done, in the past. Monique would only have to lead me down the primrose path a little, allay my suspicions...

Bertram bit his lip, hating himself for thinking such things about Monique... and her father. He consoled himself that a certain amount of professional paranoia was healthy in his line of work and proceeded, trying to think coldly, logically:

To what end would they betray their companions?

The easy answer—wealth—did not signify. They had that in abundance, and stood to gain even more with time and the exercise of the firman Dara granted the Mission. Indeed, their places at court had them daily in the presence of more portable wealth than most kings could marshal in a year.

Another answer—power—did not satisfy, either. They were just as intoxicated by the sheer challenge of this great enterprise, of helping direct the intrigues and intelligences of an empire richer and more vast than any European state, as Bertram himself was. They could never exercise such power in another court, except perhaps that of the USE, and that subject to the new laws concerning sharing of power brought to them by the up-timers.

No, they were not engaged in some enormous swindle.

But then, the target of a swindle rarely believed himself the victim until he'd been thoroughly fleeced and left naked in the cold...

His mind circled the thought, an indecisive vulture in need of assurances that the thing contemplated for dinner would not bite back.

Mission House

Rodney slammed the door behind him, rattling the doorframe and making the flame of the lamp beside her dance.

Priscilla started, looked up to see his face tight with anger. Her husband was normally very conscious of how his great size and strength could do unintended damage when he lost his temper, so any such display was unusual, to say the least.

"What is it?" she asked, putting down the needle and thread next to the piece of pork shank she'd been practicing on and stood up. Figuring the battles to come would produce plenty of wounds that required suturing, she'd been passing the time until Rodney came home from the late shift overseeing Dara's care by suturing cuts in the shank.

"Smell this," he said, tossing a length of silk at her as he stomped to the table.

Not particularly interested in rewarding his bad mood and concerned lest she contaminate it with something from the uncooked pork, Pris didn't try to catch the length of fabric. It fell to the ground as she went to the wash basin and started soaping her hands.

Behind her, she heard Rodney give one of his great gusting sighs and stoop to pick whatever it was from the ground. She finished cleaning her hands while he calmed down.

"So, care to tell me what's up?"

"Sorry about that, honey. I'm pissed."

She turned to face him, toweling her hands dry, and leaned against the table. "You don't say."

He chuckled. "All right, I deserved that . . ." He held the length of silk out to her again. "Please, smell this and tell me I don't have anything to worry about."

She took the silk and examined it. "Is this a bed hanging?"

He nodded. "From the emperor's own sleeping chamber," he said, gesturing again for her to take a sniff.

Wondering what, exactly, he hoped she would smell,

she sniffed cautiously. Stale tobacco . . . and something else . . . Pris felt her nose wrinkle as she tried to sort it out. Stale smoke and . . . vinegar?

That was it: the not-quite-vinegar tang of opium smoke underlying the sweeter scent of the tobacco blend favored by the highest echelons of the court.

"He's hitting the pipe again?" she asked.

Rodney's shoulders slumped. "Damn. I hoped I was just imagining it."

"Did you ask Dara about it?"

"I did. He lied to me, said he hadn't been smoking since we weaned him off it at Amritsar. I was close enough to see his pupils were as big as dinner plates, though."

"Oh, man. I'm sorry, Rodney."

He waved one big, thick-knuckled hand. "No, I am. Shouldn't have brought it home. Sorry."

She caught his hand, kissed the back of it as she stepped close to him. "I understand why you did. Who else knows?"

"No one, yet. I was going to get some advice from Gervais about it, but he's already in bed. John and Ilsa's lights are out, too."

"It'll wait. There's only so much we can do just this minute."

"It's got me real worried."

"I get it."

"I know you do. I'm sorry," he repeated.

"I know, Rodney. This qualifies as a really bad day, especially . . ." She kissed his hand again, the action preventing her finishing the thought. That was all right. She didn't have to. Not with him.

Rodney didn't tell everyone the origin of his concerns

about addiction, but she knew. Knew about Jimmy Saunders, his college teammate and best friend. Knew about Jimmy's back injury and subsequent spiral into addiction. He'd gone to the coaching staff with his concerns at the beginning of Jimmy's spiral and been told it wasn't something they could do anything about. How the eventual overdose hadn't been a surprise, but wounded him still. Knew how Rodney had found Jimmy in the bathroom, needle in his arm, cold to the touch. Knew his death and the coaching staff's refusal to take even partial responsibility for it were the reason Rodney had quit football and come back to Grantville. Just as she knew that, however aware he was of the dangers of painkillers, his experiences as an EMT in the aftermath of the Battle of the Crapper made him acutely aware that the suffering that would follow every battle would leave them utterly unable to relieve their pain with what little medication Grantville had brought back across time.

They held each other for a long while, found their own painkiller in each other when the embrace turned passionate, as it always did.

Chapter 17

Mission camp west of Patna

Ricky looked askance at the waters of the river... or rivers, maybe? He wasn't sure, exactly. Strand after strand of sand emerged from the slow-moving water, with occasional higher spots of forest-covered land to obscure whether a particular stretch of brown water was its own river or merely a branch of the Ganges. There was a lot of traffic on the river, most of it transporting covered loads that the boatman made sure to keep a safe distance from the shore and any other boats that came along.

There hadn't been a repeat of the attack on their camp, but they'd seen the results of what Jadu had called a pirate attack. The hacked up and looted bodies had been a sobering sight, and more than enough confirmation that the rivers were no safer than the roads in these days of confusion and uncertainty.

"I'd go swimming if the air didn't keep a fella as wet as a dip in the river," Bobby said, mopping his brow. "If there's one thing I miss, it's air-conditioning..."

Ricky gave him a worried glance, saw Bobby's brow already beaded with fresh sweat. Water he could ill-afford to lose. Bobby had recovered from whatever had been making him puke and crap with such regularity you could set your watch by it, but only recently. His recovery had been slow, and left him thinner than at any time since they'd met in middle school.

"Relax, man, I'm not going to fall off my horse or anything!" Bobby said, catching his concerned glance. He grinned. "Not today, anyway."

"Just not looking forward to crossing that..." He broke off as Jadu rode up.

The up-timers greeted their merchant-guide with smiles, with Ricky taking his reins as the older man dismounted and spent a moment stretching. Jadu had been in the saddle all day, scouting ahead into Patna.

Bobby handed the older man a skin, which he upended and drank from. "My friends, we have much to discuss—" He drank again. "Some of Asaf Khan's men have been seen around the city."

Bobby and Ricky shared a look. "Some?"

"Several hundred. An advance guard, I think."

"Why's that?"

"I am told they arrived on boats, and have since been seen to negotiate with every horse dealer in the city."

"Not the imperial officer?"

"No."

"That's unusual, no?"

"Indeed it is, Bobby. At least, it's an unusual measure for a *loyal* general to take."

"Would the imperial officers be able to supply the numbers he needs?"

Jadu looked thoughtful. "Probably not. But Asaf

Khan's arrangements have him paying for mounts out of his own purse. If he were to go through the imperial officers for even a portion of the expense, it would save him considerable coin."

"But he's not relying on them at all?"

"No." Jadu gave his beard a thoughtful tug. "It does not make much sense. He could use the imperial offices to ease the burden on his coffers and then renege on payment if he decides or has already decided to support one of Dara's brothers."

"Unless he doesn't want Dara informed that he's returning?"

Jadu nodded. "That's the only way it makes sense, but even then only if he was sure they would remain silent about the fact he was returning at all. And that's far more difficult.

"The local zamindars could be expected to cooperate with him, given even a flimsy excuse. Dara confirmed him as governor of Bengal as one of his first acts as emperor, so they should be predisposed to follow his orders." He shook his head uneasily. "But if I, on the basis of one day's easy inquiry, can discover what his men were about, then more than enough people know he's returning to make it no secret at all."

Ricky pulled his lip. "I think I follow: he isn't keeping it secret by doing what he's doing, so why not just take the horses as well and damn the consequences?"

"You have it right," Jadu said. "Perhaps I am too tired, but I cannot think why he would do things this way . . ." Frustrated, he took the reins back from Ricky and started for his tent and attendants. "I need to eat."

"Was there any opium on the market?" Ricky asked as they set out after the merchant.

"There was. I purchased what could be had at a reasonable price"—he gestured at his saddlebags—"but we're leaving the better poppy-producing lands behind if we go much farther east...at least until the foothills on the other side of the Punjab."

"Do you think we will need to?"

"What, go farther east?"

"Yes."

A shake of his turbaned head. "I do not think so. We have acquired several times what your Doctor Nichols reported would be required."

"If you got another fist-sized ball," Ricky said, glancing at Jadu, who nodded confirmation, "then we've got enough."

"We don't know for sure what the purity is, though," Bobby said, thoughtful.

Ricky caught the smell of something cooking, stomach rumbling in response. Jadu's cook was good, and it smelled like he'd been standing by for the moment his master reappeared on the horizon.

"It will have to be refined once we get it back home. That's why Doc Nichols told us to buy as much as we could in the first place. He figured we'd get some stuff that was bunk, anyway."

"Home." Bobby looked wistful, and a little sad.

"Listen to us, talking about purity and shit," Ricky said, trying to divert Bobby from the bout of homesickness he saw creeping in. Everyone on the Mission suffered bouts of it every so often, but Bobby'd had enough trouble to make Ricky want to spare him.

Bobby grinned, took up the thread: "Couple of backcountry hillbillies becoming international drug dealers."

"Just need some outfits that scream *Scarface* and we're golden."

Bobby snorted, shook his head. "Speak for yourself. I am going for the business executive look. You know, someone who doesn't get his hands dirty with such things."

"So you'll be wearing one of those outrageous starched silk collars we saw the English wearing at court?"

"Hell, no!"

"Well, what's the current fashion among European men of affairs, if not starched lace collars?"

"Shit. Guess I'll just have to have a silk tracksuit made up, get some of the gold we've earned made into thick necklaces, and touch my balls a lot during a conversation."

"You watch too many mob movies, Bobby." Ricky ducked under the tent awning, Bobby on his heels.

"Watched."

"Didn't need that particular reminder, thanks."

"Fogettabouttit," Bobby said by way of apology, sniffing and touching his crotch before throwing himself to the cushions.

Ricky joined him a little more slowly, still thinking over Asaf Khan's strange actions.

Jadu emerged from the sleeping area of the tent wearing a fresh over-robe. As if on cue, his body servant and cook entered the tent from the cook fires outside, one carrying a covered platter and the other covered bowls. They laid out the meal and departed.

Jadu waved his guests to start, taking up a large piece of naan from the platter and spooning some steaming rice and delicious-smelling curry onto it.

"Course, the way some of these nobles operate, might as well be capos straight out of *The Godfather*," Bobby said around a mouthful of food.

Ricky nodded agreement. "I think I remember Ms. Mailey saying something about their organization being straight medieval when she talked about how John Gotti got away with his crimes for so long."

"Who is that?" Jadu asked.

"The boss of one of the Sicilian organized crime families..."

"Organized crime?" Jadu asked, spooning more rice onto his shrinking stretch of naan.

"Yes."

"As opposed to unorganized?" Jadu asked, waggling his head.

"Exactly..."

"And?" Jadu asked.

"Probably need to unpack that some, Ricky," Bobby said, wiping his mouth.

"Organized might not be the best term. Say, enterprise, maybe. Groups of people working criminal enterprises." Ricky dredged his memory of history class, came up empty, and started explaining it as best he could anyway. "Some people left their homes in Europe for various reasons and came to the U.S. Most didn't leave all their culture behind, and many didn't have legitimate opportunities in their new country for a variety of reasons. Unable to make a living legitimately, some started operating businesses outside the law, either because those businesses weren't legal at all or because they didn't mind ignoring certain tax requirements, that kind of thing." He glanced at Jadu to be sure he was following.

"I certainly understand wishing to avoid taxation," Jadu said, smiling.

"Well, one such group to come to America was the Italians. Within that national group were the Sicilians, and they formed one of the longest-lasting, most successful criminal enterprises in the history of America. So successful, in fact, that there were a lot of shows on TV and film about them. That's what we were referring to: the popular fiction versions of those criminal enterprises."

"I . . . see . . ." Jadu said. Then, clearly puzzled, asked, "Were these criminal organizations not secret? Like the Thug?"

"Thug?"

"A criminal and religious organization here. Very notorious, but also very secretive as to their actual membership and methods. They are known only from camp tales."

"But you believe they exist?"

"Well, certain cults count them as enemies, and the same god is worshipped by many others, even if their practices are wildly different and they claim the Thuggees are blasphemous . . ." He trailed off, and then smiled ruefully. "I suppose I just answered my own question about the Sicilians."

"Kind of. In the States they were eventually hunted pretty hard by the feds. Ah, government." Seventeenth-century Earth didn't have anything like the FBI. "A lot of what we know about the way they handled business is from the investigations and trials of some of the families."

"Ah, so it was courts that exposed them."

"Sure. And that some turned in other members

to escape prison, offering testimony to the court in exchange for freedom."

"Oh." Jadu shook his head, eyes distant.

"What?"

"As often as I think you up-timers are so different from us, I stumble into one of these conversations that proves that you are not. That which motivates all men in this time and place holds true throughout the ages and places where the wheel of Heaven intersects with the blood and sinew of men."

The friends digested Jadu's wisdom for a little while, finishing up their meal in thoughtful silence.

Bobby broke that silence: "Huh."

"What?" Ricky asked.

"Just that bit about turning state's evidence on a family member . . ."

"Go on."

"How many kids has Asaf got, Jadu?"

"He has two sons, why?"

"I was just thinking that just because Jadu's informants saw Asaf Khan's men doesn't mean they are about Asaf Khan's business."

Jadu sat up in his cushions. "Say on."

"I mean, what if . . . with the fight between Dara and his brothers, there's some kind of parallel revolt going on? Some of his men supporting one side or another and rebelling against Pops?"

Jadu's eyes widened. "That might explain why they chose not to even try to prevail on the imperial officer for mounts. And why their attempts at secrecy are . . . uneven."

"Do you think Asaf's dead, then? That this is his subordinates fighting for their place?" Ricky asked.

"Dead?" Jadu thought for a moment, then said, "No, I can't imagine he's dead. It would be too hard to conceal . . . Ill, though?" He snapped his fingers. "Yes, that could very well be it."

"So, what does this mean for us?"

A waggle of Jadu's head. "That we have a lot of work ahead of us to confirm your very good supposition, and that we must be doubly careful about it."

"Well, since we've got about all the dope we're going to at a good price, we can focus on this . . ."

Jadu sniffed.

"What?" Ricky asked, half-smiling.

"Well, I have other trade to transact, and I'm not sure how you two can gather information. You don't exactly look like locals."

"We got eyes to look," Bobby said, a little defensive. Understandably so, Ricky felt. Aside from the night of the attack, they hadn't done much but learn a smattering of languages, do even less actual trade, be sick, and provide passable dining companions for the merchant. All this despite the fact the Mission had provided the impetus for the caravan in the first place.

"Yes, yes you do"—Jadu smiled—"and you can be seen, too."

"Sorry?" Ricky began, indignant.

"Just thinking of ways we could use your presence to attract rumors to our ears. I mean, I could just continue my quiet trade. It is widely known among those that matter that the Mission is supporting Dara. Your presence here, should it become widely known, might bring people to ask precisely what it is you are doing here. Such questioners can be learned from. Indeed, much can be learned simply from the questions they ask."

"Do we want that kind of attention? I mean, we haven't been exactly low-profile, so I imagine that anyone who wanted to know about your caravan could easily find out about the two ferenghi with you."

"Precisely. But, in and of myself"—he waggled his head—"I am of, at most, moderate interest to any trader, and of even less importance to the powerful umara and zamindars of the region. Unless we inform certain parties I know that you are here, and then see who comes calling..."

"All right, but what if they've declared for Shuja or Aurangzeb? They could just decide to kill a couple of Dara's supporters and show their loyalty to Shuja or Aurangzeb or whoever they think will appreciate the killing."

"It is a risk, I admit." Jadu shook his head, looking thoughtful. "I will see what I can learn with another foray into town tomorrow, but I think we should consider my idea. I think it has merit, and may work more quickly than waiting for some rumor to find us."

Chapter 18

Agra
Taj Mahal

The stone and marble had long since been cleaned of blood, but still Jahanara saw it—images in the mind that appeared in flashes behind closed eyelids, apparitions half-glimpsed out of the corner of the eye, like the ghosts of one of Smidha's tales. She turned onto her back, silken shift protected from the earth by the mats laid down upon her decision to rest in the shade of the gardens dedicated to Mother and Father. She looked up through the shade of the mulberry trees she'd ordered transplanted here from . . . she could not recall where, and at the sharp blue sky.

Aside from sheltering her from the heat of the sun, there was little ease to be found in the gardens around the Taj. The trees, grass, even the nodding flowers had sat mute witnesses to the killings that had claimed her father and nearly claimed her. Mute to what they had seen, but witnesses all the same.

She preferred the garden's mute witnesses to the visions of Father's blood on stone steps.

Such visions were why she retired to the gardens and let her brother speak to Father's architects and overseers without watching him. They both needed the break. He from supervision, if only for a brief moment—among men who had too much to lose should his secret come out; she from covering for his every mistake, from ensuring the secret of his condition never escaped to reach the wider world and destroy their collective future.

So much killing. And for what?

On edge, she heard the slightest jingle of Atisheh's armor. Jahanara looked at the woman who had nearly given her life to defend those in her care, found the big warrior woman tracking something in the direction of the Taj.

Jahanara tipped her head up to see what had alerted her guardian, spied Nadira's lovely form gliding across the grass toward her.

"Sister of my heart, peace be upon you," Jahanara said, her own soul still far from the peace she craved.

"And upon you, sister," Nadira answered, folding lovely legs beneath her while one hand reached for a goblet. A slave moved forward with a sweating silver pitcher and filled the empty goblet.

"How is he?" Jahanara asked as the slave retreated out of easy earshot.

"Well enough. But he has heard something, a rumor, that sorely vexes him."

"Oh? Something new concerning Shuja or Aurangzeb?"

Nadira's pretty eyes went to the southern horizon. "No. Nothing so distant, nor so important. Not yet, at least. It was a not-uncommon whisper among men, but he gives it more credence than it deserves, as close to his own heart as the subject is."

"What, then?"

"The rumor..." She trailed off yet again.

These repeated hesitations were most unlike Nadira. "So you have said, sister," she prompted.

"The rumor is about you, sister."

Jahanara sighed, tightened abdominal muscles and drew herself to a sitting position without the use of her hands. That she found the movement harder than it was a few months ago—the result of much less time spent at dancing and yoga these days—was a lamented result of matters of state taking up too much of her free time to pursue the rigorous training regimen of her youth.

"More of the same drivel about how I run the harem without your consent?" she asked, anger sharpening the words. "We wen—"

"No," Nadira said, looking at her again. The concern in that look stopped Jahanara as much as the word.

Dread stirred her heart to beat more strongly. "What is it this time, then?"

"This rumor is more personal, and more threatening."

"Do not keep me in suspense, sister. Tell me."

Nadira lowered her voice. "That you and Salim are sharing a bed."

Jahanara could not prevent the sudden heat that colored her from chest to cheeks at the thought of Salim's hard body against hers, swordsman's hands in her hair, lips pressing against hers.

Nadira's indrawn breath told Jahanara she'd seen the powerful reaction the words had summoned.

Her sister-in-law chuckled on the exhale and spoke quietly. "I can see your great beauty is enhanced by desire. But, for all our sakes, I hope you can restrain such displays in future."

Jahanara opened her mouth to protest, but Nadira spoke over her. "I know you have yet to throw yourself at him, but really, that people are speaking of you meeting him alone is bad for us." She paused, looking at Jahanara from beneath lowered lashes. "And actually meeting with him, however innocently, is a risk you should not be taking."

"How did you know?" Jahanara asked, fear making her blood run cold despite the heat.

Another chuckle. "I didn't. At least, not before seeing your reaction." Nadira glanced at Jahanara's guardian. "But that, coupled with the fact Atisheh, only just returned from her convalescence with the up-timers, was assigned to guard you through the night? You are not known to be a harsh taskmistress, and that raised suspicions."

Atisheh's weight shifted again, the faint chiming of her mail a mute version of *I told you so*.

"Whose suspicions?" Jahanara asked. "Rumors always persist about the women of the harem..."

"Mine. Your brother's. He is worried that your protection of his secrets is taxing your good sense." Nadira took Jahanara's hand in hers, met her eyes. "I do not disagree with him, in principle. I worried— worry—you feel as if you are alone in fighting for us, that in that moment of feeling isolated, you might do something careless, if only to feel like you were doing something purely for yourself."

Silenced by the painful accuracy of Nadira's words,

Jahanara brushed at the sudden tears welling at the corners of her eyes. That Nadira was so perceptive did not surprise her. It was her own lack of perception that made her heart ache.

Nadira, first-and-only-wife of the emperor, watched her through tears of her own. Wiping at them, she sniffed, said in a firm, even hard, voice, "I have told Dara that his concerns are unfounded, the rumors false. Informed him that you are a pillar of strength, and would not falter or fail him in such a way."

Shame wrenched at Jahanara's heart—that she'd believed Nadira had too much to deal with already, that she wouldn't welcome some portion of those burdens Jahanara carried on behalf of her brother, that her loneliness would remain unrelieved if she were to open her heart to Nadira, that she'd considered approaching *Roshanara!*

All that and then to discover that Nadira had already taken on a burden she did not have to: defending her honor against rumors her own brother believed.

Jahanara stifled sobs, clutching Nadira in her arms. "I have not failed to protect Dara's honor or mine. I have not given myself to Salim nor any other." She swallowed against a knot in her throat. "You have not lied to Dara." She dared not—could not—add: *not yet, at least.*

"That is good, sister of my heart…" Nadira lowered her voice to whisper her next words in Jahanara's ear. "Though I would gladly do so in partial repayment of my many debts to you, Jahanara Begum."

Startled again at Nadira's perception of her inmost thoughts, Jahanara sat back. Smiling through her tears, she said, "I hope I am not so transparent to everyone as I am to you..."

Nadira's smile was tender. "I should think your secrets safe, for now. No one else has my access to your doings, your brother, your plans, or your heart. Besides," she said with a shrug of slender, silk-sheathed shoulders, "you need never ask for my aid, Jahanara. As long as I'm aware of your need, I am here to help."

"Thank you, Nadira. Thank you. I promise I will ask for help rather than make you puzzle it out again."

"I just want you to know"—a gentle squeeze of her hands—"deep in your bones, that you are not alone."

Driven to tears again, Jahanara could only nod.

Nadira brushed her tears away with the hem of her sari and passed Jahanara her goblet.

The two had relaxed into a companionable silence over the drink, each enjoying the momentary quiet spent in company with the other.

Jahanara saw Prasad and the veil-swathed figure of Monique pass into the garden from the heavily guarded checkpoint.

Monique was readily identifiable—by the way she started removing the *purdah*-required veils as soon as possible—if not by her form and movements.

The most loyal of her eunuchs carried a bulging satchel, likely filled with correspondence, official and unofficial, that must be tended to with as much, if not more, care as the gardens surrounding them.

Even when she wasn't exhausted, Jahanara often felt like a gardener forced to tend an unruly patch of ground that sprouted tangling briars and thorns far more often than flowers or sweet fruit.

She sighed, idly—and foolishly—wishing for the days

when she'd had no responsibilities and only dreamed of having power over her own fate.

Nadira glanced up at the sound. A delicate sniff as they watched the eunuch make his way toward them. "I assume you've already seen the reports from Shuja's camp?"

"I have."

"I was utterly surprised that Aurangzeb bowed before his brother."

"As was I. None of our sources saw it coming. I suppose that should not have surprised me. He was always very careful with his trust. Even when a boy in the harem, he would not go to anyone, even Mother, with his thoughts, preferring to pray over his hurts, his concerns, his thoughts..."

"Strange that so admirable a trait should produce so odd an outcome."

"Then you do not believe his pledges of allegiance to Shuja?"

A mirthless chuckle, then: "What was that colorful up-timer expression that Priscilla used? 'Ox-shit'?"

"Bullshit, I think," Jahanara said.

Atisheh's quiet snort confirmed her recollection.

"Bull—or Ox—the pledge reeks of duplicity."

"Shuja seems to be holding his nose quite well, even so." Jahanara grinned, watching Monique divest herself of everything but the lightest, sheerest silk.

Jahanara smiled. Not so many months ago, the young ferenghi woman would have been uncomfortable showing so much skin to anyone. Now she was more practical, and much cooler for it.

"That's because he thinks he can have it all, should he hold his nose long enough," Nadira said.

On reflection, Monique was not the only one to have been changed. Jahanara acknowledged, if only to herself, that the young woman was her closest friend and confidant outside her family and those who served for decades, like Smidha and poor, sweating Prasad.

The heavyset eunuch bowed low and presented his satchel to Jahanara, who ordered him to rest and take refreshment.

"But what a performance!" Jahanara said as the eunuch withdrew.

"Indeed. What I don't get is what angle Shuja saw in accepting the lies. I mean, I understand that their combined army is more powerful for not having battled, but now each has to watch the other for betrayal at every turn."

Jahanara nodded agreement. "I would hope that such vigilance would lead to suspicion and the dissolution of their alliance, eventually. But then, I didn't think that either could keep their armies together when Dara cut off their supplies." She pawed through the correspondence, found a letter she'd been waiting for, unsealed it, and quickly read the contents.

Monique strode up, bowed and fair threw herself down next to Nadira when she gestured the Mission woman to join her.

Jahanara missed some byplay between the two women, but watched as Nadira worked the other woman's unruly curls into a short, heavy braid. Nadira preferred to keep her hands busy and while Monique's hair wasn't as exotic as Ilsa's, the Frenchwoman seemed to enjoy the attention far more than John's wife.

She suppressed a sigh. If reports were true, Nadira wasn't the only one tangling her fingers in Monique's hair of late. The twinge of unwarranted jealousy served to return her attention to the letter she'd already read once through without actually retaining any information.

"Finally!" Jahanara muttered after several minutes, rereading the pertinent section once again.

"What is it?" Monique asked, tip of her tongue protruding daintily as she concentrated on working another hank of hair into place.

"We presumed Aurangzeb and Shuja were pillaging the land as they came north, but wondered how they were able to maintain their strength, as the Deccan had scarcely recovered from the famine of a few years ago when my brothers first rode south to conquer it." Jahanara waved the letter. "Herein lies an answer: Apparently the Portuguese have made some sort of deal with Aurangzeb. They have been making up the shortfall from their lands to the west."

A disbelieving look crossed Nadira's face.

"You do not believe it?"

"It is not so much that I don't believe it entirely, but that I wonder how they have so much to give," Nadira qualified. "I'm sure Portuguese Goa has its share of productive farmland, but it's hardly the Punjab."

"When you treat the people like slaves, and keep many *actual* slaves, it is not so great a sacrifice to short your own populace for the purpose of supplying your warriors," Monique opined.

Jahanara looked at her.

The ferenghi winced, leading Jahanara to suspect Nadira had given Monique's hair a little extra tug to still her tongue as much as keep her from moving.

"Still, the passes through the Western Ghats must be full of oxen day and night to keep the army fed,"

Jahanara said as she digested what the pretty young ferenghi had said and, more importantly, Nadira's reaction. Most of the Mission had, at one time or another, and to various degrees, expressed a similar distaste for slavery. It was an odd distaste to have, let alone speak of openly. The Quran and most every other religious text she had read documented how, under certain circumstances, the practice was acceptable, sometimes even required for the betterment of all mankind.

Why should the Mission people feel that way when at least the slavery practiced in Mughal lands allowed for a slave to convert and then become free, something the indigenous caste system never countenanced. Born into a caste, one never left it, not in this life, anyway. Jahanara suspected Monique and the other down-timers of the Mission had their opinions heavily influenced by the up-timers, who claimed slavery was universally reviled in their time, and outlawed by every nation.

That it was not so—indeed that she had heard of no nation where it *was* a crime to keep slaves—in the here and now was a simple, unassailable fact of life.

If it were even rumored that Dara contemplated abolishing slavery, he would be removed from power in an instant, and not by his current enemies, but by a general uprising of every class and caste *but* the slaves.

But do I have to silence her on this point?

No, such oblique mentions can be ignored. Censuring her for it would only draw attention to their alien opinions, and possibly alienate them when we have need of them.

Besides, I would hate to stop Monique speaking her mind. Just a few years older than Jahanara, Monique was worldly in a way no inmate of the harem could ever be, and she was a storyteller of rare skill and humor.

Realizing she'd been silent for too long, Jahanara picked up the thread of the conversation and moved it elsewhere. "I am equally concerned that we only learned of this now, a month and more after this strange alliance started. We do not have enough friendly people in either camp, and fewer still that are willing to pass us information now that Aurangzeb and Shuja joined forces."

"I would think that the friction between them would make people *more* willing to inform than less?" Monique said.

"Normally, perhaps. But both enemy camps were already fairly firm in their opinion that Dara would be defeated by the prince they chose, and now they have twice the men and their supply situation is no worse than it was before. Some of those who were willing to report goings-on went silent when that happened, and more since."

"Do you think they are actively rooting out spies?"

"Of course."

Monique looked worried, and Jahanara quickly explained, "I am not speaking of what might be termed 'professional spies,' only those umara too powerful to accuse as such. Men—and women—who merely write letters to their 'friends and relations' in other camps, keeping in touch so as to hedge their bets in case of sudden misfortune befalling their chosen prince. They are the ones who have stopped writing Dara or his supporters, for the most part."

Tight, heavy braid complete and free of Nadira's grasp, Monique shook her head.

"What is it, Monique?"

"The way some things are handled here seem so reasonable, and yet there are so many things that are unreasonable, and wrong, in my view."

Wary lest Monique say more on the subject of slavery, Jahanara decided to move to a subject that would require Monique to explain the ways of European rulers rather than continue to critique those of India. "I have heard the courts of Europe are terribly quick to cry treason and execute anyone on the losing side of a dynastic war."

Thankfully, Monique took the bait, and the conversation veered away from anything to do with slavery. Soon, Jahanara had forgotten her earlier funk. Soon after that, what part of her mind not engaged in the conversation started to work over the failure of her sources to obtain even basic intelligence and, in light of those failures, began to adjust her plans to overcome the many challenges facing Dara's rule.

Chapter 19

Agra
Jasmine Court, Red Fort

Business of the day done, Jahanara shifted position in a fruitless effort to find a cool spot among the cushions. The heat of the afternoon was only made bearable by a combination of deep shade, cool fruits, and the constant effort of several slaves sweating to power overhead fans.

She cast a look at her brother, considering.

He hardly sweated, of course. He'd always been better in the heat than she, and his use of opium seemed to keep him cool, as well. Normally, the court would have retired to Kashmir to enjoy the cool air and royal gardens of that highlands region, but leaving Agra with their brothers in rebellion was impossible, so they made themselves as comfortable as possible and kept to the gardens and the shade as much as they could.

"I would ask a minor favor, Sultan Al'Azam."

"You would, Padishah Begum?" Dara asked, smiling.

Startled, Jahanara nearly dropped the grapes she'd just retrieved from the tray between them. Dara had never before called her by that great title, one usually reserved for princesses and dowager queens. It was one thing to have lesser men call her such, but to have the emperor declare it so, even in the privacy of the harem, was another thing entirely. He did her great honor.

"Yes," she said, setting aside the sudden urge to tell him everything. But some things must remain secret, even from him. Especially from him.

Far too many ears listened to every conversation Dara had to risk telling him, even here.

He gestured for her to continue, popping a pair of grapes into his mouth with a hand bearing nearly as many rings as Father, a notorious lover of such jewelry, had been given to wearing.

"Your armies grow by the day, Sultan Al'Azam, and I would see their power preserved..." She trailed off, uncertain how to continue.

He chewed, swallowed. "I'm afraid I don't follow, sister?"

"I had a thought—"

"Surely an event to cause the world to tremble!"

She gave him a hard stare. When that didn't quell his laughter, she plucked a grape from the bunch and threatened to throw it at him.

Dara raised both hands in defense of his person. "Stop threatening me with such a deadly weapon, or I shall call my bodyguard!"

"It is good to see that your sense of humor, such as it is, has returned, brother."

Dara lowered his hands. Still smiling, he gestured for her to continue. "A small joke, sister. Do go on."

"I was watching Rodney and Priscilla work..." Again she let the thread of conversation lapse, unsure what to say, or how to say it.

He nodded encouragingly. "Rodney Totman is like a magician in his skills at medicine."

Deciding on a course, she said, "And, by his own admission, his wife's needlework is even better. I would remind you that both of them oversaw the initial treatment of both Salim and Atisheh for their injuries."

He looked at the guard post leading from the garden to the harem, where Atisheh stood with the other guards, and said, "I need no reminders, sister. In addition to her healing of our wounds"—he touched the scar just out of view under his turban—"as well as those of our men, I well recall Nadira's praise for the skills Priscilla Totman showed during the delivery of our son." He took his time pronouncing the up-timer's name, clearly enjoying the way the odd-sounding name sounded.

Jahanara, moved by his suddenly serious tone, nodded and pressed on. "It was my thought that your army could be well served by them."

His brow furrowed. "What service can they do the army they do not already do me? They only have so many hands..."

"Exactly so, Sultan Al'Azam. Having only four hands, they can only do so much. I would ask them, instead, to use their minds and tongues to train others. Men and women who wish to learn the science and art of healing. Monique tells me such people, called 'medics,' march now with the army of the USE. I think your army needs such."

"Women, serving with the army?" he asked, frowning.

She waggled her head, sensing he was on the verge of denying her. "Not with the army, but here, in your capital, and in your camp, and not to treat the men. With your permission and blessing, I wish to establish a hospital where women will care for women."

And if they should be available in an emergency, and treat injured fighting men, I hardly think anyone will complain of it.

"An interesting idea. Have you asked the up-timers if they will do such a thing?"

"No, Sultan Al'Azam. I would not presume."

"Would not presume?" he repeated dryly, unscarred brow rising.

She held her tongue, unsure what he meant to imply. She searched his face but could not discover his meaning. He looked thoughtful, only.

At length Dara tapped golden rings against the heavy golden tray of fruit. "I think it a good plan. There are many among our people who cannot fight for reasons of their faith, and yet would serve. If Rodney agrees to it, I will make him an umara, and his zat will be commensurate with his contributions to our health and that of my army."

"And his wife, Sultan Al'Azam?"

He waved her concerns away. "She will rise with her husband."

She bowed her head. "As you say, Sultan Al'Azam."

"You think she deserves more?"

"I do, Sultan Al'Azam."

"Then you can give it to her. I grant you leave to establish your hospital here in Agra, or wherever the Red Tent goes. You may name whomever you please to its administration."

"Forgive me, but I believe that in order to over-come the most recalcitrant of the physicians I shall be interviewing for posts, I must ask for more. If I am to ensure Priscilla is taken as seriously as her husband . . ."

"What then?" he asked, somewhat sharply.

"Assign her a mansab, Sultan Al'Azam. Make her an umara."

"An umara?"

"Yes, Sultan Al'Azam," she said, forging onward.

He almost scoffed, but read the deadly seriousness of her expression, and quite likely thinking he would hear no end of it once his wife learned he'd had a falling out with her, Dara moderated his tone and gestured for her to continue.

"No rank of sowar, naturally. But of zat—"

"Naturally?" he asked, shaking his head.

"But of zat," she continued doggedly, "you can grant her rank just below that of her husband."

"Sister, you ask a great deal. My brothers already speak of how I plan to overthrow all that is decent in my wanton efforts to offend all religions and upend the order of the universe."

"And yet it is a small thing for an emperor to order his house as he pleases. We women, your relations, have always had our own rank, our own mansabs."

"That is different."

"Only in that she is not a blood relation. The precedent still stands."

"Not only is she not a relation, she hardly has your education, sister. Why, yours rivals my own."

"No, but what she lacks in that regard we can shore up with suitable munshis."

"Eunuchs."

"I did say *suitable* munshis, Sultan Al'Azam." Jahanara regretted her acerbic tone as the words leapt from her painted lips, but could no more retrieve them than stop the sun in its progress.

"You did, sister."

"And any munshi will have to be approved of by Rodney, of course," she lied, thinking it impolitic to mention that it would not be up to Rodney, but Priscilla herself, whether to employ eunuchs or simply the most qualified of people regardless of gender.

"You did. I have heard your words. I will consider them," he said, trying to dismiss her from his presence rather than grow wroth with her.

Knowing that what she wanted to accomplish would take a great deal of time they didn't have, she decided to stand her ground and attack. "Forgive me, brother, but time presses. Can you ask Rodney tonight?"

An angry glint sharpened the look he cast her way.

She bowed her head in humility. "Please forgive me, Sultan Al'Azam, but we have so little time to accomplish all the tasks God has placed before us, and I think now is the time for decisive action."

He surprised her then, smiling instead of showing offense. He said something in English she did not understand, then translated: "Sooner begun, sooner done," explaining the lyricism in the original saying.

"Indeed..." She cocked her head and allowed herself to be sidetracked, knowing he was convinced. "I do not think I have heard that turn of phrase before. Something the up-timers say?"

"No. Or, rather, I do not know," he said, waggling his head. "I heard it from Gervais, who said it might be a Protestant English saying, as far as he knew, so I imagine he could quite possibly have learned it from the up-timers. I do like it, however."

"As do I." Again she was assaulted by a wave of guilt. That she should keep secrets from him wounded her.

Again she put it away.

"Their language may not possess the poetry of ours, but there is an elegance there I wish I had the time to explore more thoroughly."

He sighed. "Would that I had time to pursue all my interests. I have yet to complete my treatise on the values of the varied religions of our lands, and I am afraid it will have to wait until after I have vanquished my upstart brothers."

"God willing, next year."

Jahanara Begum prayed for that very outcome.

Shores of the Yamuna

The late-morning sun had yet to heat the day as Bertram and John rode the last mile to Talawat's munitions factory. John was enjoying the cool air, if not the ride.

They cleared off to the side to give the road to a patrol heading to Red Fort. He shifted his seat while they waited, attempting to find a more comfortable position. It seemed they'd been resident at Red Fort long enough for his ass to grow unaccustomed to the saddle, and training his thighs and ass to the saddle was a hardship. And to add to his ass pain was the thought of *why* they were riding out to the factory.

He'd never been a fan of inspections: Back up-time

at the county job he'd held they were usually conducted by assholes who didn't know the job, didn't listen to explanations, didn't care at all about the people working the site they were inspecting, and went through any given job site just looking to check things off on their clipboards. It would be one thing if the inspection served a purpose other than justifying some county clerk's existence, but they almost always seemed to have nothing better to do than get in the way.

Only now, I get to play "asshole with a clipboard." The thought shored up his resolve to make this inspection as quick and painless as humanly possible. Talawat and his people didn't need anyone interfering, and certainly didn't need to hear some bullshit from a jumped-up hillbilly who didn't know half the chemistry or metallurgy they had learned in a lifetime.

He shook his head and, in an attempt to distract himself with something positive, said, "Got to say I'm surprised by how quick the Sikhs have taken to training in the new tactics and guns." Of course, the 'new' tactics were from a Civil War–era training manual—pamphlet, really—someone back home had copied off and thought to send along with the Mission in hopes it might prove useful.

"Bidhi Chand seems to have had his orders direct from Sixth Guru, and those orders must have been pretty clear: Learn everything you can, fight for the emperor the best way you can, and bring that knowledge home from the wars," Bertram said.

"That makes sense, I guess. You know, back up-time I didn't know much about Sikhs except for a vague notion they were some military-minded folks from India, but the other day Bidhi was telling me they only recently 'took up the sword.' Said they were *driven* to it by what he called 'Mughal persecution.' Said they were pacifist right up until the present guru came to power and decreed it was okay to protect themselves. Makes it easier to understand. That kind of history would motivate the hell out of me to learn all I could about fighting, just to make sure I wasn't an easy mark for any old raja wanting to take my land."

"Right. They do seem to apply themselves better to new martial practices than those who inherited the warrior ethos of their forebears."

"The Rajputs, you mean?" John asked, watching as a crane rose from the riverbank and flew across their path. He made out a red throat or partial hood on the long neck, but John didn't recognize the breed. The diversity of wildlife in India constantly amazed him. Game was more plentiful everywhere down-time, even in densely populated Europe, but India was in a league all its own.

"Them, too, but the Afghans and the rest of Dara's sowar won't get off their horses if they can help it, so they hardly make good candidates for infantry drill," Bertram clarified, not in the least fascinated by the appearance of the bird. "Interestingly, the emperor said Bidhi Chand only converted to Sikhism a few years back."

"Well, that explains his skill with the sword, then," John said, watching the crane disappear into the cover along the next bend in the river.

"Oh?"

He looked back at the down-timer. "'Cause there's no way Bidhi Chand just learned sword fighting since the guru said it was okay to defend oneself. If you watched him practice, you'd know better."

"I haven't seen that, b—"

John cut him off, shaking his head. "I mean, I've seen more swordwork than I could have ever wished since coming here, but that guy made Dara's man look like he was wading in quicksand."

Bertram continued as if he hadn't been interrupted: "Dara said he was quite the scoundrel before converting. Made his living by the sword. Some kind of bandit chieftain."

"No kidding?"

"N—" This time his reply was cut off by a thunderous explosion that made their horses rear and both men flinch.

John lost his seat. He watched, as if in slow motion, as Bertram, a far more accomplished horseman, stood in the stirrups and sawed at the reins, but lost sight of the other man as he went ass over teakettle and slammed into the ground.

Stunned by the impact, he could do nothing more than watch as his horse bolted for the stables.

Aware of the hooves of Bertram's mount flashing close to his head, John rolled to one side and got to his feet as quickly as he could.

Bertram was still trying to control his horse and John staggered out from under the threat of the horse's hooves. Once out of harm's way enough to spare the attention, John looked toward the munitions factory: a great black smear of smoke was already rising from inside the berm just over a quarter mile away. Debris was still pattering to the ground, some within a few hundred yards of their position.

All along the river, on both sides, every single duck, goose, coot, and crane had taken to frightened flight, wings clattering and beaks or bills open to hoot, quack, or honk. It would have been deafening if his ears hadn't already been ringing from the explosion.

"Jesus, the workers!" John barked. Turning to run, he staggered and almost fell, his bruised body refusing to follow the commands of his brain.

"Wait, John!" Bertram yelled.

John stopped, as much to let his legs steady as obey his friend's command, and looked at Bertram. The eyes of the down-timer's horse were rolling, but he had it under control.

"What if it's sabotage?" Bertram asked, face pale and frightened above his horse's head.

"So?! We still gotta get the workmen outta there!" The smoke was yellow beneath. Something was burning inside the compound.

"But what if the saboteurs are waiting for whoever shows up?"

Didn't think of that, John, did you? Some military man you're turning out to be.

Aloud, he said, "Ride back. I'm sure you'll meet that patrol we passed or some other troop of riders sent to investigate. Send them on."

"What about you?"

John spat. "I'll wait and watch from that stand of trees over there. Go!" By the time he finished saying the words, Bertram had already turned his horse and was clapping his heels to its flanks.

Another, less violent explosion went off inside the compound as he reached the stand of trees between one estate and another. John threw himself flat, glad his horse had run off. One fall from horseback a day was more than enough for his abused posterior.

His eyes teared up as he looked at the factory. Something was burning very hot now, flames rising above the berm. Nothing could survive in there, least of all workmen already stunned by the explosions. No, least of all some supposed saboteurs waiting to mousetrap whoever responded to help.

John dragged himself up, started toward the fire, unsure what he could do for anyone in that furnace, but sure he had to try.

He'd covered half the distance before his stunned brain recovered enough to start assessing what this disaster would mean for the war effort.

"Shitshitshit!" he chanted, staggering into a run.

Outside the munitions factory

"There were no survivors, Salim," Bertram said, visibly struggling to control his emotions as the last of the bodies they were able to recover were laid out beside the road. There were only fourteen of the hundred or so who were working within.

Salim nodded. He waved his entourage back and dismounted, walking to where John, Talawat, and Bertram stood with the patrol of horsemen that first responded. The manufactory was still smoking beyond the berms.

"What the hell was burning on the north side?" John was asking Talawat, wiping at his soot-blackened face with one hand and only succeeding in smearing the oily residue further. "Last time I was here, everything was covered in earthworks to prevent just this kind of thing."

"There was a large store of supplies laid in that some workmen were using to expand the manufactory,"

Talawat said quietly, wiping at his own soot-stained visage. "I believe the explosion was in the primer-cap manufactory and the secondary was the main powder store. It was muffled because it *was* covered in earth."

"Jesus," John said.

Talawat went on as if he'd not been interrupted. "The door to the main powder storage was off its hinges and several *gaz* from the entry. From the damage and its position, I can only imagine it was not closed when the first explosion occurred."

"Why not?" Salim asked, deeply concerned about the possibility of sabotage.

Talawat waggled his head and explained in a leaden voice, "It may have been open in the course of obtaining powder for the day's production of either shells or caps. Such would have been a bit late in the morning, but if there was powder left over from yesterday's work, I require my people to finish what they had already taken on hand before sending for more from storage."

"I am sorry for your losses, Talawat, but I need you to be more specific. Was this sabotage or an honest accident?"

"If it was sabotage, John and Bertram didn't see anyone flee just as or after it happened, and none of the bodies show any sword strokes or the like . . . which doesn't rule out the use of slow match, just makes it far less likely . . . The patrol that was first on the scene had also just come from here, so . . ." He trailed off, thoughtfully tugging at his beard.

"So, accident?" Salim pressed.

Talawat nodded, expression tight. "Much as I hate to admit it, yes. Most likely. I will investigate to confirm it, but yes, I think so."

"I should have been more on top of site safety," John said, looking at the row of bodies.

Talawat moved to interpose himself between John and the corpses. Once he had the up-timer's attention, he straightened and looked him right in the eyes. Speaking slowly, and enunciating clearly to ensure the up-timer understood his every word: "My people are very experienced at working with gunpowder, John Ennis. Sometimes these things happen. They know—knew—the risks. Don't think this is something you could have done anything about. I will be more careful in laying out the next manufactory in the future, given how this ended. I welcome your input and knowledge, but do not think to treat me or my people as children unused to the dangers of gunpowder and chemicals. We are not. We are Atishbaz!"

John winced at the hard edge in Talawat's voice, but Salim fully supported every word Talawat said.

Salim wondered at the strength of the artisan's character: that he was able to shoulder all the burdens of this disaster and still reach out and protect John from the up-timer's frequently expressed propensity for taking responsibility for events he could not possibly have done anything about.

All the up-timers were soft in some ways, and this setback would be hard enough to overcome without John wallowing in guilt, as Salim had watched him do in the first weeks after Randy's death. Perhaps it was their lack of faith that made them so attached to this life and its burdens.

Shaking his head clear of ideas that would, at the very least, offend John, Salim forced himself to consider the critical question at hand. The weapon Talawat had copied was only useful with the up-timer munitions, which could not be made by just any craftsman. The artisans working here could not be replaced, not for a generation, at least. Salim sat erect, trying to put on a brave front as another thought occurred: the remaining masters would be forced to stop production and train their inferiors or not only fail to meet Dara's needs but also risk the loss of an entire generation's acquired knowledge.

Unsure he wanted to hear his thoughts confirmed, Salim asked, "What does this mean for production of munitions for the new guns, Talawat?"

"Honestly, I don't know that we will deliver all that we need, Wazir."

"So, how much ammunition can we expect to see?" Salim insisted.

"Only about a quarter of what I promised, Wazir. There are simply too few full craftsmen to tra—"

Salim waved his protests down even as he mastered his own surge of angry disappointment. "I understand. I must inform the Sultan Al'Azam. Do what you can to salvage things here. I will be making a full, formal report to the Sultan Al'Azam as soon as you can give me an accurate assessment."

"Yes, Wazir."

John was muttering something, his eyes sliding to the corpses yet again.

Bertram was also staring at them, face drained of color.

"John, you and Bertram should ride back with me. The Mission will be concerned and there is nothing more for you to do here." Salim left unsaid that he didn't want either of them waylaid on the road, either.

The specter of sabotage had also raised the possibility of assassination as well, and he decided to speak to Jahanara about assigning bodyguards to each of the Mission members, whether they wanted one or not.

"What? Oh. Okay," John said. He walked over to one of the remounts Salim's men had brought. Bertram went to another of the horses, his original having blown itself out carrying the young man after galloping for the patrol and then returning to the manufactory in an equal rush.

John mounted with great difficulty, bruised posterior and legs making him grunt with effort and no small amount of pain, no doubt.

Bertram mounted in silence, but Salim caught sight of the young man's eyes, and was unsurprised by the smoldering anger he saw there.

Good. I fear we will need a great deal of anger and rage to carry the day against Dara's rivals now.

He turned his horse and, out of deference to John's infirmity, started at a slow trot for Red Fort. He felt time pressing on his spirits with the weight of mountains, and within moments he ordered them into a gallop.

Those guns were the single greatest technical advantage we had over the pretenders. Now, without enough ammunition to make a difference, they are only so much steel and wood—awkward clubs, really.

Dara—or Jahanara—must be brilliant, or all will be lost, because I am fresh out of ideas...

The Grape Garden, Red Fort

Jahanara hurried into the Grape Garden, her veils, the noonday heat and stress making sweat bead her brow. She saw Dara, or rather one of his nökör, rising from a full prostration before the white marble dais at the center of the four quarters of the garden. Her brother liked to rest there while enjoying the garden and whatever entertainments his wife had arranged for his pleasure.

Biting back an oath that Smidha, hurrying along in her wake, would surely reproach her for uttering, Jahanara hurried to join the cluster of women surrounding Dara.

Upon hearing the great explosion, she'd made arrangements to delay the messenger reaching Dara until she could get back from the diggings of the reflecting pool across from Mother and Father's tomb, but it would be one thing to slow an imperial messenger at the entrance to the harem, quite another to prevent one of Dara's nökör making his report to the emperor.

Jahanara watched him dismiss the bodyguard with a wave.

The jeweled pin in his turban caught the light filtering through the white silk pavilion as Dara turned his head to look at Nadira. His wife was speaking quietly in his ear, every line of her posture hard.

He did not like what she said, or was otherwise so overcome with anger that his face went purple red.

She hadn't quite made it to the dais when he surged erect, pulling away from his wife's white-knuckled grip.

His gaze fell on Jahanara as he cast about for something to break. The rage she saw in his eyes made her miss a step and stumble to a stop.

"Did you hear?!" he raged.

"Of course, Sultan Al'Azam," Jahanara said with

practiced calm, hoping the use of his title might recall him to self-control and some semblance of calm.

"I will have the culprits trampled by elephants, their skulls to adorn pillars like those of our ancestors!" he shouted, heedless of her attempt to remind him of listening ears.

He began pacing, balled fists shaking with rage.

"No, trampling will be too good for my brother! He has done this thing, destroyed our one and only hope!"

"It is not so, Sultan Al'Azam."

"What?!" He rounded on her, pointing an accusing finger. "You claim he is not responsible?" he barked, face going more livid still, something she would not have thought possible.

"I make no such claims, Dara," Jahanara said, unable to look him in the eyes. She looked at the marble at their feet and swallowed before continuing. "Sultan Al'Azam, I only wish to point out to you that we have other hopes, other chances, other play—"

His sudden collapse likewise brought her careful arguments crashing to dust and ruin. The seizure that followed made her wonder if Dara were not some sort of prophet, predicting their doom even as his damaged brain ensured the prophecy was self-fulfilling.

Somewhere amid the panic, guilt, and fear, she vowed to make the planned hospital still more grand and open to serve everyone, regardless of caste, religion, or privilege, if only God or some version of Heaven would see Dara recovered; vowed further that she would do all she could to improve the lot of the weak, the ill and the lame, the injured and the crippled.

Her vow must have been sufficient to appease, as

Dara's seizure subsided, leaving him exhausted and on the verge of unconsciousness.

Nadira held his larger hand clasped in both of hers, kissing the back of it. If Jahanara had been frightened by the seizure, Nadira was shaken to her very core, and needed every support.

Seeking control of the wild swing of her emotions, Jahanara took a deep, steadying breath. Employing the rest of the mental exercises learned from her mother and Mian Mir, she started to think more clearly.

Snapping her fingers in front of Smidha's stunned eyes, she commanded the servant to summon, in utmost secrecy, the up-timer physicians.

Once certain that what little physical aid she could offer had been secured, Jahanara knelt beside her brother and his wife, offering both all the love and support her unworthy heart contained.

Chapter 20

Burhanpur
South shore of the Tapti

Aurangzeb glared at the sluggish brown waters of the river as two of his finest subordinates rode up the near bank to join him. Half-remembered tales churned his mind. Tales Smidha—nursemaid and now advisor to Jahanara—sometimes told of the goddess who was the personification of the river. Sister to one of the gods of Death, the river goddess would carry those who died in her arms directly to her brother and a new place on the wheel or some such.

He'd never understood how the Hindu cosmology that so enraptured Dara and the Hindus at court worked, leading him, in moments of youthful weakness, to mock the odd turns their religion took and the actions those who followed it had to take in order to propitiate their false gods.

Now the Tapti mocked him in return. She was shallow in the dry season, but not so shallow that crossing her was without risk, especially for men afoot.

Coming south they had used nearly a hundred wide, shallow draft boats to ferry men, horses, and material across, but whomever the general on the other side was, he'd withdrawn them all to points unknown. The elephants had simply waded.

A scouting force of his best light cavalry had made it across after a hard-fought and fast-moving skirmish, but they'd quickly been forced to retreat back across the river.

"Can't be more than a few thousand," Shahaji said as he and the other cavalry commander reined in before the prince. Water streamed from both horses and their riders, who'd been forced to hang from their saddles and be towed by their horses on both crossings. Shahaji's mount was different from that which he'd gone across with. Aurangzeb had watched with awe as horse and rider went down when the man's original mount took an arrow. Bare instants later and the man was up on another horse as if nothing had happened.

"More than enough to grind down the numbers of any serious attempt at crossing, however," Sidi Miftah Habash Khan said, his Habshi face shining with fresh sweat under his turban. "We tried to split up and make them chase us away, but we were forced back into the river without gathering more than a general idea of what was on the other side."

"Chased, my brother?" Shahaji asked with a grin.

Habash Khan returned the smile with a cocked brow.

The Maratha placed a hand on his chest, his thin yet handsome face dressed with a sardonic grin. "*I* was not chased. I only wished to rejoin our prince here on the overlook. It is a pleasant place from which to watch the goddess sway through the land, is it not?"

Habash Khan laughed. Aurangzeb smiled as well, though not from humor so much as pleasure at commanding such fine warriors. The Habshi clan leader and Maratha chieftain had become fast friends in the last few months, much to Aurangzeb's delight. Having two excellent light cavalry commanders was a gift from God. Having two such men who worked well together without direct supervision was surely a sign that God's hand rested upon His chosen.

"We could let your brother try..." Shahaji said with a glance at Aurangzeb, hopeful light in his eyes.

"He would only send us directly at them like a hammer to an anvil," Habash Khan said, pointing to the far shore. "To weaken Shehzada Aurangzeb at little cost to himself or his favorites."

"Messenger for my brother," Aurangzeb called, pretending he hadn't heard the former slave speaking the absolute truth.

"And once we take this ford, we still have to take Burhanpur and that stone bitch Asirgarh..." Habash Khan said, the doleful words spoiled by a predatory gleam in his eye. The sack of a city meant danger, yes, but also a great deal of loot. Besides, he knew that light cavalry like his sowar were rarely called on for direct assaults, especially not with heavy infantry made up of bang-addled Rajputs and the like around to do the work.

"One river, city, or fort at a time, my friend. Eventually Shehzada Aurangzeb will bring all to heel, never fear," Shahaji said.

A man in embroidered green robes rode up, slid from the saddle and into a smooth, courtly bow.

Aurangzeb waved him permission to stand, some part of his mind not occupied with the tactical problem in front of him reflecting that when he was Sultan Al'Azam, he'd do away with the requirement that imperial messengers dismount to receive orders. Such was a waste of time. He filed the thought away with the thousand other things he planned upon once he'd ascended the throne and focused all his attention on the problem at hand.

"With my usual compliments to the Sultan Al'Azam, if you please," he said, after a moment spent putting the finishing touches on his plan of battle: calculating the route of march, the time his forces would require to get into position, and just how long Shuja could be made to wait without issuing direct orders Aurangzeb knew would make pointless sacrifices of his best fighters.

The imperial messenger merely nodded and waited for his next command.

"I am sending my fastest cavalry downriver to cross while I form up my foot, heavy cavalry, and artillery to assault the crossing. I welcome reinforcement, provisions, and prayers at the Sultan Al'Azam's pleasure. You are dismissed."

The messenger bowed again and, with a prideful display, leapt back into the saddle and sped away.

"Now, what are we *really* going to do?" Shahaji asked.

Aurangzeb looked at the men. "What I told my brother that we would..." He paused a moment, watching them. When their stares turned concerned, he went on. "...with a few slight adjustments I hope will be effective."

"So long as it does not involve those damnable camels..." Shahaji said.

"So sorry to disappoint, but it does."

"Getting them to cross water is not for the faint

of heart, Shehzada. And they're so *slow . . .*" Shahaji's tone was only half-joking.

"No, but you will want them, regardless, when it comes time to complete my orders." He waved a hand, and glanced at Kumar, one of the experienced messengers who'd been with him on the campaign south.

"You will cross at the first ford to our west, about five kos, if memory serves." He looked at the sun. "You should arrive near dusk. I want you across tonight. It's a quarter moon, but that's a risk we must take. The ford will, no doubt, be defended, but I cannot imagine they have the men necessary for more than a picket force intended to report any crossing. Ride them down, if you can. If you cannot, hound the pickets right back to their masters but don't allow yourselves to get sucked into any engagement short of this ford unless you are certain of victory."

"And the blasted camels?"

"They'll be following on at their best speed. You will wait for them to come up in support . . . they should come in just before dawn, I should think. I will commence an artillery barrage to distract them"—he considered a moment, then continued—"as it comes time for *asir* prayer." If having a reputation as an overly pious zealot could be used against him, he would, in turn, use it to his advantage.

He turned to Kumar. "Kumar. Message to Ali and his *zamburakchi*: he is to follow Shahaji and Habash Khan's forces west and cross the Tapti at the first ford upon arrival. He is to support the cavalry in their action, concentrating fire on the enemy artillery first, infantry second, and cavalry last. Shahaji is in command, this time." The Maratha chieftain was more cautious than the Habshi, and would take to heart the idea that they were not to even try and overcome stiff resistance once across the river.

Seeing Aurangzeb had finished, Komar repeated his orders, verbatim. After permission was given, the young sowar shot off back down the line of march to the zamburakchi contingent.

Aurangzeb watched him go and, turning to the men still with him, said playfully, "What, you are still here? I believe I gave you your orders. Change mounts if you must and be on your way."

Both his umara whooped, clapped heels to horses, and rode to join their respective sowar.

When he was sure no one else could see him, Aurangzeb smiled at their antics. Both men were at least a decade older than he was, but often behaved as if they barely had thirty years between them. He wished, on occasion, that God's plan would have allowed for him to act his age.

He took his prayer beads to hand, praying for forgiveness of his momentary weakness as he rode the short way to the command group.

South shore of the Tapti

The predawn quiet had yet to be broken by the army's muezzin calling the faithful to *Fajr*, the third prayer of the day, when Aurangzeb's messenger arrived and ordered Carvalho to begin his artillery barrage. A quick study of the moon's position made it clear that the order was arriving at least three hours early.

Strange, he had been clear that we were not to

begin until the muezzin began to call the faithful to Fajr. I wonder what changed.

He knew better than to send the messenger back with questions for the prince, however.

"To your guns, men!" Carvalho's command was quiet but spurred his gathered gun captains to run for their guns.

Rodrigo, his second, gave a short bow, a mocking grin, and departed at a more stately pace.

Carvalho smiled. Rodrigo knew his duty well. Besides, he had the shortest walk, and being the captain's oldest comrade had its prerogatives.

He checked the nervous impulse to verify the angle of his fire with his linstock one more time while waiting for his men to reach their guns. The fools across the river had kept watch fires going through the night, and he sighted in his guns using the excellent aim-points each made. The wait was longer than it was when he first entered service under Aurangzeb. The twenty-odd cannon he was fairly confident would not explode when loaded with powder charges sufficient to carry their shot across the river and into the enemy encampment were not even half the guns that he'd been given command of.

Despite the many difficulties of supply the march had placed on his talents, Aurangzeb had managed to expand not only the numbers of his artillery park, but the quality of the guns as well. As a result, Carvalho's command had swollen to some fifty heavy pieces and nearly a hundred lighter guns. There was no shortage of powder, either, though much of it lacked the purity Portuguese gun captains were used to when at home, as it had been looted from the many magazines of the forts and armories taken on the campaign south.

He heard the camp drums begin to rumble behind him, knowing that any chance of surprise they'd hoped to gain for the cavalry with the artillery barrage had been destroyed. Cocking his head, Carvalho listened to the signal repeated a few times before he was confident of its meaning: *troops to general assembly.* Something had changed Aurangzeb's timetable for the attack, and as it was not for the better, he assumed that Shuja had arrived and ordered Aurangzeb to attack before he was ready.

Shaking off thoughts of things he couldn't very well change—least of all in the next few minutes—Carvalho stepped to one side of the gun he'd chosen to captain for tonight, careful to keep the glowing match cord at the end of his linstock out of view from across the water. Just because Shah Shuja had spoiled the chances for surprise didn't make it wise to abandon *his* orders.

A pair of whistles, one from each end of the gun line, reached his ears.

He counted to three and lowered his dragon-headed linstock to press the match it held at the touchhole. The powder caught as he skipped aside. The gun belched fire, smoke, and thunder, setting the attack in motion.

North shore of the Tapti

"How many?" Aurangzeb asked, turning from the opening of his tent and the smoking battlefield beyond. The scene inside was not comforting, either. Several of his senior umara had been injured, and he'd ordered them placed in his tent and commanded his personal physicians to tend their injuries.

"The count is still being made, Shehzada," Painda Khan said, sweat dripping from the round eunuch's face onto the reports laid out before him.

"How many?" he repeated, glaring at his diwan.

"Forgive me, Shehzada, but we are still making our count..." The eunuch cleared his throat as he shuffled slips of paper. As if to prove his point, a clerk in his service entered and placed yet another slip on the field desk.

Aurangzeb waved impatiently.

The eunuch swallowed, but knew better than to make Aurangzeb wait further. "Our preliminary count has our losses at something less than five hundred men dead or wounded, Shehzada. Mostly wounded, of course, but we will know better tomorrow who will survive their injuries."

"Far fewer than would have died had...some other been allowed to plan this victory," Shahaji said, skirting the edge of treason.

Aurangzeb, unable to tear his eyes away from watching his personal physician pull a thumb-length sliver of wood from the hard muscles of Habash Khan's ebony flank, said, "You will speak no more of such things."

"As you command, Shehzada," Shahaji said, suppressed anger running beneath the words like a spring dwelling beneath stone.

"I would lose no more men to my brother," Aurangzeb said in a near whisper, wanting to tear his hair out, to wail and gnash his teeth, but unable to. As such conduct was impossible, given his position, he would have preferred not to utter a word. His captains had, this day, earned and more than earned an explanation.

Quietly, hoarsely, he told them: Shuja had arrived

just before midnight and ordered Aurangzeb to begin a general assault. Aurangzeb had argued with his elder brother to no avail, then delayed the transmission of Shuja's orders for as long as he dared, but ultimately he had been forced to follow orders and send his men in.

Burhanpur

Something heavy went flying into the air above Raj Ghat Gate, pieces of metal glinting in the sun above the dirty black smoke of the explosion. The sound of what must have been a great cannon barrel failing reached Aurangzeb's ears a heartbeat later, thudding into his chest and making several of his entourage's horses rear or start. His own stallion, better trained than most, flicked an annoyed ear at the racket, but paid no further mind.

Aurangzeb ground his teeth in a rare show of annoyance. The governor of the subah of Khandesh might have been bribed into surrendering the fortress-palace Father had spent so much treasure and time improving over the last few years, but Shuja had flatly refused to entertain the idea. That refusal had narrowed the many options open to them down to exactly one method of overcoming resistance. Aurangzeb had quickly established siege lines and begun the artillery assault even before the encirclement was completed.

A lower, duller rumble than the explosion echoed across to him, drawing his eyes to the wall adjacent to the gate as it slowly slumped into ruin in a cloud of dust and smoke.

Within moments, men and horses rushed to exploit

the breach, war-shouts of his heavy infantry thin with distance.

Sited on the edge of the city right beside the Tapti, the fortress-palace did not boast particularly daunting defenses, as shown by the quick collapse of the wall. But any siege action slowed their advance and not only gave Dara more time to gather his army at Agra, but also allowed the already strong garrison of Rajputs at Asirgarh to ready their defenses and lay in additional supplies.

And, unlike the fortress falling before his men, Asirgarh's defenses were among the most formidable in the empire, and garrisoned with men who, thanks to Shuja's obstinance, would know Shuja's army did not offer reasonable terms. Built atop a natural outcrop of sheer, heavy stone, Asirgarh was going to require time, treasure, and men that would be better spent in the final conflict with Dara, not in overcoming underlings who could be dealt with through fair offers of honors, position, and wealth. If Father had not died, the lines separating each of his sons' supporters would have been far better defined. Years of service, honors given, grudges settled and unsettled—all would have served to firm each camp in its allegiances. As it was, there was little to no history of leadership for each prince. Dara's already sparse military reputation—partially a result of Father never allowing him out of his sight for long—would not withstand another loss like the one the Sikhs had dealt him. That, and the fact that Aurangzeb was the most recent son to reach adulthood had left Shuja in possession of the longest record of commanding armies, though he'd done little enough with the opportunity.

Tired of running over the same ground, Aurangzeb's

hands found his prayer beads automatically. Starting silent prayers to their clicking, that part of his spirit not occupied with prayer sought answers to when, exactly, He would reveal the time and place when Shuja was to be displaced in accordance with his plan.

Shuja's camp, north of Burhanpur

The fighters circled one another as first Shuja and then his most vocal sycophants called odds or accepted bets supporting their favorites. They had until the fighters clinched to place their bets, and the two men were showing their experience by letting the purses build. One or the other would be paid far more the longer and more intense the betting became.

Aurangzeb sat rather more quietly, watching the sport while thinking of other things. Shuja's man, a thick-necked, bullish fellow with the hands of a strangler, feinted several times, grinning and spitting threats under his breath. The other fighter was more reserved, conserving energy, guard up and ready to receive the first real attack with his own. It occurred to Aurangzeb that the pair made for a fair representation of the two armies in the coming conflict.

Shuja was bound to be extravagant, and make threats. Dara, however, looked to be content to sit behind the walls of Red Fort and build the weapons his pet up-timers had provided. The weapons would likely prove effective, just as the up-timer medicine had been effective in preserving Dara's life beyond its natural end. It remained to be seen if their tricks would prove as important as the ground Dara chose to fight on. Aurangzeb believed Gwalior Fort a stronger military position from which to oppose Shuja's forces, but the political value of Agra was greater.

The heavy thud of the fighters making contact was audible over the calls of audience. Wine sloshed from Shuja's cup as he sprang to his feet, spattering Aurangzeb's sleeve as the fighters closed to the clinch.

Leaning slightly away from the probable spill radius of his brother's goblet, Aurangzeb carefully took no notice of any disapproving faces in the crowd. If anyone else thought ill of Shuja drinking to excess, Aurangzeb had spies who would report precisely which of the gathered umara expressed that dislike, just as Shuja had set watchers to observe who might express even passing approval of Aurangzeb.

The fighters grunted, hands sliding, weight shifting as each sought an advantage.

Again it struck Aurangzeb how similar the combat was to the larger conflict. Each brother had his spies, soldiers and supporters, each sought to use those tools at their disposal to break the other's grip on the Peacock Throne.

Of course, tools such as the army surrounding them could only be directed by one mind, one strong hand, and Aurangzeb had yet to see the opportunity that God would surely place before him. He knew such an opportunity was coming, as his every prayer and meditation had consistently given him to believe that His will was to see Aurangzeb made emperor.

The stolid fighter tried to slide under the guard of Shuja's man and grasp a leg. He was rewarded with an elbow to the cheek that split the skin and rocked him, blinking, onto his heels.

Aurangzeb deciphered God's message: such would be his fate if he were to take action before the moment He designated. Not wishing to give his watchers any sign what he was thinking, Aurangzeb checked a nod and resolved to pray on it at the next opportunity.

Shuja's man followed up on his advantage, grabbing the other man by his arm and pulling it into a lock that made his opponent gasp. His supporters groaned, though Aurangzeb believed the noise had more to do with fear of losing massive bets rather than any actual sympathy for the fighter.

The armlock may have hurt, but his free hand lashed out to sink deep in the other man's belly. Once. Twice. Three times.

Shuja's man bore in, heedless of the blows. Pressure on the lock eventually put his opponent on one knee, face a rictus of pain.

Aurangzeb felt his own expression tighten in sympathy.

Shuja's man howled his victory.

Too early, it seemed: The kneeling man turned into the lock, tendons visible as they ground across the shoulder into new, unnatural positions. The fighter, ignoring what had to be crippling pain, thundered home an uppercut that lifted Shuja's man onto tiptoe and prevented him getting his breath. The grip on his crippled arm relaxed enough for the fighter to break free. He surged to his feet with another punch, this one to the breathless man's bearded jaw.

A stunned sigh ran through the audience as Shuja's man fell bonelessly to earth, dislocated jaw obvious despite the beard.

The winner stood over his opponent, breath coming

in ragged gasps, injured shoulder far lower than the other.

Shuja himself, impressed with the astonishing end to the fight, roared congratulations as loud as any of his court. Seeing it safe to do so, the men who had bet on him surged forward to congratulate the winner, who swooned with pain when one idiot jostled his shoulder to congratulate him.

Aurangzeb bowed his head in silent acquiescence to God's will.

So I must suffer to ensure Your victory. I will gladly do that, and anything more that is required of me, to secure Your ends.

Part Five

June, 1636

Suppressing all the instruments of flesh
—The Rig Veda

Chapter 21

"Would have been nice to have some of this while we were watching the troop barges on the river," Bobby said, sipping at the chilled wine the household staff had laid out for them. He'd have liked an ice-cold beer, but that was not happening.

Ricky nodded agreement. "Probably too expensive for more than occasional use."

"Much as I want to keep cool in the sun, we probably can't afford it." Bobby drank the last of his wine, Adam's apple bobbing.

"Yeah, must not come cheap, all those people dying to bring ice down from the mountains at top speed."

"What did you say?" Jadu asked, a bit sharply, from the cushions across from the younger men. He wasn't looking at either of them, but had his pen poised above the paper.

Both up-timers started a bit. The merchant only just joined them a few minutes ago and, as was his habit,

269

quickly lapsed into silence to log the day's receipts and complete the daily log of expense reports to be sent off to the Mission with the next messenger.

Bobby looked at Ricky, a question in his eyes.

Uncertain what had pricked Jadu's interest, Ricky shrugged.

"We were just..." He trailed off, not wanting to give offense.

Jadu put his quill down and looked at the pair. "I am not angry. I just want to hear it again."

"Well, we were wondering how many people died to get us the ice to chill our drinks."

"Died?" Jadu asked, puzzled.

Bobby frowned. "You know, bringing it down from the mountains in this heat couldn't have been easy."

Jadu's puzzlement evaporated, only to be replaced by a stifled chuckle that soon grew to outright—and loud—laughter.

Bobby shot a questioning look at Ricky, who could only shrug and watch as both his oldest friend and his newest grew red in the face.

"What did Bobby say?" Ricky asked. He sniffed his own goblet, suspicious because Jadu had only just started drinking, having been at the market all day listening for rumors and buying on behalf of the Mission.

Wiping tears from his eyes, Jadu looked at him, but continued to convulse with laughter.

The merchant's body servant, Vikram, entered. While Vikram had served him for years, Jadu had bought the large house and hired additional servants from the locals in hopes of establishing his bona fides as a trader of consequence and thereby gain access to additional intelligence sources.

Vikram, at least, showed some discipline, and avoided joining his master's laughter. He merely poured more wine for Jadu from an unwieldy-large and towel-wrapped ewer, then offered more to the boys.

"Tell me, what's got you laughing so hard?" Bobby asked, covering his goblet to show he did not need more wine.

Bobby had spoken in English. Realizing his best friend was about to lose his temper, Ricky stood up. They'd both grown used to avoiding the use of English unless they were completely alone, having come to the conclusion it was the only way to acquire the necessary language skills in anything approaching a useful time frame. For him to abandon the habit was a sure sign Bobby was pissed.

Jadu held up a placating hand and made a visible effort to stop laughing.

The servant, taking Ricky's rising as an invitation to fill his goblet, approached. Ricky held it out, deliberately holding his arm so that it interfered with the angry eyes Bobby was sending Jadu.

As Vikram filled his goblet, Ricky caught sight of something odd about the ewer: it appeared to have an inner pitcher, the spout of which extended beyond the lip of the sealed outer one.

Jadu saw his interest and finally got control of himself, waving to draw Bobby's attention to the container as well.

Grateful for the distraction, Ricky asked, "May I, Vikram?" and held his hands out for the item.

Confused, the servant glanced at Jadu.

"Let him see it, Vikram. It will help me explain my undue mirth."

The servant handed it to Ricky, keeping the towel. The metal was quite cold to the touch, so cold the humid afternoon air quickly beaded the surface once exposed.

Holding it up, he saw what appeared to be a thermos-like arrangement: the outer pitcher was filled with water and sealed, while the inner contained the wine they were drinking.

He handed it to Bobby.

"I don't get it. Ice in the water of the outer pitcher?"

Jadu smiled and shook his head. He stood and bowed before Bobby, who waved him away, uncomfortable as only up-timers could be with all the bowing and scraping people seemed to do in this time and place.

"Forgive me, Bobby. I was not laughing at you. Your question caused a strong memory to surface." He sobered further. "One that should serve as a firm reminder to me of the perils of man's stubbornness and basic assumptions regarding reality."

Bobby's expression eased at the apology, but Ricky could read his friend's expression. Bobby still needed to know what was so funny before he'd forgive the man.

"Given the reputation you up-timers have for technological wonders, I had assumed you knew *all* the properties of saltpeter, and that those several properties were the reason you sought the substance in the first place, and why I was instructed to purchase so much on your behalf."

"Saltpeter . . ." Bobby mused, looking at the ewer. "You put saltpeter in the water?"

"Yes. Stirring a sufficient quantity of the substance into water causes it to grow quite chill, though it does not solidify into ice."

Endothermic reaction. The phrase bubbled up

from Chemistry 101. *And here I thought I'd forgot everything I ever learned in Chem.*

"So, to answer your question without laughter: no blood was spilled or lost to make your drink cool, my friend." His grin grew and he waggled his head. "A lot of piss, however, was poured."

Bobby looked uncomfortably at the ewer, making Jadu chuckle again. "They use urine to speed production of saltpeter. Vast quantities of it, from both humans and livestock.

"In fact, with every purchase of saltpeter we made for the Company, the English factor I used to work for always muttered"—he dropped into English, the King's English—"'This will drive the God-damned and Devil-loving petermen out of business for good.'"

"Petermen?" Bobby asked, interested despite himself.

Jadu returned to Persian. "To hear him tell it: Men who were licensed by the English king to enter a man's home and property to collect saltpeter wherever it may lay. They were even allowed to damage that property in order to collect the substance. Given how our own imperial jagirs are managed, I find it easy to imagine quite a few instances of corruption that might have led to my employer's low opinion of petermen."

"No offense, but I still don't see why you found my question so funny."

"Forgive me, I was recalling a similar conversation with my former employer, who was, in his own parlance, a tight-fisted bastard. When available, he insisted on purchasing ice instead of using any of the Company's wares. When it wasn't available, or too dear—which was most of the time—he went without . . ." Jadu trailed off, looking sidelong at the up-timers.

"And?" Bobby asked.

"And he died of heatstroke, sitting atop a cart containing enough saltpeter to cool a good-sized pond."

Both up-timers stood silent a second, then burst into laughter.

The wisdom of his long-ago choice to avoid the fermented grape confirmed by the antics of those he served, Vikram left the pitcher behind and departed, smiling.

Patna market

The market was busy even in the heat of the afternoon, though most of the traffic consisted of the servants of the great merchants, rather than the men themselves.

Ricky enjoyed watching the activity, if not the powerful odors that accompanied them: spices, unwashed flesh, strange incense, and weaving through it all, the moist, mud-laden scent of the Ganges.

Jadu was busy finalizing the arrangements for taking possession of another shipment of saltpeter. At least, he was supposed to be—but he seemed to be spending more time complaining, loudly and at length, of the cost. They'd run out of goods to barter with and Jadu hated, absolutely hated, spending cold, hard cash. He liked to claim that making a profit was easier when he could talk up the value of his goods and denigrate the value of those goods offered in exchange than when offering coin.

While he complained on the market side of the awning set up for his trade along the edge of the market, Ricky and Bobby were on the back side, along the stone stairs that led down to the river. They were watching the river, just as they had done for weeks, keeping track of the number of troop barges arriving from farther south and east, which was slow and stupid-boring make-work, but it might prove useful, eventually. Jadu said so, at any rate.

"What's that, you say?" Jadu barked. Voice raised, not in complaint, but in question. "You are the tax collector here?"

Bobby started to get up, but Ricky grabbed his arm and kept him still.

"And to whom will my taxes go, then?" Jadu said, just as loudly, but without the biting tone of his earlier question.

Ricky smiled. The clever merchant was speaking so loudly, not from thoughtlessness, but for the benefit of the up-timers. Bobby smiled back a beat later, and together they snuck to a position where they could better hear what was being said without revealing themselves.

"I am not saying I will not pay the tax! I only ask to whom it will be paid!"

"The governor," the tax collector said, voice tight.

"The governor, you say?"

Ricky's grin grew wider. *From his tone, you'd never guess he hates revenuers at least as much as my pa.*

"I do. Now, I will see your books, that I may make a proper assessment."

"Of course, my friend. Perhaps something cool to drink while you do?" Ricky heard the snap of Jadu's fingers.

"I would not refuse such a kindness."

"Good, good. Perhaps a seat in the shade as well? Here, take mine." A brief pause in Jadu's patter, filled with a creaking sound as Jadu's camp chair had a heavy load placed upon it, then he continued, "As we speak of kindnesses done from one to another, I would ask a small one of you. A trifle, really."

"A trifle?" the man asked, voice full of resigned suspicion. Probably expecting the usual plea from merchants, a request that Jadu be exempted from taxes just this once.

Vikram stepped into view from the front of the tent, collecting a pitcher of wine from a barrel-sized version of the ewer he'd served them from last night. The servant winked at him and bustled back to the front of the tent.

"Ah, you see, it's a small matter... Ah, our drink is here!"

Only after the wine was poured and goblets touched did Jadu resume speaking. "This small matter I spoke of..." Jadu paused again, this time the sound of his document chest being opened filling the pause, then the sound of shuffled papers. "A matter most delicate. Delicate, but minor... One that this humble servant wishes to clarify with someone of wisdom and intelligence. Someone like you..."

"What is this?" the tax man asked.

Jadu's lowered voice was still audible. "That, neighbor, is a firman exempting my trade in opium and saltpeter from any and all taxes normally levied in the empire, signed by the emperor Dara Shikoh."

"Ah."

Ricky had always wondered what writers meant when they wrote stuff like *pregnant pause*, but figured the silence that followed Jadu's statement must qualify.

"You see my problem, my good man?" Jadu asked, after a moment.

"I think I do."

"Well, have you some wisdom to share with this poor merchant?"

"I, perhaps, do."

"Please, then, share it." Ricky heard the faint clink of coins being passed. "For I know not what to do."

"Well, it is quite clear, here ... You see ..."

"Please, do tell."

"This morning, I myself was at the palace ..."

"You were?"

"Indeed I was."

"Among the exalted of the empire, then?"

"Indeed, though I do not step above my station. No, I was there to receive instruction."

"Oh?"

"Indeed. We were all told that every merchant trading in Patna was required to resume payment of the emperor's taxes."

"And, dear neighbor?"

"Well, there was no mention of *which* emperor. So, clearly, your firman takes precedence and all prudent men will abide by its terms."

"But, then, where does the money go if not to serve the emperor in Agra?"

A loud snort. "Sooner ask where the monsoon rains go as ask where the taxes paid go, in the end!"

Ricky thought Jadu laughed harder than the weak joke warranted, but the tax collector must have enjoyed it because he continued, "The money is collected by Asaf Khan's wazir at the palace."

Ricky stifled a sigh of disappointment. This they knew within hours of entering the city.

"And where is Asaf Khan and the great army he was sent here with?"

"In the east, still. Everyone says so. Though no one knows where, precisely."

"And so, who then, is this wazir?"

"And why do you ask?"

"Well, who is he, to be trusted with the revenue of so many merchants? And why now? I have not seen a single one of your fellow tax men about..."

"So interesting that you should ask, my dear friend merchant..."

Another pause followed.

This time Jadu must have retrieved additional coin from the strongbox he kept on the table, as the hinges squeaked loudly (a security measure, he'd assured the up-timers).

"Shaista Khan, Asaf Khan's son, returned two days ago. He promptly ousted the man Asaf had left behind when that most famous general sailed down the Ganges."

"Oh?"

"Shaista had the old hand whipped from the palace. I'm surprised the market gossip had not already spread."

"It will now," Bobby mouthed, grinning.

Ricky nodded back, still listening.

"Did you, by chance, learn when the legendary Asaf Khan will be returning? I saw him several times, from afar, in Lahore. A most impressive figure."

"Soon, I think. Why, only yesterday evening I recognized one of his most famous captains—the commander of his personal guard, I believe—at the horse market."

"I am impressed by your acumen, neighbor. Not every man is as aware of the comings and goings of great men. I count myself very lucky to have made your acquaintance."

"Humbly, I try to be . . . My father made sure to teach me that every man must take note of the doings of great men, if only to avoid being swept aside by their activities. I still have rounds to make, but rest assured that your firman will be honored by this humble collector of taxes . . ."

Jadu was staring unseeing at something in the distance when the up-timers emerged. Seeing he was busy, Vikram gestured them to take seats and poured them drinks while they waited.

"Never thought I would get used to drinking so much wine," Bobby said, gesturing with his cup, "but I can't remember the last time I had a hangover."

"I still remember the first time I got wasted." He dropped into English on the last word.

Bobby answered in the same language: "Me too. Freshman year. That party in the cut after homecoming, right?"

"Yup." Ricky shook his head, rueful. "God, but I got sick."

"I'd still prefer that brutal hangover to the squirts I got from just an accidental sip of the river."

"I was told the waters of England are no better," Jadu said, a defensive note in his voice.

Bobby turned to face Jadu and raised his hands. He apologized in Persian and continued in that language: "It wasn't an attack on the quality of the water here. Really."

Ricky nodded and tried to explain further. "I'm amazed we weren't sick more often when we came to this time. We were *so* used to having everything cleaned for us it's a wonder that we aren't sick all the time."

Jadu waved a hand and changed the subject. "You heard my conversation?"

Picking up on the fact Jadu didn't want to go down the rabbit hole of yet another discussion of the many differences between the time they came from and those they found themselves in, both up-timers nodded and gladly let the matter drop.

"Your thoughts?" Jadu asked, his thoughtful tone suggesting he wanted to use the young men as sounding boards.

Bobby looked at Ricky, who answered for them both. "Seems like someone must have won whatever fight was going on in Asaf Khan's camp."

Jadu's brow arched under his turban. "And what makes you say that?"

"Because we didn't see blood in the streets, or hear about fighting at the palace," Bobby said.

"Explain."

"I figure if the guy who was running things in Asaf Khan's absence thought he had a chance at a win, he'd have fought Shaista Khan to keep his spot. And, with the succession still an open question, fighting to keep your position doesn't mean a nasty letter to the boss man, but taking up your sword, ordering your boys to do the same, and sticking those swords into the fellow giving you problems."

Ricky smiled at the look Jadu gave his friend.

Bobby rarely chooses to give voice to his thoughts, but when he does, then Mom's old adage about still waters running deep comes to mind.

"What?" Bobby asked, looking from Jadu to Ricky.

Jadu recovered smoothly. "It is only that I had not expected your thoughts to mirror my own so perfectly."

"So either you're both right or both making the same errors in our assumptions," Ricky said.

"As you say, it is possible we are both wrong, but I think we are right. Especially in light of news I received from the horse market outside of town." He gestured at the notes on his desk. "It was nearly silent, not because there were no horses to be bought, but because *all* of them had been spoken for already.

"It seems that whatever infighting or confusion there was in Asaf Kahn camp is over, and whoever won is making ready to move."

"But where?"

"That, my friends, is the question."

Chapter 22

Asirgarh
The Red Tent
Shuja's camp

"I will leave behind a force sufficient to continue the siege here and take the rest to advance at all speed toward Agra," Shuja said, putting his wine cup down. He looked as if he would continue, but just then the siege cannon thundered in a lingering barrage, a stuttering roar barely muted by both distance and the heavy material of Shuja's Red Tent.

At great cost of powder, blood, and guns, their fire was slowly chipping away at the walls of Asirgarh fortress. Aurangzeb was certain there was a metaphor or something to be drawn from the ineffectiveness of the guns despite their loud bellows, but could not be bothered to pin it down, not when Shuja gestured to what amounted to his inner council and said, "I would have your advice here and now, and invite you to give me your best counsel, so that you may better know my mind and carry out my orders when I have decided upon a course of action."

Aurangzeb felt his brother's gaze drift to him as he made this pronouncement, but felt their stare as anything but an invitation to conversation.

No, he does not want to hear what wisdom I might have, not at all.

Ah well, "wish in one hand," as they say.

With a final unspoken prayer, he said aloud, "We need not press so quickly, Sultan Al'Azam."

There was a long, shocked silence at this apparent reversal of position.

"So quickly? So quickly?" Shuja sputtered, words steeped in derision. He gestured, presumably at the siege lines outside the tent, and went on: "First you say we go too slow, yet now you say too fast? Which is it, brother?" He shook his head as if gravely disappointed. "You speak like a woman: uncertain of her desires and like to change her mind with the next breeze to touch her intimate parts."

A few umara chuckled. Most simply listened.

Aurangzeb felt the sting of their amusement despite having repeatedly steeled himself against the slings and arrows of his brother's limited wit.

When he failed to answer, Shuja continued. "If we strike straight at Agra with all speed, we will prevent Dara from buying more allies like the Sikhs he has already purchased with Father's treasury, not to mention additional time for his pet sorcerers from the future to create more weapons to use against our brave sowar."

Aurangzeb nodded even as he disagreed. "He can buy all the Sikhs he wishes; they are but farmers. As to the weapons they plan to use against us, all reports indicate they are refinements of common fowling pieces, allowing one to reload from a prone position." That such would improve the survivability of infantrymen under fire wasn't worth mentioning to the emperor. Shuja spared little enough concern for his sowar, let alone the common men that constituted the majority of infantry forces.

"No, what I am most interested in is the whereabouts of Asaf Khan and the army he commands. An army that was the same size as yours is now, and that *before* Father's death. He has had many weeks to add to his forces now, and was always a competent general."

Far more experienced than all of the princes combined, if not known for any particular genius, Asaf Khan was the single greatest threat to the *dynasty*, let alone its individual factions. He was, as long as he did not declare for one or another faction, a knife at everyone's throat.

"We have received word from several friends at Red Fort that Dara does not know any more about his whereabouts than us," Shuja said, dismissive.

Fool. Ignorance does not equate with absence. He is out there, readying himself to strike.

Feigning agreement, Aurangzeb nodded. "I have heard the same from my sources."

"Well, the—" He stopped, seeing his younger brother's raised hand and waggling head. With ill grace he waved Aurangzeb permission to continue.

"What if our informants have been deceived? What if our wily great uncle merely waits to spring some devastating trap upon us?" He looked at the faces of the men of Shuja's inner circle, seeing many expressions of interest and concern. "I needn't remind any here of what he, with his experience and intellect, has proven himself capable of."

The nods this wisdom solicited among his brother's advisors were no surprise to Aurangzeb. Brother to an empress, father to another, vizier to two emperors, successful general, and favored great uncle to all of Shah Jahan's children, Asaf Khan and his extended family had cast a long, deep shadow over dynastic politics over the last three generations. His name was the perfect lever for conjuring fear and concern among Shuja's advisors.

"You shelter his sister, do you not?" Shuja asked.

"I do," Aurangzeb replied. He had expected this question, and the tone that insinuated so much.

"Nur Jahan..." Shuja mused.

"Asaf Khan and Nur remain at odds, out of communication since shortly after Asaf backed Father's successful bid for the throne."

"So *she* says."

"Indeed." Aurangzeb said nothing more, waiting for Shuja to speak himself onto the killing ground he'd prepared.

Shuja leaned forward. "As she would be bound to, given that she is reliant on you for her continued maintenance."

"Just as she was to Father, and to Jahangir before him."

"She encouraged the one to kill himself with drink and opium, and made every effort to keep Father from the throne. Successfully, the first time."

Aurangzeb hid contentment. "Yes, she did. Only to have Asaf Khan put her in her place, eventually. Something she has yet to forgive him for."

"Oh?"

"She has expressed the hope that you will strip

him of his power and position," he explained, lying for the first time in the conversation.

"And if, instead, I choose to reward him for staying out of our current conflict?"

Aurangzeb shrugged. "Then that is your will, Sultan Al'Azam. I will certainly not resist it, and *she* could not even if she wished to."

"But you do not approve of the idea?"

"Sultan Al'Azam, the approval of your vassals is irrelevant. I—like every one of your worthy umara— serve at your will."

"Of course. But you"—Shuja sneered—"*you*, would approach Asaf Khan differently?"

"If we had reliable—and trustworthy—means of communicating with him, then all my reservations regarding your stratagem would be as the last full moon, done and gone, a mere memory."

"Very poetic, brother. Yet I do not hear the alternative I know you must have hidden in your sash alongside your ever so piously simple prayer beads."

Several of Shuja's umara stirred. Regardless of their own fatih, they did not like this assault on Aurangzeb's religiosity any more than its target.

Stung despite his earlier resolve and mental preparations, Aurangzeb opened his mouth to reply.

Shuja wasn't done: "So spare me your false smiles and crooked tongue as you chivvy me down the path toward whatever end it is you seek. I will listen, but only if you drop this pretense and speak with a straight tongue."

Several men winced to hear the venom in Shuja's voice, looking from their emperor to his brother. Many were obviously thinking Aurangzeb could not ignore such a public, vicious slight. Some, Shuja's most foolish toadies included, had been looking forward to this moment in hopes they could seize advantage from the eventual break.

Others—more important men, *wiser* men—watched with carefully concealed interest, but no less avidly.

Almost there, my brother.

Aurangzeb took firm hold of his anger and his surging hopes and said simply, "As you command me to, Sultan Al'Azam, I will reveal my idea: I think the army should approach Agra with care, dispatching a column to discover the whereabouts of Asaf Khan's forces. Should they meet with that force, the leader should be of sufficient rank to treat with Asaf Khan, and wise enough to identify any potential snares laid to entrap the unwary…"

"So you think I should send you?" Shuja said, cynicism dripping from the words like honey from the comb.

"No, of course not. I make no claims to wisdom, and he is likely to still think of me as a child fresh from Father's harem. No, some other from among your umara would be more suitable."

Several of the more ambitious men among the court stirred, excited by the prospect of an independent command and the chance to win honor and glory.

The wiser among them spared Aurangzeb glances of, if not approval, then certainly respect.

The wisest were silent and spared no glances for anyone, keeping their motives and thoughts closed off from the world behind shuttered expressions of cool disinterest.

"Perhaps there is some merit to this idea," Shuja said. "I shall think further on it."

Methwold's tent, Shuja's camp

"Aurangzeb wants his aunt to address our concerns with still more empty platitudes," De Jesus muttered, eyes flashing angrily.

Methwold waited, holding his tongue until after the messenger conveying Nur's invitation to pay her a visit had withdrawn. While doubting in the extreme the man spoke any Portuguese, one's tone—especially an angry buzz like De Jesus'—could give away too much.

Once the man had gone, Carvalho glanced at Methwold, who returned the slightest of nods.

"Father," Carvalho said, "you need to be more careful of letting your anger show before these people."

De Jesus twitched at what, from the angry set of his shoulders, he perceived to be a rebuke rather than a brotherly bit of caution.

"I, of all people, understand your impatience. You know I do," Carvalho said, making oblique reference to the fact that De Jesus had informed him the viceroy and archbishop had tabled his request without proffering a decision date.

On spending more time with the mercenary-cum-nobleman, Methwold had learned to respect the man's patient intelligence far more than De Jesus' intellectual and linguistic achievements. In fact, he'd grown to suspect the man knew the viceroy and archbishop of the Estado da India wouldn't—couldn't—ever approve his request the Inquisition be barred from the Estado, but felt the opportunity to ask was one he simply could not, in good conscience, pass up. William knew he wouldn't have in Carvalho's place.

"I do not want to listen to some *woman* repeating lines she's memorized from her betters!" De Jesus said, tone that of a petulant boy. Methwold was growing to detest the priest's antics, especially in light of the man's excellent mind.

"Nur is no mere woman, Father," Carvalho said patiently.

"No matter who she is, she is not Shah Shuja, emperor of the Mughals. She is not Aurangzeb, would-be emperor of same. No, she is an elderly woman sent to insulate Aurangzeb from our righteous anger at these unconscionable delays and stall us seeking an audience with Shuja!"

Methwold, seeing this as ground already well trod, thinking it not worth his time to address the priest's tirade himself, only made a small gesture for Carvalho to continue. Perhaps his countryman could talk some sense into the priest.

"Perhaps you should remain here and write another letter to the archbishop and viceroy reiterating the humble requests I made of you?" Carvalho asked, making it obvious he wasn't as interested in mollifying the priest as he was in advancing his own agenda.

Methwold hid the smile that a glance at De Jesus' stricken expression threatened to summon.

"Nur is, by all reports, a formidable personage, having once wielded great power," Carvalho said.

"How? With the constraints of purdah, she must act through intermediaries to obtain her every need!" De Jesus said, Carvalho's reminder of his personal failures to deliver on promises not enough to silence him.

Carvalho nodded placidly. "Women of a certain age are far more free of the restraints of purdah than women of marriageable age.

"And, to answer how she remains powerful: She is still the closest female relative either brother has in camp. Mughal courts traditionally rely on their aunts and grandmothers for certain...restraints as well as courtly refinements. And, while Nur is firmly in Aurangzeb's camp, she does spend some of her time interacting with Shuja, as the emperor Shuja has only the ladies of his umara with us, and the fathers of such women require marriages before they allow their daughters to exercise such power on behalf of a man outside their family. Shuja, for whatever reason, has been slow to take wives..."

"Do you think Nur will provide us an answer for such queries?" Methwold asked, interested. He hadn't thought to apply to Nur for assistance navigating court politics. She had certainly figured large in Company fortunes on occasion, but before Methwold had ever set foot in India.

"She will surely know. She might be forbidden to answer, though."

"Interesting," Methwold said. "Perhaps I should have considered her earlier."

"Perhaps? Perhaps you did not because she is even further from the throne than the prince who keeps promising but never delivers. I, for one, will not see her."

"Shall we make your excuses, then?" Carvalho asked, expression blank. Something, perhaps the speed of Carvalho's question, led Methwold to believe the older Portuguese had intended to leave his countryman behind all along.

"Feel free. I will busy myself with more useful pursuits, like prayer."

Methwold cast a searching glance at De Jesus but the priest didn't seem to be speaking ironically nor did he seem to have noticed Carvalho's manipulations.

"Very well," Carvalho sighed. "Will you join me, William?"

"I will," Methwold replied, schooling his expression to show less interest than he felt at the prospect.

Chapter 23

Agra
Red Fort
Harem precincts

The dancers stopped, golden bangles and sweating bodies catching the light of a hundred lamps and scattering it back across.

Dara and Nadira rose to their feet, eyes shining, and sent slaves bearing gifts to reward the dancers for their exquisite performance.

Already standing, Jahanara smiled behind her veil, glad to see the pleasure the dancers she'd commissioned had elicited in her brother and his wife. Dara had been greatly upset by the explosion in the factory. Dashing many of his hopes in one blow had so upset the emperor that he'd suffered a seizure the doctors—both up- and down-timer alike—claimed was a direct result of too much stress. She swallowed past a knot in her throat at the memory of his collapse when she informed him of the incident. The guilt-ridden hours that followed had been painful, not least because, with

Dara incapacitated even for a few hours, the rest of his inner court had been hard-pressed to cover for him.

Without conscious thought, she found her eyes searching for Salim. The proud Afghan profile was easy to pick out, standing as he was among the up-time men of the Mission, none of whom—aside from perhaps the giant Rodney, and that merely a result of his prodigious size—had anywhere near Salim's presence. She caught her own smile widening to match his as he grinned at something Bertram said.

"Your promised man is a treasure, Monique," Jahanara said, turning to look at the woman she'd grown closer to than any other outside the family. Monique knew all but her most personal of secrets, and was, in fact, more deeply involved in her current intrigues than any other.

"Perhaps," Monique said, lips curling in a half-smile.

Jahanara sniffed. "As I am not in line to compete for him, you hardly need to play down his many virtues."

Monique snorted. "I do not 'play down' his virtues." The words had a surprising edge to them, so much so the princess touched her friend's hand in sudden concern.

The ferenghi covered her hand with her own. "It is nothing serious. I simply wish he could speak his heart the way he speaks his mind: freely, easily, and with the passion I see burning in him. Instead he acts like every other man: silent when he should speak, speaking when he should be silent, and seemingly deaf to how my heart beats for him."

Jahanara shook her head in wonder. "I had little idea you were such a poet, dear friend."

"Not generally . . ." She bit her lip rather prettily. "Then again, perhaps the burgeoning need to get a leg over has made my tongue more clever than is its habit."

"A leg over?" Jahanara asked, puzzling over the phrase.

Monique colored, looked away, then back up at Jahanara with an insouciant grin and broad wink.

Such was Monique's charisma that Jahanara found herself returning the grin even before she fully comprehended the foreigner's turn of phrase, which only served to increase Jahanara's embarrassment and deepen the flush that spread like fire across her skin upon fully realizing what Monique meant. As if the flush were truly flames, Jahanara felt a stab of pain that slaughtered the smile with its suddenness. Fighting a welter of tears, she struggled to keep the pain from finding expression.

She speaks so easily of . . . of . . . something I am never to have for myself, not with things the way they are. Not without crippling my brother's already tottering regime.

Perceptive in the extreme, Monique's smile was replaced with a look of concern. "I'm sorry, I should not have said anything."

"No, my sweet friend, it is not your fault that our world is nothing like that of our up-timer friends," Jahanara said, catching Monique's hands in her own as the smaller woman smoothly interposed herself between Jahanara and any potential observer.

"At the very least, Shehzadi, it was thoughtless of me," Monique said in quiet, soothing tones.

Jahanara managed a weak smile. "It is nothing, Monique," she said. Hoping to quell any further unnecessary apologies, she hugged her friend.

Head on Monique's shoulder, Jahanara had to look away, not just from Monique but also from Salim, which led her gaze to fall on Dara. The emperor had turned in their direction, likely intending to congratulate her on organizing the entertainment, and instead had seen her commiserating with Monique. Taking hold of her emotions, she smiled to see him beaming. It was an honest, almost pain-free smile the likes of which she had not seen in months.

Still, she cast about for some way to cover her expression as some passing fancy, and unable to resist tweaking Monique's nose a little, said quietly, "Perhaps your lapse is yet another result of your needs not being met?"

A snort of laughter met her sally. Monique pushed herself out of Jahanara's embrace, laughing.

If Dara had wished to, he might still have questioned her expression or the embrace, aware, as he often was, of the things that upset her, but just then Rodney and John closed in on the emperor and began speaking to him. She saw Bertram standing in Rodney and John's wake, saw also the broad wink he gave her.

"I did not misspeak," Jahanara whispered.

"Did not what?" Monique asked, laughing still.

"Misspeak."

"Oh?"

She nodded at Bertram. "He is a treasure."

Monique laughed harder, gasped out, "Please don't let him know that! He's already proud as a peacock!"

Feeling the tense, tearful sadness of a moment before retreating, Jahanara chuckled. Like the last clouds of the rainy season, tears might threaten still, but she knew they would soon disperse in the warm sunlight of friendship and chosen family.

With such friends and allies, surely we will overcome.

Red Fort, Gardens of the Harem

John didn't particularly like the music that accompanied the big dance production Jahanara had staged for Dara's amusement, but he had to admit the dance routine was impressive in the athleticism it demanded of the participants. So much so that it was almost possible to ignore the amount of flesh on display.

Almost.

He was thankful that Ilsa really enjoyed *both* the music and dancing. So much so that it seemed she didn't mind him looking at the dancers. At least, not from the way she smiled beneath her nearly transparent veil.

This social visit-cum-meeting was a new one for him. Special arrangements had been made for the various women to attend, with the unmarried ladies wearing far more in the way of veils and concealing clothing than either Ilsa or Nadira. The way the silks worked, though, he could almost see through his wife's, especially where it touched the skin. The effect made it easy to ignore the near nudity of the dancers, and from certain looks Ilsa had sent his way his attention to duty would be rewarded later tonight.

Her presence, while exciting, also calmed him. That he was worthy of such a fine woman's interest made him more confident in himself, made him want to *win*.

His eyes went to the emperor, who was looking across at his sister and Monique, pensive expression on his face.

He's a good guy, but he's been hard to deal with since the factory explosion. Temperamental and angry, even with Salim, who's been juggling everything to try and cover for him.

John's eyes slid to Salim, who had also noticed where the emperor's attention had fallen. Bertram stood beside him, and made a small gesture with his hand, asking John to intercede.

Rodney and John both moved to the emperor's side, trying to figure out what to say.

Dara saw them coming, however, and smiled, the one side of his mouth slower to respond than the other.

"John, Rodney." The emperor had taken to using their given names as a sign of his favor. It sometimes made John shake his head in wonder, the weirdness of life as an up-timer. "If you've had your refreshment and enjoyed sufficient entertainment, I would like progress reports on the readiness of our special armsmen"—he looked from John to Rodney—"and these 'medics' my sister insisted we train."

John and Rodney bowed, not nearly as well as any courtier born to it, but close enough for government work.

"How goes the training of our specials, John?"

"Shehzada, I believe they are doing well, with the Sikhs in particular taking the drills very seriously. Your public rewards for their good performance during the last review proved useful in spurring the other contingents to take it more seriously"—the Rajput commander who had replaced Amar Singh Rathore had flogged his *rasildars* for failing to earn top spot in the review—"and so they apply themselves to the drills we've established."

John carefully did not mention precisely *why* the men had found it difficult to take training with the new weapons seriously; by now, even the least sowar in Shuja's distant army knew Dara's up-timer ammunition factory was no more. Despite Talawat's heroic efforts, the situation was unlikely to change.

"And my Servants of Vāyu?"

"Rodney put the volunteers through the eye exam, and we selected thirty candidates from that. They are being trained separate from the main body of troops. We'll be testing them next week to get the best mix of spotter-shooter."

"And the breakdown of the men?"

"Quite diverse," Rodney supplied. "We had volunteers from every level of society, and that diversity is reflected in the men who passed the exam."

They both knew from reading they'd done that one of the reasons the Allies had prevailed in World War II was the Axis powers' insistence on using social elites to provide specialized soldiers like pilots, where the USA had screened *everyone* for raw ability and taken the cream off the top. So, when pilots started getting killed, the U.S. had far more replacements sitting on the bench than either the Japanese or the Germans.

So, when it came time to look at recruits, Rodney had insisted on accepting volunteers from every caste. Mostly, they'd gotten the usual Muslims and warrior-caste folks, but there'd been one or two outsiders who'd applied, even passed. John wasn't too sure it would serve to chip away at the caste system, or whether it was good for the unit they were establishing. There'd already been one barracks-room dustup he knew about, and he suspected there'd both been and would be a lot more unless they could find someone to run the unit who understood—yet could work around—the various cultural and religious landmines they were facing.

"And the ammunition?" Dara repeated, a tinge of impatience coloring his tone.

The question finally penetrating his funk, John answered: "Talawat tells me that since we don't have that many of the rifles to begin with, and we skimp on the training I wanted to put them through, that we'll have more than enough for any battle."

"Well then," Dara said with an air of satisfaction all out of order with the news, "at least in this we shall be as Bhima, and crash down upon the foe from beyond his reach with a violence undreamed of, in protection of our family."

John saw the expressive eyes of the empress shift to her husband, her worried glance even more disconcerting than the behavior of the emperor.

Rodney shifted his weight, uncomfortable with the unreasoning, bloodthirsty glint in Dara's eyes.

The movement of Rodney's large frame must have drawn Dara's attention from whatever fantasy of bloodletting he'd been having, as he asked, "And these field medics you are training, Rodney?"

Rodney bowed and said, "The volunteers are training up nicely. Everything Pris and I can remember, we've got on the syllabus, and the first graduates, the ones who will train everyone else, were as ready as we can make them. We are testing those recruits soon. Over the last months Shehzadi Jahanara has collected and issued us an enormous endowment of supplies: bandages, suture-quality thread, even opium. We are distributing them to the medics and stockpiling surplus for the field hospital."

"And how goes that particular project?"

"Very well. The tents and other materiel your sister

provided will all prove very useful, once we get our staffing situation sorted out."

"From your tone, I gather there are issues?"

"Not for the general staff; orderlies, nurses, that sort of thing, no."

Dara quirked a scarred eyebrow, inviting the man to continue.

"Well, while we've had a flood of physicians applying for positions, figuring out who is..." He trailed off, glancing at John for help.

"Qualified?" Dara said, before John could come to his friend's aid. "According to your up-time standards, I mean?"

"You understand exactly. The interview process is... tedious and slow."

Dara smiled. "Diplomatically put. I am sure they have strong opinions on the processes you require them to implement."

Rodney returned the smile. "Exactly, Sultan Al'Azam."

"And how they must have balked when they learned they would be instructed by a woman!" Dara chuckled.

Nadira, relaxing visibly, slid her arm through her husband's, her eyes smiling now.

"The Jains were slightly better about it than the rest of them, but none of them were, well..." Rodney trailed off, perhaps realizing his words might have been insulting. Knowing that the emperor was okay with statements that might be seen as a dig against some ethnic or religious group Dara favored was one thing, knowing the mind of his wife quite another. He quickly qualified: "But most doctors are snobs when it comes to where they studied, or who they studied under, even back up-time. They certainly would've had a hard time listening to some paramedic, regardless of how much experience the paramedic had."

"Really?" Nadira asked, one brow arched.

Rodney bowed again, uncertain of protocol when addressed by the empress.

John stepped in. "Oh, there was a definite pecking order, even among doctors with different specialties who went to the same school."

"The smaller our differences, the more weight most people will place on that side of the scales, if only to mark themselves as better than the others," Dara said.

Like the differences between you and your brothers? John had the good sense not to speak the thought aloud, but it still plagued him no end. There had been scant evidence he'd chosen the right prince to back, except for... His eyes slid to Jahanara, standing in the background, head together with Monique. Begum Sahib had suffered some loss of reputation with her brother since the explosion, but she was still the foremost of Dara's inner circle, and, by all accounts, working hard to keep him on the throne.

Except for Begum Sahib... Just about every good turn we've done here has been done at her urging or as a result of her direct actions.

If only...

However pleasing the image, he deliberately turned away from the thought of Jahanara Begum ruling from the Peacock Throne. Closing his eyes, he stifled a rueful grin. He could almost hear his mother's voice telling him, in no uncertain terms, "That's right, you're just a hillbilly from West Virginia, son, not any kind of king—or queen-maker."

Chapter 24

Patna
House of Jadu Das

"What was that?" Bobby asked.

Ricky groaned, wakened from deep sleep to find his best friend standing at the foot of his bed. The barrel of the Remington 870 held in his hands gleamed dully in the silver moonlight coming from the balconies.

"Wake up, there's something going on downstairs." A crunching bang from the front of the house punctuated Bobby's words.

"Wha?" Ricky mumbled, staggering out of bed only to enter into a battle with the entangling mosquito netting that wanted to drown him.

"Shhh—" Bobby's attempt to silence him was cut short by the unmistakable sound of a musket being fired nearby. There were several angry shouts, none of which Ricky could understand.

"Fuck!" Ricky hissed, finally extricating himself from the netting.

Bobby chambered a shell and moved to cover the door.

302

Ricky paused, torn between arming himself or getting dressed. He put pants on, stuffed a few extra shells into his pocket and moved on bare feet to join Bobby on the other side of the doorway. The sound of several more bangs came from the front of the house as he moved.

"Ram on the front door?" Bobby asked.

"Must be," Ricky said. "But who? And why?"

"Gentlemen?" Jadu's low-voiced query issued from the shadows across the hall.

"Jadu!" both younger men said.

"What the hell is going on?" Ricky asked, chambering a shell into his own 870.

The merchant glided out of the gloom and slid between them, a wicked length of steel clutched in his right hand shining in the moonlight filtering in from the balconies. "It seems Vikram has fired upon someone attempting to invade our home."

"But who?"

"I do not know."

"Do we fight or run for it?" Bobby asked.

"I would normally counsel running, but we have committed no crime, and worse yet, have not prepared for flight. I cannot afford to lose my inve—" A splintering crash from the downstairs door as it collapsed under the repeated battering. A barely audible clatter came on its heels. Ricky identified the sound of a musket being dropped from nerveless fingers. Torchlight, presumably from the invaders, flickered up the landing. Shouts of pain and a series of dull thuds echoed from downstairs—Vikram catching a beating for having shot at the door-crashers.

Bobby raised his shotgun. "Top of the stairs?" he hissed.

"Yes," Jadu said, "but please don't start shooting right off. We may yet get out of this if we don't kill anyone."

All three of them took up positions overlooking the landing. Ricky rested his shotgun on the stone railing and whispered to Bobby, "I'll fire a couple warning shots while they're on the stairs. Cover me, but don't shoot unless you absolutely have to."

"Right, you're doing the shooting until I absolutely have to."

"Stop your crying!" someone growled from below. "Where is your master?"

Ricky couldn't understand the reply, and, judging from the meaty thuds of fists striking flesh, neither could the questioner.

"Find them!" The way the torchlight wavered and the sound of booted feet approaching, the command, delivered by a different, gravelly voice, was followed immediately.

The boots of three armed and armored men pounded across the foyer to the base of the stairs.

Two flights to climb. Not much.

"Hold!" Jadu shouted.

The men ignored him and mounted the stairs, holding shields above their heads. More followed behind them.

Ricky aimed and pulled the trigger. Nothing happened. Belatedly remembering to take the weapon off safe, he quickly did so and *then* pulled the trigger.

The gun boomed, report biting everyone's ears. The tiles covering the landing shattered into dust as the deer shot bit, making the men hop and slow. One even yelped, perhaps catching tile fragments in his shins.

"Hold!" Jadu screamed again, as much at Ricky as the men below.

The men resumed their climb, rushing across the landing and lowering their shields to cover their vitals. Ricky glimpsed tense, bearded faces, swords clenched in armored fists.

These weren't bandits, not from their dress or discipline.

He fired again, this time above their heads.

The man on the right stopped, the man behind crashing into him and making their still-advancing companion stumble.

"Hold!" Jadu shouted once more.

Ricky cycled the action and fired again, abused ears failing to register the shells falling this time.

"We can kill you all without reloading!" Jadu cried as Ricky chambered another shell.

The men gathered themselves to resume their rush, but Ricky could see any enthusiasm they might have had for it had vanished with proof he wouldn't have to spend a moment reloading to kill them.

"Halt!" the shout came from the gravel-voiced man below.

The soldiers showed discipline—or a perfectly reasonable fear of being shot—and stopped. Boots on the next riser, they watched the men on the floor above them warily.

"Why do you break down my door, invade my home?" Jadu yelled.

"You are the merchant Jadu Das?"

"I am."

"Then I am in the correct place. I am commanded to bring you before my general."

"I have committed no crime. Why should I be arrested? Why should I have men invade my home?"

"I was not told, merchant. I was ordered to fetch you, as I said."

"And if I resist?"

"Further, you mean?"

Jadu shook his head, though the questioner could not see. "I do not understand."

"Your man at the door refused us entry, fired on us, even." The voice drew closer and the speaker, a large man with a luxurious black beard and fine over-robe, stepped into view. His gaze traveled the three men atop the stairs. "And again, here, you shoot at my men."

"If we wanted to kill them, they'd be dead." Ricky said the words slowly, hoping to overcome fear-stiff lips and his bad accent. He really didn't want to have to shoot anyone else.

Jadu tried to silence him with a look, but the man just chuckled.

"I believe you, young man. That's why we are speaking."

His men, hearing their commander's confident tone, eased back on the landing.

"What happened at the door?" Jadu asked.

"My man knocked and told your doorman we were entering. He objected. Strenuously. He slammed the door. We persisted." The man's voice was gravel on stone, but somehow light all the same.

"Vikram shot at you?"

"Who—Oh, yes, your servant. He did shoot at us, more or less." The man grinned, teeth glittering. "Like your companions up there, he didn't manage to hit anyone."

"Is he still alive?"

An unconcerned shrug of broad shoulders. "He's breathing."

"Good. He was only doing his duty to me."

"Speaking of duty: I am still to bring you to my general."

"And which general is that?"

Ricky saw the gold teeth that made the man's smile glitter this time. "You *are* new here, to ask such questions."

"I am. I do not hide the fact I am but recently arrived from Gujarat."

Another shrug of broad shoulders. "What you are hiding makes no difference to me. Whatever it is, you—and it—will come with me to see my general."

"Without knowing your name, how can I accept any sureties from you as to our safety?"

The smile grew broader still. Almost piratical. "Have I offered any sureties?"

Ricky could hear Jadu's swallow. "No, you have certainly not."

Another chuckle. "I like you, merchant. I perceive you have the heart of a warrior. Are you certain you are not Rajput? Some raja's bastard?"

Jadu stiffened. "While I appreciate the Rajputs for their martial prowess, I am Gujarati, not of the warrior caste, and quite content with my place in life."

"You tell me more things I do not need to know. Come, I see the arms of your companions begin to tremble with the weight of those repeating firearms. We must come to an agreement before they can no longer defend you."

Which was bullshit; Ricky had the elbow supporting his shotgun resting on the railing, so the weight was negligible, but he did appreciate the man's style.

"Well then, if you'll give me your name and some

sort of surety, perhaps we can bring our negotiation to a close."

"Very well. I, Mohtashim Khan, offer you my protection. You and yours will not be harmed, by me, nor any other. What happens after you are presented to my general, well, that is up to him."

Ricky almost missed the tight little smile that came and quickly disappeared from Jadu's lips.

"May I confer with my trading partners?"

Another shrug. "Of course."

"What?" Ricky whispered.

Jadu's eyes glittered in the torchlight. "I thought I recognized him. He is son-in-law to Asaf Khan. Married the sister of Mumtaz Mahal. He is a very, very well-connected man."

"Does that mean we'll be safe?"

Jadu nodded without hesitation, but then qualified: "At least until Asaf Khan decides what to do with us."

"Why not drop Asaf Khan's name immediately if he serves the big boss?" Bobby asked.

"Good question, friend. Perhaps we were right, and Asaf is gravely ill . . . And the man in his place is still consolidating?"

"Jesus, these are some deep waters."

Jadu nodded.

"I grow impatient, merchant." Mohtashim Khan's smile was evident in his voice.

Shrugging, Jadu wordlessly asked the up-timers' permission to accept the man's offer.

Ricky nodded. Bobby sucked his teeth a moment before nodding agreement.

"Mohtashim Khan, we accept your honorable surety."

Palace west of Patna

"Christ, could this take any longer?" Bobby grumbled, wiping sweat from his brow.

"Of course it could. This is Mughal India, after all," Ricky opined.

Jadu favored the younger men with an old-fashioned look meant to silence them.

Ricky stared back, his patience nearing its end. Mohtashim Khan had brought them to a not particularly well-appointed palace just outside Patna, disarmed them, and placed a guard to watch them. Nearly twelve hours ago.

Seeing the look would not suffice to silence the younger men, Jadu said, "Should not be long, now."

"How do you know?" Bobby asked.

"Because everything happens according to our dharma, our fate. And my fate is to die at home, among family and enjoying the wealth made in a lifetime of trading."

"That's some answer," Ricky said, then regretted it.

Bobby just looked as if he'd bitten into a lemon.

Jadu waggled his head. "Mohtashim Khan told us we would at least meet the diwan today."

"Another day, another diwan," Bobby grumbled, in English.

Surprise cracked Jadu's control. His snorting chuckle drew a disapproving glance from the snobby eunuch who'd been stonewalling them since arriving this morning. Ricky suspected the eunuch, like every DMV employee ever born, resented everything that was unexpected—and most things routine—about their job.

"Seriously, Jadu, this is taking too long. The armies of the pretenders will be marching on Agra if they haven't alr—" He stopped, shaking his head.

"What?" Bobby asked.

"I can't believe I just said that with a straight face. Like a line out of *Lord of the Rings* or some shit."

Bobby grinned. "Never read it, but we for damn sure ain't in Kansas anymore, Toto."

They both laughed.

The merchant sighed, stopping Ricky. He looked at Jadu, found the man's good mood had vanished, replaced by an intensely thoughtful expression. "Perhaps you're right," he mused in quiet tones. "I had hoped our trade would drive interest in our presence, and, based on last night's events, it did. But I was not prepared for this..." He gestured at the guards beside the door. "And we were done trading. I have little left to sell, having made all the most profitable trades of the season in our first weeks here... Had this court not proven so impenetrable, I would not have exposed us to this risk."

"What with the fighting we heard went on at the governor's palace, it's no wonder Mohtashim Khan and his men were primed and ready for violent resistance when they came to the house," Ricky said, equally quietly.

"Very true—" A man entering through the door behind the eunuch interrupted Jadu. He crossed the floor to mutter quietly in the eunuch's ear. That worthy stared at the slave, hissed something harsh, and started toward the up-timers and their companion on slippered feet.

"This bodes ill," Jadu said, watching thin lips turn into a pout.

"The diwan will not see you today, Jadu Das."

"He will not?" Jadu asked, glancing at Ricky as if to say, "Of course!"

Ricky cocked his head, weighing their response.

The eunuch bowed deeply. "I am afraid not."

Expecting more empty platitudes, all three of them were caught off guard when the eunuch said, "You are summoned."

"Summoned?" Ricky and Bobby blurted at the same time.

"By whom?" Jadu asked, more sensibly.

A shrug of round shoulders. "An umara of great importance."

"May I ask the name of this great personage?"

"I am forbidden to say."

"You are?" Jadu asked, incredulous.

"I am," the eunuch said, standing erect from his bow. "You are to follow that one"—he gestured at the messenger—"to the appointed place."

The messenger, still standing where he'd been left, bowed deeply. Ricky noticed he wore slippers. *So... somewhere in the palace.*

Jadu must have been on the same page, because he took one look at the messenger and said in English, "Witness the rich robes...and slippers. He's at least as richly dressed as this one."

"Yup," Bobby said. Ricky just nodded.

The messenger bowed deeper still, turned, and led them deeper into the palace.

The trio were ushered into a chamber with no less than three ceiling fans pushing the warm, moist air around.

"Be seated," the man who had fetched them said

with a broad gesture at a group of cushions arrayed around a low dais with several trays of refreshment. "Be refreshed. Your host will be with you momentarily." He departed on silent feet.

Looking about, the men of the Mission sat down. Bobby sniffed an ewer and, apparently satisfied, poured a drink. He offered the glass to Jadu, who accepted the cup.

"Think it's safe to talk?" Bobby asked, pouring another. Given they did not want to be understood if overheard, he set aside their general rule about speaking English.

Ricky leaned back and let his eyes follow the line-and-pulley system powering the fans to where they ran through openings high up in the walls. Figuring the slaves laboring to drive the fans were too distant to overhear any reasonably quiet discussion, he nodded.

Jadu was also nodding. "We are to feel comfortable speaking"—he raised his glass—"hence the absence of service."

"Did you see something?" Ricky said.

"No. Guess I was just hoping one of you two saw something I didn't," Bobby said.

"Just another wait, man."

Bobby sighed and nodded. They were just settling in when a man in fine robes strode in. He spared a glance for the trio waiting on him but sat without a word.

Ricky was struck by the feeling he'd seen the man before, but couldn't place him. From Jadu's sudden razor-sharp attentiveness, he recognized the man, too.

"You have been in Patna long, merchant?" the man said without preamble. His Persian was smooth and cultured, his accent something Ricky hadn't heard since leaving court.

"For several weeks now, Shaista Khan," Jadu said.

Oh, I see the family resemblance now ... Looks like a younger version of Asaf Khan. Supposed to be a general in his own right, and the one man Jadu believed would succeed his father. He's ... uncle to Dara and Jahanara, then? He hid a smile. *I swear these folks are just as close-knit as small-town West Virginians, all related by blood or marriage, or both.*

The man did nothing to confirm or deny Jadu's use of his name, instead asking, "And your business is concluded?"

"For the most part"—Jadu paused as if considering, then said—"forgive me, but I am uncertain what mode of address I should use?"

That drew an arched brow, but no reply.

Jadu glanced at his companions.

Ricky cleared his throat, drawing the man's gaze.

Shaista Khan's other brow joined its companion, though Ricky suspected he was not at all surprised. "You have something to say?" he asked.

"Maybe I do," Ricky said, disliking the high-handed manner of the man and, frankly, frustrated and impatient with the whole damn thing. Politics was not a game he liked to play.

"Maybe? You seem uncertain. Perhaps it is the ... irregular nature of your arrival here that makes you so uncertain?"

Dick.

"There is little uncertainty to it," Jadu said. "We are merchants, trading on a firman issued by the Sultan Al'Azam, Dara Shikoh."

"But that is not *all* you are, is it?"

Jadu's only answer was to look a question at Ricky.

"No, that isn't everything we're about." Ricky looked from his friend to the nobleman.

Fuck it.

"But if you insist on playing games, you will have to allow us our little mysteries as well."

Jadu winced, but Shaista Khan laughed.

"And if I continue to insist?" he asked, stroking his oiled beard.

"Then I suppose we'll close up shop and head back to Agra."

"You already tire of Patna?"

"As Jadu said, we've finished trading for the season. We had hoped to get some other business done, but it seems everyone wants to waste our time."

"And what other business did you have?" Shaista Khan asked, all trace of banter gone from his tone.

"Why," Jadu interjected, "to meet with your father, or his chosen representative, and discuss certain matters of mutual interest."

"I am that representative."

"Oh?" Jadu said. "I had not heard an announcement to that effect."

"No, you have not."

"Then how are we to proceed?" Jadu cocked his head.

"I am not certain, good merchant. I, too, have not heard who it is you are here to represent."

Jadu again looked at Ricky, who nodded, wondering when Jadu had decided he needed Ricky's permission to speak for them.

The merchant took a deep breath and said, "In

truth, we are here on behalf of Dara Shikoh, not only as merchants, but also in order to locate the noble Asaf Khan and, if possible, determine which son of Shah Jahan he would serve."

Again those eyebrows rose. "And why do you, clearly the senior man, defer to these youngsters?" He gestured at Ricky and Bobby.

"Simply put, Great Khan, it is they who have the ear of the emperor, not I."

"It's true the Mission has influence, but I've barely met the man," Ricky put in.

"Why not send a munshi or other senior member of the court?"

"The trade we have engaged in was necessary, and such a personage was considered, but the emperor and his counselors did not wish to display concern over your father's loyalty, and offer offence."

Shaista Khan sat back, stroking his beard for several long moments.

Jadu leaned forward, looking very much like a cat about to pounce.

"I told him to answer," Shaista Kahn said after a moment's thought, "but he has ever been slow to take counsel from his children."

"He is well, then?"

"No, not well."

"But he lives?"

"Oh, most certainly."

Chapter 25

Agra
Red Fort, harem precincts

"You really have no idea, do you?" Roshanara said, wishing she could see, and therefore read, his expression. She had many wishes, all of which looked to remain unfulfilled, at least in the near term. If she had to choose one wish she could have fulfilled immediately, it would not be to put an end to the roundabout code they were forced to employ in order to communicate.

"I'm afraid I do not, Shehzadi," the physician answered from beyond the jali. "I conveyed your requirements to the herbalist, but have not heard back as yet whether there is some new decoction ready for use."

"That is not what I wished to hear."

"Nor what I wished to convey, Shehzadi. There is also another request from the herbalist: he wished me to ask if you have specific numbers in mind."

Roshanara mastered a snarl and said evenly, "If he cannot meet my requirements, what is the point of my providing numbers? In fact, I am sorely tempted to see if the palace herbalist has made any progress, since your man seems unable to meet my rather basic requirements."

"I hope I have not disappointed, Shehzadi," he said, tone conveying a warning out of keeping with his actual words.

Which she translated as: *Don't be hasty! I'm trying, and you asking about such things might reveal what we're about.*

"I confess I am disappointed. I had hoped to participate fully in my sister's work. If I cannot provide the new poultice that, on your assurances, *I* promised *her*, well then I shall be embarrassed before all the harem. I do not know what I will do with the shame."

Roshanara quelled the wicked smile that threatened to grace her lips on hearing the clear sound of his indrawn breath.

He was silent a long time after. So long it made her wonder if she'd pushed too far.

She bit her lip. *I will not apologize to this ... this messenger. He and, more importantly, Aurangzeb, put me in this position in the first place.*

She wanted to warn them of many things, not least that she was not some petty zenana toy, paid to dance for the pleasure of others and having access only to the small secrets of the harem. No, she was a princess, with knowledge of and influence on affairs of the wider court.

They would, at minimum, promise to treat her as such if they wished to learn what she knew: that Dara's condition was still in question. That Jahanara ruled from the shade of the harem and, not content with flouting only that tradition, there were rumors she had engaged in clandestine embraces with Salim. Such rumors had doubtless already reached the ears of Aurangzeb's other spies, but those whisperers were not to know that Dara gave credence to the rumors, so much so that he had placed many spies to watch his elder sister.

There were many spies in the harem now. So many that Roshanara felt a rising paranoia. It had begun as sensible caution, but now... Roshanara's experiences of harem politics had been, up until getting caught between Nur and Jahanara, petty in nature. Harem life was always rife with intrigue, but she'd been too young to fully comprehend imperial politics when Father had vied with Jahangir and Nur for the throne. This was the first time Roshanara played for such massive, and permanent, stakes. It frightened her, but also made her feel very... *alive.* Alive in a way she hadn't felt since... she could not remember ever feeling quite this way. Certainly, there had been moments of fear; when her sister beat her, when she'd nearly fallen from the horse at pulu, and the lengthy, if low-grade terror of not knowing if she would be executed by her brother for her role in the events that led to Father's death. Those fears, however severe, were not the same as the constant state of tension she found herself in as she struggled to secure her own place in the world. A place outside the shadow of her sister or any other who wished to cast her back into obscurity.

I, too, am a daughter of Shah Jahan.

Mission House

Waiting for her moment to strike, Ilsa smiled and took another bite of tikka, watching her companions fondly.

Agra's nights were blessedly cool after the scorching heat of the day, so the Mission members had made a habit of eating together on the long gallery above the inner court of Mission House.

Everyone but Ricky and Bobby were present, though they'd been receiving reports from the youngest members of the Mission or Jadu Das on a regular basis.

Even Rodney and Priscilla, who had been busy enough they'd missed the last few such gatherings, were present. The couple had their heads together, sharing a rare quiet moment. Not that anyone complained of their absences or their lack of participation this evening, as they had been training the medical corps Jahanara had commanded into existence, and everyone suspected Dara's growing army would need trained medics before too long. Dara had created a new precedent, and named Priscilla to a military rank, admitting her to the ranks of his umara. The salary was not the equal of her husband's but it was still a substantial sum, and allowed her to pay for the medical corpsmen out of her own salary. Those she had trained directly were now themselves training the rest of the corps, which was to number a few thousand, even leaving out the staff being trained to work in the hospital.

Farther down the table, Bertram and Gervais were talking with Monique, who was clearly enjoying illustrating some fine point of politics to Bertram. Gervais gazed upon his daughter and her suitor with an air of bemused happiness. The three of them were fixtures at court, serving both Dara and Jahanara as advisors. Both men had been given formal rank and salaries, just like John. Because they were not expected to command in the field, neither man possessed the military rank and salary John had been given, but they were still very well paid on the imperial administrator pay scale, called zat.

Even Angelo Gradinego had stopped by earlier in the day. His visits had become less frequent over the last few months as Bertram and Gervais mastered the languages and politics of court. He was still friendly, but Ilsa was not sad his visits had grown infrequent. The Venetian made her uneasy, what with his easy airs and assumption of superiority to all things female. If Gervais felt the lack, he made no report of it to the rest of the Mission.

John's hand found hers under the table and gently closed on it. She put thoughts of the others aside and looked at the strong hand on hers, then let her gaze travel up his muscled forearm. The silk robe of state he wore concealed his broad shoulders and muscled chest right up to his strong neck.

The square jaw she loved so much was covered in a well-trimmed beard that left his lips visible. Lips that curved in a smile for her.

"Love you," she said, meeting his gaze with her own.

"Love you, too."

"Two, my love?" she said, holding up thumb and forefinger.

John's smile faltered slightly, handsome features showing a lack of understanding.

"Do you love us both?"

"Both? Wha—"

"I am pregnant, husband," she said, kissing him.

"What?" he said, loud enough the rest of the table grew silent.

"I am carrying our child, John Dexter Ennis," she said, equally loudly, punctuating the statement with yet one more kiss.

"Uh—buh—" he sputtered, stunned.

She touched his face as the rest of their friends stood and moved to surround them, faces bright with happiness, and congratulated them both.

"How far along?" Priscilla asked.

"Just about a week past the first trimester."

"But—" John said, still struggling with the news.

"Awww, so nice that he's forming complete words again..." Priscilla mocked, ever so gently.

"Be nice," Monique said, rapping her fan against the table.

"I didn't, I just..."

"Thought I was getting fat, did you, John?" Ilsa asked with a playful pat on his cheek.

He tilted his head against her hand, smiled and said, "Really?"

She smiled back, and nodded, feeling tears well in her eyes. "Really."

"I'm going to be a father," he said, voice thick with emotion.

Ilsa kissed him gently.

Rodney clapped him on the back with one shovel-sized hand, the other men pressing in to congratulate him.

"I'm going to be a father," John repeated.

"Yes, you are," she answered, actively refusing to consider any outcome but the one she desired for him, for herself, and for the child they would have together.

Pris couldn't help but smile at the look on John's face.

Rodney nudged her, brows raised in question, then moved aside to let Monique, Gervais, and Bertram congratulate the expectant couple.

"Just trying to find the word that best describes John's expression," she said, smiling up at him.

He chuckled. "J.D. does look pretty stunned."

"You bet he does, but I think I will settle for pleasantly bemused."

"Settle?" he asked, wrapping her shoulders with one arm and hugging her to him. "You're not one to settle."

"Well, at first I was thinking poleaxed, but I don't think one can be happily poleaxed, do you?"

Ear against his chest, she felt as much as heard his chuckle. He kissed the crown of her head and asked, "Did you know?"

Pris nodded. "She told me this morning, but I half suspected the last few weeks."

"Oh?" he asked.

"This place isn't that big."

He pulled away slightly and looked another question at her.

She shrugged. "Not so big I didn't hear her getting violently ill after breakfast every day I was home to hear."

"Oh." He shook his head.

"What is it, Rodney?"

"Just thinking how clueless I can be, even with my training."

She pulled herself back into his embrace. "It's normal. You don't have ladyparts, so you miss some clues."

"Ladyparts?" he asked.

She nodded gravely, cheek sliding across the silk of his robe and the hard muscle underneath. "The new technical term. I will spread it through the harem!"

His chuckling grew to laughter, then to great guffaws.

Ilsa and the rest left off their conversation to stare at him, which only made him laugh harder.

Priscilla stepped back from him, wondering what she'd said.

"What's got him laughing?" Ilsa asked, smiling tentatively.

"Spread—parts." Rodney gasped, tears at the corners of his eyes now.

"What?" John asked.

"I don't know. I was telling him—" Her eyes widened in shock as she figured out what had struck him so funny.

"Oh, Jesus, Rodney!" she cried, slapping him on the shoulder. Then she stifled a mad laugh herself. It was funny, but what made her lose it was his attempts to control himself, as he rarely suffered such attacks. It wasn't that he was humorless; he was constantly making her laugh with his dry humor.

Their friends waited, with various levels of patience, for an explanation. At least all of them were smiling indulgently.

Rodney sobered enough to gasp out, "She"—he pointed at Priscilla, who was still laughing too hard to speak—"threatened to spread"—he bit a broad knuckle and eventually managed to gurgle—"her ladyparts." He gnawed on his knuckle once more, then said, quite clearly, "Through the harem," and fell to laughing again.

Ilsa's bright, infectious laugh silvered the air first, quickly followed by that of the rest of their friends.

Chapter 26

Asirgarh
Nur's tent, Shuja's camp

"There is only so much I can do, Nur."

"I know this as well as you, perhaps better, Shehzada."

The look he gave her was not meant to put her at her ease, nor show understanding.

Nur, tired in her bones, accepted his disapproval without bowing to it. She busied her hands by plucking a folded letter from between her toes and proffering it, knowing early news of the explosion outside Agra would cover many sins.

He did not take it. "From who?"

"One of your many friends at court," she said, offering it again. Unsurprised that he need not bother to ask *which* court. He was very clever, this great nephew.

He took the letter in hand, but did not open it.

"You will want to read it, Shehzada."

"What I want, Nur, is assurances."

Nur fought the urge to shrug. Aurangzeb—indeed, most princes—did not respond well to an apparent indifference to stated desires from subordinates. "The ferenghi want what they want. I report to you what they conveyed to me, as you require."

He leveled a stare at her, dark eyes glittering in the lamplight.

Nur was struck by the fact he'd grown into a magnetic, handsome young man. This, despite the severe piety that drove him to suck all pleasures from life but the thin ones prayer provided.

Five heartbeats he stared at her. Five heartbeats she returned his regard. One does not show fear to the lion unless one wishes to be eaten.

He was the one who broke the silence. "There is a limit to a prince's patience, Nur, just as there is for the ferenghi whose questions you choose to convey to me."

"Of that there is no doubt, Shehzada. We are all run low on patience. I . . ." She stopped, thinking it was not yet time to make that particular offer.

"What is it, Nur?"

"Shehzada, I . . ." *He is not ready, but you've given him the opening.*

He cocked a brow. "You are not one to speak unless you wish to say something in its entirety."

"Shehzada, a question, first."

He gestured her to proceed.

Nur took a moment to marshal her thoughts, as the proposal was dangerous to even think of, let alone discuss.

"Speak. Your hesitation makes my teeth itch," Aurangzeb said.

Nur could not tell if he joked with her or not, and so continued: "I may have the means, Shehzada, to provide an opportunity . . ."

"That is as vague a statement as I have ever heard from you, even knowing your penchant for indirectness. Cease these prevarications and tell me what it is that makes you dither so."

"I have someone in a position to place something in Shuja's food or drink."

"Something? You mean poison."

Nur shook her head. "Something so obvious as a deadly poison would surely mean an end to the servant if they could be deceived into doing such a thing. And if they are caught, then more of the network I have built for you will be exposed than would be prudent, Shehzada."

"Then what?"

"If he were to become so intoxicated that he acted outside the bounds of propriety, before witnesses..." She trailed off, wondering if Aurangzeb would recognize the danger: Shuja could simply order his death in a drunken rage.

"The emperor sets the standard for propriety," Aurangzeb said, shaking his head.

"A low bar, then," she said, forcing a smile.

He did not return it.

"We would have to choose the timing most carefully," he said, surprising her.

"Most carefully," she agreed. "And yet I cannot help but think this may be the time God has chosen."

"Oh?" he said, managing his tone and expression with admirable control.

"Make no mistake, I claim no special ability to divine God's plan, but...I am ready for God to present the moment you will step forward and take what we have worked so hard to obtain."

Speaking so openly of his desire, and of the delays God had seen fit to set in their path, put a fine crack in his self-control. She, who had spent so much time observing him and attempting to gauge his mood and mind, recognized it the moment Aurangzeb looked away.

Having stoked the fires of his ambition, she set about putting any unease to bed, adding: "And I shall be certain the substance is only placed in those beverages forbidden to good Muslims, thereby making Shuja the author of his own fate..." Nur winced inwardly, wishing she'd used different phrasing...

"A man's fate is as God wills it."

Nur was relieved that Aurangzeb's correction was automatic and devoid of heat, his thoughts obviously elsewhere.

"What, then, is in the letter?" he asked, eyes falling on the note in his hand.

Smiling was less of a trial this time. "Good news, Shehzada. News that may address your concerns regarding timing..."

"Is it too much to ask that you stop playing, even for a moment?"

"What game do you believe I play, Shehzada?"

"The only one that matters."

"Then, with respect, you answer your own question, Shehzada."

Carvalho's guns, siege lines

Carvalho spat as the remnants of his second gun fell to earth about the emplacement twenty yards to his left. He didn't curse aloud, though. In truth, he was surprised they'd made it this long without a failure. The heaviest of his guns had been hard-used these last weeks, and one was bound to fail at some point.

A ragged, jeering cheer rose from within the fortress as the defenders watched the aftermath of the explosion.

Carvalho was happy he could not understand the Rajputs, but it was easy enough to guess what they were cheering about. The garrison was no doubt happy to see the gun visit destruction upon its crew after so long suffering under their fire.

"Not like you had anything to do with it!" Carvalho bellowed at the defenders as he ran over to check on his crew. He'd silenced the last of the fortress's big guns last week, and was within a few days of reducing the gate to rubble, so he only had to brave a few shots from a few long arquebuses to get there.

Rodrigo, the *mestiço* bastard who captained Carvalho's second gun, was dragging himself to his feet as his commander entered the smoking hole that used to be the gun emplacement.

"What?" Rodrigo shouted, eyes unfocused and blood sheeting down the side of his face.

Carvalho took Rodrigo by the shoulders and sat him, unresisting, on the ground. He stepped past, only to set a boot in the remains of one of the crew.

Rodrigo moaned, swayed, and fell back against the berm thrown up to protect the gunners.

"Christ!" Carvalho grunted. Slipping in gore and choking back the horror-spawned urge to vomit, he checked on the rest of the men. The examination only required a moment: No one had survived the breech explosion that sent two forearm-length shards of metal sweeping through the gun pit like twin reaping blades, removing limbs and disemboweling the man Carvalho had put his boot in.

By the time he returned to Rodrigo, the man was unconscious, though breathing. The head wound had almost stopped bleeding, too. He pulled the man up and drew him over both shoulders, carrying him out of the gun pit and toward the rear of the siege lines.

"Keep firing!" he shouted at the rest of his crews.

A ball from some skilled or very lucky arquebuser cracked against a stone at his feet, making his nuts draw up into his belly.

Fucking useless, unnecessary siege! Had I wanted this kind of fight, I'd have stayed in Europe.

No mercenary gunner—and Carvalho was still a mercenary at heart—enjoyed a siege. The daily cost in money, material and men, not just from combat, but from the sickness that often struck armies encamped for too long. And the longer the siege, the more likely an event like that which had claimed the gun and all but Rodrigo of its crew.

Rodrigo, who was with me when I jumped ship in Goa and first came to Mughal lands. Rodrigo, who saved my life twice, no, three times, at least...

Minutes later he staggered, panting, into the tent Aurangzeb had set up for the relief of wounded men. He passed Rodrigo into the hands of someone who might be able to help.

God knew he could not.

He stood in the entrance of that tent and stared at his hands. Shaking, bloody and clenched into fists, they offered no answers.

Much later, Aurangzeb found him standing there.

Found him, and, in a vastly unusual move, took Carvalho's fisted hands in his own. He said something, something that penetrated the darkness filling the ferenghi umara's heart.

The eyes Carvalho stared at Aurangzeb with were full of desperate hope.

The prince repeated himself, the words for Carvalho's ears alone, and they lit a fire in the artilleryman's heart.

The Red Tent, Shuja's camp

"The ferenghi wizards have killed themselves, and with them all Dara's remaining hopes!" Shuja gloated, wine dribbling through his thin beard and onto the naked chest of the dancing girl on his lap.

Occasioned by the news of the setback Dara's cause had suffered, the festivities had grown in intensity in the hours since, Shuja leading the debauchery with drink after drink.

"Sultan Al'Azam, may I depart?" Aurangzeb asked for the second time, striving to keep his tone neutral and his expression blank.

Shuja pretended not to hear.

Aurangzeb raised his voice slightly and again asked the emperor leave to depart, adding that it was nearing time for prayer.

That gained Shuja's attention. He surged to his feet and turned to face his brother.

The dancing girl stifled a squeak as she fell from his lap to the carpets, her lustrous black hair coming loose.

Stumbling slightly, Shuja caught himself, one boot coming to rest on the dancing girl's long, unbound hair.

Shuja smiled bitterly. "I wonder," the elder brother slurred.

Aurangzeb did not respond.

The festivities, losing momentum without the continued attentions of the emperor, stumbled to a lesser tempo, spreading silence in a circle radiating from the brothers like the ripples caused when a stone was dropped in a still pool.

"I wonder," Shuja repeated into the ever-greater quiet, "how Father sired such a bloodless pair as you and Dara. The one wants nothing but to hide behind his wife's veils and the other ... the other"—he spilled wine over Aurangzeb's crossed legs as he pointed down at him—"the other"—he hiccupped—"the other would spend his time *praying* for victory."

Be calm. God fashions each moment like stepping-stones to knowledge of His will; do not miss your step for anger or pride.

"I do not know what you mean, Sultan Al'Azam. I have only ever done as you commanded."

Another gesture of the cup made the emperor sway.

"And if I *command* you to drink?" Aurangzeb felt those of the umara who kept God's law as written by His Prophet tense on hearing Shuja's words.

Even those of the umara who were neither Muslim nor devout, but yet remained sober enough to think, had misgivings. Commanding a man to act against his religious conviction was simply not done. Certainly not by one of the descendants of Akbar.

"Then I will beg forgiveness," Aurangzeb said, hiding satisfaction.

"Of whom?" Shuja asked.

"Sultan Al'Azam?"

"Who will you ask for forgi—" Shuja's swaying reached a critical mass, forcing him to adjust his footing. One slippered foot caught in the dancing girl's hair. The emperor threw out both hands to save himself from a fall, his goblet striking Aurangzeb in the face before he could raise a hand to guard it. Wine splashed his eyes, blinding him.

The dancing girl shrieked.

When he wiped away the wine, Aurangzeb saw only the bottom of his brother's feet. One slipper had come off, and both heels drummed the carpets, along with his other foot. His gaze traveled up his brother's supine form and saw purple-red froth about Shuja's mouth.

Aurangzeb blinked in momentary confusion, mind failing to apprehend what was before his eyes.

Nur's poisoner wasn't supposed to kill him, just make him more drunk.

No. This looks like the seizures he used to have after the fall in Lahore, when I was a baby.

This isn't the result of poison, it's a seizure!

He's having a seizure, just like when he was a boy.

I thought he'd recovered . . .

Merciful God!

He sat up, aware he must seize the moment God had laid before him, and do so immediately.

The tent was now entirely silent, aside from the choking gasps of Shuja's breathing and the whimpering of the dancing girl who thought herself the cause of Shuja's fall.

Fitting, that.

"God!" someone's startled cry rent the near silence.

"No!" Aurangzeb cried, improvising as he, still on his

knees, went to his brother's side. "None shall say my brother was struck down by God! It was a simple accident brought about by too much drink, nothing more!"

Several of his followers shouted support, providing a cloak to cover his true intent.

Islam Khan, one of Shuja's more prominent, and supposedly devout, commanders, was shaking his head.

Aurangzeb pointed at the man. "You shake your head in denial, but I beg you, do not think ill of my brother! It was a simple fall, not God's justice."

Islam Khan's face, made florid by drink, went stiff under his beard as he realized that whatever he'd been shaking his head about, it had been made to serve Aurangzeb's purpose.

Aurangzeb hid exultation behind a facade of care for his stricken brother as the umara began to mutter, then declaim, then bellow at one another. For it was apparent that, despite Aurangzeb's protestations, Shuja's sudden fall and subsequent seizure were clear and obvious signs from God of the emperor's fall from grace.

Shuja relaxed into the deep, exhausted slumber that had always followed one of his seizures. Had he not been drinking, or dosed with whatever Nur's agent had placed in his drink, he might have roused, for there was danger in his slumber.

Careful not to argue too persuasively, Aurangzeb slowly gave ground and allowed himself to be convinced that his brother's fall was the sign they all knew it to be.

Pretending to rally, he called for learned men to assess the validity of the sign. When his shrinking pool of opponents challenged him further, he asked them to bring their own seer or learned men in to refute what they had all witnessed.

An hour, then. A golden hour in which the fate of the dynasty was decided.

As if there was any question as to God's intent.

There was a shift in the royal tent, a movement Aurangzeb likened to the gathering power of an avalanche. At first there were but a few small stones. After enough of them had been moved, the larger, heavier stones—the ones that carried more weight—were set in motion, falling over each other to throw themselves at Aurangzeb's feet.

Eventually, all those present—the most powerful and privileged umara of Shuja's court—were moved from the circle of Shuja's power and entered the shade of his younger, better-suited, and most pious brother's ambit.

When one of his snores grew too loud, and Aurangzeb was certain he had every umara who counted in hand, he directed Shuja be taken from the Red Tent to his own erstwhile quarters and seen to, but not before making certain that his own nökör stood guard over the fallen emperor.

Aurangzeb's tent, Aurangzeb's camp

Nur yawned behind her veil.

Humayun Lodi, Shuja's personal physician, glanced at her on hearing it. "I can give you a draught, Begum. One that will keep you awake for hours. I only offer it because women do not suffer stress as men do, being far more delicate in their constitutions."

"No, I will be fine." Nur did not like the slim Persian's airs. While he cut a dapper figure in any of the robes of state Shuja had lavished on him, the man's skills as a courtier far outstripped any medical acumen he might have laid claim to.

Years spent propping up her beloved Jahangir had taught her more about the interplay of drugs and alcohol on the human form than most physicians would ever have the chance to learn, and certainly far more than the presumptuous buffoon before her.

Another yawn threatened. She concentrated a moment, breathed deeply, and murdered it before it could betray her fatigue to Humayun once again.

The yawns might be attributed to relief. That she was here with Humayun instead of being questioned by the fool was a clear indication none suspected Shuja had fallen victim to poison. But it had also been late when word reached her of Shuja's collapse, and later still when she'd brushed aside the complaints of his servants and diwan, to enter Aurangzeb's tent—no, Shuja's now—and began her watch.

Shuja's men had proved persistent. Their complaints had reached Aurangzeb, naturally, prompting the younger prince to order them to accept her commands as from his own mouth and placing her in charge of Shuja's recovery.

Damn him and his clever head.

Such a public command placed her in a precarious position. She had thought to see if there might be some way to quietly do away with Shuja, perhaps by the administration of some toxin that would make his death seem a natural outcome of drink, his fall, and the seizure that followed.

She'd discarded the notion as soon as Aurangzeb's command had been delivered, however.

By publicly placing her in charge of his recovery, Aurangzeb had also made her responsible should the drunken idiot pass on to his reward.

Besides, he gave no specific instruction regarding such action, and I have only to think back on Mullah Mohan's fate to see what repercussions precipitous action will win for me.

No ... I need to consider carefully how best to gain advantage from this and ensure Aurangzeb does not decide he can dispense with me now he begins to see his aims met.

Red Tent, Aurangzeb's camp

Knees aching, Nur prostrated herself before the emperor in all but name. It was late, very late. There would be time to sleep when she was dead, and she counted it a good sign that he had granted her a private audience.

He had timed her audience with the same care he showed in all things, admitting her into his presence just as he was preparing to retire for the night.

As his closest female relation in camp, none should think it strange that she attend him now, especially after she had spent the last few hours nursing his brother, Shuja.

She would report the deposed emperor's status, of course. But there were other issues of import to discuss, such as how to retain enough support from the men about him to maintain the power he'd grasped today.

Dismissing his attendants, Aurangzeb gestured for her to rise and come closer.

"Sultan Al'Azam," she murmured quietly, always wary of eavesdroppers. She settled on a cushion below the raised platform where he sat.

He yawned, fatigue warring with exultation, and returned, just as quietly: "Not yet, Nur. I have yet to have the khutba said in my name nor had coins struck. Then there is the uncomfortable fact that Shuja still lives..." He looked at her with eyes rimmed red with fatigue. "How fares my brother?"

"He slumbers, and will continue to until noon, at least. Measures were taken."

"But he will not die?" he asked.

Admiring his neutral tone, she answered, "Not if this is but a recurrence of his old condition, no."

"Is it?"

"It is." Nur's answer was without hesitation, despite a twinge of misgiving. Even the best physicians often had to guess as to what ailed their patients, and for all her knowledge of intoxicants and their effects on the human body, she was no more a proper physician than Humayun.

"I thought your actions precipitated his fall."

"His seizure was not a result of what you commanded be put in his drink"—she felt it useful to remind him just who had given the orders—"instead, it was a result of too *much* drink, both tonight and over the last few weeks. In fact, what we put in his drink should have made him *less* prone to seizure, not more."

He was young enough to let his relief show. "I admit to some shock when he fell. Indeed, I had not remembered his condition until that moment." He shrugged. "In fact, I recall very little about his falling spells save that he had them as a boy."

"You were very young, and the event was a great secret. Even I am not absolutely certain of what happened, as Shah Jahan and my husband were at odds when it first happened. Jahangir told me later one of Shuja's nurses tripped and fell with him from the balcony. He struck his head and very nearly died, but the young have great powers of recuperation. His seizures did not come as often while we had you both in our custody, and I thought they had ceased entirely by now. At least, I had not heard he still suffered them."

"If it didn't resolve on its own, they kept his condition a very close secret indeed. I had entirely forgotten about it." Aurangzeb shook his head, perhaps thinking that if he had known of it, he might have tried to trigger the condition earlier.

"So, how shall we proceed?" Nur asked after a moment.

He waggled his head thoughtfully. "On which account do you speak?"

She smiled thinly. "On every account, Sultan Al'Azam. There are a great many birds need killing, and only so many stones to go about. Shall we see if there are a few that can be slain with but one stone?"

"I marry as soon as possible. Sher Shah Khan will provide his daughter."

Her smile grew. "An excellent match!" The girl had been Nur's first choice and main recommendation for weeks now. Aurangzeb had refused to approach her father out of concern Shuja would learn of it and punish them both.

He nodded, tugging gently at the thin beard trying, valiantly, to cover his chin. "I confess to some... trepidation."

"Why? Tying that family to you also signals that Shuja's most powerful supporter believes you are the one to back. When the others see him depart, everyone who thinks to remain with Shuja will have to question why they do not swear to you."

Aurangzeb waved her down. "That is not my concern—or, rather, it is one I have already planned for. No, I—" He shook his head and looked at his hands, jaw working. "What if I do not like her? Or... she... dislikes me?"

Aurangzeb's shy admission tested the experience and discipline of a lifetime spent in the courts of the perceptive and powerful. Crushing the desire to smile, she reached out a hand to gently touch his. "She is a great beauty, and will give you the sons you need to secure your throne, Sultan Al'Azam. The rest will come as God wills."

Mention of God's will soothed his troubled brow, as she knew it would.

He brightened and quickly changed subjects: discussing the day's momentous events, with Aurangzeb revealing his plans to solidify support and deny Shuja the chance to regain his power. He even asked her to advise him on what he might have overlooked in his planning.

That part of her not engaged in that process reviewed what had just transpired: *He so rarely shows his youth, it is easy to forget his inexperience.*

That inexperience is a point of exposure anyone with access can exploit. I must be certain to cover for it, even as I ensure I am in position to exploit it.

Carefully.

She noted, as she left him to his rest, that he had not mentioned how he planned to dispose of Shuja. Nur did not press the question, knowing Aurangzeb had a number of sensible reasons not to have his brother murdered.

First off, murdering one's own brother was against Heaven's law. Princes, especially among the Ottomans, vying for a throne were known to cast aside that law with regularity. Here, though, Aurangzeb's reputation for piety was such he could not execute his brother without sacrificing many of the allies his pious image had brought to his cause.

Second: as long as he was entirely in Aurangzeb's power, the threat Shuja posed was mitigated, especially as Aurangzeb was not likely to make the same mistakes as his elder brother.

Third, and most important: those who supported Shuja would be comforted by the fact that should Aurangzeb die in battle or some other incident, there was an heir who would be grateful to those who freed him from whatever prison Aurangzeb decided to put him in. Of course, once Aurangzeb fathered a son on his new wife, Shuja's life would be counted in breaths, if not heartbeats.

Chapter 27

Agra
Red Fort, the harem

"You will explain yourself," Dara hissed.

Jahanara flinched, caught completely by surprise. The sharp reprimand lacing his tone was entirely unexpected. She looked around, half thinking his tone indicated a slave must have made some egregious error and created some mess that she should have prevented. Seeing they were as alone as he ever was, she looked at her brother only to find him staring at her.

"Do not look for my wife to answer for you, sister."

"What? I do not understand the source of this sudden attack, Dara," she said, fatigue making her wilt in the face of his obvious anger. She had no idea what might have precipitated such anger in him. She'd been late joining the imperial couple because she'd been seeing to one of the endless details of government that had fallen on her since Dara's ascension.

"You have been lying to me for months." The scar of

his head injury, normally just visible as a finger-width white line against his skin, was flushed a deep red.

"I—" she began, hoping she would be given a chance to explain her reasoning. The entire purpose of the conspiracy was to preserve his throne, after all.

"Nadira—"

He cut her off once more. "My wife has retired for the evening, and even were she here, I would say she has covered for more than enough of *your* indiscretions. She will do so no longer!"

Unused to being spoken to in this manner—and from him, for whom she had sacrificed so much—Jahanara felt her own anger rising. Still, it would not do to show it. Not while there were any witnesses. She must remain the Begum Sahib.

"I know you have been"—his angry gaze darted about, presumably assessing who could hear him, as he at last lowered his voice—"meeting in secret. It will stop. Now."

"But—"

"But?" he snarled. "You dare challenge my command?" he barked, grabbing her wrist in a painfully tight grip.

"No, I—"

"Good! Because I will take away your salaries and prerogatives. Do not think I won't!"

"But, Dara! I—I—" she spluttered, tears of frustration welling. He'd not spoken to her like this since they were children.

"Don't you 'but Dara' me! You presume too much! I cannot afford to ignore such behavior, now, when everyone already watches me. When courtly tongues already mutter of my weakness!"

His words alarmed her as much as everything he'd said thus far. She'd been so sure they'd put a stop to such talk, and Nadira had confirmed that her detractors had been silenced. "Who—"

He interrupted her once more, shaking his head. "It does not matter. They see their Sultan allowing, even encouraging, you in the discharge of duties that are more rightly Nadira's, and find fault, calling me weak behind my back."

He shut his eyes tight.

She was too angry to recognize the warning sign. "It is not weakness, Sultan Al'Azam. It is only sensible—"

He cut her off once more, shaking her by the arm he held. "So you don't deny that you have met with Salim, alone, and in secret?"

He must have taken the glance she cast at her hennaed toes for confirmation of his suspicions, because his next words struck cold fear deep in her heart: "I will send him away. Your willful disregard for how your wanton behavior would reflect on me might have cost me the throne, sister!"

"Wanton?" Jahanara protested. "I have done nothing —"

"Nothing?" he scoffed. "You have ruined m—"

"Dara!" Shouting his name stopped his tirade before it could truly begin, but she found her own tongue failing her, fearful of continuing, of what her anger might lead her to say. He'd always had difficulty with accepting that his thoughts on a matter might be incorrect, and woe to the man or woman who corrected him. There was much that might be used to wound him, and so little that would correct his mistaken impressions. He had not ordered her from his presence, yet, so there remained a chance to convince him. "I have done nothing to deserve such recriminations!"

He did not answer, only sat there, staring at her.

She could see his anger was so vast that it had stopped his ears, and tried again: "More importantly, your faithful friend and supporter, Salim Gadh Visa Yilmaz has only ever acted with all honor! He would never imperil your cause! These rumors are a poor reflection of what actually transpired."

"And?" he asked at last, face so flushed and angry it dawned on her he might be on the verge of another fit.

"We did meet in secret," she admitted, hoping to mollify his anger.

"Alone?" he demanded.

Jahanara nodded reluctantly but hurried on: "But only to ensure the secrecy of our discussions, Dara."

He rolled his eyes and scoffed. "How could you be so stupid?! Can you not see how the appearance of impropriety is, for our purposes, as bad as the thing itself? No, I shall send him away and restrict your allowances..."

Knowing she must preserve Salim's position at court, whatever the cost to herself, she pretended surrender. "I am sorry. I acted foolishly and dangerously. I will suffer whatever punishment you wish to levy upon me in silence, but do not banish Salim in our hour of need. It was I who organized the meeting between us, and did not tell him we would be alone. It is I who must be held responsible."

His angry flush was, by now, impossibly dark. "And what was so important you could not discuss it with me... or even Nadira present?"

"Plans I hoped to keep from our enemies, Sultan Al'Azam."

"You will make me ask again," he said, eyes flashing dangerously as he pulled at her wrist.

"No, I—"

He struck her—or so she thought, at first. It was only as she was blinking away tears of pain that she began to understand what had happened. He was lying on the floor between his cushions, arms and legs spasming in what Priscilla termed a grand mal seizure. Her stunned brain working again, she realized his arm had twitched uncontrollably as the seizure began, savagely throwing the arm he'd held by the wrist into her face, striking her nose. She straightened, wishing she could check if the blow he'd struck her would leave a visible mark. After a single touch of her stinging nose, she put both pain and political concerns aside to order the nearest slave to fetch Rodney or Gervais.

Her brother's seizure was already slowing by the time the woman, whose name escaped Jahanara, ran from the garden. While the woman was reliable, it would only require one moment's slip of the tongue to unravel everything. She considered having the slave silenced, but had her hand stayed by the guilt she still carried over the murders she'd ordered in the first hours after Father's death. She consoled herself with the knowledge that news of a falling out between the two of them was unlikely to be believed by their opponents, as long as Dara did not carry out his threat to order Salim into exile.

Hating the need, she sent another slave to fetch Nadira. His wife would not suffer Dara to commit such folly as he'd spoken of before collapsing.

She knelt next to Dara, praying for him, for herself, and, not for the first time, a change in the way that God saw fit to bind the threads of their lives together.

Red Fort, Vine Court

"I can scarce believe it, myself," Roshanara mused, trusting the noise of the water splashing in the fountain where her sister had nearly drowned her to cover the words.

"I am sorry, Shehzadi?" Omid said, jowls bouncing as the eunuch's nervous eyes traveled the rest of the Vine Court in yet another search for listeners.

She said nothing, but gestured for him to continue memorizing the poem she hoped would convey her news to Aurangzeb but conceal it from any who should intercept it.

The sweat pouring from beneath Omid's pale blue turban dripped on the fine paper he held before him, making obvious the eunuch's desperate desire to get away from her as quickly as possible.

Wishing Doctor Gradinego were present to advise her, Roshanara sighed.

The ruse they'd used to communicate had grown too thin a cover for the frequency of their meetings, so Doctor Gradinego had introduced her to Omid just two weeks past. But even if the harem guard were smarter than he looked, Omid was too fearful of discovery to even consider offering an assessment of the information she provided.

Left with nothing save the ferenghi's assurances the eunuch was entirely Nur's creature, and could be relied upon to pass information to him, she'd sought Omid out. Since then, she had made something of a show of making Omid and several of the other senior harem servants join her in a poetry competition, all to furnish reasons for contact with the guard.

Omid shifted his bulk from one foot to another.

"You have it memorized?" she asked, realizing she'd left him to ruminate too long.

"I believe so, Shehzadi."

"Repeat it, then."

The stammer that accompanied the first few lines retreated as Omid fought to recall the hastily composed poem rather than remaining focused on the peril they were in.

When Omid finished Roshanara nodded and gave what she hoped was a reassuring smile. "You have it. Go now to your rest, you have much to do over the next few days."

"Yes, Shehzadi," Omid said, scarcely concealing relief at being allowed to leave.

"Omid, please at least *act* as if you wish to participate, if not win the competition. It will make things easier."

The harem guard glanced up at her, took a deep, steadying breath, and bowed.

She gestured permission to depart and turned back to her qulam and ink.

Omid left without another word, and with a grimace that was supposed to be a smile plastered on beardless cheeks.

Roshanara did not notice, already lost to the present trying to predict what future moves her sibling would make in response to the news.

Red Fort, west of Lahore Gate

"This is some fort, Talawat," John said, slapping the sun-heated stone of the crenellation in front of him with an appreciative hand. He'd had about an afternoon's worth of training on the state of the art in fortress-building back when he was inducted into the USE's TacRail program, and they'd gone on at length about the uselessness of freestanding curtain walls that made up most medieval castles.

The advent of cannon powerful enough to knock down such outmoded defenses had been part of the demise of medieval fortifications, but the far greater factor had been an increase in the *mobility* of cannon of all sizes.

Military architects in Europe and under the Mughals had both adopted the construction of earth-backed walls in response to the power of gunpowder. The Mughals also liked them because such defenses were less prone to undermining or actual explosive mines placed against the base of a curtain wall.

"Sure is," Bertram agreed. "Geneva's fortifications, built to defend that city from the papists over the last two generations, are the only ones I've seen that might be better, and that's only because they create a brutal crossfire by building in a star shape...And those defenses certainly lack the visual appeal of this place."

Talawat nodded but didn't comment. Instead he led the others over to one of the cannon installed to defend Red Fort. Patting the big bronze piece, he dismissed the men working to rebore it.

Knowing Talawat wouldn't speak about whatever he'd brought them here to discuss until they were alone, John looked Talawat over while the men left the parapet and Bertram bent to examine the steel borer the crew had been using on the barrel. To be honest, John was a little worried about the gunsmith. Dark rings around the Atishbaz's dark eyes showed the long hours the man was putting in.

Red Fort had a lot of cannon and a lot of mortars, but very little standardization between pieces, so the accuracy of any one gun couldn't be relied on for training on another cannon. The program to rebore some of the bronze barrels to a standard size went on despite the destruction of the munitions factory. John figured Salim had decided the work should continue as much to shore up morale as to improve the accuracy of the guns themselves.

"How many more do they have to get done?"

Talawat heaved a tired sigh. "A great many, I'm afraid. Dara's enemies have a *lot* of cannon as well as mortars."

"I thought they wouldn't be able to bring them to bear," Bertram said.

A shrug. "The largest weapons in their artillery park, the true siege guns, are incredibly heavy and difficult to transport. As their supply situation is less than generous, it is hoped they will attempt a storm before the big guns can be brought up and laid in to bring down our defenses."

"An attempt to storm us doesn't sound much better than a siege," John said, leaning on the gun.

Talawat nodded. "They have the numbers tradition claims sufficient to overcome the fortress."

"Shit. Three to one?"

"Closer to four to one."

"They have eighty thousand men?"

"More or less. It is assumed they will lose a number of them as they reduce the fortresses to our south, but their eventual arrival is why I asked you to come up here with me."

"What's that?"

"I wished to, as you say, 'pick your skulls' for possible technologies and weapons we could utilize to even the numbers, even slightly."

"Brains," John corrected.

"What?" Talawat asked.

"'Pick your brains' is the proper term." John smiled and, rather than explain further, returned to answering the question: "Can't do mines..."

Talawat perked up. "Mines? How would undermining our def—"

"No," John interrupted him, "not mines in the traditional sense. These are...a small explosive and shrapnel are placed just beneath the ground. When a man or vehicle walks over, they trigger the device, which either kills or maims them."

"A pit trap that explodes..." Talawat said, seeking clarification.

"Kind of. But making the triggers would be another drain on your skilled manpower, so I don't think it's a good idea... Plus, they're a nightmare to clean up afterward."

Talawat shook his head. "Ah. The manpower issue is a greater problem in the short term."

"Command detonated, though..." John mused, thinking about the time they'd had an explosives expert out to blow a landslide from one of the county roads he'd been trying to clear.

"Command detonated? What is this?"

John, knowing he lacked the language to convey his thoughts, looked at Bertram, who translated: "An electrical charge is generated all along a circuit. The charge ignites powder in the charges it comes into contact with, exploding it."

"No triggers?"

"No. Well, kind of. But just one or two. And while the dynamos will need a lot of copper wire, they aren't all that complex. Your people can spin wire faster than anyone else I've seen down-time, and I remember enough from the design TacRail was implementing for blasting to help out."

"How big a charge can we set off?"

John shrugged. "Big as you want, I guess. Biggest problem is they'll be one-shot weapons. Well, that and the farther you are from the dynamo and the more of charges you put on a circuit... Oh, and the longer you wait for lots of men to get into the area of effect, the more likely the wire might get cut or the circuit fail from something going wrong..."

"That's a lot of ands..." Bertram said.

"And if any of those 'ands' happen?" Talawat asked.

"No boom," John said, appreciating the man's razor-sharp focus.

"Hmm... Shrapnel from the ground just becomes so much hard rain. Could we use something lighter?"

"Like what?"

A shrug. "Oil? Perhaps?"

"I guess so, but then you have to make sure it ignites."

Talawat nodded thoughtfully but didn't say anything more for almost a minute.

John, thinking the gunsmith was trying to figure out a way to tell him the idea sucked, said, "Talawat, I don't know. It's probably not worth the time and effort to experiment with it."

Bertram waggled his head. "I don't know, John. Might be a horrible surprise for an enemy, especially if placed at the base of the wall while men were trying to climb."

John shrugged. "What do you think, Talawat?"

"Shit," Talawat opined, in a near-perfect West Virginia accent that startled a laugh from both Bertram and John.

"Don't—" John gasped, but another burst of laughter made him cut off.

"Don't what?" Talawat asked, smiling impishly.

"Please don't say that in front of Ilsa." John shook his head, wiping away tears. "She'll have my head."

Talawat's smile lost none of its brightness. "I will be sure to watch my language, John. In the meantime, do you think you could draw a diagram of this, what did you call it, 'dynamo'?"

"That's it, yes. And if you want me to, sure."

"I do. Even if your exact idea does not work, I may be able to think of other uses for it."

John nodded. "If anyone can, you will. You have to be one of the smartest people I've ever met."

Talawat ducked his head, cheeks above his beard darkening as he looked at his feet. "You do me too much honor."

"No, I do not, Talawat. Your work is outstanding, and if we are going to win, it'll be because of you and your people."

Talawat turned abruptly away. "My thanks, John." Wiping his face, the gunsmith said over his shoulder, "I will go now. Please send the diagram on when you can."

John looked at Bertram, who shrugged and turned to lean on the crenellations. "Will do, Talawat. Hope I helped."

"More than you know, John, more than you know," Talawat called.

John stood up and joined Bertram at the parapet. He leaned elbows on the hot stone and looked out over the plain to the south.

"Think we can win, Bertram?" he asked, watching a patrol ride south.

"I do, John," Bertram said without taking his eyes off the horizon. "Why do you ask?"

"I guess I can't help but think we're in way over our heads."

"Might be. But we have the tiger by the tail now, so there's not much to do but hang on."

"True enough." John turned around and folded his arms across his chest. He watched Talawat walk from the shadow of the ramp that accessed the upper defenses. "Sure am glad that guy's on our side."

"Talawat?" Bertram asked.

"Yep."

"You were right to compliment him," Bertram said.

"Just telling the truth..."

"But it's nice to hear someone say, anyway."

John cocked his head. "Doesn't seem too comfortable with compliments."

"Perhaps not." Bertram sniffed. "But comfort is one thing, appreciation another. He's being worked rather hard."

"Too hard, you think?"

"Oh, I doubt it!" Bertram chuckled. "I'll wager he's the happiest he's ever been."

"Happiest?"

"Look, back before the Ring of Fire, when I was at university, I had befriended an incredibly intelligent and accomplished fellow. The rest of the students, my other friends, we all knew he was destined for great things. He wasn't wealthy, though, and needed a patron. Thing was, he hated the nobility and most other wealthy people generally struck him as grasping and lacking in vision. For these and other reasons, he was unable to find a patron. As a result, his ideas languished or failed for lack of money to fund his experiments."

"Oh?" John asked, unsure where Bertram was going with this.

"The last thing he said to me was that he wished he'd found a king or duke or even a merchant to serve, so that he could use the wealth and access such a patron provided to follow through on the promise of his many ideas. To apply the full measure of one's mind, experience, and skill upon problem after problem. To see the material results of one's vision prosper, be given physical form?" The young down-timer shook his head. "Surely that is a reward unlike and greater than any other for a man with his gifts."

"I'm sure all the cash Dara is throwing his way doesn't hurt."

Bertram laughed aloud. "There is that, my friend. He does pay well."

"Sure does. You see the robe Talawat was wearing? All those gemstones?"

Bertram nodded, still chuckling, and added, "And the stone stuck in his turban would choke a horse."

Hell, my own wardrobe is starting to look a lot more Liberace than The Man in Black.

The pair of men, far from home but still with loved ones near at hand, laughed long and hard.

Part Six

July, 1636

Joys of the sense, delights of eye and ear
—The Rig Veda

Chapter 28

Asirgarh
Red Tent

"It is done, then?" Aurangzeb asked. He had only just come from morning prayers and, as ever, was feeling refreshed, reinvigorated, and ready for the day. He had decided, on Nur's sound advice, to make a habit of granting private audiences—on short notice—to his diwans and others whose characters he wished to directly assess. And with the need to placate and fully seduce his brother's supporters to his cause, Aurangzeb thought carving out the time necessary to do so was time very well spent.

"It is, Sultan Al'Azam," Ghulam Khan answered.

"That was quick work." That the tall, darkly handsome and freshly appointed diwan of the Imperial Mint did not have an actual physical mint to direct did not signify. All things happened at the place and time mandated by God, and God *would* provide. In the meantime, Aurangzeb had promoted Ghulam, one of Shuja's many erstwhile supporters, to the post. The move had been

359

carefully considered, as Ghulam was well connected with other umara, but not so well connected he must be given a field command. Thus, he'd been raised to the nearly empty office yet given the prestigious task of creating the silver rupees that would mark the regnal year of Alamgir Aurangzeb according to his specifications.

Aurangzeb seated himself and waved permission for Ghulam to do the same.

"Your *kharkhanas* had several worthy silver smiths and engravers ready and eager to practice their craft on your behalf, Sultan Al'Azam," Ghulam Khan said as he sat at the proper distance and artfully arranged the gem-encrusted robes Aurangzeb had awarded him upon promotion to the post. That done, he removed a slim sandalwood box from one sleeve.

"They were able to read my calligraphy, then?" Aurangzeb asked, gesturing his body slave to retrieve the box.

"Of course they were, Sultan Al'Azam. Your skill with the qulam was recognized by all the court." Ghulam smiled at Aurangzeb as the slave returned to his master with the small box held before him.

Do not think I fail to see how that smile does not reach your eyes. Upstart. Fakir.

The experienced courtier must have read something in the emperor's eyes, because he quickly bowed his head low. "I have said something to displease you, Sultan Al'Azam?"

"It is nothing," Aurangzeb dissembled. "Only that I must be cautious of letting such flattery incite unseemly pride." His slave knelt to one side and slid the small box open in front of his master, revealing its contents. Aurangzeb ignored it, staring at Ghulam Khan.

"I beg forgiveness, Sultan Al'Azam. I merely intended to make you aware of the esteem not only I, but many other members of your court, hold you in. Not just for your piety, which everyone recognizes as a fine example, but for the small things..."

"The small things?" Aurangzeb asked.

"Indeed, Sultan Al'Azam," Ghulam said, bowing again. He waited, head bowed.

Aurangzeb could not decide if the humble pose was genuine, decided it did not matter. "Say on," he commanded.

"My father, before fleeing that country under the present sultan, was one of the many courtiers who served the court of Shah Abbas, Sultan of Persia. There, he claimed to learn that one could judge a sultan's character far better from the small works they produced than the great ones."

"How so?" Aurangzeb was intrigued. He had not planned on giving much more of his valuable time to this interview, but found his interest snared by the man's smooth manners and articulate speech, even in the face of displeasure from his emperor.

"The small works, the ones from a ruler's own hands, from his own pen, those are examples of what matters to the man seated on the throne, while the large works, the ones visible to all, and commanded into being by them, tend to represent the concerns of the monarchy, not the man. So, when I see the fine calligraphy laid down by your pen"—he gestured at the open box between them—"and the thoughtful selection of the sura you choose to place upon your regnal coins, I believe I see something of the man the Sultan Al'Azam is."

"And if a ruler should avoid creating things by his own hand?"

A smile. "Then he may avoid such assessment... and possibly, any feeling of fulfillment in life."

"And what does my calligraphy show you is in me, then?"

"A man of many parts."

Aurangzeb sniffed. "Hardly an answer."

"Forgive me, Sultan Al'Azam. The tongue is slow to articulate the thoughts of the mind."

Aurangzeb, disinclined to play the man's game any longer, said, "Then perhaps you should simply say what is on your mind."

"As you command, Sultan Al'Azam, so shall it be. I believe you to be quiet, alert, serene, and thoughtful as you prepare... something like a lion waiting for the proper moment to strike, or perhaps a falcon on the verge of stooping..."

"And what did you compare my brother to when you served him?" Aurangzeb said, staring at him with the blank expression he'd cultivated.

"Shah Shuja has ever been inclined to indolent pleasure. You do not give in to such pleasures of the flesh..." The man's mask of affable calm slipped and his voice trailed away as Aurangzeb continued to stare.

After a long, uncomfortable moment, Ghulam cleared his throat. "It seems I cannot please. What I intended to say was that I was never in a position to observe any of Shuja's accomplishments."

"Accomplishments, you say?" Aurangzeb said, feeling a smile threaten to break his firm demeanor. "I think that might be the very first time anyone has mentioned my brother and accomplishments in one breath."

Ghulam, fighting to keep a smile off his face, said, "And there is the first reason I serve you and not him today."

"God willed it," Aurangzeb said, retrieving the coin and rolling it across his knuckles to examine both sides.

"God willed it," Ghulam Khan confirmed.

"This is excellent work. Convey my congratulations and contentment to the craftsmen."

"I shall, Sultan Al'Azam. Thank you."

Feeling he had the man's measure, Aurangzeb dismissed his newest diwan.

He sat a moment, brow furrowed in concentration, as the umara departed. Shuja was much on his mind. A prickly problem that would not, could not, be resolved comfortably.

I can't exile him. He would only return and drain my strength as the first group of umara disaffected with my decisions would rally around him, not to mention what the Safavids might do with a pet pretender to the throne in their hands...

Yet, there has to be a solution that does not include fratricide, even at the hands of those not specifically ordered to it, as Father's umara presumed to when Father ordered his cousins imprisoned. Besides, I am not in a position to leave him in some fort where my own best supporters might repeat history and ki—

The firing of one of Carvalho's guns interrupted his thoughts. Not in anger, but signaling the dawn, as one of his first commands as emperor had been a cease-fire and an invitation to talks with the garrison commander, Lahore Raja. The man was a Rajput, and considered prickly in his honor. He was older than any of the imperial family, but not by much, yet had obtained a fine martial reputation for good service with Father's forces from Bengal and the Afghan territories. The Rajputs wouldn't have been in the fort, but for Shuja's insistence on reducing Burhanpur when he could have negotiated a settlement and moved on, pressing the timetable...

But he is in the fort. A loyal, proven general. One of the few Dara has at his disposal.

Aurangzeb paused. Felt his way around the edges of an idea, gently nudging it rather than trying to seize it and lose it all.

Oh.

Of course.

Shuja cannot die in my *custody. Not at the hands of* my *supporters.*

Aurangzeb considered the idea, bringing all his mental resources to bear. And still could not find a flaw.

God inspires.

He praised God and called for Nur.

There was much to organize, and time was in short supply.

"The boy wants *what*?" Amar Singh Rathore said, twisting one end of his majestic Rajput mustaches into an even tighter curl.

"The *emperor* Aurangzeb only wants to be your friend, Amar Singh Rathore," Nur corrected, her enjoyment of the moment unsullied by Rathore's weak attempt to belittle Aurangzeb by calling him a boy. Amar Singh's mother had been a member of Jahangir's court when the prideful Rajput princeling had been but a spoiled and somewhat sickly child, so she knew better than to engage him further on a point they both knew to be of very little import. No, she was enjoying herself too much.

That negotiating on behalf of kinsmen was a traditional role for senior Mughal women made little difference. The exercise of *real* power was the only thing that mattered, the only intoxicant that enticed her. These moments were as the pipe was to the opium addict: a tool to reach the place where the gods dwelt.

"He wants to be my friend, you say?" he asked.

"He does, and I do," Nur replied, waving off a slave presenting her with a tray laden with food. Her host had already offered refreshment and been refused, but the repeated offerings were Rathore's attempt to gracefully indicate the fortress was in possession of all the stores necessary to last any but the longest siege.

According to Aurangzeb's reports, he was also overstating the garrison's supply situation, but such was expected of a besieged commander.

She was less sanguine about the finger he waggled at her. "Does he think me so without honor that I would abandon my sacred duty simply for the mere promise of coin? Because it is just that, a mere promise. He has no mint, barely a treasury to supply cash payments, and no access to the proper imperial bureaucracy in order to administer and distribute the jagirs he claims to possess. Even the experienced men of his personal staff have less than a decade in service."

"All true. You are most perceptive, Amar Singh." She kept a straight face as she delivered the words. She was here to broker a solution, not pour oil on a fire, and flattering a man's wisdom could be almost as effective as flattering his manliness.

He sat back, trying to cover a suspicious glance with another drink.

Nur smiled. He was fairly astute, but young. She would best him as she had so many others.

"Your suspicious glances lead me to believe you think I but flatter you. I do not. Nor do I dissemble or seek to inflate your sense of self-worth. Everything you have said about the current state of the emperor's court is true..." She let the statement trail off. Best to let the prey think it freely ran its own path than know the huntress lay waiting.

"What, then?" he asked, expressionless once again.

She waggled her head, made a face as if eating bitter melon. "As if Rajput honor could be purchased with coin!"

His smile was sly. "So he would give me title to more *zamin*?"

"No." She pointed to Heaven with one hennaed hand, gold bracelets clinking. "For what is receiving land but coin in a different purse, and therefore beneath men of honor?"

Amar's first genuine expression of the day was a smile that made his mustaches quiver at their waxed tips.

"No, Sultan Al'Azam Aurangzeb bears too much respect for you and your followers to ask you to betray his brother."

"What, then, is the purpose of your visit, if not to entice me to abandon honor?"

She found his betel-stained smile less than fetching, but returned it nonetheless. "We return, then, to the friendship and love of the Sultan Al'Azam, Aurangzeb."

"An emperor whose friendship and love will prove expensive to Rajput honor."

She pretended ignorance. "In what way?"

He sighed, set his goblet down. "He must ask that I abandon honor if I am to surrender this *garh* to him, whatever he told you to tell me."

"And if I told you that Aurangzeb knows the predicament honor and duty place you in?"

"I would not be surprised. He may be young, but I remember no talk at court of him ever playing the fool."

"No, never that."

"Well, then?"

"He has come upon a solution that preserves honor and does him great service."

"I will not abandon—"

Nur waved him down, not wishing to allow him to verbalize—and therefore reinforce—the position he had already claimed to hold. "Such will not be required. No, Aurangzeb has something different in mind, something rather... brilliant."

"Brilliant, you say?"

"Indeed. It has to do with prisoners—"

"I have taken no prisoners from his army," he interrupted, picking up his drink with an air of disappointment. "So I have none to exchange."

Nur smiled again, knowing she—and Aurangzeb—had him. "The Sultan Al'Azam does not have an exchange in mind."

"Oh?" he asked, no longer trying to hide his thoughts, which were obviously bewildered.

"What if I were to tell you that all Aurangzeb wishes of you is that you follow Dara's orders and hold this fort for him?"

"For him? Aurangzeb?"

"No, Dara."

"But that—makes no sense..."

She could see his confusion, and it warmed her heart.

"God willing, there will come a time when you will serve Aurangzeb, but for now, he requires only that you continue in your duty to Dara. And one thing more."

His smile grew wry, dark eyes glittering with humor. "And here is the moment where you ask for the first small transgression. The one that hardly counts, being so small," he said, delivering the words as though he were a would-be lover asking a reluctant bedmate for some special, forbidden act to show her love.

She hid her pleasure at winning against such a game opponent and sat up straight, as if offended at the very notion. "Nothing of the sort, I assure you. Indeed, Aurangzeb believes that, should you agree to this thing, your duty to Dara will *require* your continuance in your duties at the fortress here."

He shook his head, confusion on open display. "I confess, I do not understand what it is he desires, and cannot see any way a warrior can serve two masters honorably."

"Not two. Just one. Dara has commanded you here in order to garrison the *garh* and hold it against all enemies, no?"

"Of course."

"And if some of Dara's enemies should fall into your hands, what would Dara's orders require of you?"

"That I keep them until such time as he decides their fate."

Trench lines outside Asirgarh

"He denies us audience?"

"Only for the time being," Carvalho said, and not for the first time this morning. Methwold suspected the Portuguese gun captain's patience grew less from any practiced virtue than the distraction provided by the goings-on at the foot of the fort. If so, the Englishman did not think poorly of him for it. It was hard to ignore the pomp and ceremony of the ritual going on in the no-man's-land between the fortress and the entrenchments it had cost so much time, treasure, and blood to build.

De Jesus was scowling. "How long must we endure this?"

"As long as necessary," Methwold snapped. He regretted speaking so harshly the moment the words escaped him, but the papist's constant petulance set his teeth on edge. "We are closer now than ever before to getting what was promised."

Carvalho turned his gelding's head toward camp and without another word, rode off.

"What has him so surly?" De Jesus asked.

Oh, I don't know, perhaps your constant whinging?

"It seems the fortress, so long his nemesis, has fallen, and not under the weight of fire from his guns culminating in a storm, but to a simple overture from Aurangzeb."

"Oh?"

"With respect, my young friend: if you complained less, you might hear more," Methwold said, striving to keep his tone light yet convey some urgency.

The priest opened his mouth to answer only to clamp it shut with a wet clomp. From the deepening color of his cheeks, Methwold surmised the priest was struggling to contain a bitter retort.

He turned away, ceding the priest a moment to master his anger and hoping—against all previous experience—the man would learn something from the experience this time. The imperial panoply on display provided excellent distraction: elephants, banners, streamers, drums, all of it made for a most impressive show. He squinted, but the scene was too crowded to determine who was at Aurangzeb's side as he greeted the garrison commander, a Rajput named Lahore Rathore.

Perhaps it was Nur Jahan with the fresh-made emperor. It was rumored she'd been instrumental in the negotiations. He looked for the great beast with the ornately decorated howdah Nur used perched on its broad back. Sure enough, the enormous bull elephant Aurangzeb had gifted her upon her escape from Agra was partially blocking their view of the proceedings.

On second thought... He squinted bad eyes, and when that proved insufficient, shaded them from the unrelenting sun with one hand. The lady's howdah had the heaviest of its curtains drawn back to reveal a vaguely feminine silhouette seated within, leading his thoughts to linger on her...

It was rumored Nur was as beautiful as she was clever, having survived the turmoil in the wake of the deaths of two—no, *three*—emperors now. Certainly her voice and manner had been cultivated and graceful, leading his thoughts astray when Carvalho had secured audiences with her. Then there had been her eyes.

The delicate scent of her. And her shape, even under the layers of silk decorum demanded even of elders and widows. Most intriguing.

"Do you think Shuja dead, then?" De Jesus asked, the quiet question jolting Methwold from pleasant daydreams of lovely women of experience in perfumed gardens exhibiting a healthy interest in *him*.

The bloody papist probably never thinks of women as anything but the whores, mothers, and saints contained in scripture.

"No, though he might as well be, as his every breath is at his brother's whim now," he said aloud. He shrugged. "Still, it does seem a great risk, keeping him alive."

"The infidels keep some honor," De Jesus allowed.

"Indeed," Methwold said.

"Do you know how this was accomplished?" the priest asked, his wave taking in the fort and the gathering going on before it.

"Not the particulars of the deal, no. I do know that as soon as he seized power, Aurangzeb ordered a cease-fire and began negotiations."

"Was one of their holy men sent to handle the negotiations?"

"No." He considered stopping there, but decided the priest might learn something if he told all. "I am told it was Nur Jahan. I gather she is some relation or other to the commander of the fort. An aunt or some such."

"They do seem to place great store in family ties. And even these barbarians recognize that women are to be protected... Now, just who is that?" the priest asked, standing in the stirrups and shading his eyes.

"Who?" Methwold asked, unable to make out any details. De Jesus' eyes were much better than Methwold's, especially at a distance.

"Someone is being handed over to the garrison commander, but I didn't think we had any prisoners to exchange, did you?"

"No . . . What does he look like?"

"Richly dressed. Young. Perhaps twenty? Looks a lot like Aurang—Christ preserve us!" the priest cried out in astonishment.

"What!?" Methwold said, unable to bring the distant details into focus.

"They are handing Shuja over to the garrison commander," De Jesus said.

Methwold could see for himself that a small group had detached from the main body and was walking toward the gate of the fortress. "Loyal men following the deposed emperor into his ex—no, not exile, but prison?"

"Not warriors, surely," De Jesus said.

"Not likely, but certainly his body slaves and those servants judged too little a threat and too loyal to be trusted anywhere else."

"But, to hand over a very real threat to your rule over to a man who, until just hours ago, was your enemy? It exceeds imagination!"

"The Holy Bible urges good Christians to turn the other cheek, does it not?" Methwold said, unable to resist taking a poke at the priest's pious maunderings.

Realizing he might have undone any good work training the man to patience, Methwold tried not to laugh at the look De Jesus cast his way. A lifetime's experience of trade negotiations stood him in good stead, allowing him to keep some semblance of serenity plastered on his face.

"As an infidel, he is doomed already. That he asks the lion to lie down with lambs under the false banner of his religion only makes it more certain he will end in the flames of hell..."

How did this man ever survive among the heathens? Because, if ever there existed a man unable to see the forest for the trees, it's Father Cristovao De Jesus.

Chapter 29

Agra
Diwan-i-Khas

Salim released a slow, silent breath as the last of the petitioners filed from the hall of public audience. The day had been challenging, with rumors that Shuja's army had declared for Aurangzeb confirmed while the Sultan Al'Azam had more than an hour of overseeing the daily durbar to get through.

The court had early warning of the news, of course, but only by an evening. Aurangzeb's army was a mere two weeks' travel away, and that at a comfortable pace. Salim did not begrudge the rumormongers or the news writers who had sold the information in the meantime. Such information was of great value, and there were many willing to pay a premium for it. But, to make matters worse, while Dara sat the Peacock Throne before the wide court, additional reports arrived concerning the pretenders. Those reports, announced before the full court, indicated Aurangzeb had taken possession of his brother's army, suspended active siege operations of Asirgarh, and then sent Nur Jahan to begin negotiations with Rathore Singh.

That the messenger bearing that information had brought the news before all the court rather than wait for the end of the public audience had been either a boldly calculated move purchased by Aurangzeb's supporters in Agra or the stupidity of an imperial messenger wagering that his post rendered his person inviolate even against an emperor's wrath.

Salim tried not to sigh again. He'd been half tempted to send Iqtadar or another of his cousins to catch the messenger and beat some sense into him.

From the icy anger in Jahanara's voice the few times she'd contributed to the proceedings, she might have already ordered something to that effect.

And Dara had not taken the news at all well, mumbling through the final proclamations in a rush to get away from the scrutiny of both needy petitioners and tense public. He'd barely allowed the master of protocol to announce the end of the durbar before departing the throne for the harem precincts.

Taking full advantage of a moment of semi-solitude himself, Salim leaned back and closed his eyes, silently reciting a swift prayer to God that all would be well with Dara. As he prayed, one of Dara's champion elephants trumpeted from the ground between the river and the fortress. Jahanara had scheduled elephant combats for Dara's enjoyment this afternoon. Indeed, Salim imagined the balcony overlooking the fighting ground was where Dara's inner circle would be found. Knowing he'd delayed for too long already, Salim repeated a final prayer and opened his eyes.

He found the harem diwan, Firoz Khan, approaching

on slippered feet. The eunuch's robe was fine, alternating patterns of light and darker blues creating a pleasing contrast to the sash that bound the robe across the eunuch's ample belly. Embroidered with row upon row of freshwater pearls and tiny gold coins, the sash fairly shouted "expensive" if not "good taste." On second consideration, Salim was probably not as well qualified to make fashion choices as the eunuch.

Salim smiled encouragement at Firoz. Appointed just a short time before Salim had arrived at court, the portly umara was a perpetual favorite not only of Jahanara and Nadira, but also of Dara. The potbellied diwan had managed to impress Salim with constant good humor and a strong work ethic, qualities which were often in short supply in the harem. The eunuch was also among the most intelligent people Salim had ever met, let alone had the pleasure of working alongside.

The two servants of the emperor greeted each other warmly and with what Salim hoped was a mutual respect.

"Forgive the intrusion, Wazir, but the Sultan Al'Azam requires your presence in the harem," Firoz Khan said.

"Very good," Salim answered, rising to his feet and gesturing for Firoz to accompany him. Something in the eunuch's round, sweat-dampened face caused his instinct for trouble to itch.

"What is it, Firoz?" he asked in a quiet voice as they set out.

"He is most wroth."

"And well he might be! To have today's news so public was annoying, to say the least."

"It is not simply that..."

"Then what troubles you, Firoz?"

"I am uncertain..." Again the diwan let his statement end unfinished.

"Be assured that anything you choose to tell me will be held in strictest confidence," Salim said, projecting as much reassurance as he could.

"His relations with Begum Sahib have been strained of late. He has been in a *mood*..." Firoz lapsed into silence as they entered one of the heavily guarded checkpoints securing the harem from the outside world.

"What mood is it, friend?" Salim prompted as they left the immediate vicinity of the guards and started across the garden courtyard.

Firoz did not immediately reply, waiting until they were near enough the burbling waters of a fountain to cover his reply from casual listeners. "It seems this... mood... has affected his relations with Nadira Begum as well. To the point the royal apartments have not been loud with cries of pleasure in some days."

Salim glanced away, uncomfortable with that particular bit of knowledge. His gaze fell on a group of veiled women of the harem some distance away. One woman, possibly Roshanara Begum, was supervising a game or lesson of some sort.

"I understand, friend diwan," he murmured, looking back at Firoz. "Is there anything I might do in order to help you rectify the situation?"

The elephant bugled once again, this time answered by the bull challenger brought to the field.

The diwan's wide brow creased in worry. "That is just it, dear Salim: I had hoped you might be able to advise *me*. I am at my wit's end, and the doctors have enough to do without my asking stupid questions about the moods of the Sultan Al'Azam."

Salim considered that a moment, then shook his head. "I don't think they will think your questions stupid. Like ours, the up-timer medical practitioners seem to take an interest in all aspects of the body and how it might affect the mood."

"They do?" Firoz looked skeptical.

"Well, they are not concerned with the spirit, at least as we define it, but they are concerned with the mind and how it might affect recovery, even in the case of injuries not involving the brain. So it stands to reason..."

"Good. I will consult with them." The worry-knot between Firoz's brows eased. He waved Salim to proceed him across the threshold into the royal apartments.

"Happy to be of even so small a service, my friend."

Firoz smiled. "I regret that I cannot reciprocate with help timely enough to save you from the Sultan Al'Azam's *current* mood, however."

"Your warning is all a man could ask, Firoz."

"Still, if I could stand between you and his anger, I would gladly do so. Even though he would make even my steely heart flutter with trepidation."

"Such a warrior," Salim said with a smile.

"Indeed I am," Firoz said, pausing to take a warrior's stance that looked slightly absurd from the soft little palace eunuch. "I will shield you, if I can."

"And if you are overmastered, then I shall be a warrior myself, and weather his anger with whatever might I can muster."

"Surely my stout defense will render any such attempts superfluous."

Salim grinned. Reflecting that the bantering friendship they'd enjoyed almost from their very first meeting must have seemed unlikely to any outside observer.

A battle-hardened adventurer and a slippered palace servant enjoying each other's company? Pah!

He was still smiling when Firoz led them through the royal apartments and out onto the balcony overlooking the fighting grounds.

Harem precincts

"What are you smiling about, Salim?" Dara asked as Salim and Firoz approached the slightly raised dais the emperor sat upon to watch the fights.

"Sultan Al'Azam?" Salim asked, stopped in his tracks by the emperor's tone. He glanced about, relieved there were only four slaves in earshot of the conversation, though all of them were visibly tense.

Dara's expression was stone. "You smiled. I ask what it is you are smiling about."

Salim bowed, deeply. "Sultan Al'Azam, I smile because I am happy in your service."

"You are, are you?"

"Indeed I am, Sultan Al'Azam."

"Sultan Al'Az—" Firoz began, attempting to deflect the emperor's wrath.

"When I want you to speak, eunuch, I will command it," Dara said, glaring at Firoz.

Firoz prostrated himself. "Forgive me, Sultan Al'Azam," he mumbled.

Dara ignored Firoz to focus his anger on Salim. "So, what is it about serving me that pleases *you*?"

Reeling a bit from the sudden vehemence of Dara's

attack, Salim struggled to find words that would not make him sound like a sycophant. "I have found many challenges in your service, Sultan Al'Azam."

"Such as dishonoring my sister? Mocking my hospitality?" the emperor barked.

"Your s—" Salim began.

"Yes, my sister: Begum Sahib. No doubt you found it a grand challenge to sully her with your touch. First to suborn my servants then to inveigle me into pliant placidity."

The war elephant chose that moment to trumpet once again, making everyone but Dara flinch. Salim could only shake his head, stunned at the scope of these baseless accusations. Had he not known better, he would have thought someone had been whispering vile rumor into the emperor's ear.

"Say this, at least, of Salim Gadh Yilmaz's honor: he made no effort to lie to me when confronted with his shameful impropriety."

"Lie? Suborn? Impropriety?" Salim asked, anger cutting through his surprise and making each word louder and sharper than the last. "I have not lied. I have not touched your sister. I am your faithful and obedient servant. I would not disrespect you nor your sister!"

Dara scoffed. "I know you met. I know you desire her."

Unable to answer that without betraying his feelings for Jahanara Begum and condemning himself, Salim took a deep steadying breath and said slowly, "Sultan Al'Azam, I am not your enemy."

"Then what are—" Dara's angry retort was cut short by a groan. He surged erect, walking toward the edge of the dais. Salim's gaze caught Dara's contorted expression. No longer angry, it was bewildered, eyelids closing unevenly. Then, the emperor's entire body convulsed. Moaning, he toppled forward, falling atop one of his body slaves with a heavy thud that frightened Salim more than the unreasoning anger of a moment before.

While Salim struggled, first to comprehend what had happened, then to thank God Dara had not fallen over the balcony, Firoz leapt into action. He pulled the emperor from the tangle of slave and silks.

Salim broke free of his stupor and barked at a slave, "Find Gervais or the up-timer physicians!"

Firoz eased Dara onto a set of cushions and commanded some order out of the trembling slaves.

Bertram and Gervais arrived quickly, Rodney a few minutes later.

As they took over Dara's care, Salim sought solace in the teachings of Mian Mir. Slowly, and with great difficulty, he asserted control over both the rate at which his breath filled his lungs and his unruly thoughts, and was rewarded by the feeling of his scarred hands uncurling from the killing fists they had balled into during his confrontation with the emperor.

It was only later, when the emperor was being treated for his collapse, that Salim realized that even if the slaves present did not reveal everything they had seen, his shout had been loud enough to be heard throughout the harem.

Jahanara appeared, dressed and veiled in accordance with propriety, despite the heat and urgency of the situation. Salim tried not to think at all. Tried not to remember the emperor's snarl as he made his allegations. Allegations that were true only in Salim's heart.

Do I want her?

Of course.

Would I have sacrificed honor and position for her?
Quite possibly.
And yet, despite these desires, I have not.
Not yet, at any rate.
Yet Dara is ready to punish me for acts I have not committed.
Something must be done.
Soon.

Red Fort
Jasmine Tower

"Amir Gadh Yilmaz, there is much we must discuss. Please, be seated," Jahanara said, gesturing at the cushions across from her.

"This is most unwise, Begum Sahib. We should not be meeting like this again," Salim said, declining to sit.

"You sound like Atisheh," Jahanara said, repeating her wave for him to be seated.

"Then Atisheh gives sound, correct, and timely advice," Salim said, avoiding her gaze and still refusing to sit. Not that she minded overmuch. She liked looking up at him. He was wearing a fine saffron-colored robe of silk with a turban of slightly darker hue pinned with a large silver brooch studded with small diamonds and a central emerald that complimented his eyes. Beyond his dress, there was something about his confidence that filled a room without being overbearing, and his every movement spoke of a lifetime of training at weapons-work and horsemanship.

Deciding not to press further, and genuinely glad to focus on something other than what his body might feel like under that silken robe, Jahanara spoke as if he had not contradicted her: "I wanted to discuss today's events and how we might retrieve something of value from the situation."

Salim looked down, bearded cheeks darkening.

Assuming he was still feeling the embarrassment brought on by Dara's outburst, Jahanara pretended not to notice. "I received intelligence that I think we must act upon, and that works with our current circumstances."

"Something that will save me from your brother's wrath?" he muttered.

Jahanara gently cleared her throat to make him look at her. "The information alone is not so valuable as that. It is what we will do with it that will, God willing, serve to assuage Dara's anger and confound Aurangzeb as well."

She had Salim's full attention now, making her suddenly, unaccountably anxious, proof of which was finding one hand toying nervously with one of the tassels of the cushion she knelt on. An effort of will stilled it. However fiercely his gaze made her heart hammer, she wanted his eyes on her. For what she wanted to see in them. For what she wanted to tell him without words.

Would he risk everything for so little guarantee of reward?

And really, she feared his answer would not be what she wanted to hear. Or, worse yet, Salim could only tell her what he thought she wanted to hear.

She took a deep breath and said, "Dara wishes to exile you . . ."

Salim muttered something inaudible, something she thought was English.

"What's that? I don't understand that particular English idiom."

He shook his head. "Only that is the very least I expect him to do, Begum Sahib," he said, though she'd had the distinct feeling there was one of John Ennis' favorite words in there.

She decided it wouldn't serve to get distracted, and went on without pressing the matter. "Rest assured, Nadira and I would not normally allow him to make such a rash move, but we will not pressure him to do the right thing in light of the intelligence just received from Aurangzeb's camp."

Salim was silent, handsome features thoughtful instead of fearful. "What news is it that will stay your hand and see me exiled, then?" He somehow managed to ask the question lightly, without rancor.

Quelling the desire to tell him how much she admired him, she explained, "We have confirmed the rumors that the Portuguese are supporting Aurangzeb with supplies and food brought through the passes of the Western Ghats from the interior of Goa. Only with great effort and expense, I might add."

"And they've been successful, otherwise Aurangzeb's army would have ceased to exist."

"You are correct. What is important—and not so well known—is that my brother the pretender has been slow to reward them for their service and his Portuguese and English allies are represented by an angry Christian priest and the Englishman, President Methwold."

"Methwold is a skilled diplomat. I would not underestimate him."

"I do not think we do, but from all reports he's representing the junior partner in the enterprise."

Salim waggled his head. "Understandable. Given Shah Jahan's revocation of the English Company's firman, they could hardly be expected to offer support to equal the Portuguese."

"True, though I believe they are trying to make up the lack using goods and treasure taken in acts of piracy against the Hajj pilgrims traveling to Mecca."

"God forbid," Salim said.

"God forbid," Jahanara agreed.

"Still, I am sorry, Begum Sahib, but I fail to see how these disparate things—my exile and Aurangzeb's support—connect to our advantage?"

"If you are exiled, you will naturally be expected to take your followers with you. News of the departure of Dara's strongest umara with his many sowar will surely be welcome when it reaches Aurangzeb's camp."

Salim gave a slow nod. "But my exile will be a ruse?" he asked, rubbing his beard. "And instead of riding north I will be attacking . . . ?"

". . . Aurangzeb's supply lines between here and Bombay."

"Bombay?" he asked.

"A minor Portuguese port, though the up-timers tell me it became an enormous metropolis and trade center during the British Raj that, God willing, will never come to be."

"God willing," Salim repeated. He fell silent, looking thoughtful, then said, "If we can keep it secret, and not just from the court, but from the scouts he will certainly have covering his advance, it might work. Might work very well indeed. But then he will just forage for what he needs here, will he not?"

"There is little left to gather. We have not been

idle in bringing supplies into the fortress, and this heat makes grazing hard to find."

"True. I need a map..." he mused.

Jahanara pushed her map box toward him and gestured at the cushions once again.

He sat with a rueful smile.

She watched him as he rifled the contents of the box and selected several maps for consideration. Pretending an ease she did not feel, Jahanara busied herself loading the water pipe with fresh tobacco. In truth, she was anything but relaxed. Dara's rage had continued, even after he'd slept. Even Nadira's calm presence had scarcely appeased the emperor. Would that what had made him so angry had no foundation in fact. She could barely admit, even to herself, that everyone, from Smidha to Atisheh to Salim himself, had been correct: she should not have been taking these insane risks to meet Salim alone. And now she had to worry that her efforts to retrieve the situation would merely make things worse.

He was watching her when she looked up.

"What vexes you, Begum Sahib?"

Those eyes. So perceptive.

"Am I so transparent?"

"To the eye, no."

She smiled.

"But your sighs are perhaps more audible than you intend." He gestured at the water pipe. "That, and the pipe you pretend to work upon has been ready to smoke for some time now."

She bowed her head, thankful for her veils as she felt a flush creep up her neck and color her cheeks. "Perhaps you should not make me sigh, then."

"What fresh error of mine upsets you, Begum Sahib?"

She swallowed fear and blundered on. "You are so very handso—"

He came to his feet, interrupting her. "Begum Sahib, forgive my interruption, but what you are about to say will lead to exactly the kind of situation your brother raged against. His imaginings about what we did last time brought on his collapse..."

"If I may finish, Salim?" she asked, more shortly than intended, more gently than he deserved.

"Apologies, Begum Sahib," Salim said, eyes sliding to hers and then leaping away. His glance carried gentle rebuke, and the regard of those grass-green eyes made her heart thump even faster in her chest.

She recovered, said, "First: be seated. I should not have to crane my neck to speak with you."

"If I..." he began.

Jahanara resorted to one of Mother's favorite ploys to gain compliance: she sat entirely erect, squared her shoulders, mustered her most imperious expression, and raised one brow in question.

He bit off his next words, glanced at the place she had indicated and eventually settled among the cushions.

Hiding a smile, Jahanara Begum watched him as he complied with her command. The technique had performed admirably upon her father, recalcitrant princes, and palace servants alike, so she was not surprised he complied. The grace and strength of every movement of his swordsman's body made it difficult to look away.

God help me, but just watching him is enough to fill the chambers of my heart to bursting!

"That's better," Jahanara said past the catch in her throat. "As to what caused me to sigh: the reasons I gave at our first private meeting are even more valid in light of this afternoon's events. Dara's unreasoning rage can be of service."

"Unreasoning?" he said. "I have known men of power who incited their tribes to kill their neighbors for less insult to their honor than your brother's suspicions."

"Suspicions aside, you are his faithful servant, your only transgression to meet with me upon my command."

He grimaced. "Yet that meeting is all the grounds the Sultan Al'Azam needs. Indeed, none would call him tyrant if he were to have me executed, not merely exiled."

"Dara Shikoh would not dare punish you for acts you have not considered, let alone committed," she exaggerated. In truth, her brother had grown erratic enough she could no longer tell with absolute certainty what he might dare. Indeed, if he were to learn of *this* meeting, he might very well order them *both* executed.

"Considered?" Salim said, his tone bringing her back from dark thoughts. "Would that I was so pure in thought that I could truthfully say I never considered what"—he swallowed, taking his lovely green gaze from her face again, and continued—"your brother believes already accomplished fact."

She blinked, the admission catching her off guard. So much so that she had to shake her head to clear away the implications.

"My . . . I . . ." She let the words trail to a stop, unable to find those that would serve to convey the depth of her feeling.

"I know I am not wort—" he began, misinterpreting her mumbles and the shake of her head for a denial of his feelings for her.

"No!" she said, interrupting him with one hennaed hand atop his larger, scarred one, willing him to look at her and *believe*. "Salim, no! I . . . I have—wanted—thought . . ." She could not finish the statement, despite all her experience of court, of exchanges of witticism and poetry. She could no more tell him her heart than conquer him in a contest of swordplay.

He smiled down at their joined hands, turning his own palm up to lace his fingers with hers.

She sighed, reveling in the strength and warmth of his hand, the rough ridges of a fighting man's callouses. She let one finger trace the thin ridge of a scar that ran across his first two fingers, knowing the injury had been earned in the battle at Mother's tomb.

He opened his mouth, on the verge of saying something, but then stopped.

"What is it you wish to say?" she asked, voice suddenly as husky as if she'd smoked for hours.

He shook his head. "Nothing."

"Oh?" she asked, unable to keep the disbelief from her voice.

"No, I . . . mean it, I wish we could remain this way forever. That nothing would change. That nothing would have to be said."

Jahanara felt tears well.

"Oh, no . . . I didn't mean . . . I have never claimed a courtier's tongue, but rarely have I proved so incapable of finding the words to serve my heart, even when the purpose is to avoid hurting you."

"No, I do not cry because I am hurt—or rather because it is so bittersweet—I cry because you say exactly what is written on my heart."

"I do?" he asked gently, running a thumb across the back of her hand.

"You do, Salim. I, too, wish this moment could

last." She sighed, knowing that, however much power she might exert from the harem, no one could stop the natural advance of time. There was only this moment and the next, on and on until God received her soul—or didn't.

Seeking solace from thoughts of the future and the state of her soul, she lifted his hand under her veil and kissed his knuckles.

His hand trembled, or perhaps hers did. She could not tell.

Their eyes met. She knew she shivered this time, the sensation running along her spine to her every extremity like the long grass bending in the wind that presages the storm.

Jahanara Begum, Princess of Princesses, reached up and pulled her veil away. Lips yearning to meet his, she pulled herself to him by their clasped hands.

"We cannot—" he began, hunger in his eyes vying with the desperate control evident in his voice.

She buried his protest under the press of hungry lips, glorying in the feel of his beard, his lips, the taste and smell of him. The ache she had sometimes felt when thinking of or looking at him exploded, a wildfire that consumed all thought and robbed her lungs of breath.

Chapter 30

Asaf Khan's camp west of Patna

"What the hell is going on?" Bobby asked as another troop of sowar marched out of Asaf Khan's tent and down the hill.

"I ain't got any more information than you, Bobby," Ricky said, wishing the rainclouds building to the south would arrive and relieve some of the heat.

Bobby turned to look at their host. "What about you, Jadu?"

Jadu waggled his head. "We're supposed to be presented to Asaf Khan, that is what I know. I admit that this fresh activity is worrisome. I had thought Shaista Khan had settled matters, but perhaps something has occurred to change how things stand."

"You seem awfully relaxed, Jadu."

"I believe I mentioned dharma before," the older man answered, smiling. Ricky noticed a bit of sweat just trickling from beneath the merchant's finest turban, however.

"What is it, Jadu?"

"What? Oh, nothing."

"You sure?"

"I am," Jadu said absently, waving the up-timers to silence as Asaf Khan's diwan appeared at the opening to his master's tent.

The diwan summoned them with an imperious gesture. He then walked back into the enormous tent Asaf Khan resided in.

"Here we go," Ricky muttered.

"About fucking time," Bobby groused under his breath. "I about sweated through these robes Jadu made me buy."

"Want some cheese with that whine, Bobby?" Ricky asked as the guard standing just inside the entrance told them to disarm.

"Now you sound like J.D."

"There's worse people to sound like," Ricky said, gladly giving up his sword.

"Sure are," Bobby said, handing over baldric and blade with his own contented smile. Both up-timers were happy to be rid of the trip hazard a scabbarded sword proved to be, if only for a little while. Who knew that simply wearing a sword was so hard? Like swordsmanship itself, it proved to be a skill neither of them had mastered nor cared to master. They wouldn't have been wearing swords at all, but Jadu had insisted the bearing of such arms was necessary for anyone wishing to be taken seriously.

Which makes me think...

"Jadu, why did we have to have swords for this audience if they were just going to take them away?" he asked.

"Because all things are observed and remembered," Jadu replied.

Ricky, thinking there was a warning in Jadu's tone, bit his tongue.

Jadu handed his own scabbarded sword and dagger to the guard.

Each of the party was given a small wooden chit with writing on it. Ricky assumed they would be used to collect their arms when the audience was over.

One of the guards went through to the next chamber, presumably to check with someone higher up the food chain whether they were ready to receive the mission party.

"Can you be less cryptic?" Bobby said, once it was clear they would be spending a few minutes cooling their heels.

"I meant that we must keep up appearances, because every one of these people serves someone." He waved one beringed hand to include the surrounding camp. "Serves...and makes observations of our behaviors, of our dress, of our character, our place in life, in the order of things. You are expected to appear and behave as emissaries and umara of the Swedish king's court, late of the court of Sultan Al'Azam Dara Shikoh. So, the more things that are out of place or do not correspond to the expectations of the observer, the more excuses those who control access will find to hinder our cause, either directly by denying us communication or through delays such as we have faced these last few weeks.

"So: Just as I made sure you both had the fine robes Bobby complains are making him sweat, I made certain you both had swords. Swords that, when the guards asked for them, you had to give. All so that your appearance and behavior do not raise questions as to whether we should be allowed in the presence of power in the first place. Such is the way of things in the halls and tents of the powerful."

In the thoughtful silence that followed Jadu's patient explanation, Ricky felt another surge of appreciation for the man. They would really not have accomplished a God-damned thing if not for Jadu's immense store of knowledge, experience, and ability to simply talk to people. Thoughts of how much they owed the down-timer made him feel a sudden surge of—he supposed it couldn't be called homesickness—but he did miss the rest of the Mission folks something fierce. Things had been easier when he and Bobby hadn't been out here with only the one guy, however capable, they could count on as friend and ally among all these strangers.

The guard returned shortly after, and ushered them through the next set of hangings and into the presence of Asaf Khan.

The brother to one empress, father to another, and grandfather to the current crop of competing claimants to the throne reclined on cushions set upon a low dais at the far end of the chamber. Shaista Khan sat below him at his right while the diwan who'd summoned them was behind one of the little low writing desks the locals used on Asaf's left.

Ricky didn't know if that was significant, and didn't have a chance to ask Jadu, as they were announced just then.

Ricky checked the old man out as they advanced together and made their bows. Asaf Khan did not look well. The white in his luxurious beard made the unhealthy pallor of his skin obvious, even at a distance. His eyes were sharp, though, flitting from one member of the mission to another.

The man behind the desk bade them sit and had slaves offer them food and drink. All three gratefully accepted drinks. The day was scorching hot, even in the shade of the tent.

"You are here on behalf of which of my daughter's sons?" Asaf Khan demanded. The man's voice was rich and strong, though his accent challenged Ricky's shaky comprehension. Ricky assumed the accent was a result of the man being an actual Persian, rather than learning the language in order to fit in at the Mughal court.

"Dara Shikoh, ghazi," Jadu said, bowing deeply.

"I see. And what would my daughter's eldest son have of me, that he sends a *Vaishya* to my tent like I need more trinkets for my wives?"

Jadu smiled serenely in the face of the unsubtle reference to his class and the gulf between their stations.

"As I have told your fine son, ghazi, Dara wishes only to affirm the mutual friendship, love, and regard he holds you in."

"Well said. Of course, a Vaishya would know that to peddle tawdry goods, one must speak with a smooth tongue."

Ricky saw Shaista Khan twitch, but Jadu's expression might as well have been carved in stone.

The uncomfortable silence that followed went on too long, making Ricky sweat.

"You do not speak?" Asaf Khan said.

"Father," Shaista Khan cautioned.

But Asaf ignored his son to smile at Jadu. "My

son would have me be polite, but tell me, is the lion polite to the jackal?"

"If he wishes his dinner brought to him, perhaps?" Jadu said, returning a disarming smile.

Asaf Khan snorted. "Keeping one's nerve in a trying situation is yet another trait of the best merchants."

"I had no idea you knew so much about merchants, Father," Shaista Khan drawled.

Asaf Khan waved at Jadu but spoke directly to his son. "You forget that my father—your grandfather—brought us to this land of opportunity from our homeland in order to sell his wares. That both he and my mother were of storied lineages made no difference to him, as he was forced to succeed as a merchant!"

"And faced many, many challenges, not least of which was the loss of all his stock," Shaista Khan said, with an air of someone who had heard it all too many times. "I forget nothing of our origins, Father. I am impatient to learn what my cousin wants of you."

"Indulge me. I only test the mettle of this man, the one Dara Shikoh chose as his . . . messenger?" Asaf Khan asked, returning his attention to Jadu.

"When the usual messenger fails to obtain a response, there is work for the unusual," Jadu said, waggling his head.

"And what does Dara want of me, *unusual* messenger?"

"Only your continued love and affection," Jadu said.

"Meaning he wants me to come pull his toes from the fire."

"It is more than his toes in the fire, ghazi," Jadu said.

"Ah, the greatest truth is spoken at last."

"I have only spoken honestly."

"Honesty is not truth," Asaf said, dismissively. "One can speak clearly and in complete honesty, yet speak falsehoods the Adversary would be proud of."

"Could you *please* allow him to speak, Father?"

Asaf's chuckle ended in a coughing fit. Ricky watched Shaista Khan's expression shift from mild annoyance through deep concern, before settling back into the courtier's mask.

With a start, Ricky realized that Shaista was staring directly at him.

"You, up-timers," Shaista Khan said. "I have heard that you can cure the sick. Have you brought some miracle cure to treat my father?"

"We cannot work miracles," Ricky said carefully. "And neither of us are as deeply trained in medicine as those that saved Dara."

"And what are you trained in?"

"They are road builders," Asaf put in. "They attempted to sell such skills to Shah Jahan." He coughed again, but only a few times.

"Your father is right," Ricky said. "But we do know some basics about medicine that might be helpful, if you will allow me a few questions?"

Asaf waved permission, wiping his mouth with a handkerchief.

"Do you smoke?"

Asaf nodded, another coughing fit silencing him.

"Stop."

"But we were advised that it helps with the digestion," Shaista Khan said.

"It might, but is a gut problem killing him or are his lungs?" Ricky said.

"His physicians say it is a combination of things,

and they recommended smoking a mixture of opium and hashish to calm his—"

"Jesus!" Ricky blurted.

"What?" Shaista Khan asked.

"Are you in much pain?" Ricky asked Asaf Khan directly.

"Only when I cough," Asaf Khan said.

"Well, I am no physician," Ricky said, "but the doctors back hom—er, up-time, were very certain that smoking *anything* was bad for your health. I mean, so sure about it they managed to pass a bunch of laws about where and how you could smoke regular tobacco. Not in West Virginia—some parts of the state were too dependent on tobacco as a cash crop—but out in California, they were working to make it damn near illegal."

"Cali—"

"A state in the . . ." He shook his head. "There is too much to tell in one night. Please trust me when I say, the physicians of the future all agree that smoking is bad for you."

Shaista looked at his father. "No more bhang for you!"

The older man grinned. "Deny a dying man his pleasures, will you?"

"I will, if it means you'll be around a bit longer."

"Ricky," Bobby said, looking uncomfortable.

Ricky looked a question at his old friend.

"Withdrawal?" Bobby said, in English.

"Shit," Ricky answered in the same language.

"What is it?" Shaista and Jadu asked at the same time.

"My friend reminds me that . . . Well, how much are you smoking?" he asked Asaf.

"Four to six pipes a day," Shaista answered for his father.

"All right, then . . . you should drop that off by, say, one pipe a day each week for the next five weeks. The . . ." He racked his brain for the Persian word for withdrawal but couldn't figure it out and had to work around it. "The absence of opium may make him very ill if you cut him off completely."

Shaista did not look surprised by this revelation. "I had wondered. We are familiar with the illness that comes after long use of opium."

"Meaning: you were testing me." Ricky said the words carefully, hoping to avoid giving offense.

"Of course I was, and will be," Shaista said, equally neutral. "Whatever proofs were provided to Shah Jahan were not provided to us. We would be fools to simply take you at your word."

"And no one ever took Asaf Khan for a fool," Jadu said.

"God willing, there is still time," Asaf Khan said.

They laughed together, and Ricky felt more hopeful about their mission for the first time since arriving in Patna.

Chapter 31

Agra
Red Fort, Harem

The balcony was crowded with harem inmates, everyone watching as more than a thousand horsemen rode away from the fortress. Jahanara and her favorites were notably absent. There was much muttering and some consternation, but no tears.

Shedding a tear for an exile, no matter how important he was thought to be, would not be politic. Not in light of Dara's commands. Roshanara had to hide a feral, vindicated contentment behind a bland expression and false utterances of worry for their future.

For there was much for Dara's supporters to be concerned about. The palace had been abuzz with rumors of Aurangzeb's approach for days now, and every road out of Agra was swollen with people fleeing the conflict and siege everyone knew would not spare the city, so the gathered women watched and worried as Dara threw the best part of his forces away.

To an outsider, the exile of Amir Salim Gadh

Yilmaz must appear the absolute pinnacle of folly, but to those who knew the first thing of life at the imperial court, it was quite clear Dara had been left with very little choice. Rumor or not, an umara, no matter how highly placed, having—or even attempting to have—relations with an inmate of the imperial harem was a matter of honor that must be treated with the utmost seriousness. It did not matter that the woman was not a wife or concubine of the emperor, for any harem was meant to be sacrosanct, the sole preserve of the man for whom it was sanctuary. The merest rumor of impropriety had been enough to shake the court to its very foundation.

Exiling the man was excessive only if Dara were *absolutely* certain the rumors about what had gone on between Salim and Jahanara were purely a fabrication, a dark fantasy concocted by their enemies at court and beyond.

But he could not know. Not for certain. That was the deadly brilliance of it. Roshanara spent a giddy instant wishing she had been the author of such a daring play. But then reconsidered in light of the great stakes at risk, and was glad enough she had not tried to spread such talk.

Which set her to thinking... Roshanara knew Nur, for one, would have been overjoyed to use her allies in just such an effort. To discredit the Afghan so thoroughly and disrupt the court to such an extent was a victory worthy of Nur's skill and experience, but Roshanara had no proof that it was the older woman's intrigues that had led to Salim's exile. She was certain someone had made the story up, though, because if such a rumor had held even the tiniest grain of proof,

Salim would not have ridden from Red Fort with his head, let alone the sowar sworn to his service.

That last was a surprise. She would not have thought so many men would choose to remain with their exiled leader when he was unable to pay them. Salim Gadh Yilmaz had been a penniless adventurer before entering imperial service, and so had no great personal wealth to support his followers out of his own coffers. Dara had revoked all Salim's ranks—zat and sowar alike—and made certain, by royal decree, that the proceeds and title to all jagdirs given to the outcast Salim Gadh Yilmaz were to revert to the imperial offices. He must be quite the leader, to inspire so many to follow him into exile.

Unless...*the umara were so certain of Dara's defeat that following Salim into exile was far preferable to remaining here?*

That thought made her bite her lip to stop a joyful noise.

I simply must *pass this on.*

Red Fort, Delhi Gate

Ilsa paused on exiting the shade of the interior gateway of Delhi Gate, casting about for the escort John and Gervais had arranged to protect Mission personnel on their travels between Mission House and Red Fort.

She sighed. It was the changing of the guard, and, if they were even here, the men of her small escort were lost in the sea of two-hundred-odd men occupying the courtyard. John had said the design of the courtyard—which required a hard left turn from her position and then a hard right turn and shallow descent in order to enter the outer gatehouse—was not only intended to prevent an elephant from making a full-speed charge at the inner gate, but to force the creatures to advance one at a time, all while being stung by arrow and shot from defenders on all sides. She glanced at the shadowed gateway she'd departed, shaking her head. If one of the majestic giants were killed there, its massive corpse would block the passage as well as any boulder.

Shaking her veiled head free of thoughts of the siege that was to come, Ilsa looked again for Ahmed and her escort. The smell coming off the court was a pungent mix of sweating men and stale horse piss that made her queasy.

Her hopes rose momentarily, only to be dashed when she spied what she thought was Ahmed's signature dirty green turban, but the wearer turned out to be an imperial messenger walking a short string of horses to the stables lining one edge of the courtyard. The man stared at her when he caught her looking at him. Veiled or no, these people had a real problem with women who went out in public without an escort.

Ilsa sighed again. She understood the need for them, but didn't like the way the men the Mission had hired behaved around women in general and her in particular, so the last thing she wanted to do was wander in search of *them* among other men who clearly saw her as an interloper at best and a game animal at worst.

A stable hand approached. She asked for her mount and spent the next few minutes letting her eyes travel in a fruitless search for Ahmed or one of the other guards she knew by sight.

I'll be damned if I'm going to walk among them in search of him, no matter how badly I want to get away from here.

Harem life had become oppressive in the days since Salim's exile, and while Dara didn't treat the married women of the Mission any differently, Jahanara, and, to a lesser extent, the other unmarried women resident in the harem like Monique, were suffering from Dara's displeasure with Jahanara. It all led to an atmosphere of distrust and uncertainty in the harem that set everyone's nerves on edge. She'd remained as long as she could, but her pregnancy already made Ilsa uncomfortable and tired, so however much she might want to support her friends, she had to take care of herself, too.

On top of which, she wanted to be alone with John as soon and as much as possible before the siege, and there was only so much time remaining to them before Aurangzeb and his army arrived to make privacy next to impossible for everyone. The rumors had it that Aurangzeb was approaching Gwalior, and if that fortress fell as quickly as Burhanpur, then they would be under siege in months if not weeks. In light of the approaching threat, John's schedule had grown even more difficult. Training, drills, and long war councils with Dara consumed nearly every waking moment of John's day. He'd arranged for this time only by taking the men into the field for the day on something called "close-order drill."

"Heading back to Mission House?" Atisheh asked from above, startling Ilsa from her musings. The warrior woman was already mounted on a fine bay gelding, and armored cap-à-pie.

"I am," Ilsa said. "But my escort is nowhere to be found." She gestured up at the surrounding walls and the many fighting men in the tiered galleries overlooking the killing ground.

"If you like, I will escort you to Mission House."

"If it will not take you away from some other duty?" Ilsa said, grateful for the woman's offer.

"Hammerfall needs exercise," Atisheh explained, patting her horse's neck. She nodded at the stables. "And so does your mare, from the look of her."

Ilsa turned, watching Flower, the deaf mare she'd preferred since that fateful day in the hills, as the horse was led from the stable. She did look out of shape.

"I've barely ridden her except to get back and forth between the palace and home," Ilsa admitted, feeling a twinge of guilt. Her teamster father, were he alive, would have given her one of *those* looks.

"You can have the diwan of stables exercise her for you," Atisheh said.

"I can?" She was not used to the level of service Red Fort provided even temporary visitors to the palace. None of the Mission members were. Perhaps if one of them had been nobility in Europe, they might have been. But none of them had been remotely of that class, so they tended not to think that they should be waited on hand and foot.

"Indeed. They should have offered, really, but someone was obviously being lazy or..."

Ilsa mounted. "Or what?"

"Just a passing thought," Atisheh said with a shrug of armored shoulders, setting her horse in motion without apparent command.

The soldiers parted for her as meat from a cleaver.

Flower was not so well trained nor her rider so confident, and required Ilsa to put heels to her flanks before she would advance into the milling mass of men. Even then, the mare tried to follow in Atisheh's wake rather than carve her own path through the men.

"I would know your thoughts," Ilsa said as they rode into the shade of the gatehouse.

"Are you certain? It's really not that important."

"Not important, but you do not wish to tell me? These things, as my husband might say, 'does not compute.'"

"You mean like a mathematician?" Atisheh said as they exited the gatehouse into the heat of the afternoon sunlight.

Ilsa squinted. "John says it's a line from a show, supposedly said by a very complex machine that does computations."

"A machine?"

"You'll have to ask John. I never watched the show, so I don't know the details well enough to explain."

"Perhaps I will," Atisheh said, spurring her horse to a canter as they cleared the traffic lined up to enter the fortress.

Flower, given her head, gamely set out to catch the bigger gelding. After a few furlongs she began blowing hard and Ilsa reined her in.

Atisheh, instead of immediately reining in to a matching pace, rode a wide circle before returning to the road and Ilsa's side. Watching the warrior woman ride, Ilsa realized Atisheh hadn't answered the question she'd posed.

"Fine day for a ride if it were not so hot," Atisheh said.

"And for avoiding answering questions?" Ilsa said it lightly, not wanting to alienate the big warrior woman.

Atisheh grunted, then shrugged. "I merely wanted to be sure you were . . . certain you wanted to know."

"I am."

"There are those at court who resent you and the rest of your companions for your rapid rise to the pinnacle of power. Some of those resentful fools play the usual petty games, cutting at you with minor inconveniences, such as refusing to offer proper care for your mounts and circulating foul rumors behind your back."

"You've heard such rumors about us?"

"No, not me. But then I am known to be an ally to you and yours, not to mention to Jahanara Begum, so I would not be a likely target for those looking for ears to pour such poison into."

"But you know such rumors circulate?" Ilsa asked, hating how veils, even chain mail ones, made it so hard to read expressions.

"They always do. Do not take it personally."

"I don't. Just interested to confirm it's been going on."

They rode in silence for a little while, then Ilsa twitched the reins as an alarming thought occurred. Flower tossed her head in irritation.

"We aren't a liability for Begum Sahib, are we?"

Atisheh looked across at her. "No, not at all."

"Good," Ilsa said. Even as she said it something pricked at her mind. Something in the other woman's tone that was less than reassuring.

"How goes recruitment?" Ilsa asked, more to give herself time to think than out of any real interest.

"More slowly than I would prefer." Atisheh's immediate answer told Ilsa the issue had been weighing heavily on the warrior woman's mind. "My tribe is not as large as it was in my youth, so my kinsmen have taken to recruiting from among clans that are not counted among the friends of my own kin."

"Things are that desperate?"

"Desperate, no." Atisheh said, then sniffed. "But even in my tribe, women like me are not common."

"No, I don't think anyone could ever call *you* common," Ilsa said, laughing at the thought. "God broke the mold when He made you."

"You should have known my aunt. I am but a rough-hewn imitation." Atisheh's voice was thick with emotion, surprising Ilsa.

"She must have been a most formidable woman," Ilsa said quietly.

"She taught me everything I know about riding and fighting."

"Not your father?"

Atisheh sniffed derisively. She was silent a moment, then said harshly, "When he was not drunk, my father was, at best, a passable swordsman, though he did know a thing or two about horseflesh and riding."

"My father taught me a great deal about horses, too," Ilsa said, hoping to navigate the sudden angry turn the conversation seemed to have taken.

"Oh, he didn't teach me anything. The only and best thing he did for me was sell my services, and that only because he was paid handsomely by the recruiter."

"How long ago was that?"

"Fifteen—no, seventeen years ago now."

"That would have made you, what, ten?"

Atisheh snorted. "I was fully sixteen. Old enough my father despaired of finding me a husband..."

"And here I thought you only in your twenties."

"When I was younger, I'd hoped a facial scar or two might make me look less a child, but none of the men I've fought with live steel have landed blows on my face. But then, I am here to complain of it and they are not."

Ilsa's smile made her glad of the veil, for once. "I know we were all so grateful for the skill at arms you and your sisters showed that day. I don't know if I, personally, expressed my gratitude for your her—"

"Please, I only did my duty. And by one measure, failed, miserably."

"But—"

"Oh," Atisheh interrupted her, "I know I am not responsible. But, when one has dedicated one's life to defending a man and all that he loves, it hurts to see him murdered, even if it happened beyond the reach of my sword."

Ilsa nodded. "Understandable, that."

Another chuckle.

"What is it?"

"The back of my neck heats as if my aunt had just slapped me."

Ilsa looked a question at her.

"She had a habit of doing that when I would complain of how hard a lot in life I had or when I failed at some task she'd set for me. Which occurred, judging from the number of slaps I received, far too often for her liking."

"Sounds as if you miss her a great deal."

"Every single day." Atisheh chuckled again, and waggled her head. "Though I have little desire to relive those stinging slaps."

They rode the rest of the way to the city gates in a reflective, friendly silence. A mob of people were at the gate, most of them waiting for loved ones trying to get out of the city. The press of people was loud.

A richly dressed man Ilsa took to be the captain of the gate was standing on the rampart. He was looking down at them and shouting some query Ilsa couldn't comprehend.

Atisheh must have understood him despite the crowd noise. Rather than shout back, she simply gave an exaggerated nod.

The man barked a command.

Men with long batons emerged from the gatehouse and started to push the crowd back from the gate with their staves. A few minutes of shouting and shoving opened a narrow passage to the gate and emptied the mouth of the gate itself.

Ilsa would have said something about the lack of care the men showed for the well-being of the people shoved aside, but her baby-sensitive stomach roiled at the smell of all those sweating people and their varied diets crammed together in so small a space.

The pair of riders approached the crowd, which Ilsa thought remained far calmer than any equivalent crowd of Germans would have been under similar circumstances. A small group of men escaped the cordon to one side of the gate, forming a knot in front of it. Atisheh rode slowly through them, seeming unconcerned by their presence.

Ilsa, not so sanguine about their presence, watched them closely. One of the men seemed to reach up at Atisheh as she passed into the shadow of the gate. She opened her mouth to shout a warning but the man withdrew his hand so quickly Ilsa doubted the evidence of her own eyes. By the time she managed to urge Flower up next to Atisheh, they were through the gate, past the crowds, and nearly home. Ilsa was going to say something then, but the city was too quiet, the silence oppressive in a way the heat alone could not explain. She wanted to mention that man, but opened her mouth only to clamp it closed as a light breeze assaulted her nostrils with a new stink. Instead she spent several minutes struggling to keep her lunch in its proper place, unable to answer when the Mission House guards challenged them.

Atisheh glanced at Ilsa and, no doubt observing how green her companion was, answered for them both.

John and Monique walked up as she dismounted in the inner court. He was dusty and looked worn out from the day's work. Probably smelled a bit, too. Still, she loved the way he walked, broad shoulders and narrow hips moving in a way that never failed to catch her attention. Sure, most accomplished swordsmen had similar moves, but they also had the bandy legs of the born horsemen. She preferred her man's straight legs.

"Hey, how are you?" he asked them both, leaning over for a kiss.

She pecked him on the cheek. He did smell: his own brand of healthy sweat and horse, which she didn't find at all offensive.

"I am well, Mr. Ennis, Monique," Atisheh said, nodding at the pair from the saddle.

Taking Atisheh's horse by the bridle, Monique looked up at the warrior, thick curls bouncing. "Staying?"

"I must return," Atisheh said.

"Thank you for escorting my wife, Atisheh," John said.

"It was nothing. A pleasure," the harem guard answered.

John nodded and looked at Ilsa. "Shall we?"

"Of course."

As she and her husband walked Flower to the stable, Ilsa reflected how odd her pregnancy was. She remembered her mother claiming she'd been sick all the time whilst pregnant with Ilsa, but hadn't mentioned what, in particular, had made her throw up. For her own part, Ilsa didn't vomit very often, and then it was usually as a result of some everyday smell seeming ten times as powerful as it had been before her pregnancy.

And then, there's the fact that when I'm around John, I'm randy as a stoat—not that I wasn't before! Speaking of which...

Glancing over her shoulder to see the guards attending to their duty and looking out over the city, and Monique and Atisheh deep in conversation, she gave John's muscular bottom a squeeze.

Surprise made him hop. He grinned down at her and placed his hand on her posterior as well.

So, so randy.

Chapter 32

Gwalior Fort
Aurangzeb's camp
The Red Tent

"Carvalho, you are to proceed north once you have rested and the remainder of the artillery train has caught up," Aurangzeb said. The heavy guns had a hard time keeping up with the army, and were only going to find it more difficult the longer the campaign continued.

"As you command, Sultan Al'Azam." Carvalho's answer was quick despite the expression of surprise that flashed across his face. And, among his officers, Carvalho had the most justification for that surprise: Aurangzeb's artillery corps commander had lost more men at Burhanpur than anyone else, so he was naturally more concerned about committing to another siege, and certainly more so than the light cavalry commanders standing to either side of the ferenghi captain.

"The men here, they will not resist us?" Sidi Miftah Habash Khan inquired, gesturing at the massive defenses of Gwalior Fort.

Aurangzeb hid a smile by bowing his head. It boded well that even his trusted men could not foretell his actions. Of course, they did not have access to the sources of information that he and Nur had cultivated.

His good mood soured as he watched water drip from the edges of the awning set up before the Red Tent. His trusted umara attended him in an informal council of war while the first steady rain of the season offered liquid proof of how little time remained for the young emperor to bring Dara to battle and defeat him. The rains would not stop his army but they would slow it, and, more critically, greatly reduce the speed and efficiency of the banjari network transporting the necessary supplies from Bombay port. So much so that most of the fodder would rot or be eaten before arriving at the men and horses it was intended to serve. The relief he'd felt upon receiving the message last night had put him on his knees, driving him to offer fervent prayers of thanksgiving unto the Almighty for many hours. The grain stores of Gwalior, when emptied, would serve to keep his army fed and mobile for a month or more, despite the weather.

Aurangzeb decided he'd left the question unanswered for long enough. "To be sure, were I to offer them insult or the sword, they would deny us the fortress for months, if not years."

"You bought another commander, Sultan Al'Azam?" Shahaji asked, grinning.

Aurangzeb leveled a sober stare at the man. "No, I did not."

Shahaji's smile faded only slightly, and Aurangzeb found himself forcing down a matching grin that threatened from the corners of his own mouth. Such would be an unseemly public display.

He sniffed. "In fact, I had been much distressed with concerns over how we might take Gwalior without spending blood and treasure I can ill afford," he admitted.

"Blood we would gladly spill for you, Sultan Al'Azam, for your cause has God's favor," Sidi Miftah said.

"Indeed. God, in His wisdom, did correct me in my doubts. He provided, as always. Ahmad Khan sent a messenger with an offer to capitulate. I accepted."

Piratical grins greeted that news. From everyone but the Habshi, who tugged at his densely curled beard.

"What is it, Sidi Miftah Khan?" Aurangzeb asked.

"Forgive me, Sultan Al'Azam, but how can you trust this commander? Forgive me, but I do not even recognize the name you give us. Lacking that name recognition, I know this man cannot possess an honorable reputation to match Lahore Rathore, and therefore is not likely to be worthy of remaining in our rear without the necessary assurances." He raised a brow in question. "Hostages and the like?"

"I will not take hostages from men whose only crime was to be loyal servants of the imperial court."

Everyone seemed dismayed at this revelation, so Aurangzeb took great pleasure in revealing his next bit of news: "But he—and his entire garrison—will not remain here. They will ride north with us. I will install my own garrison there on the morrow," he added, pointing at the citadel.

When Sidi Miftah looked unrelieved, Aurangzeb gestured for him to speak his concerns.

"Sultan Al'Azam, please forgive me any impertinence in questioning you, but why this sudden collapse of Dara's support? I am thankful to Almighty God, of course, but it almost seems too good to be true."

"As it did to me, before I had confirmation from other sources."

"Confirmation of what, Sultan Al'Azam?" Sidi insisted.

"Thanks be to God," Aurangzeb said, "Dara has removed his most powerful supporter from the court, exiling him."

"Exiled?" Sidi Miftah asked, eyes wide in his handsome face.

"Indeed. My brother is so lost to morality he has allowed my sister, Jahanara, to have relations with the upstart Salim Gadh Yilmaz. And then, to add to his shame, only exiled the pig instead of killing the wretch as he ..." Aurangzeb let the words trail away, pretending a pain he scarcely felt. The news was too good for his cause to truly feel regret. That his eldest sibling had been so lost to honor that she had tarnished the family image in such a way was ... useful.

The gathered men's shocked mutters stopped when Sidi Miftah went to his knees before his ruler.

"Sultan Al'Azam," he said, "may I be the first to offer my blade to avenge your family honor? Let me seek this man out and kill him like the pig he is!"

Aurangzeb froze, surprised at the passion in his follower's words. He found his voice after a moment's consideration, and said, "If he should be so foolish as to come to us thinking to take service despite his transgressions, I will avail myself of your kind offer. As it is, I doubt very strongly we will be seeing him again. By all reports, he flees to Gujarat, and thence to Mecca."

"You are certain? I would follow him to the ends of the earth to expunge this stain."

"I am certain, Sidi Miftah," Aurangzeb replied, though he did not feel half as certain as he tried to project.

"As you command, Sultan Al'Azam," the Habshi said, reluctantly climbing to his feet.

Aurangzeb called for a drink, using the moment to assess the men's response to his report. The other captains seemed content with both their companion's offer and their commander's response, but if the Habshi's response would be paralleled—or even exceeded—among the common sowar serving him, was he missing a potential liability...or possibly an opportunity to either strengthen their ties to him?

"Sultan Al'Azam, may I ask a question?"

"Of course, Carvalho Khan," Aurangzeb said.

"You have not told us what reason, specifically, the commander gave for his defection. I understand a certain level of fear, but the Afghan was only one man, not a proven general such as yourself, from a family of no great consequence."

"You are correct, he was not a proven leader, but he was the man trusted to employ the technology of the up-timers to best effect. Then the common sowar see the explosion destroy the manufactory set up for the production of the advanced up-timer weapons. Each is seen as a possible foretelling of Dara's failure in battle. Then we take Burhanpur, and Asirgarh capitulates far more quickly than anyone predicted. And now this last proof of Dara's moral failures. While not weighty as a military matter, it proved the straw that broke the camel's back, at least for the commander up there." He pointed at the vast fortress. "Indeed, I am told that some who had been whispering that Dara's cause might be cursed now speak openly of his personal failures and the obvious corollary: the imminent failure of his cause."

Even as he offered the captains his assurances, Aurangzeb wondered, not for the first time, if he was not falling into some trap laid for him by the Adversary.

It would have helped to have someone to speak to candidly regarding his concerns. Other than God, of course, He was consulted at every opportunity. No, just someone to listen and offer commentary would be helpful.

Much to his surprise, he felt her absence was a detriment to his decision-making. Nur would have offered her opinions, but she had taken ill the night before last. Unsolicited as those opinions might be, Nur Jahan was the only person in the world with both the political acumen and sufficient awareness of his plans to comment with clarity on the repercussions of his decisions.

Suddenly irritated that he should have become reliant on anyone, let alone Nur, he turned his attention to the task at hand and rattled off the next day's order of march.

The Red Tent

"Greetings, Sultan Al'Azam," Methwold said, rising from his bow. He could hear De Jesus' robes rustle as he climbed to his feet as well. Methwold hoped the priest would control himself at this, the first formal audience they'd had with Aurangzeb since he'd declared himself emperor of the Mughals.

"You requested an audience?" the emperor asked, entirely without preamble.

The gathered umara stirred, interest piqued. Supplicants were rarely admitted without the emperor knowing precisely what they wanted from him.

Feeling De Jesus tense behind him, Methwold quickly spoke: "Indeed, Sultan Al'Azam, we only wished to congratulate you on your victories. Surely the speed with which you have accomplished them is testament to the favor God shows you."

Again he felt De Jesus stir, and again Methwold prayed silently—and without much hope—for the priest to keep silent. De Jesus had complained bitterly and at length that Methwold was not being assertive enough with their claims on the emperor before, and now that Aurangzeb had taken Gwalior and its vast food stores, the emperor was far less reliant on the Europeans for their maintenance. It had taken every bit of Methwold's diplomatic skill and experience to talk the priest into allowing Methwold to take the lead in the audience.

"While I appreciate the sentiment, it is premature to offer such congratulations." The emperor's expression remained impassive as he spoke, though his gaze did slide from Methwold to the priest and back again.

"We pray God your victories will be repeated until your final triumph, Sultan Al'Azam."

Again De Jesus stirred.

Damn the man's religious intolerance.

The emperor had not missed the movement. "Your priest does not seem as certain of God's will as you are."

"I am not his—" De Jesus blurted.

Methwold spoke over his companion. "As you know, Sultan Al'Azam, Father De Jesus and I are not of the same church."

An expressionless nod of the young man's head. "I did know that, though it seems Father De Jesus wishes to speak for himself."

"As he says, President Methwold is . . ." De Jesus

paused, ". . . not a member of the Mother Church. I will not vouch for the efficacy of his prayers for your cause . . . Sultan Al'Azam."

Bloody hell!

Methwold thought he saw a hint of a smile playing at the edges of Aurangzeb's mouth. Though what, exactly, he found humorous in the priest's statement was beyond the merchant.

"What, then, brings you before me?"

"Sul—"

Aurangzeb's raised hand stopped Methwold. "I would hear it from Father De Jesus."

William Methwold closed his eyes and began a silent prayer.

"As President Methwold states, we are here to congratulate you"—Methwold dared hope, opening his eyes—"and to see you make good on the promises made to our patrons in exchange for their assistance!" De Jesus finished in a rush, too loudly to be ignored.

Methwold stifled a fearful groan.

Aurangzeb's slow blink was disconcerting. "Have you not received our words on this matter?"

"We have—"

"Certainly, we have, and we are gr—" Methwold tried to interrupt, but Aurangzeb again raised his hand. "Do continue, Father," he said, dropping the hand.

Oblivious to the trap he was setting foot into, De Jesus went on. "But that is all we have received, Sultan Al'Azam."

His courtiers began to mutter angrily, but Methwold was made far more nervous by Aurangzeb's seeming calm. By comparison, Shah Jahan had been an easy read. His son was cut from a different cloth altogether.

"And what would you have of me now, priest?"

De Jesus wasn't stupid. He caught the change in the emperor's address. He was, however, young and far more of a hothead than his superiors had thought.

"Simply that you grant the firmans promised in exchange for our support...As well as provide for the protection of priests traveling in your lands."

"All are—or will be—protected on the emperor's roads, so I do not see why it is you see fit to make a point of it."

Methwold opened his mouth to reply but stopped when Aurangzeb sent a sharp look his way.

"Of that I have no doubt, but—"

"You forget yourself, priest. I have yet to win this war." The emperor's delivery was mild, but only a fool could mistake the words that followed the interruption for anything other than a threat and a promise: "When I do, all who have been steadfast and true to their salt will see themselves rewarded and raised up in station and regard."

"And when will you declare your victories sufficient to deliver what was promised?" De Jesus spat, proving he was a bloody idiot. "When you've conquered all of Hindustan?"

Methwold tried to silence the priest with a look, but De Jesus was glaring at the emperor with an expression so dark and flushed with anger it seemed he must burst at the seams.

The tone of the priest's words was so disrespectful the guards to either side of Aurangzeb tensed, armor chiming faintly as they anticipated a command to seize the bloody idiot priest.

The command did not come. The emperor's regard

was silent and calm, prompting Methwold's guts to churn all the more. The priest might forget, but the merchant knew damn well the deadliest adder lies silent until it strikes. He drew a ragged breath, trying to think of something to say to break the tableau.

He was just clearing his throat to deliver he knew not what platitude when Aurangzeb looked at him and broke the collective silence: "From his color, it seems Father De Jesus isn't feeling well. I think you should take him and retire to think on what has been said here today." Aurangzeb's voice was calm, but the iron command of his words was not to be ignored.

How can one so young maintain such a passionless facade? At his age I wasn't even aware my face could be read like a book, let alone be in control of it...

Part Seven

August, 1636

Excellent chiefs, commanders of my line
—The Rig Veda

Chapter 33

Horse trader's enclosure
Camp of Asaf Khan

The more or less constant drone of bidding stuttered to a stop, gaining Ricky's attention. He looked for the source of the interruption but, unable to see anything for the press of bodies, had to step to the bottom rail of the fencing around one paddock.

Just as he started to look around someone shouted, "Dead?!"

A general hubbub started then. Ricky was unable to understand anything more than the fact someone of importance had died. Praying it wasn't Dara, he stepped down from the rail and listened intently, trying to pick up more details. Far fairer and slightly taller than the average, he stood out as a ferenghi despite long since having abandoned up-timer clothes in favor of the locals' comfortable dress. Even amongst the cosmopolitan horse traders his appearance set him apart from others. Unsure where to place him in the pecking order of caste and religion, most folks just ignored him.

"Mourn, for the old lion is dead!" a cooper wailed.

"Who's dead?" Ricky asked the nearest buyer, fairly certain it was Asaf Khan they were talking about, but wanting to be sure. The man looked him up and down, but didn't deign to answer before walking away from the ignorant ferenghi.

"He is dead!" Others took up the cry. Some began to openly weep.

"Who?" Ricky asked. Having no response, and realizing that a group of competitors who assumed everyone knew what they were on about were not likely to be forthcoming with information, Ricky started jogging back through the mud to their tents. His legs were heavy after the first hundred yards or so, mud from the nonstop rains of the last couple days clinging to his boots. The sun had yet to dry the camp's thoroughfares despite what had to be temperatures in the nineties, but it was doing a good job of drying him out. He paused to mop sweat from his brow. Sticking his bandanna back in his pocket, he decided cleaning his boots now wouldn't get him across the huge camp any faster. While impressed with the organizational planning of the Mughals, he still wished the horse trading enclosures were closer to the tents for traders in fine goods, but supposed it wouldn't do to have the stink of horseshit vying with the delicately scented goods some of the luxury traders were peddling. And the sheer volume of horseshit was breathtaking. Of course, not all horseshit came from the south end of northbound horses: there were a ton of charlatans and snake-oil sellers amongst the legitimate merchants, not to mention fakirs and other assorted holy men of different stripes all spouting various levels of nonsense to any that looked prosperous or paused to listen. A couple such men approached him when he paused, forcing him to shoulder past them.

They didn't take offense, just turned and sought someone else to sell to. Before he'd made it another ten strides he noticed a change in the noises of the camp, a murmur that rose to a more general wail.

Figuring such generalized wailing was only done for great men, Ricky picked up the pace. Not that Jadu needed them there, but he'd been sent to gather information at the horse market, and this was as big a bit of news as they were likely to get.

Tent of Jadu Das
Camp of Asaf Khan

"Ricky, good timing!" Bobby called as Ricky came to a sweaty halt in the shade of the awning set out before Jadu's tent.

"Not really," Jadu Das said, waggling his head as he stepped out from behind the larger up-timer's back. "Very little time remains for him to change into proper court attire."

"Wh-What?"

"We are summoned to Asaf—pardon, Shaista Khan's tent."

"So soon?" Ricky asked, mentally nodding as the older man confirmed his suspicions.

Jadu nodded, expression unreadable.

"But why?"

"Best get changed, buddy," Bobby said. "The messenger didn't explain shit to us."

Ricky turned toward the tent he and Bobby shared and saw Vikram emerge from it, the chest the up-timers used to store their finery carried between him and another man.

Cursing the sweat he knew would start staining the fine silk robes the moment he put them on, Ricky entered Jadu's tent and sat on the carpet. He'd barely gotten one boot off when Vikram entered and deposited the chest next to him.

The servant went to the rear of the tent and returned a moment later with a goblet of cold watered-down wine. Ricky thanked him and drank it in a few gulps before opening the chest and putting on his Sunday best, as he jokingly called the array of bejeweled silks.

He was putting on baldric and blade when he heard Bobby stage-whisper: "Hurry up. The guy Shaista Khan sent is coming back, and he doesn't look patient."

Tent of Shaista Khan

The faint smell of corruption greeted Ricky's nose on entering the tent, but there was no sign of Asaf Khan or his corpse.

Shaista Khan was in his father's position on a slightly raised dais at the other end of the tent's largest chamber, and waved them forward without comment. There were only a few of Shaista Khan's favored sowar present, and all of them were studiously ignoring the presence of Ricky and his companions. A quick glance confirmed that none of the bevy of usual attendants were around.

Making this as private an audience as we're ever going to get. I hope he isn't going to have us killed for

*advising them to wean his father off of the opium. I
assume Mughal malpractice suits are prosecuted a little
more harshly here than they ever were back up-time.*

Ricky glanced at Jadu for guidance, but the merchant had already stepped forward to bow before
Shaista Khan.

With a nervous glance at one another, Ricky and
Bobby followed suit.

Shaista Khan gestured for them to be seated, the
expressive face drawn and, if Ricky was any judge, sad.

"Our condolences on the passing of your father.
He was a great man and will be missed by all who
knew him," Jadu said cautiously.

Shaista Khan accepted the merchant's condolences
but quickly moved on: "We have little time to settle our
business, Jadu Das. I accept the conditions set forth in
the documents you provided and will be henceforth supporting Dara Shikoh as the rightful emperor of India."

*What conditions? I didn't know we'd presented
any offers for there to be conditions?*

Ricky looked a question at Bobby, who gave a tiny
shake of his head. They both shifted their gaze to
Jadu and tried to divine what the hell the down-timers
were talking about.

"Indeed," Shaista continued, unaware or ignoring the
consternation his answer had sparked in the up-timers,
"I look forward to seeing my intended once more. We
have a great deal of catching up to do, but for now
I must see to my father's funeral arrangements." He
paused, seemed to consider, then asked, "Will you be
staying with us as we march to support Dara or riding
ahead to report to him of our arrival?"

Jadu bowed his head. "We are at a disadvantage at

this moment because I do not have a great deal of intelligence regarding how things stand in the greater political arena."

"Gwalior Fort has fallen—or rather, been handed over to Aurangzeb's forces."

Jadu's dismay was evident despite the man's excellent self-control. "When was this?"

"Not a week." A sad smile appeared from behind the beard. "It seems my cousins are in a hurry to discover who should rule."

Ricky tried to mentally calculate exactly how far away Gwalior Fort was from Agra, but couldn't.

Jadu waggled his head. "By the time we could return with our goods, it is likely Red Fort will be besieged. I would hate to travel all that way only to be taken prisoner and my goods seized."

"And I would hate for you to be taken, what with you bearing word of my plans."

"We could ride ahead," Ricky suggested, gesturing at Bobby.

Shaista looked at the up-timers and waggled his head. "I did not know you up-timers could ride so well."

"So well?" Ricky asked, confused.

"Aurangzeb's army is certain to have many outriders, among them the best light cavalry in the world: Maratha, Persian, Afghan, Turkic, every man of them born in the saddle, or as close as makes no difference. And they will have superior mounts as well as remounts."

Jadu leapt into the momentary pause: "And I am loath to leave my baggage unprotected." He waggled his head. "Did you know, Shaista Khan, that my friends almost single-handedly fought off a bandit attack on our way here?"

Shaista looked from the two younger men to Jadu. "I did not."

"A local zamindar thought to obtain my goods. These fine men sent his entire troop packing, those few that remained after they started shooting, that is."

Why is Jadu talking us up? We only did for a couple of the guys.

Another slight smile. "They do not look like sowar."

"No, they do not. Indeed, I believe you'll not find a bandy-legged horseman among the up-timers. They're bad riders, but veritable demons in a fight. That said, I think we'll travel with you, if that is acceptable?"

"It is. We are mere weeks from Agra."

"You will proceed with your foot and baggage?"

"Of course," Shaista Khan said, a slow smile spreading across bearded lips, "How could I be sure you, your wares, and your friends could keep up, otherwise?"

Jadu bowed.

"Now, if you will excuse me? I must see to the arrangements . . ." Shaista Khan let the statement trail off, his smile fading to a grim line and eyes welling with tears.

"Of course," Jadu said, forestalling any responses from his companions.

"What the hell is going on, Jadu?" Bobby asked as soon as they were clear of Shaista Khan's tent.

Jadu motioned him to silence but Bobby wasn't having any of it. "I walked in there thinking that maybe we would be killed for having changed the old man's treatment, only to find out you've been running some kind of game behind our backs."

Ricky saw Jadu frown but wasn't about to stop Bobby asking the hard questions.

"Jadu, what is going on?" Bobby asked again.

"Salim asked me to arrange certain diplomatic niceties on behalf of Dara Shikoh," Jadu explained. "I was not to inform anyone what I was about. That included you, my friends. I am sorry that duty required that I remain silent, but I had promised to keep silent."

"Salim? Why wouldn't he trust us to know?"

Jadu sighed. "I do not know. I can guess that there was some concern that one of your companions in Agra might have spoken out of turn and thereby allowed Dara's enemies to know what it was we are about."

"Jesus," Bobby said. "We left Agra months ago, you could've told us after we left."

Jadu shook his head. "Do you not write letters back to the Mission? Granted, you two write nothing like the volume of letters that I do, but surely you understand the need to ensure you did not accidentally reveal some portion of Dara's plan in your correspondence."

Ricky missed a step. "Wait a second! What exactly did you arrange? What is it that Dara's planning?"

"I acted as the emperor's envoy in this."

Exasperated, Ricky grabbed Jadu's wrist and made him stop. "And what, exactly, is this?"

Looking around, Jadu said, "Not here. Please, let us get to my tent and we will discuss it."

Ricky shot a glance at Bobby, who nodded. Releasing Jadu's arm, they resumed walking.

The uncomfortable silence that followed in the wake of the confrontation persisted until they entered Jadu's tent. The merchant sent his servants from the tent and sat, inviting his guests to do the same.

Bobby remained standing but Ricky took a seat across from Jadu.

"Where to begin?" Jadu asked.

"How about with the truth?" Bobby snarled.

Ricky shot another glance at his friend, but Bobby was too pissed to notice.

"I, perhaps, deserve your anger. But you must know, my friends, that I took on this duty and obligation before I knew either of you. It pained me to keep the truth from you but there it is."

Ricky shook his head.

Jadu tossed his head, asked, "What is it, Ricky?"

The up-timer smiled. "Just that you still haven't told us what the hell it is you were doing."

"Can you guess?"

Bobby grumbled something inaudible, but Ricky thought back to the conversation. "He said something about intended, didn't he?"

"Exactly so." Jadu nodded. "I was sent on behalf of the emperor to negotiate Shaista Khan's—or, rather Asaf Khan or his heir's—support. Part of the inducements I was authorized to offer was a royal marriage."

Ricky rocked back on his cushion, considering the ramifications of that.

"But, he's like, forty," Bobby said.

Jadu gave a soft chuckle. "Interesting that your mind immediately leaps to marrying one of the princesses."

Bobby shook his head. "I keep forgetting you all are polygamous."

"Not *all* of us," Jadu corrected. "Not even most of us. But the royal family, yes."

"So he's got a daughter he wants to marry to Dara?"

"Not one of marriageable age, no. I just thought it interesting that you immediately thought *he* would be marrying."

Bobby growled again, but Jadu held up a hand. "Need I remind you that we are at war? When I say I am intrigued by your responses to my statements, I am trying to figure out what it is that our enemies would deduce from the information you have. Neither of you is an idiot, yet it seems the deception Salim asked me to practice upon you worked. And if it worked on you, who became intimately familiar with me and how I behave, then does it not follow that our enemies would have even greater difficulty in divining our intent?"

"You people think in circles."

"I am but a humble merchant. I am not entirely used to thinking in these ways myself. It was my honor to do this service for Dara Shikoh and the throne, but I am not used to thinking in terms of espionage and spies. At least not on this scale and with this much at stake."

Smiling, Ricky shook his head. "So what Bobby said still stands: Shaista Khan is at least twenty years older than Jahanara Begum."

"It is not so uncommon these days, my friend. And if I recall correctly, he is not yet forty."

"Wait, if Asaf Khan is their grandfather, isn't he her uncle?"

Jadu shrugged. "It's not that unusual, even among those who have nothing so important to keep in the family as the Peacock Throne."

"And people used to make cracks about us hillbillies!" Bobby said, disgust evident.

Ricky fought against his own revulsion. He often forgot how different down-timers were in general, and those of different religions and cultures were an even greater departure for a hillbilly from twentieth-century West Virginia. Add to that the fact the family they were discussing was perhaps the richest and most powerful in the world. So powerful he could still recall the high school history lessons that taught him that when people in the twentieth century said "music mogul" and the like, they were talking about the merest shadow of these folks and the very real power they wielded over the lives of millions.

Jadu smiled questioningly. "What?"

An irritated shake of the head, then Bobby said, "It's just . . . People from West Virginia mining towns were seen as backward and inbred by those who lived in big cities."

Jadu's brows rose to meet his turban. "Astounding. I suppose I should not be surprised that people still try and find someone to look down upon, even in your time."

"Damn straight," Bobby said.

A brief silence descended on them.

Ricky grinned, shaking his head in wonder.

"What makes you smile, my friend?" Jadu asked.

"You still haven't told us just who you arranged to marry Shaista Khan."

"I haven't?" Jadu asked, voice and gaze full of entirely false innocence.

Chapter 34

Countryside east of Agra

"Are you certain it's safe?" asked Sidi Miftah Habash Khan.

Aurangzeb smiled. "Are you not certain yourself? You are commander of scouts, are you not?"

"I am." The Habshi smiled, white teeth dazzling against his dark skin. "I am certain *I* could escape, but then I am counted amongst the greatest horsemen who have ever lived. I am not so certain about you, Sultan Al'Azam."

Aurangzeb snorted and barely stopped a peal of laughter escaping dry lips by focusing on an annoying fly that flitted about the mane of his horse.

When he was confident he could keep a straight face the emperor said, "I believe we are safe enough. My brother cowers behind the walls of Red Fort. And I . . . I need to make sure to pay my respects at the tomb of my parents. Too long have I been denied the opportunity to show them the devotion a son owes."

"Ah, but then there is the possibility of hidden assassins waiting for you at the tomb. Please allow us to conduct a thorough search of the grounds before you enter, Sultan Al'Azam. The loss of one Sultan Al'Azam there was sin enough. I would not see another lost, however beautiful the setting."

Aurangzeb waved permission and the Habshi rattled off a series of orders to his subordinates. Messengers on fast horses shot away from the column and rapidly disappeared into the distance. No doubt they were eager to sack the city, but discipline held for now. Especially given that they all knew it would happen.

Rather than try and restrain them entirely, Aurangzeb had commanded that they only loot the city and leave the Taj Mahal untouched.

Nur had nodded sagely when told of his designs for overcoming that minor challenge. Far better to swim with the current than try and resist. The men of Aurangzeb's army would get an opportunity to enrich themselves at the expense of the residents of Agra, but only when given leave to do so by Aurangzeb.

Simply knowing they would have that chance at wealth made the army compliant to his will.

And that army was less than ten kos from the tomb and Red Fort, both of which were visible against the light pall of smoke shrouding Agra just beyond the tomb.

A strong feeling of . . . Aurangzeb wasn't sure what it was that he felt as the long-foreseen conflict with his eldest brother grew closer with every hoofbeat. Tension, certainly. He did not want to see his brothers dead, but could not suffer Dara Shikoh to rule from the Peacock Throne. Dara had forever been a fool for whatever courtier or fakir had most recently spoken in his ear. Nor was Aurangzeb about to lie down and be murdered as his uncles had been when Father ascended the throne. No, this was the only way to safeguard the dynasty in the future and prevent the European Christians from overrunning all the world. With such weighty matters at stake, who was he to try and fight the obvious tide of God's will?

His gaze slid to Red Fort. Dara had sent no messengers, nor had he taken the field in any capacity. Word from within the Fort was that even his garrison was starting to lose its nerve. All as a result of the departure of Salim Gadh Visa Yilmaz. Interesting that an adventurer but recently elevated at court could have carried so much weight of regard with both the umara and sowar of Dara's forces. Then again, Mullah Mohan had been driven to near madness by the mere presence of the Afghan at court, so was it so hard to imagine that such a forceful personality could inspire a great many, especially in light of Dara's ability to alienate his greatest allies and best field commanders?

He blinked, finding his eyes on the Taj again.

Mother, Father: forgive what I must do. I will do what I can to spare lives, but only when such restraint fails to interfere with God's will. Feeling the weight of massive responsibility, he looked up at the sun to gauge how long he had to wait for prayers. By his estimation it seemed that he would arrive at the Taj within a quarter hour of afternoon prayer being called.

Yet another sign of God's favor.

Red Fort
Agra

"Why isn't Aurangzeb's army setting up for the siege already?" Ilsa asked, gesturing at the long column of cavalry and elephants riding toward the Taj. "I would have thought they'd be in a hurry to sack the city."

"And miss the opportunity to display the size, discipline, and power of his army?" Jahanara answered. The inner circle of her court were watching events from the balcony overlooking the river, the Taj, and, most recently, the vanguard of Aurangzeb's forces.

"I suppose not," Ilsa said.

An uncomfortable silence descended on the party, each aware their loved ones would soon be fighting for their very lives against that distant army.

"Will they?" Priscilla asked, breaking the silence.

"Will they what?" Jahanara asked. The up-timers were a constant fascination and distraction, one she sometimes craved like Dara craved his opium; yet, at other times she wished they and their disruptive ideas and prescient history had never come to court. Today, however, she was glad for the distraction.

"Loot the city?"

"Almost certainly, though I am told most of the easily portable wealth has already been removed by the owners."

"Good. I feel bad saying it, but I'd hate to think we stripped Mission House of all our property and moved it in here if we didn't need to," Priscilla said, looking uncomfortable.

"Oh? Feel bad?" Jahanara asked.

"I don't know that much about sieges and sacks, but I assume the people of Agra will suffer a great deal? Those that couldn't leave before the army arrived, I mean."

Jahanara nodded. It spoke well of her friend that she considered the plight of all folk, low-caste Hindu and Muslim alike. Most she knew would not have—or given it no more than a passing thought.

"Yes, those who fail to get out of the way will suffer at the hands of Aurangzeb's army, and their property will be seized by whatever sowar get his hands on it. Do you do things differently in Europe?"

Priscilla glanced at Ilsa, who answered, "Europe is almost precisely the same, though often people do not have as much advance notice nor the ability to move away as many residents here seem to."

"Were things different in your time, Pris?" Jahanara asked, ignoring the fact that her people didn't really find it easy to move out of the way of princely armies, they just knew better than to try and retain their goods at the cost of their lives.

"Only in the particulars. War-torn regions produced a lot of refugees and I think looting was supposed to be illegal, at least for the professional soldiers of most countries."

"Looting, illegal? How did they prevent it?"

"With really harsh punishments for those soldiers who did it, I think. But regardless of the law, a city that became a battleground was not a place anyone would want to be. Not by a long shot."

It took Jahanara a moment to deduce the meaning of the expression *not by a long shot*. And as was often the case when talking to the up-timers, Jahanara found more questions in the answers. "Professional soldiers? Like our sowar?"

"Similar...I guess. Seems to me that your sowar are paid out of their umara's pocket instead of directly from the coffers of the empire?"

Jahanara nodded. "The umara are paid a fixed salary by the crown, out of which they must pay not only their own maintenance, but that of a specified number of sowar. They are given the tax proceeds to do this, but they often skimp on pay with promises of loot. Regardless, an individual sowar's pay is often low, especially if they do not provide their own weapons or horses. It is a complicated system of ranks for umara... which I think I heard Ilsa's John call them officers?" she asked, looking at Ilsa for confirmation. When Ilsa nodded, she continued, "But there is little distinction made between horsemen who are not umara."

Priscilla looked again at the army, but this time Jahanara had the sense that she was trying to avoid saying something she thought would upset the princess.

"What is it, my friend?" she urged.

The up-timer shrugged. "My uncle, he used to brag that one of the reasons we won the World Wars was because we didn't rely on nobles to lead us."

Ilsa put an arm around the taller up-timer woman. "These umara aren't quite the same as our nobles in Europe, Pris."

"I know."

"How are they different?" Jahanara asked.

Ilsa gave a delicate snort. "To start with: our nobles are mostly born into their station without having to earn *any* part of it. I suppose in the past they might have been warriors, but many noble families do not produce reliable leadership—military or otherwise—these days."

"Fascinating. You have been here long enough to see how much better our system works, haven't you?"

Both Priscilla and Ilsa looked away this time.

"What is it? What did I say?" Jahanara asked, confused.

It was Ilsa who looked at her and said, quite cautiously, "John says your umara are a good sight better than the nobles he dealt with in Europe."

"But?" Jahanara said, annoyed that she'd asked the question in such a demanding tone. She was unused to having friends, and it was difficult to keep a lifetime's habit of command from straining her relationships with these women.

"But we just don't know, Begum Sahib. He says your ideals of military leadership and ours are quite different."

Jahanara drew a steadying breath. "But we will soon find out, won't we?"

Both women nodded. Another uncomfortable silence pervaded for a little while.

This time it was Jahanara who broke it: "I would hear more of your American military, if you would, please?"

Priscilla smiled uneasily and shrugged. "I'm not really a student of military matters, so take what I say with a grain of salt. My dad used to complain about the draft..." She trailed off, obviously uncertain. After a moment's thought she resumed, "Thing is, until coming through the Ring of Fire, I'd never seen a battle or, hell, even real life-and-death violence up close. Most Americans hadn't. For that matter, most Americans never had an opportunity to watch our soldiers at work. Oh, we might watch movies and TV shows about it, but we really didn't know what it was our military did for us—or, more accurately, *how* they protected us."

"How can that be?" Jahanara asked. Much of court life revolved around military ceremonies; the granting of rank, investment of command, even governorships were all military matters. Beyond the ceremony, she had been witness to many battles, both for and against Jahangir. So many that she felt she knew more than she wanted to about the sacrifices involved.

Priscilla shrugged. "I guess we were lucky in that most of our wars were fought defending our allies or our interests far from home."

"Where?"

"Oh, the Middle East, Europe, Africa, and Southeast Asia. I don't even know some of them qualify as real wars, but our soldiers died fighting them."

"Never in India?"

"To my knowledge, no. Not even Pakistan."

"I heard mention of this Pakistan. I gather it is the northern part of the subcontinent?"

Priscilla's lips curled in an uncertain smile as she shook her head. "If I recall correctly, after the English pulled out they left two states south of Afghanistan: one primarily Muslim, and one . . . not. Pakistan and India, though I'm almost certain I am way oversimplifying things . . ."

"Fascinating. You mentioned that looting was illegal. How then did the common soldier make his fortune?"

"They didn't often make a fortune. They served for duty, honor, family tradition, because it was a good way to pay for an advanced education, and even because some people just didn't have any better options."

"They didn't often make a fortune?" Smidha asked, confusion echoing Jahanara's own. Salim himself was a fine example of the warrior-adventurer most common at court. Granted, he was far more successful than most.

"They were paid, but there were safer, better paid jobs out there to be had." Priscilla snorted, shook her head. "*When* there were jobs to be had..." She again shook her head in evident frustration, saying, "Sorry, these waters run deep, and I barely have the experience or knowledge to do the subject justice, dammit."

"Why 'dammit'?" She asked the question gently, pronouncing the unfamiliar English word carefully.

Priscilla pulled at a strand of hair, obviously searching for the right words. "I'm frustrated because the experience of American armed services were so foreign to my day-to-day existence yet I recognize that their service formed an intrinsic part of precisely *why* my childhood and the childhoods of so many generations of Americans did not contain daily concerns about things like invasions or having our cities being made battlefields. So, yes, it upsets me that I feel all this gratitude yet cannot easily describe for you what motivated the men and women of my country to protect us and our way of life." She nodded at the army in the distance. "Especially in light of where and when we find ourselves."

"I think you said it quite well," Jahanara said.

Priscilla looked down at the elephant fighting ground and didn't answer.

Jahanara let her be, filing the implications of the conversation away for future reference and consideration.

Smidha left her side for a moment, retrieving a packet of messages, quite possibly among the last few to arrive at Red Fort before Aurangzeb invested the fortress. She was sorting them as she returned to her mistress's side.

"Anything I need act on immediately?" Jahanara asked, eyes on her brother's army as the older woman flipped through the folded notes. The distance made his army a serpent swimming in dark waters, its head visible but body shrouded in the dust of its own passage.

"Nothing pressing..." Smidha turned over another missive. "Though you may wish to look at the latest report from your diwan regarding the income from your jagirs in Surat."

Jahanara nodded on hearing the code phrase. Talawat was ready. Salim was well on his way. The plan was coming together. All that remained was news of Asaf Khan's army. That, and Aurangzeb cooperating. Oh, and Dara not suddenly developing a desire to assert direct control over events and disrupting all her carefully laid plans. Of course, allowances had been made for just such circumstances, but it would be far easier on everyone if he were to remain silent, regal, and ready to command the defenses rather than ask uncomfortable questions concerning what was to come.

Much as she loved Dara, he could not be allowed to interfere with her defense of his throne.

No one could. One delicately hennaed hand clenched into a hard-edged fist. She had been losing weight these last months, stress gnawing at her appetite until she barely ate.

I will see to it, my brothers. For a better future for all those we govern, I will see to it.

Taj Mahal

Completing the ritual cleansing of face and hands, Aurangzeb took a moment to look around Mother and Father's final resting place, noting the fine work accomplished in his absence. The craftsmen employed by Dara had not shirked their duty, not in the least detail. Delicate tracery and fine Koranic script flowed along every surface not embellished with floral designs, Father's dream and tribute made manifest in stone, lapis lazuli, and filigree. Thousands of gemstones caught and cast the light of lanterns, making the interior seem a star-studded dusk. It was beautiful, solemn, and bittersweet. A true monument to Mother.

Aurangzeb struggled to contain a bitter anger that suddenly welled, threatening to overtake iron control. While he had been on the march north, concerns of a rapidly dwindling treasury and insufficient supply a constant burden, Dara not only had enough cash to fritter away a fortune on the disastrous attempt at manufacturing up-timer weapons and recruiting as many warriors as would serve his flawed rule, but the vast treasury Father had amassed provided sufficient cash on hand to continue work on the vastly expensive tomb complex. Work that had continued right up to his arrival. The exterior was not yet complete, and the full complex was not yet half-finished. But here, where Father had seen to Mother's final interment, it was complete, its perfection marred only by the seeming afterthought of Shah Jahan's own stone sarcophagus, off to one side. Even with that flaw, the tomb was a fitting tribute to the immortal love his parents had shared. Mother had, even in death, always sat at the center of Father's world.

All reports had Dara's army weakened by Salim's exile, in possession of no ammunition for the up-timer weapons, and was less than a third the size of Aurangzeb's own. Indeed, Dara's force was, according to all intelligence, a mishmash of foot and dismounted sowar suffering from low morale stemming from reports of Aurangzeb's rapid advance and Dara's own poor decisions. Aurangzeb's advisors agreed that Dara's forces would not withstand a determined assault despite Red Fort's substantial defenses. The agreement between his sources should have eased Aurangzeb's concerns, but they remained.

For one, despite the stores in Gwalior Fort, his supply situation was not good and the Europeans daily grew more and more impatient for the rewards he had promised. Just thinking of the Portuguese priest made Aurangzeb angry. The thin scholar's impertinent and repeated requests that the Europeans be allowed to proselytize their faith among the citizens of the empire was proving an annoyance he could not shake.

Frustrated that the ritual cleansing had washed neither his anger nor his concerns away, Aurangzeb strove for calm. It was elusive, however. Thoughts of the upcoming showdown and plans for what would come after continued to crash into the nagging feeling his cause might not be quite as just as he would prefer.

But he was here to offer his respects to Mother and Father, not plot his future. Yet a small voice from a dark corner of his mind whispered, *You have ever and always plotted your future. Such a habit is why you are here, poised on the verge of victory.*

"Not my victory, but God's," he murmured.

Distorted echoes of his words returned to his ears from the dome above, mocking his justifications, his certainty.

Tears welled, grew, and raced toward oblivion along his cheeks to wet his thin, adolescent beard.

"God's will or not, I only do what I must," he choked out.

The sibilant echoes of this whispered admission returned to his ears as more a plea for forgiveness than the statement of certainty he'd intended.

As was often the case in such moments, Aurangzeb found solace and a measure of calm in the mere feel of the wooden prayer beads under his fingers. Taking them in hand, Aurangzeb knelt upon the simple prayer rug and began his prayers, asking forgiveness of his parents and God for what he must do.

Gardens of the Taj Majal

Nur Jahan knelt in the shade of the garden, marveling at the work her grand-niece had accomplished in her absence. Fruit trees from all corners of the empire and beyond its borders flourished where they had only just been planted when she left. She could not help but think there was a message there: Jahanara, young though she was, had flourished in the absence of both parents and her eldest living relative. Eldest, now, because Asaf was gone: the brother who had alternately supported her, challenged her, protected her, betrayed her, and, ultimately, been responsible for the death of her only son, was dead.

A tear slowly welled in the corner of her eye. She dabbed at it with a silken kerchief, annoyed that she should show such feeling for him. Putting away her annoyance, she examined the source of her feelings as rationally she could.

Despite all the conflict that marred their history—or perhaps because of it—he had always been her favorite. Present for almost every single major event of Nur's life, he, more than their father, had been the measure by which all men were judged. Judged, and found wanting. The current crop of male relatives were but pale shadows of Asaf Khan, and would have been dancing to his tune had he been healthy and, perhaps, closer to the throne when Shah Jahan was assassinated.

Even Aurangzeb, gifted as he was, would have been no match for the peerless politician Asaf Khan had been. Shah Jahan had ruled well and wisely, but he had been given that opportunity as much through the efforts of his father-in-law as his own military—or political—prowess.

Aurangzeb was gifted, certainly, and she had helped him bridge the gap between experience and training. But he had yet to face failure, and therefore could not be trusted to overcome it. For if there was one thing Nur's long career had made her certain of, it was that failure at some point was always certain. And it was always a better measure of someone's character to fail and rise again to the challenge that defeated them. She worried that, given his supreme faith that God was on his side, Aurangzeb might fracture under the strain of any significant failure. That could lead to disaster, both in the current conflict and in the future to come.

Not that she felt particularly averse to someone reining Aurangzeb in. He could be blithely inconsiderate of others.

Or perhaps he was not being inconsiderate but deliberate?

He was capable of great subtlety and possessed no little patience, something rare in someone so young. So it was not outside the realm of possibility that Aurangzeb had summoned her to attend him here, in the place she had fled so many months prior, in order to put her off guard.

And that bloody afternoon was, while not the worst she'd endured, certainly not forgotten. She did not need reminding of it. Not here. Not now.

As uncomfortable and irritated as she felt waiting for him in the garden, she had to assume the provocation was entirely according to Aurangzeb's design.

She heard him before he came into view. Or rather, Nur heard his entourage before seeing the Sultan Al'Azam himself. Leaving them atop the plinth, he quickly descended the steps only recently sheathed in the white marble that was going up all over the monument to her niece. He came alone, certain in the protection of his guards. How she envied that light step, the boundless energy he expressed with every movement, and the sure certainty of youth that promised he would not, could not, be overcome.

He paused at the base of the stairs and glanced around, searching her out. She nodded when Aurangzeb's gaze fell on her. He returned the gesture and strode quickly to her side.

"Sultan Al'Azam," she said, lowering her head.

"Nur. Thank you for coming. I know you must

be fatigued from our journey, but I had something important to ask of you."

"You have but to command me, Sultan Al'Azam."

He looked around, studying the garden a moment before continuing. "Was it here?"

Nur could not prevent her jaw clenching in sudden anger. "Pardon, Sultan Al'Azam?"

"My father was attacked here, in the garden?" he clarified, still not looking her in the eye.

"No, we heard the fighting up there first," she said, pointing with her chin at the plinth he had just descended from. "It wasn't until after a few moments had passed that the guards separating the garden from the plinth were set upon and overcome. It happened very quickly."

"Yet not so quickly that you were unable to escape." His tone was not accusatory. It was simply that of a son trying to grasp the circumstances of his father's untimely death. Of an emperor determined not to suffer the same fate.

"As I told you, Sultan Al'Azam, I did not see him fall, only heard the resultant lamentations. And I was, at the time, as much a target for those assassins as your beloved father."

Aurangzeb turned to look at her. "It seems I am to place you in danger once more."

"Oh?" Nur asked, arching one brow.

He looked away again. "Although, it should be safe enough."

Nur waited in vain for him to continue, was eventually forced to ask, "What shall I do for you, Sultan Al'Azam?"

The emperor cocked his head. "I would have you meet with my sister and negotiate on my behalf."

Nur gestured at the distant bulk of Red Fort. "Negotiate? For what, exactly? Surely you have sufficient forces to overrun the fortress."

"For the lives of my sisters, to start."

"But he has made no threats to their safety..."

"I am too young to remember it myself, but I think it was at Murad's birth that a cannonball launched from some fortress Father was besieging made it so far as to penetrate the Red Tent and threaten the lives of both Mother and Father."

Nur, remembering the incident, suddenly understood. It would do his reputation no harm to show concern for the safety of his sisters. Indeed, it was a clever move. One she should have foreseen and, perhaps, suggested. If only she had been less preoccupied with memory and, she had to admit, grief over the death of her brother.

Shaking off dark thoughts, Nur realized he was gazing at her in expectation of an answer.

"Of course, Sultan Al'Azam. You are wise to consider the safety of your sisters."

"Good." He looked away again, eyes traveling over the monument to his mother.

"What may I offer in these negotiations?"

"He will not accept it, but offer him safe passage to Mecca should he abandon the fortress and abandon his claim to the Peacock Throne."

"Anything else? Perhaps something less...stark?"

"For my brother, nothing but that offer. Jahanara, she may do as she wishes short of marriage. I cannot afford her marrying some ambitious umara, especially before I have had a son. Roshanara, well, the negotiator need not know what we will give her as compensation for her support."

"And Murad?"

Aurangzeb sighed. "I offer him the same terms as Dara. I hope he will be made aware of the offer and know it for the genuine sacrifice I make in order to offer it to him. Allowing him to go into exile is opposed by everyone."

"They are right to oppose it, Sultan Al'Azam," Nur said, more harshly than she intended. Her daughter and son-in-law had not been offered such leniency, but knowing why was no salve to her broken heart.

"I am aware he and his heirs will forever pose a threat to me and mine, but I cannot, in good conscience, see him imprisoned with Dara because of my older brother's preventing him from joining my just cause. He is but eleven years old."

And you hope—no, pray—that he will not be made aware of the offer.

Nur was sure that, at least on the surface, Aurangzeb told himself that he wanted his youngest brother to take up the offer. But deep inside he had to know what a threat that would be. The Persians, the Turks, or some internal enemy would make a puppet of Murad and use his cause to strike at the very heart of Aurangzeb's rule.

There was little room for mercy when the Peacock Throne was at stake.

Chapter 35

Agra
Red Fort, Diwan-i-Khas

"What do you mean it's impossible?" Dara hissed. He looked around his circle of counselors. "Aurangzeb has yet to completely encircle Red Fort. Surely we can get someone out under cover of darkness. On the river, perhaps?"

The late afternoon summons to the Diwan-i-Khas had served to pull John from his vigil. Not that he was alone in watching Aurangzeb's army begin its encirclement of Red Fort; everyone with sufficient status to claim a spot on one of the many balconies had watched as the rain-soaked banners and tents of Aurangzeb's umara sprouted like mushrooms from the rain-veiled landscape just beyond the reach of the fort's guns.

"Sultan Al'Azam, I fear such a mission would be wasteful. I have only just heard that Asaf Khan is dead."

Dara pounded an impotent fist against the jeweled side of the Peacock Throne. He looked up, an air of desperation about him, and said, "His son, then. Shaista Khan was always easier to speak to than Asaf Khan."

"Sultan Al'Azam, I beg forgiveness, but getting to Shaista Khan's camp is the greater problem. Sending one man will surely fail, and sending more will merely serve to reduce our already thin garrison."

"Is there no one? No brave warrior who will take up this task and be made a hero in the doing of it?"

The silence that followed his questions was telling. The emperor's jaw clenched, muscles under his beard bunching. The scar peeking from beneath his jeweled turban stood out against the darkening flesh of his face.

"Husband," Nadira's calming voice came from behind the jali. "Your sowar and umara are all ready to become heroes, but Shaista Khan has made clear by his lack of response to your generous offers and diplomatically worded messages that he believes he can stand aside in this conflict between brothers." A brief pause, then, "Surely the Sultan Al'Azam can see that it is only his desire to save lives on both sides of the conflict that leads him to ask such a thing of his loyal warriors."

That was well said, John thought. *Hope it works . . .*

Dara was still incensed, glaring about at his inner council in search of someone to vent his spleen on. Dara's counselors avoided meeting his eye. For his part, John concentrated on memorizing the latest training report he'd generated for this meeting. He hated speaking in front of any crowd, especially in a language he still felt uneasy with, and these meetings were torture for him. Even without Dara losing his composure.

Dammit, I'm a hillbilly from West Virginia, not some Renaissance man to be speaking a language I hadn't ever heard a word of before coming here. If I speak with a horrible accent or use the wrong words, they can just suck it up.

Dara's wife gave a delicate noise that might have been a clearing of the throat, John wasn't sure.

Whatever it had been, the sound was enough to remind Dara of decorum, because the emperor, instead of barking at his subordinates, leaned back and took a deep breath. Then another. He even spread the fingers of both hands flat across the silk cushion covering the monstrously heavy gold-and-gemstone-encrusted Peacock Throne.

The hopeless atmosphere permeating the hall eased slightly. Dara might not be as charismatic as his father had been, but he still projected his moods well enough to make everyone aware of his displeasure. So far no up-timer had taken the brunt of such outbursts, but John was sure it was only a matter of time.

Firoz Khan spoke into the quiet. "I believe John Ennis has a report to give, Sultan Al'Azam."

Dara, steadier now, gestured for John to make his report. It wasn't actually his work, not entirely. He'd always sucked at paperwork. Thankfully Bertram was a fair hand at just about anything he decided to put some effort into and Priscilla and Ilsa had gathered up the various reports and edited the flowery language out, rendering it into something he could deliver in less than an hour.

Hoping to keep the emperor calm, John began with the positives: "First off, the medical corps report. Every one of the men who volunteered for and completed medical training has been issued the standard medical kit Begum Sahib and the Totmans developed and put into production. They've been dispersed amongst the garrison and the triage centers along with stretchers and bearers. The operating theaters have been prepared, equipped, and manned, and the hospital reports they have the supplies you mandated, Sultan Al'Azam."

He departed from the report to speak from the heart. "Sultan Al'Azam, I have to say I've seen a lot since coming to this time. The United States of Europe has done a many great things with the knowledge that came with us from the future, but this drive to provide medical services to the masses that Jahanara Begum has led, it might be the best thing to come from our arrival." Realizing a better courtier would have given Dara more credit, John looked down at his report for inspiration.

"You are kind to say so, Mr. John Dexter Ennis," Jahanara's voice rang across the hall of audience. "But nothing would have happened had my brother, Sultan Al'Azam Dara Shikoh, not seen some wisdom in my humble suggestion that we provide for the sowar and, once the battle to come is won, the peoples of his realm."

"My wife and my sister are wise," Dara said, standing. "And, like all women, have a care for those less favored by fate than themselves." He turned and bowed to the jali. "Their wisdom should be an example to all, their charity an example to the cosmos of our good intentions."

Their approval of—and display of that regard for—the royals dispelled some of the gloom that had clung to the court and, frankly, to John's own mood.

Thanking God that the princess was on their side, John turned to face the jali and bowed as well. The court followed suit.

"Your Master of Fortification's report shows he is prepared. Work has been completed removing or restoring the decorative balconies as necessary to the design of your defensive works. He also reports the fletchers and bowyers of your factories have met their quotas, as have the Atishbaz powder and shot makers."

What John didn't want to talk about was the status of the up-time weapons and their ammunition: there weren't enough of either to go around, not by a long shot, so he moved on quickly. "The cisterns are at acceptable levels and all predictions"—he was not about to give the astrologers and soothsayers cited in the report any credit—"indicate heavy rains arriving over the next few weeks. That should actually provide more water than we consume. He also reports that we have provisions sufficient to provide full rations for more than a year at our current numbers—"

Dara interrupted a thankful John with a wave. Wondering why, John cast about for the source of the interruption.

A man in messenger greens was just leaving Firoz Khan's side. The portly eunuch was opening an official-looking set of papers with several seals and such hanging from it.

John glanced back at the emperor, found him watching impatiently as his diwan and personal munshi read the document through.

Firoz, suddenly aware that John had stopped speaking, looked up. Scrambling up with the document in hand, the eunuch bowed deeply to the emperor.

"What is it?" Dara said.

"Sultan Al'Azam, Aurangzeb sends a messenger."

Dara snapped his fingers, gesturing imperiously.

John was impressed Dara hadn't barked at the eunuch for stating the obvious.

The message had hardly been in his hands for more than a few seconds before Dara had read it through. John suspected Dara's background as a religious scholar stood him in good stead when it came to reading that fast, but idly wondered if the emperor shouldn't be taking his time with something so important.

"The pretender to my throne asks me to send him someone to negotiate on my behalf. He says he will offer sureties they will not be harmed, and to make certain, he says, 'As it was for our ancestor, Akbar,' he and his men will all refrain from being present. He asks that I select one of my sisters to meet with Nur Jahan at the tomb of our parents.'" He paused, reading something from the document once more. Shaking his head, he tossed it aside.

"Just what he presumes there is to negotiate, I do not know," he said, his voice an angry growl.

"My love," Nadira's calm voice issued from behind the jali again, "you must send Jahanara to treat with Nur Jahan regardless. Your sister may be able to learn something of his intentions, even if, as you rightly suspect, Aurangzeb does not intend to negotiate in good faith."

Dara's head swung around. He glared at the jali. "I cannot see him doing *anything* in good faith. His continued insurrection against my rightful rule provides all the proof anyone needs that he is both a faithless son and perfidious brother."

"Perhaps some concessions can be earned for the people of Agra," Nadira continued. Judging from the calm tones of her voice, she was singularly unfazed by the nasty look her husband had sent toward the jali. "God willing, Jahanara may learn just what has happened with Shaista Khan and the army of his father."

Dara's gaze softened as he considered her words.

"Brother," Jahanara's voice issued from behind the jali once more, "I would ask Nur Jahan of the events leading up to Father's death. I want to know what she knew. I want to know why it is she fled, don't you?"

From the way Dara's expression darkened, John thought he was going to launch another tirade, this time aimed at his sister, but Dara only bit his lip and stood silent. Or almost silent. The emperor was breathing deeply.

After a moment, he simply nodded once, firmly. The emperor Dara Shikoh looked to his diwan. "Coordinate with my sister. See it done."

"Your will, Sultan Al'Azam!"

Well, that's one way to avoid giving a report full of bad news, anyway . . .

Approaches to the Taj Majal

It was raining, though it was dry enough beneath the awning carried by four of Dara's mounted harem guards. At least for those riding tall horses. Those on shorter mounts had to contend with wet legs. The rains had begun. Or, if some of the court astrologers were to be believed, the gods were weeping for the strife to come. From the pair of howdah-capped elephants standing to one side of the awning, Nur had not had to get her feet wet at all.

Atisheh emerged from the Taj's grounds, effortlessly

leaping to the back of her horse and beginning to canter back to Jahanara and the rest of her escort.

Aurangzeb's forces had purposely left a gap in their lines to allow her party to access Mother's tomb, but Atisheh could not be persuaded that scouting was an unnecessary waste of time. Still, she supposed, dealing with Atisheh's security concerns was another way to avoid obsessing over which of a half-dozen stratagems would work best to secure the ends desired, namely that she reveal less of their situation and plans than Nur and, if lucky, plant a seed or two of disagreement – and anger, hopefully—between Nur and Aurangzeb. She'd spent much of the night before seeking counsel from her advisors, Nadira, and even the up-timers. All of them had counseled caution, but Jahanara was willing to exploit any advantage Nur exposed. Indeed, she intended to ruffle more than a few of the courtly feathers Nur used to armor her intent and conceal her actions.

Atisheh, mounted on a fine horse, splashed her way back under cover and to Jahanara's side. "Everything is as agreed to, Begum Sahib. Her guards cover the other half of the garden. We are ready to take up positions opposite them on your command."

"Make it so," Jahanara said.

"Your will, Begum Sahib." Atisheh gestured with one hand. Those guards not carrying her awning rode ahead to take up positions along the perimeter of the garden.

"What, there are no assassins waiting under every bush for me?" Jahanara asked the question without thinking as they plodded along in the wake of her guards.

"No, Begum Sahib. At least, none that I could see." Atisheh's expression was stony, but Jahanara could see her grip on the reins tighten.

Jahanara felt shame color her cheeks. She had suffered no injury in the attack, her only loss that of Father; while Atisheh had been gravely wounded, lost numbers of both blood kin and warrior sisters, and been forced by her injuries to miss the funerals of her fellows.

"I apologize, Atisheh. You do your duty well, and do not deserve the brunt of my foul temper." The apology forced Jahanara to admit, at least to herself, that she was suffering more anxiety about the impending meeting than she'd allowed. Nur, with her towering reputation for manipulation, cast a vast shadow. A shadow made both darker and longer by the uncertainty shrouding her involvement in Father's assassination. Jahanara knew she lacked the breadth of experience that Nur had gained over a lifetime of politicking and could only hope that her experiences since Mother's death had given her the tools necessary to overcome.

"No apology is necessary, Begum Sahib." Atisheh waved at the clouds and rain. "These conditions are not good. And to be forced to talk of important matters of state with a woman who, if I can be forgiven for saying so, deserves nothing better than torture until she confesses."

Uncomfortable with the ease with which Atisheh would condemn Nur to torture, Jahanara opened her mouth to silence the warrior woman, but Atisheh cut her off.

"Almost, you lost a sister in the attack," Atisheh

said to the woman bearing the left front pole. "If Begum Sahib were to command it, would you not enjoy carving the flesh from the bones of those who ordered it? I know I would. For sacred honor, if not the blood of our kin."

"God forgive me, but I would do so without hesitation," the lithely muscular Armenian answered, crossing herself. Jahanara saw the woman's counterpart holding up the opposite corner of the awning nodding agreement.

A fresh wave of shame swept over Jahanara. She hadn't considered how deeply affronted her guards were by the continuing lack of certainty as to who was responsible for Shah Jahan's death. Not that she wasn't plagued with doubts herself, even knowing what she had learned from the torture of Mullah Mohan. And she could hardly admit, tacitly or otherwise, to the torture of a man of God, even amongst her closest guardians. Atisheh knew, of course. But, from her statements, Atisheh had no more believed Mohan's claims than Jahanara herself. In truth, it was easy to lay some portion of the blame for Father's assassination at Nur's feet, especially when she had so conveniently disappeared from Dara's court only to reappear in Aurangzeb's camp weeks later.

Instead of trying to suppress the feeling, Jahanara embraced it. Made it one more coal to feed the flames of her desire to reveal the truth of Nur's—and Aurangzeb's—involvement. Father deserved no less. The warrior women, father's nökör, and the eunuch harem guards who died protecting the family deserved no less.

I *deserve no less.*

Gardens of the Taj Mahal

Jahanara dismounted, transitioning from beneath the awning carried by her guards to the open-sided pavilion without getting wet. She took a moment to gather herself. It was important that certain things be accomplished in this meeting, and her opponent was a fierce and dangerous foe.

Atisheh and the rest of her escort withdrew to another pavilion some distance away, leaving her alone with Nur. More alone than she'd been since that night in the Jasmine Tower—

Savagely, she pushed thoughts of Salim away. Now was not the time.

"Greetings, Jahanara," Nur said, voice pitched to not only carry through the constant patter of the rain striking the pavilion above their heads, but also convey a warmth Jahanara doubted her adversary actually felt.

"Greetings, Nur Jahan," Jahanara returned, crossing the carpets to meet her kinswoman among the pillows set out for them to sit upon.

"You are as lovely as ever, Begum Sahib," Nur said, inviting Jahanara to sit with one hennaed hand. The scent of roses, delicate and ephemeral, trailed Nur's gesture.

"And your beauty is ceaseless," Jahanara lied, accepting the seat. In truth, Nur appeared tired, drawn. Her eyes remained bright, however, and Jahanara would not put it past Nur to pretend exhaustion in order to cause an opponent to underestimate her. Certainly the smooth grace Nur exhibited as she took her seat argued against severe fatigue.

Nur offered refreshment, which Jahanara politely refused. There followed a rapid exchange of news regarding the health of the royal family. Jahanara could not discern any interest in news of Roshanara beyond that expressed for Murad or Gauharara. News that Aurangzeb was healthy, in good spirits, and recently married was neither surprising nor pleasing.

The preliminaries concluded, Jahanara decided to come directly to the point: "I am here and ready to represent Dara in these talks, though it was not made clear to us what Aurangzeb hopes to accomplish with them."

Nur smiled. "Good. God willing, we shall show these men a path to peace."

Jahanara returned her own smile, though she put a blade in it. "That path finds an easy end. Aurangzeb need only relinquish his claim to the Peacock Throne."

Nur cocked her head, seemingly unfazed by either Jahanara's hard-edged smile or blunt words.

Silence descended. Jahanara refused to break it. She had learned that much.

"You know he cannot do that. He—"

"Do I?" Jahanara interrupted, deciding it was time to show some of the anger seething in her heart. "Do I know he cannot turn from this course of insurrection, betrayal, and blood that he has chosen?"

Nur did not so much as blink as Jahanara flung words at her. "I am not here to discuss the choices already made by those we have agreed to represent, but to reach agreement regarding the future for you and the rest of the siblings not directly involved in this conflict."

"And we are to trust you, and him?"

Nur's eyes narrowed. "You question whether I will bargain in good faith on behalf of Aurangzeb?"

Carefully directing and controlling her anger, Jahanara said, "No. While I have many questions I would ask of you, that is not one. I know you will represent Aurangzeb to the best of your considerable ability. At least until he does something you do not approve of."

Nur's smile lit the gray afternoon. "What would you ask, then?"

"Why did you goad Mullah Mohan into killing Father?" Jahanara asked, hoping to wipe the smile from the older woman's face.

It worked: Nur's mask, usually so perfectly controlled in every detail, slipped. "I did no such thing. That creature had his own hates, and acted on them independent of all reason, let alone any influence from me."

"Yet you admit to knowing him well enough to be intimate with his state of mind? Interesting," Jahanara said, hoping to capitalize on her apparent advantage.

"He supported Aurangzeb." Jahanara watched as Nur reasserted her habitual control of her expression, though she noted the older woman's eyes glittered fiercely. "I supported Aurangzeb, as I supported all my brother's grandchildren. It was Aurangzeb who brought us together in order to coordinate the recruitment of his forces for Shah Jahan's invasion of the Deccan. I could not deny a request from such a one."

"I see. I do not recall the court being made aware that you had decided upon a career as a recruiter of sowar."

Nur smiled again. "I have ever sought to serve the crown."

"Ever? Really? I do believe my brothers can do without service such as you rendered the crown whilst you attempted to place Shariyar ahead of Father on the throne."

Nur's smile remained in place as she spread her hands. "You do not spend much time looking in the mirror, do you?"

"I reflect upon my actions always, Nur."

"And the difference between what you do and I have done is?" Nur asked, cocking her head a little.

Jahanara could have slapped her. "I am helping him to fill the role Father envisioned for him from the moment Dara first drew breath to Father's last."

"And Shariyar was not chosen by *my* husband before his unfortunate death? I was there, child."

"I am no child."

A twitch of silk-covered shoulders. "Perhaps not, but then, I have found that only children feel the need to declare that they are not children."

Jahanara marveled at Nur's skill even as she reveled in letting her righteous anger show. "Yes, and Father let you back into public life, and the way you chose to repay him was to allow his murder."

"Allow?" Nur asked, reproachfully. "You give me too much credit. I had no control over the actions of either Mullah Mohan or your father. How, then, should I be named responsible for the fate of either, child?"

"Save your condescension for one who must suffer it. I am Begum Sahib, Jahanara Begum, Shehzadi and first born of Shah Jahan and Mumtaz Mahal. I am your equal in every way that matters."

"Are you? Better that Nadira had been given the task of treating with me. She, at least, is a mother.

She, at least, would know the stakes for which we contend and not blithely assume the false superiority you cling to."

Jahanara laughed. "Nadira, more wise than either of us, said you would attack me not only on that front, but using those exact words. I will be sure to let her know exactly how prophetic her predictions of your behavior proved."

"These attacks resolve nothing," Nur snapped.

Suspicious of a trap, Jahanara did not immediately capitalize on her opponent's loss of control.

Nur took a steadying breath but Jahanara found her tongue before she could reply: "But they're providing such sport, Nur. It is a rare treat, this exchange of words with the woman all the world knows had a hand in Father's death. I shall be certain to record this day's conversation in my diary."

Nur's control slipped further, as evidenced by the flaring of gold-studded nostrils.

Jahanara watched, that part of her not reveling in the accomplishment worried the older woman would lash out at her with something other than words.

Much to her surprise, Nur did not attempt to strike back with either words or actions, merely repeated her earlier claims in a soft voice. "I had nothing to do with the death of your father. I was, like him, a target of Mullah Mohan's assassins."

"So you keep saying. As if repetition would make your story any more believable."

"I say it because it is the truth." Nur looked down, then muttered, "But I can see it is no use trying to convince you of it."

"I'm sorry," Jahanara said with the honey-and-vinegar

tone of a harem instructor correcting a wayward student, "I couldn't understand your words just now. Please enunciate."

"Perhaps we should get on with the business we are sent here to conduct?" Nur grated.

Certain she had her opponent off balance and at a disadvantage, Jahanara agreed.

As Nur began laying out Aurangzeb's position, Jahanara let her thoughts wander, knowing Aurangzeb was exceedingly unlikely to authorize the offer of any substantial concessions, not when he seemed so close to victory. He had offered this meeting more out of concern that he be observed by everyone to have kept the forms rather than any sincere desire to come to terms with Dara or his supporters.

Still, Jahanara must remain alert to some advantage she may yet squeeze from these talks.

Please God, let Salim strike true, and soon.

Chapter 36

Agra
Red Tent, Aurangzeb's camp

Aurangzeb set aside the golden chalice of julabmost he'd been drinking from and reread the report he'd been looking at but failing to comprehend for the last hour. The report was not so complex it defied comprehension, it was simply that he was impatient for Nur's return to camp. He'd watched from the shelter of his tent as Jahanara rode to meet his chosen representative, but had retired before he gave the men the impression he was overly concerned with the outcome. The last thing those under his command wanted was a negotiated disposition that prevented them pillaging Agra. Not that he expected Dara to agree to any of the terms Aurangzeb was offering—but God was known to work in mysterious ways.

He blinked. He'd reached the bottom of the page yet again without actually absorbing the information contained in the report.

The messenger entered and placed a fresh packet on the table set aside for Aurangzeb's correspondence.

I'm going to need a small army of highly qualified munshi soon. It's one thing to command an army with but my own skills at administration, quite another to rule the empire.

He stood and paced over to the table. Rifling through the latest messages, one caught his eye. Snatching it up, he returned to his seat. A few moments later he had decoded the message within. He had no trouble focusing on its contents. This time he checked his cyphering as well as rereading the message, wanting to be certain he hadn't read only what he wanted to learn from the message instead of picking up what he wanted to hear.

A slow smile spread beneath his thin, almost-adolescent beard. Roshanara's report confirmed, from inside the harem, that Salim's banishment did not appear to be a ruse. Even the up-timers were upset with Dara over the exile of their patron. And they were not the only ones. His sister reported that all the court seemed to have lost heart with his departure. Jahanara had also lost reputation in the exchange, Dara blaming her for some transgression that Roshanara took some glee in reporting, as it was reportedly sexual in nature.

Thoughts racing, Aurangzeb sat back.

Briefly, he considered dispatching a messenger to Nur with this new information. News that Dara's court was in such disarray might prove useful, but the fact that certain members of the court intended to capitulate meant nothing when Jahanara was negotiating in their presence. No, jogging Nur's elbow at this late hour would do nothing to benefit his cause.

Was it an opportunity, though?

Perhaps some demonstration before the walls of Red Fort was called for? Some final plea for Dara to surrender? Those umara of questionable loyalty serving Dara might be convinced to betray the pretender if he could find the right words to sway them. But shouting at the walls did not seem the proper way to convey the necessary image of unassailable power and gravitas so essential to his image as a better, more mature ruler than his elder brothers.

No, the value of any piece of information was based not only on the facts, but timing as well. Roshanara's message had come too late for maximum value. The best Aurangzeb could do with the information now was plan for the defense to collapse rapidly if and when his own army appeared to be so overwhelming, and in such a position that any assault would surely doom the defenders. As any collapse of the defense was already predicated on such shows of force, the intelligence hardly affected the plan.

That need in mind, Aurangzeb turned his attention to considering the disposition of forces at his command. The first assault would be given every chance of succeeding, if only to spare the lives of his followers.

Carvalho was still shepherding the heaviest of the artillery train's guns a few days to the south, the rains having made progress hellishly difficult. Even after he arrived the guns would take nearly a week to work into positions where they could even start to reduce the walls, a process which would take weeks he did not have. No, they would make do with the lighter pieces to support the assault.

Unfortunately, there were fewer contingents of

infantry among his followers than he'd like. The Rajputs were the best of his heavy foot, if a bit oblivious to tactics more complicated than charging directly at the foe.

Most sowar did not generally approve of being told to dismount and fight on foot. And they were even less inclined to assault fixed defenses when dismounted. That said, the prospect of loot and glory would make no few sowar serviceable infantry just as they had on the many sieges and assaults of the campaign to conquer the Deccan.

Their horse-bows were almost as problematic. Composite weapons did not suffer damp conditions well, and some would certainly delaminate in the coming weeks—the obvious solution to that particular problem being a rapid conclusion to the siege.

He had less than a thousand musket-armed men under his command, and most of them were scattered amongst the retinues of his umara. Some were sowar but most were infantry of uncertain quality drawn from the various zamindar he'd affirmed in their estates. And here again the wet would prove a detriment to their effectiveness. Damp matchlocks were prone to misfire and failure. But then the defenders would have similar problems.

He ruled elephants out right away. They were too big, too slow, and too prone to mayhem when injured. And they *would* be injured—the defenses of Red Fort had been specifically designed to counter any attack on the gates by pachyderms. And any elephant slain at a gate would slow or even prevent the passage of successive waves of attackers, an unacceptable risk.

The camel corps, on the other hand, might prove

useful. Deployed to shoot over the heads of the infantry as they made their way to the walls, the zamburakchi should serve to keep the heads of the defenders down along one wall. He made a note to include them.

His supply situation was, if not comfortable, acceptable. So much so that he had already considered ridding himself of the troublesome priest, but it was a poor general who thought current circumstances would continue without regard to the efforts of his opponent. Already the fodder coming north was at risk of deteriorating in the wet conditions that would prevail for the next few months. So long as the priest did not repeat his public stupidity, Aurangzeb would continue to accept European assistance and, eventually, have to honor his debt to them.

A night attack? No. On balance, in the unlikely event Dara proved so incompetent a general that he failed to plan for a night attack, the surprise won by such a move was outweighed by the difficulty of getting troops where they needed to be in order to follow up and exploit any advantage gained from that initial surprise.

Between the Taj Mahal and Aurangzeb's camp

Nur seethed in silence as she was helped into the howdah for the ride back to Aurangzeb and the Red Tent.

Taking her seat among the pillows and silks, she frowned down at what looked like blood soaking the hem of her sari. The sight made her heart race, casting her mind back to the desperate days following the death of Jahangir and the battle she'd commanded from the back of an elephant no less mighty than the one that bore her now. The howdah she'd ridden in on that day had been far less decorative though no less heavy, weighted as it had been with two of Jahangir's favorite harem guards in addition to Gargi and herself. With bow and blade, the three of them—Gargi had been untrained at arms—had fought across the river and into her betrayer's camp. Faithful, deadly, scarred Nadia had bled to death on the floor of that howdah, an arrow through her neck. It had been her blood that soaked Nur's clothing that fateful day, the battle when she'd lost all control and power over her future.

Blinking, Nur struggled to control the sudden, sharp surge of revulsion she felt and think clearly.

Looking closer, she grunted in disgust and tossed the hem back at her feet. The stain was not blood, but some of the paint her mahout had used to decorate the vast bulk of Bheem with great whorls of red and gold to match his livery. The rain must have fouled the art to such a degree the paint had begun to run and, as she was lifted into the howdah, her sari must have trailed along the beast's flank, soaking up the paint.

One crisis of misapprehension dealt with, at least for the moment, Nur felt the hooded cobra of her anger rise again. Allowing herself to be bested by that stripling of a girl with all the advantages she'd had going into the meeting? Folly!

The sole consolation she drew from the outcome was that it was only the two of them who witnessed her failure to control the course of the conversation. That, and, she admitted after a moment's reflection, the fact that neither party had truly been there to negotiate in good faith.

She couldn't even blame Jahanara for her lapse. In fact, Aurangzeb's eldest sibling had impressed Nur with her skill and nerve. No, Nur was angry with herself for having lost control, for having responded to the verbal goads and barbed tongue of the young princess, however skillfully employed. She should have allowed for each of the gambits Jahanara used, prepared counterattacks and traps to capture her prey. Instead she had barely set foot on the playing board before being slapped down, forced onto the back foot for the rest of the meeting. That their efforts were doomed to failure made no difference. Those they represented had set the price too high for their offerings, and no one wanted to pay again for goods they believed already owed. Nur could scarce remember the last time she'd been bested so handily.

A flash of memory: Gargi advising her to avoid mentioning certain matters to Mumtaz, and Nur, so certain of her course and power, ignoring her servant's caution only to regret it later. A fresh wave of loss and regret washed over her. Had Gargi been here to help her prepare, things might have been different. Then again, Nur was forced to admit to making an occasional habit of ignoring sound advice during her long career at the pinnacle of Mughal politics.

Shaking off thoughts of what could never be again, Nur began to plan how best to make her report to Aurangzeb.

One thing Nur had gleaned from the experience: Dara—or at least Jahanara—blamed Nur and Aurangzeb for Shah Jahan's death. Jahanara would not be shifted from certainty on that one point, despite Nur's efforts to convince her otherwise. While she admitted to some fault for the creature's anger, Nur had not directed Mullah Mohan to act against Shah Jahan. As far as she knew, that had been purely motivated by the Mohan's fanaticism. A fanaticism that had, as such religious fervor often did, driven the man to respond violently to the perceived threat to his religion posed by Shah Jahan's lifting of the *jizya*. Nur had maneuvered Mullah Mohan into attacking the Englishman as they departed under Shah Jahan's protection, true, but when Mullah Mohan had struck back at her by having Gargi murdered in Agra, Nur had possessed neither the means nor the inclination to treat with the fanatic. Indeed, she'd feared Aurangzeb would punish her for interfering with his supporters.

Nur ground her teeth in frustration, the pressing need to focus on casting her report in the best light possible warring with a strong desire to wallow in dark memories and attempts to justify her loss of control. Perhaps it was her long exile from the halls of power that had rendered her so sentimental, so vulnerable.

She sighed.

Or perhaps it was just growing old that made her maudlin. Shah Jahan. Mumtaz. Jahangir. And now her brother Asaf, every single opponent, every foe she'd contested with—and learned from—in her quest for power over her own fate was now gone to dust.

Shah Jahan's children, just now coming into their own, would render her irrelevant if she let them.

Somehow she must find a path that would allow her to avoid such an ignoble destiny. Once already she had been cast into the shadows. She would not suffer it to happen again.

Two days south of Agra
Tent of Carvalho

Methwold started, nearly spilling his wine, when one of Carvalho's men shouldered his way into the tent.

The scarred veteran barely waited to be recognized before letting loose a rapid stream of Portuguese Methwold was hard-pressed to understand: "My captain! The priest is making a scene again. He ordered his tent to be taken down and sent his messenger boy to command an audience with the Sultan Al'Azam."

Carvalho glanced at Methwold, who shrugged helplessly. "Thank you, Fernando. We will see to it."

The gun captain nodded, turned, and left the tent almost as quickly as he'd entered.

"Jesus Christ, but that man's temper is an embarrassment to my people. I don't think I've ever met a more intemperate countryman in my life!"

Knowing precisely what the artillery captain meant with his outburst, Methwold did not think it politic to mention that De Jesus was not likely to share any of the Jewish blood flowing through Carvalho's New Christian veins. Besides liking Carvalho a great deal more than the priest, it simply would not do to offend the man who'd seen them safely to this point.

"I wonder what set him off this time?" Methwold wondered, drinking more of the wine he'd barely saved from spilling.

"Most likely fresh news and orders from the Estado."

Methwold bit back his own urge to blaspheme. Despite repeated attempts to get De Jesus or the messengers employed by the Portuguese to wait until he or Carvalho were present to hear firsthand the news from Goa, the priest continued to receive and read orders from his superiors in Goa privately. Methwold understood why the priest's superiors might want him to receive such orders and news alone, but as their ally and compatriot in this endeavor he resented being saddled with an intemperate priest they were forever winding up with their unreasonable demands.

So much so he'd been driven to report De Jesus' various imprecations and errors to the viceroy in no uncertain terms. Methwold discarded the unlikely possibility that De Jesus' current fit of temper was a result of learning of his report, as the viceroy's response had been rather terse. Only very slightly paraphrased, it left the message quite clear: *Deal with it, Englishman.*

Carvalho finished his own glass and set it down on the silver camp table with an air of resigned finality. Taking his cue from his host, Methwold did the same.

He held out a hand across the open space between them and, when the heavier mercenary took it, they levered one another up to stand facing each other.

Methwold stepped back and retrieved his sword belt from one of the tent poles. Carvalho snapped his fingers, the sound summoning a slave from the back of the tent, a pale puce over-robe held at arm's length for his master. Freshwater pearls glistened in the subdued light as the slave dressed his master. A gift from Aurangzeb, the robe of honor was worth a good deal more than Methwold's annual salary from the English Company. Intricately carved ivory toggles inlaid with silver wire closed the garment over Carvalho's wide chest. Impatient, Carvalho waved the slave away and finished closing the robe himself.

"Let's see what set him off this time, shall we?" he said, picking up his own baldric and blade.

Methwold nodded and, with the last wistful look at his empty glass, led the way from the tent.

The sky above the camp was overcast, the air hot, and humid, and it was very soon to rain if the ache in his joints was any indication. Still, the contrast between the shaded darkness they'd come from and the afternoon light was enough to make Methwold first squint and then sneeze.

"Health!" Carvalho said in his native Portuguese, already striding toward the tent being disassembled some thirty yards away.

Methwold set out after him. Already beginning to feel the heat, the Englishman spared a thought for the sweating slaves and servants toiling to set up the tent only to have the priest command they take it down scarcely an hour later.

A red-faced and sweating De Jesus appeared from behind a pair of horses.

"Father De Jesus, what has you out in this heat?" Carvalho said pleasantly, neither voice nor expression betraying the angry frustration he'd displayed just moments before. "The guns will move no farther today, much as I wish they would."

De Jesus looked at the approaching pair and visibly steeled himself for a confrontation.

"What news, Father?" Methwold added, hoping to discover what had the priest so agitated.

"I am required to meet with Aurangzeb and secure the promised rewards pledged to my superiors," the priest said as the pair stopped before him.

"What—*now*?" Carvalho asked, incredulous.

De Jesus' eyes narrowed. "Immediately, yes."

Beside him Carvalho had gone very still, only the faint rattling of pearls betraying his unease.

"May we see these orders?" Methwold asked.

"Certainly." The priest recovered a packet from his horse and handed it over, saying, "I have already sent a messenger to Agra, so please do not attempt to dissuade me from seeking redress for the complaints. My superiors insist upon them."

"Please tell me you did not *demand* an audience with Aurangzeb," Carvalho said.

The obstinate priest lifted his chin. "I did. Moreover, I did it at the express command of the archbishop himself."

"One does not *demand* anything of a Mughal emperor, least of all when the only outcome for your demand is to waste more of the man's time whilst he prepares for the battle he must win in order to secure that which he promised us in the first place!" Carvalho's even, reasonable tone was replaced by an ever-increasing volume and anger as he delivered his opinion of De Jesus' actions.

"Perhaps it is not too late to—" Methwold began.

De Jesus cut him off. "I will not allow you to countermand the orders of the archbishop."

"Be reasonable, Father."

"I believe the same was said to the Lord our Savior before he entered the temple and cast down the moneylenders for their perfidy. I can do no less than follow his example."

"Jesus Christ!" Carvalho grated. Hands balled into fists, Carvalho looked down at his own robes and then back up at the priest, shaking his head as if the desperate need to knock the man flat warred with the instinct to preserve his rich, courtly dress.

Methwold considered putting a restraining hand on his friend's arm but decided he wanted the priest shut up more than he cared for the already-frayed alliance between them. If Aurangzeb thought Carvalho and Methwold involved in these demands, they were at risk of being punished along with the priest. Then again, Carvalho was at least protected by the fact that his guns and crews were necessary to Aurangzeb's plans. An English merchant named Methwold was most definitely not.

"Blaspheme as much as you want, but I will not do other than I have!"

Carvalho's punch was, to Methwold's experienced brawler's eye, nearly perfect in its execution. It certainly lifted the thin priest from his feet. De Jesus was unconscious before he hit the ground.

Chapter 37

The Western Ghats

Salim quieted his horse and returned his gaze to the outcropping above, only to see the lookouts signaling.

He raised the sword Jahanara had given him. A curving length of beautifully worked wootz steel, the sword was the finest he'd ever held, much like the woman who'd given it to him. The responsiveness of the blade to his hand made him feel powerful, strong, much like he had felt holding Jahanara in the circle of his arms.

Blinking away thoughts of Jahanara was more difficult than it should have been in these circumstances. The caravan below was almost perfectly positioned for the ambush he was about to unleash. Just a little while longer and he would lead his five hundred men out of the box canyon and down the alluvial fan spreading across the valley floor into the enemy.

The midday sun reflected from a lance point rising above the saddle of earth separating the two canyons. Slowly the lance tip climbed, its wielder coming up the rise.

All that remained was timing...

The hand holding the lance appeared just as the turbaned helmet of the owner crested the rise.

The caravan's individual guards might be competent, but their leadership left something to be desired. Unfamiliar with the territory they were passing through, the Europeans in charge of the caravan would not pay the bribes to the local tribesmen necessary for accurate information about bandit activity in the area. At least, that's what Salim had been told when *he* had offered such bribes.

Lacking such paid informants, the guards had to scout each pass and valley before the caravan passed by. The commander of the guards had sent pairs of his men to check the higher valleys, thinning their numbers and tiring their horses. It was a time-consuming enterprise, making sure each notch in the hills did not contain enemies ready to sweep down and attack their patron. Just such a pair of ill-fated guards were making their way to the mouth of the canyon where the force under Salim's direct command was hiding.

Salim leaned forward in the saddle, dropping his sword level with the shoulder as his mount leapt forward.

Iqtadar and Mohammed charged after him up the few gaz of slope that concealed them from the lower valley, followed by the rest of his sowar.

The pair of riders wore matching expressions of astonishment as Salim and his men topped the rise and rode down upon them, an avalanche of silk, steel, and flesh.

Mere heartbeats later Salim struck at the exposed thigh of the right-hand guard, desperately struggling to turn his mount. Riding past, he felt the blade catch and slide as dirty cotton and the flesh beneath parted at the merest touch of the curved edge of his sword.

Knowing the wound was, if not fatal, likely to spill the man from the saddle and under the hooves of his sowar, Salim paid him no further attention.

The caravan, stretched out over the better part of two kos, had yet to react to their sudden appearance. That would not last. But every moment that passed without a reaction from the caravan counted in their favor, allowing Salim's force to get that much closer. He bent over the braided mane of his horse and urged the sturdy gelding to greater speed.

It appeared the commander of the escort knew his business, when, scarcely a few breaths after the attackers hove into view, he began shouting at his remaining riders to join him in an effort to delay the riders descending upon them. Of course, commanding a response and getting it were two different things. Most of the caravan guards, shocked into panic by the sudden appearance of riders hell-bent on mayhem, failed to answer the command of their leader.

Those who did were too little, too late. The horse archers among Salim's sowar loosed. Arrows fell amongst those men who kept their wits and were organizing to meet Salim's charge. Horses screamed and blood flowed, the wounded men and mounts adding to the confusion among the foe.

Salim found himself shouting wordless excitement over the pounding of horses' hooves. Not long now. He raised his sword just as another flight of arrows sank home. More screaming. More blood. One horseman, felled by an arrow, panicked his horse, which fled at a gallop. Other horses, seeing the example set, thought better of standing around waiting to get bit by the deadly rain falling from the sky. Ignoring the shouts, spurs, and whips of their riders, many of the remaining horses bolted.

Howling, Salim and his men rode among those who managed to retain mastery over their mounts, carving them from saddles and this life.

Dragging his sword across the face of one man, Salim shifted his seat and leaned over in the saddle to avoid the desperate stab of a spear from some enterprising footman. Looking about, he realized his headlong charge had carried him past the last bit of organized defense and among the caravan proper.

A touch of the reins and his horse wheeled right. Seeing no threats, Salim stood in the stirrups to check the progress of the rest of the skirmish.

Sunil's men had emerged from the canyon on the far side of the valley and were hastening to cut off any retreat for those fleeing the caravan's fate.

Mohammed and the horse archers were riding parallel to the caravan, loosing arrows at anyone still bearing arms. Dead guards spotted the ground in their wake, each sprouting arrow shafts like obscene flowers.

Salim again flicked the reins, turning back to face where he'd penetrated the defender's lines. The other men who had followed them into the melee had routed the remaining opposition and were starting to celebrate with shouts and ululating war cries.

"Take it!" Salim shouted, waving his blood-edged sword at the carts, wagons, and pack animals of the caravan. "Take it all!"

The bellowing of livestock and frightened cries of

their drovers did nothing to stop the looting, though Salim did manage to restrain most of his men from needless killing.

Three things helped maintain discipline in this regard: firstly, it helped that none of his men felt any particular anger towards these people, who had been, after all, easily overcome. Secondly, who would carry all their loot if the drovers were put to the sword? Thirdly, Salim and their horses could hardly eat all of the food and fodder captured in the raid and no man Salim chose to ride with would wantonly destroy food and fodder when so many of them had grown up knowing the belly-gnawing pain of hunger and the ever-present specter of famine.

He was meeting with his subordinates to count the losses and gains when one of the scouts he had set to watching their back trail rode in on a foam-flecked horse.

The rider, a painfully slim youth in a sweat-soaked robe, brought his blown horse to a staggering halt directly in front of Salim.

"Amir, a war band!" the youngster gasped. "They came out of the hills. We killed a few of their fastest riders but there are at least several hundred, perhaps more. I could not stay to watch."

"How long until their main force arrives?" Salim asked, thinking to order his men into their earlier ambush positions.

"An hour before dusk, I think," the scout answered, sliding from his horse and pouring water into his hand.

Not enough time to clean up the signs of their attack and reset the ambush, then.

Unaware of his commander's thoughts, the boy

continued speaking: "My brother and uncle should give us warning. They sent me on ahead, as I am the lightest."

Salim and Iqtadar shared a look. There would be no more warnings. The scout's kinsmen had sacrificed themselves to ensure word reached the main force.

"Any idea who they are?" Salim asked, not ready to reveal to the young man his suspicions.

"I think my uncle..." The boy swallowed tears, some inkling of what his kin had sacrificed for him dawning in his brown eyes. "I think Uncle said something... some curse about Bhonsle dogs."

The big Gujarati, Sunil, spat. "Maratha are bad enough, but the Bhonsle clan are a plague on trade in these hills."

"But which emperor do they fight for?" Salim asked.

The Gujarati laughed. "Last I heard, Shahaji was taking Aurangzeb's coin, but the Maratha are ever faithless and fickle. Indeed, I imagine some of the coin you spent on informers made certain that word of our presence found its way to their ears."

Thinking the Gujarati's assessment of the character of the Maratha was quite similar to most of settled India's opinion of Afghans, Salim considered the lay of the land between himself and the Maratha force. On any other ground he would be confident of victory between his sowar and any smaller force, but here, on ground they knew intimately and he did not, he could not be sure of the exact size of the force he would face in a battle.

"Amir, I don't relish the idea of blundering around in the dark with this great herd of idiots among us," Mohammed said, waving at the beasts of burden only just being forced into some semblance of order.

"Nor do I," Salim agreed. "And there's no telling whether or not they have another group of riders to our west. Damn."

"Parlay?" Iqtadar suggested.

"At the very least it would allow us some time to prepare..." Salim mused.

"And perhaps scout a line of retreat?" Mohammed said.

"Both," Salim said decisively. "Start sending the caravan west ahead of us."

Mohammed shook his head. "We'll lose the lot of them if they're ambushed."

"Send some of your best herdsmen with them. At the first sign of an attack have them stampede the oxen and buffalo. We might get lucky and the livestock will kill a few of them."

"And," Iqtadar said with a wolfish grin, "it will certainly distract them, having all that loot charging by."

Salim nodded, matching his cousin's expression.

Sunil was not smiling. In fact, from his aggrieved expression, Salim could almost believe they'd been discussing giving the Gujarati's firstborn son to the enemy.

"What is it, Sunil?"

"I had a thought, Amir."

"Oh?" Salim prompted.

"I merely reflect upon a truism spoken of among my people..."

"Oh?" Salim asked, impatience making an order of the question.

"You can take the hillman out of the hills," the lowlander said, crooked teeth showing in a smile, "but you just can't take the hills out of the hillman."

Western Ghats
East of the ambush site

The enemy chieftains met as the sun was rising, just as they'd agreed to the night before.

Three men led by a fellow in a jeweled robe rode into the valley from the east while three more, one on a horse with an obvious hitch in its step, rode in from the west. The two groups met on the slope above Salim's camp and spoke at length before descending to the agreed-upon site for the parley. And, it seemed to Salim's tired mind, they had spoken angrily as well.

Two of the men who'd come from the west were scowling, including the one riding the injured horse. That man winced as they dismounted, favoring his left leg. One of the other men he'd come up the pass with looked as if he'd been knocked on his side in the dust.

Salim hid contentment. The stampede that cost them the lion's share of the caravan loot had not been a waste, then. His men had reported success in causing it, but were forced to retreat without observing the results.

Bread and salt were eaten by all present, allowing everyone to relax, if only slightly. Rites of peacekeeping were not universally observed, but most warriors respected them.

With his counterparts so angry, Salim was just as glad to be meeting them under truce. His scouts had reported not just one force surrounding him, but five, each numbering hundreds of men. He could certainly overcome them in a straight fight, but war was only a straight fight when both sides were either idiots, had erred enormously, or both. Besides, he could not afford to lose any men, and he would lose a great many, especially if the Maratha chose to do to him what he was trying to do to Aurangzeb, and taxed his supplies by conducting lightning raids on his forces. Granted, Salim had very little in the way of supply train, but he could not afford to lose his remounts, not if he wished to travel fast himself.

"You wished to speak to me?" the Maratha chieftain asked in Marathi, eyeing the Afghan warily.

Thanking God for a youth spent guarding caravans and learning tongues, Salim answered in the same language. "Assuming you command those who seek to block our way, indeed I do." He studied the richly dressed man in turn. From the scars seaming his jaw and crossing the backs of his hands, this man was no stranger to fighting, however richly he chose to dress.

"I command here."

One of the men to the man's right, the one with the injured leg, allowed his frown to deepen.

Something I said? Salim wondered. *No, something he said.*

"Regarding what matters?" the man said, either ignoring or unaware of his companion's deepening anger.

Salim paused, considering. No, he'd bet a lakh of rupees the finely dressed fellow was perfectly aware of the other man's rising ire.

Deciding to see where it led, he extended the preliminaries in hopes of capitalizing on some outburst from the anger in the air. "I have been remiss, it seems. Forgive me. I am the Amir Salim Gadh Yilmaz and I lead these men..." Salim said, watching the faces of their counterparts as he introduced each of his men.

"I am Shahaji Bhosale, and I command here in Aurangzeb's name."

The lip of the man to Shahaji's right curled in a silent snarl as his head whipped around to the younger, better dressed man.

Affecting disinterest, Shahaji continued, "You are here on the pretender Dara's orders?"

"All the world knows I am not!" Salim said, forcing a laugh. His men joined their laughter to his, lending credence to the falsehood.

Shahaji's brother chieftains all looked to Shahaji, who cocked his head as a mongoose does upon spying a cobra.

"I do believe you lie, Amir."

As his own men tensed, Salim leaned back and laughed once more. He smiled at Shahaji once again, and, edging his voice with careless disinterest, said, "Fascinating as that may be to you and"—he waved dismissively at the other chieftains—"Aurangzeb's other lackeys, I don't give a fig for your thoughts on my honesty."

"We are not his—" The injured man's angry words were cut off as Shahaji's dagger appeared at his throat.

"Hold," Salim barked at his own men, not wanting any blame to be leveled at his own people for the blood he hoped was about to be shed.

"You agreed, Koyaji, to me speaking on behalf of the people," Shahaji said, once certain there would be no interruptions from Salim or his men.

"I did, but only after you assured us *he* was here to suppress the people on Dara's behalf."

Salim was impressed by the chieftain's nerve, doubting his own ability to say anything with such clarity with a blade pricking his Adam's apple. Two of the other Maratha chieftains grumbled agreement, while the others maintained a facade of indifference.

The neutrals were either better at schooling their expressions or were genuinely unconcerned that Shahaji might kill Koyaji, it was hard to tell.

"No free Maratha here agreed to serve Aurangzeb! Just because you and your band of th—" Again Koyaji's tirade was stopped by another movement of Shahaji's blade. This time the richly dressed man laid the blade along his companion's cheek, point resting on the soft flesh just beneath the eye.

Salim, grateful that his men obeyed him better than Shahaji's brother chieftains, remained still.

The careful hunter bided his time, waiting for an opportunity to strike. If this squabbling was not some ruse, then his position was far stronger than he'd expected. The chieftains did not seem to care that he was watching, which could mean they were trying to deceive him for some reason, but Salim couldn't figure out what advantage they might gain by it.

"Say what you will of me, Koyaji, but you know better than to insult my men in my presence."

One of the impassive chieftains spoke: "My wife's cousin spoke out of turn, Shahaji. His injuries make him short of temper."

Shahaji turned his head to level a gimlet stare at the speaker without lifting his blade from Koyaji's face. Indeed, the blade did not betray so much as the tiniest tremble.

"And you think we should make allowances for his clumsiness?" Shahaji asked in honeyed tones.

The cheek not covered with the blade lifted in a snarl, but Koyaji made no other reply.

"He was injured playing his part in your plan, Shahaji," the other man said with a shrug.

"Had he not charged in, he would not have lost any men nor fallen from his horse."

"I don't have to explain my actions to the likes of you," Koyaji grated.

"Did someone ask you to explain, Koyaji? I think not. I know what you and your clansman think of me and mine. The fact remains that had you followed my commands you would not have been injured nor lost any men. You but reaped the whirlwind of your own greed. No, what you're really angry about is that while my people and I have prospered in service to Aurangzeb you have...well, *not*. Did you not lose one of your clan's redoubts to the Bhoite?" he asked with a glance at one of the other men who had yet to speak.

Salim would've thought it impossible for someone to look even more angry, but Koyaji managed the feat.

"You prattle about how Maratha do not serve," Shahaji continued, "and I tell you this: there is much to learn from our enemies. You complain about the gains the Bhonsle have made under my leadership, calling us lapdogs and worse, but only beyond our hearing."

The man's thin smile held nothing of humor as his voice rose in deadly serious tones. "And that is all right with us because, you see, while you spend your breath in idle complaints, we *act*. While you fight amongst yourselves for the scraps from one another's tables, we *conquer*. While you rush in foolishly, we *prepare*."

"I've been told olive oil can help with that," Salim said, having picked his moment with care.

"What?" Shahaji's expression was the very picture

of surprise as he turned to face Salim, unconsciously lifting the knife from Koyaji's face.

"Well, while I have no personal experience of such acts, I've heard that if you bend over and oil up, it's easier for your master to have his way with you."

"Dog!" Shahaji shouted as he bolted to his feet. Forgetting Koyaji entirely, he reached for his sword.

Salim rolled away, scrambling to his feet but keeping his hands well away from his weapons.

Koyaji, for his part, had certainly not forgotten Shahaji. The older chieftain, having risen to his feet, appeared to punch Shahaji several times in the back. So fast were the man's movements that it was only when Shahaji turned to face his attacker that Salim could see the blood staining the Maratha's back and realized Koyaji had a knife in his hand.

"Dog!" Shahaji repeated. The sword he'd thought to cut Salim down with rose and fell. Koyaji deflected it with the knife, drawing his own sword.

"Hold!" Salim shouted at his own men in Urdu, retreating a few steps from the combat with his arms up and spread wide in hopes of appearing nonthreatening enough to preserve the pretense of a truce.

The other Marathas scrambled back, forming a circle that gave the combatants room.

Salim could hear shouts from their respective camps, but it would be some time before anyone was able to get to them. Things between the rival chieftains would be concluded long before anyone was able to interfere.

Shahaji launched a series of slashes the older man deflected or dodged. The bladework of both men was commendable. All other things being equal, Salim would've picked Shahaji as the victor. Things were not equal, though—Koyaji had seen to that with his first blows.

The spreading stain of Shahaji's blood now soaked his robes to the hips, more than making up for any stiffness or bruises Koyaji suffered from his earlier mishap.

Koyaji feinted twice and struck at his opponent's exposed thigh.

Shahaji rolled his wrist and parried at the last instant, following through with a straight punch. Weighted with his sword pommel, Shahaji's fist crushed Koyaji's aquiline nose with a crunch audible some distance away.

Koyaji's head snapped back. He staggered, nearly losing his feet.

Instead of following up on his success Shahaji reached back with his off hand and felt at the wounds.

The older chieftain steadied, glared at Shahaji and snuffled through his broken nose.

"You've killed me," Shahaji said in disbelief, rubbing thumb and forefinger together in the blood wiped from his back.

"True Maratha do not serve any but the gods!" A gobbet of blood fell from the man's nose as if to punctuate his shout.

Shahaji lunged forward, sword a blur.

Once, twice, three times Koyaji parried the impossibly fast, desperate attacks of Shahaji. The fourth, though, crashed past the knife in Koyaji's left hand to bite deep into his side.

"We are," the older chieftain coughed blood, "free men . . ."

"Free to die," Shahaji said, spitting in Koyaji's face as his opponent slumped to earth.

A long moment later the victor stooped and wiped his sword on his opponent's corpse. With a grunt of effort he stood and turned to face Salim.

Salim returned a respectful nod.

Shahaji smiled bitterly. "Did not Veerabathira say I would die in the hills of my homeland, a victim of my own pride?" He sighed and started to sag. The chieftain who'd claimed kinship with Koyaji was first to the younger chieftain's side, putting an arm around his chest to keep him standing.

"Well played, Salim," Shahaji said, slurring as if drunk. "Well . . . played."

Salim did not reply. He was too busy searching the faces of the other men for signs they contemplated violence against him.

"Stabbed in the back . . . Dattaji, can you believe it?" Shahaji snorted weakly.

Easing Shahaji to the ground, the man called Dattaji spoke too quietly into Shahaji's ear for Salim to hear. The wounded man sighed and did not draw another breath.

Riders from both camps were, by now, approaching at the gallop.

Salim cleared his throat.

Dattaji looked at him, conflicting emotions warring openly across his face.

"I have kept the truce," Salim said, hands still as distant as he could keep them from his weapons.

Dattaji thought about that for the space of a few heartbeats. The earth was starting to tremble under their feet as hundreds of horsemen from both camps converged on them.

Salim was about to arm himself when Dattaji stood up with raised arms and shouted for his warriors to stop.

Relieved but aware he might have only postponed the battle, Salim turned and did the same to his own men. There were a few horses injured as his sowar complied with his sudden order to stop their charge, but no blood was shed and the truce stood unbroken.

Trying not to let wild hope cloud his judgment, Salim started thinking about how to turn the truce into something more substantial. The Maratha had no love for Aurangzeb—or any Mughal for that matter—so he would pursue his goals along that broad path.

Thanking God for the story Jahanara had spun to explain his departure from court, Salim considered how to best capitalize on the animosity he'd seen on display and any of the greed Sunil said claimed their hearts. That the supplies came from Portugal should help. The Europeans held less and less sway the farther one traveled from the sea, their only true protection being the Mughals. And, as long as the empire was at odds with itself, those who enjoyed its protection would be fair game.

It might—just might—even be possible to *enlist* them in raids on Aurangzeb's caravans coming north from Gwalior. Raiding and banditry were something of national pastimes for the Maratha, just as it was for his own people. Failing that, there was a far better chance he could buy these men off or otherwise convince them to stay out of his way than he would have originally believed.

He said a brief prayer to God, thanking Him for this chance.

Chapter 38

Red Fort
Diwan-i-Khas

Jahanara gathered herself as the last rolling beat of the drums announcing her presence settled into silence. She had spent the ride back to the fort in silent, furious thought. The rain had let up by the time she left the garden, giving way to a stunning sunset of burnt umber, ocher, orange, and gold she could not enjoy. Her thoughts were fully preoccupied with planning how best to give her report to Dara, with how to strike just the right notes, hit the exact tone necessary to bend and unify Dara's umara behind Dara. She must not only speak before all the court, but gather them to hand, thorns and all, in order to forge a strong sword and shield that Dara could wield against his brother. Thankfully, Nur had unintentionally given her the exact course Jahanara believed would best secure her ends.

"Well?" Dara asked the question without preamble, giving voice to the question that everyone present, from the lowest slave to the greatest umara would have answered.

Grateful for the jali that prevented the eyes of so many from staring at her, Jahanara took a deep breath of rain-washed evening air before responding, "It went as expected, Sultan Al'Azam. He requires your abdication and offers safe passage to Mecca and exile for both you and little Murad. He even presumes to offer a small stipend for your maintenance in Mecca."

Dara nodded, impassive. Jahanara was happy to see her brother in control of both his expression and, apparently, his faculties. She hoped it would continue. All the court were watching. Everyone needed reassurance that Sultan Al'Azam Dara Shikoh could lead them, would defend them, and would overcome his enemies.

"And you, sister?" Dara asked.

"Your sisters," Jahanara saw no harm in including the others, "are offered safety beyond his lines, even should we remain faithful to your cause."

"Even should you remain faithful?" he sounded incredulous. "Why should he offer such a thing?"

"It was claimed that our safety in the battle to come is of great importance to the pretender. Nur claimed that Aurangzeb was very concerned for his, and I quote, 'powerless sisters' who had been 'led astray' by 'honeyed words and the foolish promises of my elder brother.'" Jahanara allowed some of the scorn she felt to permeate her words, carefully avoiding mention of Nur's reminder of the cannonball that, when fired from a fortress Father was besieging, had nearly taken Mother's life when she was in labor. That incident occurred when the Red Tent was set at what was thought to be a safe distance from the battle, not the focus and target of it. That they were all in danger was certain. No need to add to the atmosphere of fear already creeping like a clinging mist among the umara.

"And after?" Dara asked. "What did he propose to do with you then, loyal sister?"

"The pretender Aurangzeb cannot possibly throw a tantrum strong enough to prevail against you, Sultan Al'Azam Dara Shikoh, so I hardly listened to his childish foolishness." Jahanara injected her voice with every bit of her mother's remembered disdain for the occasional childish tantrum of her sons.

Nadira, standing beside Jahanara, stifled a giggle with one hand. Several other women of the court were not so quick to control themselves, their laughter dispelling the fearful mood. *There is nothing like the laughter of their women to put steel back into the spines of men*, Mother had told her once.

Smidha, sitting in silence to her right, still managed to radiate intense approval.

The wider court beyond the jali began to stir.

Dara's masklike expression slipped, a tiny smile curling his lips.

Wait, brother. Let me finish setting the playing board for you.

"Aurangzeb's prattle only regained my interest when Nur mentioned your son."

Dara, instead of reacting negatively, cocked his head to one side as if listening to a diverting story instead of the proposed fate of his son. The gesture filled Jahanara's heart with the certainty she had chosen to support the right man.

"Just what did he say regarding my boy?" he drawled.

"Aurangzeb claimed that your son would be allowed to go into exile with you. When I questioned the veracity of that particular claim I was told Aurangzeb is so certain he shall have many strong sons that he need not be concerned whether they will be able to defend their own claims to the throne." She paused, judging her moment.

"Not yet, I told Nur," Jahanara said, deliberately pausing in her narrative.

"Not yet?" Dara repeated, his nonchalance slipping a bit.

"Nur asked precisely the same question, Sultan Al'Azam. I explained to her that unlike the Sultan Al'Azam Dara Shikoh, Aurangzeb has no sons. Furthermore, it is well known that, for whatever reason, he keeps no other women but our elderly aunt in his harem, who is quite past her childbearing years. How then, I asked, did she know he would father children, let alone the mythical multitude of strong sons Nur claimed?"

An openly giggling Nadira turned shocked eyes on Jahanara as the rest of the court chuckled, snorted, or laughed outright.

Letting a smile creep into her own voice, Jahanara continued, "I told him perhaps it was better to retire until such sons were born and fully grown before trying these walls, since Sultan Al'Azam Dara Shikoh and his faithful umara were warriors fully grown; with sons already honorably born—sons who are strong, healthy, and blessed to grow in the sheltering power and grace of Sultan Al'Azam Dara Shikoh's shadow."

The gathered court's amusement changed tone, becoming a feral delight in an insult well delivered.

Looking around, Jahanara could tell the subtext of her reporting the insult had not been lost on the wiser members of the court: Aurangzeb may have proven himself a general, but Dara rules, and had already guaranteed the future of the dynasty by presenting a son to the court. Such matters were important to those who took the long view. And, as Smidha had pointed out, the larger group of umara, lacking the wisdom and refinement of their betters, often enjoyed making sport of another's lack of virility.

Nadira reached out and took Jahanara's hand in hers, whispering, "I have something to tell them, Begum Sahib."

Dara's next question prevented Jahanara asking her sister-in-law what she was to say. "And Nur? Did she offer anything but false rationales for betraying us?"

"Regrettably, no," Jahanara said, holding up a finger of her free hand to delay Nadira. "She claims to have had no part in Father's assassination, insisting she had nothing to do with Mullah Mohan's plot. I can almost believe her on those points, but when she claims to have no idea why the mullah wanted him dead, I cease believing anything that flows from her mouth."

"So you'll stay with us, dear sister?"

"Of course! I would not miss your victory, not for all the jewels in your treasury nor all the silver and gold of the throne God placed beneath you." It could not hurt to remind the more mercenary of the court of the vast wealth Dara could dispense to his loyal supporters when he emerged victorious.

Dara smiled benevolently at his court. "It seems Aurangzeb has offered much that he does not have to those who would not have it. All present know my generosity, that I will reward each man for their part in the coming fight." He paused, scratching his beard as if in thought. "Indeed, I shall offer one lakh of rupees to the man who succeeds in killing the greatest number of my brother's sowar." Dara suddenly surged to his feet and drew his sword. "But warn your men, warn them well! I intend to personally kill so many of my brother's men as to make it possible to walk from the top of the wall to the ground upon the backs of his dead."

The Hall of Public Audience went mad with shouts and growled cries of "Da-Ra! Dar-Rah! DahRahhhhh!" until the shouts blended into one long, aggressive growl of barely suppressed passion.

Jahanara felt a fresh surge of hope that Dara might be well enough recovered to be the leader they all wanted, needed him to be.

Jahanara winced, hand suddenly squeezed so hard she thought the bones might bend. She looked at Nadira, found her weeping, the hand not crushing Jahanara's stuffed in her mouth to stifle great, racking sobs.

"Nadira, what is it?" Jahanara asked, pulling Nadira into a hug. Those closest to them converged to offer comfort as well.

Her sister-in-law took long moments to respond, and even then her strangled whisper was as much tortured sob as coherent statement. "God will take him from me, I know it . . ."

Shaken by the certainty in Nadira's voice, Jahanara still had the presence of mind to pull her into an embrace tight enough to stifle the other woman's words.

"I won't—*we* won't let that happen!" Jahanara whispered fiercely, willing Nadira to a silence she had no right to command and acceptance of the promise she had no true power to keep.

The Rose Court

"Where are you taking us, Bertram?" John asked, yawning. It had been a long day and he still wasn't done. With Salim gone he'd been made Dara's de facto adjutant, and he'd been making the rounds to all the different captains to reassure them all was right with the world, even when it wasn't.

"I don't know, precisely."

John looked sidelong at the down-timer. "What you mean you don't know? You asked us to come with you. I have things to do, Bertram."

"Look, John: I don't know exactly where we're headed, I only know my bit."

A heavyset eunuch shuffled out of the darkness carrying a lantern before John could reply to that bit of mystery. Gestured to silence, they were led through the perimeter of the harem.

John looked again at Bertram, but while the down-timer looked uncomfortable, his expression revealed nothing else.

Led down deserted halls John assumed must have been cleared expressly for them, he wished again they hadn't lost the powder factory. Not only would he have liked to have seen what the massed fire of Talawat's copies could have accomplished, watching Aurangzeb's army take position outside the walls made him certain they were going to need all the firepower they could get.

"Jesus," he muttered.

Bertram looked a question at him.

John shook his head and said quietly, in English, which he assumed the eunuch couldn't speak, "Just can't believe I'm in charge of some part of a battle, let alone a damn siege. Not only that, but one it sure as shit looks like we can't win."

"Take heart, John," Bertram said. He looked as if he was about to go on but the eunuch silenced them with a glance.

Looking around, John realized he didn't know this part of the fort. They'd gone down several flights of stairs and around so many corners he wasn't really sure where he was relative to his quarters.

He was about to ask the eunuch just what the hell was going on when he made out a light ahead of them. His feet slowed involuntarily as he realized that in the party around the light stood Atisheh, Monique, Gervais, and, on closer inspection, Jahanara as well.

"John Ennis, welcome," Jahanara said with a nod. Ilsa had described how beautiful the princess was, and even from the little John could see of her because of the veils, he could believe it. He'd never tell Ilsa, but he found Jahanara's voice sexy as hell too.

"Begum Sahib," John answered with a bow.

"I fear I must beg your forgiveness and forbearance for a few moments more. Not all of those summoned are present just yet."

Puzzled, John nodded. Questioning glances at Bertram and Gervais went unanswered. Monique, though, seemed both nervous and...triumphant?

Seeing as no answers were forthcoming from his companions, John checked out their surroundings. The hall was getting a little cramped, at least as cramped as any part of the palace he'd been to. Atisheh and one of the other guards John didn't know by name were standing beside a heavy ironbound door.

Another eunuch appeared out of the stairwell, closely followed by the imposing figure of Bidhi Chand, who appeared ready for an ambush. The former bandit was weird that way, always prepared to fight, but still conveying an air of relaxed confidence, even happiness, that John wished he could project.

John met the warrior's eyes and nodded. The set of Bidhi's shoulders relaxed fractionally. John hid a smile.

Not so relaxed he wasn't thinking he might be about to be betrayed to the enemy! But then, who wouldn't think that when summoned in the middle of the night?

John shook his head.

Jesus, I've been here so long I'm even starting to think like some kind of medieval warlord.

Beneath Red Fort

Jahanara did not fail to observe the exchange between Bidhi Chand and the up-timer. Upon consideration, it stood to reason the two might become friendly. John had, after all, been responsible for training Dara's forces in the weapons and tactics of the up-timers. Even after Talawat's factory exploded and took all hope of producing enough ammunition for the guns with it, Bidhi had quietly insisted John continue to train his Sikhs in the formations necessary to maximize the impact of the arquebus and muskets they did have at their disposal.

And now, she would reward his insistence. Rather, they would all reap the benefits of his stubborn refusal to give up on the idea that disciplined fire was preferable.

"I apologize for this late-night excursion, but I wanted to be certain that what I reveal here tonight comes as a surprise to Aurangzeb. I'm afraid I must also apologize for deceiving most of you as well. Some to such an extent that you will be justified in being quite angry with me. I hope you will forgive me, as I could see no way to avoid the necessity of lying and deceiving you."

She swallowed, surprised at the depth of emotion she felt in asking these disparate people to forgive her. Unwilling to watch their reactions, Jahanara turned and beckoned Atisheh to open the door. The warrior woman smiled and turned the key in the lock before shoving the heavy door open.

Jahanara made a final check to ensure there were no open flames among the party. Seeing none and gently chiding herself for the caution Atisheh had assured her was unnecessary among the new tools Talawat had made, Jahanara strode through the portal and into the chamber beyond.

The lantern Smidha held revealed only a portion of the contents of the room. Freestanding wooden racks positioned back-to-back two tiers high stood directly across from the entry and marched into the darkness, each tier loaded with twenty Damascus steel shotguns. Every weapon had a wide leather bandolier containing twenty shells hanging from where the barrels met the racks. Boxes stacked along the walls to either side of the door they'd entered through contained thousands more shells. In the darkness beyond the lantern light were forty more boxes, each containing copies of the special cannon shells copied from the two the USE ship, *Lønsom Vind*, had furnished.

Talawat's towering achievement was made all the more impressive by the fact that all this had been done in nearly complete secrecy. Setting up a manufactory in the abandoned city-fortress of Fatehpur Sikri had beggared her personal treasury, but the additional layer of secrecy between the project and the Imperial Civil Service had been well worth the investment.

At least, she prayed it would be, as she heard the collective gasp from her guests as they finished filing in behind her. If she had surprised them, then there was a very good chance the products of Talawat's manufactory would catch Aurangzeb and his men completely flat-footed.

A prideful little smile began to play about her lips.

"What the hell?" John blurted.

Smile dying, Jahanara turned to face him.

Jaw working, the up-timer leveled a stare at Jahanara that was so hostile that Atisheh moved to interpose yourself between her princess and the man.

The princess held up a restraining hand. "I should have known better than to ask for forgiveness before revealing the nature of my transgression against you. I can only repeat that no one beyond the tiniest circle of people knew what I was about. I could not risk Aurangzeb discovering my deception and refusing to make the direct assault we need him to make so we might employ these weapons to maximum effect. A prolonged siege is not enough to secure victory for us, even should the other part of my plan succeed.

No, we need to show his followers that Aurangzeb is not and never will be chosen by God to rule the empire." She paused, uncertain whether or not she was getting through to John.

Bertram and Gervais must have been concerned as well, because they took up positions on either side of their friend. John cast a reproachful look at both men, shaking his head in disbelief.

"All those people ... How could you, Bert? How could you agree to killing all those people?"

Bertram's face crumpled. "John, I didn't know they were going to kill anyone."

"No one was killed in the explosion," Smidha said forcefully.

"I saw the bodies," John snarled.

"The bodies were the corpses of people who had expired quite naturally in the city the week before," Smidha explained, scandalized at the tone John was taking with Jahanara.

"Bertram wasn't aware of that portion of the plan," Jahanara amplified. "I, and I alone made the decision that he could not know if he was to be with you when the explosion happened, not if he was to keep you safe *and* behave sufficiently surprised to deceive any spies that watched you in the days that followed."

"Jesus, lady. Here I was thinking I was starting to think like one of you. Damn, but I was wrong! Just who the hell is this spy you're so worried about, anyway?"

Gervais touched John's shoulder. When the younger man looked at him he said quietly, "Gradinego, for one. It shames me to admit it but he's been serving up information on the Mission and the royals to whomever will pay him."

John made a face. "But Gradinego hasn't been in on any of the councils? So how is he getting any information—"

Gervais cut him off. "Roshanara and a few others: servants, guards, slaves, even a courtier or two. Luckily we found them early enough to cut or control some of the leaks."

Jahanara took up the thread. "But the court, as you no doubt have learned, has no greater pleasure than gossip and rumor. If all sources of information were to have dried up, Aurangzeb and certainly Nur would have been suspicious of everything they observed. So I gave them their pleasures. Fed them. Fattened them. Now comes the time of slaughter."

She drew a deep breath. "I do not ask forgiveness for what I have done, but for the necessary hurts I inflicted in order to accomplish it."

Jahangir's palace

"I'll understand if you don't want to do this, Gervais," Bertram said as they walked across the jasmine-scented garden leading to the massive edifice of Jahangir's palace. Previously Shah Shuja's lodgings while in residence at Red Fort, the capacious palace had been divvied up among those umara of the court who served the Sultan Al'Azam or his immediate family but didn't have entourages of their own to speak of.

Aurangzeb's former palace, on the other side of the fort, had similarly been given over to the families of the more prominent and powerful umara.

"Don't even think of leaving me out," Gervais said.

"I want to know what he knows, and when he learned it, besides. I can't think anyone else will be able to get him to talk."

"And if he gets out of hand?" Bertram asked.

"Then I'll put him down with less remorse than I would a mad dog. Just don't get in my way," he said.

Wary of the angry intensity of Gervais' response, Bertram let the subject drop. They walked in silence for a little while, Bertram considering how best to do the job Jahanara had, through Monique, ordered them to undertake.

Gervais suddenly sighed, stopped, and turned to face his future son-in-law. "I apologize, Bertram. I am angry. Have been since you and Monique uncovered this betrayal."

Bertram put a hand on the older man's shoulder. "No need to apologize. He's the one should be begging forgiveness."

"And will be, when I get my hands on him," Gervais said.

"Will he fight?" Bertram asked.

"I doubt it. Usually that only makes things worse." He shrugged. "But then this isn't just stealing from your crew—which can be a deadly-enough affair. This is an entirely different level of betrayal."

"Should I have sent a runner for Atisheh or one of the others?"

Gervais shook his head. "The fewer, the quieter, the better, I should think. Besides, while I may talk a good game about mayhem, I'm fairly certain Atisheh would actually enjoy cutting his guts out and using them for garters."

Bertram chuckled and squeezed his friend's shoulder.

They resumed their march, intentionally avoiding talk of what would happen to the traitor once they handed him over to Dara's people.

The guards at the palace entrance allowed them entry without a second glance.

"How do you want to handle it, then?" Bertram asked as they mounted the stairs.

"I think I'll try and convince him we're going to give him a chance to run. Play it like I needed convincing he was spying on us and might be convinced to let him go."

"Just let me know when you want me to step in. If he does not want to come with us, I don't have anything less lethal than my knife. You?"

"Just this," Gervais said, pulling what looked like an elongated leather pouch from his sword belt. The fat end of the cosh looked heavy, and bulged as if loaded with stones. He smacked it into his off hand and said, "Lead shot. Good for stunning guards and the like, should work well enough on an unarmored man. I suppose we can use a sash or something to tie him up."

Bertram pulled a pair of up-timer handcuffs from inside his robes. "I've got these, a parting gift from Don Nasi," he said, intentionally leaving out the caveat his kinsman had offered when presenting them: *In case one of the Vieuxponts does something to risk the mission.*

Gervais looked sidelong at him. "Interesting. I had wondered how you got them."

"You don't pretend you didn't know I had them?"

A crooked smile. "A good swindler knows what tools are at his disposal at all times."

"At your disposal? They were in my baggage!"

"What's yours is ours and what's mine is mine," Gervais said, grinning.

Bertram chuckled and put the cuffs away, then added, "Just so you know, I'll likely fumble around a bit putting them on."

"Come to that, I'll enjoy beating him into submission."

Bertram began to chuckle, then thought better of it. If the traitor decided to flee, there was no telling to what lengths he might go to get away.

By unspoken agreement the pair stopped talking as they entered the hall fronting the chamber they sought. In seconds they were at the door and Bertram was producing the key Monique had supplied. Gervais tickled the lock with quiet finesse and, pausing only to fix a smile on his face, entered.

"Angelo! I need you to see something!" Gervais shouted, striding into the room as the door banged against the wall.

Bertram closed the door behind himself and stepped a little behind and to Gervais' right. Content to let the older man take the lead, he looked around for avenues of escape or weapons.

The chamber was poorly lit, a lone oil lamp beyond a red silk hanging casting a dim, red-hued light on floor cushions. There was a scattering of low brass tables covered in the various paraphernalia of everyday life, and a water pipe with enough stems for four people to partake at once.

A light breeze from the open windows flanking the balcony opposite the entrance made the hangings sway and shift. It also carried the residual odor of recently smoked opium from the pipe's grill.

There was a clatter and grunt from behind the partition, followed by a sleepy, "Who—er, Gervais, why are you here?"

"I thought we might talk for a bit. For old times' sake," he said, angling toward the center of the room.

"Old times—What are you on about, Gervais?" Gradinego asked.

"Good times, Angelo. Good times," Gervais answered.

Angelo walked barefoot from behind the hangings wearing a thin set of trousers drawn at the waist with a silk cord and nothing more. The Venetian ran one hand through salt-and-pepper hair and had a sleepy—or perhaps drug-fogged—expression. He smiled when he saw Gervais but it slipped a bit when Angelo saw his old friend was not alone.

"You say that like the good times won't come again, my friend," Gradinego said, gesturing for his guests to take seats as he came to a stop beside the hookah.

"Did I?" Gervais asked, ignoring, like Bertram, the implied invitation to sit.

Angelo shrugged hairy shoulders. "Perhaps tired ears misinterpret."

Bertram watched as Angelo's gaze flicked between Gervais, Bertram, the door, and the balcony.

"Perhaps that's because I worry," Gervais said.

"Worry about what?"

"There's word that you sold us out, Angelo."

"Sold you—" Angelo began, voice rising.

"Don't act so indignant. Just tell me the truth and I can see what I can do for you." He gestured at Bertram. "That's why it's just me and Bertram here, so we can get you out of here if that's what you want to do."

"I don't know what you're talking about." Angelo

said the words calmly, but Bertram, watching him closely, saw the weight shift onto the balls of his feet.

"Please don't, Angelo."

"Don't what?"

"Try and play me."

Angelo spread his hands. "I am not playing."

"No, I suppose not." Gervais sighed. "You stopped playing games when you decided to sell us out."

Angelo hung his head, but Bertram could see the tension in his shoulders and neck. *Not surrendering, then, just acting.*

"How could you, Angelo? My daughter. She deserves better."

"Deserves?" Angelo snorted. "You and your precious up-timers were going to get us all killed. I did what I had to do to save us!"

"Save us from what?" Gervais asked.

"From falling for the swindle."

"What the hell does that mean?"

Angelo's hands balled into fists. "Jesus Christ in heaven! What happened to you? These people you so blindly follow, they manufacture a few works of literature, some 'records' of supposed future events, and you *believe* them?"

Gervais grunted like a gut-punched man. Such was his skill at acting, Bertram wasn't sure if the sound was a legitimate result of anger and pain. The thought was sobering. Gervais claimed Gradinego was nearly as skilled a player as he.

Angelo wasn't done: "No, not just any fool, but a true believer, so hopeful of salvation they'll believe anything. When their powder factory went up in smoke, still you believed. When Dara ran off the best part of his army and the one man who might just have had a chance defending his throne, *still* you believed!"

Well, thank you, Angelo. Good to know both those particular misdirections were believed, at least at your level.

"What's even more laughable is your calling the tune for the royals, making them think you and they were people to be listened to!" He laid a hand against his hairy chest. "Do you think they might have allowed me such access without you laying that foundation? Do you?"

Gervais was shaking his head.

"So look me in the eye, Gervais, and tell me again who fooled who!"

Gervais refused to meet his old companion's gaze, looking instead at his hands. His face was red with suppressed anger and no little sadness.

"When?" he hissed, still looking at his hands.

"When what?"

"When did you decide to play the other side?" Gervais snarled, stepping close to the other man. Bertram admired how the older man used the distraction of his movement and harsh words to retrieve the cosh from his belt.

Angelo snorted. "I never stopped playing the odds just because you showed up, Gervais. It's the only way to prosper in our line of work."

"So you're the one gave Aurangzeb copies of the papers from Grantville?"

"No, I gave those to *Nur.* Hard work, too. Translating English is not easy."

"So she's the one who placed you at Aurangzeb's service?"

Angelo shrugged, perhaps belatedly realizing how much he'd admitted, and to whom.

"Thank you," Gervais said.

"What?"

Gervais' answer surprised both Angelo and Bertram: He swung the cosh overhand at the Venetian's head. Angelo's attempt to pull away resulted in the shot-filled sack striking where the neck met the shoulder.

Angelo groaned and stumbled backward.

Gervais followed, swinging again, but the traitor managed to interpose a hand between skull and descending blow. He yelped as the cosh broke what sounded like a few fingers.

Turning to flee, he tripped on another cushion, tangled in a hanging, and staggered a few steps before getting his feet under him.

Worried the man might try and leap from the balcony, Bertram kicked a cushion out of the way and followed.

Gervais raised the cosh again, but Angelo punched him in the face with the arm that wasn't numbed from Gervais' blow. Off-balance as he was, the Venetian's punch didn't do much more than slow the Frenchman.

Retreating still, Angelo snatched up a dagger from a table before heaving it over in front of his pursuers.

Undaunted, Bertram lowered his head and charged. His headlong rush caught the older man around the waist. He tried to throw Angelo from his feet but one boot slipped, either on the brass plate that had served as the tabletop or one of the carpets, he wasn't sure.

Angelo stabbed down at Bertram with the dagger, hitting him above the kidneys, hard. Thinking himself already done for, and determined that Angelo wouldn't hurt his friend, Bertram heaved and pushed for all he was worth. The pair staggered, swayed, and stumbled out onto the balcony.

Bertram shoved, managed to make enough space to grab the wrist holding the dagger and pin it to the stone balustrade.

Gervais was there again, sweeping the cosh sidearm just inches from Bertram's sweating brow. It crashed into Angelo's temple and knocked him sideways, senseless.

Right over the balcony railing.

Angelo's wrist slid through Bertram's sweaty hand. Bertram clamped down, trying to save the man from the fall, but only succeeded in grasping the dagger.

Angelo Gradinego, thief, doctor, swindler and spy, fell to a final, hard stop on the flagstones two stories below.

In the shocked silence that followed, Bertram looked down at the hand that had failed to save Angelo and realized the Venetian hadn't had time to unsheathe the dagger he'd been stabbing with.

"God, but I thought I'd been killed," he panted.

"You'll be all right. Bruised, probably, but no worse."

With a gasp that sounded—even to his own ears—suspiciously like a sob, Bertram nodded. "And you?"

"I'll be all right," Gervais said, turning from the balcony. He gave a very Gallic shrug and added, tears forming in his eyes, "It's just that . . . I already miss him . . . Or rather, the memory. I didn't really want him dead. Not really."

Bertram let that sit a moment before offering, "Better this than trampled by elephants, which is how the emperor would have dealt with him."

"Perhaps," Gervais said. Clapping the younger man on the shoulder, he smiled wanly. "Let's get someone to clean this up and make our report, then I want to get stinking drunk."

Chapter 39

River crossing to the west of Kanpur

"What river is this again?" Bobby asked, trailing one hand in the water over the side of the barge. He didn't seem to recall having asked the question not twenty minutes ago.

"The Ganges again, I think," Ricky said absently, drawn from his examination of the far shore and the men and horses reuniting there by the repetition. He glanced at Bobby, worried. His oldest friend's face was flushed and sweaty, despite the relatively cool air of the early morning. For two days now Bobby hadn't quite been himself. Ricky didn't think it was malaria, but then again he wasn't any kind of doctor.

"Where the..." he said, looking for Jadu Das on the barge behind them. One good thing about river crossings was that Jadu Das made certain that his goods were loaded and unloaded according to his specifications and desires, and could usually be found easily enough. The merchant had been distant since Shaista Khan started his army on the trek west, often spending all day in Asaf

Khan's tent only to return quite late at night, so it was a relief to know the older man was near at hand. Ricky just hoped he knew some kind of remedy for whatever had Bobby feeling poorly. One of his friends had already died here, and he didn't want to lose another.

It was two hours or so before they were fully disembarked from the barge. Bobby just sat the entire time, sheathed in sweat, eyes glassy and responses slow and uncertain. At least Bobby didn't seem to have any trouble keeping food and drink down, and eagerly accepted water from Ricky's canteen.

Ricky left him to search for Jadu Das, but settled for Vikram when he saw the servant supervising the off-loading of goods from the barge he'd thought Jadu was on.

"Vikram! I need Jadu to come take a look at Bobby."

The slightly built servant bowed to Ricky. "I'm sorry, but Jadu Das has already departed for Shaista Khan's tent. Is there anything I might do?"

"I don't know, Vikram. Bobby is sick. Some kind of fever?"

"Is he throwing up or . . . ?" Vikram asked, his normally sunny disposition clouding over with concern.

"No, he's not having any kind of digestive problems," Ricky said, feeling better just having somebody to tell his worries to.

"I will send word to Jadu Das and make sure that cold compresses are laid by when we camp this evening."

Ricky nodded, wondering if they shouldn't just camp now so Bobby could rest.

Vikram, sensing Ricky's unease, said, "Or perhaps I will look at him now and have some icewater made up for him."

"Thanks, Vikram," Ricky said, meaning it. "I'm really worried about him."

The servant delegated a few tasks to others and sent a messenger for Jadu, then organized the copper bowls for making cold water.

Ricky, relieved to have any help, didn't mind waiting. The up-timer's camp gear and equipment had been off-loaded on the upstream side of the landing, so it shouldn't cause too much of a backup for the subsequent barge-loads of soldiers, livestock, and gear.

His anxiety spiked again when they got back to the piled goods Ricky had left Bobby sitting on. His momentary panic eased quickly enough when they found a shivering Bobby wrapped in a couple of blankets among the folded bulk of their tent.

"Jesus, Bobby. Should've told me you were feeling this bad."

Bobby opened fever bright eyes. "C-c-couldn't f-f-f-find you, R-r-r-andy," he said through chattering teeth.

"Bobby, it's me, Ricky."

"F-F-fuck! Y-y-you d-d-d-d-ead too?" Bobby asked.

"We ain't dead yet, Bobby. Just real uncomfortable. Man up and drink something," Ricky said, quoting just one of their old Little League coach's many oddly inspirational sayings.

Bobby's smile nearly broke Ricky's heart.

He looked up at Vikram and asked in a voice that sounded thick to his own ears, "When will that cold water be ready?"

"Just as soon as possible, Ricky. We must keep him cool if we can. I will order the tents raised."

"You know what he has?" Ricky asked, annoyed at how scared he sounded.

Vikram shook his head. "Only that we should keep his temperature down. Otherwise, even if he survives the fever he might be addled."

A barge full of armed men was just touching shore. They stared with disinterest at the sick man and his companions.

"Can you carry him?" Vikram asked, pointing with his chin at the soldiers. "We need to get out of their way."

"I will."

"Right, I'll see to things and send you some men to set up camp and see. to his comfort and yours."

"Thanks, Vikram."

The servant turned and left, quickly disappearing in the swirl of men on the shore.

Ricky stooped and picked up his friend, carrying him a little ways up the shore to a point where they might pitch the tents without being overrun by the rest of the column marching with Shaista Khan. He sat there shading Bobby for a little while. The servants Vikram sent arrived and quickly started to set the camp up around them. Vikram himself arrived with several cold compresses and the copper rig used to make more before the tents were fully erected.

West of Kanpur
The Mission's tent

"Any idea what it is?" Ricky asked as Jadu stepped from the "bedroom" of the tent and into the common area.

"Not really, though I think the fever has peaked. You did well to cool him off."

Ricky eyed the older man. Jadu looked tired and, for

the first time in Ricky's experience, anxious. "Rough day with Shaista Khan?" he asked. "Sorry, just worried, you know?" He gestured to a seat.

Jadu accepted a goblet of wine from Vikram, and then sat down. "I do indeed." Jadu sighed. "Today was . . . difficult."

"Oh?"

Jadu waved with his goblet. "You know where we are?"

"Sure: we're just north of . . . I'm sure I'm not pronouncing it right, a place called Kanpur."

"Correct. Is that name not familiar to you?"

Ricky thought a moment. "Can't say that it is."

"Did you get a chance to study any of the histories of India that came back with your town?"

"Sure," Ricky said, nodding. It occurred to him to ask where Jadu had gotten access to the history that came back with Grantville but wanted to hear the local out before asking his own questions.

"*India Britannica*?" Jadu asked.

"No, but the title sounds familiar. I think someone checked it out and hadn't returned it to the library. I remember because Ms. Mailey was super angry, muttering about the special hell that had to wait for people who check books out of the library and don't return them." He snapped his fingers. "Is that the book Salim used to . . . Holy shit, it is! That's why Shah Jahan kicked the English out."

Jadu was looking at him in the way that down-timers had when considering how to unpack a statement made that was so laden with up-timer lingo that it was hard to know where to begin. The merchant drank instead of asking Ricky to clarify, then asked another question: "Did you read about the Sepoy Rebellion?"

Ricky nodded. "Yeah, I remember the name even if I can't remember much of the particulars. During the British Raj the governor or somebody pissed off the indigenous portion of his military and kicked off a mutiny. The mutiny got out of hand and became a rebellion. Lots of Brits got murdered and there was some kind of atrocity the English claimed was committed by their former soldiers."

Jadu leaned forward. "And do you remember where the atrocity took place?"

Ricky had to think about it for a minute but eventually remembered some part of it. "Crawnpoor or some such?"

"Kanpur," Jadu corrected, finishing his drink. "The fort on the hill overlooking the town," he said, holding the glass up as Vikram entered with a fresh pitcher.

Ricky held his own out, not really thirsty but happy to have a distraction. Worrying about Bobby sweating out whatever sickness he'd caught made him feel helpless.

"That fort—or at least a future version of it—was where the mutineers slaughtered a great many Englishmen after a siege."

Ricky considered that as Vikram refreshed their drinks, then said, "So how did that make today...?"

"Shaista Khan had word today that Aurangzeb has completed his siege lines and cut off Red Fort from all supply."

"Shit," Ricky said, suddenly feeling guilty that it seemed all his friends were facing danger while he sat here, healthy and safe, drinking wine.

"But that is not all."

Jadu drank, then said, "Our friend Salim is somewhere in the Western Ghats, hopefully on his way somewhere safe."

"Salim left Red Fort? Why?"

Jadu waggled his head. "The court is abuzz with rumors that he and Jahanara Begum had some kind of inappropriate contact. Dara exiled him. Things do not look good."

Fearing for his friends both near and far, Ricky did something he very rarely did since leaving home: said an earnest, if silent, prayer for their well-being.

"Did Shaista agree to pick up the pace or anything?" he asked.

"The Khan was considering his options even as I was called here." Jadu took another long drink and shrugged. "His army is certainly large enough to make a difference. It's his political position that's weak.

"That was the debate he was having: On the one hand it grows stronger with Dara the longer he delays. On the other, if he waits too long and Dara is defeated before he arrives, especially with little loss to Aurangzeb's forces, he will have a great deal of explaining to do in order to justify his refusal to answer Aurangzeb's call."

"But he already declared for Dara, didn't he?"

Jadu nodded. "Indeed he did. The one thing any new-made Sultan Al'Azam cannot ignore from any of his subordinates is a failure to take sides with *someone* in the royal family."

"Someone?" Ricky asked, then realized what it was Jadu was telling him. "Wait, I get it. Whoever wins will want to know why their nobles didn't pick a side..."

"Almost," Jadu said. "They will already know, in their hearts, why. It is well known that anyone who does not support one of the princes is planning to take power themselves, something the dynasty cannot and will not countenance."

"Right." Ricky felt a sudden need for more drink. When he'd refilled his cup he asked, "So, any idea which way he was leaning?"

"I believe the only sensible path open to him is to make better time, to hurry and support Dara. That is what I advised him to do." He finished his wine again and shrugged. "But then he said my thinking was a victim of my own hopes in the matter."

Sudden worry stabbed Ricky. "My calling for you here didn't screw things up with Shaista Khan, did it?"

Jadu shook his head. "No, I've been kept waiting at least as much as I have been allowed in to see him. Though I suppose telling him one of you had fallen ill may not have been the best thing to do."

"Why not?"

"In our previous conversations I put great stock in your up-timer technology, skill, and wisdom to shore up an image of Dara's camp as stronger than it might otherwise appear. Specifically your medical acumen. I'm afraid I might have made you out to be signs of divine favor upon Dara's cause."

Ricky shook his head. "And it's hard to look like a messenger from God if you're sick."

Jadu nodded. "I should not have said anything. I apologize. I've grown quite fond of both of you. The wine makes me morose and stains every word dark. The important thing is that Bobby get well. The rest of it is just politics and will work itself out, one way or another."

"One way or another," Ricky agreed.

Part Eight

September, 1637

All mounted on their shining chariots!
—The Rig Veda

Chapter 40

Agra
Red Fort, palace of Akbar

The lamps were burning low as John and Ilsa sat. Gervais had asked for the meeting, but their busy schedules had only left this after-hours window in which to meet. The palace was quiet. Even the servants had retired for the night, dismissed after setting up the chamber.

John was tired, wrung out in a way he'd rarely felt before. It had been a long evening spent in private counsel with Dara, where the emperor had dropped yet another bombshell on his closest advisors. The stress was enough to put him off his feed. Even the collection of fresh fruit and wine laid out for their refreshment held no appeal.

He tried not to grind his teeth as Bertram, Monique, and Gervais finally entered. He'd found it hard to accept that the people he'd trusted with not only his life, but Ilsa's and that of their unborn child as well, had been lying to him.

Ilsa greeted them cordially. She'd always been better at hiding her anger. Then again, she'd said she was more disappointed than angry, when John had gone off about it. She'd expressed her disappointment, sure, but hadn't shown one tenth the angry hurt he felt whenever he thought about it.

The trio looked around with fatigue-fogged interest before picking spots amongst the cushions in the center of the chamber. The Mission personnel had all been given quarters in what had been Aurangzeb's palace, but John and Ilsa had been too busy and tired to investigate their new digs, and John assumed the same was true for the rest of them.

Preparations for the siege likewise hadn't given them much time to think, let alone discuss recent events, and John had been on a slow boil the last few days, stress and anger eating at him.

"John, Ilsa," Gervais said, nodding at each. He didn't act like he was even aware the couple might have reason to be angry.

"Gervais," Ilsa said, her light tone polite enough to make even John wonder if she was angry.

John was saved from having to respond when Priscilla and Rodney entered. Both of them looked like the walking dead. Priscilla stopped and yawned so hugely a hint of tears came to the corners of her closed eyes. Led by one of Rodney's great mitts, she found a seat across from John and Ilsa.

Looking around, John saw the rest of the Mission were more or less equally divided between yawning or, like him, stifling one.

"Hey, all," Rodney said.

Everyone's responses were muted.

John felt Bertram looking at him but, not trusting his temper, refused to meet him eye to eye.

"Sorry this had to be so late, but I wanted to make sure we all had a chance to talk," Gervais said.

"About what?" John said, barely restraining a snarl.

"I certainly hope we're here to talk about the big fucking elephant in the room," Ilsa said.

Everyone turned to stare at his wife, not least of all John.

Her smile was so lovely it made his heart stumble through a few beats. Ilsa did not see his response, as her eyes were on Gervais as she answered. "You should have brought us in, Gervais. You know it, and you should apologize for it now, profusely, so we can all get along again."

"I—I—" Gervais stammered, usual eloquence deserting him.

Monique said in his stead, "To be fair, Ilsa: it was discussed and at very great length. Jahanara vetoed it."

"Is Jahanara a member of this USE mission? A special envoy of the USE?" Ilsa asked. "As she is not, it should have been obvious who you were duty bound to report to."

The con man flinched. What she was describing was perilously close to treason, something Gervais had just lost his oldest friend to. "I—"

Ilsa cut him off: "I am not done yet: You knew who you were supposed to report to and confer with and you didn't. That's not something you can just ignore."

Gervais rallied. "The fewer people who know the details of—"

"To hell with that, Gervais! You needed John and Rodney, and to a lesser extent, Priscilla and me, to act hurt and despondent, and rather than trust our ability to perform in your little operation, you actually *hurt* us. I can excuse the hurt to me. I can't be so sanguine about what you did to my husband." She smiled again, coldly this time. "Now, I understand there were reasons for doing what you did, I truly do. But now is not the time to defend yourselves. Now is the time to make it as right as you can. That in mind, I, for one, would like to hear an abject apology from each of you to each of us. Once you've all done that, I would have you explain one thing more: tell me that all the *shit* you were driven to do was worth it."

John, blinking in the wake of his wife's use of profanity, looked from Ilsa to Bertram then back again.

"And you, John, don't look at me like that," she said. "Just because I dislike such language doesn't mean I do not know how to employ it in order to impress upon our friends just how *fucking* important this is to me."

Ilsa settled back in her cushions, looking at each of the others in turn.

All three of the other down-timers looked stricken. If John hadn't been so angry and tired, he might have felt sorry for them. As it was, he could only sit in mute silence.

"Damn straight," Priscilla said, all traces of her earlier drowsiness gone.

She looked at Rodney, who was nodding agreement. "Better said than I could manage," he rumbled.

Gervais opened his mouth to say something, but Bertram beat him to it. "I am sorry. Truly sorry. Ilsa is right, we should have trusted you. I knew it from the moment I heard about the corpses in the manufactory."

Monique's hand found Bertram's, squeezing it. "I am sorry, too. We should have done better." She looked at her father. "Could have done better."

"Well, experience tells me I should smile and make some excuse to cover for my errors..." Gervais trailed off, one fine-fingered hand rubbing his bearded chin. "But no, not this time. In my life, I have used any number of rationalizations to excuse my behavior. To the public, to myself, to my daughter, to her mother. I have watched others do the same, and get away with acts barbaric and cruel. I find, at this late date and"— he swallowed—"and only after the recent example of my friend's failure to see the harm he did, that I am tired of rationalizing, of excuses." He raised his head and there were tears in his eyes as he said, "I am sorry, John, Ilsa, Priscilla, Rodney. I am deeply sorry."

Wanting to believe their apologies were sincere, yet uncertain how to trust again, John looked away.

"As to the other part," Bertram said, taking up the thread and looking directly at Ilsa. "I suppose the battle to come will provide the only real answers to whether Jahanara's subterfuge and the lies we told to maintain it were worth it or not. Early indications are good, though. If he was planning a siege, Aurangzeb's forces would have started digging trenches as soon as they first encircled us. As no one we've seen has even picked up a spade, it looks as if little brother plans to try and overrun us in one go. That means the impact of the weapons will be far greater than those killed or injured by them."

"Surprise is in the mind of the enemy," John muttered.

"Exactly." Then, probably because John had yet to acknowledge their apologies, he said, "I'm really sorry,

John. Should have told you right from the start. Or later, when we were with Talawat on the walls."

Bertram was looking at him again, eyes pleading.

John, throat tight, looked down at his lap. When he looked up again, it felt like everyone had joined Bertram in looking at him.

"Look, I understand why you did what you did, and why the princess asked you to do it. I still think the men she had me issue the guns to would be a *lot* better trained if I could have given them some live-fire training, but I see the value in making the enemy believe we were out of options. Problem is, *I* thought we were out of options. I can't see how deceiving your general up to the eve of battle is even an option . . ."

"Salim was in on it from the beginning, and he was to be Dara's second," Monique said.

John just looked at her.

"He ain't here," Rodney said.

"But he is still fighting for Dara!" Monique said. "His exile was part of the attempt to make us appear weak so Aurangzeb will attack head-on."

"We *are* weaker without him than with!" John said, a little louder and angrier than he'd meant to.

Rodney stirred, then spoke. "Dara was already cutting Salim out of the picture, you know. He thought the pair of them were knocking boots, and wanted Salim exiled. It was a weird fixation he had. Every time he started coming down with one of those brutal headaches he would start in about it."

Gervais nodded and added, "Jahanara made use of the only option that both removed Salim from the court, as Dara wished, *and* retained his services, and in the process deceived Aurangzeb. It was an elegant solution to a potential disaster."

"I don't disagree, Gervais. Thing is, when you play these kind of games with people, your mileage may vary. What if I was so pissed I just took Ilsa and we rode for the God-damned hills like the men who snuck out after Salim left? What then?"

They had no answer for that, and all of them had the good grace to look guilty. A part of John figured he'd said enough, but couldn't help continuing, "Look, we already know we aren't going to change everything about these people or this place, and we all learned exactly how dangerous court politics can be when they killed Shah Jahan. But I'm not going to sit by and idly take that crap for normal!"

Rodney and Priscilla were nodding agreement. Monique and Bertram both looked like they wanted to say something, but John plowed on. "Don't get me wrong, I'm not talking about taking her on right now. It's too important that we get through these next few days without the men realizing there's been yet another reason to worry. But once we get through this, *if* we get through this, there will be a God-damned reckoning." His voice was shaking by the time John stopped talking.

"John, we're gonna make it," Rodney said.

"I sure hope so, but Rodney, you've been neck-deep in setting up the hospital with Pris, so you don't know what we've been going through on my end since Salim left." He glanced at Bertram. "And you didn't get a chance to hear what Dara is planning now."

"No?" Rodney said, blinking.

"He wants to sally."

"Sally? You're kidding," Ilsa said. He'd not told her

the news before the meeting, more because he hadn't the heart than from any real lack of time for it.

"Nope. No joke at all. Dara said that once we've stalled the attack at the walls, he will lead a couple thousand sowar out and 'sweep them before us like leaves carried on a cleansing wind.'"

"Jesus," Rodney said.

"Right?" John said, catching Ilsa's frown at Rodney's casual use of the name. For some reason her expression struck him as funny. So funny he had to hide a foolish grin. *Foul language allowed, just no blaspheming, thank you very much.*

"Tell them the rest, John," Bertram said.

Memory killed the smile. "I argued about it—as much as I dared—and he's dead serious. I said we couldn't afford to lose him or that many fighting men and he laughed. Said we wouldn't, that God was with us. You know how he gets. I gave the signal to Bertram and things went from bad to worse from there."

Bertram sighed. "When it seemed we were going back over the same ground and Dara remained unconvinced, I told him to send for Bidhi Chand, thinking an experienced warrior would add his voice to John's wisdom."

Gervais tutted. "Didn't I teach you better, *mon fils*? Never, ever ask anyone else's opinion unless you coached them on it yourself."

Bertram's cheeks reddened. "How was I to know he'd fully endorse the idea?"

John laughed bitterly. "That wasn't the only opinion Bidhi had. He offered the services of his men in the sally."

"But they're infantry," Ilsa said. Far better at organizing than her husband, she had been a great help to John in planning and implementing the training regimen for the garrison. "Won't they deploy too slowly to make a difference?"

"Exactly what I said," John muttered.

"And his response was along the lines of, 'John, we will be like the wind, and take the fight to them, provided the preparations you and Talawat have arranged do their job and stop the storm at the second wall.'"

"But, how does—"

"He and Bidhi say they can get outside the gates in quick time. Dara will lead"—he had to pause to let the gasps of surprise die—"the horse straight out and at the retreating backs of the enemy while Bidhi follows out the gate and wheels parallel to the walls and start mopping up. They are confident of accomplishing a great slaughter."

"But if they are retreating, won't they all be out of range of the infantry?" Ilsa asked. "And what happens when they recover? Won't the Sikhs be caught against the wall? And if they're pursued as they try and return through the gate?"

"All valid points I made sure to bring up," John said. "He didn't listen. Bidhi was even worse, he just smiled and said he was ready to face whatever challenges were placed before him by God and the enemy."

"Was Talawat there?" Rodney asked.

"Yes, but he wasn't the voice of reason I've grown to expect. He was grinning like a madman."

"What did you do?" Monique said.

"I tried to convince them not to throw away our best men in an attack that would likely fail and only serve to put his own life at risk." He shook his head. "They didn't listen."

"John may have pulled off a minor miracle by convincing Dara to only sally if it was clear that any attempted storm was a failure on at least two fronts." John didn't miss the admiration in Bertram's tone.

"But then he's the one decides what constitutes success and failure, so he might order the sally on a whim." John lowered his voice and dropped into his fastest Amideutsch. "Frankly, dude is hurt and I worry he might fall out under pressure."

Rodney and Gervais shared a concerned look.

"Oh, I think he'll be all right," Gervais said.

Rodney snorted. "For certain values of all right. His blood pressure is down, and I think he's chasing the dragon again, because he's nowhere near as high strung and hasn't shown any signs of another seizure despite being under what has to be a huge strain..."

"He is," Gervais confirmed, then held up his hands to ward off Rodney's anger. "*I* didn't give it to him, Rodney."

"I asked today and apparently Jahanara authorized it when their brother arrived," Monique explained.

"I might just have to talk to Jahanara about interfering with patients," Priscilla said angrily.

Ilsa looked from Priscilla to Rodney. "Do either of you know if he'll fall out again?"

"Can't say for sure. He hasn't had another seizure, and he was sure angry enough to bring one on when Aurangzeb showed up..." Rodney shrugged wide shoulders and looked at his wife.

Priscilla nodded. "He's been working out, trying to get his strength back, and hasn't had any episodes, but there's just no telling. Not with certainty. If you want, Rodney and I can work to convince him and Nadira riding to battle is a bad idea, but it sounds like he's ready for those arguments and I worry he'd stop listening to us on everything if we push too hard."

John nodded. "Yeah, add to that the need he has to be seen leading."

"Aurangzeb doesn't lead from the front, does he?" Ilsa said.

"No, but his brother has a history, however short, of victories. Dara doesn't."

"Seems a huge risk for 'might.'"

"The warriors like the idea, though," Gervais said.

John nodded agreement.

"Oh?"

"I asked Atisheh what she thought of him fighting with them on the walls. Her response was one of those hard stares that make you feel like you're about to get cut, if you know what I mean."

John smiled. He knew the look very well.

"But when I persisted, eventually she muttered something that sounded like, 'About time!' and left."

"She's quite the social butterfly, is Atisheh," Priscilla said, grinning.

"So delicate and dainty," Monique chuckled.

They all shared a brief, tired laugh that served to dispel some of the worried atmosphere they'd been struggling through.

"Back to the point, though: The idea that Dara be seen leading was something Salim mentioned before. He said it was critical to his eventual rule, and I have to believe he's got the experience and wisdom to know," John said.

"So do we try and stop him riding out or not? Trying to stop him after he's announced that he will makes the decision irrevocable, so we need to get on it before the next durbar," Gervais said.

"I don't think so," John and Bertram said at nearly the same instant.

"And why not?" Ilsa asked, looking across at Bertram.

Bertram nodded at John to go first.

"I don't think he can afford the hit his credibility would suffer if word got out that he'd wanted to but his doctors told him 'no.' The court is already leery of how much power, privilege, and attention we've been receiving from Dara and Jahanara."

Bertram nodded. "Much of the correspondence we were reading before we rolled up the network was complaints about how much power Dara was allowing us and"—he looked at Monique—"how he was a fool for, as they saw it, 'making himself a slave to his sister's unnatural lust for power.'"

John yawned hugely.

"I'm sorry to have kept you so late, but I wanted to clear the air if we could," Gervais said.

Wiping tiredly at the tears forming at the corners of his eyes, John nodded.

"Did we, John?" Bertram asked, leaning forward on his cushions and staring intently at John.

"Did we what?"

"Did we clear things up? I know my apologies are late, but I count you among my very best friends, and hate that I hurt you with this."

John thought about it another moment, then nodded. "We have, Bertram. Wish it hadn't happened, and I hope it never does again, but I accept your apology." He lifted his head to look at Monique and Gervais in turn. "All your apologies. I understand your reasons and accept them. Just wish we could have done better."

Chapter 41

Aurangzeb's camp
Nur's tent

"Damn him," Nur hissed. Crumpling the report in one small, hennaed fist, she threw it from her in a fit of anger.

Tara, just entering, was struck in the chest. She bent with the graceful suppleness of youth and retrieved the crumpled piece of paper from the carpets. She knew better than to try and open it, however.

"I disappoint, mistress?" she asked.

Nur shook her head. Taking a deep, cleansing breath and expelling her anger with it, she said, "What word?"

"You are to attend Aurangzeb in the Red Tent an hour before sunset."

Seeing the glitter of delight in her advisor's eyes, Nur raised a questioning brow.

Tara approached and knelt. "That pet priest of Carvalho's was making a scene again. Rumor has it Aurangzeb is going to put a stop to the Christian's complaints at last," she said, excitement obvious despite the low tones used to convey the message.

"I see," Nur said. She despaired, some days, of training Gargi's replacement to a more dispassionate manner. The young woman's intelligence was undeniable, but it was too often colored by passions that Gargi had assured Nur would be tempered with experience, leaving an intellect that was not only sharp, but flexible. Of course, when they'd discussed her eventual replacement, both of them had blithely assumed there would be plenty of time for Gargi to properly mentor and train Tara before the young woman would be forced to take over the position.

Now was not the time to take the young woman to task. No, not now.

Thinking hard, Nur plucked the message from Tara's unresisting hand.

She did not have to unfold the paper to review its contents: Shaista Khan had declared for Dara. Delayed by the death of one messenger and the failure of another to find suitable transport, the missive had been dated the very same day Asaf Khan passed to his reward. Nur's informant was unable to discover what the exact terms were that had secured her nephew's service, but had said a pair of up-timers had been presented to Shaista and Asaf shortly before her brother's death and those same men had been summoned to audience with Shaista immediately after Asaf's death.

This information, combined with Tara's news about the breakdown in relations between Aurangzeb and his European supporters, was worrisome.

The supplies Aurangzeb had been able to secure at Gwalior would only stretch so far. It occurred to Nur that Aurangzeb might be counting on taking Red Fort quickly enough to use the vast stores of the palace to supply his army, but it seemed a risky proposition. What if Dara decided to torch Red Fort rather than allow it to fall into Aurangzeb's hands?

No, she reflected, Aurangzeb must be convinced to give the Europeans another chance. But from Tara's reaction to the news, the priest might get his come-uppance if he had made a public outburst that could not be ignored, forcing Aurangzeb's hand.

If only there was a way to silence the priest. Car-valho was Aurangzeb's man through and through, and the Englishman, Methwold, was an eminently reasonable man.

"Does the priest have any known faults beyond an inability to control his tongue?" Nur asked, hoping for something she could use to have the man killed without the death seeming an obvious result of some courtier currying favor with Aurangzeb. Not that such gossip would be terribly difficult to overcome, but Aurangzeb had yet to endorse *any* murder, and Nur was certain she did not want to be the first to test the young man's for-giveness for unsolicited acts that reflected poorly on him.

Tara thought a moment before replying, "None that are known to me. He drinks, of course. But not to excess. He did arrive in camp with a massive black eye. Neither Methwold nor Carvalho are with him."

"That is to be expected. They are overseeing the arrival of the bulk of Aurangzeb's artillery train."

"You are correct, mistress. However, I am told by reliable sources that Carvalho is only a few days away. Given that there are no major obstacles to the transport of his guns..."

"It follows that he could have made the trip had he wished to," Nur finished her advisor's thought.

"Exactly so, mistress."

"Do we know if any messages arrived from Carvalho to Aurangzeb?" she asked.

"Only his usual daily progress report, and it caused no undue stir that I am aware of."

Nur nodded, turning her thoughts to what, exactly, Aurangzeb knew about Shaista Khan's declaration.

The Sultan Al'Azam had made no announcement condemning his cousin nor had he dispatched any of his army to deal with the threat. From previous experience with the young man's deep thinking and devious turn of mind, she considered it likely that Aurangzeb planned to deal with the most immediate threat as quickly as possible and then turn his attentions to the more distant, lesser one. And regardless of whether he knew or not, she also knew from previous experience that he would not appreciate any delay from her in conveying news that might affect him.

"We shall go early, and hope the Sultan Al'Azam will see us privately."

Nodding, Tara snapped her fingers.

The servants summoned by the sound bore one of the robes of honor Aurangzeb had given Nur a veil of translucent silk that was set off her eyes.

Tara's fits of temper frequently disappointed Nur, but she had to admit that supervising—and vetting—household staff was one of the young woman's exceptional strengths, especially when it came to the body slaves and those responsible for her mistress's appearance.

Nur supposed that, being raised from the position

of harem guard, Tara knew the value of preparation and proper equipment for battle. Armed with this knowledge, she rarely missed a beat when it came to ensuring Nur's servants and slaves had appropriate garb prepared for any foreseeable need.

So it was that it required mere moments before Nur emerged from her tent armed and armored for her own kind of war.

Red Tent, personal quarters of the Sultan Al'Azam

"You wished to see me before the public audience?" Aurangzeb said. His body slaves were dressing his slim frame with robes of state that, while a sober dark green in color, were trimmed and accented with thousands of peridots.

"I did, Sultan Al'Azam," Nur said, careful to keep out the hint of a mothering tone that threatened to creep into her voice on seeing him so thin. While she approved of the boy's fashion sense, she felt he should eat more. No man of her family had denied himself food the way Aurangzeb did.

"Regarding?" Aurangzeb asked, checking his image in the massive mirror some courtier had given him. "I'm told the priest continues his complaints?"

"He does," Aurangzeb said. "I have agreed to let him speak one last time today."

"May I ask why?" Nur said, disquiet rippling through her at the emperor's choice of words.

"I have been more than patient with the fool but I can countenance no more of his complaints. My umara will begin to think me weak if I do not put him in his place."

And if you would have given him what he asked for in the first place we wouldn't be here.

"Would you allow me to . . ." She let the request trail off unfinished, unsure how to proceed.

"To what? To speak to him on my behalf again?" Aurangzeb shook his head. "While I have no doubt of your experience and skill, the fool is so unreasonable even your abilities would prove insufficient to retrieve him from the folly he is bent on."

Knowing she could scarcely correct his assumption she wanted to talk to the man with a request to assassinate the priest, Nur asked, "But what of the men he represents? Can you afford to give up the supplies the Portuguese are sending?"

He nodded, the gesture more indicative of his approval of the question than an answer to it. He slapped the hands of his body slave away and put the last toggle through the embroidered loop himself.

Sensing his irritation, Nur waited for the emperor to speak his mind.

"I have considered the possible ramifications." He turned to look at her. "At least all those I'm aware of."

He knows.

"I do not wish to be presumptuous but—"

"There is information you think I do not have," he said, interrupting her.

"Say, rather, I wish to make certain you have it, as it might affect how you choose to deal with De Jesus."

He gestured as if to say, "Get on with it."

"I only just received word that Shaista Khan moves against you with an army of twenty thousand."

"It's closer to thirty thousand. And his advance scouts are less than a week from Agra. But beyond that, one of the men loyal to Shahaji reported his death this morning."

"Oh?" Nur prompted when Aurangzeb said nothing further.

"Apparently we were deceived. The Amir Salim Gadh Visa Yilmaz attacked and sacked a supply caravan from the Europeans. When Shahaji and his men went to hunt the Afghan down, he enlisted the help of other Maratha. One of these men attacked and killed Shahaji in front of Salim Yilmaz, who took no part in the slaying."

"But why?" Nur asked.

Aurangzeb shrugged. "The Bhonsle, Shahaji's clan, have done very well through their cooperation with the throne, gaining much wealth and no little power over their rivals for control of the region. This other chief resented those gains as well as Shahaji's high-handed assertions and manner during truce talks with Salim. Shahaji apparently drew a knife and threatened the other chief in front of both Salim and the Maratha chiefs. A duel ensued. Shahaji won that duel, but died shortly after the victory."

Nur heard a note of sadness in the young man's voice and felt a strange, sudden, and quite powerful sense of relief.

A moment's reflection unearthed the source of the sensation: aside from the occasion of the death of his father, Aurangzeb had rarely revealed any feelings for his fellow man. A ruler must, of necessity, remain aloof from most common feelings of camaraderie and the like, but to be entirely free from such emotion was to be a monster. And such a monster sitting the

Peacock Throne would truly be in a position to devastate the world.

"He will be missed," Nur said.

Aurangzeb nodded but said nothing, hands smoothing his robe unnecessarily.

"But does it follow, then, that the Afghan works for Dara still?" Nur wondered aloud, seeking to move the Sultan Al'Azam from such thoughts.

"Does it matter?" Aurangzeb asked.

Refusing to rise to the bait and thereby give the young man reason to ignore her advice, Nur looked away.

Aurangzeb noticed, as he did most things. "Speak your mind," he commanded.

"Your will, Sultan Al'Azam. It seems to me that everything matters, the hearts of those poised to be either friend or foe more than anything else."

"I have no knowledge that he is poised to be anything to me other than a nuisance. He may have been acting solely as a bandit: having seen easy prey, he seized it." Aurangzeb raised a finger. "He might equally have been acting on Dara's orders. We cannot know. What I do know is that his actions denied me both a valuable retainer and supplies for my army. In the end, these two setbacks benefit Dara. In light of these facts, I think I might be forgiven for thinking he is working for the pretender."

Nur, having come to the realization that it was this information, rather than news that Shaista Khan was so close, that precipitated Aurangzeb's decision to rid himself of the priest, hid a smile. If the Afghan was sacking their supply caravans en route to the army, then enduring his petulant and insulting presence was no longer necessary.

An example could be made.

Once again, she felt the cold satisfaction of having chosen the proper prince to back.

Inclining her head in genuine admiration, she said, "Like a dervish, you dance ahead of your enemies. Truly, God has favored you. I see my warnings and information were superfluous. Forgive me, Sultan Al'Azam."

A more natural smile graced his thin lips, making Aurangzeb appear his age for once. "Have you not just finished telling me that all intelligence is useful? I simply seek to make best use of all that God provides. That precept in mind, the departure of the priest will be made useful to me in binding my umara further still to my cause and the will of God. Once that is accomplished, I shall reveal the true reason I called the public audience this evening: not simply to deal with one recalcitrant Christian priest, but to announce the plan for storming Red Fort."

Nur nodded. "Your will, Sultan Al'Azam."

Aurangzeb sniffed. "What, no cautions? No assertions that I am being precipitous?"

"Not this day, Sultan Al'Azam. I believe I understand perfectly why you must take Red Fort as soon as possible. And if I don't, I'm sure you'll explain in sufficient detail that both my ignorance and any reservations I might have would be dispelled."

"God willing I will dispel the ignorance and reservations of all my followers so easily," he said. From anyone else the statement would have come laced with undertones of black humor. From Aurangzeb it held nothing but a fervent prayer and the sincere conviction that the prayer would be answered in time.

Red Tent

"I have heard much of your complaints, priest. What I have not heard are cries from those of my peoples you claim clamor for the opportunity to practice your faith."

De Jesus opened his mouth to reply but Aurangzeb spoke over him: "Wait! Is that...?" The Sultan Al'Azam placed a hand next to his ear as if listening intently.

The court held its collective breath. Nur, watching from behind the jali, smiled, her misgivings slowly easing.

After a moment Aurangzeb dropped his hand and shook his head. "No, it is but the taunts of my enemies, not the cries of the peoples of my dominion. I have been listening, and yet no one has come forth begging for you and your priestly brothers to show them how to give their souls to the man in Rome who claims to sit at the right hand of God!"

The court stirred, umara growing restless and murmuring angrily amongst themselves.

Seeming to ignore them, Aurangzeb leaned forward, placing one elbow on a knee. "But then, you come from Goa, where I hear they are now burning some loyal subjects, saying they are not Christian *enough*. Is it any wonder you have no idea what it is that the peoples of India desire?"

"They—" De Jesus began.

"The question," Aurangzeb interrupted, "was rhetorical. The many peoples of India have their own religions and do not need priests deciding their faith, *whatever it may be*, is false or insufficient to meet some artificial standard set by the Pope in Rome."

Nur's spies had sent word of the burnings. It had started as something to do with New Christians being hidden Jews, but the local population was now suffering the burnings as well. She hadn't thought to use the knowledge to discredit the priest, though she heartily approved of Aurangzeb's choice of tactics. If the Christians would burn those newly converted in the Estado, would they not seek to do the same within the empire?

The Sultan Al'Azam leaned back and gestured with both hands at the gathered court. "Just look about you, priest. Muslim, Hindu, Jew, and Zoroastrian. You can find these faiths and more here at my court. None are punished or preferred over another. None are burned at the stake for not being faithful *enough*. No, whatever the faiths practiced by those taking shelter in the shadow of my power, they themselves will choose those articles of faith and worship as their religion dictates."

"Then our agreement is ended," De Jesus said when at last Aurangzeb allowed him to get a word in. That he did not immediately point out that nonbelievers were taxed under Muslim law proved De Jesus was not *entirely* an idiot.

"Only because you wish it so, priest. I sit here on the eve of victory, but your naked ambition and religious bigotry could not suffer waiting but a few more days. Young as I am, be glad my advisors implored me to delay rewarding you for your service so we might better assess your character and intent. Now, your complaints and bitter attacks upon me have grown to the point I must remove you and all your goods from our camp. Go tell your master the archbishop I hold him responsible for sending a creature such as you to treat with me, who only wished peace and beneficial relations between our peoples."

De Jesus bowed stiffly and began to retreat. Nur could not tell if it was fear or anger that caused the slight tremors in the priest's hands.

"I have not given you leave to depart, priest." The words, calmly and evenly delivered, were more frightening than a barked rebuke would have been from such a young man.

"May I leave, Sultan Al'Azam?" De Jesus grated through clenched teeth.

The priest's tone was unacceptable. Nur looked at Aurangzeb along with most of the court.

Unlike the rest of the court, she knew Aurangzeb did not want to make a bitter enemy of Goa, something that must surely happen if Aurangzeb made a martyr of De Jesus. The Portuguese still controlled too much of the sea trade, and could easily make the sea route for the pilgrimage to Mecca nearly impossible for his Muslim subjects, which would only play into the hands of the Persians, who controlled much of the land route.

"You may leave, priest. Your horses, goods, and chattel will remain with the camp, a fine for your miserable manners and insolent words. Walk home. None will help you. None of my subjects will harm you. Get out of my sight."

The court heaved a collective sigh. Not born of fatigue, but with the contentment one felt when long-held expectations are finally met.

The priest fled in the wake of the Sultan Al'Azam's dismissal.

Nur made a mental note to have the man watched

as he made the long trek to the coast. Some courtier might seek concessions from the Portuguese by helping the priest, and Aurangzeb would want to know the names of such opportunists.

Sudden movement from the Sultan Al'Azam drew everyone's gaze from the priest's retreating back. Aurangzeb had stood to face his court, eyes glittering in the lamplight. It seemed, even from beyond the shelter of the jali, that the Sultan Al'Azam stared into each and every soul present. Those small hairs on the back of her neck rose to stand on end under that forceful regard.

He let the silence stretch.

"Tomorrow. After morning prayers. We shall storm Red Fort and cast down the pretender."

He drew the sword from his hip and, raising his voice only slightly to make them lean in to listen, continued, "God willing, those who have indulged his poor, weak character and led him astray from all that is good will fall under our righteous swords, their remains trampled under foot!"

The varied bellows, shouts, cries, and yells of approval for this pronouncement merged into what seemed a single long, impossibly loud cacophony that gave Nur a headache within moments.

Chapter 42

Red Fort
Lahore Gate

There were a lot of men lingering in the outermost courtyard of Lahore Gate when John and Bertram exited the middle gate.

"What are they doing?" he asked, thoughts of betrayal making the words sharper than intended.

One man, wearing an expensive robe that positively glittered in the lamplight, challenged them in angry tones. At least, John thought it was a challenge. His exhausted brain wasn't up to trying to translate beyond noting the fellow looked like someone had pissed in his porridge.

Bertram answered the challenge in Gujarati, maybe? Whatever he said must have been the right thing, though, as the man smiled and waved them on, talking all the while.

"He said he and his men have been ousted by a bunch of Sikhs. He's counting on you, Great General, to set them straight."

"You're pulling my leg," John said, but then saw the deep bow the man was offering as they passed into the outermost gatehouse.

"Not by much," Bertram said, taking a lamp from another warrior. "He is, as you might say, 'a mite pissed.' It seems Bidhi Chand came in a few hours ago and asked them, rather pointedly, to leave while he did something. There was some argument. He believes you were sent in answer to the messenger he sent to Dara regarding the matter."

John shook his head. Hoping to ease the pain of protesting shoulders, he adjusted the sling his rifle hung from. The Winchester itself wasn't that heavy, but combining it with the shoulder rig bearing Ilsa's Beretta and the chain shirt Dara had given him and Ilsa had insisted he wear, his shoulders and knees were groaning. Not as loud as his feet, mind you, but plenty loud. He thought about exchanging it for the Remington but the shotgun wasn't any lighter. Besides, Talawat and Gervais had assured him the fireworks they'd prepared would shed enough light to make the rifle's greater range useful in a night battle.

He chuckled, wondering what kind of dharma led a twentieth-century hillbilly from West Virginia to lead a mixed force of seventeenth-century warriors in battle against one of the largest armies he'd ever heard of, let alone laid eyes on. Because the closest he'd ever come to staff school was watching *Patton*. Judging from that film, asking what Patton would do in any given situation found an easy answer: *Attack! Attack! And then attack again if you have to!*

Oh, and piss off your fellow generals where possible . . .

John had vowed not to add fuel to the already-low-burning fuse of the garrison's fragile morale. Part of fulfilling that vow was making sure the various ethnic and religious groups of warriors—he couldn't exactly call them real soldiers, though the Sikhs were furthest along in that regard—were recognized and made to feel good about their contribution to the defense.

All of which translated to long nights on his feet for one John Dexter Ennis, Dara's chosen adjutant. John and Bertram covered nearly every yard of the walls of Red Fort at least once a night.

Bertram turned the corner and led the way up the last flight of narrow stairs leading to the roof of the outer gatehouse.

John stifled a sigh. He'd intentionally left the gatehouse for last as Bidhi Chand had asked him to meet here in the last hours before dawn.

"No light," someone hissed in Punjabi-accented Persian John barely understood.

"What the hell?" John muttered, stumbling to a halt.

"Something's going on," Bertram said. He turned off the small lantern he'd been carrying.

Thanks, Captain Obvious.

"Quietly. Come."

John and Bertram cautiously made their way up the last few steps and out into the night air above the gatehouse. The moon had set some time earlier, leaving only starlight to see by. There was a rhythmic sound John couldn't immediately identify coming from the edge of the tower. Once his eyes adjusted to the darkness he made out a group of men hauling on a rope that passed through one of the crenellations topping the wall.

A few seconds later, a turbaned and veiled warrior climbed into view only to drop lightly to his feet on the roof.

It wasn't until a squinting John heard the men with the rope congratulating their commander that he realized the warrior was Bidhi Chand. An instant later he realized the warrior had been outside the walls scouting. Without telling anyone, of course.

John moved to join the Sikh umara. The big warrior saw the up-timer coming and stepped from among his men. Unhooking the chain veil, his teeth shone white in the starlight.

"Rejoice, friend John! No more waiting! Aurangzeb sends his men against us this night."

"What?" John said, stunned by the contrast between the content of the message and the tone of barely suppressed glee in Bidhi Chand's voice. The man was a maniac.

But at least he's our maniac.

"Aurangzeb's men are blundering about out there"—he hiked a thumb at the darkness beyond the walls—"getting into position for an assault."

"How many?"

"The lion's share of his forces, I think. I could hear the jingle of their armor some way off, and the stink of smoke from the bhang the Rajputs smoke is hard to miss on a still night like tonight."

"You judged their numbers without laying eyes on them?" Bertram asked.

Bidhi Chand did not immediately respond to the question as he was speaking into the ear of a messenger. Only when he had finished giving his orders and the runner sped away did he return his attention to the up-timer and his companion. "Of course not! I killed a few and then joined them. It is the best way to get a feel for numbers at night."

"You killed..." Bertram mumbled.

John might've been as shocked as his friend but he'd been around Bidhi Chand enough to know better. No one built a legend that large without there being substance behind it.

Bidhi slapped the younger man on the back, the blow rocking him up onto the balls of his feet. "Don't worry. Plenty more where they came from, Bertram."

"Any idea how wide a front they're going to attack on?"

The Sikh's smile disappeared. "That I do not know for certain. I think that it will be a general assault with a particular focus on this gate and the wall to our immediate west. Delhi Gate is too strong without being reduced by artillery, so I cannot think he will hope to breach the defenses there, as it would be wasteful and stupid. Aurangzeb is not rumored to be either."

John nodded agreement. "General attack on all but the walls on the riverside, then?"

A slow, thoughtful nod. "I believe so. Though I suggest we do not to pull too many men from those defenses until dawn makes it clear they are not planning to sneak men across the river."

"How long?" Bertram asked, looking nervously out into the dark.

"Oh, we have some time yet." Bidhi waggled his head, loose chain veil chiming gently. "It is far more difficult to move men into position at night than most commanders would believe. They will be lucky to be in position to attack before dawn." He shrugged. "If they've already been given orders to begin the attack at a certain time regardless of whether or not they are in position, we may see some action earlier than that."

John decided not to comment on how cheerful Bidhi sounded, as it would only encourage him. Then again, if every one of Dara's men had a leader like Bidhi to look to, then Aurangzeb would be well and truly screwed.

John knew better, though. All he had to do was look at how poorly suited his own experience and training was to leading men in battle. Yet, here he was: second-in-command to an emperor whose sole previous battle had resulted in defeat and capture.

Thoughts making his belly churn, John realized there were things he should be doing about their situation rather than standing here admiring Bidhi Chand and feeling inadequate in the comparison.

"I assume your man"—John hiked a thumb at the stairs the runner had departed by—"was sent to tell Dara about the results of your scouting mission?"

"He was," Bidhi said. "He will also return with my armor."

John gestured a question at the chain shirt the man was already wearing.

"What, this?" The Sikh thumped his chest, smile flashing in the starlight again. "This is but a nightshirt, friend John. For the real heavy work, I dress myself in plate armor made by the finest armorers in the Punjab and touched by Guru Hargobind Singh himself."

John and Bertram just stared at the big Punjabi warrior.

"You might have seen it when I led Guru's men into the fort on the day of our arrival? I must say

I cut quite the dashing figure. At least, the dancing girls of the city seemed to think so."

"I remember," John said, smiling despite himself. Dark thoughts found it hard to linger around Bidhi. The man was like a force of nature, always ready to take on whatever the world put before him.

"John, we probably ought to join Dara," Bertram said.

Bidhi nodded. "I will join the rest of my men when I have donned my armor. We will be ready for the sally when the horn sounds."

"Be safe, Bidhi," John said. He raised his voice slightly and addressed the rest of the men, hoping they understood his Persian. "All of you, fight well and keep safe."

"Do not fear for us, John Ennis," Bidhi said. "Fear for the enemies of Sixth Guru Hargobind Singh and Dara Shikoh, Sultan Al'Azam!" As if sound itself responded to his desire, Bidhi's low-voiced declaration carried like thunder to the edges of the gatehouse roof and no farther.

John was shaking his head in wonder as he and Bertram clattered their way down the stairs.

"That man is something else, isn't he?" Bertram said.

"Damn straight," John agreed. He laughed a moment later, making himself a bit breathless as they rounded the last flight of stairs.

"What is it, John?" Bertram asked.

"Just glad I'm not the only one with a man-crush on him," John said, cupping the butt of his rifle to avoid scraping it against the inner wall of the stairwell.

"A man-crush?" Bertram asked the question an instant before deciphering the meaning for himself, if his laughter was any indication.

John was still grinning as they pounded across the courtyard from the outer gatehouse to the inner. Then he heard a high, shrill whistle. Another. Then the throb of drums.

"Shit."

Red Fort
Pavilion of the Healers

"Dara was sent for?" Jahanara asked, attempting to see past the walls and through the veil of night.

Firoz Khan nodded. "And the messenger found him already armored and on his way to Delhi Gate, Begum Sahib. Speaking of which, Shehzadi, I must don my own if I am to prove more than a passing nuisance to any who would threaten you."

Jahanara looked at the eunuch and raised her voice so the rest of the harem women gathered to render aid to the wounded could hear. "I must apologize for denying you the opportunity to test your blade skills against the enemy. They will not make it past our defenses. Dara and the husbands of the fine women gathered here will see to it."

Some of the worried expressions among the noble-women changed, some firming with resolve, others deepening as worries for loved ones about to fight made mockery of her words.

Firoz returned the look with the terribly put-upon expression she had only ever seen when Murad had destroyed the diwan's carefully prepared correspondence with a careless kick that had upended an ink well.

"What is it?" she asked, lowering her voice.

"You agreed, Begum Sahib."

"Agreed?" Jahanara said absently.

"Please do not pretend I am a fool, not today," Firoz said, voice full of gentle reproach.

Jahanara looked again at her advisor. "Whatever do you mean, Firoz?"

"You know very well what your diwan means, Begum Sahib." Smidha was far less careful with her tone than Firoz Khan. "You promised Dara if you were allowed to contribute the ablest of the harem guards to the common defense, you would stay well away from the fighting and allow your servants who had experience at arms to don armor and weapons in your defense."

"I did, did I?" Jahanara said, pretending a lapse in memory she did not suffer.

Lowering her voice, she quickly added for the benefit of her closest advisors: "If you insist on doing this, very well. But do so quietly, one at a time. Do not make the ladies of the court unnecessarily fearful for their safety. Some are pregnant, and should not be put under any more strain than is absolutely necessary." She carefully removed the hand that had slid to cover her own womb as she spoke, regretting the strange intensity that made the statement more of a threat than intended.

"Your will, Begum Sahib," her advisors said in unison. Firoz sent two of his assistants to arm themselves.

The drums beat upon her nerves. The shooting had yet to start, however. No wounded had been brought to the great pillared pavilion she had caused to be constructed at nearly the center of the great fort. Fully staffed, the hospital was as ready as the up-timers and Jahanara could make it.

Many of Father's guards had died after his assassination, not because they had suffered wounds that could not be treated but because there had been no healers near at hand to suture wounds and stem the bleeding. This battle, and all battles to come, would be different if she had her way.

"Ilsa," Jahanara called as the lovely ferenghi appeared from deeper within the pavilion. "Are you well?"

Ilsa made her way through the crowd of women to Jahanara's side before replying, "I am well, Begum Sahib. And you? Did you get any sleep?"

"I did." The lie came easily to Jahanara. It would not do to show weakness before the women of the court. Not before the battle. Not during the battle. There would be time enough later for allowing fear to show. For now she must find some way to convert the creeping fear that threatened to overwhelm her into the kind of example that showed the way for those in her care.

She lowered her voice. "Smidha, it is time you carried out your special orders. See to it."

"Your will, Shehzadi." Smidha leaned in. "Shall I bring the ferenghi?"

Jahanara nodded. "Monique knows already, it is just the timing of the thing. Ilsa may accompany you if she wishes."

Ilsa's puzzled glance slipped from Jahanara to Smidha.

"Where?" the blonde asked, when neither responded to her look.

"To collect my sister."

Ilsa's puzzled look disappeared, to be replaced by a look Jahanara didn't care to interpret. "I will go, Shehzadi."

The drums continued their remorseless beat.

"Where is Pr—" Jahanara was silenced by a hundred sudden streamers of light leaping from the walls protecting Red Fort. It was as if Shiva had raked nails across the early morning darkness to allow the light of the cosmos entry into the realms of men.

Almost every streamer exploded into an even brighter ball of light some twenty or thirty gaz above the walls.

Gunfire erupted from every quarter but the river as soon as Talawat's fireworks shed enough light for the Atishbaz and other firearm-equipped men to see their targets.

"Dear God," Ilsa breathed as the cannon added their roar to the battle for the Peacock Throne.

Red Fort
Delhi Gate

"Merciful God," Dara breathed as the light of Talawat's flares revealed a veritable carpet of men rushing toward the walls to either side of the gatehouse he had chosen to command the defense from.

"He is sweet mercy." Talawat's answer was rote, hands and mind busy with yet another check of his work. The Atishbaz sorcerer had chortled with glee as he and his apprentices had launched the flares. Dara was almost afraid to learn what the man would do when his next surprise was unveiled.

Glancing around, Dara realized the men atop the gatehouse were waiting for his command. Archers and arquebusiers in the adjacent towers were already raining death on Aurangzeb's army.

Feeling his quickened pulse throb in his scar, he took a deep breath and shouted as loudly as he could, "Death! Death to those who think to take what is yours!"

His men leapt into action, bowstrings and matchlocks snapping. Each type of arm releasing its own particular hail of death to reap his brother's sowar.

"Breathe, Sultan Al'Azam. Steady your breathing. Keep calm," Talawat whispered from beside him. "Just like shooting the long gun, this."

Dara nodded and complied, not wanting another seizure. Succumbing to such weakness in this moment would be disastrous for his cause.

"I'd probably be a better example if I wasn't scared out of my mind, too," Talawat added as the cannon roared again.

John climbed into view and trotted over to Dara, up-timer rifle clicking against his mail. "Sultan Al'Azam, it doesn't appear as if Aurangzeb plans to assault the River Gate."

"Good," Dara said, peering down the length of the wall. Aurangzeb's men were, despite losses, about to surmount the undefended outer wall that ran parallel to the heavier, taller, and thoroughly manned inner.

"Good," he repeated. "Are you ready, Talawat?"

The gunsmith's smile was so broad it seemed his face would split in half. "I'm always ready to make things go boom, Sultan Al'Azam."

"John?" Dara said.

"Wish there was a little more light," the up-timer said, readying his rifle.

Talawat's snicker was gleeful. "'Wish there was more light!' he says."

Chapter 43

Siege lines
Grand battery

Carvalho was just finishing his report for Aurangzeb when the night sky above the walls was lit by a constellation of stars that rose to challenge the darkness.

A heartbeat later the quiet was rent by hundreds of gunshots, followed closely by the screams of wounded men.

The fire from the walls of Red Fort reaped a red harvest as the defenders opened up on those struggling to cross the ground between the deep ravine and the moat. The walls and towers of the fort erupted in smoke and what seemed a glittering silver rain as arrowheads caught and scattered the flarelight. Hundreds of men fell in those first moments, killed in a hail of arrow and ball.

Carvalho felt for them, even as he was glad his guns were out of reach of bows and aimed fire from the defenders. He had brought the guns of the grand battery to well within three hundred yards, the range he could be confident his own battery could reliably damage earth-backed walls and even aim with some precision once the sun rose.

Carvalho focused, projecting outcomes with the dispassionate eye a lifetime of conflict had trained him to. He wouldn't have delayed, but had to decide if this surprise merited a change to his report.

More of Aurangzeb's men rushed forward, a seemingly unstoppable flood. Such was the pressure of their numbers the men nearest the dead and dying were shoved forward over their unlucky comrades whether they wished to advance or not.

A minute passed. Another. The men continued to rush headlong into the killing field at the base of the wall.

"Go!" Carvalho shouted, deciding the flares were insufficient cause to substantially change the disposition of his guns. They simply decreased the wait he would have to begin accurate fire. He turned his face away as clods of earth pattered around him, shot from beneath the hooves of the messenger's mount.

Talawat had been very clever. The fireworks they were using cast their light farther and far longer than anything Carvalho had seen before. Light enough he could see his own guns were nearly ready.

A grin stretched Carvalho's lips. Unintended consequences made the Fates smile: the flares also allowed the attackers to clearly see their targets. Carvalho's guns would soon punish the defenders for the gunsmith's creativity.

Carvalho checked the positioning of his battery. They had used the light to good purpose, aligning on his own.

Satisfied, Carvalho blew on the match cord.

"Fire!" Carvalho bellowed, touching the red coal clutched in the stylized dragon's teeth at the end of his linstock to powder.

One after another, all of his grand battery belched smoke, fire, and death at the walls of Red Fort. The men bent to the task of reloading as Carvalho assessed the damage wrought by his guns and the progress of Aurangzeb's infantry.

Their fire did little but serve to keep the more fearful of the defenders from showing themselves for a few moments. Moments the infantry used to advantage, scaling the outer wall.

The defenders resumed firing down on the heavy infantry, dropping perhaps one man in five. It was hard to tell exactly how many were wounded but did not fall as the Rajputs' use of opium-infused bhang in battle made them virtually immune to pain.

Men died, those who fell serving as fuel to fire the anger that sent men over the wall regardless of the cost, the danger, the pain.

The first man was over the wall. He died, was replaced by ten more, then twenty more Rajputs followed.

"Up!" his second yelled, when the great bronze piece was reloaded. Attention drawn by the shout, Carvalho set about aiming the gun when the wall disappeared in a sheet of flame.

The space between the outer and inner walls of Red Fort became a hell on earth as flames and screams rose to the heavens. No doubt seeking to quench the flames burning the flesh from their bones, men flung themselves from the top of the outer wall to perish on the rocks below.

Carvalho flogged his brain into some semblance of coherent thought: *Some new type of mine. Stands to reason Talawat wouldn't be caught idle when his original plan died in the explosion of the munitions factory.*

Hoping there remained enough Rajputs to carry the wall, a sweating Carvalho pressed the linstock to the touchhole. He skipped back and out of the way as the cannon fired, sending its shot to slam into the red sandstone of the middle gatehouse. His careful aim was rewarded, as two of the crenellations topping that portion of the structure nearly perpendicular to his position exploded in red dust and flying stone fragments, killing the men shooting from within and dropping much of it into rubble. The murderous fire from the Sikh defenders slackened, at least for the moment.

Well drilled, his crew leapt to their tasks. A wet leather swab went hissing into the barrel. The rest of the men strained and heaved to drag the heavy gun back into position, began loading her.

Carvalho bent over the gun but spared a glance at the rest of the crews of the grand battery. Three gun bellowed as he watched, closely followed by the auditory assault of guns four and five, then number six. Number two was still not in position to shoot again. The reason became apparent an instant later when the gun captain slumped over, the contents of his chest smeared over the barrel of his gun.

"Up!" his second shouted, letting his distracted captain know they were ready to correct, but Carvalho was still trying to figure out what had hit the man at the next gun. He'd carefully sited his guns to be outside the range of arquebusiers and bowmen on the walls and in a position to be fired upon by only two of Red Fort's cannon. Laying out the path and final positions had been difficult, but they should have been safe from any but a freak shot from the walls.

Another crewman from gun two fell screaming, struck in the back by a heavy bullet. Carvalho sought the source of the fire, found an absurdly long plume of white powder smoke projecting from what appeared to be a single man's gun above the gatehouse.

Must be one of those up-timer weapons I heard so much about. Thank God they don't have more than a few of—

A man holding a similar weapon joined the first. Then Carvalho made out two more.

Mouth suddenly dry, Carvalho screamed at his men to adjust aim. More heaving and cursing had the gun lined up in time for Carvalho to see six or seven men armed with the up-timer weapons discharge their guns. A heartbeat later the maddeningly long-ranged guns began reaping Carvalho's men like so much blood-soaked wheat.

Every fiber of his being screaming at him to hurry, Carvalho took his time and carefully lined up the shot. He could see the defenders rise up from behind the shelter of the parapet, leveling their long guns and fiddling with something on top of each weapon. He finished, powdered the touch and stepped aside just as the men atop the gatehouse disappeared behind a cloud of powder smoke.

He nearly missed the touchhole with the linstock as every man of gun three perished in a hail of bullets.

The cannon belched, firing true. A portion of the

parapet jumped as the heavy ball shattered sandstone to embed itself in the brick backing beneath. One of the outsized crenellations that sheltered a defender buckled and fell outward from the gatehouse, dropping him four stories to the hard ground amongst the rubble of his former protection.

Carvalho again watched his other guns as his crew repeated the complex, carefully orchestrated dance the machinery of war required when one was in a race to see who could kill more, faster. The other gun crews, hurrying to match his aim and get off a shot before the deadly weapons of their opponents could be reloaded, hardly matched his accuracy. Two struck too low to repeat the effect of Carvalho's shot, burying themselves in the sandstone gatehouse without visible effect. One sailed high, disappearing from view. The fourth, either by some freak stroke of luck or the gun captain's skill, raked the top of the perpendicular wall that had been their initial target. Sandstone, men, and masonry shattered amid great clouds of dust and smoke.

Another series of flares rose above the walls, though by now dawn was more than a gray suggestion to the east.

Two gun's reduced crew, struggling heroically to position their weapon for another shot, died at their gun. The lone cannon that could bear on them from Red Fort had found them with a shot that skipped from the ground some forty yards in front of their position and then barreled into the gun, savagely shoving it sideways and breaking it from the limber. Carvalho could see no one alive in its wake when the weight of iron and bronze settled to earth.

The grinding lethality of battle continued: the crew

of gun five perished under the lash of the up-timer long guns before they were ready to fire again.

Sweat pouring from his lean frame, Carvalho made certain of his aim one more time and unleashed another shot. Another paltry few Sikhs were injured. It seemed for a moment that their bawling cries could be heard even at this remove.

Then the camel corps loped past his battery, screaming zamburakchi whipping their bawling mounts relentlessly toward the sound of the guns.

"The Sultan Al'Azam sends his regards!" someone shouted from behind Carvalho.

The Portuguese mercenary turned and saw a man in messenger greens sitting a fine tall horse that looked as if it would rather be anywhere but smelling camel.

"The Sultan Al'Azam commands y—" the man started to say, but pitched backward over saddle when one of the heavy bullets of the infernal up-timer weapons struck him in the chest. The horse, predictably, bolted back the way it had come.

"God. Hates. Me," Carvalho muttered. There being nothing else to do and unable to spare a man for clarification of his orders, he shouted for his men to continue firing. They would fire as long as they could.

The artillery captain cursed God, cursed Aurangzeb, cursed his brother umara, but most of all he cursed the spies who had failed to uncover the truth. Based on their reports, everyone from the emperor to the least soldier of Aurangzeb's army had been dead certain the explosion that claimed the munitions factory had cost Dara the ability to produce ammunition for the up-timer weapons.

They were paying for that failure now with their lives.

Aurangzeb's command group

Aurangzeb ground his teeth as yet another Rajput fell, an arrow sprouting from his chest. If the man yelled or cried out to his gods, the sound was lost in the distant roar and crackle of the battle taking place at the base of Red Fort's walls.

It had been hard to tell how things were going until the defenders had set off the fireworks. Until then, Aurangzeb had been fairly sure most of his men had made it, if not into position, then close enough, by the deadline the plan called for.

The light of the flares had revealed the shambles his carefully thought-out timetable had been reduced to. Some areas of the defenses were almost entirely uncontested while others were faced with masses of men packed so tightly they got in each other's way.

Worse yet, Aurangzeb's subordinates, commendably eager to come to grips with the enemy, fed men into the assault without carefully lining the troops up to minimize the time they would spend under fire from the defenders. It was less than perfect.

A messenger rode up as his artillery began firing.

The Sultan Al'Azam nodded. He had given no order to begin the cannonade, but he approved of Carvalho's initiative. The initial plan had called for the artillerist to move his mobile pieces up under cover of darkness and then only fire at dawn, when it was hoped there would be enough light to avoid striking the attacking men. The flares gave him the opportunity to do just that, and, rather than wait for Aurangzeb's permission, he'd opened fire.

Aurangzeb waved for the messenger to speak.

"Carvalho reports his guns are in position and he is firing, Sultan Al'Azam."

"Understood." Aurangzeb smiled, admiring the ferenghi's style. Making certain the emperor could not interfere with the best application of his guns even while he sent a messenger to mollify his superior smacked more of the experienced courtier than hardened mercenary.

The messenger's horse twitched, trying to move farther from the loud noises, but the rider was too accomplished a horseman to allow his mount to embarrass him before the Sultan Al'Azam.

Aurangzeb considered cautioning Carvalho, but decided against it. Repeating himself would do no good, and only serve to insult the touchy ferenghi as he'd issued complete orders to the mercenary-cum-umara in a face-to-face audience. The artillerist knew his craft, and would only fire so long as he could be reasonably assured his pieces would not strike Aurangzeb's own men.

He gestured for the messenger to retire and rest his balky mount.

While he'd been considering cautioning his captain of artillery, the infantry had pressed forward into the attack. Successfully in some areas, though the Rajputs in front of him attempting to take Lahore Gate were slowed by the deep ravine and rain-swollen creek they had to cross under the arrows of the garrison. Despite their shields and heavy armor, it seemed to Aurangzeb a great many of them had fallen even before they set ladders to the outer walls adjacent to the outermost, and lowest, gatehouse.

"Messenger to Samir Khan," Aurangzeb said.

The next in line of his royal messengers came forward.

Aurangzeb did not look at the man as he rattled off his commands. "He is to deploy the camel corps in front of Carvalho's battery and try and keep the heads of the garrison down. He should focus his fire to the left of the gate and on the left of the gatehouse proper." He spared the man a look. "Repeat it."

The rider flawlessly repeated his orders and Aurangzeb waved him to his duty.

Relative silence descended as the rider galloped away.

"Sultan Al'Azam?" Habash Khan said.

Aurangzeb looked to the Habshi, barely visible in the predawn murk, waving permission to speak.

"Something strange is going on..." the man said, eyes distant and expression slack as he regarded the fighting.

Aurangzeb returned his gaze to the battle, seeking those details that had made his umara call for his attention.

Why do their cannon not fire? He would have thought Carvalho's guns were caught in the light of the flares as well and would prove a good target, but they had been silent since the beginning.

They watched in silence for a little while, Aurangzeb wary of disrupting the other man's concentration. Father had once claimed to have developed a sense for the ebb and flow of battle, and insight for when and where to strike or withdraw. Aurangzeb knew he lacked the experience to have fully developed such a talent, but, he hoped, was wise enough to recognize it when he saw it. Unable to find it himself, he looked again at the Habshi and then followed the line of his gaze.

Sidi Habash Kahn's attention had settled on the battle surging at the base of the walls to either side of Lahore Gate.

Aurangzeb's Rajputs were over the low wall and dragging ladders into the space between it and the high inner wall. Hundreds of men, packed shoulder to shoulder... He cocked his head... sensing something... off.

"Ah!" Habash Khan sat bolt upright next to him. "They do not shoot as much as they might... Almost as if they want our men to... Merciful God!"

Aurangzeb understood then, too. He opened his mouth to shout for messengers when the gray-black of the last minutes before dawn suddenly lit with fire and light so intense it seemed the sun rose at the base of the wall. In the moment that followed, the young emperor felt his heart skip a beat before stuttering back into its normal pulse just as a muted, thunderous, evil roar reached his ears. Dara had mined the space between the walls! Men ran, made human torches when their hair, clothing, their very flesh, started to burn. Even those God chose to spare trembled at the thought of fighting on. Some broke, fleeing the horror. Aurangzeb did not even blame them.

The reinforcements Aurangzeb had sent slowed their rush to the walls, understandably reluctant to expose themselves to whatever hell lay in wait for them.

All but the Rajputs. They, incensed by—rather than fearful of—the garrison's weapons, redoubled their efforts to climb the walls and come to grips with the enemy.

But whatever the flame weapons had been, they were not the only nasty surprise Dara had in store for his brother's warriors.

The relative silence that persisted after the hellish mines had gone off was broken by a resumption of sharp cracks from the walls and towers of the fortress.

In the hell-light cast by the burning residue of the mines, Aurangzeb saw a defender level an odd-looking arquebus in the direction of a battery of Carvalho's guns. The gunners went about reloading, sure in the knowledge that nothing but another cannon could reach them. A moment later a long plume of smoke shot from the end of the gun.

A measurable heartbeat later, one of Carvalho's gunners folded.

Aurangzeb ground his teeth, but ordered another of his umara into the assault. So they had one or two of the weapons modeled on the up-timers' guns, but they would not be enough to make any difference.

Two more artillerymen fell at almost the same time. Then an entire gun crew went down within the time it took to take one breath.

Stunned, Aurangzeb watched as four other men, easily found by the cottony plumes of gun smoke, manipulated their weapons, dropping fresh twinkling things into the breeches.

Another series of smoky plumes. More men fell at their guns, struck down from a seemingly impossible range.

Carvalho's cannon kept firing. Retreat under fire was a death sentence as certain as staying, and fighting men such as those the Portuguese gun captain surrounded himself with would rather strike back than be killed while running from battle.

Two of Carvalho's guns spoke at the same time. The fortifications topping the middle gate disappeared in a cloud of dust. The rumble was audible even over the other noises of battle.

The battle went on unabated. Still Dara's cannon had not fired. As if his observation had summoned evil from them, the muzzle of the first of Dara's guns belched smoke.

Expecting the cannon to be targeting Carvalho's battery, Aurangzeb closed his eyes and said a brief prayer for the already-beleaguered gunners. He opened them to see his prayer had been too specific. Others had needed God's protection: the men approaching the outer walls had been targeted by some fresh outrage created, no doubt, by the up-timers or that devil Talawat. It seemed as if the men had splashed in a horrific fan of bloody remains. It looked almost as if God, in his righteous anger, had reached out and pulped the men who strove to take the walls.

Dara had waited until Aurangzeb's men were too close to retreat, too densely packed to do anything more than die screaming. Then, and only then, Dara had unleashed this new outrage. And, if the frenetic activity around guns of the fortress was any indication, Dara's pets had provided the means to repeat the outrage.

Aurangzeb's eyes desperately sought some positive sign, some development that would confirm that God was still with him. But God, instead of showing him favor, revealed yet another hateful weapon from the future.

Despite the fires, the devastating swarm-projectiles Dara's cannon fired, and the still-falling hail of arrows, several hundred screaming Rajputs had not only successfully set their scaffolds and ladders at the base of the redoubt west of Lahore Gate, they were about to crest the inner wall.

Some twenty Sikhs appeared atop the next redoubt thirty gaz away and leveled weapons that looked suspiciously like those already used to such good effect against his artillery.

Aurangzeb's fist clenched upon his prayer beads.

It seemed as if the entire body of Sikhs fired in the same instant. All of them certainly disappeared in a cloud of gray-white gun smoke.

An unbelievable number of Rajputs perished from that one volley, torn from the wall like the leaves of some flesh-and-blood ivy uprooted by an angry giant. It was worse than the new munitions Dara's cannon fired; no man who stepped in the line of fire of a cannon could fail to know the risks involved. No, these handguns that killed so many with one discharge were the work of the Adversary. While their effect was even more devastating, it became clear these weapons were not the same as the longer-ranged ones almost immediately after they fired. These new ones did not project their gun smoke as far from the barrel and, more terrifying, fired once more without the manipulations the other weapons seemed to require.

Surely it would be too much, even for Rajputs of the warrior caste.

Aurangzeb weighed his options. Even if they broke, the scaffolds and ladders the Rajputs had fought into place remained up. He still had nearly ten thousand men between him and that section of the wall, men who could, properly led, exploit the opening the Rajputs seemed to have carved in the defenses.

Carvalho had already called forward the guns the

night attack had forced him to leave behind. Their heavy projectiles would give any defender at the wall pause, make short work of the gates, and with God's favor, bring down the walls as well.

Aurangzeb found his prayer beads rattling through his fingers at an ever-increasing pace.

God willing, the dawn would allow them to win through. Thoughts of God and the rattle of the beads reminded him that he'd nearly forgotten *Al-Fajr* prayers.

The young emperor made to dismount, causing a stir amongst his messengers and bodyguards. Caught off guard by his sudden need to pray, those who were slow to part for him were pushed aside by those who knew better. Unrolling the carpet and performing the ablutions with his habitual care settled his spirit. Within moments he was kneeling to face Mecca and adding his unworthy praise to that of countless others in the world.

So fervent was his heart's desire that God hear him that the sounds of battle—not the cannon, nor the arquebusiers, nor even the distance-thinned screams of men dying to serve His ends—were unable to disturb his prayers.

Chapter 44

Red Fort
North wall

Atisheh nocked another arrow, drew on the powerful bow, and leaned over to lose it through the loop. She grinned as the fletching tickled her cheek, timing the release to skewer one of the men struggling with a ladder they planned to plant at the base of the outer wall to the right and below her tower. She added her arrow to the storm falling along the attackers.

"There are so many you barely have to aim!" one of her fellow guards shouted, echoing Atisheh's sentiments exactly as the target folded around her arrow.

She reached for another arrow, found the pannier mounted to the wall next to her empty.

"Runner!" Atisheh shouted as she turned and pulled another sheaf of arrows from the supply at the center of the tower.

"Yes?" the boy said from not two steps away.

"Tell the diwan we'll need more arrows, then find

Talawat and tell him I take back everything I ever said about his art. Those flares are working very, very well."

"Wait until you see what the new guns do!"

"Off with you, boy!" Atisheh grunted, already nocking another arrow.

The Grape Garden

The sounds of battle penetrated the palace complex as Smidha led Monique and Ilsa to the Grape Garden. Slippered feet found their way without thought as Smidha fretted over the wisdom of Jahanara's decision to seize Roshanara.

For one, the harem was already perilously short of guards. So much so, Smidha felt the need to improvise.

For another, while the younger princess was certainly a traitor, she had been under very close observation for months and made no effort to do anything more than pass information to Aurangzeb. Indeed, Smidha was as certain as one immured in the politics of court life could be that Roshanara had made no attempt to bribe, coerce, or even contact any of Dara's commanders, and certainly not any placed in charge of the gates.

And Smidha's informants had been eager to report Roshanara's *every* move. A reputation for capricious violence against servants and slaves alike had made recruiting people to spy on the princess absurdly easy. The difficulty had been discovering those who would not make up vile rumors as a means to strike at the young woman.

On the other hand, Jahanara had made clear to

her sisters that the royals were to present a united front to the nobles of the court. Roshanara, true to her reputation, was not complying. Indifferent to her duties to the royal family, Roshanara had decided to come here instead of joining the rest of the noble ladies and her royal sisters when the shooting started.

As Smidha, Monique, and Ilsa walked from the covered galleries and into the jasmine-scented night, they could see Roshanara had installed herself on the central platform of the garden where she had apparently rousted a number of her brother's dancing girls and a pair of blind musicians and commanded them to perform for her.

Her thoughts were interrupted when Roshanara, her back to Smidha and the Mission women's approach, flung a goblet at one of the dancers for no other reason Smidha could see than it entertained her to do so.

The goblet clipped the side of the girl's head, sending her sprawling in what Smidha hoped was a welter of wine, not blood.

Roshanara's drunken laughter filled the garden as the dancers stopped abruptly.

Disgusted if not entirely surprised by the princess's behavior, Smidha shook her head. Where Jahanara had stopped indulging in temper tantrums once she came of age, Roshanara had frequently indulged even the slightest inconvenience by beating her nurses.

Slowing, Smidha's heart swelled when her gaze found two particular women among the dancing girls. Glad neither had been Roshanara's victim, she gave each woman a tiny nod. Both gave somewhat more obvious nods in return, but Smidha doubted very much that Roshanara would notice.

Setting herself as if to carry a heavy load across uneven ground, Smidha stopped a few steps from the platform and cleared her throat.

The musicians, their performance already drowned by the constant arrhythmic percussion of the battle and Roshanara's behavior, stopped playing. They were long accustomed to taking such inaudible cues from Smidha.

"Roshanara Begum, you will come with me," Smidha said.

"What is this?" Roshanara asked, refusing to turn and look at her.

"You will come with me," Smidha repeated.

"I will do no such thing, *servant*."

An angry Monique stepped up next to Smidha and, before the older woman could stop her, said, "Jahanara Begum commands it, Roshanara."

The outburst got the princess's attention. She turned her head and glared at Monique. "I don't care if you are Jahanara's pet ferenghi, you will not speak to me in such tones. I'll have you whipped."

Monique smiled. "You are welcome to try."

Roshanara's expression slipped from angry hauteur to angry suspicion before she mastered it.

"Come with me, *now*," Smidha said.

"You think you can threaten me?" Roshanara asked, voice rising as she got to her feet.

Smidha laughed. "Threaten? Why would I threaten you?"

"I—"

"When we can just *make* you come along?" Smidha interrupted, lifting her chin.

The two dancing girls rushed the platform and, vaulting it with the smooth grace born of hard training, grabbed the princess.

"Unhand me!" Roshanara screamed. "I have done nothing wrong!"

Smidha tutted, raised a forefinger before the princess's face and waggled her head as if instructing her. "You have done a great many wrongs, Shehzadi; we are just seeing to it you do nothing wrong for the next little while."

Roshanara screamed again, struggling to free herself from the dancing girls, to strike at Smidha.

The response from her captors was immediate and, from their smiles, something they rather enjoyed: one thrust a knee into Roshanara's gut with an economical move Smidha presumed she'd learned defending herself from highborn bastards thinking they could take advantage. When Roshanara reflexively folded over her abused belly, the other girl wrenched the arm she held behind the princess's back.

"I would not give these young women yet another excuse to mistreat you, Roshanara."

"I have done nothing!" Roshanara gasped.

Smidha sniffed and regretted it. Roshanara's breath was redolent with wine. Nonetheless she pointed at the girl who was being helped to her feet by the remaining members of her troupe.

Roshanara followed the line of Smidha's finger to rest on the dancing girl. She tossed her head, dismissive. "That, that's nothing!"

"No, Roshanara, *she* is someone. *She* is the girl you hurt out of petty spite, for no other reason than you could."

"No, *it* is *nothing*. Nothing compared to what I will do to you once Aurangzeb rules!"

Smidha hoped she kept the sudden thrill of fear she felt run down her spine from reaching her face and asked, "You admit to working for the pretender?"

"Pretender?" Roshanara scoffed. "Can you not hear the sound of his guns? He is the strongest!"

Smidha shook her head and passed the nearest dancer a length of silk cord to bind their prisoner with.

Roshanara's struggles were more violent but no more effective this time. She ended up facedown on the grass and gasping for air as the girls bound her hands together behind her back.

"Here I was, worrying Jahanara's order to confine you might be excessive." Ilsa's tone was light as she stepped close to Roshanara, but Smidha did not miss how one hand cupped her belly and the baby growing there. "But now I wonder if we shouldn't just throw you to your brother? Perhaps from atop the nearest tower?"

"Ferenghi bitch!" Roshanara spat. "You and yours will be first to die!" A sudden heave bounced one of the dancers off her back.

"That's not very nice," Monique said, straddling the princess with a length of dark silk in one hand. Leaning down, she ground an elbow into the small of Roshanara's back.

When the princess's head came off the grass, Monique slipped what turned out to be a silken bag over it.

"You seem entirely too practiced at that, Monique," Ilsa said.

Monique grinned. "Papa was right: there is no such thing as a misspent youth."

"Really?" Ilsa asked.

Monique shrugged, still grinning.

Smidha shook her head. These people were almost

as strange as the up-timers they had chosen to make their lives with.

Strange, but on our side, thankfully!

Pavilion of the Healers

"Here they come," Rodney said.

Gervais looked up from his preparations to see his friend was correct. The first few sets of stretcher-bearers were crossing the big courtyard from both the north and south, field medics trotting beside the wounded. The patient coming in from the north had an arrow protruding visibly from the juncture of her neck and shoulder.

"We are ready for this, my friend," he said, thoroughly drying his hands and then inspecting his nails. It wouldn't do to have one catch on a man's wound or stitches.

"I sure hope so."

"We are better prepared than any army other than that of the USE itself," Gervais said, with what he hoped was perfect confidence.

The bearers from the south were the first to arrive, hustling their charge into Rodney's operating room.

"See you when it's over," Rodney rumbled, following them.

"See you then, Rodney."

Gervais went to his own station, giving a reassuring nod to his team. Several women were not only present, but integral to the team. Two of them would make better doctors than any of the current crop of male candidates, but Gervais knew better than to pursue their elevation too soon. Pushing too hard and early had resulted in far too many swindles going sideways on him. The more people thought a given thing their own idea, the easier they were to bring around to your purpose.

The second set of bearers entered. The patient was fully conscious and looking at Gervais with interest and no little fear under sweating brows.

"Single wound. No exit. Patient hasn't lost a lot of blood," the medic was saying, "but it seems the shaft of the arrow may have broken on penetrating. I thought it best to leave it in place and bring him to you."

Brow cocked above her veil, Sunitra held up the opium pipe.

Gervais nodded to her but spoke to the medic, "Well done. Don't forget to resupply before you go back out."

Sunitra lit the opium pipe and thrust it at the wounded warrior.

"I don't need this," the warrior said, pushing the pipe away with his good hand.

"Not yet," Gervais said, lifting one of the larger surgical knives, "but when I start cutting on you with this, I think you'll be glad of it. Now shut up and suck on that pipe."

The man's eyes went comically wide. When Sunitra held the pipe out again, he grasped it, quickly stuffing the stem between his lips to draw, hard, on it.

Gervais gestured. "Move a little onto your side, if you please, and let me take a look at that."

He had to cut the cotton tunic away from the man's back, as the arrow hadn't penetrated it. From the look of it, the arrowhead was indeed broken off.

He could see the nearly blunt cylinder of the arrow shaft pushing the skin at his back up.

"Do you know what happened?" Gervais asked. He needed to let the opium work on the boy before cutting anyway, and if the fellow could tell him where the arrowhead was, it might just help.

"I'm not sure. I was at the loophole firing. I heard a clatter, felt like I got punched, and was nearly spun off my feet. My brother said the arrow hit the wall and then me."

"Which probably saved your life. Of course it doesn't really help me figure out whether or not the arrowhead's in you or sitting at the bottom of the loophole you were defending from, but still..." He pressed gently on the would-be exit wound. When the man barely responded, Gervais glanced at one of the men and gave a sharp nod.

That man, a burly fellow selected for his muscles, gently took the patient's wrists in his own hands.

"Use the ties, that's what they're there for."

The orderly did as he was told. The next few minutes were lost to Gervais as he explored the wound and eventually extracted the arrowhead with a minimum of cuts that he was quite pleased with.

"Doctor Vieuxpont, I can finish here."

Gervais paused, hand halfway to picking up the suture needle. He looked up and saw there were three more patients waiting for his attention.

He dropped his hand. "Please do."

The burly orderly and Sunitra left with the first patient, the lovely local already marking the point where she would suture the wound.

"Next!" he called as another woman entered carrying

a tray of fresh surgical knives. As she exchanged the
trays he dropped the scalpel he'd been using on the
old one.

"You're welcome, Doctor." Gervais flinched, recognizing the voice. Veiled and dressed in one of the
nondescript robes that were provided to hospital workers
because they could be easily laundered or replaced, he
could hardly be blamed for having mistaken Shehzadi
Jahanara for a servant girl.

"My thanks, Begum Sahib."

"You are most welcome, Doctor." The princess left
without another word or backward glance.

Shaking his head, Gervais lost himself again in
the treating of wounds and the healing of bodies, a
skill and calling he would never have had the chance
to practice had he remained in Europe rather than
coming to this exotic, beautiful land.

Lahore Gate

John coughed as the stairwell filled with blinding,
choking dust. The gatehouse shook so violently he
stumbled, barked a knee on the next stairs. He was
dragging himself upright when another colossal pair
of impacts made his ears ring.

Something caught on his rifle, dragging him off
his feet and sideways. Something hard and heavy hit
his other shoulder and upper chest. A noise like a
freight train passing within inches of his ear rumbled
and clattered to a crescendo. He blinked, shot his
arms out in an attempt to grab something that wasn't
moving. An interminable, horrifying scrabble later, he

lay prone on the uneven steps of the gatehouse, rifle somewhere below.

He coughed again, started to wipe at the dust-caked eyelashes that glued his eyes shut, but stopped as his shoulder throbbed a protest. He switched hands, managed to clear his vision enough to look around in the dust-tinged predawn light.

The entire upper works of the middle gatehouse's western side had been shattered and fallen outward. When it went it had taken the wall to his right with it. He looked down, saw rubble and bodies strewn like some giant child had a tantrum in front of the gate.

John decided then that sandstone was fine for most purposes, and looked pretty, but he would have preferred granite, especially for the outer defenses. The outer and middle gatehouses of the Lahore gate complex weren't backed by earth like the inner gate, making them eggshells in comparison. It was like sitting in a thin stone box while someone hammered it with steel sledgehammers.

Comparisons between his current predicament and the storied race between John Henry and the steam drill came to mind, making him chuckle.

Don't matter one bit to the stone whether it's muscle, steam, or black powder driving the sledgehammer.

His mad chuckle ended in a dust-choked cough that made something grate in his chest.

Guns started to speak again as he looked for a way down from his perch.

Either that or his ears had recovered enough to hear such noises over the ringing.

He looked over at the sound of the guns and saw a few of the silvery tips of Sikh helmets working over the long barrels of Talawat's .45-70 rifles. Long plumes of gunpowder reached out from the walls.

Hope those guns shoot as good as they look... Never did name 'em... His thoughts sluggish, like molasses in winter, John shook his head.

What was I doing before the gatehouse fell on me?

"Bertram!" he croaked. The down-timer had been just behind him on the stairs. He spat. Hacked. Spat again. There was blood in the mud that dribbled from his mouth.

He tried again: "Bert!"

"Doan... call... medat."

John looked around, but still couldn't see Bertram. "What?" he said.

A coughing fit gave away Bertram's position.

A shiver ran down John's spine. Bertram was about ten feet *above* John. How he'd ended up there, John didn't even want to guess.

"Don't. Call. Me. Bert."

"Okay, I won't."

Something slashed through the air beside John's head and buried itself in the stones between him and Bertram. Both of them spent a moment stupidly watching the arrow quiver like a flower reaching for the sun.

"Move, John!" Bertram yelled.

John was already crawling across the broken stone toward the uncertain safety of Bertram's perch as fast as his injured shoulder, brutalized lungs, and the unstable surface would allow.

Another cannonball struck nearby, making the stones beneath him shiver. Much more abuse, and there might be another collapse.

He had more immediate threats to concern himself with, though, as arrows and the occasional bullet cracked and clattered around him. He slipped, or the rubble he was climbing shifted.

I am not dying here.

John crawled faster, ignoring the pain in his shoulder as he kept losing ground. The crawl became a mad scramble as the falling rubble seemed to pick up speed, sliding from beneath his hands, his feet.

He started to fall.

Shit, I might die here.

Bertram was screaming, reaching for him.

John reached, missed.

Bertram did not. The down-timer's hand clamped on John's arm, slid to his wrist as the full weight of the falling up-timer came to bear.

They both screamed.

"Quick, for God's sake," Bertram gasped.

John didn't need encouragement. He grabbed Bertram at the other armpit and started to pull himself up. Ignoring the increasingly vicious pain in his shoulder, he climbed.

With a final heave he collapsed atop Bertram.

"Get. Off," Bertram gasped.

John flopped onto his back, breathless and giddy with the narrowness of his escape.

"John, you need to lose some weight," Bertram groaned.

"For you, Bert, anything," John returned, coughing again. He took it as a sign of how much pain Bertram was in that the down-timer didn't bother to comment on or correct John's abbreviation of his name.

He coughed again and, wheezing, rolled on his side.

After a few careful breaths, John figured he was relatively intact, and ought to consider contributing to the battle raging around them. He looked around to find the dust was settling, the smoke clearing, and the sun rising.

Or perhaps the sun had been up for a while. How else had he seen Bertram? It hurt his head to think.

He shook his head. The sun wasn't the only thing rising: several hundred of Aurangzeb's men were scaling the inner wall to the west of the gatehouse. They were using what looked more like a scaffolding than a ladder, men without the saffron robes and heavy armor of the warriors assembling the structure with astonishing speed.

The tower to the east of them still had archers manning it, if the arrows that fell among the climbers were any indication. He watched an arrow strike home through a man's saffron kaftan, his chain mail, and exit the other side of his thigh. The stricken man merely leaned out from the ladder and used one hand to snap the arrowhead off before resuming his climb.

"Jesus," he breathed.

"The Sikhs, John!" Bertram called.

John saw them at the same time: two rows of about twenty helmeted men appeared atop the bastion. Their officer raised his scimitar. The first rank lowered their shotguns and took aim. The scimitar dropped. Twenty barrels belched fire, smoke, and buckshot at the men scaling the scaffold not twenty yards distant. The man John had seen struck by the arrow fell at last, his seeming immunity to pain rendered irrelevant by trauma and blood loss from the weight of lead from several shotguns.

The officer's sword turned, blade flashing in the

dawn light. Obscured by gun smoke and distance, John could only imagine the trooper's fingers shifting to secondary triggers as they'd been drilled endlessly in the last few months.

The sword rose, fell. Another volley, another tide of men ripped from their perches to fall in the deepening pile of corpses at the base of the walls.

"Jesus," Bertram said, surveying the ruin just twenty men had made.

John didn't want to see more dead men, and so kept his eyes on the shooters.

The front and rear ranks exchanged places with well-drilled precision. Once behind the front rank, brass bases twinkled in the dawn light as the spent paper shells were ejected high into the air. The entire unit disappeared behind the growing cloud of gun smoke in the next instant as the front rank fired.

Another cannonball roared by to slam into the tower supporting the Sikhs. About a foot square of the sandstone face shattered, the surrounding yard or so of material cracked as well, but the impact went almost entirely unnoticed by the defenders manning the redoubt.

"The difference between earth-backed and free-standing defenses sure is clear," John muttered, eyes sliding from the undamaged tower to the collapsed outer gatehouse.

"What?" Bertram called, wiggling a dirty finger in his ear.

"Nothing!" John shouted back.

Hoping Aurangzeb could see the hopelessness of continuing his attack, John rolled over and looked out on the plain.

The ground for almost a mile from the wall positively heaved with men, horses, and even camels. Most of the men seemed to be either advancing into the meat grinder of the defenses or shooting at the defenders, but he spied a few backs among them as men retreated, too.

One of the crazy camel-mounted guns belched, the one-pound ball whistling as it whipped overhead to crash into the upper works of the left-hand tower of the gatehouse beside one of the snipers, who flinched back behind cover.

That made John look for the cannon that had dropped the outer gatehouses. A moment's search revealed all but two of them were silent, their crews dead or fled. More were being rolled forward, though, and these looked bigger. The leading ox of one dropped, red stain growing against the white hide between its horns.

Someone started wailing.

He glanced back at the tower where the sniper had been perched. From the gun smoke lingering around him, he was the one who did for the oxen. He was fumbling through a reload, wailing tearfully the whole time.

Hindu. Probably thinks he's going to be reincarnated as a slug or worse for having killed a sacred bull.

Save it for later, bub. Gotta survive this shit, first.

He looked away.

Closer to hand a group of military laborers were working to fill in the creek that, running from the southeast to the northwest a hundred yards or so from the gate, made a natural, if shallow, moat in the rainy season.

"Dammit, man, where is Dara?"

North wall

They had been killing for more than an hour by the time the enemy broke and began to flee the space between the outer and inner walls below.

"They're falling back," Damla gloated, her face triumphant in the morning light filtering in from the eastern loops.

Atisheh wiped at the sweat leaving muddy trails in the dust caking her face, her breathing ragged and fast. She tried to answer but found she could only nod as she lowered her bow. She ached everywhere, but the shoulder where she'd been wounded defending Shah Jahan was a pulsing lake of fire from neck to elbow. She'd worked to strengthen it, but clearly hadn't spent enough time with the bow.

"What, tired?" Damla asked, offering a waterskin.

Atisheh's nod turned into a roll of her head and then each shoulder. Her hand shook as she took the waterskin and raised it to her lips.

"Already? We didn't even get any bladework in."

"Cousin," she gasped when she'd slaked her thirst, "I'd make you eat those words if I didn't know you'd just spew more foolishness the minute it gallops into that empty gourd you call a skull."

Damla grinned. "And I would take such threats more seriously if you weren't barely standing."

"Atisheh!" Yonca yelled as she raced into the tower. Atisheh forgot her pain on hearing the fear in her subordinate's voice.

Standing straight, Atisheh schooled her breathing and said, "Speak, do not shout."

Yonca lowered her voice. "Messengers, Atisheh. Delhi Gate is secure. The river gate has not been attacked. The Sikhs are massing. Lahore Gate is still hard-pressed."

"Good." She turned to Damla. "Quit grinning at me like an idiot and find out how many we lost. If the numbers are as expected, have the walking wounded remain at their stations and every third warrior join you."

"I go," Damla said, running up the stairs and out onto the upper bastion.

"Send them to Delhi Gate!" Atisheh shouted after her.

"We sally?" Yonca asked.

"If that madman Bidhi hasn't already."

"Already?"

"He does love a fight, that one." High praise, from Atisheh, whose reputation had grown in her absence.

"If only he were as pretty as you," Yonca purred.

Atisheh glanced at the younger woman, who was studying her with frank appraisal.

She snorted. "Later, if at all."

Yonca had the good grace to look away, ears reddening. It reminded Atisheh to pull her chain veil across her face. It wouldn't do to offend some of the more conservative men while she did the killing they could not. There would be no end of whining if they saw an unmarried woman's face.

"Run ahead and let the master of horse know we come," she said, making a show of checking her bowstring.

"I go."

Once she was alone, Atisheh groaned and leaned

heavily against the wall. Wanting nothing more than to do nothing for a few months, she pushed off the wall and staggered up the stairs.

The groom who tended her horses sprang to his feet on her arrival. She looked around and, seeing few witnesses she cared for, gestured at him. He obediently squatted beside her horse with his hands cupped, helping her mount.

She barely suppressed a grunt as the muscles in her shoulder decided to fold themselves into an agonizing cramp the likes of which she'd never felt before. She sat the horse a moment, stretching her shoulder, then gently kneed the mare into motion.

She was feeling better by the time she saw the serried ranks of Sikhs waiting to be led from the gate. Never one to publicly admit that a firearm was anything other than dead weight in the making, she secretly admired the "shotguns" the men carried at the shoulder. The amount of sword-grade wootz steel Talawat had used was a sin against all that was holy, but the weapons did look very fine, especially when massed in a solid block of nearly a thousand fighting men.

Beyond them were more men, perhaps another two thousand, with more traditional arquebuses and a level of training and expertise she knew to be less than professional. Still, they were here to make good on their duty to the Sultan Al'Azam.

She rode across in front of the men to where the Sultan Al'Azam, Dara Shikoh, sat a magnificent Marwari stallion that had been caparisoned in chain and silk.

Behind the Sultan Al'Azam, several hundred sowar sat their mounts, each armored and armed in the fashion of their people. More were riding up every moment from those walls where the fighting had finished, gathering around their individual umara; commanders of one hundred, even fifty.

A glance at the men surrounding Dara Shikoh confirmed her belief she was the highest ranking umara present. A lowly commander of five hundred sowar the senior ranking warrior? That was a problem. Mughal tactics did not rely on discipline so much as bravery and something John called "volume of fire," but Dara and John's plan did require they engage superior numbers at a specific moment in time that depended on some confusion in Aurangzeb's army to work.

To her mind, this chaos was not conducive to success. *Men.*

Dara's impatience was palpable. The emperor's horse, sensitive to his rider's mood and already prepared to fight for dominance of the growing herd about him, tried to bite the head from a messenger who stepped too close while reporting to Dara. The messenger dodged aside, but the horse took some hair along with the man's turban.

And it wasn't just Dara's horse that was threatening to get out of control. The lack of organization among the riders was an almost painful contrast to the disciplined stillness of the Sikhs. Someone needed to get control of this...what was the word John used that so disturbed his wife?

"Clusterfuck..." she muttered.

Such was her luck, however, that as she uttered the word there came one of those silences that happen at the most inopportune moments. It seemed to her that even the distant guns stopped firing in order to reveal her words to the emperor.

"What was that, Atisheh?" Dara asked. His jaw was set, and there were rings beneath his eyes that bespoke sleeplessness.

"Sultan Al'Azam, forgive me, I was asking where John Ennis is?" She felt no guilt for the lie, as there was no time to explain the saying.

"I sent John to Lahore Gate, where we are sore pressed."

And what lunacy possessed you to send the sole commander of five thousand within these walls to stand a post like a common sowar?

She swallowed bitter anger, remembering that John was no horseman, and therefore unqualified to lead this sally anyway.

"When do we sally, Sultan Al'Azam?" she asked, trying to convey with her tone that *now* would be better than later.

"Bidhi Chand has yet to arrive," Dara said, oblivious to the nuance of her message.

"Sultan Al'Azam, please heed me. Some of his best men were at Lahore Gate. Is it possible that he took personal command there when the fighting grew thick?"

Dara was nodding, but his eyes had that vacant look they got when he was having one of his spells. His mailed hand tried to steal to the scar at his temple but bonged against his helmet instead.

Another messenger ran up and bowed.

Dara managed a slow nod for him.

"Commander of one thousand, Bidhi Chand begs leave to sally, Sultan Al'Azam."

"Where is he?" Dara asked, looking at the motionless block of infantry.

"Over there, Sultan Al'Azam," the messenger said, pointing.

A man emerged from the infantry and waved his sword.

"Well, bring him here," Dara said.

Gritting her teeth, Atisheh hauled on her reins and turned her horse for the Sikhs. Dara might complain that she hadn't asked for leave to depart, but she could feel the weight of time they didn't have fleeing from them like water from between the fingers.

A moment later she was reining in before the man the messenger had pointed out.

He was not Bidhi Chand.

"What is going on?" she asked.

"Bidhi Chand is fighting at Lahore Gate"—the man's Persian was unexpectedly fluid and almost without accent, more cultured than her own had been when first she arrived at court—"and gave orders for us to go without him should he fall or otherwise not be among us."

"And who are you?" she asked, suspicious.

"A common warrior of my people, sister, chosen, like you, to lead others into battle in defense of what we love and cherish," the man said, smile emerging from a thick, luxuriant beard.

She liked his voice, though it seemed, from the length of his answer, that he liked it well enough for the both of them.

It was then she noted the man wore two of the full-length swords in the style the Sikhs preferred.

Merciful God! How long has he been here?

She swallowed, said respectfully, "I will inform the Sultan Al'Azam you are ready to march, Guru."

"I trust you will do so without mentioning me by name or title?" he asked with a waggle of his head. "I do not wish to steal any glory from Dara Shikoh."

"As you wish," Atisheh said.

"Go with God, sister."

"And you," she returned, the benediction somehow more meaningful than ever. Atisheh turned her horse again and galloped to rejoin Dara.

"Bidhi Chand begs you to begin the sally, Sultan Al'Azam, before it is too late!" she shouted as she rode up, figuring the more public the pressure, the more likely Dara would be to act without questioning.

Yonca and Damla and thirty other harem guards had joined the sowar surrounding the emperor in her absence. She was comforted by their presence even as she mourned the empty saddles of women and eunuchs she knew would have to be either wounded or dead to miss the glory that was to come.

Dara's lip curled in an unconscious snarl, but his anger must have helped him cut through the mental fog he'd suffered, as he gestured curtly to the drummers, who immediately signaled attention to orders.

No man nor horse trained to fight with the Mughals could ignore the spine-deep jolt that particular roll of the drums wrought. Relative silence fell, the only noise the slow thunder of cannon.

The Sultan Al'Azam of all India stood in the stirrups and raised his voice, first at the gates and then at his men: "Open the gates! We ride straight out to strike the camp sitting astride Delhi Road! The infantry will follow, then turn and strike at the dogs attacking Lahore Gate. We sowar will retire from the camp to cover their flank when we have set them to rout!"

He paused, drew a deep breath, and bellowed the last: "Ride! Ride to victory!"

"Victory!" his sowar cried. The drums began their roll as close to two thousand sowar rode past the infantry and down the ramp leading to the gates and their fate, the sound of their hooves thunderous in the close confines of the gate.

Chapter 45

Siege lines
Aurangzeb's command group

Aurangzeb had scarcely risen from prayer when one of his messengers was shot dead a few hundred gaz to their west.

"Who?" he muttered aloud, returning his gaze to the men following the Rajput spearhead at the base of the outer wall.

"Mohammed, Sultan Al'Azam," the first messenger in line croaked from behind him.

"What?" he asked without turning, constant motion of the prayer beads in his hands stuttering but not stopping.

"The messenger's name was Mohammed, Sultan Al'Azam."

"No"—Aurangzeb turned on the speaker—"I meant, whose message was he delivering?"

The man in messenger greens wilted under his stare. "I-I think Mohammed was assigned to Alam Shah, but I am not certain, Sultan Al'Azam."

And was Alam Shah trying to report success or failure on his assault?

Does it matter?

Aurangzeb turned back to the battle raging around Lahore Gate. The men he'd sent in to exploit what tenuous foothold the Rajputs had bled for were at the base of the wall and beginning their own climb.

Men were dying. *His* men were dying with every heartbeat, as if he were wounded and they his life's blood, spent to keep the body of his ambition advancing in tune with the desires of his heart and soul.

If Alam Shah had failed to carry the walls, he'd still tied down a large number of defenders who would have otherwise been used to reinforce the gates.

He glanced toward Delhi Gate, where, as expected, that part of the attack appeared to have failed. That gate was, quite possibly, the strongest part of the fortress, overlapping and layered earth-backed defenses making it stronger even than the walls ringing Red Fort, despite being pierced by gates.

He briefly considered sending one of his trusted men to rally the retreating warriors, but men forced to retreat from an assault were uniformly tired, frightened, and dispirited, especially if their umara was counted among the dead. Proud men might not obey a stranger in the best of circumstances, and they certainly wouldn't when ordered into another attack by some fellow who told them it was Aurangzeb's will.

No, those men were no longer effective as fighters. Not for a few hours, at least. Thinking they would not be useful until the morrow, Aurangzeb put them from his mind with a mental note to ensure the elevation to formal rank of whatever men the warriors chose to put forward as their new leaders. Time enough in the future to weed out the disagreeable and inept. Service, or at least survival, must be seen to be rewarded, otherwise men would refuse to be led.

Aurangzeb's eye fell on the heavy artillery being dragged into position and thanked God the fire from Lahore Gate was falling off in the face of the fire from his camel guns and arquebusiers.

Even the infantry assault seemed to surge forward and upward as the defenders were forced to keep their heads down.

Closer than the walls, but still some distance closer to the walls than the oxen and men towing the heavy pieces, Carvalho's original battery had only enough men standing to crew two cannon, one of which was Carvalho's own. As Aurangzeb watched, the more distant of his cannon fired, showing that crew, at least, was still willing to fight.

Thousands of men were pressing forward, trying to come to grips with the enemy. Some, pausing to loose arrows at their tormentors, had trouble raising their weapons, such was the press of so many bodies in the tight space.

It seemed to Aurangzeb the guns that had so devastated the Rajputs on the wall did not have a real range advantage over the weapons his own men carried, but the infernal weapons were capable of a depressingly high rate of fire. In an open field engagement the smoke of their own fire would have limited their accuracy, but with the mob below them, even firing blind was bound to hit some ghazi God wished to meet face-to-face.

Still, it did not appear there were enough of the

weapons to arm the number of men needed to prevent Aurangzeb's men carrying the wall.

But then, appearances can be deceiving, as my brother and sister have so recently proven.

Or am I become like the snake-bite survivor, frightened of every tuft of grass because I was once struck by a viper?

He forced himself to look at the bodies at the base of the wall, to count the cost of ambition. So many.

The beads rattled between his fingers.

Haunted by the possibility his ambition was not the simple expression of God's will he'd taken it for but something manufactured of his own pride and hubris, the young emperor searched his heart for an answer.

It beat, steady and fast, but gave no other wisdom.

Meanwhile, men died, regardless of the answer. If there was one, he did not hear it.

The prayer beads stopped their rattle.

"Send in the reserves," Aurangzeb said.

Two messengers rode hard for two wings of five thousand sowar each that he'd set aside to exploit any opening.

That decision made, he turned his attention from the base of the wall and looked to Carvalho's battery. His two remaining guns had only a fraction of their original crew remaining, forcing a far slower rate of fire than they had at the outset of the battle.

He considered ordering them to withdraw, but discarded the idea as worthless. Carvalho would consolidate his remaining men with the larger guns being brought up—or not, according to God's will. Indeed, as he watched, the first of the heavier guns was drawing into position to fire, its thirty-man crew struggling with the mighty weight of metal.

Drums sounded the advance. A moment later, ten thousand sowar rocked into motion, the rumble of their hoofbeats drowning the drums. They would be at the walls in minutes.

"God willing, we will have an end to this, brother," Aurangzeb breathed. This time, his messengers remained silent.

Gun line

"Can't shift her, Captain," Farshad said. "Not without more men."

"Still more of Dara's bastards to kill where she lays," Carvalho said, pitching in to reload. The next minutes were occupied with hard, sweaty work.

Finished, he stepped back and pulled his linstock from his belt. The cord had gone out, drowned in his sweaty robes. He bent to shelter it as he struck grinder and flint. A bullet whizzed by in the space he'd occupied, making him sweat all the more.

He put the dragon to the touch and skipped back as the powder caught and the charge exploded. He missed where the ball struck, the target lost in dust and smoke and the chaos of battle.

The next long while passed in a blur of reload, fire. Reload. Fire.

Sometime later, something reached through the raw repetition and roar of battle. Something felt in his bones, not heard. He staggered from the gun and wiped the sweat from his brow. It was then that thousands of horsemen rode past his position, charging toward the wall and battle. Even at speed, it took the better part of two minutes for the mass of men to ride by.

"Only enough powder for a few more shots, Captain!" Farshad croaked.

An oxen's low turned him round in hopes of seeing a supply cart laden with powder and ball. Instead it was Islam's *Whore of Babylon*, the largest of Aurangzeb's guns to arrive in camp before the attack.

"Get that great big bitch into line and start shooting, Islam!" Carvalho yelled. Another round whistled by his head, too close to bear thinking about.

"Yes, Captain!" Islam yelled back, eyes gone a little wild.

With a sound like two great wood blocks being slapped together, the lead oxen of the team dropped stone dead, skull pierced by a sniper's bullet.

"Jesus!" he screamed. "They must have had every Atishbaz from here to the Himalayas making powder and shot for those damn weapons! How did we not know?"

Busy commanding his men, Islam did not respond to the question. None of the rest of the gunners seemed inclined to offer an opinion either, being busy cutting the ox from its traces.

Frustration and rage vented and ignored by an indifferent God and universe, he gestured for his remaining crew to join Islam's men.

The backbreaking labor that followed caused him to lose track of time, but it passed nonetheless, and at a cost: two more oxen were killed and a man wounded. That cost paid, they had the great beast of a gun in position.

Carvalho stood back, panting.

Islam's men were more efficient, or at least less tired: they immediately set to loading. The powder went in quickly enough, but the two huge, muscle-bound men carrying the first ball from the wagon struggled to lift it to the muzzle.

"Well done!" Carvalho yelled as the men stepped back.

A smiling Islam ignited his linstock and stepped to the touch.

Carvalho looked expectantly at the wall but the cannon did not fire.

Carvalho looked back to see Islam on his knees, blood pouring from his mouth and a red stain growing beneath his breastbone.

"God!" Carvalho cried as he ran to Islam's side. He was too slow, and Islam's face struck one of the monstrous wheels of the gun carriage as he fell forward.

Grinding his teeth, Carvalho snatched the still-smoking linstock from the dead man's hand and laid it to the touch.

The cannon roared his anger and rage, propelling the nearly fifty-pound ball across the intervening distance to crash into the wall. The red sandstone facing of the wall sloughed away, the top bucking before dust and smoke obscured it from view.

Aurangzeb's camp
Tent of Nur Jahan

Nur opened the next message and brought it to the light. It did no good, however. It was her attention that was lacking, not the light.

She had not slept well, having had a strange dream in the night. It had started well enough: seeing Jahangir as he'd been when she first knew him, powerfully handsome, with eyes that pulled her in and held her in their regard. He'd been riding a white stallion across a vast plain of wind-waving grasses, riding to join her. Nur had enjoyed watching this young Jahangir ride to her, a shadow of the thrill she used to feel on seeing him rising up her sleeping spine. He was yelling something she could not comprehend. She did not mind the yells, at first, thinking he was only as excited to see her as she was to see him. But then the wind turned stiff and cold, plum clouds stacking higher and higher on the horizon and making the grass ripple wildly, as if in the wake of half a hundred unseen tigers.

The darkness closed in.

Sudden fear raked her soul. Those invisible predators caught her husband, drew Jahangir and his brilliant white mount down in a welter of blood, his voice ringing in her ears even as she startled awake.

Like all nightmares, it was far easier to remember the fear than any message, but her mind had eventually unraveled the words her love had been screaming. So she had risen, prayed, and returned to her tent.

Methwold had been waiting for her. He had been trying to see her since arriving at camp. She had consented to a morning meeting last night mostly because she knew his presence during the most important battle of Aurangzeb's fledgling reign would help distract her from her inability to influence the battle. For his part, Methwold had been so eager for an audience he'd been waiting for her. Still, she'd made him wait, had him made comfortable and served refreshments while she read the latest correspondence from her spies and servants.

He shifted slightly. That was the first sign of impatience he'd shown in the hour and more she'd made him wait. She reread the missive she'd been failing to comprehend and, failing to get any more from it than she had the last three times, looked at him.

"What is it I might do for you, President Methwold?" Nur asked, cocking her head as much to listen to the sounds of battle as what her guest had to say.

"I wish to ask a favor of you, Nur Jahan," he said.

"Oh?" Nur was disappointed that he'd opened with precisely what he was here for. She'd been hoping for more . . . more intrigue, more distraction. She glanced at him. He was squinting into the dawn's light. Nur's eyes fell again on the report, noting the light had improved enough the lamp she'd been reading by was superfluous. Craving warmth, she turned her own face to the dawn, glad of the whim that had made her command the tent be placed just so. She had an excellent view of the red-yellow brow of the sun as it began to peep over the horizon. It also prevented her from seeing the walls of Red Fort and the battle being waged there while the great awning sheltered them from the morning dew.

"The arrangement the Company had with the Estado da India ended the moment they cut ties with the Sultan Al'Azam."

"And as it ended badly, you will suffer for having agreed to it?" she asked, eyes closed, wishing she could feel the sun on her lips.

"I don't know that 'suffer' is the right term, but I will certainly have some explaining to do if the

Sultan Al'Azam does not see my efforts as worthy of compensation."

"You are unusually direct today..." She allowed the words to trail off, inviting him to fill the silence as she watched him once more.

He smiled and accepted the invitation: "I suppose it is the battle and my own impatient desire to learn its outcome that makes me so."

"You were not inclined to take to the battlefield yourself?" she asked, tossing her head to indicate the walls behind them, beyond her tent and, if not out of mind, then at least out of sight.

"Carvalho refused my offer to join him."

"He did?" She turned her face to him, entirely focused now. "What grounds did he give?"

"He thought it best I was not with him at the guns. I am not known to his crews, and so would have been in the way as they took up positions in the night. Besides, I am not gifted at the artillerist's art and he assured me he had men enough to handle Dara's defenses."

"I think the young wags all agreed the fighting would be over by dawn," Nur said. *They were fools.*

"Well, Carvalho was not so sanguine as all that," Methwold said.

Something clicked into place behind Nur's eyes. Something she had studiously avoided considering so the back of her mind could unravel it.

She allowed a small frown to edge her lips and spoke while things moved behind her eyes. "He is far wiser than most of Aurangzeb's umara, then." A louder explosion rent the air.

"It does not sound as if they were entirely correct,

does it?" Methwold's eyes were on her tent as if trying to peer through it.

"No, I'm afraid not."

"Shall we go and see for ourselves?" The Englishman's impatience to see what was happening was apparent.

"Perhaps later. First, though, what is it you want me to do with regard to your situation? Do you want me to ask the Sultan Al'Azam if he is inclined to provide compensation for your services?"

"If it isn't too much trouble. Or, if you think he might rather hear it directly from me, I could make the request myself."

"I will see to it he learns you hope for clarification of your position."

He smiled. "I bow before your greater experience."

"And the Company?"

"I am sorry?" Methwold asked.

"With the Portuguese firmly against him, it may be useful for the Sultan Al'Azam to retain the Company and its ships as friends."

The smile grew broader. "My thought precisely."

She nodded.

"I must tell you how happy I am that you are here, working on behalf of Aurangzeb," he said.

Nur allowed her own smile to greet his. "It can be hard to avoid coloring your perceptions when events appear to serve your self-interest."

He shrugged. "There is truth in what you say, but that truth is not the only one. However gifted, the Sultan Al'Azam is young and impressionable. He needs people of experience about him, ready to lend him their wisdom and experience. I have watched you provide sage counsel these last months—"

She spoke over him before the Englishmen could repeat himself. "While I have striven mightily to aid Aurangzeb in his struggles against his brother, I have no wish to hear more praise for my efforts."

Methwold drew breath to protest.

Nur stopped him with a raised finger. "Oh, I know what and how I have contributed, but the time when I let myself preen in response to such flattery is long past. I will do what you request because I appreciate you as a man of quality as much as I see the benefit in retaining such a relationship with the English Company."

The Englishman's skill at hiding his feelings failed him this once, his fair complexion coloring at the compliment.

They sat in silence a few moments. For her part Nur did not feel the need to add to the noise of the battle nor force him to acknowledge the fact she'd scored against him. She used the time to actively consider what her subconscious had been working.

Methwold grew impatient, and spoke before she was able to unearth the meaning. "If we are done complimenting one another, perhaps we can go see what progress the forces of the Sultan Al'Azam have made?"

Something surged forth to her, startling Nur.

"You may. I do not think I will." Her smile began as an attempt to reassure him, but ended on the bitter surge of emotion that threatened to close her throat.

Nur thought she caught a glimpse of an incredulous look and, driving down a sudden surge of anger, said, "What is it, President Methwold?"

"Only that your reputation would have you watching, avid to see the results of your work."

His answer was so direct, and so disarming, Nur knew she had covered the flash of emotion quite completely. Still, it struck a chord in her—a wellspring of anger Nur had thought herself immune to. She had been at or near the center of power and politics for the majority of her life.

One would think such remarks would no longer sting so.

"Reputation?" she mused.

"Please forgive my impertinence." Methwold clearly saw he'd made some kind of error, and struggled to recover. "But I can see the utility of a certain kind of reputation at court." An apologetic smile appeared while his eyes searched hers for some sign of either an impending explosion of temper or agreement.

Feeling no need to bury her anger before this perceptive foreigner, Nur spoke directly from the heart. "Who better to know the reputation I have built than I? I, who built it with acts of deceit large enough to mislead entire nations and small enough to pluck the strings of my lover's heart, one contest of wills at a time? Oh, I know what my reputation is, and what it has cost me. I also know what it means to hold the reins of power and lose them."

She smiled. "I much prefer them near to hand, President Methwold. One price of that proximity is a reputation that has, in the past, worked against me as much as for me. But then, I have lived a long time, and no one builds a reputation—for good or ill—without experiencing life. When I went to bed last night I thought that the outcome of this particular contest was a forgone conclusion. This assumption on my part was based upon the relative reputations of the involved generals, but now...Now I begin to question the validity of not only my reputation, but that of Dara and Aurangzeb as well."

Methwold nodded slowly, opening his mouth to comment again, but she silenced him with a shake of the head. "Is it possible for one night—nay, just one unpleasant *dream*—to so shake and shape one's thoughts?"

"Would that not depend upon the dream as much as the dreamer?" he asked.

She looked at him sharply. "Spoken like a guru, President Methwold. It seems you have learned more than most ferenghi in your time among us."

"You are kind," he said, clearly relieved her anger had gone, if it had ever been present.

"Am I? Truly? I think not. The life of the true guru, whatever their reputation, is rarely comfortable."

Methwold was so distracted by the sounds of battle, and his desire to see it for himself, that she was almost certain her words did not register with the younger man.

"With permission, Nur Jahan, I will take my leave of you, and discover for us both how our hopes fare..."

Nur waved him on.

He fairly sprang to his feet and was gone in an instant, leaving Nur with the residue of nightmares, dreams, and unfinished business.

Chapter 46

Red Fort
Lahore Gate

John coughed, hard. Then again, so hard he bent double.

Something very heavy shrieked through the air and crashed into the wall just below the crenellations with such weight and power that the stone construction buckled and slowly slumped outward, away from the wall, carrying two screaming men with it.

Ignoring fear, fatigue, and the dangerous footing, John lurched across the last section of wall toward the door. He and Bertram had, with a handful of other survivors, fled the middle gate what seemed like hours ago.

Knowing that, if everything had gone to plan, the inner gate had long since been completely blocked up by the defenders, they'd been forced to run the gauntlet of fire that flailed the wall that defended the courtyard between the middle and inner gates. The iron-sheathed door that would get them off the freestanding structure and into the relative safety of the earth-backed walls to the west of the gates seemed, when glimpsed through the dust, smoke, and madness, to always be just a little farther away.

Drifting clouds of smoke and dust obscured everything for a few steps, bringing their progress to a crawl yet again. They were feeling their slow way forward when Bertram hit something and staggered backward into John's injured shoulder.

Biting down on the urge to scream and shove Bertram, John saw the down-timer had run blindly into their goal. Wanting to weep, he stepped past his friend and thumped his good fist against the iron-shod wood.

No response.

"The password, John!" Bertram shouted, levering himself up.

John leaned his forehead against the cold iron, unable to recall his own name, let alone a password he'd tried to memorize over breakfast yesterday.

He was saved from further frustration when the door swung slowly open under his full weight.

Inside, a sweating Gujarati stood blinking at him, shaking arms pointing one of the long-muzzled guns at John's chest.

John opened his mouth to greet the man.

The arquebusier pulled the trigger.

Without thinking, John stepped inside and thrust his hand between match and pan.

Three things happened then. The match snapped down to burn his hand, his shoulder told him in no uncertain terms what it thought of violent, sudden movement, and his left fist connected with the man's hairy jaw.

The arquebusier fell unconscious at John's feet.

"Shit!" John said, the grating pain in his shoulder

making it a very bad idea to try and shake the still-smoldering coal from his hand. Dropping it might let the cord strike powder and result in a discharge, so that was out. He instead reached across with his other hand and yanked the match cord from the snaphaunce.

Bertram pushed past, the remaining men filing in behind him. John handed the arquebus to one of them.

"Don't you need a weapon?" the man asked, retrieving the match cord from the floor.

"I have one," John said. Suddenly scared he'd lost it, and utterly without thinking, he reached for his armpit to where his wife's 9mm had been holstered when the shooting started.

Something popped in his shoulder, making him moan.

"You need a medic, John?" Bertram asked.

"No," John wheezed, blinking. "I think it just popped back into place."

"Good..." Bertram muttered. "If true."

Gingerly, John returned his hand to the holster, unsnapped, and pulled the gun free. He made a push check as he'd been taught and, as the slide traveled smoothly, figured it was intact.

While he was feeling the spare magazines in the other armpit for any sign they'd been bent out of shape, Bertram coughed to clear his throat, then hiked a thumb at the door opposite the one they'd come through.

Switching to Persian, the smaller man eventually continued, "Because it sounds like the fighting is still going on"—the stuttering crash of a volley penetrated the door—"and I don't think Bidhi Chand will ever let us live it down if we don't take *some* part."

The fighting men with them, their hands busy reloading, checking weapons or rendering aid to the injured, chuckled.

"Right," John said. Mopping sweat from his brow, he straightened and took a deep breath. Bertram bent and picked up the unconscious man's sword.

A new sound, muffled better by the door, joined the gunfire: the steel on steel of a melee.

"Shit." John went to the door and shot the bolt.

John was about to push it open when the men he was supposedly leading shouldered him aside and, screaming, charged blindly out. Blindly, because the morning rays of the sun had momentarily cut through the smoke to shine from blades, helmets, and shields.

Blinking, John stepped into chaos. It was...beautiful in a way a train wreck could be fascinating. Each instant both a cause and an effect trailing after a thousand others that terminated for some men but allowed others to travel to the next.

The man he'd handed the gun to raised it to fire at a warrior who'd climbed into view and paused to draw a heavy curved sword from his hip.

The gun banged.

The swordsman staggered, arms windmilling as he fought for balance. He was given no opportunity to recover as the defender reversed his weapon and swung it by the barrel. The butt of the gun clipped the man's knee, dropping him like a stone. And, like a stone, he rolled and fell to the earth below.

Careful of his aim, John lined up a shot at the head of a warrior appearing between the crenellations. The man's bearded face disappeared before he could pull the trigger.

Another of Aurangzeb's warriors leapt at one of John's

companions, *katars* in each fist. Dara's man went down in a welter of blood. Crouching over his victim, the man slashed at another warrior who skipped backward to avoid losing a limb.

John shuffled sideways away from Bertram to get a clear shot. He let the sight settle on the man's chest and pulled the trigger twice. The first shot sparked through the man's mail, the second, taken while the pistol was still climbing from the recoil of the first, ripped into his throat below the beard.

The man staggered but didn't go down.

Bertram rushed forward and drove his sword home in the man's pelvis just as another man scrambled over the wall behind the first.

John shot without taking careful aim and lost track of how many times he'd pulled the trigger when the guy finally fell screaming.

Bertram was already blocking the sword of another man.

There were a good twenty enemies amongst almost the same number of defenders now. Their proximity prevented the Sikh platoon on the far redoubt from firing at them for fear of killing their own.

John's movement had left him next to the long ramp leading to the ground level inside the fort. He spared a glance down it, praying reinforcements were already on their way.

His relieved sigh was drowned as a mass of heavily armored warriors began to scream, "*Skanda! Skandaaaa!*" as they charged up the ramp and among the men struggling along the wall.

The next few minutes passed in a panting blur of fear, anger, and violence. When it ended, there was a lull John used to reload and look around. The nearest gun crew, much reduced from its pre-battle numbers, was already hard at work loading one of the shells copied from the *Lønsom Vind*'s stores.

"You've been cut, John," Bertram grunted, nodding at John's right arm as he tried to regain his breath.

John glanced down, saw a shallow wound he didn't remember taking lining one forearm. It was already scabbing, so John left it alone and returned his attention to the battle.

There were thousands more men swarming across the open ground toward the stretch of wall between Lahore Gate and where the wall turned out of view in its progress toward Delhi Gate.

His gaze fell on the nearest redoubt, the one where the Sikhs had been shooting from and stood slack-mouthed in wonder.

Bidhi Chand, dressed in what looked like plate mail out of some geek's D&D character fantasy, danced from one crenellation to another, seeming to ignore the deadly drop on one side as he stabbed and slashed anyone crazy enough to climb into reach of his blade.

"Would you look at that?" John said.

"What?" Bertram asked, tying off a bandage around his calf.

"That crazy fucker," John said, pointing at the leaping figure.

Bertram followed John's hand and shook his head in wonder.

"Shit," John said.

"What?"

"While Bidhi and his men are fighting hand to hand, they can't shoot at—" He stopped speaking and risked a quick glance over the wall. A fresh wave of attackers was within feet of the parapet.

"Get ready!" he screamed.

He pushed out over the wall again, leading with the pistol this time. Two shots at each climber in view emptied the magazine in no time. As he pulled back to reload an arrow flashed by within an inch of his face.

Putting discomfort and fear from his mind, John put his back to the tower wall. Dropping the empty magazine into his off hand and stuffing it into his belt, he slapped the last magazine into the well. He had more 9mm back in his quarters, and the bandoliers he was strapped with still had a lot of .308, but the rifle was among the ruins of the middle gate and he couldn't exactly shout *time out!* and run to his room for more ammunition.

"Just where the hell is Dara?" Bertram yelled, stabbing downward at an attacker who got too close.

"Good question!" John snatched up a fallen sword in his off hand. Lousy with a blade, John was young, strong, relatively healthy, and about to run out of ammo. Better a sword in hand than buried in his guts.

He glanced again at the redoubt to the east. Bidhi Chand continued to dance between arrows and swords, shining in the sun as he cut men down with grace and astonishing speed.

Fucking Conan, that guy!

"John!" Bertram's desperate scream snapped John's reverie.

A bandy-legged warrior had Bert's blade locked with his and was steadily pushing the smaller man over backward. There was no way he could shoot from his current position without hitting Bertram.

Never too close to miss.

John strode forward to press the pistol to the man's head just below the turban and pulled the trigger. The man dropped dead, smoke drizzling from the contact wound.

Bertram shoved the corpse from him, screaming, "*Where the fuck is Dara?*"

Panting, John didn't answer. Indeed, he was happy enough to surrender all attention to surviving the moment. That way he didn't have to think about any of what he had done—or would do—in order to survive the next few heartbeats.

I will hold Ilsa again.

Pavilion of the Healers

"Begum, it is not proper or right!" the physician said in scandalized tones, despite all the times all of the hospital staff had been warned that Priscilla would be treating the wounded.

"Damn your ideas of what's right, these men need treatment and she can treat them!" Jahanara raged, waving at Priscilla. Jahanara had been walking the up-timer to the operating room she was to use when a tall, rangy physician whose name she could not remember exited the chamber and blocked the way.

The up-timer, both hands up and raw from scrubbing, nodded.

Did the idiot think they'd been lying to him this entire time? All of the staff had been trained on the procedures, and those procedures had Priscilla as the overflow surgeon in any situation where urgent cases outnumbered the other physicians.

The physician—Jahanara could not remember his name beyond thinking it was a convert's—was one of the traditionalists she'd felt she had to keep in service as she built the medical corps, if for no other reason than his connection to the project would make the umara, and therefore their men, more comfortable with the idea.

A poor bargain, if this is the result!

She considered calling for a guard, but wasn't sure how many would answer. Rather than show such weakness, she lifted her chin as a new thought occurred to her. "Why are you here instead of seeing to your patient?"

"I-I was getting fresh bandages."

Liar. She could smell the fear on him.

But fear made him strong—and foolish—in the face of her anger. "Begum Sahib, I beg you, reconsider. These men will die or not, as God wills, all in accordance with the natural order of things."

Two women appeared behind the physician. Wives of her brother's umara that she had drafted to serve the physicians as orderlies and nurses. One—why could she not remember names this day?—waved a hand at a corpse lying on the table in the operating room, pointed at the physician's head and pantomimed breaking a stick between two fists.

So, madness and fear drive this creature, not moral outrage! Typical.

"They can make penance in future. Get out of the way."

He shook his head. "I'll not allow it."

"*Allow* it?!" Jahanara snarled, drawing herself up. The anger burned in her so brightly she thought surely he would boil away under her gaze. "Get. Out. Of. Our. Way. And. Get. Back. To. Work."

But the man's fear rendered him immune to threats as well as reason. He shook his head again, beard bristling, and shrilled, "I will not let you endanger their souls!"

Jahanara drew breath to call a guard to put an end to this idiocy, but Priscilla stepped between them, surprising her.

"Fuck this," Priscilla said. Without breaking stride, she kicked the wretch, *hard*, in the crotch. So hard, the man went up on tiptoe. The way his expression went from utter surprise, to fear, to pain, might have been comical under other circumstances. As it was, Jahanara was too surprised, both by the man's obstinate idiocy and Priscilla's violent solution to do much more than stare as Priscilla walked daintily past the man who, on striking the marble floor, folded up and vomited.

Sensing Jahanara had stopped following her, Priscilla turned to face the princess, who was still staring.

"What?" Priscilla said, raising her hands. "I'm scrubbed in and wasn't about to wash up again just so I could punch him." She touched his shoulder with a toe. "Besides, I was always better with my feet than hands."

Pressing her lips together to avoid loosing a mad giggle, Jahanara joined her friend, skipping across the physician's curled legs to avoid the small pool of vomit.

Priscilla waved goodbye as she backed into the operating room. Another wounded man was being brought in as the door swung closed behind her.

Jahanara motioned the two women over. Perhaps it was fatigue, but she could not dredge up their names.

"Would one of you find Firoz Khan and ask for help removing this creature, please?"

The women looked at one another. The shorter one nodded but it was the taller who spoke. "Begum Sahib, it will be our pleasure to drag this dog out ourselves. That was our cousin he failed to save."

"I am sorry," Jahanara said, her heart heavy and slow in her chest. She took a deep breath, reaching for calm. A princess must appear collected in such circumstances.

"May we?" the woman repeated.

"Please," Jahanara said, releasing the miasma of ill-feeling the encounter had engendered with the exhale. "Tell Firoz this man thought he could physically bar my way and countermand all the hard work of the last few months simply because he is a man and I am not. Firoz will know what to do with him."

"Yes, Begum Sahib," the pair said. They bent and, none too gently, batted aside his feeble attempts to prevent them grabbing his arms.

He started to find his wind, however, and burbled some further complaint until one of the women slapped him as one would a wayward boy. Not to hurt, just to remind the fool who was in charge.

Say one thing about the women of Dara's court: if the men would not or could not handle the challenges of the moment, the women were ready to handle anything.

"Begum Sahib?" Smidha said.

Jahanara turned to find her advisor staring down at the still-writhing physician, several taller women behind her. One, richly dressed in a beautifully dyed sari, had a black silk bag drawn over her head. Two muscular dancing girls stood to either side of the hooded figure.

Jahanara blinked. "Merciful God, but did she have to resist?" she asked, pinching the bridge of her nose.

"A monkey is ever a monkey," Smidha said.

"Is this how you treat your sister?" Roshanara barked from beneath the bag.

"You put a hood on but didn't gag her?" Jahanara asked.

Smidha waggled her head. "She was quiet for the walk over here."

"Saving it up for me, was she?"

Smiles lit all faces in response to her mild attempt at humor. The smiles Ilsa and Monique gave were far more predatory than humorous, making the princess briefly wonder why their expressions were so hungry.

Roshanara, as was her wont, killed the moment. "Jahanara, I am no dancing girl or slave to be manhandled this way, I am a princess of the blood, just as you!"

"True," Jahanara said, nodding encouragement at the two dancers. "And were you to start acting like one, perhaps you wouldn't be treated like an ill-bred falcon."

"I will have your—"

"Guess I *should* have gagged her," Monique said, removing the long, colorfully dyed scarf she used to tie back her heavy curls.

"You don't say?" Jahanara opined, the words freighted with irony.

"Your pet ferenghi won't silence me!" Roshanara yelled.

"Want to bet?" Monique said, slipping the scarf

around the shorter woman's head and pulling it tight around her nose.

"My nose!" Roshanara cried, which proved precisely the thing Monique had been waiting for. She let the scarf slip off the nose and pulled it savagely tight as soon as it was between Roshanara's open lips. Then, began tying it off.

Smidha arched a brow. "You seem quite...practiced at certain things..."

Monique's shrug revealed indifference to any censure in Smidha's tone.

Shaking her head, Jahanara looked at Smidha. "I had hoped we would not have to imprison her, but I think we must?" She looked for confirmation from Smidha.

"Hear that, spying bitch?" Monique punctuated each word with a hard jab of two fingers into Roshanara's breastbone.

Surprised at the feral anger in the gesture, Jahanara opened her mouth to ask what had Monique so angry, but saw Smidha's hand motion asking for silence.

"I believe that's an excellent idea, Begum Sahib," the old servant said.

"Very well," Jahanara gestured at the dancers, "escort my sister to the Jasmine Tower"—she glanced at Monique and Ilsa, gauging how they would respond to her next words—"and see to it she has no harm done to her."

Neither woman appeared ready to object, though Monique was still staring angrily at Roshanara.

"Then see Firoz Khan for your reward," Smidha added.

Jahanara nodded. "Yes, do tell the diwan I am most pleased with your service."

"Yes, Begum Sahib," the pair said.

Monique made to go with them, but Smidha caught her wrist. "Bide with us, please. You as well, Ilsa."

The two Europeans stood glaring as a whimpering Roshanara was led away.

Jahanara stepped over the mess Adnan Dashti—that was his name!—had left behind and joined Smidha.

"Where are the rest of your ladies, Begum Sahib?"

The princess gestured widely at the pavilion. "Those who are not caring for their own elders or children are at the tasks set for them when they volunteered their service."

Smidha nodded.

"Let us go to the veranda. We could all do with some news from the battle and perhaps a drink," Jahanara said, knowing Smidha wanted some time to think before she spoke what was on her mind.

"Not for me, thanks, I already have to pee too often!" Ilsa said, covering her belly. Her expression, at least, had none of the anger of a moment before.

Chapter 47

Ground outside Red Fort
Delhi Gate

Atisheh grimaced as she let fly with another arrow, felling a man who had thought to oppose Dara's lightning charge. There were fewer men willing to do that because Dara's sowar were in among the tents of the enemy, cutting down wounded and bewildered men as they sought to cause as much chaos as they could, as quickly as possible.

In fact, things were on the verge of getting out of hand. Dara needed—

The Sultan Al'Azam, as if hearing her thoughts, reined in. He shouted, "Drummer, signal: on me!"

Atisheh didn't immediately slow, as she'd been hard-pressed to keep up with the emperor over the last few minutes. Not only did he have the better mount, he'd barely used the magnificent bow he carried, and so did not have to slow in order to provide the stable platform necessary for accurate archery.

She had to admit he was a fine horseman. The

speed of his mount was impressive, but it was the rider who lent a horse both heart and mind. Dara had hardly slowed when leaping the creek that ran parallel to the walls of Red Fort. Where many sowar had to fight their mounts to get them to attempt the crossing at speed, he'd simply braced in the stirrups and given the horse his head.

She rode past Dara as the drummer began the signal and, finding another target among the tents, loosed. The target didn't immediately fall, but gave a satisfying yelp before disappearing in the chaos of silk and livestock that every camp throughout the long, dark history of war inevitably sank into when unexpectedly attacked.

She kneed her horse into a tight circle and looked back along the way they'd come. Many, many men lay dead or wounded along that path, but Aurangzeb had a great deal more men to spare than Dara. She wasn't sure how many fighters Dara had lost, but he could ill afford more than a pittance.

The drums started to roll.

Atisheh slowed and came to a stop near Dara, who was shading his eyes and looking with concern to the southeast and the great mass of men struggling to overcome the defenses of Red Fort.

That she was chief among his harem guards was the only reason Atisheh did not get more resentful looks from those few of his courtiers surrounding him who were not part of Jahanara's inner circle.

"Are we late, Atisheh?" he called.

"The Sultan Al'Azam arrives when he deems appropriate," she said with an immediately regretted shrug. Now that she had time to breathe, her shoulder ached with the fierce insistence of a lover too long absent.

The chuckle that followed was as manly a noise as she'd ever heard from him.

Groups of his sowar began to rejoin the messengers, musicians, and courtiers surrounding the emperor.

A crashing volley echoed across the killing field.

"I do believe we made enough room for Talawat's guns to do their work," Dara commented.

Atisheh sniffed.

"You do not like them?"

"Oh, they kill well enough." Not being able to shrug without pain was cramping her style.

Dara stood in the stirrups when the majority of his men seemed to have returned. "What do you think, my sowar?" he shouted. "Shall we help those who have to get their own feet dirty rather than ride steeds of beauty and power like ours?"

The men roared their approval.

Atisheh was impressed. Suffering as he did from the horrible headaches brought on by any kind of stress or setback, she had rarely seen Dara this strong or well-spoken of late. Never one to pray overmuch, Atisheh sent one winging up to Heaven in hopes that Dara would remain healthy and fully in control, at least for the duration of the battle.

As she opened her eyes, she saw one of Dara's battle servants dispensing sheafs of arrows among the men. She gestured for him to join her and, as he was loading her quivers, looked south and east toward the clouds of gun smoke and constant, regular beat of massed gunfire that marked the Sikh advance.

And they were advancing. The men had already covered a hundred gaz or so, even after marching out in the wake of Dara's sowar and deploying in a double file. Atisheh could now see the point of John's endless drilling of the men: their advance was steady and their fire killed or wounded hundreds of warriors with every volley. But there were thousands more behind them, pressing into the space between the creek and the walls.

Aurangzeb's warriors were caught in a bind. Too many men crowded into a limited space. So many that the sowar were forced to dismount on the far side of the creek and walk the remaining distance to the walls. The vast herd of abandoned horses were driven to the edges of the crowd of men, obscuring the advance of Dara's much smaller force.

Atisheh's smile was predatory beneath her veil.

The lions will soon be culling the sheep.

Dara shouted at the drummers. Several thousand sowar rocked into motion, heading back the way they'd come. A short time later they were approaching the edge of the shallow ravine and beginning the turn to the right.

They were, by now, approaching the extreme right of Dara's infantry. A double line of arquebus-armed infantry was lining up along the creek to cover the Sikh flank and the sowar when they were eventually driven back by Aurangzeb's superior numbers.

While planning the sortie, John had said the infantry formation would resemble one of the Latin alphabet's letters, an "L" with the base toward the enemy.

She looked forward and realized they did not have far to ride before starting the wheel, loosing arrows at the point closest to their targets in the fashion that had delivered death to the enemies of nomadic horse archers since the days of Genghis Khan, if not long before.

Of course, not all of Dara's horsemen were archers. A few hundred or so bore lances and wore heavy armor, preferring to charge home among the ranks of their enemies. Not unaware of how suicidal such tactics would be under the present circumstances, they kept to their orders, riding with the larger circle of horse.

The drums changed beat, signaling the wheel. Atisheh pressed her horse's flank with her left knee, and stood in the stirrups as the first of the enemy rotated into view. Riderless horses were stampeding away from the wall, crushing men and panicking the mounts of Aurangzeb's men trying to come to grips with Dara's sowar.

Aurangzeb had packed so many men into the attack that Atisheh loosed, reloaded, loosed, reloaded, and loosed again before the circle had moved her beyond view of targets. As she stood down and rode round again, she watched the wall to see if the wheel had advanced or not.

They had not. There were too many men to kill, and too few warriors to kill them.

Still, the wheel went through two more full rotations and half of one of her large quivers before suffering their first losses. She could not tell from the mess of tangled horseflesh and men whether the two riders had been shot or simply collided, but the wheel rode on, heedless. Another spin and she heard, over the pounding of hooves and the gunfire of the Sikhs, the signal to advance.

The slower rotation brought about by the advance and greater penetration into the ranks of the enemy gave her time to loose four arrows before she could find no target.

She'd started her second quiver by then, and her horse was sweating. They were even with the Sikhs now and caught a glimpse of a man riding hard and fast toward them from Delhi Gate. She blinked, realizing the boxes lashed to his horse and the two following it contained the paper and brass shells Talawat's weapons required.

Didn't they have bearers among them?

The wheel brought her around again. Atisheh ignored fatigue and pain to pick a target, draw, and loose.

I know they did. She drew and loosed again. *They went through that many shells already?*

She drew and loosed once more before the cannonball ripped her horse from beneath her and killed the next three sowar behind her.

Gun line

"God! Where did they come from?" Carvalho breathed. He'd been busy with reloading, and had missed the appearance of an orderly line of men around the shoulder of the redoubt to the north and west of the mob Aurangzeb's men had become as they tried to cross the creek and carry the walls of Red Fort.

The newcomers leveled long guns like those that had been killing his men and opened fire. Dozens of men died in that first volley, and many more were wounded. That was bad enough, but then they fired again without reloading. The line of men behind them stepped forward and repeated the process. By the time they were being replaced by the first rank, a thousand men and more lay dead, dying or wounded on the field.

Then, just to be certain the artillerist knew he was no longer loved by God, at least a thousand horsemen rode into view on his side of the creek and almost immediately began to rain arrows on the mass of dismounted men and riderless horses milling in confusion. Men fell dead, or screaming, on this side of the river too.

"Reset to the west!" he screamed, thanking God the *Whore of Babylon* was already loaded.

Islam's crew heaved, struggling to get the massive weight of the gun lined up with the new target. The cannon was not made for such small targets as men, even mounted men, but by God, he would do his best.

He signaled the other guns to continue firing at the gatehouse while the crew worked to shift the *Whore*. There was risk enough of striking their own men with a ball from one cannon but he wouldn't allow the guilt for such a mishap to fall on another man's shoulders.

No-man's-land

Atisheh heard muffled screams of men and horses. Some of them had been her own, she thought. She drew breath and coughed. Something rolled her into the light of the flares . . . or maybe daylight, she wasn't sure. Everything had a reddish cast she could not blink away.

The ground trembled beneath her. Many horses striking the earth. A steady thunder, as of drums, penetrated her many aches and no few pains, the paired sensations waking her to the idea she should be doing something other than lying on her back, bleeding.

Ignoring the pull of chain mail on tender flesh, Atisheh wiped at her eyes with the backs of her hands. They were tacky with blood, but she eventually cleared her lashes of most of it.

Blinking in the increased light, she watched mutely as a horse, flat on its back and its guts strewn about, flailed beside her with its hooves kicking at the dawn-reddened sky. Atisheh looked away from that horror, saw fletching catch the light as arrows whistled through the air above her.

Instinctively, she began to move.

A part of her wondered how the horse had managed to roll over her without crushing her. Atisheh scrambled aside and climbed to her feet. Indeed, despite her many aches and pains, nothing seemed broken.

Smoke carrying the stench of burned horsehair, sulfur, blood, offal, and seared pork that could not be pork drifted across her position, making her gag.

Atisheh winced as she moved her veil aside to spit the taste of vomit from her mouth. Fresh blood flowed. The chain mail had grated the skin off her nose and one cheek despite the silk winding meant to protect her flesh.

The regular beat of the Sikhs' shotguns discharging in volley fire was audible from somewhere fairly close by. The sound cut through the other noises of the conflict raging around her, but she could not see the men themselves.

Someone she didn't recognize came wheezing out of the smoke toward her, only to fall a few paces away, an arrow sprouting from his neck.

A pang of regret flashed through her as she realized her own bow was lost in the wreckage she lay in, if not destroyed. The regret made her examine her other weapons. Her sword, scabbard and all, had been bent degrees by some impact. Perhaps the steel had protected her from the rolling horse? Her daggers, one at the top of her boot, and one in her wide belt, were still in place.

The smoke cleared for a moment. Freed of the stench, Atisheh spat and quickly took her bearings. She had somehow ended up standing on the far lip of the ravine that paralleled the wall. Idle considerations like how she'd managed to move twenty gaz from where she estimated she'd been when the cannonball hit fled before the scene below her. The creek bed was filled with men in tangled heaps, some struggling, most forever stilled. She raised her eyes and saw the ground from the ravine to the walls was similarly covered in men, though the dead and dying were less visible, being trampled underfoot by the thousands of men trying to get out from under the fire lashing at them from the walls and one flank.

She flinched as one of the cannon on the wall coughed smoke and fire in her direction. The air filled with the sound of angry wasps and then the sound of hammers striking wet flesh as the men between her and that great muzzle were flailed by dozens of lead shot. Each individual projectile was nothing compared to the heavy cannonballs usually fired by such guns, but the up-timer shells packed dozens of balls that spread to wreak their own destructive path.

Dara's horsemen were a bit more than a hundred gaz to the west, arrows still flickering from their wheel and overhead at . . . she turned her head to the right. Perhaps it was the fact she was on foot and closer than before, but the milling mass of men and horses they'd been loosing into when she fell appeared neither better organized nor shrunken despite the losses she knew Aurangzeb's men had to be suffering under the killing rain of arrows and gunfire.

Those few men on the near edge of the mob who were not already panicked were starting to raise bows toward their tormentors. Realizing the danger she was in, Atisheh turned, searching for either a mount to carry her away or some protection from the arrows— from both enemy and ally alike—that fell around her.

Those riderless horses closest to her were far too panicked to hold still while she approached, let alone mounted. She had just started to curse God for leaving her in this predicament when a handsome mare emerged from the smoke at the gallop, charging toward her.

Heedless of her many hurts, Atisheh staggered into a sprint perpendicular to the horse's path. The mare saw her at the last moment and swerved, but Atisheh sprang for the cantle, grabbing at it. She missed, but her leap carried her arm over it, and she managed to hook it in the crook of her elbow as she started to fall away. Quickly adjusting position, the horse barely slowing despite her weight and awkward positioning, she gripped the cantle in hand. Shoulder protesting every jarring step, she flew one giant stride and then another before using the gathered momentum of her next touch of the ground to bounce up and into the saddle in a move even her aunt might have complimented her on.

While the mare had barely slowed, it had run in a slight arc as a result of her added weight. Seeing she was charging in the right direction, Atisheh giggled with pure relief before realizing the men she was heading toward might not recognize her.

No sooner had the thought come to her than the first arrow flew past her head.

"Damn stinking dogs!" she screamed. "Can't you see it's me?"

The warriors ahead were still in the wheel of death, though, which was hard enough to do without worrying about whether you recognized the idiot charging toward you from the enemy's direction. Giving up on yelling, she hunched over her horse's neck and tried to think herself and the horse as small and nonthreatening as she could.

The next several moments were among the longest of her life.

She saw a horseman lower his aim upon her and knew she was dead, but the eunuch who rode beside him recognized her and jostled his arm. The arrow went wide, the bowman cursing the eunuch as they whirled from view. All the while the steady beat of hundreds of shotguns firing in near unison grew louder on her right.

She turned her head to face the wall and saw the Sikhs. The formation looked exactly to plan: a long line of men three deep facing the ravine while the remainder made the same formation perpendicular to the wall in what looked like a Latin letter "L." She passed the short end of the L, looking down the lines of men extending from the ravine's edge to the outer wall of Red Fort.

The short end was the source of the crashing volleys, each rank firing a barrel and then, a scant moment later, the other. A slightly longer pause as the second rank leveled arms before firing. The only reason she could see them at all was the wind carrying their gun smoke east toward the sun and their targets. The front rank stood and retreated behind the third, while the second, now first rank, leveled their weapons and fired. The middle rank closed breeches over fresh shells. The movement was as machinelike and frightening as it was beautiful; a complex dance of hundreds of men and weapons orchestrated at the will of one man.

That will shouted something she did not need to speak Punjabi to understand.

She was past then, riding parallel to the long axis of the formation. The men in the first rank were kneeling, guns up, the second standing with their weapons pointed over the shoulders of their comrades. More than five hundred guns pointed in her general direction was a threat even her intense dislike of gunpowder weapons could not mask.

Again the bellowed order.

She was close enough now—or far enough from the great cannon—to hear the lower officers relaying the command for their men.

Looking to her left, Atisheh swallowed and, if she hadn't already decided it was past time to flee for her life, clapped her heels to her stolen horse's flanks on seeing the horde of sowar riding toward Dara's cavalry.

Certain she would die once the Sikh officer ordered his men to open fire, Atisheh considered hanging from the side of her horse, but knew she couldn't count on battered limbs to support her weight for an instant, let alone a hundred gaz and more between her and the relative safety of Dara's men. Assuming her prayers would be drowned out by those from more pious throats, Atisheh instead lay as flat as she could over the saddle and croaked encouragement to the mare.

She looked right. The range was closing fast. The infantry would be in range about—

B-b-b-bam!

No more the near-perfect drumbeat of volley fire, this was a long, drawn-out stuttering crash of each man waiting until she was clear of their immediate front before opening fire.

A lump formed in her throat; not of admiration for their action—checking fire for a lone warrior of unknown allegiance was not wise—but for their discipline. That those men were not only able to hear but also execute such a foolish order with complete precision in the heat of battle was a testament to their leadership and drill.

She looked again at Aurangzeb's men. Many of the leading horses had gone down under the Sikh fire, taking their riders and, more often than not, those following too closely behind as well. The charge she'd thought would kill her stalled as a result, allowing her a chance.

Atisheh counted it a minor miracle none of Dara's sowar plugged her with arrows as she covered the last few gaz and rejoined the wheel. Her mare nipped at another horse that came too close. Wishing she had the energy to match, Atisheh looked for Dara.

He was there, somehow having lost his helmet and the magnificent horse he'd been mounted on when she last saw him, but he was there. Still in command, not only of his senses, but of the men. He yelled something and the drum changed cadence, sounding the withdrawal.

The infantry was on the move as well, withdrawing with the same choreographed precision as before. Now that the men had no obstruction to their fire, they resumed volley fire once more.

Damla was suddenly beside her, dusty hand extending a swollen wineskin to Atisheh as they rode.

Atisheh took it with a grateful nod, ignoring the painful protests of her shoulders and arms as she raised it to her lips. She coughed up as much as she was able to get down, but still felt far better for having something to wash the blood and fear from her mouth and throat.

"Yonca?" she asked when she could speak again.

Damla shrugged. "Dead, I think. Same ball I thought killed you."

"The others?"

"More alive than dead," Damla said with a shrug. "We'll count the cost when we're behind the walls again."

Atisheh noted Damla hadn't said, "when we're *safe* behind the walls," but from the looks of things, Dara's sortie had proven extremely effective. More than she'd dared hope it would be.

She prayed Dara's luck would hold.

Gun line

Carvalho was pressing the dragon to the touchhole for what seemed like the thousandth time when his luck ran out. A round from one of the devilishly long-ranged up-timer weapons spanked from the cannon and whirred into the meat of his left hand.

Cursing, he dropped the linstock to grab his bleeding hand instead of stepping out of the way. The gun belched its load, rocking up and dropping its weight on his left boot.

The world went white, then away.

He came to on the ground, looking up into the dark, smiling face of Sidi Miftah Habash Khan. Sidi, not yet fully recovered from the injury suffered at Burhanpur, had become the leader of Aurangzeb's remaining light cavalry in the absence of Shahaji, though what he was doing here was a question.

"What?" he tried to ask, but his jaw was so tightly clenched he could not move it.

The smile disappeared. "I said, that looks like it hurts. I am sorry, my friend, for what must come next."

Before Carvalho could figure out what Sidi was apologizing for, the former slave-soldier-now-umara grabbed his hand, the wounded one, in a tight grip.

Carvalho screamed, reflexively pulling back to punch Sidi, who nodded at someone out of view.

The weight on his foot was removed.

The pain slapped him like a typhoon-driven wave. Carvalho had never felt the like, but he didn't pass out, not this time. Not with Sidi's distraction.

"Sneaky, filthy, shit-eating Mohammedan bastard!" he grated in Portuguese, more because cursing helped him deal with the pain than any real anger at Sidi.

The grin returned. "Now you sound like Father De Jesus."

"You speak Portuguese?"

Sidi's smile grew fixed. "Who do you think sold me to these people?"

Their conversation was interrupted as another round

from those infernal weapons ricocheted from the cannon and *whir-whir-wheeted* its way through the air.

Sidi flinched. "The pig-eating vermin think we're trying to get the gun back in play."

My men.

Carvalho tried to raise his head, but Sidi pushed him down. "None of that. Can't have you looking at it."

"My men," Carvalho grated.

"Are being seen to," Sidi said.

Such was the pain and disorder to his thoughts that Carvalho didn't think to ask what, exactly, the man meant until he was being lifted from the ground and thrown over the back of Sidi's horse.

Just a glance revealed far more than he wanted to see or could ever forget. Great wounds gaped in the flesh of his men, men he'd known since taking service with the Mughals almost a decade ago. Men who would no longer answer his call to arms, fight beside him, make him laugh, make him proud.

He tried to wipe his eyes but only succeeded in making his vision blur with more blood, sweat, and tears.

Chapter 48

Red Fort
Redoubt west of Lahore Gate

"Did we win?" Bertram wheezed, a coughing fit bending him double behind the parapet.

"How the hell should I know?" John asked, waving the broken—*and how did that happen?*—sword in his right hand at the chaos raging along the ravine. Nothing moved immediately below the walls, nothing but flies and the occasional twitch of things that might have once been whole men. Indeed, the walls to either side of their position were relatively quiet, the men too exhausted and stunned to do anything other than, like John, take stock.

Then one of the cannon fired, making everyone but the dead and deafened twitch. The Sikhs outside the walls were still shooting, the sound like an angry god's metronome, and John could see the dust and catch an occasional glimpse of horsemen riding out beyond, but details were scant.

Or maybe he was just too tired to see clearly. The

last hour of battle had already become a terrifying blend of images in the mind's eye, by turns fearful, angry, exultant, painful, and brutal.

Bertram spat something thick and red.

John glanced from the bloody mess to his friend, suddenly worried Bertram had been wounded.

More wounded.

No, more *seriously* wounded. They both had a number of shallow cuts and scrapes, but spitting blood was something worse. Maybe fatal.

"You okay?" John asked. Bending down, he hissed in pain. Something hot and wet spread down his back.

"I—One"—Bertram spat again—"of them..."

"One of them what?"

"I got blood in my mouth."

"I see. Do you hurt?"

"Of course I do." Bertram wiped at his mouth. He looked pale. "I hurt all over, but I didn't mean my blood." He went paler still. "Though I suppose some of it is probably mine."

"Oh," John said, feeling his gorge rise.

"Yeah."

"Fuck—" John leaned over the parapet and threw up—well, down, actually.

"Jesus, John! You're cut!"

"So are you," John said, straightening and wiping his lip with the back of his sword hand. There wasn't much more than a foot of blade left on the weapon, but he wasn't about to let it go. Sixteen or so inches was better than squat. "I'll get someone to stitch us up."

"What, this?" Bertram asked, pointing at a long scratch on his forearm.

John nodded.

"It's nothing compared to the big rent in your mail," Bertram said, taking John's arm.

"Huh. Didn't even notice—" John slid to the ground, legs suddenly weak. Now, he did let go of the sword.

"Medic!" Bertram screamed.

Pavilion of the Healers

"So, my sisters, whence comes this sudden anger?" Jahanara asked. The rumble of distant gunfire continued.

Is it my imagination or are there fewer cannon firing now?

They should have a few moments of relative privacy while the runner she'd sent for word on the battle's progress returned.

"Whatever do you mean?" Monique asked, sipping the julabmost Smidha had summoned for them once they were on the veranda.

Ilsa, less inclined to answer diplomatically, said, "I'm tired of tolerating the political games that put us at risk."

"You mean the spying my sister did for Aurangzeb?" Jahanara asked.

"For one, yes." Ilsa's tone was light, but the undercurrent of anger was still audible, like stones beneath the surface of a smooth-flowing stream.

"You worry she will escape punishment?"

"I do."

"*We* do," Monique said.

Jahanara looked at her. "You, at least, knew my plans. Nothing has changed with regard to my intentions regarding my sister's fate."

Monique shrugged.

Ilsa looked from Jahanara to her, eyes narrowing. "More secrets?"

Monique didn't answer her directly, instead addressing the princess. "I remember. And I trust you will carry through with your plans, and I even thought that would be enough. But now John and Bertram and everyone else is out there, risking everything for your brother's throne, and it made my blood boil to hear her speaking as if the sacrifices of so many would mean so little."

"She has a knack for saying maddening things, my sister," Jahanara said. Smidha knew her well enough to identify the bitter irony, but doubted the other women could hear it. "We have done much, and more, in hopes of ensuring Dara's victory. It is in God's hands now."

"No," Ilsa said, surprising them all with the venom in that single word.

Smidha opened her mouth to reprimand the ferenghi, but Jahanara stilled her lips with a surreptitious gesture.

"No," the blonde repeated, one hand still protectively curled around the baby growing within her. "It is not just in God's hands. It's in the hands of men like Monique's fiancé, my husband, and the many thousands of other men doing their damnedest to make sure Dara has a fighting chance of keeping the Peacock Throne. But are these deceptions the method you will use to retain power once his throne is won? Is there no better way to honor the sacrifices of all those who die today?"

"Dear God," Monique mumbled, suddenly white with fear. "Please don't let him die."

Ilsa's free hand took the younger woman's in her own, but her eyes did not leave Jahanara's.

The princess looked away, embarrassed that she had no ready answer. There *was* no easy answer.

"I can only do so much to change the stage upon which we all dance. I am trying. God knows, I am trying." Jahanara Begum, princess of princesses and power behind the throne of the Sultan Al'Azam, her brother Dara Shikoh, bent her head. Tears came to her eyes, and then her cheeks.

Smidha saw the gentle hand Jahanara curled about her midriff and wondered at what caused the gesture. Her puzzlement lasted only an instant, the answer coming in a landslide of implications and rising terror. She felt her face drain of all color.

A young man in messenger greens—hardly more than a boy, really—strode up onto the veranda and bowed.

Smidha shot to her feet, worried the messenger would see what only she had the experience to identify. But the boy paid her no mind, indeed did not seem to take note of anything but the report he seemed eager to make.

Jahanara took the hand from her waist and gestured him leave to speak.

He bowed again. "Begum Sahib, the Sultan Al'Azam remains outside the walls, but lightly engaged with the enemy. The sally went according to plan: The Sultan Al'Azam's sowar brushed aside the foe between the walls and the camp nearest Delhi Gate. The Sikh infantry rolled up the flank of those of the pretender's forces still trying to carry the wall west of Lahore Gate and are beginning their withdrawal. The infantry withdraws under cover of the Sultan Al'Azam's sowar, and the bulk of Aurangzeb's remaining men appear disinterested in continuing the fight."

"The men on the walls?" Ilsa asked.

The boy messenger glanced from the ferenghi to Smidha to Jahanara, unsure what to do.

Smidha and Jahanara both nodded at the youth.

He addressed the princess but answered Ilsa's query: "Lahore Gate is intact, but with what seems heavy losses. It is too soon to know who is alive and who is dead."

Both Ilsa's and Monique's eyes closed and their lips moved. Smidha thought it the first time she'd seen either ferenghi pray.

"Go, obtain the latest reports and return to us with fresh news," Jahanara said firmly, eyes on her friends.

Another messenger appeared as the first made ready to leave, this one from the interior of the pavilion.

"Yes?" Begum Sahib said.

This messenger, far senior to the first, began his report even as he bowed. "Priscilla begs leave to send in the stretcher-bearers and medics held in reserve."

Smidha had forgotten they were to send them in where the battle dictated a need.

From Jahanara's frown, she had forgotten as well. "Go directly to them and command them to go first to Lahore Gate and thence to wherever there are the most wounded in need. Then return to Priscilla and extend my personal thanks for her foresight and memory."

"Your will, Begum Sahib," the man said as he bowed.

Redoubt west of Lahore Gate

"Jesus Christ," Bertram said, turning John's fall into a slide. A heave rolled the heavier man sideways and onto his front.

"Medic!" he yelled again. When one did not immediately appear in answer to his desperate summons,

Bertram took a breath and tried to remember his first aid training. Kneeling over the up-timer, he started the assessment.

John was breathing normally, a good sign. He was pale. Not a good sign. There were a number of scrapes and bruises visible on his face, hands, and lower arms. But all of them seemed superficial. Ignoring the big wound he could see, Bertram felt for others. Finding none, he examined the wound in John's back. It was perhaps the length of a hand and gaped a few fingers wide while the rent in the armor was far bigger, and the padded silk undergarment was stained red with blood. He shook off idle questions of exactly how and when the cut had been made. He couldn't pull the armor off, so he had to do his best to check beneath the belt and around John's waist by feel alone. Lots of blood in the fabric, but he didn't find another wound.

"Medic!" he shouted again. Standing, he opened the pouch at his side and promptly stuck himself in the hand with the tip of the pre-threaded needle as he rummaged for it.

Cursing softly, Bertram bent, the needle ready to punch yet another hole in his friend's back.

Chapter 49

Battlefield outside Red Fort

Watching the milling mob of his reserves begin to retreat, Aurangzeb knew the day was, at best, a draw. He still had perhaps four times as many men as his brother, but Aurangzeb's losses had been greatest amongst the most aggressive of his warriors. It was, perhaps, the natural outcome of any attempt to storm prepared defenses, but it was still one he could ill-afford. Unlike a regular siege, his best artillerists had died almost to a man while at their guns, felled by the infernal up-timer weapons with little to no gain.

Sternly, Aurangzeb repressed the fury he felt toward Nur Jahan and his sister Roshanara, whose supposed intelligence had proven so faulty. He would deal with them later, but for now he forced himself to accept that the fault was ultimately his and no one else's. He'd tried to be clever and forced the matter too quickly.

He considered ordering the most powerful of his remaining umara to rally their men and make another attempt, but wisdom learned from Father stayed his tongue. A true leader did not issue an order when he knew that order would not be obeyed. Doing so led those who heard it to question not only your orders but also your authority to give them. No, the men would not—could not—be organized for another attack. Not today. And to ensure the men would fight tomorrow, he would have to arrange a truce to collect the dead and wounded who fell today.

Dara had won the day—and perhaps many days still to come. Despite all Aurangzeb's prayers. Despite his every effort to live and plan according to his understanding of God's will.

Aurangzeb glanced about his greatly thinned command group and sighed. None of his more powerful umara would be returning soon. Even if the battle had left them unwounded and not facing a challenge to their right to lead, none among them would wish to face their Sultan Al'Azam after failing to secure the victory, even though it had been Aurangzeb, not they, who had promised the win.

No, they would not serve, and none among those remaining with him was of suitable rank to treat with Dara or his representatives.

Briefly, he considered using Nur, but dismissed the thought almost as soon as it came to him. She had proven herself untrustworthy, whether from error or treachery.

His eye fell on President Methwold. Dimly he remembered the man joining the command group sometime after dawn. Now the Englishman was gray-faced with worry as he watched Sidi Khan's retreat from the guns, concern for Carvalho writ large on his pale features. He wore ferenghi garb today, making him stand out among Aurangzeb's silk-and-jewel-studded courtiers. Such garb would also mark him out on the battlefield.

"President Methwold," he said.

There was no response.

"President Methwold," he repeated, louder.

The Englishman started in alarm, but controlled his mount's reaction without conscious thought. "Sultan Al'Azam!"

"Approach," Aurangzeb said, deciding the Englishman would serve.

Methwold did as he was told, ignoring the stares of Aurangzeb's kokas and umara.

"I require a service from you," Aurangzeb said.

Methwold nodded and said, with admirable calm, "Then I am at your service, Sultan Al'Azam."

Aurangzeb looked again at the battlefield. "Ride to the pretender's commander and offer a truce to recover the dead and wounded. The truce to last until"—he glanced at the sky—"tomorrow at dawn."

The Englishman nodded, expression unchanged despite any surprise he might have felt at the request.

"And if they request more time?"

Aurangzeb did not hear the question. A figure approaching from the east had caught his attention. A messenger, his greens stained and mud-spattered, his mount's hide flecked with sweat. The rider himself sagged in the saddle.

This bodes ill.

Most long-distance messengers, when delivering news that was not critical, stopped for a time to clean themselves and their mounts so as to make the best presentation possible. Imperial messengers were, first and foremost, required to uphold an image as indefatigable *riders*. Reporting to the Sultan Al'Azam while appearing exhausted, travel-worn, or weary was simply not done.

"Bide a moment, President Methwold." He gestured at the messenger. "This news may influence the particulars of your task."

"Of course, Sultan Al'Azam," Methwold said.

Aurangzeb gestured for an opening to be made for the messenger, who slid from the saddle and stumbled a pace before catching himself.

"Report."

"Sultan Al'Azam, Shaista Khan approaches with near fifty thousand sowar," the messenger said, wearily pulling his satchel around to present it.

There was a stir around Aurangzeb at the news.

"How far behind you are they?" Aurangzeb asked, ignoring the mutters as he pulled the only thing the satchel contained: a hastily sealed letter.

"I barely escaped, Sultan Al'Azam. Remounts were scarce, as many imperial servants have abandoned duty or declared for Dara and therefore refused me remounts and supply."

Another wave of mumbles and mutters from amongst his men.

"How far?" Aurangzeb repeated.

"A day. Two at most, Sultan Al'Azam. They have no cannon with them, and travel quickly as a result."

Aurangzeb broke the seal and read the contents of the letter. Mohammed planned to harass the much larger force as he retreated, but a commander of five thousand, no matter how gifted, could scarcely be expected to stop a competently led force numbering ten times his own. And Mohammed's competence was apparent in the next lines of his report: His force lacked the remounts necessary to maneuver out of the larger army's way and then return to raid Shaista's rear, so he planned to withdraw as slowly as possible before it in an effort to screen Aurangzeb's army. His men would mount a monumental effort, no doubt, but would ultimately fail as they had here today. Not through any fault of their own.

Aurangzeb struggled to hide his fear. Not of losing the war—what God willed was inevitable—but for his personal understanding of that will.

Where he had always found comfort in contemplating God and His design, he only had raw, bewildering questions he'd never thought to ask before:

How could my understanding of God's will be so flawed?

Where was my error?

What did I do wrong, God?

When did it become necessary to teach me this humbling lesson?

Who is Dara that you have chosen him and his heretical ways over me? I have strived to be a good Muslim whilst he courts false gods and godless men!

Mastering the urge to curse angrily and give his rage free rein, Aurangzeb said, "Take your ease, messenger. You have done good service and will be rewarded."

"Yes, Sultan Al'Azam. Thank you, Sultan Al'Azam."

Aurangzeb waved the man away, mind already racing across the ground between here and Shaista Khan's force. There were no good options for a set piece battle that would not leave his rear exposed to Dara's garrison, even if he managed to get the bulk of his army turned and ready to face Shaista Khan in time.

The certainty of a few hours before had entirely deserted him, leaving in its wake a hollow desperation and fearful anger. He struggled past it, trying to think quickly and clearly.

Slow Shaista. Whip the men into some kind of order. You had the strength to take on all comers. If you appear weak now, you will lose more than today's casualties. Men will desert you for Dara.

Damn him. How did Dara bring Shaista over to his side?

The answer came easily enough, when considered.

He had not. Dara could only offer money and station, and that no more than Aurangzeb could have.

Jahanara. She accomplished it with promises of marriage, no doubt, of opening whore legs for our ambitious cousin to have children that could rise to the throne themselves, in time.

I pray you will live to regret your perfidity, Jahanara.

His eyes traveled back to the walls of Red Fort, where much of the smoke had started to clear. Dara's cannon and those terrifying long-range guns were killing those of Aurangzeb's men still in range, but at a greatly reduced rate. The Sultan Al'Azam suspected more because they were running short of armed targets rather than ammunition.

Many of the fleeing sowar had thrown away their weapons, if only to lessen the weight tired legs—their own or their mounts—must carry. Sidi Khan's men were the exception. Their return to camp appeared as orderly as such light cavalry ever showed, though their opportunistic nature as raiders had certainly shown itself in the number of remounts they had procured from among the riderless horses roaming the field. Aurangzeb hoped they'd found time to save some of Carvalho's gunners while they collected the horses of dead men.

"Summon Sidi to me," he said to the drummer. He would send the Habshi and his men to bolster Mohammed's force, redirect his efforts to establishing a defensive position from which to stand that threat off and still breach Dara's defenses. All that and God granting a miracle or three, he might still win.

Methwold quietly cleared his throat.

Aurangzeb found the man looking at him with a carefully neutral expression in place.

Racing thoughts came to a halt, clicking into place like the playing pieces of one of the games his sisters so enjoyed.

"President Methwold," he said, glancing at the sky, "offer the truce as instructed, but inform the pretender's commander in the field that any truce agreement will end at noon today."

Aurangzeb ignored the uneasy murmurs that rose from among the men of his bodyguard. A truce that short would not provide enough time to collect the wounded, let alone the dead.

Let them complain. I no longer have time, patience, or the men to spare.

"Sultan Al'Azam!" someone shouted.

Dara Shikoh craned his neck around, shoulders and neck aching from the unaccustomed archery.

"Atisheh!" he croaked, surprised. He'd thought her dead some hours ago and was glad to see her still among the living. He tried to add a happy greeting, but his throat was caked with dust. But no longer tight with fear, at least.

She maneuvered to join him. When close enough to speak without yelling, she said, "Sultan Al'Azam, from the looks of things, Aurangzeb will not make another attack."

"Are you certain?"

She shrugged, gesturing with a hand at what little of the battlefield they could see. Even that small slice of the fields was carpeted with dead men and horses. "The men who most wanted a fight were the vanguard, both in the assault of the walls and when Aurangzeb sent his reserves against us. The ones still alive and unwounded have already fled once, and won't have the stomach to fight again, if they had it to start with. Even the brave men among them will not want to tread upon their own dead to come to grips with us, even if enough could be found and organized. At least, not today."

Dara spat again. He looked around, saw the signalman had been replaced by a boy barely out of the harem and croaked. "Sound the walk..." As the horses and men slowed, Dara took stock of his own hurts. On top of a throbbing headache that God, in his infinite wisdom, had decided to visit on him in the last few minutes, the fingers of his right hand felt shredded from the bowstring. He knew the pain was a result of too many hours spent bent over paper with the qulam and too few at archery. His horses and warriors, being in better condition than their leader, made no complaint, but he could tell the mounts were vastly slower than they'd been even during the last rotation, and the men were reaching into empty quivers for arrows already sent at the enemy.

They slowed to the walk with little of the brave show they'd had when first they'd sallied.

And the sally had been far more effective than anyone but Dara himself had believed it would be. Dara felt a pride that made all his pains diminish to a dull ache. *His* plan had killed a great many of the enemy today.

Still, Aurangzeb had so *many* men. And there was so much dust, despite the light rain that had fallen the evening before. Enough, almost to make him wish he'd stayed atop the walls to better see the progress of the battle.

But all his hurts, all his fears—they were as nothing compared to the feeling of leading men in battle as his great ancestors had done for generations. Back unto Babur, back unto Timur—back unto Genghis Khan.

They were as nothing.

And the Sikhs! They had, in the last hours, killed many, many times their number. They alone had broken the charge of Aurangzeb's reserves. Aurangzeb's thousands of sowar had gambled their lives against the very real threat on their flank in hopes of killing Dara himself. Unfortunately for those brave men, their charge carried them at an oblique angle across the front of the Sikh firing line, prolonging their exposure to fire. The result had been a murderous slaughter. Nearly half of them were dismounted or killed by the time the first warrior saw sense, turned, and fled for his life. The ignominious stampede to safety that followed would have made his ancestors proud, Dara was certain.

He patted his horse's sweaty neck with his hand, wincing at the painful protest from abused fingers.

The wheel slowly brought him round to the creek side. The Sikhs were withdrawing toward the gate by sections. Dara could not—would not—call it a retreat, not with the orderly ranks the Sikhs displayed. And it was a proud display: the men, heads held high under saffron turbans, were singing as they were given orders to march toward the gate. Bidhi Chand was not among the singing men, of course. Dara had sent him to Lahore Gate.

The Sultan Al'Azam glanced over his shoulder as the slowed rotation carried him around once again. The outer works of Lahore Gate were a smoke- and dust-wreathed ruin, bodies heaped at the base of the walls and even atop the parapets. He'd been so busy with the fight there had been no time for fear—at least beyond the momentary fear for one's own life—for the lives of others, like John and Bidhi Chand, that he'd ordered into battle.

The Sultan Al'Azam hoped Bidhi and John had at least lived to see the effectiveness of the tactics they'd taken such pains to impart to the men. The up-timer may have used a book of what he called "old-ass tactics" to train Bidhi Chand and his men, but all the book learning in the world would have meant nothing had the men themselves not been disciplined and willing to adopt the new formations, weapons, and tactics Bidhi Chand had drilled them on with such relentless fervor.

He raised a hand to signal the men to slow to a walk and could not help but see the bodies of men—both his and his brother's—who had fallen and would not rise again, would not grow older, would not sing nor pray, eat nor drink, nor love a woman. If the coin of

sovereignty was the blood of such brave men, had he
the stomach to pay the price of victory over and over
again until the war was won?

Did Aurangzeb?

And was that what this was? Victory?

There were so *many* dead.

His mouth tasted of ash and blood.

So many wounded.

Is this what victory looks like?

"Sultan Al'Azam?" Atisheh said, interrupting his
fugue.

Dara glanced at his bodyguard and found her
craning her neck to look toward Aurangzeb's lines.

"What—" He cleared his throat. "What is it?" he
asked, unable to see what had caught her eye.

"A messenger."

"From the pretender?"

She peered at the approaching rider before replying, "So it would appear, Sultan Al'Azam, though they
are dressed like a ferenghi. An Englishman, I think."

The elation he'd felt not long before was all gone
now. *My brother is sending a messenger to me, the
traditional acknowledgment of defeat, yet I can think
of nothing but the cost ... the pain ...*

The headache was growing with every beat of his
heart. Dara put away such thoughts and tried to focus
on what he must do to retain the upper hand.

First, it would not do to appear or sound less than
kingly before the messenger. Dara unhooked his chain
veil with a hand that shook rather more than he liked
and leaned over to spit. The lean threatened to turn
into a fall. He jerked back, making his unfamiliar
horse prance sideways with uneasy fear.

Atisheh reached out with an almost absent gesture and steadied her monarch, eyes still on the approaching messenger. "It *is* an Englishman. The one called Methwold."

Dara patted his horse's neck and, considering it best to appear the general before anyone coming from Aurangzeb's camp, began issuing commands. "The Sikhs are to continue the withdrawal." He paused, winced at the number of walking wounded among the infantry. "The wounded are to be given priority to pass through the gate. The Sikhs to rest until the next time my brother thinks to challenge my defenses."

"Yes, Sultan Al'Azam!" one of his men said. The rider turned and set his tired horse in motion.

Dara turned a gimlet eye on Aurangzeb's messenger. It was, indeed, Methwold. The man kept his eyes up and trained on Dara, probably to spare himself future memories of the dead and dismembered.

"You were exiled by my father, Englishman."

The man had the good grace to blush. "I was. Your brother saw fit to pardon my transgression."

"You address the Sultan Al'Azam! No other can lift your exile!" Atisheh growled.

Dara wished she had not. It only added to the throbbing pain in his skull.

Blushing scarlet, Methwold bowed his head in recognition of the point. "Forgive my error, Sultan Al'Azam."

Dara waved the apology away. "Your message?"

"Th—" Methwold caught and corrected the error rather smoothly. "Aurangzeb declares his intent to agree to a truce to collect the wounded and the dead. Such truce to last until noon today."

Atisheh's chuckle was menacing and cold, yet managed to convey good humor. Dara glanced at her, uncertain what summoned the sound from her lips.

Meeting his eye, Atisheh punched her chin at the battlefield.

His thoughts were sluggish, but he understood the meaning of that gesture. While Dara's wounded and dead could be easily recovered in the time covered by the truce, Aurangzeb's far greater losses would require days, not hours, to see to.

Not making allowances to see to the dead and dying was bound to make his men unhappy. Why push such a timeframe, then?

Dara closed his eyes against the pain and wished his thinking unimpeded by his many hurts. Seeking an answer that made sense was hard enough when dealing with court politics, but now...

It can't be that Shaista Khan approaches and Aurangzeb wishes to deny me a delay that might give us a chance to coordinate...

Hope soared in his breast, only to crash to earth.

No, we have heard nothing of Shaista, and just because I wish it true does not make Shaista's arrival any more imminent. No, relief—if there is any—will not arrive in time to threaten Aurangzeb.

Is he that short of provisions?

No, with what the traitor gave him from Gwalior Fort, surely his army can hold for weeks, not days.

What, then?

Dara's lip curled as he stumbled on what he felt must be the reason. Aurangzeb wished to make him appear heartless and cruel. Telling his men one thing whilst he sent this man to make a different offer, only to later blame Dara for his refusal to show courtesy to the dying and dead.

"President Methwold, did my brother not say why he wants his truce so short?" Dara asked, watching the man closely.

"No, your brother did not choose to reveal to me his reasons," Methwold answered, expression giving nothing away.

Despite the clangor within his skull, Dara raised his voice and waved with feigned nonchalance at the battlefield. "He must not wish to see the great many dead his pretensions to generalship have caused this day, lest they ask him with their silence, 'Why must we die to serve your false claims?' No, my brother is fearful of the mute dead, not to mention the voices of his living wounded. *That* is why he seeks such a short truce."

Dara's sowar were moved by his words, some even shouting angry contempt at Methwold, who sat stone-faced through their cries and Dara's diatribe alike.

Raising tired arms for a silence he ultimately decided he could not wait for, Dara shouted, "Tell my brother that, in direct proportion to his faithless nature, I will show mercy to those he would trample under the indifferent hooves of his ambition!"

The old wound throbbed with every shouted word, a saw-toothed dagger trying to carve his thoughts to bloody offal. He closed his eyes, sucked a deep breath in, let it out.

Dara's men were silent, waiting, watchful.

The Sultan Al'Azam Dara Shikoh opened his eyes and locked gazes with Methwold. "By my command, my physicians will treat *all* those wounded this day, regardless of who they chose to follow into battle!"

Dara heard the expected protests from among his own men. They were not unreasonable fears: the wounded would be additional mouths to feed and possibly become a significant internal threat if inclined to repay his mercy with betrayal.

"Those whose only crime was to be led astray by the honeyed promises and false piety of the pretender," Dara said, addressing their complaints but pointing at his brother's position, "need not suffer under his hand any longer. My closed fist, having struck so many down today, is once more opened—opened to offer succor to the wounded and friendship to the friendly."

The concerns of the few were drowned out as most of the men roared their approval. They even began chanting his name.

Dara very nearly spoiled his gains just then by throwing up. A veil of pulsating, painful blackness menaced from somewhere beyond the corners of his eyes, ready to rend and tear his sanity.

He did not actually hear Methwold's response, nor was he conscious of what was said to give the Englishman leave to depart. It was all he could do to remain upright in the saddle and not beg for a pipe to ease his pain.

Chapter 50

Red Fort
Pavilion of the Healers

"Who are these men?" Jahanara asked. From the quality of his bloodstained robes and fine armor, the patient was clearly a Rajput umara of some note and likely someone she should know, but Jahanara could not place him. He might have been any age, really, so much of his face was covered in savage burns.

"One of the sons of Samarjit Khan, I believe," Smidha supplied after a moment's thought.

The veranda had become a triage area for the wounded. Three quarters of the pallets set out in preparation for the injured were already full, and the men out here were those the medics deemed would survive without immediate care. The stretcher-bearers of the corps had been bringing them in, first in a trickle, but in the last hour the flow of wounded had become a continuous stream.

"I thought they'd all declared for Aurangzeb," Jahanara said.

"They did." Monique had just entered the pavilion proper. "Your brother has decreed all wounded will be treated for their injuries, those who served the pretenders just as those who fought for Dara."

Like her older brother, Jahanara considered herself a student—even a disciple—of the teachings of the great Sufi saint Mian Mir. So she could appreciate Dara Shikoh's mercy while at the same time stifling a curse at his impracticality. Their medical capabilities were already on the verge of being overwhelmed, just treating their own wounded. If they had to treat those of the enemy as well...

She thrust that issue aside. They would just have to do as best they could. At the moment, she was more concerned over her brother's own well-being.

"Have you heard anything of Dara?" she asked Monique. "He's alive, or he couldn't have given that order. But is he injured himself?"

The young Frenchwoman shook her head. "No, I haven't. But—"

A stir at the entrance to the pavilion drew their attention. Another stretcher was being brought in. Pushing his way ahead of the stretcher-bearers was a man whose vigor indicated that the blood that covered much of his armor was not his own. Not most of it, at least.

When he looked up, searching for a space to set down the stretcher, Monique could see his face.

"Bertram!" she cried out, rushing toward him.

Bertram fended off her attempt at an embrace. "Careful! You'll get blood all over you."

Most of the blood was already drying, but he had a point. So she satisfied herself by leaning forward to give him a quick kiss. To hell with Mughal notions of propriety. She could manage that because he wasn't wearing a helmet any longer.

Unless—

"You *did* wear your helmet out there, didn't you?"

Bertram ignored the question. "Where can we set John down?"

For the first time, Monique looked down at the man on the stretcher. Sure enough, it was the up-timer John Ennis. He was very pale and didn't seem conscious.

By then, Jahanara had arrived. "Over there," she said, pointing to an adjacent pavilion whose entrance was flanked by two of her personal guards. She'd kept that in reserve for wounded men of high rank, not so much due to concerns over status but simply because the survival of such men and their quickest possible recovery was likely to be important. She'd stationed two of her best medics there for that reason also.

Speaking of best medics...

She looked around and spotted Priscilla in a corner of the main pavilion. Turning Monique in that direction with a hand on her shoulder, she pointed. "Get her," she commanded.

When Ilsa saw her husband lying on the medical bench where the stretcher-bearers had placed him, her face grew tight but she gave no other indication of concern other than a quick hissing intake of breath.

Priscilla arrived just moments later. She turned to Bertram. "Where is he injured? Injured worst, I mean."

Before Bertram could answer, John himself did. "My back," he mumbled. But his eyes remained closed.

"It's a wound in his back," Bertram confirmed.

"Help me turn him over."

Once Pris got a good look at the wound, the expression on her face seemed to ease. "It's bad," she said, "but I don't think it's fatal, although if infection sets in it will get nasty. Ilsa, see what you can find in the way of disinfectants."

After Ilsa left, she turned back to John. "Can you move your legs?"

His left leg shifted a bit, then his right. "Sorta. Hurts, though." He managed a soft chuckle. "Of course, they *already* hurt. Everything hurts."

Pris wasn't surprised. The wound in John's back was the worst one he'd suffered, but there were several others. More than anything else she'd seen, that drove home to her just how savage the fighting must have been. He was lucky that no vital organs seemed to have been pierced, even if he'd lost a lot of blood.

Thankfully, she had plenty of one of the trade goods they'd come to India to find.

"Opium," she commanded.

What she was actually handed by an orderly was what would have been called "laudanum" by Americans—those of them who knew their history, anyway—although it didn't bear much resemblance. It was a tincture of opium in distilled palm wine, a reddish-brown liquid that was roughly eighty proof in terms of alcohol content.

And *very* bitter.

"Shit, that stuff is horrible," John complained.

"Take another swallow," Pris commanded. "What I'm about to do is going to hurt."

John did, grimacing.

"And another."

Despite his anxiety as he watched, Bertram was a bit

amused at this further example of Mughal tolerance—
perhaps flexibility was a better term—when it came to
Islamic prohibitions. In theory, only non-Muslims were
allowed to drink any sort of alcoholic beverages. But the
empire had a history of looking the other way given any
sort of reasonable excuse. A bitter drink taken to help
a warrior recuperate from his wounds easily cleared
that rather low bar.

Bertram was glad he wasn't the one who had to drink
it, though. The stuff tasted *awful*.

"And another," Pris commanded again.

Aurangzeb's command group

"You have no choice, Sultan Al'Azam," said Sidi Khan. He
pointed to the battlefield that was becoming more visible
as a breeze cleared away the gun smoke and dust. "Our
losses are great, the walls of Red Fort still stand, and
we no longer have Carvalho's experienced gun crews."

Aurangzeb's jaws, already tight, grew tighter. He
glared at the abandoned guns before him.

"We no longer have Carvalho, for that matter," added
Sidi. He gestured with his head toward a group of men
some distance away who were tending to the wounded.
"I think he will survive, God willing, but his wounds
are enough to end his life as a soldier. He will lose the
foot, for a certainty."

Aurangzeb started to shift the glare onto Sidi, but
managed to restrain himself. The Habshi leader was
simply doing what any good subordinate would, giving
his best advice to his commander. After a moment, the
young Mughal prince exhaled.

He hadn't even been aware that he'd been holding his breath. At the end, it turned into a soft sigh.

"Yes," he said. "But where do we retreat to? Our men are too exhausted to build fieldworks—and I don't trust my brother to keep the truce he agreed to."

The truce was to hold for hours only, at Aurangzeb's own insistence. Had that been another mistake?

"Gwalior," said Sidi. It was more of a statement than a suggestion.

Impertinent, perhaps, but Aurangzeb didn't bridle. Today, after his blunders, he had no right to resent advice.

"We can't all fit into Gwalior," Sidi continued, "but it will shelter us well enough. It's a very strong fort, and—"

He pointed again at the battlefield. There were bodies everywhere. Some were moving, some even with vigor. But many were not.

"—Dara Shikoh has suffered losses of his own."

It was a good suggestion, Aurangzeb decided. Gwalior was no more than a two-day march, or perhaps three. There was no chance of pursuit, he thought. His brother's strongest forces had been those damned Sikhs, and they were mostly infantry.

That left—

"What about Shaista Khan? Can he intercept us?"

Sidi shifted his shoulders slightly. The gesture was a shrug, but not one of uncertainty. It was that of a man dropping a weight from his shoulders.

"He's coming from the east and we'll be going south. Not impossible, maybe, but . . . not likely." The Habshi's chuckle was dry—harsh and cynical. "He's not moving quickly. At all. I believe he intends to keep his own army intact and untouched to further his agenda."

Aurangzeb nodded. That made sense. Shaista Khan would be able to negotiate the best possible terms for himself if he had forces that were still strong and unbloodied. The bastard.

"We will do it," he said. "To Gwalior."

That left some unfinished business. "Bring Nur Jahan to me."

Aurangzeb's camp
Nur's tent

"Whatever you wish done must be done now, Nur Jahan," said Tara.

She did not give any explanation for the statement, but none was needed. Nur squinted toward the battlefield, wishing she had eyes that were thirty years younger. Her sixtieth birthday had been in May and everything at a distance was no longer very clear.

Then she turned her gaze toward Red Fort. That, at least, she could still make out well enough. The walls were imposing both in size and color. The striking red sandstone that Emperor Akbar the Great had used in its construction a few years before Nur's birth shone wet with blood in places where it wasn't shattered by cannonballs.

"There," she said, nodding toward it. "We will go there."

Tara turned in her saddle. "You are certain, Nur Jahan?"

"I have no choice. Lahore is too far away. If we try to reach Shaista Khan, we will be intercepted."

That last wasn't certain, but it was not a risk she

was prepared to take. And judging by Tara's head nod, she was in agreement.

Nur didn't bother to explain the rest. Tara knew more than enough to understand the peril she was now in.

Perils, rather. There were at least two in Red Fort—Jahanara as well as Dara Shikoh. Both had reasons to want her dead. But she might be able to negotiate something with them. Whereas with Aurangzeb...

Now? After the disaster—which is what the battle was, even if the boy didn't understand that yet because of his pride—which he was sure to blame at least in part on her faulty advice?

And it *had* been her failure, incorrectly assessing the information she'd obtained. Her own pride resisted the admission, but her intelligence would have none of it. She had been fooled—badly fooled—by Dara Shikoh and Jahanara.

Mostly by Jahanara, she was sure. Only the most powerfully confident woman would be ruthless and brave enough to risk her very reputation for the sake of a daring military maneuver. It was a wonder she'd managed to persuade her brother to allow it.

Nur had no chance with Aurangzeb. Not now; probably not ever again. He would surely have her executed.

"Get me to Red Fort," she commanded.

Red Fort
Pavilion of the Healers

Jahanara had not stayed to watch Priscilla clean and sew up John's wounds. By now, the pavilion was spilling over with wounded men. There were no benches or cots left. The newcomers had to be placed on the floor—and then on the ground in the gardens outside. She found herself doing what Priscilla called "triage," knowing full well she didn't have the medical training or knowledge to do more than make rough estimates of what a man's chances of survival were.

Inevitably, she was more inclined to give the benefit of the doubt to their own sowar rather than to those of the pretender. And if that strained the spirit of Mian Mir's teachings, so be it. Rulership had its demands as well as its privileges. Whatever Dara's faults might be, she had no doubt—had never had any doubt—that he would make a better emperor than either Shah Shuja or Aurangzeb.

There was another commotion at the pavilion's entrance. She came over to find out what was causing it, but could not see over the heads of the guards clustering there.

"Follow me, Shehzadi," said Firoz Khan. The armored eunuch started pushing his way through. Strong as well as fat, he had little trouble opening a way forward. Those who turned to snarl or curse at being pushed aside fell silent when they recognized Firoz—and she who came in his wake.

Moments later, Jahanara was past the throng at the entrance and into the garden beyond.

"Dara!" Her brother was sitting astride his warhorse, both hands clutching the ornate pommel of his saddle. His expression seemed vacant, his eyes staring at . . . nothing, so far as she could see.

She hurried forward, with Firoz Khan now following in her wake. "Dara!" she said, more loudly.

With a bit of a jolt, her brother's head turned to

look at her. His eyes seemed to come into focus. "Jaharana," he said. That was almost a murmur; she could barely hear him.

She came alongside. From a quick examination, she was relieved to see that he seemed to be uninjured. She could see no blood, at least. He might be bruised somewhere. Probably was.

"Dara—"

"I can't move," he said, again in that semi-murmur. "If I try . . . I will fall off the horse. I'm . . . exhausted."

Judging by the strained look on his face, Jahanara thought her brother was more than just "exhausted." He seemed as brittle as thin glass.

She turned to Firoz Khan. "Can you . . . ?"

The eunuch came forward. Jahanara stepped aside to give access to the emperor. Firoz Khan raised chubby hands and more or less lifted the emperor out of the saddle. It might be more accurate to say Firoz gave the appearance of assisting the emperor by turning Dara's collapse into some semblance of a dismount.

Jahanara was pleased. Her brother's dignity had been protected. Well enough, anyway. No one watching would think poorly of Dara; certainly not sowar who had their own experiences with battles.

"Get him into a litter and to the harem," she said softly. "I will find Priscilla."

Priscilla was where Jahanara had left her, still working on the wound in John's back. Ilsa was there as well, hovering with her fists balled as if she might beat her own impotence into submission.

Jahanara was struck by memory then. Father as he stood waiting for the physicians to ease Mother's pain, her cries growing steadily weaker and weaker until that horrible silence came.

Blinking tears and memory away, she crossed the last few steps to the trio.

"I need you," Jahanara said to Priscilla. "Now."

She turned toward Ilsa. "I am sorry. But . . . my brother. I must have Priscilla examine him."

Ilsa drew breath, no doubt to shout a refusal, but Priscilla interrupted her, "Ilsa, you can handle the rest of it. The sutures are finished. None of what's left requires me."

She came to her feet. "Lead on, Shehzadi."

Chapter 51

Red Fort
Harem

After rubbing her eyes to provide some ease, Jahanara looked back down at the note she'd started reading. It was perhaps the hundredth—so it seemed, anyway—she'd gotten from various commanders in the field or on the walls. Most of them were addressed to her brother, but Dara Shikoh had been in no condition to give any coherent responses, so Jahanara was handling it for him. Her eye strain was certainly not for lack of light—a sunlit balcony was always easy to find in the harem—but rather the result of poor penmanship from most of Dara's subordinates. Usually they would use a munshi, but the crises of the last few days made everyone wish to use their pens, if only to hurry their reports along. Few such reports were directly military in nature, and those that were almost always addressed the needs of the fortress itself. Logistics was a subject she was quite confident she could handle—better than Dara Shikoh himself, actually.

The fighting had ceased entirely. While the cease-fire had ended the day before, Aurangzeb had begun withdrawing a few hours before it was over. Not thinking it wise to disturb her brother, Jahanara had ordered his officers to avoid any clashes unless they were directly attacked. Only two minor tactical questions had been raised in the missives, and in both cases her reply had been *do what seems best to you*.

None of the replies were sent in her own hand, of course. After she wrote them out, they were passed along to Dara's munshi for copying and distribution. The officers would readily accept orders written in his hand, where they would question anything written in Jahanara's. Most of them wouldn't even recognize Jahanara's handwriting unless they'd had commercial dealings with her or their wives had furnished some of her poetry for their pleasure.

It was an irritating subterfuge, but she had no choice. Dara Shikoh's sally had gained him great prestige and stature among the umara and, perhaps more importantly, his sowar. Indeed, that he had gone against his advisors and prevailed was also a sign to Dara's followers the emperor was his own man. For all intents and purposes, the shadow cast over him—not quite a stigma, but close—by his defeat the year before at the hands of the Sikhs had been erased. Completely erased, she thought; the fact that the Sikhs had proven reliable and incredibly effective allies had helped a great deal in the restoration of Dara's military reputation. So much so that she expected some of Aurangzeb's people to begin making discrete overtures to Dara soon.

Was it true that the Guru himself had been in the battle? she wondered. Rumors were spreading that he had been. Whether true or not, those rumors also helped Dara's reputation.

But however much better her brother's reputation was today than it had been before, it would come under severe stress if it became known just how fragile his health remained. Dara Shikoh had become almost comatose after he'd been brought into the harem. Priscilla had told Jahanara that none of his injuries were dangerous, physically speaking. He was simply beyond exhausted, the demands of his condition and recent days having drained him of the meager reserves of strength he'd managed to build since Father's assassination. And Dara had never been one to seek exertion even before his injury.

She looked down over the river and toward Mother's tomb, glad of the moment of solitude she'd obtained by the simple expedient of sending her body slaves to assist Nadira.

Jahanara heard Firoz Khan's slippers pacing the dense carpets. Looking up, she saw that Smidha had entered the chamber. She seemed very tense. Her eyes flicked back and forth from Jahanara to the eunuch.

"Leave us, please, Firoz," Jahanara said.

Firoz bowed and left. When the sound of the eunuch's slippers faded from hearing, Jahanara looked back up at Smidha. Gesturing to a nearby cushion, she said, "Sit. You look tired."

"Tired!" Smidha folded herself onto the cushion. "Tired of folly, perhaps! When were you going to tell me?"

Jahanara frowned. "Tell you what?"

Smidha turned her head and looked at the doorway, then peered at the shaded alcoves where Jahanara's body slaves usually lingered. Apparently, to satisfy herself that no one was listening. Finding they were as alone as they were likely to ever be, Smidha turned back and nodded her head sharply. The gesture was...

She was pointing with her brow, Jahanara realized. At Jahanara herself.

No, at her midriff.

"You're pregnant." The words were soft, but the tone was not. It combined accusation, exasperation and... sorrow, perhaps.

"I *told* you it was folly to meet with Salim alone. At least, if either I or Firoz had been there we could have restrained that... that... *adventurer!*"

Jahanara's mouth opened and she waggled her head a little. Part protest, part denial, and part acknowledgement that Smidha was correct about the pregnancy.

Smidha sniffed, a lifetime's experience with the princess letting her read Jahanara's expression. "Fine. We could have restrained *you*." She threw up her hands. "Both of you!"

Realizing she'd raised her voice, even if only slightly, Smidha turned her head again to peer at the balcony entrance. Then, not satisfied, she replaced her veil, climbed to her feet and looked out over the balcony, then moved to the entrance.

"No one," she muttered, returning to her cushion. After she was seated, she said: "So, an answer. When were you going to tell me?"

By then, Jahanara had regained some composure. "Ah... soon."

Smidha sniffed again. "When your belly was showing for all the world to see?"

"I was going to tell you... maybe tomorrow. Or the day after." She gestured at the pile of missives still stacked before her. "I have been very busy! Dara is in no condition to handle such matters now."

"He's well enough to order your death once he discovers the truth."

Again, Jahanara opened her mouth and shook her head. But no protest came forth. Smidha was probably right, she knew. Her brother might, if Nadira had her way, spare Jahanara herself—though she'd certainly be imprisoned—but there would be no such mercy for Salim. None at all.

"I don't know what to do," she admitted, hanging her head.

"There is the dancing girl's remedy. The up-timers probably know better and safer ways to do it, and I think we could trust them to keep silent. We certainly cannot rely upon any of the old guard at court."

Jahanara had already considered that option herself. For hours, now, she had only pretended, even to herself, to be fully occupied with her brother's correspondence. So when she shook her head, the gesture was firm and final.

"No. It is impossible."

"Nonsense. Not until one hundred and twenty days after conception—and don't tell me you don't know what day that was. We still have plenty of time."

Jahanara knew that herself, because she'd studied the matter once she realized that she was pregnant. The Koran said nothing directly about induced miscarriage, so guidance had to be found in the Hadith—which, for Sunni Muslims like herself, meant the words, teachings and actions of Muhammad and his companions. The Hadith could be construed in different ways, however. So, over time, four major schools of Islamic law had emerged: the Hanafi, Maliki, Shafi'i and Hanbali. The Mughals followed the Hanafi, with some modification.

She had one hundred and twenty days from conception, when the law did not consider a fetus to have a soul and thus be a human.

"I will tell you what *is* forbidden," said Smidha. "Suicide is forbidden—and that applies just as much to killing yourself by inaction as doing it directly."

Jahanara knew that also. The fourth Surah said it clearly: *And do not kill yourselves, surely God is most Merciful to you.*

"No," she repeated. "*I* forbid it." She placed her hand over her womb. "I will not kill my child. Who is also Salim's child. *No.*"

"Stubborn, like your mother." Smidha sighed.

Jahanara glanced at her advisor.

"Oh, don't look at me so. Your mother didn't have to keep bearing children, not after supplying Shah Jahan with four sons! She could have let one of the others run those risks, bear those burdens."

"But, she loved us. Loved being mother to us all."

Smidha nodded, face pinched with sorrow. "She brooked no competition for Shah Jahan's love, either."

Knowing what Smidha said was true, Jahanara had no reply.

"In truth, I was afraid you'd say you wanted it," Smidha said, placing her hands on her thighs and leaning back a little. "There is only one other option, then. We must place you in seclusion—and for months. But how? Where?"

Jahanara heard Firoz's approach first. Smidha, despite her nervous disposition today, was older, with an older woman's ears. The scuffed heaviness of the eunuch's slow tread was a signal to Jahanara. The eunuch's tread was normally as light as could be, given his weight. Firoz wished her to know her privacy was about to be interrupted.

Smidha recognized the signal also, of course.

The two of them fell into a cautious silence.

A bull elephant trumpeted, answered a moment later by another.

The eunuch joined them on the balcony and approached. His obeisance was perfect. He came erect and said, "The Sultan Al'Azam requires your presence."

Jahanara was relieved to see that Dara seemed alert. That could be a mixed blessing, of course—and judging from the scowl on his face, it probably was. He was in his private chambers, seated comfortably among cushions, and attended only by Nadira, who had sent everyone away with her son upon her sister-in-law's arrival. That he was not abed was surely a good sign, though his glower was not.

So she was surprised when his first words were not a reprimand. "Nur Jahan is at the Water Gate," he said. "She begs for sanctuary, having taken a boat from Agra proper."

For an instant, Jahanara's mind blanked. Among all her present concerns, projections, plans, and worries, Nur had been distant and of little import. And for the woman to be approaching from Agra when Aurangzeb's Red Tent had been south of Red Fort?

Nur Jahan. Here? *What could she possibly be thinking?*

The answer came on the heels of the question,

and she spoke it aloud. "It follows naturally on Aurangzeb's bold attack. The misinformation he had from the Venetian spy, Gradinego—what she was deceived into believing was reliable information—led him astray." She'd almost added *and from Roshanara* but stopped herself in time. As furious as she was at her younger sister, Jahanara had better use for her alive than as a corpse.

Dara Shikoh grunted. "Your doing." That sounded more like an accusation than the compliment she deserved for the sacrifices she'd made to bring off his great victory. Yes, there would be a reprimand coming soon.

But not yet. Her brother left off scowling at her and his glare softened as he looked at Nadira, seated close enough to hold his hand. Then, looking back at Jahanara, he said, "I don't want Nur Jahan anywhere near my wife and son. She's too dangerous. In fact, I'm inclined to simply execute her and have done. But . . ."

Jahanara gently shook her head. "Make use of her instead: employ her as your mediator with Aurangzeb."

"So *he* can be her executioner?" Dara ran fingers through his beard. "I suppose that would be better. She is Jahangir's widow, after all. An empress in all but name, in her time. So let her imperial blood be on his hands, you're saying?"

"Possibly. But that might be the least beneficial outcome. What I am primarily thinking is that the way Aurangzeb deals with her will tell us a great deal about his state of mind after his defeat at your hands. His self-restraint, especially."

Dara had not invited her to sit, so she remained

standing even though after all the hours she'd spent the day before overseeing the work in the healers' pavilion her feet still hurt. She didn't mind the pain so much as the distraction. She'd be able to think better if she weren't forced to hover on aching feet.

"What do you propose Nur should tell him, beloved?" Nadira asked.

Dara was still running fingers through his beard, as he often did when deep in thought. He glanced from his wife to Jahanara. "What is your advice?" His jaws tightened. "As angry as I am at you, I do not—cannot—deny that you are shrewd. Very much so. So what do you think?"

"Offer him the governorship of the Deccan," Jahanara said, ignoring his tone to concentrate on achieving her ends.

"He will only use such a position to strengthen himself," protested Nadira.

Jahanara nodded agreement, even as she outlined her reasoning: "And yet, over the last ten years, the Deccan has been ravaged by famine, plague, and, of late, the vast armies of your brothers' comings and goings. What remains is a war-torn and famine-ravaged region without the resources that you command here—and we also can strengthen ourselves further given the head start you have obtained for us. It will be what the Americans call an 'arms race' in which we have all the advantages."

She waggled her head. "It is either that or resume the war. Time will work to our advantage, not his."

"Aurangzeb is not stupid," cautioned Nadira. "He will understand we offer a flower thick with thorns."

"Yes, of course. But . . ." She *really* wished she could

sit. Her aching feet were muddying her thoughts. Not so much making them murky as slowing her normally quick mind.

After a moment seeking her inner calm, the game pieces came into sharp focus, the board before her clear. "The thing is, I don't believe Aurangzeb has much choice. You gave him a great bloodying out there, brother—and the fact that it was *you* who did it—in person, leading from the front—makes it all the worse. He has suffered a great blow to his prestige and is already losing men. Some will have lost any taste for fighting and will leave for home, but others will begin exploring their options, begin to make overtures to you. His army might remain larger than ours should his key umara remain loyal, as I expect them to, but he will not resume fighting again. Not by choice, and not for at least a year. His army is a bent blade, and he needs time to mend it before bringing it to battle again. And in that time, you will further strengthen your position, forces, and technology to the point any fool will see who is the rightful Sultan Al'Azam."

A few heartbeats passed. Enough that Jahanara worried she might have overstepped, said too much, but then Dara lowered his hand. "Do it, then. Instruct Nur Jahan"—he smiled thinly—"on her new duties."

She almost said, "What—me?" The last thing she wanted to do was undertake the walk down to the Water Gate. Firoz Khan could provide her with a litter, but she did not want to show any weakness before Nur. And besides, the pain would be some small penance for the lies and lives she'd spent.

So be it. Without protest, she turned and left.

Red Fort
Water Gate

"Aurangzeb will have me beheaded!"

Jahanara nodded, pitiless. "Yes, that is quite possible."

Nur glared at her. "And that is your intent."

"No. That is a *possible* outcome—and one I have no difficulty accepting. But I would actually prefer it if he spared you and sent you back with a reply."

"He might send my head back with a reply—a reply carried by another emissary."

Jahanara found herself enjoying Nur's fear, and strove to suppress the feeling. Mian Mir would not approve of that. Nor did she herself, in her better moments.

"Yes," she said. "That would also tell us something."

Nur Jahan shifted her glare to the boat where her few remaining guards and servants sweltered in the sun, as did she herself. Jahanara had insisted on conducting this meeting in the open, above the dock that had been thrown up in the wake of the battle—where she was being shaded by a parasol in the hands of a large eunuch.

It was *hot*.

Nur had no choice, and she knew it. At least she had the satisfaction of knowing she hadn't been bested by Dara. No, it was another woman who had come up with this clever and cunning scheme. Bad enough to have a man cut her head off; worse still if she were forced to explain to the man exactly why and how he'd been maneuvered into the action in the first place.

"Very well," she said between gritted teeth.

There followed a rather long period of instruction,

wherein Jahanara explained to a sweating Nur exactly what was expected of her.

"I will carry your words to Aurangzeb . . . I will return in two, perhaps three days. If I return at all."

She didn't bother to add any curses. The young princess she'd so badly underestimated would probably deduce something from those as well.

Jahanara had certainly come into her own. She was . . .

Impressive.

After Nur Jahan boarded her boat and was being poled to Agra, Jahanara watched her for a while—not so much to be sure the woman was leaving, but simply because she was reluctant to start walking again. Her feet were still very sore. She had gotten little exercise for quite a while now because of the demands of the crisis. Even when her life had been more active, that had usually meant she was on horseback. She'd spent all day on slippered feet yesterday, from dawn to well past midnight. There hadn't been a single day in her previous life when she'd ever done that, so far as she could remember. Not even as a child.

When Nur Jahan's boat was a mere speck on the river, Jahanara blew out a soft sigh and began to turn back toward the gate. Looking down at the wide Yamuna, a thought came to her. A wish, really. To be able to sail away. She stared down at the slow-moving waters of the great river winding toward the sea, mind racing.

Of course.

Red Fort
Harem

As soon as Jahanara returned to Dara Shikoh's private chambers, her brother burst out angrily.

"You have done nothing but deceive me!" With a sharp jerk of his head, pointing with his chin, he indicated his wife. "And you drew her into your schemes as well! You talked me out of executing Salim on the grounds that I needed to be merciful. The teachings of Mian Mir, you said. But all the while you and your lover were scheming!"

Her own long-suppressed anger boiled over. "Scheming? Scheming to do *what*? All Salim and I did was plan a maneuver that would cripple Aurangzeb's supply lines from the Portuguese! A maneuver which may have preserved the Peacock Throne for you!"

This time she wasn't going to wait for any invitation. Even after resting on the litter Firoz had summoned for her, her feet were still sore. She folded herself down on a cushion. "And it is a lie that Salim is my lover!"

That itself was what Priscilla's husband Rodney would call *a bald-faced lie*, but she was too furious to care. "I am tired of your false accusations!"

Nadira tried to intervene. "Husband, everyone is crediting *you* with what Salim did. 'A masterful stroke,' some have been heard calling it."

"Oh, splendid!" Dara Shikoh threw up his hands. "So now you have ruined my reputation as well as hers! Everyone thinks I have no respect for my own honor, now."

Jahanara had calmed down enough to speak in a

level tone. "Brother, the supposed 'honor' of an emperor means less than nothing if he loses the throne, his family, and his means of bestowing honors on his subordinates. Every diwan, umara and zamindar with any experience knows that—and all but a handful will admire an emperor who knows it as well. Better still, an emperor who knows it and is willing to act accordingly. If you did not let your emotions cloud your good sense—"

She bit that off. Dara was clearly about to explode again. "Let us be done with this! I realize there is a problem and the solution is clear and obvious: I will go on Hajj. As soon as possible."

Dara's mouth, which he'd opened to shout, was now simply agape. So was Nadira's, although she managed somehow to do it prettily.

"Hajj will solve everything, I think. Even your issue with my contact with Salim. Even though there is and was absolutely nothing scandalous or improper in my conduct with Amir Salim Gadh Visa Yilmaz—none whatsoever and never has been!—"

She hoped it was not pride that led her to believe she was actually as good at telling the bald-faced lie as recent experience had made it seem. Perhaps it was Nur Jahan's influence; certainly her interactions with her eldest female relative had proven she'd some ability at dissembling.

"—if it is obvious to everyone that I no longer have any contact with him, for most of a year, then rumors should die down." She nodded respectfully at Nadira. "And my absence will make it clear your wife is in unquestioned and complete control over your harem."

She fell silent. Saying anything further, she thought, would be a mistake. And she hoped . . .

Nadira did not fail her. "You see?" her sister-in-law exclaimed, gesturing with her hand toward Jahanara. "You should be ashamed of yourself, husband! Your sister has never done anything except in furtherance of our needs and interests, in the interest of preserving our son's life and chance to rule. Ashamed of yourself, I say! Ashamed!"

Shame did not come naturally to Dara Shikoh—or any Mughal royal, being honest about it, including Jahanara. But his wife's vehement censure caused him to close his mouth and flush. At least a bit.

Jahanara decided the moment was ripe. It was probably the only chance she had.

"I have one condition," she said. "You have treated Salim disgracefully, and must make amends." She held up her hand stiffly, as if to ward off any dispute. "I will be gone, so there will no longer be cause for foul rumors and idle gossip. And you can put what remains to rest by appointing Salim governor of Gujarat."

She lowered the hand and began counting off on the fingers. "That will accomplish several things. First, it will make clear that your exile of Salim was merely your clever subterfuge of war. Second, it will help clear my name and honor, since you would certainly not give the Afghan such responsibility if you had any doubts or suspicions about him. And finally"—she stopped counting on her fingers and lowered both hands into her lap—"he will be a good governor. You know it as well as I do. And the Das family will assist him in rooting out those who might retain some vestige of loyalty to the pretenders. He has proven very capable at everything he puts his hand to."

Including me. She forced the smile brought by that memory to go into hiding.

Dara was running fingers through his beard again. A good sign, she thought.

"Very well," he said, after a minute or so. "But!"

He raised a cautioning finger. "Salim is not to be told until after you have left for Surat. I want no further encounters between you!"

"Of course, brother," she said, trying to sound as submissive as possible. "By all means, do not make the announcement until I have left Red Fort. By the time he can get to Surat, I will already be crossing the sea."

Unless he's a superb horseman with a string of superb horses.

Chapter 52

Sinhagad Fort
Western Ghats

"Well, at least we should be safe enough here," said Iqtadar, leaning over the wall and looking down at the steep hillside below. "Need to clear away some brush, though, if we're going to be here for very long."

He turned away and looked at Salim. "Just how long *will* we be here, Amir?"

Salim spread his hands wide. "I have no idea. Hopefully, not long. But..."

Standing to his left and also looking over the wall, Sunil chuckled and did a fair imitation of Salim: "My return is dependent on the whims of the emperor. Will he decide to reward me? Shorten me by a head? Who can say?"

Both of Salim's other lieutenants smiled. "What do you think, Iqtadar?" asked Mohammed. "Should we bet on it?"

"Enough," said Salim. His tone was mild, but his

subordinates obeyed instantly. By now, Salim's authority over them was unquestioned, in fact as well as in theory.

He had chosen this fortress as the place to quarter his troops because he himself had no idea what Dara Shikoh intended to do with him. The Bhonsle clan had agreed to let him take possession of Sinhagad, since they were not using it themselves. Indeed, taking possession of the fortress had required ousting a band of outlaws who had been living there, but that hadn't required any fighting. As soon as the bandits saw Salim and his sowar approaching, they had fled hurriedly.

They would find a refuge somewhere else, easily enough. This whole region of the Western Ghats had been a harsh, chaotic landscape for years. In 1630, in the course of their war with the Sultanate of Ahmadnagar, an army of the Sultanate of Bijapur had razed the city of Pune about twenty miles or so northeast of Sinhagad. Salim knew that Shah Jahan had made plans to seize the area for the Mughals and rebuild it, but his assassination and the subsequent war of succession had ended that plan, at least for the time being.

"We wait," said Salim. "We have provisions enough for a month, two with some foraging. By then we should know something."

And what will I do if that "something" is a summons to answer for my errors in Agra?

A summons that would most likely end in his death, if Dara still polished his anger. Salim might even be trampled by elephants, a traditional method of execution. Jahanara would try to intercede for him, but it was possible her brother might remain angry enough to have her executed as well. That would be done privately, though, not as a public spectacle.

But . . . perhaps not, also. Dara Shikoh was another adherent to the teachings of Mian Mir.

Still, that left exile. Or immurement.

A reward of some sort was even possible. Salim had, after all, done the Sultan Al'Azam many services.

"We should be quite secure here in Sinhagad," he said firmly.

Which means I'll have plenty of time to brood.

Stop. It.

He'd think of Jahanara instead. Those memories were worth dying for. They were the best of his entire life.

Agra
Mission House

"I'm not going to lie, folks," said Bobby, sprawling on a pile of cushions. "I'll be glad to get back home. India was . . . well, interesting, for sure. But I can't say it was all that much fun."

"At least we're *going* home," said Ricky. "Which Randy ain't—not even his body."

Bobby made a face. "Yeah, I've thought about that. But even if we dug him out of the Catholic graveyard here, how would we get him home? We're talking months at sea."

John grunted. "The British Navy managed it, back in the days of sail. I read about it in a book once. They wouldn't do it for common sailors, of course, but if it was a big-shot captain or admiral they'd—" He glanced over to where his wife and the other women were chatting, to make sure they weren't in hearing range. "They'd gut him—pull all out all the innards—and then ship him home in a casket of rum. Pickled, sort of."

"Oh, you're not doing that to Randy," said Bobby, looking green around the gills. The effect was even stronger as the young man was still sickly-looking after his repeated illnesses on the road. They made quite the pair, the wounded "soldier" and the sickly "trader."

"Hey," John said, raising his hands in surrender and wincing as the motion pulled at his many, many stitches. "I'm not proposing we actually *do* it. Just giving everyone a history lesson."

"And thank you for sharing." Bobby smiled to show he held no grudge and cocked his head quizzically. "Are you sure about this, John? Staying here, I mean."

It was John's turn to make a little grimace. "Am I *sure*? Hell, no. But . . ." He reached up and ran fingers over his scalp. "Rodney and Priscilla are dead set on staying, and Ilsa's inclined that way, at the very least until our baby is born. I can't see leaving the big guy and Pris here alone, even if I could talk my wife into it. Besides . . ."

He paused again, and the grimace faded away. "Look on the bright side. Where else would a West Virginia country boy whose only qualification was as a county roadworks crew supervisor wind up an imperial general, ennobled, earn a vast fortune, and be entrusted with the safety and security of an emperor I'd never heard of before the Ring of Fire?"

Ricky had a skeptical look on his face. "This might be a good time to remember that old saying, 'Pride goeth before a fall.' It's from somewhere in the Bible."

"From Proverbs," said John. "And the exact words are 'Pride goeth before destruction, and a haughty spirit before a fall.' I don't honestly think that describes me, guys. Proud—yeah, sort of. I think we can all be proud of what we've done here. But I'm not what you could call haughty, and in any event"—here, he returned Ricky's look of skepticism—"do you really want to try matching Biblical saws with me? My mom taught Sunday school, remember. And she was damn firm about her kids attending religiously. No pun intended."

Smiling, he added: "I'm sure there's something from Ecclesiastes, especially if I paraphrase a little. How about 'a time to be humble, and a time to accept awards'? Or—"

"Never mind," said Ricky, waving his hand in a gesture of surrender. "I'll give you this: the Mughal idea of a formal dress uniform is waaaay fancier than anything the up-time U.S. Army ever came up with."

Hating the jeweled robes something fierce, John hastened to change the subject. "So when are you guys leaving? Have you decided yet?"

Bobby shrugged. "It's mostly up to Jadu Das. He's the one putting together the caravan."

"Is he really planning to go all the way with you? Back to the USE, I mean? Not just Surat?"

"Are you kidding? *Jadu Das?* If you think that man would give up the chance to set up and profit from a new trade network—with people from the future, no less—you don't know him the way Ricky and I do."

Ricky nodded. "He's dead set on it, and having him not only along, but in charge, makes a lot less work for me and Bobby. We're pretty much just"—he patted the silk cushion under his butt—"sitting pretty until he tells us he's got all the goods packed away and we're ready to go and what's taking us so long anyway?"

Monique came into the room. "John, Ilsa wants to talk to you."

Ennis climbed, a bit laboriously, to his feet. The Mission had chosen to follow the local custom of sitting on cushions rather than chairs in those rooms that might host informal guests. Mughal furniture could be very ornate, certainly, but it wasn't particularly comfortable, especially for someone who'd been so recently sewn back together.

"See you later, guys." Gauging the subtleties of Monique's expression, he added, "Probably quite a bit later."

When he entered the chamber that served the Mission House as a formal meeting room, John came to an abrupt stop. Monique, who'd entered ahead of him, took a seat at one end of the table, but John's attention was on the people seated at the other chairs.

Four of them: Bertram, Ilsa, Rodney and Priscilla.

"I thought you said my wife wanted to talk to me," John said, in a mild tone of voice.

"I lied," said Monique. "Well, left a few details out."

"I do want to talk to you, John," said Ilsa. "But this involves everyone here."

"And no one else," said Priscilla. Her tone of voice wasn't mild at all. You could even call it steely. John didn't think he'd heard her take such a tone ever before. She gestured at the empty chair on the side of the table next to Ilsa. "Sit. Please."

Shrugging a little, John did as he was told. After gingerly seating himself, and smiling at Ilsa's helping hand, he said, "Okay, so what's this about? And why aren't Bobby and Ricky—or Gervais—invited to join us?"

Rodney chuckled, but there wasn't much humor in the sound. "Haven't you ever read a spy novel? It's called 'need to know'—and they don't."

"They *can't*," Priscilla corrected her husband. "What we're about to discuss needs to be kept secret. I mean, really, really, really secret—and no bullshit about it."

She looked at Monique. "Tell him."

"Jahanara is going on Hajj."

"Yeah, I know. Cut to the chase." John didn't bother explaining the idiom. An Indian wouldn't have understood it, but by now Monique and Bertram spoke completely fluent and idiomatic American English, even, in Bertram's case, without a trace of an accent. Not that John minded Monique's French-accented English. He quite liked it.

"She wants us to come with her. By 'us,' I mean me, Bertram, Pris, and Rodney." She nodded toward Priscilla, who was seated at the other end of the table. "Especially Pris."

"What the hell for?" John demanded. "None of you are Muslims. And while I wouldn't mind seeing Mecca—or even participating in the whole thing, just out of curiosity—they won't let you in. The whole city's off-limits, right?"

Rodney shook his head. "I did some research and: not really—not in this day and age. That was true in the when-and-where we came from, because the Saudis were strict about it. But today the city—the whole Hejaz region—is under Ottoman control, although in practice they let the emir of Mecca pretty much run the show locally. From what I've heard, they're pretty slack on the subject of keeping infidels out of the holy city. Probably all it would take to get in is a cover story and a bribe."

John was getting impatient. "I said, cut to the chase. What is this all about? Why does Jahanara want you along?" He looked at Monique. "You, I can understand. You're probably the best friend she has—insofar as she has any friends at all. But why 'especially Pris'? She doesn't look sick, so why does she need to drag our best medical person out of here?"

"No, she's not sick. But she saw firsthand how much of a difference Pris made when Nadira gave birth. And she doesn't want to lose her own kid—or her own life, for that matter."

John stared at her, his mouth open. "Huh?" was all he managed.

His wife made an exasperated little snort. "What is so surprising?" She leaned back from the table and ostentatiously curled both hands around her growing belly. "She's young, healthy and in love. Or thinks she is. Maybe it's just lust, who knows? Salim is as pretty as they come. So she got pregnant. It happens. Even to princesses. Even in Mughal India."

John now stared at her. "But—"

"Close your mouth, dear. You look silly."

Flushing a little, he clamped his mouth shut. Then, between clenched teeth: "Jesus H. fucking *Christ*."

Ilsa smiled. "Now that is some serious blasphemy. You should be ashamed of yourself."

John shot her an irritated glance. "Blasphemy be damned. We're talking about *Jahanara*. Do any of you have any idea what's likely to happen when Dara Shikoh finds out? We ain't in West Virginia anymore, kiddies. The worst you'd get back home was a shotgun wedding. Here ... *Shit* ..."

He grimaced. "You can start with Salim—we are

talking about Salim, I assume—staked out on a field with an elephant trampling him into chunky ketchup. It's even possible Jahanara will be staked out alongside him. Probably not—she's probably just in for a brutal beating and then being walled up for life somewhere really shitty—but you can't rule it out. For the love of—"

His mouth snapped shut again. After a second or two, he added: "Oh."

Ilsa shook her head. "He's usually quicker-witted than this. Yes, dear, that's why Jahanara's going on Hajj. In case you hadn't noticed, that girl is one smart cookie, to use one of your silly American expressions. The Hajj will take her out of India for most of a year. She leaves next month, before she's really showing yet, and she has to stay in Mecca until May because that's when they do the annual ceremony this year. Luckily for Jahanara. The timing's perfect."

John was feeling out of his depth again. "The date of the Hajj changes every year?"

Monique laughed. "You've been in the Mughal empire for this long and still haven't figured out local customs? No, the date of the Hajj doesn't change. It's always the first ten days of the month of Dhu al-Hijjah, which is the twelfth and final month of the Islamic calendar. But it's a lunar calendar, so over time the days and months shift compared to the calendar we use. This year, it starts in late April and runs through the first week of May."

"The *point*," said Priscilla, "is that by the time observance of Hajj begins in earnest, Jahanara will have given birth. She told Monique she's pretty sure she conceived early in July."

John glanced at Monique, frowning. "She doesn't know for sure? How many times did she and Salim—"

"I didn't ask," Monique said. "But I'm sure it was more than once. Let's just hope she conceived the first time because if it was later in July—might even be in early August—then the timing might get sticky. She can't very well be waddling around the Kaaba for seven circuits—that's how many are required—and still keep her condition secret."

"How is she going to keep it a secret anyway?" John asked.

"Us," said Pris, pointing to herself and her husband and Monique and Bertram. "And there'll be others. Smidha knows already, so does Atisheh—and if Atisheh tells the staff to keep their mouths shut you can be damned sure they will. No one will go up against the *Nagini* of Red Fort, not after her repeat performance in defense of the emperor."

"Nagini?" John said.

"Female naga," Pris said. "A serpent-man of Hindu mythology. In her case, like a cobra crossed with a woman. Which isn't too far removed from the truth, judging from the accounts I've heard."

"Firoz Khan might know already," said Rodney. "If he doesn't, Jahanara or Smidha will tell him by the time we reach Jeddah."

John scratched his chin. "Will all of them—I'm especially thinking of Firoz—keep the secret? They could collect quite a reward if they told Dara."

"Jahanara's not worried about informers, at least not profit-motivated ones," said Monique. "First, because she believes they're completely loyal to her—and for what it's worth, I agree with her. Second, because telling her brother is likely to get your head cut off immediately after he hands you the reward. The last thing Dara would want is for his sister's condition to become public knowledge. And finally—"

She laughed again. "Who do you think has been managing the empire's financial affairs? Leaving aside the fact that Jahanara has her own incomes from trade, jagdirs, and endowments from her mother that make her something like the fourth or fifth richest person in the *world*. Why would any of her entourage go to Dara for a reward when they know that Jahanara will take very good care of them anyway?"

John leaned back in his chair before thinking about it. The pain was sharp, and a stark reminder of the consequences of failing to recognize a backstabber. Sitting unnaturally erect, he spent another few seconds studying the table while the pain subsided. Jahanara had commissioned the large piece of furniture along with the accompanying chairs for the Mission, another reminder of her power. The princess had used the craftsmen of her own establishment, the same ones who provided the many palaces of the dynasty with furniture.

Mom had been into antiques. He had no idea how much it had cost. The wood itself was very fine teak, and it seemed as if every inch of it including the tabletop was covered with intricate carvings of geometric designs. It was probably—literally—worth a fortune. So were each of the chairs.

Worth a fortune to *most* people. Monique was right about that much, at least: to a princess of one of the two or three largest, richest and most powerful empires in the history of the world?

Pocket change.

"Okay, I can see that," he said. He looked around the table and issued a soft, dry chuckle. "What the hell? She's trusting us, isn't she?"

He frowned again. "She could trust Bobby and Ricky just as much." He gave Monique a slightly—very slightly—apologetic glance. "Okay, probably your father too. Besides—and I can't believe I'm saying this—I just got done being royally pissed off at Gervais"—he looked from Bertram to Monique—"and you two."

"Need to know," said Rodney, shrugging. "Which none of them do because none of them need to. And before you get all upset about keeping secrets from Gervais, Bertram, and Monique the way they did from us, it's not treason for the head of the Mission to keep his subordinates in the dark for security reasons. So it ain't the same, not including them in the . . . what do we call it? 'Conspiracy' seems a little . . . I don't know. Underhanded."

Priscilla shrugged. "That's because it is." She shook her head. "It is what it is. Which is, yeah, a conspiracy—but it's in a very good cause."

She looked around the table. "And by 'good cause' I don't just mean keeping a woman—Salim, too—whom we all like and admire alive and doing well. It goes way deeper than that. Jahanara and Salim already have a lot of trust and confidence in us, and they listen to us. A year from now, we'll have even more influence on them."

She took a deep breath and let it out slowly. "Which, I don't know about anybody else, but I damn well plan to *use*. I want the Mughal empire—hell, all of this subcontinent—to start changing. I've gotten attached to it, being honest. But it needs to *change*."

She took another deep breath. "Starting with a man and a woman who love each other being able to get married, for Pete's sake. Starting with a family being able to settle an inheritance without brothers having to murder each other." Her voice got a bit shrill. "And not executing people by having them stomped on by elephants!"

"What she says," said Monique. She laughed again, more loudly than before. "And who do you think is most likely to get some of those changes made? Or at least get started. My money's on the most capable—ruthless, too, when she needs to be—member of this whole damn dynasty."

John shook his head. "They don't allow women to rule here."

His wife laughed. "What difference does it make what these men *allow*? You will recall Nur Jahan? The woman who, in her heyday, was the empress of India in all but name. Jahanara..."

She said the next words softly. "I think that young woman—she's still only twenty-three years old—can do nearly anything she sets her mind to."

"And she's got a pretty impressive boyfriend too," said Bertram stoutly.

John ignored Bertram and focused on Ilsa. "But what about our baby? If Pris and Rodney are on Hajj, who's gonna look after you?"

Ilsa's smile made her even more radiant. "My mother had six children without a single issue, and your mother gave birth to you on the way to the hospital, John. I've had no issues so far, and if something should happen, I have every confidence in the physicians Pris has trained."

"If they're so great, let them take care of Jahanara," John mumbled weakly, knowing he'd already lost the argument.

Her gaze softened the words that followed: "Were you not listening before? Allowing them to treat her places Jahanara, and therefore us, in way too much danger. It is far safer this way."

John bit his lip, worry for his wife warring with pride in her strength and wisdom. Ultimately, it was her health, and therefore, her choice. Not trusting his voice, John just nodded.

Chapter 53

Red Fort
Harem precincts

"You have no right to do this to me, Janni!" Roshanara wailed, setting Dara's son to crying.

Jahanara ignored both her sister's histrionics and her familiarity. "I have every right, Roshanara Begum. I am senior of the bloodline, and have arranged everything."

"And before you think to ask me or Dara for relief from it, we *fully* endorse the marriage," Nadira said, handing her son off to one of his milk mothers. The servant took the squalling child and retreated.

"But, *she* should be marrying him, not me!" Roshanara cried, gesturing at Jahanara. Her face was a bitter fist, as if she'd devoured a lemon whole. Perhaps Shaista Khan could make her happy, but Jahanara sincerely doubted anything could. Some people were bent on bitterness.

"I wanted you trampled for your treasons," Smidha snarled from behind and to Jahanara's right.

"Silence, you—you . . . witch! You have no right to speak here!"

Smidha continued remorselessly, "You should be grateful to your sister. To have a third opportunity to properly serve the family, despite your history of treason! And to be well-married in the bargain? I should think you would be overjoyed at the opportunity to live."

Nadira and Jahanara both sat stone-faced. Their very lack of expression indicated their complete agreement.

Seeing no one would silence Jahanara's advisor, Roshanara fell forward on her hands and knees, then, and started to blubber.

Letting her sister's noises wash past her in a wave that did not touch her, Jahanara reflected on the fine works the Das brothers had accomplished on her behalf. The merchant had not only negotiated the bride price, he'd preserved the very particular wording of her offer: be awarded the very highest of ranks in both sowar and zat, and marry an imperial princess for your service to the throne. Jahanara would have married Shaista herself, had he arrived in a timely fashion instead of delaying in search of some advantage. Such a marriage was completely out of the question now, even if her uncle had made all speed to ride to Dara's aid. No, her pregnancy had narrowed options, but then she'd made allowances for Shaista failing to show proper support for Dara. Rarely had anyone been so glad of any such precaution taken in dynastic politics as Jahanara had been since the moment her menses stopped.

"Such a child!" Smidha threw up her hands. "Gauharara is twice the lady you are, and she's not even ten!"

"Are you done, sister?" Jahanara said the words softly.

"I—I—I can't, Janni."

"Oh, stop it! You know you can. And stop trying to play on my affections by using my nickname. We both know you detest me."

Roshanara sniffled, wiped her nose, peeked out at her sister with one red-rimmed eye. "I do not detest you, not really. I—I—*fear* you. No one should have been able to pull such a monumental victory from Aurangzeb's grasp. He was emperor for nearly fifty years in the times your pet sorcerers come from!"

Momentarily stunned that Roshanara should be the one to fully recognize just how Jahanara had made the rest of the family dance to her will, Jahanara slowly shook her head.

"Do this and you will have nothing to fear from me, ever again."

Roshanara sat up, blinked a few times.

Jahanara let the statement sink in for a moment before continuing, "Shaista Khan is older, certainly, and from all accounts, most generous with his wives. You will have all that you do here, and be treasured by him as befits your station. Better still, you will get away from me and from the shadows cast by your previous bad acts."

"But"—Roshanara wiped at her face—"Father was always against princesses of the family marrying."

Jahanara knew she had her sister's tacit agreement then. A legitimate appeal to tradition from Roshanara was like a tiger asking for tea—fanciful in the extreme.

"He is no longer amongst us," Jahanara said. She left out adding the words *because you helped his assassins*, which very much wanted to leap from her lips.

"But what does Dara say about this?"

"He mentioned execution, but I was able to convince

him this was the better alternative," Nadira said. "Smidha was not joking. You could have very easily been staked out for the elephants to crush. Or beheaded, at least."

That penetrated the last of Roshanara's reticence. And well it should have. Dara had wanted much the same fate for Shaista Khan, truth be told. The only thing that had stayed the emperor's hand—well, aside from the problem of having to fight another battle—was the death of Asaf Khan. He'd even said, huffily, "I wouldn't have put it past the crafty old lion to have died just to advance his son's designs. I can't very well have him executed for attending to his father in Asaf Khan's last days and hours."

Jahanara had not offered an opinion on that, just let Nadira carry the argument.

And here they were.

Jahanara shook her head.

May God grant that the two of them come to love one another. Or, if He should deem it appropriate, kill one another. Either would serve the rest of us equally well. God, I'd be satisfied if they just stay out of the way.

Agra
Mission House

"*Everything?*" asked Rodney. "All of the saltpeter, too?"

Bobby nodded. "That's what Jadu Das tells us."

"But he said—"

Bobby waved his hand dismissively. "As the man says, *that was then, this is now.* 'Now' being after he sweet-talked Jahanara into giving him a big—huge, he calls it—consignment of her own goods."

Ricky was grinning. "Which, of course—seeing as how we already had enough of our goods to fill the *Lønsom Vind* and then some—would require adding another of her ships to the flotilla going to Jeddah."

"To Jeddah and *beyonnnd*," added Bobby, who was now grinning himself. "That's one of the *new* ships we're about—the ones modeled on USE designs that Jahanara has been building in Surat. She's even going to let one of them accompany the *Lønsom Vind* all the way home. And we get one fourth of her hold capacity."

"I thought those were all warships," said John, thinking the youngest men of the Mission had matured on their trip east. "And are you telling us she's already got three built?"

"The third one's still a few weeks away from being completed—but it'll be finished by the time we get to Surat." Ricky shrugged. "And, yes, they're warships, by seventeenth-century values of 'warship.' They all double as troop carriers—or cargo haulers—although they don't carry as much as a pure merchant ship could. But that's enough for our purposes. Except for the saltpeter, everything we're bringing back is high value, low volume."

"I'll be damned. That woman is . . ." John started to lean back and then stopped, wincing. Sitting straight up on cushions put some strain on a spine accustomed to chairs with backrests, but the pain his sutures still caused was worse.

"Efficient," he finished, through teeth that were a bit clenched.

His wife had something of a smirk on her face.

Seeing it, John's lips twisted. "Hey, thanks for the sympathy, dear."

Ilsa shook her head. "I wasn't smiling at you in particular, I was smiling at all of you. *Men*. It doesn't seem to matter what century you were born in, either."

Priscilla was smiling also. "A Begum Sahib's place is in the kitchen, right?" She shook her own head. "When are you dimwits going to finally figure out that if Jahanara had this era's idea of the proper genital equipment as well as being the oldest of the siblings, *she'd* have become the emperor the moment her father died. And not one of her brothers would have dared to contest the issue. Well, maybe Aurangzeb would have. He's a damn sight more gifted than the rest of the bunch and certainly stubborn enough."

Another headshake. "Back up-time, they called Margaret Thatcher the 'Iron Lady.' Ha! They had no idea what the term really means."

"Okay, okay," grumbled John. "You've made your point. You don't need to rub it in." Gingerly, he reached back and poked the edges of his worst wound. "Ouch."

A servant came into the chamber. "You told me to tell you when you needed to start getting ready for the wedding. For the women, that is now. Not yet for the men."

John grimaced. "Even in a litter, that trip's going to hurt. Dammit, do I really need to go to—"

"*Yes*." That came from everybody. Except the servant, of course. She kept properly silent, although she might have hid a smirk.

Ilsa, Priscilla and Monique all rose to their feet. "Stop bitching," said Pris. "At least you don't have to spend hours and hours getting all hennaed up."

She didn't sound all that aggrieved, though. None of the men could prove it, but they all suspected the women of the Mission—up-time and down-time both—enjoyed the excuse to put on the elaborate makeup and skin decorations that were Indian custom for such occasions.

None of them said anything, of course. They weren't *that* dimwitted.

Red Fort

"And they make jokes about hillbilly marriages," Priscilla said to Rodney, in a half whisper. "I don't know about your family history, but none of mine ever had a girl marrying her uncle."

Rodney smiled, although he kept it on the thin side. "Hey, they do it in Europe too, y'know. If she hadn't run off, the archduchess of Austria, Maria Anna, would have married her uncle, Duke Maximilian—and even as it was, she ran off to marry her first cousin Fernando."

His wife made a face, but, like her husband, she kept the expression on the subtle side. In the interests of diplomacy, you might say. She wore a water-silk veil that concealed her face from anything more than a few feet, but it paid to be careful.

Not that anyone would be likely to notice. An imperial wedding ceremony like the one they were attending was what anyone would call a gala affair. Nobody was paying any attention to what a couple of peculiar westerners were saying or doing—and if they had paid them any attention, it would have simply been because of Rodney's size and the couple's proximity to the emperor. Even so, the vast mustering field of Red Fort had been made over into a confection of silk pavilions populated by bejewelled and perfumed nobility, so there were plenty of distracting views.

"Royals will be royals, I guess," she murmured. "Being fair about it, the Mughals are more broadminded than most European monarchs. Jahangir's wife—Shah Jahan's mother—was a Rajput princess. A Hindu, to boot. Certainly more broad-minded even than folks seemed to be about religion back in our time."

Rodney nodded. "Akbar the Great did the same thing. In fact, she was Jahangir's own mother. Yeah, I grant you they're not snotty that way—and won't be, so long as Dara Shikoh stays in power. If Aurangzeb ever takes the Peacock Throne, though..."

He winced, and made no effort to hide it. "Be a different story altogether, then. He's what you could call a Saudi type of Muslim. Intolerant as all hell."

"And here comes the bride," murmured Pris. "At long last."

Rodney smiled again, this time making no effort at all to keep it subdued. No reason to: everyone else was smiling widely also. That much, at least, was exactly what would have happened at a West Virginia wedding when the bride made her entrance to the pavilion.

"Could be anyone under those veils," Priscilla said, startling Rodney.

"But it is Roshanara, right? She couldn't pull some stunt or something, right?"

"Oh, it's her, and she'll be gone as soon as this performance is over. But I can't help feeling that, like a bad rash, she's sure to be back."

Rodney coughed to cover a laugh.

"Are we there yet?" said Pris, merciless in the face of her husband's self-control. "My feet are starting to hurt."

"Not hardly, dear. Royals will be royals, remember?"

Chapter 54

Red Fort
Agra

"Aurangzeb had agreed to accept your offer to become the governor of the Deccan," said Nur Jahan.

Dara Shikoh leaned forward, his hands planted on his thighs. "What was his demeanor? Sullen? Resentful?"

Nur shook her head. "He had none, Sultan Al'Azam. None that was visible, at any rate. You have not had any direct dealings with your brother in some time now. He has become..." She paused, searching for the right term.

"More mature?" suggested Dara.

Nur took a slow breath and then seemed to shrug a little, as if to resign herself to whatever might follow. "I was going to say 'imperial.'"

Dara stared at her for a few seconds, and then leaned back. Jahanara was relieved to see no signs of anger or impetuousness showing. Dara's moods fluctuated a great deal—far more than an emperor could afford. In a way, Nur's statement had been a subtle warning to him. They could not afford to underestimate Aurangzeb.

Yes, they had beaten him—because the youngster had been rash. But he learned from his experiences and maintained self-discipline.

Not for the first time, Jahanara was reminded of what an asset Nur Jahan could be to a ruler who listened to her. No woman in the history of the Mughal empire had ever wielded as much power as she had, in her prime. The last of Jahangir's wives had been a co-emperor in all but name. She'd often held court with him jointly, and when he was ill she'd hold court on her own. Coinage had even been struck in her name—which had never been done before or since in Mughal history. A very scandalous situation! But what Nur had demonstrated was that scandal was not all-powerful, not when the person who generated the scandal had enough power of his own—or her own.

"Did he threaten you in any way?" Jahanara asked.

Nur shook her head. "No. He said nothing about me. I would have been surprised if he had, given that he agreed to meet with me as your emissary. If I had come on my own . . . or been brought to him . . ."

Her lips twitched. "He would have said nothing to me. Made no threats. Just ordered my execution. I probably would not have been brought into his presence at all."

Jahanara nodded. That spoke to an impressive degree of self-control on their younger brother's part. That was dangerous, in the long run. But for now, it meant that they could be reasonably certain Aurangzeb would accept the new situation. For . . .

Dara seemed to be reading her thoughts. He turned to look at her. "Perhaps a year, you think?"

"Probably longer—but almost certainly a full year. It will take Aurangzeb at least that long to restore his authority over his supporters and assemble enough resources in men and materiel to resume the civil war."

On an impulse, she looked at Nur Jahan and asked, "Do you agree?"

"Yes." Nur squared her shoulders a bit. "There is one other thing. Aurangzeb has a request."

"Which is?"

"He says we have a soldier of his here. A European—Portuguese—whom he employed with his artillery. He was badly injured in the battle. He requests if the man is still alive and able to travel that we send him back to Europe. He has done Aurangzeb good service and is owed that much."

Jahanara almost blurted out *he is owed that much by* you—*certainly not us!* But she left the words unspoken. This was not a time for pettiness.

"And how is this to be paid for?" she asked.

"If the man—his name is Carvalho—is alive and able to travel, Aurangzeb will send over his belongings. There is more than enough there to cover the cost."

Jahanara glanced at Dara. He nodded his acquiescence.

"I will find out if the man survived," she said. "If he has, we will do as our brother wishes. Is there anything further?"

Nur shook her head. "No."

"Not true!" said Dara. "There is still the matter of what is to be done with you."

Nur's jaws tightened a little. "I did as you bade me."

"Yes, you did. But that still leaves the issue of what we are to do with *you*. You are dangerous, Nur Jahan. I do not trust you at all."

Dara shook his head firmly. "I will not send you back to Lahore, to your own estates. Who knows what mischief you will get into up there?" He gestured toward Nadira. "And I do not want you anywhere near my wife and child. That leaves only one option."

Now he turned and looked at Jahanara. "She is going on Hajj. Very soon. You will go with her."

"I have already been on Hajj," Nur pointed out. "Twice."

Dara shrugged. "So? The Prophet set no limit on the number of times someone may make the pilgrimage." His jaws tightened a little. "I will brook no argument on this matter. The one person in the world whom I trust to keep you under control is my sister Jahanara."

Jahanara was doing her best not to let her dismay show on her face. Her *great* dismay. How was she to hide her conditions from Nur Jahan over the coming months, if they were in such close proximity? But she could think of no response to her brother's argument.

In the corner of her eye, she caught a glimpse of Smidha making a small gesture. Glancing over, she saw that her advisor was fluttering her fingers slightly. The meaning was clear enough: *Say nothing. We can deal with this.*

How? she wondered. But she kept silent.

Mission House
Agra

"Absolutely not!" Gervais proclaimed. "You are not getting out of my sight until the two of you are properly wedded." His stern almost-glare shifted back and forth between his daughter and Bertram.

Monique threw up her hands. "And how are we to

do that, Papa? In case you hadn't noticed, there are no Christian clergy in Agra."

"Probably none in Surat either, by now," said Bertram. "We could find some in Goa, of course, but..." He made a face. "That would present us with another set of problems. Probably *big* problems."

"Such as arrest," muttered Monique. "Auto-da-fé."

"The solution's simple," said Rodney. Everyone seated at the meeting table turned to look at him.

"Rune Strand," he said. "Remember him? As captain of the *Lønsom Vind*, he has the authority to marry them."

John frowned. "Does he, though? Yeah, in our day and age he would have, but does that custom apply in this one?"

As it happened, Priscilla knew the answer to that question. She'd run across it once in her voluminous and somewhat scattershot reading. The answer was:

No, captains in the seventeenth century did not have the authority to conduct marriages—any more than they did up-time. The whole thing was a myth promulgated by romance authors.

But she saw no reason to clean up waters that her husband had sufficiently muddied for their immediate purposes. They could deal with it one way or another once they got to Surat.

Harem quarters
Red Fort

"But what will we do, Smidha? We can't keep my condition hidden from Nur Jahan for almost a year!

Even the most dull-witted woman in the world would figure it out—which she's anything but."

"We can certainly keep it hidden until we get to Surat, at which point our options will be much greater. You have great power in the port city, don't forget, because you control so much of the commerce that passes through it. One thing we can certainly do is see to it that Nur is placed on a different ship than yours. She will not see you for the whole voyage."

"And then?"

Smidha threw up her hands in a little gesture of exasperation. "And then we will see! If nothing else—"

She broke off that line of thought. She didn't think the princess was ready for that yet.

If nothing else I am bringing several poisons with me, Nur Jahan has no bodyguards, and Firoz Khan is quite strong enough to pitch her over the side on a dark night.

So was Jahanara herself, for that matter. Smidha might even be able to do it.

She reached out her hand and gave that of her mistress a reassuring little squeeze. "We will figure something out, I am sure of it."

Sinhagad Fort
Western Ghats

Salim braced his shoulders, his hands clasped behind his back. He recognized the face of the umara—one of many he'd encountered at Dara Shikoh's court—but couldn't recall his name. "Am I summoned to Red Fort? And if so, do I bring my men with me?"

The emissary from the Sultan Al'Azam shook his head. "No, Amir." He withdrew a scroll from his tunic and handed it to Salim.

"This contains your orders in much greater detail. The essence is that you are appointed the new governor of Gujarat and are to establish your headquarters in Surat." The umara glanced around at the large number of Salim's forces who were visible on the nearby walls of the fortress. "Take all your men with you. They will form the core of your forces until you can recruit more men.

"Which you will need," he continued. He tapped the scroll with a finger. "As you will see, the Sultan Al'Azam is providing you with plentiful funds. He instructed me to emphasize to you that he wants you to concentrate on building a navy for the empire. He is tired of the insults and depredations of the ferenghi flotillas."

Salim stared at him. *Build a navy ... ?*

The Mughal empire had always been a land power, not a seagoing one. For at least the past century, they'd relied on the various European naval forces to keep piracy suppressed in the Arabian Sea.

More to the point, Salim himself was an *Afghan.* What he knew about building, maintaining—much less properly using—naval forces amounted to practically nothing.

He tightened his jaws to keep his mouth from sagging open.

The umara seemed to understand at least some of Salim's disquiet. He leaned forward and said softly, "The Sultan does not expect you to be the expert on the subject, Amir. Those we already have—and in greater numbers than you probably realize. For some time now, the Begum Sahib has had our shipbuilders in Surat designing war vessels based on not just European but up-time designs. None of them will be there when you arrive, for the Begum Sahib is taking all of them to Jeddah."

"Jeddah?" He tightened his jaws again, lest he look like an outright fool.

The umara nodded. "She is going on Hajj. By now, she will have already left Agra. Two of the new vessels will continue on from Jeddah to Europe, in order to expand our trade. She will bring the other two back with her when she returns. So as you can see, you will have considerable resources available to you when you arrive in Gujarat, and still more by sometime next year."

He handed over the scroll. "My congratulations, Governor."

On the road to Surat
Southeast of Agra

"I'll say this—" Priscilla used a forefinger to move aside one of the curtains concealing the interior of the howdah from outside view. She didn't move the curtain very far, though. "It can get a little stifling in here, especially in the middle of the day, but it's not an uncomfortable way to travel. At least once you get used to the..."

She used her hand to mimic the rolling, swaying motions of an elephant's back.

Jahanara glanced up at the canopy covering the

howdah. "I can have more water spread on the cloth, if you like. That will cool us."

Priscilla shook her head. "It's not that bad." She left unsaid that every time the caravan stopped, it seemed to take at least an hour to get it underway again. She was a little surprised, actually, that Jahanara seemed very willing to make such stops. The woman was normally given to driving projects through with great energy.

"At least we're traveling at the right time," said Monique. They had now entered India's best time of year, the cool and dry season called rabi. That season would last about four months, until well into February, before the heat of garam arrived. By then, they would have crossed the sea.

"Really," said Jahanara. "I can have the howdah stopped so we can have more water sprinkled on the canopy." She made a little fluttering motion with her hand. "It is not a problem."

Sinhagad Fort
Western Ghats

"I leave you in charge of the sowar, Sunil," said Salim. "I am instructed to take command in Gujarat as soon as possible."

His subordinate officer frowned. "Surely you can wait a day or two. The Sultan's emissary seemed in no great rush when he left us yesterday."

Sunil glanced over at the small force Salim had assembled by way of an accompanying guard. "Twenty men is not much."

"It is enough. With as many good remounts as we have, no bandits will undertake a pursuit anyway. I repeat: *I must be off.*"

He frowned, very sternly. "Duty calls. And that call is relentless, as always."

A moment later, he was up in the saddle and leading his little troop on the road north to Surat.

Part Nine

October, 1637

Troubled no longer by the priestly lore
—The Rig Veda

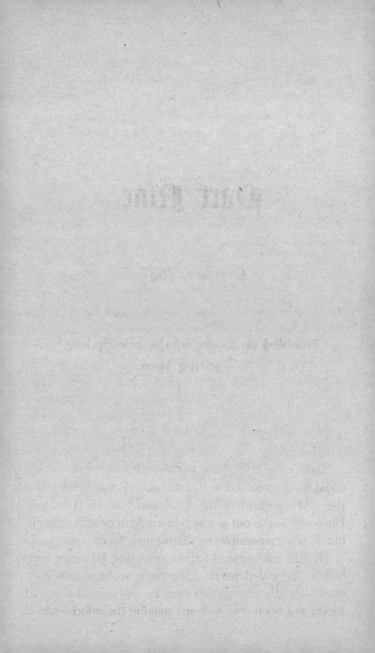

Chapter 55

Surat
The Gulf of Khambhat

By the time he rode onto the quay at Surat, Salim knew he was too late.

Barely—but still too late. Drawing up his horse at the end of the stone pier, he watched the flotilla sailing with the tide down the Tapti River toward the Gulf of Khambhat. He had no doubt of the identity of the four ships, since they were quite distinctive in their design. Even a landsman like himself could tell the difference.

They were still quite visible, although few details could be determined at the distance. For one, they flew the odd standard of the USE and that of Hamburg. He could make out a few human figures well enough, but it was impossible to distinguish faces.

He did not curse. In truth, meeting Jahanara here before she sailed would have been an enormous risk, even a deadly one should they be discovered. He had simply not been able to resist making the effort—which had gained him no favor among the men of his escort. He had driven them very hard, and for many days, even using up some of the remounts.

He could hear their horses' hooves clatter on the stone quay as they joined him upon it, could feel the sullen fatigue in their stares on his back.

They'd live. Hardships had benefits of their own, after all.

After staring at the distant figure of the lone horseman at the end of the quay for a moment, Jahanara looked around the rear deck of the *Lønsom Vind*. The ship's captain—she couldn't remember his name at the moment—was but a few steps away, facing downriver and seeming happy to be on his way.

"Monique," she said. "Would you ask the captain if I might use his spyglass?"

Monique was back in a few seconds with the telescope.

It took Jahanara more effort than she thought it should to bring the device into focus, but soon enough . . .

She spent several minutes gazing upon the figure of the horseman, until distance and the slight haze covering the waters made the effort pointless.

"Thank you," she said, handing back the spyglass.

She was suffused by a great warmth. In truth, she was surprised he had made such good time. Even so, she could only delay here for so long without raising suspicions, and Dara Shikoh would not have sent Salim his new instructions until he was certain the Amir could not possibly reach Surat before she departed.

Jahanara would miss him. Begum Sahib dare not show it.

Stifling a sigh, Begum Sahib turned to Priscilla, who was standing silently beside her at the rail. "We shall be together for a long time now, with many opportunities to speak. Of many things."

"Yes," said Priscilla, eyes on the distant shore.

After a while, Jahanara added, "There are many things I think it would be good to discuss. With a woman from the future."

"Oh, yes," said Priscilla.

Glossary of Terms

Akbarnama Book of Akbar, one of the great Mughal Emperors.

Atishbaz Caste-workers who manufacture rearms and cannon.

Begum Princess.

Begum Sahib Princess of princesses.

Betel A leaf containing stimulants that is consumed in Southeast Asia, noted for causing staining of the teeth in regular users.

Caravanserai Way station on a caravan route. Often paid for out of royal coffers.

Chakram Sharpened throwing rings of thin steel hurled like a Frisbee.

Dastak A scepter, specifically a symbol of diplomatic status and protection of the sovereign.

Deccan	Plateau in north-central India.
Diwan	Royally-appointed manager for some specific trade or bureaucratic entity.
Diwan-i-Khas	Hall of public audience.
Diwan-i-Am	Hall of private audience.
Doab	A tract of land between two rivers.
Ferenghi	Foreigner, usually European.
Firman	Written permission or order. Necessary for trade.
Qalam	Writing instrument.
Gaz	Distance, much like a cubit or yard.
Howdah	Passenger compartment on an elephant, sometimes enclosed.
Jagir	Income property rights, not usually overseen in person by the holder, a Jagirdir.
Jagirdir	Holder of a jagir.
Jali	Ornate stone or wooden screens to preserve purdah.
Julabmost	Nonalcoholic fruit drink.
Jizya	Muslim tax on nonbelievers.
Katar	Triangular double-bladed punch dagger.

Khalat   Robes of state, embroidered and decorated, that were given as gifts to umara who pleased the powerful.

Khan-i-Saman   Manager of a harem's dealings with the outside world, usually a eunuch.

Kharkhanas   Craftsmen collected by a royal, the product of which can be many things.

Khutba   Friday prayers. In this instance, Friday prayers proclaiming a new emperor.

Kokas   Milk-brothers. Those warriors of the inner circle of a prince who "shared the milk" of their mothers, meaning they were to be trusted in all things.

Kos   Length of distance equivalent to approximately 2.25 miles.

Maghrib   Afternoon prayers for Muslims.

Mahout   Elephant handler and trainer.

Mansab   A set of jagirs, often scattered throughout the empire.

Mansabdar   A holder of mansab.

Mihmandar   Person responsible for the upkeep, care, and security of an envoy visiting the Mughal court.

Nizam	Mughal title for foreign princes and sultans—a way to avoid admitting in writing that another could hold the title of sultan.
Nökör	Personal guard of a prince.
Pulu	Polo.
Purdah	Separation of women from men in accordance with cultural and religious norms.
Shehzadi	Princess.
Shehzada	Prince.
Sowar	Cavalry trooper. Also one of two rankings in the emperor's court, this one denoting how many actual sowar were paid for out of the rank-granter's treasury. Inspections were common.
Sultan	King.
Sultan Al'Azam	High Sultan, the emperor's honorific.
Umara	Nobles of the court.
Wazir	First advisor, minister.
Zamburak	Camel gun, small cannon like a swivel gun aboard western ships.
Zamburakchi	Camel gunners.
Zamind	Land rights settled region.

Zamindar   Recipient of land rights to a region, usually resided in or on and defended by the zamindar himself.

Zat   Courtly rank, strictly a sign of the emperor's favor, compensated with cash allowances and jagirs, but no troops.

Cast of Characters

The Mission

John Dexter Ennis USE TacRail veteran and titular leader of the Mission. Technology specialist for the Mission.

Rodney Totman NUS Army Medic, former college football player. Medical expert for the Mission.

Priscilla Totman Paramedic, married to Rodney. Medical expert for the Mission.

Bobby Owen Maddox Up-timer and USE 2nd Lt of TacRail Unit, security specialist for the Mission.

Ricky Wiley Up-timer and USE 2nd Lt of TacRail Unit, security specialist for the Mission.

Ilsa Ennis	Down-timer, married to John Dexter.
Gervais Vieuxpont	Down-timer and onetime con man, skilled linguist and father of Monique. Disgraced physician.
Monique Vieuxpont	Down-timer and onetime con woman, skilled linguist and daughter of Gervais.
Bertram Weimar	Down-timer, spy for the USE, and distant relation to Don Nasi.

Lønsom Vind Crew

| Captain Rune Strand | Danish captain with experience at the Dutch trade in the Far East. |
| Mate Loke | Long-service Danish sailor, Rune's second. |

The Mughal Royal Family

Nur Jahan	Widow of Jahangir, former emperor and Shah Jahan's father.
Jahanara Begum	Eldest daughter of Shah Jahan and Mumtaz Mahal.
Dara Shikoh	Eldest son of Shah Jahan and Mumtaz Mahal.

Shah Shuja	Second son of Shah Jahan and Mumtaz Mahal.
Aurangzeb	Third son of Shah Jahan and Mumtaz Mahal.
Roshanara	Second daughter of Shah Jahan.
Murad	Fourth son of Shah Jahan, child.
Guajara	Third daughter of Shah Jahan, toddler.

Umara and Other Notables

Asaf Khan	Great-Uncle of the emperors, governor general of Bengal.
Shaista Khan	Son of Asaf Khan, brother-in-law to Shah Jahan, and uncle to the emperors.

Dara Shikoh's Camp

Nadira Begum	Dara's wife and cousin.
Suleiman	Dara's infant son.
Amir Salim Gadh Visa Yilmaz	Afghan adventurer, student of Mian Mir, and general.
Talawat	Gunsmith, part of Dara Shikoh's princely establishment.
Firoz Khan	Chief harem eunuch.

Kwaja Magul	Eunuch advisor employed by the emperor to serve Dara.
Mohammed	Captain of Dara's personal guard, appointed by Shah Jahan.
Smidha	Jahanara's eldest and most trusted advisor.
Atisheh	Chief among the female harem guards.
Prasad	Eunuch, harem slave entrusted with Jahanara's personal messages.
Sahana	Harem slave purchased by the court from Jadu Das to serve as translator.
Gopal	Jahanara's Mahout.
Sabah	Turkic warrior woman placed as guard over Roshanara.
Damla	Cousin of Atisheh.
Yonca	Warrior woman of the court.
Iqtadar Yilmaz	Afghan cousins of Salim and his lieutenant.
Tariq Yilmaz	Afghan kinsman of Salim and his lieutenant.
Angelo Gradenigo	Venetian con man, doctor, and now servant to the court.

Jadu Das	Hindu merchant in Agra, old ally of Salim.
Dhanji Das	Hindu merchant in Surat, sibling of Jadu.
Sunil	Gujarati Lieutenant to Salim.

Aurangzeb's Camp

Mahabat Khan	A captain of cavalry troop.
Carvalho	Portuguese artillery captain and mercenary.
Samarjit Khan	Rajput commander and zamindar.
Ghulam Khan	Persian umara, made diwan of the imperial mint.
Nur Jahan	Great aunt of the emperors and princesses of the various courts.
Tara	Chief advisor to Nur Jahan and onetime bodyguard.
Shahaji Bhonsle	Maratha chieftain and umara, commander of contingent of Aurangzeb's light cavalry.
Koyaji	Maratha chieftain.
Dattaji	Maratha subordinate to Shahaji, member of the Bhonsle clan.

| Sidhi Miftah Habash Khan | Habshi chieftan and leader of light cavalry for Aurangzeb, former enslaved person. |

Sikhs

| Hargobind Singh | Sixth Guru of the Sikh religion. |
| Bhidi Chand | Disciple of Sixth Guru. |

Portuguese Goa

Conde do Linhares, Migeul de Noronha	Viceroy of Goa and the East.
Archbishop Francisco dos Martires	Franciscan priest in Goa.
Father Christovao De Jesus	Franciscan priest sent to Aurangzeb in the Deccan on behalf of the Archbishop and Count.
William Methwold	Erstwhile President of the English Company Factory at Surat, now at large in Goa.

ERIC FLINT

ONE OF THE BEST ALTERNATE HISTORY AUTHORS TODAY!

THE RING OF FIRE SERIES

THE RING OF FIRE ANTHOLOGIES
Edited by Eric Flint